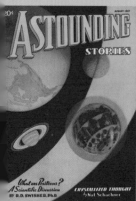

# SPIDER
# ISLAND

# By Jack Williamson

## The Collected Stories of Jack Williamson

Photograph first appeared accompanying the article "Horror Yarns—Double Action" in the August 1937 issue of *The Author & Journalist*. Later used alongside a variety of biographical sketches and editorials in *Thrilling Wonder Stories* and *Startling Stories*.

# SPIDER
# ISLAND

## The Collected Stories of
## JACK WILLIAMSON

### Volume Four

*Foreword by*
*Edward Bryant*

# HAFFNER PRESS
### ROYAL OAK, MICHIGAN          2002

# FIRST EDITION

Published by arrangement with the author
and the author's agent, The Spectrum Literary Agency

ISBN 1-893887-14-6 (Trade Edition)
ISBN 1-893887-15-4 (Limited Edition)

Library of Congress Control Number: 2001088982

Printed in the United States of America

# Acknowledgments

This is the fourth volume in a publishing program dedicated to collecting the short fiction and unreprinted serials, less than four parts, of Science Fiction Grand Master Jack Williamson. The contents of each volume are presented in order of publication date and, aside from typographical corrections, are taken from the texts as they originally appeared. Some stories are amongst the most reprinted and anthologized tales in the genre, and others are appearing for the first time in book form.

For their assistance in the preparation of this work the publishers wish to acknowledge the contributions of Richard A. Hauptmann for his Hugo Award-nominated bibliography of Jack Williamson's career, Gene Bundy and his staff at the Jack Williamson Science Fiction Library at Eastern New Mexico University's Golden Library, Eleanor Wood of The Spectrum Literary Agency, Scott Lais of Dell Magazines, and "Big-Hearted" Howard DeVore.

Special recognition goes to George Flynn for his stellar job in proofreading the manuscript, to Edward Bryant for his exceptional foreword, and of course, to Dr. Jack Williamson.

*To*
*Stephen Haffner*

# SPIDER ISLAND

# Contents

# American Gods, American Dreaming

FADE IN:

EXTERIOR - NIGHT

We're looking down at what we later discover is prime New Mexico wilderness, circa 1915. We see sand dunes, ridges edged with eerie radiance from the rising moon.

CAMERA CLOSES IN on campsite. There is a covered wagon of the traditional design with a vintage hack parked behind. The team has been unhitched and is grazing, along with a roan riding horse.

REVERSE ANGLE to the night sky. The southwestern stars have never appeared more brilliant. We see an EXTRAORDINARILY SHINING LIGHT moving relative to its companions.

BACK TO the campfire by the wagon as the CAMERA closes in on the family seated around the flames, a man, a woman, two young boys, one about three, the other, seven. The mother is consoling the younger boy, rocking him in her arms.

> LUCY
> Sleep now, Jim. Another three days, we'll all be home.

The boys' father shakes his head.

> ASA LEE
> Four days, we're lucky.

In the background, coyotes howl. CAMERA moves to the periphery of the firelight. The older son, the seven-year-old, lies on his back with his head propped on a rolled horse blanket. He's staring up at the sky.

REVERSE ANGLE again to the sky. The mysterious light is brighter now, moving faster.

We hear the older boy's off-screen voice.

> JACK
> (o.s.)
> Look! I see something.

His parents look up, expressions not registering what Jack is obviously captivated by.

> ASA LEE
> The moon, some stars. It's pretty. Get some sleep, son. You're gonna need it.

LUCY

It's beautiful, Jack. But your father's right. Sleep. (hesitates) Dream.

CAMERA ALTERNATES among the sky, the campfire, Jack's enraptured expression.

Jack says nothing, but his eyes widen as the bright light descends toward him from the sky.

And there are SOUNDS, the coyote howls blend with a rushing as of a great river, and voices, many and varied, all indistinct as yet.

The LIGHT radiates into Jack's wide-open eyes and his face glows.

The wood in the campfire crackles, for a moment all by itself in the night, then is subsumed into the growing river sound.

None of the rest of Jack's family seem to notice what's going on, but there are concerned nickers from the horses.

The LIGHT seems to flow out of the boy's features now, as if exploding from every pore. His expression is one of complete and utter wonder

as the LIGHT intensifies to an almost painful brilliance, beginning to wash out the whole rest of the FRAME.

There is nothing now but the LIGHT. And the voices of the river.

*All right already with the filmic conceit,* you may be grumbling. I mean, what's the likelihood of a Jack Williamson bio-pic opening in your suburban multiplex in the near future? Oh, say with Vincent D'Onofrio playing his dad and Renée Zellweger his mother?

There are stranger things, Horatio . . . I'm just remembering 1996 when the critically well-received *The Whole Wide World,* Dan Ireland's wide-screen version of Novalyne Price's memoir about Robert E. Howard, hit the screen. The *New Yorker's* old editor, Harold Ross, to the contrary, sometimes people do want to see involving drama about writers' lives.

And no, I'm not presently pitching *Wonder's Child* to Paramount as a major feature for the Christmas after next. I don't have the Hollywood clout. But a fellow can dream, can't he?

Which brings me back around to Jack Williamson, the guy who wrote the fiction in this thick volume you're presently holding in your hands.

I hold the same reaction to Jack and his work that many musicians have to the most accomplished of their profession. There are guitar gods. Here in science fiction and fantasy there are writing gods. Some of them are distinctively American, and that seems to define Jack to a *T.*

He is an American god. He is a wonder and a legend and a role model for me and any other decent writer I know. Or at least he should be. In some areas, the word is slow in percolating out.

But Jack's taken his time. He's seen and experienced more than most of the rest of us in our entire lives. All we can do is play catch-up. Jack saw Halley's Comet—twice, so far. The first time was in 1910 when Halley's ushered Mark Twain out of this world. Jack's been alive through the *Titanic* disaster, the rise of aviation, two World Wars, the first wartime nuclear attack, the Lunar landing and the rise and subsiding back of the space program, the cybernetic age and the advent of the personal computer. He's keenly keeping track of nanotechnology and every other innovative phenomenon on the horizon.

He married a lovely woman and reared a family and earned a successful and honored career as an academic. But mainly for our purposes here, he's been a professional writer since 1928.

And he still is. To be a professional in one's chosen field over a span of nine different decades is pretty darned impressive. But what's even more terrific, is that Jack's never even thought of retiring. He still publishes at least one new novel per year and those books are not a matter of perfunctory coasting. Jack's work continues to be vital, intriguing, energetic and entertaining. His titles are published on merit, not momentum.

That's one of the reasons he's a role model for so many of us. It's a writer's consummate fantasy to be writing and doing good work in our later years. Of course for most of us, our "later years" optimistically mean something like our seventies. Jack's so far beyond that and showing little sign of slowing down, one could speculate he's a concealed member of a benign, long-lived alien species residing here on Earth.

My home in Denver is full of books and shelves, and those shelves are dotted with Williamson books. It seems as though there are too many to consolidate in one location. I stick a single new volume on a fresh and uncluttered shelf. Before I know it, there's a second, a third, a vintage title I've finally tracked down, a nonfiction work. I swear, they proliferate like exotic alien lifeforms.

My reading life has never been without Williamson fiction. While my family didn't move to New Mexico in a covered wagon in 1915, we did move from New York to a desolate section of Wyoming in 1946 in a battered DeSoto. I grew up in an isolated world of ranching that, though not yet completely gone, is fast vanishing. It was a world of loneliness and alienation much of the time, so becoming an avid reader was my primary salvation. After that came the writing. I'm one of the many people who, if pressed, will admit that science fiction saved my life.

So I discovered the worlds of Jack Williamson early on. When I finally gained access to a Carnegie public library nearly thirty miles from our ranch, and when my family eventually moved into town and I attended a school with more than a dozen students, I quickly was seduced by the school system's TAB Book Club, discounted access to mass market paperbacks. Science fiction titles were prominently featured.

I know I read an anthology reprinting Jack's "With Folded Hands . . .," that tale of the perfect robots who protected humanity absolutely perfectly from human foolishness and risk, with—to me—utterly sobering results. The story did things to my mind. I spent many days pondering the issues it raised, and then more time dealing with the horror of a future of perfect repression.

The library turned up a copy of *Darker Than You Think,* Jack's speculative novel of lycanthropy that did for werewolves what Richard Matheson did for vampires with *I Am Legend*. Many years later I used Jack's novel as the touchstone for trying to explain to the assembled multitude at a Horror Writers Association Bram Stoker Awards Banquet in Manhattan why it was that HWA was awarding Grand Master status to Jack Williamson.

*But he's not a horror writer!* You could see it in some wary eyes. Writers themselves can sometimes be especially obstinate in regard to accepting the reality that writers are not always categorizable in neat pigeon holes A, B, or C, but are simply writers who do a lot of different things and create broad spectra of creations reflecting their complex personalities and interests.

So why not the HWA Grand Master Award for Jack? Made sense to me, and still does.

I think I was about twelve, probably in the sixth grade, when the TAB Book Club delivered a paperback of *Star Bridge* by Jack Williamson and James E. Gunn. To this day, I refuse to understand why this novel is not accorded the same classic status as *The Stars My Destination* or *The Moon Is a Harsh Mistress*. I opened that volume and encountered Horn, the hired gun and disillusioned rebel who's riding an exhausted buckskin pony through an immense desert on a far future Earth; his mission, to assassinate one of the prime executives of the Eron Company, the Microsoft of transportation and communication in a massive future interstellar empire. As much as any other piece of sf I read in my formative years, *Star Bridge* taught me about romance and sense of wonder.

The seeds of that romance and sense of wonder are abundantly scattered through the tales in *Spider Island*. See? I may wander far afield, but I always get back to the point.

The tenor of Jack's early fiction in *Spider Island* is what critic John Clute, not one ever to issue empty kindnesses, calls in the Jack Williamson entry in *The Encyclopedia of Science Fiction*, "rough but vigorous."

That's not a bad thing. I think "vigorous" translates to the concept of infusing a story with genuine passion. There are plenty of writers who can never do that even in their sixth or eighth decade of writing. And "rough"? Well, Jack cut his literary teeth during the pulp era, and it was the pulps that constituted his early professional markets. Literary polish was far less valued by the editors than colorful characters and hyperkinetic plots. So far as I can see, Jack's always been a writer who has learned as he's gone along, and he's never been satisfied to plateau on a level that's significantly less ambitious than another he knows he can achieve with some sweat and elbow-grease.

Along with the pulp ingredients that keep the stories herein spanking along splendidly, you'll find examples of both the vaulting imaginative imagery that lends classic sf a memorable grandeur, and snatches of poetry in the prose of a writer finding his way to matching his own notes with the key to the music of the spheres. All of which is a way of saying the contents of *Spider Island* give us readers an evocative portrait of a talented writer continuing to find his true voice.

Particularly intriguing in *Spider Island* are the tales for *Thrilling Mystery,* along with the essay "Horror Yarns—Double Action" in the appendix. Imagine the challenge for a writer attempting to set up a fully convincing supernatural fantasy or science fiction scenario which he knows he must eventually rotate 180 degrees to complete rationality, all without jerking the reader, screaming and kvetching, from the story's own internal reality. It's amazing—or in this case, thrilling and mysterious . . .

So get to it, readers. This is one of those "great, square books" that will furnish you plenty of diversion.

Now mix your media. Sit down, lean back, let the lights dim. Did you remember to fix some popcorn and mix up a home-brewed Italian soda?

```
                    FADE IN:
                    EXTERIOR - NIGHT

        We are the CAMERA and we are looking
        down at a clean, sharp, but mostly
        sleeping small university city in
        eastern New Mexico.

        There are moving lights on the thor-
        oughfares and in the air, and we un-
        derstand the time is SOMEWHERE WELL
        INTO THE 21ST CENTURY.

        We hear fragmentary SOUNDS that
        clarify as snatches of NEWSCAST.
```

Borderless electronic video screen flickering slightly as it floats in center of frame. A 50-something WOMAN NEWSCASTER looks up as if she can engage us eye to eye.

> NEWSCASTER
> ...widely viewed as portents of a potentially terrifying but nonetheless astonishing future. The millions who have witnessed the mysterious lights in the sky...

CUT TO:

The nightscape of the small city from the air.

SOUND is the rush of river voices, all combined, all a powerful choral effect, akin to the SOUND we heard in the first scene, save that now the voices suggest a meaning we can begin to make out.

Off to one edge of the urban lights, a single light in particular begins to wax. It pulses ever brighter.

MONTAGE OF FACES which includes young and old, male and female, many races, many ages, one or two more exotic countenances that beg description as Homo sapiens. In other words, aliens.

Tears shine in some eyes. Happiness transforms others.

> YOUNG MAN
> His work? I can't tell you . . .

> YOUNG WOMAN
> . . . loved it forever. It's taken me
> . . .

              OLDER MAN
. . . places I'd never even conceived
. . .

           OLDER WOMAN
. . . a weaver of dreams . . .

           UNIQUE ALIEN
. . . so for a time, we will borrow
him back . . .

We see a long shot of the city from
above, as the LIGHT gathers and
flares more intensely, then offers a
final pulse and rushes upward, trailing white-hot sparks. It's a coruscating tower of brilliant flame.

REVERSE ANGLE as the light and the
river-rush chorale of VOICES dimin-
ish and vanish into the brilliant
canvas of the heavens.

           UNIQUE ALIEN
              (o.s.)
But just for a short time . . . And
all of you . . . you've caught on to
this dreaming thing . . .

        HOLD on the stars.

        FADE TO BLACK

           and

         FADE OUT

              Edward Bryant
              July 11, 2001
              Denver

# The Ruler of Fate

*Weird Tales, April, May, June 1936*

## 1. To Avert a War

'LO, KID."

The warm, quiet greeting came out of the dark beyond the opening door, suddenly. The girl, sitting in the pool of light in the middle of the big room, had not heard the door. She was startled. Her wide-browed face drained white, and one hand clutched at her throat.

Shiela Hall was tall for a girl, and she sat very straight in the swivel chair behind the battered desk. Usually Shiela appeared the very efficient secretary for the Montel Foundation that she was. Beyond her trim, secretarial efficiency, however, welled up eternal surprize.

Her waved hair was commonly a pale, tawny brown—until some trick of light unveiled glories of unsuspected gold. Her eyes were usually brown, level eyes honestly quizzical—until quick emotion flooded them with purple. She was ordinarily composed, serene—yet sudden feeling could, as it had now, bleach her skin to an unflawed, telltale transparency.

Kane Montel came through the door, into the large, bare of-

1

fice. A hastily walled-off corner of a larger interior, it had never been finished. The floor was bare concrete, the walls sheet metal and fiber-board. The ceiling was crossed with dusty girders.

Kane Montel was a slim-waisted, big-chested giant. He stood six-feet-two, weighed two-twenty. He was limping a little, now, upon one bandaged foot. One big arm hung in a white sling. His square jaw was crossed with plaster. Keen gray eyes smiled beneath the bandage around his forehead. The hair above it was black.

He came from the door to the big desk. He sat down on the corner of it, to swing his injured foot clear of the floor. Under the bandage, his gray eyes looked warmly down at Shiela Hall.

She was still staring up at him, with the purple in her eyes. One white hand was still pressed to her throat, and the other, on the desk, was convulsively crushing a sheet of paper. But she was beginning to smile, faintly, and a slow pink was coming into her blanched skin.

"Matter, kid?" Concern spoke through the lightness of Kane's tone. "Look as if the skeleton in chains had walked in on you. Shouldn't be here so late, kid—you work too hard."

She swallowed, and the hand came away from the white column of her throat. The brilliance of a sudden smile transfigured her face, and she breathed, softly:

"Oh, Monty!"

Kane Montel bent a little toward her, over the telephone on the desk, his gray eyes drinking in her loveliness.

"Most amazing kid, Shiela," he whispered. "Always pretty. But sometimes, just a moment, you're so perfectly, blindingly beautiful that it hurts. Tell me—what scared you?"

"Thank you, Monty."

Her wide eyes were looking up at him, ,steadily, candidly, still purple.

"Somehow, Monty," she said slowly, "the sound of your voice made—this afternoon—all come back." Her voice fell to a shaken whisper. "Somehow, just for a moment, I was back there at the edge of the field. I saw the flyer rise again.

"For a moment, then, I was so glad, Monty—even if I was afraid for you. As the flyer lifted, I could read her name—*Spirit of Man*. It made me proud and happy, for a moment, because I was a human being, and because you were on the flyer, going out to the moon.

"And then that horrible, horrible instant! Shining in the sun, the flyer had come up like a bright, living thing. And suddenly it was dead. It tilted a little, and fell.

"There was a dreadful, hanging silence as it came down, and then the terrible grinding crash when it struck the field. My feet felt the shock of it. And that was about all I did feel, for hours. I thought you were—were—dead, Monty.

"Somehow, your voice made it all come back."

"Just luck I'm not. Or I'm such a big brute you can't kill me." His lean face twisted grimly. "Others are, who had more right to live than I do. Harper—and Benning."

"Farris?" she asked, mechanically.

"Hospital," he said. "Nine bones broken. Punctured lung. Docs won't say.

"But, kid, what are you doing at the shop at midnight? Think you are a robot secretary, or something? Hadn't realized what a shock the—we must have given you. Ought to be home in bed, kid."

"I WAS waiting for someone," she said. "An important visitor."

"Who—"

"The phone rang this afternoon, just before the ambulance came. It was Mr. Grenfell."

"The senator?" His gray eyes narrowed with surprise. "Thought he was in Washington, staving off the dogs of war."

"He was. He's coming down from Washington tonight, by plane. It's about the moon flight. You have to go, he says."

"Have to, maybe," muttered Kane. "I used to think that. But luck says not." He bit his lip. "Must be important, if Grenfell's coming himself, by air. Old friend of Dad's. But I haven't seen him for years. "

He looked at Shiela.

"Why didn't you let me in on it? Haven't I anything to do with the Montel Foundation? Or is a flying visit from Grenfell just routine?—Grenfell being just now a bigger statesman than the President."

"You were in the hospital, Monty—for a week, the surgeon told me." Her wide eyes, golden again, were deep with reproof. "You shouldn't be here tonight, Monty."

"Oh, nothing the matter with me." He shrugged unconcernedly, and tried to conceal a wince. "No bones broken, anyhow—unless in the foot—a few strains and bruises and a cut or two—"

Under the bandages, his lean face twisted grimly.

"Nothing much," he muttered. "When I think of Harper and Benning and Farris—I was the leader; it should have been me, under that motor, instead of poor Harper—"

"Oh, Monty, don't say that!" the girl pleaded, deeply agitated. "I couldn't have endured living, if you had been killed—"

"Sorry, kid," he said quickly. "Shouldn't talk that way. But after all, what's left for me to do?"

"Plenty," she told him, earnestly. "You've as fine a body as ever grew—when you get well—and the brain to match. You're just twenty-seven, Monty. You have ability to do a great deal, and the world needs you to do it.

"Why," she reminded him, "the biggest man in America is coming here tonight, to give you a job."

"A job that can't be done," be murmured, gloomily. "Shiela," he said grimly, "I've been trying for seven years to get off on the moon flight. Can't be done. Luck's against me. Circumstance. Always some little thing, something we couldn't foresee—such as that flawed control gear, today."

"Next time—" she began, hopefully.

Kane Montel shook his bandaged head.

"Next time won't come," he sighed, wearily. "Thought I would find some way, when I started back here from the hospital tonight. There's none. Light in the head, I suppose.

"Flyer wrecked. Harper and Benning and Farris all out of the running. Money all gone. The Foundation's last cent went for oxygen, yesterday." Abruptly he asked: "How long since you've drawn your salary, Shiela?"

"My salary doesn't matter," she said. "I wanted you to succeed."

"Thanks," he said. "Nice play I made. You've no business being generous to a Foundation, kid. You'll get your pay, though, if we have to sell the impulse-flyer for junk metal—"

"Junk metal, do I hear?"

The crisp, low voice spoke from the open doorway.

"Nothing of the kind, Montel! The Bull-Montel impulse-flyer must make a successful flight to the moon. You must carry on, Montel. It is necessary—vital!"

They turned to look at the man who had come into the light.

S ENATOR Martin Grenfell was a small man, slender, very erect. Grave and reserved of manner, he was yet pervaded with a singular aliveness. He was never still. Arms, shoulders, head moved in continual support of his swift speech. He rarely sat down, never stood completely still.

He gave, however, no impression of abruptness or unease. His whole body, rather, was integrated with his quick, cultured voice, his small-featured, mobile face, in one organ of expression. His face was oddly fluid, mobile, expressive of as many emotional overtones as his voice. His eyes were a kindly blue, twinkling, sympathetic; wide with the generous innocence of a child's eyes, yet somehow wise with the wiles of international diplomacy.

"Montel," he said, "I've come tonight from Washington to tell you that the moon flight must be carried out at once—at any cost. A crisis is upon us. Your success is the only hope that I can see, for America and the world."

Speaking, he had come to the big, scarred desk. He stood beside it, with the tips of his small, sensitive fingers resting on its battered top. His quick blue eyes looked keenly down at Shiela Hall, sitting before a mass of papers; and then across at Kane Montel, resting wearily on the corner of the desk, with his hurt foot swung off the floor.

"We tried, today," Kane told him, his voice low with hopelessness. "Last time. Flyer smashed. Money all gone—not enough left to pay Shiela's salary. Harper and Benning killed; Farris crushed. No—last chance is gone."

"The thing has to be done," said Grenfell. His eyes went briefly up to the dusty girders high above. "What has been your trouble, Montel? Your father once told me that your success was certain."

"It looked so," said Kane, bitterly. "If any big thing had stopped us—any scientific difficulty—it wouldn't be so hard to take. All our troubles have come from small things, accidents, freaks of bad luck. This afternoon, a flawed gear that somehow got past the X-ray tests."

"Then you still consider the flight feasible?"

"It is," said Kane, promptly, "if luck would give us a break. The impulse wheel is a success. You know the principle: equal action and reaction between slung weights in the wheel. The momentum of one is transmitted by springs as a forward impulse to the ship. The momentum of the other—the reaction—is converted into heat of impact, in the multiple hammers.

"The reaction, you might put it, is diverted into the fourth dimension of heat, and gives us the first contained drive in history. We don't need a boat's reaction against a resisting medium, nor a rocket's waste of material, for reaction.

"And Dad's iron-vapor disruption tube gives us power for the wheel. A few pounds of iron ribbon would supply electricity to take us out to the moon and back, if," he finished bitterly, "fate would let us go. "

"You have to so, Montel," said the little statesman, gravely. "For America's sake—for humanity's."

"Why?" Kane asked him, puzzled.

A bitter weariness descended suddenly upon Martin Grenfell. The quick vitality seemed to flow out of his small body. His blue eyes were clouded with despair. His small face drooped hopelessly.

"War," he sighed.

Leaning listlessly on the edge of the big desk, he looked abruptly old to Kane, exhausted, useless. But his limpid, restless eyes, lighting upon Shiela's face, seemed to find there the seed of strength.

D RAWING his shoulders square, with grim determination, Martin Grenfell said:

"War is upon us, Montel. No nation has any reason to fight, really. Even the individuals who hope to profit by it should know that war has become too monstrous to be profitable. Even the munitions-makers should be able to see the collapse and the ruin and the famine ahead—death for them, with the rest of us.

"But war is in the air, Montel. It is a kind of madness. It won't let a nation—or a man—stop to be reasonable. It is a kind of emotional poison, that drives mankind to mass-murder.

"No man or group of men is completely to blame—though the munitions firms are piling fuel on the fire, with their usual propagandizing skill. As you say about the failure of your flight, it has been fate—trivial circumstance.

"Yesterday, for instance, an oil line burst. A transport plane went down into the Baltic, flaming. It carried a poet, a national hero, to death. And today one people is accusing another people of murder, and clamoring for revenge. A jingoistic press, subsidized by the munitions interests, is screaming that a secret heat-ray brought down the plane."

He shook his small head, glumly.

"I don't know where it will stop, short of a world in flame." Martin Grenfell was silent a moment, his blue eyes resting gravely upon the bulk of Kane Montel. "But you can do more to stop it, Montel, than any other man living."

"By planting my bones on the moon, you mean?" asked Kane, puzzled. "I don't see how that—"

"It's no material necessity driving us to war, Montel. It's a psychological complex—the emotional accumulation from a hundred such circumstances as that broken oil line. It is a kind of temporary insanity, fostered by men who blindly hope to make money out of war.

"Your success, Montel, is the one way that I can see to break that complex. Through the past seven years, all the world has been eagerly following your attempts, sharing in them. All the world feels kindly toward you, because of your father. Cheap atomic power has done a great deal for mankind, and it could do a thousand times as much, in a peaceful world.

"Go out to the moon, Montel." His voice was ringing, now. "Mankind will follow you, with a sense of common effort, of common victory. All mankind will be greater, because one man has crossed space, to conquer another planet. The public attention will be lifted above the confusion of narrow hates and blind fears that hold it now. By the time you return, Montel, the war psychosis will have been forgotten."

Kane looked at him heavily, with no light in his gray eyes. He began to speak, in a slow, lifeless tone.

"Seven years ago, it looked easy," he said. "Harry Bull had worked out the impulse principle, decades ago. I had designed the wheel. We had Dad's tubes, for atomic power. The impulse flyer was a fact. Space was already conquered—on paper.

"We had plenty of money. Dad left his whole fortune to the Foundation, you know, for the conquest of space. The royalties from his tube were still coming in. Millions of dollars a year.

"All changed, now," he muttered. "Failures cost money. Patents expired, royalties stopped. Corporation taxes and the recent capital levies have eaten up out resources. This afternoon, Senator, we came to the end of the rope."

"Montel," said Martin Grenfell, his urgent voice low, tense with electric energy, "you don't know what war will mean. Let me tell you what one of our observers—if you will, spies—reported to

Washington not a week ago.

"The scientists of one foreign power have worked out a new application of the Montel equations—of the equations from which your father developed his tube. Your father gave mankind the greatest gift of science: power unlimited. And these men, potential enemies of our nation, have made it a power of destruction.

"These new atomic bombs will desolate a country, a continent, a planet—hideously, and for ever. The process is slow. It is a gradual disruption of the iron atom in the soil. It follows the same principles as the break-down of atoms of iron vapor in your father's tube. But, once started, it cannot be controlled or stopped. And the emitted radiation, will destroy all life in the area affected.

"Think what that means, Montel! If war comes, those bombs will be rained upon America. It will be transformed for ever into a desert of terrible, destroying dust.

"And our laboratories are working furiously, now, to develop the same agency for use against the possible enemy—the madness of war is as terrible in America as anywhere else.

"Let me tell you, Montel."

A terrible, desperate earnestness pleaded in Martin Grenfell's voice.

"War will certainly mean the collapse of civilization. Quite possibly, it may mean the end of humanity."

FOR a little time he was silent, while his eyes traveled back to the dusty girders above.

"It is a kind of dreadful jest," he said, somberly. "We have come to the threshold of a new age. Modern technology, with its climax in your father's discovery, has made it possible for man to step out of the snarling, struggling animal, into real humanity.

"I have dreamed of a time, Montel—and fought for it—when there should be a universal happiness such as the world has never known. Your father was my friend, Montel. We had the same ideals, we struggled toward the same goal. And now it seems that the Montel equations are to be the means of utter ruin, annihilation.

"Unless," he finished, "you go out to the moon, Montel."

Kane Montel's big shoulders twitched, beneath the whiteness of the sling. Brightness of sudden tears glittered in his gray eyes.

His lean, square-jawed face was abruptly twisted, gaunt and terrible with pain. He gulped noisily, and whispered:

"If it can be done—"

Then the telephone whirred beside him on the desk, and Shiela reached mechanically to pick it up.

Gripping the instrument hard, her white hand began to tremble. Kane saw the color flowing away from her loveliness. Listening, twice she said yes. Without having spoken again, she set the telephone back on its stand.

Her wide eyes looked up at Kane, with purple shadow coming into them.

Kane asked, "What is it, kid?"

She started a little, and said, in a dull, weary voice:

"That was the secretary to the chief of staff of the American army. He called to notify us that the President of the United States is just issuing an executive order, forbidding the flight to the moon. The impulse flyer is being commandeered, under the National Safety Act, for military use.

"Army officers, he said, and engineers from the Bureau of Standards, will be here at Maple Hill in two days, to take possession of the flyer, together with all the records and equipment of the Foundation.

"You are to stay on, Monty, to help develop the impulse flyer as a fighting arm, a bombing machine."

## 2. "Red Ruin . . . upon Us!"

"TWO days."

Kane's voice broke the grim, long silence that followed Shiela's words.

Martin Grenfell swung toward him quickly, across the big desk, with eager approval lighting his small, expressive face.

"Then you'll go?"

"I'll try it," said Kane, simply. "If luck will give me half a break—" His big hand rubbed the cross of white plaster on his jaw. "I'm not superstitious," he said, "not in theory, anyhow. But I can't help feeling, somehow, a malicious purpose in our failures. Fate is jesting with us, always moving to defeat us. Sometimes I'm ready to quit. But I'll try."

He looked down at Shiela's silent loveliness, and his gray eyes were suddenly brimming with tears. He flung up his bandaged head, and swallowed, and said to Martin Grenfell, in a loud, hoarse voice:

"Two days—not long; can't waste time. Must have three things: money, equipment, men. Foundation has come to the wall."

He was looking at Shiela again, and she said:

"I've just been going through our balance sheets. There's not an asset left; not one item that we could sell or offer for security—except the flyer itself."

Martin Grenfell spoke up softly.

"My own personal fortune is at your disposal," he said. "It isn't large—I've given my life for other things than money. I could rake up perhaps twenty thousand."

"Thank you," said Kane, soberly. "Might be enough. But a lot of expensive instruments are smashed—have to be replaced.

"As for the equipment, I'll go down to the wreck, tonight. Check over the damage. Instruments. The snapped control gear. Motors torn loose from their brackets—one of them got Harper. Tube batteries smashed, dead.

"Hull's well built. Can be repaired—test it for leaks with compressed air. Landing-gear wrecked, when we cracked up. Have to raise the hull, rebuild it.

"Tonight I'll find what we must have. Get off orders for the instruments and parts. Get a crew to clearing up the wreckage."

Shiela was protesting, with concern on her face:

"Monty, you mustn't! You ought to be in the hospital this minute."

"Got to carry on," he said, grimly. "Now or never. Few caffine tablets will keep me going." He tried to grin. "By the way, kid," he said, "call up the War Department. Tell them we wrecked the flyer today. Tell them we're beginning repairs at once. Considerable undertaking, tell them, and their experts needn't hurry.

"Needn't say what we think of the President's command."

She nodded.

"And that," Kane told Martin Grenfell, "brings us to the third item: men. A problem. Four is a full crew; two can handle the flyer. But I don't know a single man to get, on short notice. Takes training. Sane man wouldn't go," he finished bitterly, "when he saw the list of those I've killed."

Martin Grenfell hesitated, doubtful.

"I myself should volunteer," he said slowly. "But I'm not an engineer. And I dare not be away from Washington too long—"

Shiela Hall was rising slowly out of her chair. Her fair skin had drained again to milky white. Her eyes were expanding to purple pools, and she was breathing swiftly. Speaking with difficulty, in a low, strained voice, she said:

"Monty—I'm—I'm going with you."

"Shiela!" His voice was astonished. "Mustn't think of that, though it's mighty good of you." He bent toward her, earnestly. "No picnic, kid. Rocketing off in a machine already wrecked. Just half a crew. No time for tests or complete preparations. Suicide!"

"I'm going, Monty," she repeated.

"Can't let you, kid," he protested, desperately. "You might be—like Harper—" He choked and swallowed. "Nobody knows what's going to happen."

Wide and purple, her eyes stared up at him, out of the whiteness of her face. Her hands, resting on the desk, were quivering. Her voice trembled.

"That's why I'm going, Monty," she said. "I didn't realize, until the ship fell, this afternoon. I couldn't bear to go on living, Monty, after you were dead or gone. Don't you see, Monty?"

He was staring at her, and yet seemed not to see her white loveliness. His gray eyes were blank with a kind of fascination. His lean face had become a stiff mask. His upper lip was twitching.

"You know I can do the work, Monty," she insisted, earnestly, when he failed to speak. "I helped with the drawings, and watched you in the shop, and kept the lists and inventories. I know more about the flyer than anybody besides you. And I have to go, Monty. Don't you see? To stay would kill me."

A tear started down his lean check. He ignored it. His face broke slowly into an odd, stiff smile. He tried to speak, and swallowed, and said:

"Of course, kid. I understand. I feel the same way. We'll try it—together."

His big hand reached across the desk, and touched her arm.

The telephone whirred again.

"We'll go down to the flyer, right away," Kane told Grenfell. "See what must be done."

Shiela had picked up the telephone.

"A call for you, Mr. Grenfell," she said, and handed him the instrument.

"Yes, Higgins, Grenfell speaking."

The little statesman listened silently, with increasing agitation upon his small face.

"My secretary," he said, in a slow, abstracted tone, replacing the instrument. "I must hurry back to Washington." His thin, nervous fingers were tracing the lapels of his coat. "Sometimes, Montel," he said, "I feel that I'm the only sane man left in the world.

"The message," he explained, "was guarded. But I understand that the President himself suggested in conference today the advantage of a surprize attack, to anticipate our enemies with the atomic bombs.

"The world is mad, Montel. Red ruin is upon us. I'm alone, in Washington. But I'll try to hold the war off, long enough to give you a chance—"


### 3. THE DWELLERS ON THE MOON

S UNSET on the second day following, the *Spirit of Man* still lay where it had fallen, on the testing-field of the Montel Foundation, at Maple Hill. It was now supported, however, upon a hastily erected scaffold, and the landing-skids had been repaired under it.

The bright steel hull of the impulse flyer, washed now with sunset crimson, was spindle-shaped, tapering, somewhat less thin seventy feet long. The big, enclosed disk of the impulse wheel, projecting above the hull, made a hump on the middle of its back. Entry to the double hull was through a small air-lock, set in the level deck forward of the hump.

Men were busy, within the hull: technicians testing the newly installed batteries of Montel tubes, located in the tail; electricians completing the connections to the six big motors mounted on either side of the impulse wheel, geared to it; men with acetylene torches repairing an airleak, where the hull had been strained in failing.

Kane Montel was in the control room in the flyer's nose, just forward of the narrow, compact living-quarters. His lean face was a little haggard, a few bandages were still on his big body. He was trying and adjusting the new navigation instruments, as

Shiela unpacked them carefully.

Slim and boyish in white coveralls, her pale, tawny hair held close to her head with a little white cap, Shiela was silently efficient. Her golden eyes were happy. Once she told Kane, softly:

I'm glad I'm going with you, Monty. Whether we get back safety, or not—I'm glad."

He paused a moment, and caught up her hand, tenderly.

Alertly, she kept peering up through the small, thick lenses of the observation ports.

"A plane, Monty!" she called, suddenly tense. "A big tri-motor, with the army insignia."

Kane raised his eye from the ocular of a new heliocentric theodolite.

"Our military friends," he announced, looking at the big plane wheeling down toward the testing-field, "with their scientists from the Bureau of Standards, to take possession."

He stood silently for a moment, his gray eyes resting on Shiela's trim white figure.

"Well, kid," he said, "this is the word to go."

She moved a little toward him. Her breath quickened. A little wave of color came into her face, and it was illuminated with a smile.

"I'm glad," she whispered.

They gripped hands a moment, solemnly.

Then Kane's lean face broke into a grin.

"So am I," he said. "But we're crazy, kid! I'll have to run the men out, now, and seal the air-lock. Just have to hope that the hull is patched so our air won't be gone before we get out of the stratosphere, and that the new batteries are wired so they won't burn up the motors."

He laughed suddenly, almost harshly.

"Fools," he muttered. "We're fools to tackle it. Always before, we've tested every part of every instrument, spent months, checking every detail and failed! What will happen to us now?—trying to get off in a wreck just half repaired!"

"But we're going to try," said Shiela, serenely.

"Yes, we have to try," he said grimly. "Code wire from Grenfell, this afternoon. War clouds blacker. President has ordered a secret mobilization of the air force. But if we don't move, these officers will have us mobilized, too."

He turned aft.

Shiela followed him out of the control room, saying:

"I'll be warming the batteries."

The military plane came down on the field and taxied to a halt a hundred yards below the *Spirit of Man*. Men in uniform tumbled out. An officer, seeing the closing air-lock of the impulse flyer, seeing the men standing away from it, emitted in angry shout.

With uniformed men streaming along behind him, he lunged toward the flyer, waving an automatic.

Dropping down the companion ladder beneath the air-lock, Kane ran back into the little control room.

"Ready, kid?" he called into a telephone.

"Aye, Captain," came Shiela's cheerful reply. "Tubes hot, sir, ready at full potential. All motors set for starting. Wheel clear, brakes disengaged, axis of lift at ninety degrees. All ready, sir."

"Thanks, kid."

Kane's big fingers brought down a series of levers.

Baffled rage twisted the countenance of the running officer. His black military mustache quivered angrily. His mouth flew wide as he bawled unheard orders.

The high-pitched whine of racing motors filled the *Spirit of Man*. Her bright hull quivered to the beat of the accelerating impulse wheel. It trembled to the swiftening impacts of the leaden surfaces of the multiple hammers, that diverted reaction into heat.

T HE long, humped spindle of her hull stirred upon the scaffolding. It lifted clear. With increasing, amazing velocity, it drove upward into the blue abyss of the evening sky, A bewildered military man stared up at it, cursing fervently, waving a futile pistol.

The sun, which had set beyond the village, came up again, red above the shadows of the wooded hills. Its redness fell away like a veil as the flyer drove upward. Its naked face was left, a supernal blue-white disk in a sky of utter blackness. It was pitilessly bright, peering between the delicate wings of its corona.

But Kane Montel, in the control room, shaken with unbelieving elation, was watching not the sun but the moon. The full white face of it had come up out of the hills, opposite the sun. It grew ever brighter, and the star-dusted sky behind it blacker. It seemed to shrink a little, yet every marking upon it became harshly, blindingly dear.

A cruelty was in the grim, rugged nakedness of its wild craters; somber mystery shadowed its "seas". The white net of Tycho's rays became a puzzling, sinister web. The moon looked down upon him with a pitiless face of blinding enigma and ominous promise.

And Kane, for all his incredulous elation at the successful start, was suddenly afraid.

"Well, kid, we're off," he told Shiela, two hours later, when she came for a little while into the control room. "Funny that nothing should go wrong—when everything should. Luck is having another joke at our expense."

"You're developing a kind of complex about luck, aren't you, Monty?" Shiela asked him, soberly. "I thought you didn't believe in any—well, supernatural interference with human affairs."

"I don't; at least I shouldn't," Kane told her. "But circumstances have defeated me so many times. Trivial circumstances. The flaw in that gear. A month ago, a drunken driver, who ran dawn Marston on the day he was going to take off with us. The time before, some factory mistake in assembling the multiple hammers, so that the wheel shook itself to pieces.

"But you know the sort of thing. It's always some small, unpredictable accident that stops us. I can't help feeling a purpose behind it—grim, malicious, jesting." He laughed at himself, bitterly. "Foolish idea, I suppose."

He scanned a row of dials.

"Doesn't it look like a joke?" he asked. "Here we are, in a wreck that shouldn't have been able to leave the ground. But the tubes are generating at full potential. Motors running perfectly. Old wheel drumming along smoother than she ever did in a test. Even the hull is holding—we haven't lost an ounce of air.

"No, when fate decides to let us reach the moon, kid, we could make it in a tin can.

"Be there, now, in about seventy hours."

He pointed through a thick quartz lens, and they paused to look about.

Earth, visible in the reflectors, was behind, a vast disk of darkness blotting out the unwinking splendor of the stars. The sun's rays ringed it with supernal radiance, fading outward from a band of deepest scarlet, to fairy wings of delicate opalescence.

All about, in a sky of utter, frosty darkness, burned the still glory of the stars. They did not twinkle. Each shone with a pure, steady light, very tiny, very bright. In color they varied from pale green to violet blue and hot scarlet. Out here, beyond the veil of the atmosphere, their brilliant hordes overwhelmed the familiar constellations. Kane felt half lost amid their brilliant myriads.

The moon flamed ahead of them, a full, mottled disk, cruelly bright against the blackness of space. The perfect circle of Tycho's ringed plain was pitilessly distinct at the center of its spreading net of dazzlingly white rays.

"See the rays of Tycho!" whispered Shiela. "I can trace them across all the moon now."

"I always wondered," muttered Kane. "Greatest mystery of the moon. Straight white streaks, crossing mountains, craters. Plains. Cast no shadows. Most prominent at full moon. Strange, how much more distinct they seem. Well, in seventy hours we may know."

A little silence, and Shiela asked:

"What's the program on the moon? We got off in such a rush—"

"Main thing—what Grenfell wants—is just to land, and get back to Earth with proof that we did. Have cameras, instruments for observing physical conditions, heliograph for attempting communication. And that space-armor; go out in that to get rock specimens, and so on.

"Want to land near Tycho. See what those rays really are. Since Dad give me a telescope, when I was twelve, I've wondered—"

THE *Spirit of Man* drove on toward the moon. The even whine of the motors never faltered; the drumming of the impulse wheel was steady as the beat of a great heart. Standing alternate watches, Kane and Shiela found time for rest. Both felt much recovered from the ordeal of departure.

After three "days," the flyer dropped upon the naked lunar plain, five miles north of the great annular wall of Tycho.

Southward, that crater wall plunged mightily into the star-shot blackness of the sky, abrupt, tremendous, a hostile overwhelming barrier. Its peaks, in the sun's radiance, were spears of blinding light, thrust from chasms of infinite darkness.

The plain about the flyer blazed with merciless sun. It was scarred with the queerly black shadows of a million pinnacles, of naked, jagged boulders, of miniature craters. It was cracked, splintered, fused.

"Looks like some weird battlefield," said Shiela, shivering a little with dread at its marks of tremendous cataclysm. "Torn up by a million big guns."

"So it has been," said Kane. "Meteors. No air to shield against them. No erosion to remove their scars."

In the clumsy, heavy fabric of the space suits, they had climbed up through the little air-lock. They stood side by side upon the small deck, forward of the great bulge of the wheel. The quartering sun fell upon them out of a black sky with a dazzling, stinging power. Every surface it touched was a burning, merciless white. And every shadow was night-black, cold, mysterious.

Even behind the tinted lenses of their helmets, their eyes streamed tears from the savage radiation.

"Half blind," muttered Kane. His voice was carried by telephone across a short wire between them. "Let's just stand still until our eyes get adjusted."

"I feel—queer," came Shiela's voice from the receiver against his ear. "Dizzy."

"So'm I," he said. "Light in the head. It's lack of gravity. Get used to it. Awkward walking, but the shoes are weighted. We'll get a few rock specimens. Photographs. Then get over to that ray—just half a mile or so."

They stood silently for a moment, both making little movements, getting the feel Of the unfamiliar suits, testing the effects of muscular efforts against lunar gravitation.

S HIELA was peering across that terrible plain at the strange horizon of dead black and eye-searing white, of mountains incredibly wild, cragged and cruel and precipitous beyond imagination.

Then, through the stiff, inflated fabric of his suit, Kane felt the abrupt pressure of her hand against his arm. He heard her voice in the receiver, low with breathless wonderment, trembling with vague apprehension.

"Monty!" she was whispering. "The ray—look at the ray!"

He looked quickly at her and saw that she was pointing with the swollen sleeve of her space suit.

"Something," she whispered. "It's something more than a surface marking."

The tiny, flat plateau where the flyer lay was half a mile eastward of the wide, snow-white ray that Kane had planned to investigate. He turned and looked toward it now. And beyond the tortured, blazing, motionless lunar plain, below the black sweep of the star-drifted sky, he saw a singular thing.

"It's like a wall of light," he whispered, amazed.

Straight out from the titanic buttresses of Tycho's barrier ring, it marched along the cragged horizon. It was a changeless wall of white opalescence, a thrusting arm of milky radiance.

"It's like a real ray, shining out through the crater ring," breathed Shiela, "like a ray of some queer—energy, but it doesn't change. And it shines through mountains."

Standing on the low-railed deck, beside the girl, Kane gazed at it until the pitiless light of the moon-scape blinded him with tears. Burning wonder welled up in him, and he chilled to the touch of a nameless, puzzling dread.

Shading his streaming eyes until he could see again, he looked at Shiela. Within the bulk of her helmet he could glimpse her face. It was white now. Her eyes were wide and purple, fascinated.

"Stranger than I ever dreamed," he said. "Can't get an angle on it." He touched the sleeve of her suit with his. "May be dangerous," he said. "Somehow—makes me afraid. But I want to investigate. Mind?"

"I'm going with you," she said.

"No," he protested. "Might be somehow—deadly. Wait—"

But the girl was already scrambling down the light accommodation ladder toward the white-lit, pitted plain.

The opalescent, enigmatic wall of the ray was often lost to sight as they struggled across the scarred plain. They moved awkwardly, planting weighted shoes with care, keeping muscular effort to the minimum that prevented spectacular leaps and dangerous falls. At last, assisting each other out of a miniature crater, they found themselves within fifty yards of the ray.

A straight, motionless wall of milky light, it burned high against the blackness of space. Its strange radiance hid the stars. Its edges seemed oddly sharp, definite—as if it had been a luminous white fluid, poured into invisible walls.

"Queer! Queer!" Kane whispered. "Must be radiation-energy. But what penetration! Drives through the mountain ring of Tycho!"

He led the way forward, across the last intervening yards of level rock.

Shiela stopped him abruptly, clutching his arm.

"Monty, wait!" she cried, with a mute terror in her voice. "Don't go any closer—please! You're—shining!"

Kane held up his gloved hand and saw that violet fire was glowing about the thick fingers. And he saw a violet-green spark leap silently away from his body into the white, ominous barrier of the ray.

"Static potential discharging," he murmured. "Then the thing is real energy. No illusion. Represents power—tremendous power."

Shiela was tugging at his arm.

"Come away, Monty," she pleaded.

"Coming, kid." He followed her,

"Kill us, probably, to go closer. But I wonder—"

"Look!" The sharp alarm in her voice cut off his words. "Above the mountains yonder."

Staring into the blackness of the star-shot sky, above the looming, overwhelming, fire-white and night-black ramparts of Tycho, he saw what the girl had seen. Above the highest pinnacles, which bit like white fangs into the black sky, was a moving object.

It was a small globe, silvered. The rays of the sun, burning upon its upper surface, made it look like a little half-moon floating in the ebon sky above the peaks. A small globe-but swiftly growing. It drove past the highest summits and then sank a little, still expanding.

Panic closed its cold iron fingers on Kane's chest.

"A ship!" he muttered. "Some strange ship coming toward our flyer. Fool that I am—leading you off here!"

"Can we get back," Shiela whispered anxiously, "ahead of them?"

"Doubt it."

B UT they started to return. They tried to run. Their efforts carried them above the surface in grotesque bounds. Again and again they fell, sprawling awkwardly, painfully.

"Dangerous, kid," Kane warned. "If you tore the fabric of the suit—"

The picture of death by suffocation, by internal explosion, as the air in the suit rushed out into the near vacuum of the moon, was so painful that he choked off his voice.

They plunged down into the inky shadow of a depression.

The white, humped spindle of the impulse flyer was lost from sight. Leaping ahead, stumbling in the frigid darkness, they watched the bright globe descending amid the stars. It was near now. It looked huge. It vanished, sinking in the direction of the impulse flyer.

When they had toiled out of the crater end and come again within view of the *Spirit of Man,* consternation stopped them. The white bulk of the sphere lay motionless beside the flyer. Its shimmering, riveted mass overwhelmed the little spindle-shaped machine.

"It *is* a ship!" muttered Kane. "What kind of life on the moon—"

"See—" whispered Shiela.

A great valve had opened in the side of the globe. Little figures were tumbling down a ladder. They scattered across the rocky plain. A few approached the impulse flyer. They were diminutive, Kane then realized, by comparison only.

"Men!" he breathed, astounded. "They we men. Have on space suits like ours."

"They're trying to catch us," whispered Shiela, voiceless with fear. "Already we're cut off from the flyer. And now they are spreading out to hem us in against the ray."

### 4. The Machine of Destiny

"YES, they've got us," muttered Kane, wearily. "Look how they travel—leaping like kangaroos! If we had that knack, we might get away. But no chance. Outnumbered. No weapon. Not a chance."

He looked at Shiela's helmeted head. He could see a stray wisp of hair, a flame-bathed brown against the whiteness of her brow, and her eyes, wide with apprehension, purple-shadowed.

"I'm a fool, kid," he said bitterly, "to let you come. And then blunder out here with you, to be caught like a rat."

"No, Monty," she said, and her low voice rang with a curious serene strength. "I wanted to come. Remember that. No matter what happens, I'm glad I'm with you.

"And there was no reason to expect hostile life on the moon. No use blaming yourself."

He gripped her thickly gloved hand for a moment, silently.

"I love you so much, kid," he said abruptly. "Why must circumstances always wreck our happiness? On Earth this moon-flight was always a river to cross. And now we're here—"

His eyes went back to the two argent ships, the leaping figures.

"Let's make a break for it!" he urged, desperately. "They're trying to surround us. Can't outrun them, but we might hide in some little crater."

He was tugging at her arm. She resisted quietly.

"It's no use, Monty. You know that. They have the flyer already. If they want us, all they have to do is wait until our oxygen tanks are empty. We may as well surrender.

"Anyhow, they may not intend us any harm."

"Of course," he said. "No reason why they should."

Yet, despite his words, wild fear was leaping in his heart. It came from the wild, cruel malice of the moon's face, from the terrific enigma of the white, blazing ray behind them, and from the swift, well-planned movements of the leaping figures closing in like wolves on helpless prey.

Fear it was, not for himself but for the girl at his side. His mind was fogged with scarlet intuition of danger mounting over her. He felt nerved to any rash attempt that might save her. Yet his reason told him there could be no escape—not now.

"No reason," he repeated.

Grimly he strove to still his dread with the calm of scientific curiosity.

"Anyhow," he said, "we should learn if they are really men, and how life exists on the moon in defiance of all the astronomers. And we may learn the how and the why of that flaming ray!"

They moved forward deliberately toward the two dissimilar ships that shimmered upon the white, pitted plain.

The leaping, bulky-suited figures gathered around them as they advanced. Keeping a cautious distance, they menaced Kane and Shiela with long spears and with odd little devices like golden needles. They herded the two toward the ladder that fell from the air-lock of the huge globe. Kane led the way up the ladder and into the air-lock.

The outer valve clanged behind the two, ominously.

Kane and Shiela waited in the bare, cylindrical metal chamber. Air was hissing in about them noisily. The inflated fabric of their suits collapsed slowly as the outside pressure increased.

They were clasping hands.

"Remember, Monty," Shiela whispered once, "I'm glad I came with you."

The hiss of air at last ceased. The massive inner valve opened. A man walked through it toward them.

Gaunt he was, tall, lean of frame, yet erect and powerful. He was all in black: odd, long tunic and high, skin-tight hose of black, lustrous, silken stuff. The hands hanging from his black, tight-sleeved arms were thin talons, corded, powerful.

The hair upon his bare, angular head was long, fine, completely white. His face, long, thin, high of brow, was wrinkled as if with extreme age; yet the skin had the healthy pink of youth. His eyes were dark; they gleamed with quick intelligence; within them lay the shadow of deep and ancient melancholy.

Within the valve he halted, his somber eyes resting upon the two. He bowed a little, gravely, without mockery. He spoke, and his voice came through the fabric of the space-suits distinctly. It was a low, deep voice, measured, deliberate.

"Shiela Hall and Kane Montel," it said, "I convey to you the greetings of my master, Aru, who styles himself Lord of Destiny. And I congratulate you upon your intelligence in yielding without attempting to cause us difficulty.

"You may remove your space-suits now. You need them no longer. Do so and come with me. Many things await you.

A T THAT first somber-toned word, Kane's sense of reality crumbled. His world dissolved bewilderingly into chaotic, conflicting illusion. He was seized again by the helpless bafflement which lately had so often overcome him. Again he felt that he was but a puppet dancing on the strings of a jesting fate.

In dumb silence he waited until the tall man had done speaking; then a dazed, wondering impulse in him framed the question:

"You knew we were coming to the moon?"

Somberly the gaunt man nodded.

"All things on Earth," he stated gravely, "are ordained by my master." Solemnly he repeated his request: "Remove your suits now and follow me within. Much is waiting for you."

Kane was grappling with an incredible possibility. The question burst from him incoherently:

"Our failures—when luck was holding us back—was that—"

"The desires of men," said the man in black, "conflict often with the supreme will of my master."

Kane turned to the silent, motionless fabric that cloaked Shiela beside him.

"I believe him," he muttered. "Thing's impossible. But I do. I've felt a will, a purpose, in fate." His voice sank to the faintest whisper. "Frightens me, kid. Such power. Absolute power to rule men—without their even knowing. And it's a cruel power, malicious, dreadful. I wish you were safely back—"

Steady!" her serene whisper came to him "Remember what I said." Her hand touched his arm. "After all, this is just a man. Probably his master is only another man. Things look mysterious and terrible, but that's probably just because we don't understand.

"Ask him a few things: what his name is—how he knows English—how he knows about us. When we understand—"

Kane turned toward the man in black to meet his grave, measured voice:

"Me, you may call Vethlo. Please remove your space-suits and come with me. You shall soon see how I know your language, your names—how I am aware that you came to the moon because a man named Martin Grenfell was foolish enough to think that your flight would avert a war.

"Come."

Numbed with apprehensive bewilderment, Kane turned to Shiela. Pale, trembling with uncomprehending dread, she had mechanically begun unfastening the catches of her helmet. He assisted her out of the clumsy fabric. Then, in the freedom of her trim white coveralls, she helped him unfasten his own.

And they followed the man in black into the ship's interior.

I N A curiously shaped chamber whose curving, fluted walls were illuminated with pallid, flowing lights of violet and green, he made them sit upon a deep, oddly fashioned divan. Seating himself opposite, he waved a thin, powerful hand.

Silent servants in white appeared at once, kneeling to offer crystal goblets of some fragrant purple drink, and deep silver bowls filled with unfamiliar, delicately textured ruddy fruits, and platters of small brown cakes.

"Refresh yourselves," said Vethlo. Seeing Shiela about to decline the purple glass, he suggested gravely: "The drink brings strength, of which you may soon have need."

Kane found his goblet pleasantly stimulating. It revived his courage, cleared a little of the numbed incredulity from his mind. When it was empty, he leaned toward the man in black, asking:

"Just where do we come in? Your master—this Aru—what does he want with us?"

"The Lord of Destiny willed that you should reach the moon," said Vethlo, solemnly, "because he has a deep purpose for you." His dark and ancient eyes rested upon Shiela's white-clad form, full of somber and veiled speculation. He modified: "For one of you."

Whiteness flowed over the girl's fair skin. Her eyes dilated with sudden, shrinking fear, to dark pools of purple. Shuddering a little, she moved instinctively closer to Kane.

Fiercely protective, Kane's big arm went around her trembling shoulders. Savage, helpless rage was touched off in him by the leering significance he read in Vethlo's glance. His voice harsh and rasping with emotion, he demanded:

"What is Aru's purpose—with Shiela?"

Gravely, Vethlo said:

"That will be revealed to you in time."

Muscles trembling in his giant shoulders, Kane pushed himself forward, half out of the seat.

"Do what you please with me," he muttered grimly, "but nobody's going to touch Shiela! That clear? Anybody lays a finger on her—I'll smash him."

No answering resentment touched the long face of the man in black. His grave calm was unruffled. In the same weary voice, heavy with age-long sorrow, he said:

"I beg you to control your emotions, Kane Montel. You must realize that the will of my master overrules the desires of men. His purpose will be revealed to you.

"First, however, it is my task to convince you of his power, You are now to be allowed to see the instrumentality which directs the destinies of Earth, the machine by whose means my master rules every act of every dweller upon your planet.

"When you have seen what I shall show you, you will know how pitiful, how helpless, are your desires against his will. Perhaps you will then more willingly accept the fate my master has ordained for you."

Leaning forward, Kane whispered breathlessly:

"Who—or what—is this—Lord of Destiny?"

"You shall come before him," said Vethlo. "But first I must demonstrate to you the mechanism of his power."

His dark eyes fell to a panel of small instruments set in the arm of his seat.

"The ship has lifted with us," he said. "We have passed back over the summits of the mountain ring you know as Tycho. We are descending, now, through a shaft, into a space beneath the central peak. In this space is the instrumentality that I must display to you—the machine which rules your world."

"Machine?" echoed Kane, incredulous. "A machine, on the moon, that controls happenings on the Earth?" He laughed at himself with a sound almost harsh. "You had me going," he said. "But a machine that rules fate! It's impossible—"

"A scientist," said Vethlo, gravely, "should be slow to use that word."

He gestured again. Again servitors came silently to offer cakes and fruits and frothing glasses of the purple drink.

"My task of explanation will be simpler," he said, "if I begin by recalling certain instruments which my master has allowed your scientists to devise upon Earth.

"The harmonic analyzer is one of them. It can separate the functions or components of any curve. That means that it can isolate the factors that bring about events.

"The product integraph is another twin instrument which multiplies together any given curves. It combines functions, integrates elements. That means that it can predict the events that will be brought about by certain factors.

"Decades ago your scientists devised crude apparatus of this type to predict the tides on the seas of Earth. The Great Brass Brain, it was called. By the process of harmonic analysis it obtained the value of each harmonic constituent for a given time. The addition of all these constituents gave the tide at that time.

"Your own scientists have since been allowed to go far beyond that crude beginning."

"The weather machines, you mean?" asked Kane.

He was beginning to be absorbed in the quiet voice of the man in black, in spite of the shadow of wonder and apprehension still upon him.

Gravely, Vethlo nodded.

"From predicting the tides to predicting the weather was but a step—though a long one," he said. "The periodic factors involved are much more numerous, much more difficult of analysis. The project, as you know, involved the construction of thousands of automatic relay stations, which automatically observe and report innumerable such factors as solar radiation, barometric pressure, wind movements, humidity; temperature. And if the Great Brass Brain performed integrations beyond the power of the human brain, your new analyzers, synthesizers and integraphs are a thousand times more complex.

"Weather control," he said, "might be the next step—if my master chose to allow you to undertake it. Certain of the elements with decisive influence upon the weather are comparatively infinitesimal. A few propellers mounted on the towers of your relay stations, to start small currents of air, a few heat bombs to create small changes in temperature—small things mold circumstances."

Vethlo paused. Somberly his sorrowful eyes rested upon Shiela and Kane, dark with some enigmatic speculation. Slowly he sipped from a tall purple glass.

"Yet all that is simple," he said, "childish toys—beside the machine of destiny."

He set down the goblet and looked again at the little dials beside him. Deliberately he rose.

"The ship is at rest," he said. "Come, and you shall see the machine that rules your world."

Icy feet of dread raced again along Kane's spine. And Shiela shrink back into the divan, trembling. Her face was bloodless, her eyes distended with premonitory horror.

"Come," repeated the weary, sorrowful voice of the man in black. "It is my master's will."

And they rose and followed him.

5. "THE WORLD IS A TOY!"

"THE subsiding magmas of the cooling moon left many such cavernous spaces as these under Tycho," Vethlo informed them.

They had descended the ladder beneath the air-lock of the spherical ship. Their apprehensions momentarily overcome by amazed wonder, Kane and Shiela were staring about, breathlessly.

The thin, cool air about them was filled with a pale, violet light, as if it were itself slightly luminous. The sourceless radiance shone upon the dark, looming, cragged walls, upon the oppressive roof, of a cave incredibly vast. Vastness brought no relief from the sense of crushing, overwhelming mass above. Farther spaces extended away into purple gloom.

The cavern floor was covered with thickets and fields of curious vegetation. It was fungus-like, or fern-like, or totally strange. The predominating color, beneath the sourceless, enigmatic light, was a weird blood-red.

Looking into the darkness of a far, unlit space, Kane saw a distant structure towering luminously, It was a cluster of thin, lofty cones, fluted spirally. They shone with deepest blue, and each high point was tipped with purple flame.

The eldritch mystery of it, burning against the violet dark, held him with a timeless fascination. Beside him Shiela shivered, clutching at his arm.

"That is the dwelling of Aru, the master of destiny," Vethlo informed them. "I shall take you before him, there. But first you must witness the machine."

He led them a little aside, so that they could view a thing that had been hidden by the bulk of the ship. Kane gasped with amazement, and Shiela cried out.

It was a machine they saw, but a machine incredibly huge. Its supporting girders towered up, against the rough black walls of the volcanic cavern, a full mile. Carried amid the girders was a maze of intricate mechanism from whose complexity the mind recoiled in dismay.

Set above them was a crown of tremendous, curved tubes, which burned with lurid, flickering hues of scarlet and green.

Flung out from those tubes was a net of rays. Flaming swords of white, unchanging opalescence, they stabbed into the black cavern roof.

"The rays, Monty!" whispered Shiela. "The rays of Tycho! They come from here up through the surface of the moon."

"Exactly," said Vethlo, gravely.

But the extreme penetration," murmured Kane. "I don't understand—"

"Those rays," the thin man informed them, "represent an order of energy which my master has not allowed you scientists to investigate They curve out beyond the moon, invisibly. Earth is caught in their impalpable net.

"Their sensitive fields serve as detectors for the harmonic analyzers, here. No act of any being on the planet, no word spoken,
escapes those delicate fields. The effect of every falling leaf, every
insect sound, is carried here to the moon, recorded."

His thin, black-clad arm gestured at the crown of white rays.

"They serve also as a means of control. At any point upon the
planet, the rays are so weak that men have never detected them;
yet their influence is everywhere. The forces they exert are always slight: a tiny electric charge, imparted to a rain drop; a few
electrons liberated, in some neurone cell in a man's brain.

"But that slight force has been calculated by mechanisms a
million times more complex than the human brain. And it shapes
results as a pebble starts an avalanche.

"The machine analyzes all the elements of every situation,
which are picked up by the fields of the ray. Then, again through
the ray, those few tiny factors are changed, which must be
changed to make the resulting events obey my master's will."

Shiela was still clutching Kane's big arm, trembling.

"The machine knows—everything?" she whispered, "It has all
power? Like a mechanical god?"

She shuddered.

"Come," resumed the weary, sorrowful tones of the lean man
in black. "Words are but words. You will not feel my master's
power until you have seen."

He led the way toward the tremendous, looming mountain of
the machine. Kane and Shiela followed, silent with the pressure
of numbing dread.

At last across the strangeness of the scarlet garden, they came
into the machines glistening bulk. Vethlo guided than along a
narrow, railed walk that pierced its heart. In mute wonder, Kane
gazed about him at the mass of equipment carried upon the
cross-members between the soaring girders.

The individual units looked delicate and precisely made as the
parts of a fine watch. Tiny spheres of white crystal, rolling slowly
upon curving crystal surfaces. Silently spinning disks, sliding levers, rotating cams, styles tracing grooves in moving plates. Flashing lights, interlacing multicolored rays, curved mirrors, lenses.
The only sound, from all of it, was a faint rustling whisper. It was,
Kane thought, the perfect mechanism.

Into an open, circular space they came, walled with the

machine's intricacy. Looking upward, Kane saw the red-and-green flicker of the crown of tubes, visible at the top of a great shaft.

The space was paved with hard white metal. At its center was a ring-shaped table, ten yards in diameter. The surface of its curving, yard-wide top was set with a maze of gleaming instruments: levers, key's, buttons, dials, knobs. It was the control board, Kane immediately guessed.

"Here is the earth," said the solemn voice of Vethlo.

His thin fingers played skilfully over keys and dials.

A pallid arm of silver radiance fell down the mile-deep shaft, from the crown of flaming, colossal tubes.

K ANE drew in his breath sharply, staggered with surprise. Out of the ray was born an image of the earth. No more than twenty feet in diameter, it hung within and above the ring-shaped table. Only in image, it must be, he knew, created at the focal point of the ray by some unguessed miracle of optical science. But its impression of solid, material reality was overwhelming. Every detail of continental outline, of mountain and river and forest and polar cap, stood out sharply, down to the limit of his vision.

"Why," Shiela gasped, "why, it's like a toy world!"

"It is," said the thin man. "The toy of the machine."

He moved a little around the table, to a white screen, four feet high, framed in intricate mechanism. Its surface had an odd, granular luster, as if composed of millions of microscopic, luminous cells.

"Here," said Vethlo, "we may have a closer view."

His hands ran over the dials and keys below the screen. Behind it, the image of the earth turned a little. It stopped with western America toward them; with the light gray blur of San Francisco, Kane saw, at the apex of a metal cone behind the screen.

Upon the screen, sharply dear, faithful to every vivid hue of sea and land and sky, appeared the Golden Gate and the city's familiar bay-front façade.

"It—it's real," whispered Shiela. "I was born there."

"So you were," said Vethlo.

Again he touched the controls.

The city shifted, raced toward them upon the screen.

And Kane was looking suddenly, upon a weathered, shabby two-story house on the slope of a hill, behind a wide yard red with autumn leaves.

"Our house!" breathed Shiela, in awed recognition. "Where I was born—"

Her words halted, as the door opened and a slender girl in red-and-white street pajamas came running down the leaf-strewn walk.

"Shiela!" gasped Kane.

It was indeed the girl beside him, as she must have been at fifteen.

A heavy, smiling man in business gray, finishing a black pipe, strode briskly into the picture.

"Dad!" whispered Shiela, voiceless.

"Daddy!" her own voice echoed from behind the screen, from the lips of that Shiela of the years ago. "You're late. Do hurry and wash for dinner. I helped Mildred fix it, today. And there's sherbet. Do hurry—"

The clear voice faded, as Kane felt a shudder of uncanny wonder mount along his spine.

"Poor Dad," whispered Shiela, her voice husky with remembered grief. "That was just before he took sick-"

The scene shifted again. They were looking through an open window, into the shabby house. They saw the heavy man, now lying in bed, flushed, haggard, smiling up at the slender, troubled girl, who stood at the bedside with a tray. The girl was Shiela again. Her voice came from the screen, ringing with forced cheer:

"Of course you are, Dad. Buck up. You're going to be as well as anybody."

"The screen went white again, and the weary voice of Vethlo said:

"But my master willed otherwise."

He looked at Shiela. She was biting her full lip to keep back a sob.

"Perhaps," he said, "you two recall the day when my master first brought you together."

The image of the earth turned again, behind the screen. And on the screen abruptly appeared the shops and the testing field of the Montel Foundation, at Maple Hill, A battered taxi stopped before the buildings. Shiela got out. She was four years older now, taller, trim in a business suit. She paid the driver from a thin purse. Anxiously, diffidently, she walked to the door.

Kane himself opened it for her, a powerful, black-haired giant in white overalls. His gray eyes lit at sight of her. A quick smile broke on his lean face.

"I'm looking for Mr. Montel," said Shiela's doubtful voice from the screen, "I'm the secretary he asked the agency to send."

Kane repressed an inward shudder of uncanny wonder as his own voice answered cheerfully.

"Good. I'm Montel. Come in." He made way for her. "Handle technical dictation? Getting off some factory specifications today." He looked at her weary face, and smiled again. "Had lunch, kid? Sandwiches back here, and a jug of coffee."

The picture faded, and Kane whispered, wonderingly:

"Three years ago."

"Time is nothing to the machine," said Vethlo, "save that it has already fixed the past, while the future is fluid, still, to be molded by the machine to my masters will."

His thin fingers ran over the controls. The bright globe of the earth spun behind the screen.

"I must show you now," he said, "how events are shaped."

S AN FRANCISCO was on the screen again: Market Street. Traffic was stopped by a cordon of police. The pavement was jammed with a waiting throng. A white sea of faces looked up toward an empty balcony.

Then a man was on the balcony, speaking eloquently.

"Senator Grenfell," whispered Kane.

Martin Grenfell it was, slender, erect, immaculately clad. He was gesturing as he talked. The movements of his mobile, small-featured face, of his whole body, as always, emphasized his words.

"The madness of war has seized upon us," the soft magic of his voice came from the screen. "I appeal to you, my fellow human beings, to fight it like a fever. Keep your sanity. Keep your feet on the ground, your eyes on the facts.

"The war can bring no good—not to any man living. The era of war for profit has passed. Every one of you must know the horror locked up in the new weapons that other nations have ready, and that America has ready. You must have read of the new atomic bombs, that can turn the green wealth of your fertile state into lifeless, burning dust.

"The war will kill civilization—perhaps kill the human race."

A desperate, terrible urgency had come into Martin Grenfell's ringing tones. Kane could read the fatigue upon his face, the bitter despair hidden under his words. He realized that the little statesman was throwing his last resource of effort into a grim, hopeless battle.

"And there is no need of war," the urgent voice went on. "This fever of war is simply mad emotion, born of blind circumstance. We must see the truth. We must recognize the war psychosis for the needless horror that it is. We must break the web of emotion, escape that psychosis.

"I had hoped that Kane Montel and Shiela Hall might help us, when they flew out to the moon, a month ago. Surely the pride of such a magnificent achievement would save the human race. Mankind could not conquer space, and then fail to conquer its own blind madness.

"But the two did not return. The *Spirit of Man* must have been lost in—"

As Martin Grenfell spoke from the screen, Vethlo had drawn a small instrument from a socket below. It was a small needle, set in an ebon handle. Its sharp point glowed with a sinister scarlet incandescence.

With an odd, sorrowful reluctance of manner, with pitying dread like a shadow on his long thin face, he pressed the dark handle into Shiela's hand.

"Touch the man Grenfell," his low voice commanded. "It is my master's will."

Shiela shrank back unwillingly, trembling.

Grasping her fingers in his thin, powerful hand, Vethlo pushed them forward, so that the ominous red point of the needle touched the breast of Martin Grenfell upon the screen.

"The will of Aru," said Vethlo, in tones that rang with dread.

From behind the screen came the sharp, repeated crack of a pistol. The urgent, appealing voice of Martin Grenfell was abruptly cut off. His arms were flung suddenly wide, in a gesture of convulsive agony. Then his small body staggered forward, collapsed. It hung limp and lifeless over the balcony rail.

Morbid excitement stirred the horror-stricken crowd below. Sudden confusion surrounded a man struggling wildly toward the balcony, waving a revolver.

"I killed him!" he was screaming, in tones of insane emotion.

"Damned pacifist! Grenfell was trying to bind America had and foot, and betray us to the enemy. I killed him. I'm glad of it!"

And then, as the scene faded, a policeman was taking away the gun.

"One illustration of the power of the machine of destiny," remarked Vethlo. His voice held a dull, weary regret. "Among other decisive factors in the shaping of this event, the rays influenced an unbalanced brain, by the release of a few free electrons in one neurone fiber."

He turned slowly to Kane, who was still dazed and speechless with horror.

"My master, Aru," he said, in the same tone of lifeless, hopeless regret "wills that you should participate in another illustration."

H E TOUCHED the intricate controls again. San Francisco retreated, until the Golden Gate was once more visible and the green-clad hills that framed the city and the bay.

One thin finger indicated a red button, upon the curving table, which gleamed like a malefic eye.

"Touch that," he said. "Aru commands it."

Voiceless with numbing, helpless dread, Kane mutely refused.

"Then allow me," said Vethlo, bleakly. "I do it upon your behalf, at the will of my master."

He depressed the crimson button,

Above the white city, Kane's eye caught the gray, fleeting motes of airplanes, wheeling high above the futile bursts of defending guns. He saw the little spurts of orange flame, the fountains of white dust, where bombs fell. He saw white buildings collapse and burn; he watched gray destruction consume the green upon the hills.

Dust lay where the heart of San Francisco had been. In patches of leprous ray, it shone oddly with prismatic glints too faint for the eye to analyze. It spread. Trees and buildings crumbled into it, consumed. And the last green, the last hint of life, was presently gone from the barren gray slopes above the empty bay.

Gray dust swirled and shimmered, down to the water's edge.

"That is six months in the future," said Vethlo. "The war, of course, follows the death of Martin Grenfell. The special factors eventuating in the destruction of San Francisco involve an electronic disturbance in the brain of an American general, and a consequent forgotten command which results in the annihilation of the Pacific fleet."

Kane and Shiela did not speak. Clutching hands, they looked each at the other, seeking mutual strength to sustain them against overwhelming horror.

"Now," the thin man asked them, "are you convinced of the power of Aru, through his machine?"

Numbed, shuddering, the two mutely shook their heads. A deep inner conviction told Kane that the horror of that last scene had been no trickery, no illusion, but dreadful truth. The omnipotence of the machine overwhelmed him.

Then we shall go to the dwelling of Aru," Vethlo announced. "From his own lips you will learn the fate he has designed for you."

His dark eyes rested upon Shiela's white beauty, somberly dreadful with a leering, half-hidden speculation.

### 6. THE LORD OF DESTINY

"DESCEND," said Vethlo.

He paused above a railed opening at the edge of the circular floor.

With Shiela beside him, Kane went down a short flight of steps, into a small, box-like chamber of white metal. Following, Vethlo motioned them to seats. He touched a knob on the wall. Kane swayed to sudden motion.

"Sort of subway," he commented.

The motion stopped. Vethlo rose.

"Follow me," he said. "Above is my master's dwelling."

At the top of the steps, Kane and Shiela came into a singular room. It took up, evidently, all the interior of one of the blue cones which they had seen burning against the dark remoteness of the cavern. Its curving, overhanging walls shone with a deep and eldritch blue.

The circular floor was vast and largely vacant.

In its center was a ring-shaped table, studded with intricate mechanism—the duplicate of the one they had just left. Within and about it, sharply focused, hung another image of the earth, a miniature planet, vividly real.

"A second control board," murmured Kane.

Vethlo, deliberately led them across the wide floor, and around the circular table, and so brought them face to face with the huge room's one occupant.

"Master," said Vethlo, in a humble, half-fearful tone, "these are the two adventurers from Earth."

Before the control-board, the man was reclining upon a long, luxurious divan. He was inordinately fat and the white, bulging rolls of his flesh were swathed in sheer fabric of fine-spun silver, woven with strands of scarlet. His hair was straw-colored, and fine as a woman's, and braided in an elaborate jeweled coiffure which capped the huge sphere of his head.

His features were all but lost between the pink-white masses of his checks. His small, half-concealed eyes were a light, hard blue-green, They twinkled maliciously. They were cunning, cruel eyes. And they were veiled with a baffling inhumanity that made them strange, unreadable, as the eyes of some animal.

He looked at Kane and Shiela, indolently, without moving to rise. He began to laugh. The heavy white masses of his flesh, beneath the silver-and-scarlet gown, quivered like jelly. His tiny, red-lipped mouth opened to a perfect round, and his gasping breath hissed through it.

The uncontrolled laughter went on until Kane's ragged nerves drove him forward.

"Aru?" he questioned grimly. "Call yourself Lord of Destiny?"

The laughter subsided a little. The bright, hard eyes were uncovered again. They stared at Kane. Then they leered across at Shiela, with a brutish obscenity in them that rocked Kane forward on his toes. His heart drummed in his big chest, and a white wrath urged him to sink his fingers in this soft flesh and rend the lecherous life from it.

"Recall yourself," spoke the low, weary voice of Vethlo.

Glancing at him, Kane saw that he gripped a small sphere, from which a thin golden needle projected menacingly.

Still quivering with rage, Kane restrained his hot lust to slay.

Harshly, he demanded of the inert man: "What do you want of us?"

Aru spoke. His voice was soft as his body, high-pitched as a woman's, cruelly caressing.

"Of you," he said, "only the joy of crushing you, with amusing agony. Of the woman—more."

The glittering, greenish eyes dwelt upon Shiela, indolently, in-

solently, burning with a singular, passionless avidity. The girl
shrank against Kane's arm, trembling. The rose of shame flooded
her fair skin, and then drained away until she was ghostly pale.
And her eyes were deep with the purple of terror.

Kane felt his muscles tensing. His gray eyes measured the
short distance to the divan, flashed a glance at Vethlo. One instant, to sink his hands into the white, shuddering thickness of
Aru's throat—

"Watch!" the soft voice called to Vethlo.

The thin man's weary voice spoke to Kane:

"My weapon is less insignificant than its size might lead you to
suppose. Its discharge of free electrons could burn you to a cin-
der, instantly."

"You should be warned of another thing, also," said Aru. His
fluid tones were limpidly sweet. "My life is guarded by the machine, so that fate will let no man strike at me. And the machine
is set, also, so that if any man should strike from an unguarded
sector, and harm me—his own doom will immediately find him.
Thus, Kane Montel, my life is doubly guarded. And my slayer
shall instantly die."

"Might be worth it," muttered Kane.

"Allow your weapon to convince the man," cooed the soft
tones, to Vethlo.

VETHLO'S thin hand grew tight on the black sphere. The
golden needle, pointed at Kane, glowed. It spurted purple
flame. Kane reeled to an avalanche of burning agony. He spun to
the floor, paralyzed by the torturing shock, his big muscles knotted with uncontrollable convulsions.

"Good," gasped Aru, through his laughter.

Kane staggered back to his feet, beside Shiela, his outraged
body quivering. His skin smarted cruelly where the force of the
weapon had struck; he caught a little odor of burnt flesh.

"I could have used a thousand times more power," Vethlo
informed him

"Well," muttered Kane, harshly. He looked grimly at Aru, who
was trembling and gasping with amusement. "What do you
want?"

Aru controlled his heaving laughter.

"You are convinced now," he asked softly, "of my power? Of
your helplessness?"

Kane bit his lip, grimly silent.

"Then," Aru's voice caressed him, "I shall tell you of my purpose for the woman. I shall tell you why your flight to the moon was impossible until Shiela Hall was upon the flyer, and then easy."

Kane and Shiela stood together, staring at him, They were mute, fascinated by the menace of his power and the pitiless beauty of his liquid voice.

"The earth," he said, "has been a game. Humanity has been a jest of mine. It has amused me long. But one tires of a game. The best jest wearies, if the point is too long delayed. And therefore the jest must reach its end.

"The war whose beginnings my servant has showed you will wreck the toy you call civilization, within this year. The atomic bombs—the gift of your father to the world, Kane Montel—will spread deserts of eternal flame.

"For a whole generation, a few men will linger on, always fleeing before the spreading terror of the dust. Then, when the last man is overtaken by the desert of atomic flame, in his stone hut by the polar sea—jest will be done.

"The jest on Earth," he said caressingly.

The pale greenish eyes rested upon Shiela again with a keenness that stripped the garments from her white body. The pink rolls of flesh hid his eyes, and his gross body quivered to gasping laughter.

Kane swung upon him, driven by resistless anger. But Vethlo was waiting, wearily alert, a yard behind Kane. The agonizing prod of his electron-ray stopped him again with its merciless paralysis.

Aru's laughter ceased, and he said:

"Yet one would grow weary indeed, with no jest at all, and no game to play. And therefore I have devised a new game, more clever than the old. This woman, Shiela Hall, is to play against me. Her beauty is to be the prize. Her hatred of me, her remembered love of you, Kame Montel, will give spirit to her play.

"It will be no brief game. It may last as long as the game of humanity has lasted. For I can give her life as long as mine—however unwilling she may be to accept it. Her beauty I can make eternal—a greater prize to play for.

"Nor will it be a simple game. I have devised intricacies—intricacies as delightful as the death of mankind by your father's gift, Kane Montel, which he believed to be life and happiness.

"But you, Kane Montel, have no further part in the game—save as you may live in the memory of Shiela Hall and make her playing keener. Therefore, if you will now bid her farewell, my servant will conduct you back to your doomed flyer—its name is part of the jest—so that you may attempt to return to the earth."

"Yes?" rapped Kane, staring at him with a curious fixity. "Yes?"

A dull blankness filled his mind. He was beyond emotion. Fear and horror and despair had been thrust from him by the grim necessity of mental self-preservation. His gray eyes gazed at Aru, with no light in them, and his numbed brain was hardly aware of the thing he was doing.

Vethlo was standing a yard behind him, with the deadly golden needle steady, covering him.

Kane's foot came up abruptly, kicked straight back at Vethlo's knee.

He heard the thin man's mute little cry of unendurable pain. He heard the dropped weapon clatter on the floor, even as he lunged forward toward the inert grossness of the monster on the divan.

The exultation of unexpected victory, for one sweet instant, rang loud in his brain. His fingers were already tensing, to sink into the fat throat of Aru.

But the puffy white hand moved a little on the divan's ornamental arm. And a sheet of crackling, greenish flame burst upward from a suddenly glowing ring in the floor, surrounding Aru with a shining wall.

Kane's headlong lunge carried him into that wall—and into an inferno of pain. His body was racked and twisted with the agony of a strange force that seemed to sear every nerve-fiber in his body. His joints cracked. Every muscle jerked into a tortured knot. The breath drove out of him. Fiery darkness blinded him.

He knew, in that instant of ultimate pain, that he had fallen across the abruptly glowing ring, inlaid in the floor, surrounding Aru. Agony completely paralyzed him. He was helpless to move out at the wall of greenish, consuming flame which rose from it.

He knew that the flame was killing him. For one long instant he struggled vainly to roll out of it. Then darkness cut short his agony.

When he came slowly back to awareness, he knew first that the strange fire no longer burned him. And he sensed a curious, silent tension that now filled the huge room.

As his mind rose slowly out of the abyss of pain and oblivion, the tones of a singular voice kept ringing in his memory. It was a woman's voice, but strong and deep. It rang with a melodious, golden power.

Out of the darkness it had come, urgently commanding:

"Stop the flame. He must not die."

That unfamiliar voice was like a golden thread that drew him back to life—and to the silent conflict that filled the room.

### 7. SHE—FROM THE SHADOW

WEARILY, Kane threw himself back upon his haunches and lurched heavily to his feet. He stood swaying, fighting away dizziness and nausea and pain. His skin was blistered, smarting, where the wall of flame had seared it. Every muscle in his big body ached from forced, agonizing contraction. And the fog of blindness still pressed in upon him.

"Stop the flame. He must live."

That strange voice of living, vibrant gold rang still in his mind. He peered about, drunkenly, trying to see who had spoken.

Dimly, he knew that Shiela was close beside him. He could feel her cool, tender hands against his tortured body, her quick strength aiding his lurching efforts to stand.

"Monty?" her low voice was in his ears, anxious, appealing. "Monty? How are you, Monty?"

"All—all right," he gasped hoarsely, through the leaden mists of pain. "Who—spoke?"

He was trying to see. Dimly, he could see the blue depths of the curving walls. He made out the brilliant disk, that was the image of the earth, floating above the ring-shaped table. Then his clearing eyes saw Aru, inert on his couch, not laughing now. And he saw the dark, thin form of Vethlo, sprawled moaning on the floor, nursing the knee that Kane had kicked.

His eyes found the white beauty of Shiela's anxious face, close to him. He smiled at her, feebly.

"Who was it spoke, kid?" he gasped again. "Who stopped—the flame?"

"There, Monty!" The girl spoke in a queer, awed voice. She pointed. "There—I don't know who—what—"

Kane looked where she pointed. He saw a thing so strange that at first he thought it an aberration of his disturbed vision. For a long moment he stared, until the sharpening detail convinced him that he looked upon reality.

Suspended just above the floor was a shape like a tremendous jewel. It was a faceted mass of purple shadow, three yards through. And within that bulk of shining shadow stood—or floated—a woman.

Or was she woman?

Kane shaded his uncertain, aching eyes, peering at her. Surely no woman ever looked so strange as she. Just as surely, none ever looked more womanly.

She was tall and slender and straight Her skin was golden, not yellow merely, but truly golden, and textured with the glowing, unwrinkled softness of eternal youth. Her hair was the pure white of silver, and abundant, and very long. Bound in scarlet, it hung behind her back.

Her eyes were large, long, somewhat oblique; they were black with the darkness of midnight.

She wore a long, sheer gown of lustrous black, touched here and there with crimson. Molded to the full rounds of her breasts, to the perfect columns of her thighs, it hid no curving beauty of her.

Kane searched her regular, classic features, pointed, elfin face, small, red-lipped mouth, straight nose, with delicately flaring nostrils. Something in them hinted of the immemorial past.

Yet nowhere could he find the key to her strangeness. No, the oddness of golden skin, snowy hair, archaic face—they could not account for it. There was some deeper, more elemental strangeness. Deeper—yet not so deep as her womanhood.

If she had belonged to some elder human species, he thought; human, certainly, but not *homo sapiens*. . . .

Then she moved. She touched a hot purple orb that clung to one long finger of her left hand—a singular ring. And the purple shadow fell away from her. It dissolved, vanished, like the ghost of a purple jewel.

The woman sank lightly to the floor. She swept toward him, with a walk that was pure, delicious rhythm

"Kane Montel," resounded the magic chime of that deeply golden voice that had saved him from the flame, "I cannot heal you now, but my hands can soothe your pain."

And her hands touched him. They were the color of pale gold, and slender; the fingers very long. They brushed his cheeks. They moved across his shoulders, down his arms, down his sides to his knees. They left a curious tingling coolness that blotted out the agony of his scared skin.

Kane's eyes fastened upon her ring. The white band was very thick, with six little knurled studs projecting from it. The huge set was purple, with its own inner fire. Its facets, he saw, were like the facets of the shadow-jewel that had enveloped her.

Was the ring a machine? Had it brought her here?

R ELAXATION crept over him in the wake of her easing hands. The wonder left him. He swayed backward a little, his eyes closing for an instant.

"Thanks," he murmured.

"Athonee!"

The name leapt from Aru's lips with the venomous suddenness of a striking snake.

"Athonee! Leave that carrion. It has played its part in my game. I have done with it. But I shall destroy it as I please, without aid from you, my mother."

His small eyes stared at her, insolently. A ruddy color was mounting into his gross flesh. Aru had been frightened, Kane realized, by the sudden apparition of this strange woman—by whatever means had brought her within that ghostly jewel-shape.

His blustering courage was just returning.

"By what right, my darling Athonee," his liquidly soft voice inquired, poisonously caressing, "do you return from the lower caves? Do you forget that I sent you there for ever? Do you forget that I am the master, that the power and the knowledge of the machine are mine?"

"I do not forget," replied the deep, golden voice, "that I created the machine long before that ill day when my reckless passion brought you into being, my son. I do not forget that I have one secret that gives me power over you, and that it is a secret which the machine can never tell you."

Aru heaved uneasily upon his divan.

"The machine," he blustered, "gives me all knowledge."

"Not all," said Athonee. "For it warned me of this day. And it gave me the secret that is today my strength. And, forseeing this day, I changed the machine. One sector of knowledge is closed to it, so that it can never reveal to you the secret, nor destroy my secret strength.

"There is one factor in your life, my son, a ruling factor, that the machine can not read to you—and can not change. The key to your doom I have kept to myself, against this fatal day. The cup of your life is in my hands, to spill as I choose."

Aru was staring at her. His skin had gone a sickly yellow-white. His pale greenish eyes were wide, protruding. His gross mass was trembling again, not with laughter but with fear.

Then he seemed to recover himself. With a swollen arm, he heaved himself upright upon the divan.

"My dearest mother," his liquid voice caressed the golden woman, maliciously sweet, "the key of my fate may be in your hands. But the machine his told me this: you will never destroy me. For you love me, Athonee—the machine told me that.

"Hate and rage and scorn you may mingle with that love. Yet always it will be strong enough to stay your purpose to destroy me."

His gross bulk quivered again with laughter.

"Perhaps you have power to destroy me, Athonee—though I believe in my heart that your secret is but a clever lie. But an old love makes you helpless. And now again I ask you why you came here. Perhaps you wish to play in this new game of mine?"

The woman Athonee had turned away from Kane and Shiela to face the man upon the divan. She stood very straight. A faint, ruddy glow had come into her golden skin. Her small, red mouth was hard with angry scorn, and her long black eyes were flashing.

"I have come to stop your cruel game, Aru," her golden voice pealed out, "or to change the rules of it. I have endured much of you, my son. But this new thing you call a jest is monstrous cruelty. The mad horror of it is enough to kill my love for you— and with it, you.

"I have come to forbid you to slay Kane Montel. And to forbid you to take this woman, Shiela Hall, for your monstrous game, unwillingly."

With the barrel of his silver-robed torso propped upright upon the divan, supported by the great soft pillars of his arms, Aru stared a long time at her. His veiled, greenish eyes were contemptuous, mocking. Presently he began to laugh again, so that he gasped and shook.

"You say unwillingly, my mother," his soft voice inquired, when the tremors of laughter had stopped. "But if Shiela Hall should come to me willingly, to play the game as I choose—what then?"

The golden woman slowly turned. Her long black eyes rested upon Kane and Shiela. Framed in the snow of her hair, her elfin, pointed face was softened with tenderest pity. A glitter of tears brightened her eyes.

She swung abruptly back to Aru.

"My son," she said, "if anything will make this woman surrender her lover, and give herself to you, then I will know that my life has failed. I will know that humanity can never rise above the machine. My greatest hope will be dead.

"Yes, my son, if Shiela Hall abandons her lover, to give herself willingly to you, then I shall return to the lower caverns—for ever. I will give you the secret that is my power over you, and unlock the sector of your fate closed to the machine. I will creep into the crypt that I have made to hold my bones, and die."

Very tall and very straight she stood, the red-bound silver of her luxuriant hair falling behind the darkness of her gown. The rosy light was higher in the gold of her smooth skin. Her fine shoulders quivered a little with emotion, and her long black eyes were burning.

"I made the machine when I was alone, when my last fellow-being was dead, here on the moon. I made the machine to lift your kind from the jungles to civilization, Kane Montel, and to guide it past the pitfalls of weakness and passion that destroyed my own kind.

"I failed, in the beginning, to take account of the weakness of my ill-fated kind, in myself. Yet I struggled ever to build finer qualities in the new race. And if I have failed, you must perish, Kane Montel and Shiela Hall, and your kind with you."

Her eyes swept back to Aru.

"Therefore, my son, I submit. You may test this woman as you choose. And if her love of this man is a thing so weak that you can break it with the machine, the she and her race are fit only to die. And I will give up my secret and go into my mausoleum."

## 8. "You Have Chosen . . . Go!"

A RU stood up.

Watching the gross, quivering bulk of him upon the divan, Kane had thought it hardly possible that he could stand, even against the feeble lunar gravitation. But the mountain of his white flesh held an unsuspected strength. He stood without support upon the great shuddering pillars of his legs. One massive arm pointed at Shiela Hall.

The girl shrank away from him—away from the inordinate grossness of that pointing arm, away from the coldly avid, mocking leer in his small, greenish eyes, Trembling, she drew close to Kane.

Aru spoke in venomed tones of honeyed caress.

"Shiela Hall, my darling," he said softly, "since my mad mother demands it, I will change my plans for finishing the jest of mankind, and for playing my new game with you. And I will offer you a choice."

He paused. Malicious promise glittered in his hard eyes.

Shiela quivered in the hard curve of Kane's big arm The beat of her heart against his side, seemed light and rapid as a bird's. She was breathless, tense, straining. All the color had ebbed out of her milk-white skin. Her wide eyes were staring at Aru, fascinated, purple with dread.

"Come to me, if you choose, Shiela Hall," cooed the limpid tones of Aru. "Give to me your beauty. Take me for your master, and accept my will in everything.

"Give yourself to me, and so long as your lover shall live, you may be mistress of the machine of destiny. You may guide the *Spirit of Man* safely back to Earth, with Kane Montel upon it. Upon the earth, you may order his fate—and the fate of all men— as you please.

"So long as Kane lives, you may rule destiny. You may give him anything you like: fame, wealth, position, continued health. Anything—save yourself. You may give him, if you will, another woman, to take your place in his memories."

Aru's laughter came again, softly malicious.

"I know that your thoughts are largely of Kane. Yet your power will extend over the lives of all men. You may, if you will, stop the threatened war. You may order for humanity such in era of peace and achievement and happiness as the earth has never known—for so long as Kane may live.

"For your own comfort. I offer you the freedom of my dwellings on the moon, and the full service of my retainers, the full enjoyment of my possessions.

"But when Kane is dead, I shall be free to finish the jest of man—and the new jest I plan for you—in the way of my choosing.

"That, Shiela darling, is one alternative."

Aru swayed ponderously forward. His gross arm still pointed at Shiela. His huge body was yet quivering a little with malicious laughter.

Crouching against Kane's arm, Shiela drew breath with a painful little sob. She watched Aru silently. Her eyes were still dilated with the purple of terror.

"The other alternative, my dear," the dulcet tones flowed on, "is to return to Earth with Kane Montel. Through the machine, I shall see that you reach Earth alive. I will promise you both life— for so long as either of you may desire."

Softly, mockingly, he chuckled.

"But let the machine picture for you the fate that shall be yours if you choose to leave me."

Aru turned. He lowered himself heavily into a sitting position upon the divan. The divan glided smoothly forward until his thick arms could reach the ring-shaped control table. Not without skill, his thick fingers moved over the innumerable keys and dials and levers.

Above the table, the vivid image of the earth slowly spun. And a screen before him glowed with colored life.

Kane and Shiela moved silently to face the screen. Stately, golden Athonee came to stand beside the divan. Vethlo, still lying on the floor, caressing his injured knee, looked up with weary darkness in his tragic eyes.

"Your return, my dear ones," the voice of Aru caressed Kane and Shiela.

K ANE saw upon the screen a dark horizon of tossing gray sea, misted with spindrift, whipped with sleet and rain. Heavy with sullen clouds, the sky was lurid with angry lightning.

Out of that mad sky, the silvery, humped spindle of the *Spirit of Man* came driving down. It plunged into the wild, green water. It sank and rose in a geyser of froth. It drifted. low in the water, sluggish. Evidently it was crippled, sinking.

Rocks loomed ahead, dark fangs shredding the sea to white ribbons. The impulse flyer drove down upon them, helpless. It was lost in a smother of snowy spray. It was tossed high, impaled on a spear of stone.

Kane glimpsed Shiela's white-clad slenderness, his own hard bulk. For a moment they were clinging to the low deck-railing, battered against the hull. Then they were carried away into the madness of the sea.

"Both of you, my dears, shall survive," the honeyed poison of Aru's voice assured them.

"Mark that well. Yet the elements shall separate you then—for ever. You, Kane Montel, shall reach the shore, swimming. And you, Shiela Hall, shall be picked up by a fishing-boat, and carried to the city of San Diego.

"Neither of you shall ever see the other again.

"Each of you, however—not quite believing me, for your love is stronger than reason—each of you shall ever hope to find the other.

"Your lives shall be long—full long. I think that neither of you shall ever wish to die—your irrational hope will be too strong for that. But even if you should, the machine can guard your lives for me. It can break the noose, and turn the blade from your throats.

"I need not show you all that awaits you, back upon the earth. A glimpse will be enough."

His gross fingers went back to the dials.

"Let us see Kane Montel," he said, after five years."

Upon the screen, with the same startlingly vivid distinctness, appeared the roaring canyon of a street in some great city. Chill twilight filled it. A bleak wind swept it with fine snow. A certain strangeness in the attire of the rushing crowd, in the design of the swiftly gliding stream-lined vehicles, convinced Kane that it was indeed a vision of the future.

He saw a man, stumbling against the human tide. Powerful he was, and yet half broken. His great shoulders sagged wearily. His hard face was drawn, lined, haggard. His thinning hair seemed prematurely white. His sunken eyes were burning wells of hope and grim despair.

His clothing, Kane saw, was pitifully ragged, inadequate

against the freezing blast that whipped him. The pinch of hunger was on his lean face, the blue of cold on cheeks and gnarled hands. His body was scarred, twisted, from old injuries.

Fighting the wind and the pressure of the hastening throng, he was lurching forward. His hollow, burning eyes peered anxiously into every woman's face, and ever they looked on again, with renewed hope and renewed despair.

Kane gazed at that tortured figure for a long moment, with pity welling up in him, before he recognized it for—himself!

The man turned toward the pavement. Lighting with abrupt joy, his eyes fastened on a passing vehicle. Crying out in hoarse eagerness, he leapt toward it. It paused. The woman in it seemed to have the form of Shiela. But when she looked out, her face was coldly strange.

The vehicle leapt ahead again. The man reeled upon the pavement, dazed with new despair. He staggered back, too late. Another rushing vehicle grazed him, flung him down motionless upon the pave, glided on.

Shiela, her terrified eyes fixed on the screen, cried out in pain.

"Never fear, my darling," the voice of Aru softly reassured her. "Your lover shall be hurt many times, through the many decades that he shall search for you. But killed—never.

"And now," the pitiless sweetness of his tones went on, "let us see the woman, Shiela Hall, when a few years more have gone."

His thick fingers moved with a curious, astonishing deftness over the intricate controls. Within the circular table, the bright image of the planet once more spun and shifted.

"The final war is ending now," said Aru. "For ten years the world has been devastated with atomic bombs, until no nation has the men or money or machines to make more of them. Everywhere are growing patches of gray, flaming dust—the leprous cancers upon the planet that were the gift of your father, Kane Montel. Yet in the twilight of man, there is war still—even if it must be fought with weapons less noble than atomic bombs. And we now look upon a battlefield of the dying planet."

T HE screen shone again.

A flat plain filled it, desolate and vast. All the background was filled with a smooth sea of dust. It was leprous gray. And it shone with a faint, prismatic glow—with the eternal destroying fire of disintegrating atoms of iron.

Beyond that plain, the sun was setting. Its blood-red disk rested upon the straight horizon. It barred the evening sky with rays of sinister scarlet, and washed the dead plain with a terrible, ominous illumination.

Upon the plain lay the rain of a city. It was dead, and the dust had overwhelmed it. Here and there loomed vast, dark piles of debris. Black, bare girders crossed the face of the sinking sun, like the naked ribs of a skeleton.

In the foreground, at the bottom of the screen, was a little barren, rocky eminence that the consuming dust had not yet reached. Among its gullies and boulders and gnarled thickets, Kane saw, were scattered the bodies of men newly dead.

Here and there was a smashed rifle or a broken sword. But no serviceable weapon or useful article had been left. The white, mutilated corpses were stripped of clothing. No wounded man had been left alive. Upon the hill was no movement save that of the black wings of vultures; nor any sound save their raucous cries.

Then a living human figure came into the scene. It was a thin woman, haggard with suffering and privation, bent with weary pain. She wore tattered rags. Her gaunt body was hideous with the scars of disease and injury.

Trembling with weakness, she staggered up the hill. She crept from one nude, silent horror to another, searching The sun sank. Red, dreadful twilight shrouded the leprous plain, the dead upon the hill, the vultures, the woman.

Quivering, his very soul ripped with the stark talons of horror, Kane drew his arm tight around Shiela's body and swung her away from the screen—for the woman had been Shiela.

"Don't look any more, kid," he muttered. "Too much."

"I think," said the liquid voice of Aru, "that you have seen enough.

"You shall have three days together as the *Spirit of Man* returns. Enjoy them well," he chuckled, "for you shall be separated when it falls into the sea. Through the rest of your lives—and they shall be long lives—you shall search, each for the other.

"You shall search, through the crumbling wreck of a doomed world. Cities shall be overwhelmed about you, nations burned in atomic flame. Horror and ruin and death shall creep upon you daily. Both of you shall know fear and injury and pain. Yet neither of you shall die—until I will it.

"Perhaps, Kane Montel, I will let you be the last man alive—overwhelmed when the dust reaches that stone hut by the polar sea. And perhaps Shiela Hall may be the last woman, searching for you among the dead of another continent."

The divan rolled back from the curving control-board.

Aru once more heaved himself upright A quivering mountain of gross flesh, he stood looking down at Shiela. She was still crouching close against Kane.

Again his swollen arm pointed at her.

"Now, Shiela Hall," came the high-pitched sweetness of his Voice, "You may choose.

"Remain on the moon, to be mine. Send your lover back to Earth, and be mistress of his destiny—and of all Earth's fate—for so long as Kane may live. Send all the good things you will to your lover; and peace and progress and happiness to all the earth.

"Or return with Kane. Enjoy three days with him, and lose him when you reach the earth. And spend a long life searching for him, ever hoping, ever frustrated by fate—by the machine of destiny. Search for ever, vainly, in a doomed, dying world. And die, when I allow you, with your lover never found."

S ILENTLY, Shiela's white face was lifted to Kane's. Her purple, terror-distended eyes dwelt in his. He took her tense shoulders, and swung her a little away from him, and looked long down into her face. No words passed between them.

Athonee was standing a little apart from them. Slender and erect and tall, she was a statue of pallid gold, striking in the scarlet-shot darkness of her revealing gown. Her pointed, elfin face wore a look of tenderest pity. Her long black eyes were fixed upon the two, big with suffering compassion.

Shiela looked up at her, suddenly, with quick, pleading inquiry upon her pain-drawn face. Some ray of understanding, Kane thought, passed between them But Athonee shook her snowy head.

Her golden voice pealed out, vibrant with pity:

"I cannot help you, Shiela," she said. "You must choose."

And Shiela looked back to Kane, and seemed to find in his lean face a serene strength.

She swung quietly to face Aru, and moved a little toward him, and told him, in a strong composed voice:

"I will go back with Kane.

The white mountain of Aru's flesh, for a moment, was perfectly still. His gross features sagged slowly. His mouth opened to a small, perfect ring of surprize. His greenish eyes widened unbelievingly.

Then, as he understood, rage mounted within him. Red flamed in his skin. His huge body trembled. His great hands doubled convulsively. His face was drawn into a buttery mask of fury that left his eyes greenish, malevolent slits.

"You choose to return," he gasped shrilly, "after all you have seen?"

"I do," said Shiela quietly, "because I love him."

"Then go back," said Aru.

The softness of his voice had turned to strident, dreadful rage.

"And you shall be torn apart when the flyer is wrecked. And you shall search for each other for ever. And the machine of destiny shall send upon you every agony, every extreme of suffering and despair, that it is possible for you to endure.

"You have chosen. Go."

## 9. THE SECRET OF THE CRYSTAL URN

"**W**AIT!"

The voice of Athonee pealed out, arresting, electric.

Aru wheeled ponderously upon her, his thin voice snarling—no caress in it now!

"And what now, my mother?" he demanded. "Have I not given her her choice?"

"If she had chosen you, my son," the stately golden woman replied, with strangely mingled elation and pain, "I should have said nothing. I should have opened to you the secret sector of your fate, and gone back to my lonely place to weep and die.

"But Shiela Hall chose her lover. Her love triumphed over the machine. It revealed a human power stronger than circumstance. It showed me that the machine is not the ruler, absolutely. It proved that my hopes for mankind have not been in vain."

Then the triumph in her tone seemed to stumble over despair. Her voice caught. She swayed toward Aru's couch. Her golden, statuesque form was suddenly tense with suppressed sobs. Her long black eyes rested upon Aru, and Kane saw in them a great devotion, and a greater agony.

"Aru!" her strong voice rang out, heavy with emotion. "My son!"

Her slender arms went out toward him.

Aru was heavily resuming his seat upon the divan. The anger had gone out of his puffy face. He looked up, slowly, indolently, at the stricken loveliness of Athonee, and laughed.

"See, my darling mother," his soft voice mocked her, "you love me still. You can never destroy me—the machine told me that."

"I do love you, Aru," breathed the golden woman, brokenly; "for you are my only son—the only son of all my race."

She paused a moment. Her long eyes watched him, glittering with tears.

"But Shiela Hall," she said, "has shown me how blind is my love for you, how selfish and weak."

She straightened against her burden of pain.

"I will not allow you to send these lovers back to Earth, to the dread fate you have pictured. I am going to take them with me, back to my own dwelling."

Aru's gross flesh went crimson again with rage.

"You cannot," he shrilled. "Remember, I am the master. You gave me the machine, and all its power."

Athonee lifted her slender golden hand, to show the thick white ring, with its tiny knurled studs, and the great, flaming purple jewel set in it.

"You cannot stop us," she said, "now."

Aru stared around him, and down at Vethlo's thin, black-clad form, still helpless on the floor. Under the jeweled crown of pale, fine hair, he shook his big head, in apparent baffled anger. But Kane had seen the fleeting little movement of his hand, on the divan's arm.

"Not now, perhaps," he shrilled. "But I can follow. And I will follow, my dear mother. I shall take them back—and mete out what doom I will to them and their race of crawling vermin. And you—"

For a moment he gasped incoherently, speechless with nameless passion.

"And you! I have had enough of you, and enough of your threats, that kept we from working my will upon you, long ago. Your secret power is a lie; I see it now—the machine tells me nothing of it."

His white, swollen fingers were writhing like thick snakes.

"Yes, my darling mother," the shrill edge of his voice cut at her, "I shall crush your body with my own hands, as I have long desired to."

"Come," Athonee had whispered to Kane and Shiela, while Aru still spoke. "Swiftly, before his slaves are here to stop us."

She drew them away from the divan, the table. Her long fingers were twisting the little studs upon the ring. The purple stone lit with a new, cold fire, and the magnificent ghost of it abruptly surrounded her, a faceted bulk of purple shadow. She mounted, floated within it, above the floor.

"Leap," she called. And her golden arms reached out to Kane and Shiela.

K ANE had seen Aru's covert signal. He was not surprized when the big room under the cone was swiftly thronged with armed men. Attired in gray garments fashioned like the black of Vethlo, they carried pikes and swords and the golden electron needles.

Aru screamed at them shrilly, in a strange tongue. Feet came drumming across the floor.

Kane lifted Shiela into the purple shadow. She floated out of his arms. He leapt upward. The golden hands of Athonee caught him, lifted him. And then he was drifting beside the two women, weightless, in a shining purple mist.

Athonee's golden fingers were again upon the tiny studs of the ring. The flame burned colder in the jewel's purple heart. The shining mist grew thicker. The blue walls of the conoid room grew dim. The charging men in gray were blotted out.

Kane drew Shiela behind his body. He shuddered, expecting a pike or a blast of electrons to come probing through the purple haze.

"We are safe—for the time," Athonee reassured him. "We are no longer in the dwelling of Aru. We have come upon a way where he cannot follow."

"We are—moving?" demanded Kane, incredulously, for he had felt no sense of movement.

"Not in the way you have known motion," said Athonee. "But we are now in the lonely place where I live."

She was twisting the studs upon her ring. The purple haze grew thin. The slight lunar gravitation embraced them gradually, drew them slowly down to the floor of a strange room. The shadow about them vanished, and the cold light died in the purple stone.

Kane was staring in mute wonderment at the ring.

Athonee, reading his curiosity, said:

"This is one heirloom I have from the scientists of my lost race. A small thing, it is yet the key to vast energies. It unlocks the way to a space beyond, from whose vantage-point distance is no barrier, but a bridge.

"Upon the way of the ring, the star you name Capella is as near to me as you are. I have stood upon the twilit strangeness of its seventh planet, and in many another far place—that was in the old, lonely days, before the machine was made, when the call of the new and the far came strongly to me."

For a moment she was silent, and a shadow was in the depths of her eyes. She wiped it away with a slender hand.

"My dwelling," she said, with a simple gesture of a slim golden arm. "You are welcome."

Kane looked away from the jewel, about the room.

Its paneled, many-angled walls were the green of jade. They were translucent, glowing with a deep, soft radiance. The vaulted ceiling was a high, flawless sky of green. The simple, oddly fashioned furnishings were silver and black—couches, small tables, heavy coffers.

On one table was a vase filled with crimson sprays of fern-like leaves. Beyond the wide arches of the unglazed windows lurked the wild darkness of the lunar cavern; black, cragged volcanic rocks, washed with a pallid violet light; dimly lit fields of scarlet, fungoid growth.

"Rest," said Athonee.

She pointed with a stately dignity to a couch; and Kane and Shiela sank into it, gratefully.

"We are all fatigued," she said. "I shall bring refreshment, and a lotion to aid the healing of Kane. We shall have need of all out strength and courage, when Aru comes."

"Then he can follow us—here?" asked Kane, anxiously.

"He can," said Athonee. "He will. But he and his slaves must trace the labyrinth of the lower caverns. The passages are too small for their ships. They must finish the journey on foot. They cannot arrive for a little time."

"Have you any weapons?" Kane demanded. "If I had a gun—"

Athonee shook her white head, slowly.

"None," she said, "save the secret that is my power over Aru. With that, I could destroy him.." She hesitated, reluctant, doubtful. "Yet, in my heart, I know that the machine has told him truth.

"Aru, for all his monstrous nature, is my son, my only son, and the only son of my dead race. I love him, despite all that he has done. I must forgive his cruel weakness, his mad passion, because I know they came from me. In my heart, I know that I con never destroy him, nor give my power to another.

"But I will show you the secret of Aru's doom, when we have had refreshment To prepare it I must leave you, for I dwell alone in this place of exile."

She glided from the green room.

K ANE took Shiela's hand in his. She relaxed beside him, sighing. Her eyes looked up at him, full of a weary, deathless joy.

"I'm glad you chose as you did, Shiela," he whispered.

"And I am, too, Monty," she breathed, "no matter what Aru does."

He tensed. His gray eyes stared through the green arch of a window, at the cragged black precipices looming above a dusky scarlet slope.

"Aru will do enough," he muttered, grimly. "Vicious. And powerful. Our hostess won't do anything. I suppose you can't blame her, since he's her son. I'd give a million for a good automatic."

Gray eyes darkened somberly, he shook his head.

"Wouldn't be any use, though, I suppose. Not against that monster, with his hands on the wheels of destiny. Not against that electron gun." He bit his lip. "Anyhow, the machine had this all settled, ten thousand years ago."

He squeezed her hand again.

"Nothing for it but to stick together, kid. See it through, best way we can."

Athonee returned, with a basket. She gave Kane a jar of fragrant ointment, and he went behind a screen to rub it on his seared, painful skin. When he had finished, he found a small table spread with such food as Vethlo had given them upon the ship: small scarlet fruits, brown cakes, purple wine.

A THONEE served Shiela and Kane, and relaxed upon another couch, opposite. Sipping wine, she looked at them thoughtfully. Presently, in a sober, deliberate tone, she began to speak.

"Before Aru comes," she said, "I must tell you the story of the machine of destiny, and of the lives bound up with it. A part of it you know already. And I must make the telling brief; for Aru will soon be here, to destroy me, and to drag you away to the cruel doom he plans."

Kane leaned forward anxiously.

"We can't fight him?" he demanded. "There's—nothing—"

Athonee shook her snowy head. Her long eyes dwelt somberly upon the two.

"My race is not your race," she went on, "though we are kindred species, cousins. Your fathers were yet brutes of the forest when my people reached their pinnacle of achievement upon the earth. Your fathers had not even the secret of fire, when my people had fashioned science into a perfect tool, when they had mastered natural forces yet unsuspected by your savants."

She touched the purple-jeweled ring upon her finger, and Kane bent forward in eager wonder.

"This ring is but one marvel they created. Its energy-field taps the cosmic forces of a higher dimension to bend the space in which we dwell. It makes distance but an imaginary concept."

She looked away from the ring, and a shadow fell upon her pointed, elfin face.

"But for all the wonder of their science and the splendor of their cities, my people never overcame the heritage of the brute. Their united strength was ever sapped by a strain of selfish emotion. And their new machines left them too little work to do, left too much energy to be spent in passion.

"Hatred gripped their civilization. Reason fell before animal selfishness. The tower of their accomplishment was overwhelmed in the red flood of war. And not one of my species, upon all the earth, survived the final war.

"A few of us, however, escaped the holocaust. We fled to the moon upon the power of the ring."

Her black eyes looked moodily past the two, back into the mists of time.

"Nearly a score of us came here, before the war was ended," she said, "both men and women. We should have found happiness. We came to carve out a new dwelling-place for our kind.

We brought the finest treasures that science had given our race—even the last great discovery, that came in the midst of the final war: the secret of life.

"We might all have lived here upon the moon, happy, secure, eternal. But we brought the curse of our kind to the moon; and after our dwellings were prepared, in these great caverns, our selfish, animal energy ran to mad waste. I need not tell the dreadful story of rivalry, jealousy, hate, murder."

Dark fires slumbered in her eyes.

"At last," she said, after a moody silence, "but two men were left—and I. One man was my lover. The other slew him, for jealousy. That man I slew, for revenge. Then I was alone upon the moon, and the last of my race."

Athonee was silent again for a little time, with pain upon her golden face. Her eyes still gazed into time.

"I was impelled to join my lover in death," she said slowly, "yet I had the desire to live. And the secret of life that we had brought from the earth made death needless, so I lived. And time passed by; and presently, to fill the emptiness of my life, I took up the science of my lost race, and went forward with it.

"And the day came when I conceived the machine of destiny. At first I saw it only as a means to knowledge, a window to the past and the future, a key to unlock the last hidden secret of the universe. And then I saw the possibility of control.

"The fathers of mankind were yet in the forest, then. They were peering ahead, but still held down by the chains of the brute. I built the machine to free them, and to lead them up the mad of civilization that otherwise—so I read from the machine—they could never have found.

"Through the unsensed, universal influence of the machine, I guided your race upward. Step by step, I aided them. I gave them fire, tools, metal, writing art. I would carry them, I thought, safely beyond the pitfalls of animal selfishness that destroyed my race.

"And thus I brought men to the state that is dimly recalled in your traditions of Atlantis. Upon a continent that has been overwhelmed, I lifted them to almost the level that my own people once reached. And I planned to lead them higher, to the perfection that I had dreamed of, in the ages of my lonely life upon the moon.

"But the weakness of my selfish passion rose again before me, as the machine had warned me that it might.

"Looking upon the earth, upon the race that I had lifted from the brute, I saw a man. I loved him. I consulted the machine, and it foretold all the terror that might be born of our love. And for a time I allowed the man to remain upon the earth.

"But in the end, animal selfishness overcame me. The ring carried me into the chamber where the man lay with a daughter of Earth in his arms. And presently he left her willingly, and came with me. I brought him with me to the moon, and gave to him the eternal youth, which only violence can destroy.

"You have seen that man," said Athonee. "His name is Vethlo."

Kane's mind went back to the thin man in black, with such a weight of suffering in his age-weary eyes.

"Here upon the moon, in the dwelling where I had been alone and lonely through ages so long, we loved. The machine had told me what our child would be, the hybrid of two races. But passion swept us on, and Aru was born.

"I knew all the sorrow and the pain that he could bring to us, and to his father's race upon the earth. And because of that, I prepared the thing that now gives me power over him. But Aru was the crown of my selfish love, and I could not bring myself to stop his evil course.

"ARU sought power as he grew up. He plotted to seize the machine, to make his father a slave, to exile me here—he wished to destroy me, but fear of my secret restrained him.

"All the selfish passion, the animal stain, of both races, seemed distilled into Aru. He was a creature of pure, malignant hate. From the beginning he knew that he was a monster, like no being that ever lived or ever would live. He knew that he must dwell for ever alone, and that he could never beget his kind.

"His loneliness, his monstrosity, filled him with bitterness for all others. He hated his father. He hated me for giving him birth. He hated all men, because they were unlike him.

"Therefore he plotted to humble me and his father, and to degrade and destroy humanity. I knew of his plot. But I loved him; I pitied him in his monstrosity and his pain. I could not move to stop him. And Vethlo had ever feared him.

"So he took the machine, and made his father a slave, and sent me here.

"And that is all—save that I will show you my secret."

Athonee rose. With majesty in the sweep of her walk, she

crossed the room, and knelt to open a long coffer. Her slender golden hands laid back soft wrappings. They lifted a tall, frail urn.

Slowly, handling the urn with utmost care, Athonee brought it back and set it upon the low table.

Kane and Shiela cried out together at its beauty, at its slender grace. It was of some milk-white, opalescent crystal, inlaid delicately with black and with scarlet.

"I fashioned this urn," said Athonee. "And I wove its life into the life of my son, upon the loom of fate. The breaking of the urn will start the machine of destiny, and the machine will forge a sword of fate to destroy my son.

"And when that was done, I closed a sector of life to the machine, so that it can never reveal this fact to another, and so that it can never cut the thread between the urn and my son.

"Many times, as Aru humiliated me and degraded his father, and destroyed the civilization that I had been building so long, as he overwhelmed the fair continent that you know as Atlantis, and played at his cruel jests—many times I have been moved to hurl down the urn upon the floor.

"And yet I cannot," her voice choked; "I cannot destroy my son."

And she set the urn farther back upon the table, as if to shield it from any accidental mishap.

Then her small, pointed face went rigid with surprize. Her red mouth opened to a tiny circle. For a moment she inclined her snowy head, listening. In the distance, Kane heard the rattle of a dislodged pebble, the clatter of metal, the tramp of many feet.

Consternation mounted to Athonee's face.

"Aru!" she whispered, voiceless with dread. "Already he, comes, with his slaves—to destroy me, and to drag you away to the fate he plans."

## 10. "My Son . . . Destroy Me!"

K ANE'S gray eyes fell speculatively upon the slender beauty of the crystal urn. Was it possible that the life of the jesting master of destiny was bound up with this delicate perfection in white and black and scarlet, so that the end of the one would doom the other?

His mind put aside the strangeness of it, to accept the fact. For it was no stranger, after all, than the machine of destiny, and the wonders he had seen within the machine.

His gray eyes narrowed a little, suddenly. His lean chin set and his big body abruptly tensed.

Athonee's quick glance read his thought.

"Kane Montel," she swiftly warned him, "do not touch the urn. You could not break it. Attempting to harm it, you could only destroy your own life. When I fashioned the urn, fearing that it might be shattered by another, accidentally or maliciously, I safeguarded it with the machine of destiny.

"You should know, too, that the life of my son is guarded by the machine; and that whosoever slays Aru shall immediately be stricken down."

Kane sank back wearily upon the couch, beside Shiela. His lean face was haggard with baffled desperation.

"Nothing," he muttered bitterly. "Nothing we can do. Everywhere we turn the thing was all settled, ages ago, on that accursed machine."

The swift tramp of feet was louder, now. Kane heard low, quick voices, ringing through the green arches of the unglazed windows. Athonee rose. She faced the broad doorway, looking out upon twilit scarlet garden and soaring volcanic cliffs.

The doorway was suddenly filled with men.

"Salutations, mother, darling," the liquid voice of Aru floated into the room. It was soft, mockingly endearing.

Kane and Shiela sat motionless upon the divan, staring at the door. Kane's arm was about the girl's shoulders. She trembled against him. For a desperate, frightened moment, her eyes looked up at his face. They were wide and purple with fear.

Athonee stood near them, watching the doorway. Her tall, slender body was rigid. Despair had fixed her golden, pointed face. Her long black eyes were molten with pain.

Aru led the men crowding through the arch of green crystal. He had changed his sheer robes for fine, linked mail of gleaming purple. He was a ponderous, lurching mountain of puffy white flesh. His small, greenish eyes glittered with malevolent amusement from the white rolls of his face.

Fifty men followed him. They wore close-fitting gray. For weapons they carried swords, pikes, golden needles of flaming death. Behind Aru they spread out across the floor, alert, menacing.

Among them, Kane saw Vethlo. The thin man's knee, evidently, was still hurt from Kane's kick; for he was sitting upon a crude litter improvised from pikes, carried between two men. In his lean fingers Kane glimpsed the golden needle of his electron gun.

So this somber-eyed, white-haired man, then, with his singular look of mingled youth and age, was the beloved of Athonee, and the father of Aru. Watching him, Kane saw his eyes fasten upon Athonee's golden loveliness. A sudden warm eagerness flooded them. And that warmth was instantly chilled with cold despair.

The dark, sad eyes crossed Kane's. There was a little flicker of greeting in them, but nothing of resentment. And Kane knew that the man harbored no ill feeling for that painful kick upon the knee.

Vethlo looked from Kane to the purple-mailed bulk of Aru standing just before him. Kane was puzzled by the swift motion that filled the dark eyes of this weirdly ancient man, as he looked upon his son.

There was love, Kane thought; in agonizing tenderness. There was fear, a humble, shuddering dread. But there was something beyond these, and greater—a slumbering flame, intense, yet veiled, hidden. What could it be? Resentment, Kane guessed. A smothered hatred, ancient and bitter.

Breathless, speechless, stricken, Athonee stood eyeing Aru.

He swayed across the green room, toward her. He stopped, when there was only the small table between them, with the peerless grace of the crystal urn resting upon it. Heavily, he planted himself. He braced himself with a long staff, jeweled, scarlet-lacquered.

His small, hard eyes looked across the urn, at Athonee. The buttery masses of his white face were twisted into a leer of peculiarly brutal, malicious triumph. His inadequate scarlet mouth opened, and he began to laugh. The grossness of his flesh shuddered against the tight purple mail.

"My darling mother," he gasped, as the spasm of laughter subsided, "have you no tongue to bid welcome to your only son, when he comes after so long to your dwelling?"

His words faded again into pitiless, mocking laughter.

THE quivering restraint of the golden woman broke abruptly into choking sobs. She swayed unsteadily around the small table, to Aru.

"My son," she cried, in the low, dead voice of heart-break. "Aru, how can you be so, when you are my only son?"

She reached him, and tried to throw her slim, golden arms about him.

The ponderous thickness of Aru's puffy arm came slowly up. With deliberate, brutal strength, his great white hand struck the woman's face. She reeled backward from the blow, and stumbled, and fell headlong to the floor.

Aru laughed softly.

"So, my dear mother," he said, "you love me still. The machine tells me that you love me too much to destroy me, even if indeed you have this boasted secret, which I believe is a lie."

Glancing at the thin form of Vethlo, drawn half upright on his rude stretcher, Kane was amazed at the agony that twisted his long face. His mouth was twisted, trembling with some inner conflict. His dark eyes were pools of pain.

Pale and silent and quivering, Athonee gathered herself upon her knees. She made some little effort to rise, and then sank back to the floor. Her pointed, small face looked up at the purple-mailed bulk of Aru, haggard with ultimate despair.

"My son," she whispered brokenly, "destroy me if you will. I cannot use the secret."

Aru wheeled ponderously upon his scarlet staff .

"The machine told me that, dear mother," he said, in fluid tones of malicious caress. "And the machine is master of events, and I am master of the machine.

"I am going to destroy you, my mother, as I should have done, time and time again, but for my foolish fear of your lies. So, my darling, compose yourself to die. And prepare yourself to endure in dying a little pain, for I shall slay you with my own hands, in a manner whose sweetness I have long foretasted.

The golden woman shuddered a little, on the floor. Her black eyes remained fixed upon the face of Aru. On her face was mute agony, and she made no sound.

Aru turned slowly. He looked at the lean, black-clad form of Vethlo, heaped upon the stretcher, clutching the golden needle of his weapon. And the thin man, Kane saw, brushed the conflict and the agony from his face as Aru turned, so that only the shadow of old pain was left for Aru to see.

"My father," said the sweet, high voice, "may live on for a time, and serve me. He shall remain my slave and the master of my slaves. For he fears me, the machine tells me. He knows that my slayer will die with me. And the machine has not warned me of danger from him."

He turned to Kane and Shiela. They were still upon the couch, trembling in the silent embrace of despair.

"When my mother is dead," his venomously sweet voice assured them, "I shall take you both back to my dwelling. And I shall seek in you the cream of my jest with mankind."

Releasing Shiela, Kane surged up from the couch. Bare hands clenched, he lunged savagely toward Aru. He realized the blind futility of the attack. But his restraint could endure Aru's torture no longer. Outraged senses drove him forward, heedless, unreasoning.

Aru moved his white hand. Indolently, he signaled. Vethlo lifted the golden needle of his weapon. Purple, crackling flame leapt from it. Kane was hurled to the floor by a resistless flood of pain.

Aru chuckled softly.

"Kane Montel," he said softly, "it is well that you struggle against me. It amuses me. You are playing your part in the jest, as I planned that you should play it, long before the day of your birth.

"You may have the pleasure of resisting me again, and many times, in the years to come, as we finish the jest—you, and Shiela, and I."

He chuckled again.

Kane sprawled on the floor. His mind was numb with despair. His twitching body was paralyzed with pain beyond endurance. Shiela dropped to her knees beside him, seeking in vain to ease his agony

Aru looked slowly away.

"Now," he said, "I shalt kill my mother—"

"No!" the word rasped from Kane's tortured throat.

His muscles trembled and cramped as he struggled in vain to drag himself back to his feet. The flame from Vethlo's golden needle struck him again, and hurled him beck into helpless; agony.

"I know that my mother is beautiful," said Aru, softly, "and ever it his pleased me to destroy beauty." His hard, small eyes were gloating upon the tall grace of the crystal urn. "This trinket," he said, "my mother his long treasured. And I have long wished to destroy it, because it is beautiful, and because it is precious to her.

"Now I shall shatter it, as I shall shatter her beauty."

Deliberately, he picked up the flawless urn. His great, puffy hand held it high. Glittering with malevolent amusement, his small greenish eyes went to the crouching form of Athonee. He chuckled mockingly.

Desperately, Athonee was shaking her white head. Her lips moved frantically, but emotion held her speechless.

"Does it please you, darling," Aru inquired softly, "to see how you are to die?"

"Stay, my son!" the urgent appeal broke forth at last. "Don't break the urn! Your doom—"

A GLEAMING miracle in crystal, opal-white and ebon and scarlet, the urn had already left the fingers of Aru. It spun down toward Athonee. It struck the floor, and dissolved with a musical, tinkling crash into a momentary spray of bright fragments.

"My son!" moaned Athonee.

Aru was striding heavily toward her, his huge, white, thick-fingered hands were twitching with a hideous avidity.

Kane heard a gasping, muted cry of agony from Vethlo. He saw the thin man come rigidly erect upon his stretcher. Vethlo's long face was contorted with the agony of a supreme conflict. In the instant that Kane looked, that conflict was resolved. Agony gave way to grim purpose.

The thin, knotted hand brought up the golden needle. Held steady and true, it pointed at the striding bulk of Aru. A blinding torrent of purple flame gushed from the needle's point.

Aru, within his tight mail, stopped, stricken. His big body was driven a little backward. It shuddered convulsively. Purple flame enveloped it. Smoke burst from the jeweled crown of fine, pale hair. The odor of burnt flesh swiftly filled the room. The big body slumped and fell heavily upon the floor.

Aru lay motionless, a mountain of seared flesh, smoking.

"My son!" wailed Athonee. "He is dead."

A strange, hoarse cry of terror drew Kane's eyes to Vethlo. Agony twisted his long face. He tried vainly to hurl away the black globe of his weapon. It seemed to burst in his upraised hand. Kane heard a loud report. Vethlo was enveloped in a momentary flare of violet flame.

For an instant afterward, he sat erect, quivering with hysteria.

"I have killed Aru!" he screamed, shrilly. "I killed my son, and I must die! The machine has decreed that the killer of Aru must die!"

Then pain and weakness overcame him. His thin body tensed for a moment, and then fell limply back upon the stretcher. The shattered globe of the electron gun fell from his inert fingers. In a low, broken voice he gasped:

"Athonee, my love! Come to me, before I die. I love you still, Athonee. And I am dying, because I killed our son, for you."

Pale and silent, the golden woman got uncertainly to her feet, and walked unsteadily to the stretcher. Vethlo reached out his hand, as she came near, and she took it. His lips moved. A brief, hoarse sound came from his throat. Then his thin arm stiffened and relaxed, and Kane knew that he was dead.

Athonee stood holding the limp hand. "How blind I was," she wailed. "His hate was the hidden factor that the machine could never reveal."

She stumbled back to Aru, and dropped beside the inert mass of his body.

"My son!" she sobbed, her voice high and dreadful with grief. "My son is dead."

### 11. "MIGHTIER THAN THE MACHINE!"

KANE and Shiela were walking, many hours later, in the scarlet, unfamiliar garden below the green, domed mass of Athonee's dwelling. They were bathed in a cool, violet dusk. Beyond the strange, graceful plants loomed the black and rugged cavern walls, broken here and there by the mysterious darkness of farther spaces.

Kane's big body was bandaged. He walked a little stiffly, and winced now and then from the pain of an unaccustomed movement. But his lean face was smiling, and his mind was less upon his injuries than upon the laughing girl beside him.

"It's hard to realize it, Monty," she whispered once. "But it's all over, like a bad dream. With Aru dead, it must be."

Her hand closed on his, with a quick, light pressure.

"Does seem queer, kid," he said, "to think we can have each other, for keeps, without fate making a joke of us. Hard to believe."

Then he saw Athonee, coming through the delicate scarlet fronds.

Her tall, golden slenderness was once more erect. She had put on a simple robe of the same snowy whiteness as her hair. Her small, pointed face was still marked with grief, but it was composed. Her long dark eyes smiled a little, as she greeted the two.

"My dead are put away," she told them quietly. "The servants of my, son I have sent back to his dwelling. I shall follow them soon, to take my old place beside the machine of destiny."

Still holding Shiela's hand, Kane faced the golden woman earnestly.

"What's going to happen, now?" he asked her. "All those dreadful things that Aru showed us—must they take place? The death of Martin Grenfell? The War? Must the world be destroyed with these atomic bombs?"

"About Monty and me?" asked Shiela, her voice low with anxiety. "Must our lives be what Aru showed us? Must we be separated when we get back to Earth? Must we spend all those terrible years searching for each other? Must we endure all that suffering?"

Athonee smiled a little, and shook her white head.

"The machine still rules the future," she said. "I can change all that Aru showed you. I can save the life of Martin Grenfell. His efforts, and your triumphant return from the moon, will avert the threatened war.

"I will send lasting peace and new happiness with you, back to Earth."

Her somber eyes went past them, into some far space of the lunar caverns.

"I will not let the machine into another's hands, again," she said. "I will make it serve its first purpose, of lifting your race to true manhood."

"A terrible interlude this his been, since I surrendered the machine to my son. But I think the terror and the pain of it have burned all the weakness and passion and selfishness, all the animal, out of me. I can go ahead now, untroubled, toward my old aim."

"But we two?" asked Shiela, apprehensively.

And Kane said, "What of us?"

Athonee smiled again, quietly.

"I shall now carry you back to your flyer," she promised them. "And I can assure the *Spirit of Man* a safe flight back to Earth, and a happier landing than my son showed you.

"And I shall send you happiness on Earth that will be full reward for all your sufferings. You both deserve reward," she said softly, with a tender radiance in her long black eyes, "for it was your choice that won the victory. It was your love that proved mightier than the machine of destiny, and changed the course of fate."

THE END

# Death's Cold Daughter

*Thrilling Mystery, September 1936*

## CHAPTER I

### "They Kill With Cold"

SEND MAN WITNESS TRIAL NEW STRATOSPHERE
ROCKET PLANE STOP SENSATIONAL DE-
VELOPMENTS EXCLUSIVE STORY ASSURED.
LOGAN FERRIER, SECRETARY
STRATOSPHERE EXPLORERS ASSOCIATION
BLACK MESA, NEW MEXICO

THE TELEGRAM CREATED A LITTLE STIR IN THE EDITORIAL OFFICE. "Denny," the chief said, "nobody ever heard of this association before, and maybe I'm sending you on a wild goose chase. But we've checked up on Ferrier, and he's well known. Seems he knows more about the liquefaction of gases than any other scientist in America. He's too big to ignore. So you're going to New Mexico."

Dennison Trevor accepted the assignment with enthusiasm. The lean, dark-haired young newspaperman was eager for this first trip west of Philadelphia. His newshawk instincts sensed in the telegram a promise of adventure.

Dr. Logan Ferrier met his train at the lonely Black Mesa station. The scientist seemed queerly excited. His slight, stooped body was tensed as if to some grim expectancy. In the strained frown that puckered his thin, pale face Denny Trevor thought he glimpsed the shadow of an unholy dread.

In the waning purple and gold light of the desert dusk, Ferrier drove him in a small roadster out across the flat brown waste of the mesa. The lonely road was a straight, dark ribbon. It ran on and on, across a lifeless tableland, toward jagged, far-off purple mountains.

"What's up?" Trevor asked curiously at the first opportunity. "Tell me about the Stratosphere Explorers Association."

At the wheel, the little man started nervously, and then explained.

"The association was formed two years ago. Jimmy Adcock was the organizer. You may have heard of him—used to be a barn-storming pilot. He has invented a rocket motor that can carry a plane above the stratosphere. Two years ago he made his first rocket flight, in an old crate of his own. He made a remarkable discovery, that until now we have kept from the press. He brought back pictures of a fragmentary solid or semi-solid stratum above the stratosphere. With his story and those pictures, he got four of us to join with him in forming the association, for the purpose of developing the rocket plane and making a more ambitious flight."

"A solid stratum!" murmured Trevor. "Another flight—when?"

"You are late," Ferrier informed him. "Jimmy Adcock took the new stratoplane on its first flight this morning. He may be down before we get back to the field."

The field was a level stretch of the lonely mesa. At one side, beneath a green beacon blinking on a metal tower, was a little group of buildings: a huge sheet-metal hangar, shops, laboratory, garage, and a sprawling adobe residence. Beyond, the flat desolation of the mesa was broken with dark outcroppings of age-shattered stone and the knifelike gashes of dry arroyos.

THE three remaining members of the association, in a little group with four mechanics and an aged Chinese cook, were waiting at the edge of the field for the ship to come down. Mild, slight Dr. Ferrier presented them. Arthur Randolph, Chicago financier, hawk-faced, harsh-voiced. John Lane, big, booted Westerner, in vest and white Stetson; the owner, Trevor understood, of all the reach of desert to the railway and beyond. Alan Morridon, tall, silver-haired, a precise-voiced Boston attorney.

Night had come as they waited. Cold and motionless the stars burned in the moonless desert sky. But suddenly two among them moved, a red star and a green. And down from the frosty dark rolled an increasing thunder of supercharged engines.

"It's the stratoplane," cried Ferrier. "Lights!"

Floodlights drenched the field, and the great plane dropped out of the night. It touched too hard, bounced, came with roaring motors toward the hangar. Dark and ominous against the lights as some mighty bird of prey, it stopped. Four great engines coughed and died; four mighty propellers flickered and stood still.

Trevor was foremost in the little eager group that ran to meet the ship. The silver wing spread high over him, like a vast roof. He reached up to touch the sealed, streamlined cabin. Its white duraluminum was colder than ice. It stung him with the deadly chill of outer space.

The newshawk stepped back, rubbing his cold fingers in the palm of the other hand. The stratoplane was like a monstrous living thing from a metal world of cold. It seemed for a moment no willing tool of men, but a creature of alien menace.

The little crowd waited, tense-faced, silent.

"Trevor," whispered Ferrier, "those are the rockets." His thin hand pointed at the flaring muzzles jutting from the edge of the great thick wing. "Adcock's invention."

His voice stopped at a little sound from the cabin. The group surged forward anxiously as a small sealed door opened in the glass-and-silver hull. A lank man swung out.

Eager confusion greeted him.

"Adcock! How'd you make it?" . . . "Rockets work?" . . . "Find anything in the sky?" . . . "odd work, Jimmy! Come on, tell us, what did you find—"

Moving with the slow heaviness of exhaustion, the rangy pilot swayed to the ground and carefully locked the small door behind him. His hand with the key shook. He was shivering in his bulky togs.

"Fire!" came a croaking rasp from his blue lips. "Got a fire? Cold—"

His voice faded to a papery rustle. He toppled stiffly forward, and Trevor caught him in his arms. Lane, the big rancher, took his feet, and they carried him off the field into the thick-walled adobe dwelling.

In the heavy-beamed living room, before a roaring blaze of piñon logs, they stripped off the flying togs. Jimmy Adcock was a long, lean-stomached redhead. His bony extremities were blue and goose-pimpled with cold. Trevor and Lane rubbed his body, before the crackling fire. The Chinese cook, Charlie Moon, brought hot water and Ferrier began to pour it, mixed with whisky, through the pilot's lips.

A ND Jimmy Adcock at last opened dare-devil greenish-blue eyes. He tried to grin, and sat up uncertainly on the couch they had dragged before the fireplace. He shivered again.

"Cold," his blue lips whispered. "Never been so cold—" He took the steaming tumbler of whisky-and-water out of Ferrier's hand, and gulped it thirstily.

Trevor caught the greenish eyes, as he turned. Something in them chilled him to the soul. It was the shock of pure, overriding terror. Those eyes had seen something that had seared them forever!

Trevor was glad when they looked back into the fire.

The pilot crouched toward it. He thrust out bare shivering arms as if to embrace the blaze. The others were all retreating from the fierce scarlet radiation. But Adcock seemed to drink up heat like a sponge—and he was still cold.

"Cold!" his whisper rasped above the crackle of the fire. "I've been to a world of cold!" His greenish, horror-chilled eyes flashed to the others again, from the fire. "This time I've got the proof. Solid, material proof!"

Excitement whispered through the little group. There was an eager motion forward against the savage radiation from the fire.

"Proof?" Arthur Randolph's voice was harsh and anxious. "Proof of what?"

"Proof of all I told you when you were putting money in the association; proof of all my pictures showed," said the flier, in a calm, weary voice. "There is a world of crystal frost above the stratosphere. It is inhabited—by weird, uncanny intelligences of pure cold! Cold. . . . Things of cold. . . ."

The voice sank away, the terror-seared eyes looked back to

the fire.

"They almost had me," the ghostly rustle of his whisper came again into the strained, expectant silence. "It was a close thing. They nearly got me. . . . They kill with cold. . . . But I got away with the proof. It's out in the plane."

His white face seemed to congeal with horror, as he sat for a moment silent. He shuddered abruptly, then whispered:

"But they are furious, those creatures of cold. They'll follow, if they can. And they kill—!"

Ferrier was holding out the tumbler again.

"Drink it, man!" snapped Arthur Randolph harshly. "Drink it, and get yourself together. Tell us what happened. And then we'll have a look at your proof."

The pilot accepted the steaming glass with a steadier hand, gulped it, and once more turned his horror-filmed eyes upon the listeners.

"I'll tell you what happened," his tired voice said. "I must, some time. Then you can go and look in the plane. What I have there will remove any doubts."

"Your rockets?" A curious anxiety sharpened the precise Bostonian accent of Alan Morridon. "They performed satisfactorily?"

The redhead nodded wearily.

"Up to ninety thousand feet," said Adcock, "they did. I went higher after that—but I didn't have time to watch the instruments."

"And you actually found," put in the mild, insistent voice of Dr. Ferrier, "that there is a solid stratum above the stratosphere?"

A GAIN the pilot nodded heavily. "I found drifting masses solid enough to land a plane on."

The pale little scientist clenched his hands excitedly.

"That justifies my theory of the molecular cohesion of gases at extreme lows of temperature and pressure!" he exclaimed earnestly. "My theory of gas crystals will be the beginning of a new physics, a new chemistry. It opens the way to a world where new laws of science prevail—"

"Pardon, Doctor!" broke in Arthur Randolph's voice abruptly. "Shall we listen to Adcock's story?"

"Of course! At once!" said the mild little man, eagerly. "I'm sorry if my enthusiasm carried me away, but this thing is tremendous! Please, Mr. Adcock, go on!"

The chilled greenish eyes came slowly from the fire.

"I'll tell you about it," said Jimmy Adcock. "But I'm sorry that I must. Because you will believe me, after you have seen the proof. And nobody who believes me will ever feel very secure again— not on this earth." The haunted eyes flashed toward the door. "There's real danger. I told you—they will follow, if they can. I don't know whether they can, for the air here must be as hot to them as a furnace is to us. But I know that they have descended far enough, before, to carry off a human being. I *know!*"

## CHAPTER II

### THE WORLD OF FROZEN FEAR

J IMMY ADCOCK relaxed wearily against the end of the couch. His eyes were still filmed with that disturbing terror-glaze. Hawk-faced Arthur Randolph had drawn up a chair. John Lane squatted on boot-heels, automatically manufacturing a brown cigarette. The others, white-haired Morridon and little Ferrier, Trevor and Charlie Moon, and the four mechanics, stood in an intent semi-circle, eagerly waiting.

The pilot's low, husky voice spoke with a taut, tired haste, as if the thing he told were an agony that he hurried to escape.

"I tested the air equipment and our other devices as I rose," he said. "The self-adjusting props worked admirably, and the super-chargers got me to forty thousand feet. I cut the motors there, and opened the rockets.

"I reached eighty thousand before I saw anything. The world had become a pit of blue-grey mist under me. Everything beneath was lost, mountains and all. The earth was just a ball of blue haze. There above the stratosphere the sky was purple-black, except for a pale circle around the sun. Stars were coming out above the horizon.

"I knew what I was looking for. And I saw a glow of faint blue high in the distance, like a wisp of pale cloud. I climbed toward it, with the full power of the rockets. It became more distinct as I climbed; yet it remained somehow unreal, like a world of frozen blue mirage.

"I remember when I passed ninety thousand feet. The rockets

were functioning perfectly. Outside the cabin it was a hundred below, but the defrosters kept the windows clear and the heaters kept me comfortable enough—it was afterwards that I got cold."

He shivered, and leaned toward the fire.

"I'll never forget the sight of that frozen world, when the plane came up over its rim. A drifting island, scores of miles long—I don't know how big. A congealed mass of gas crystals. I guess Ferrier's theory about the upper regions is all right.

"At any distance it is transparent, almost invisible. It still looks unreal as you get close. The landscape is the weirdest you can imagine. Crystal. Everything is crystals of pale, glittering blue—crystals of pure cold. It leaps into spires and peaks and jagged pinnacles. Sharp edges and cruel points jut at you. There's nothing level or smooth or soft anywhere. It's a world fanged with frost.

"At once I knew that it was the same island where I took the pictures two years ago. In the distance I recognized the same blue mountains. They are ragged and precipitous as the mountains on the moon.

"I flew over them, toward the hidden place where I got the picture of the girl. The place where *they* live! Beyond the mountains there's a sort of temple—if you can imagine a temple larger than any building on the solid earth, its pillars and soaring arches all of ghostly blue frost. Cold haunted that temple like a hostile, deadly spirit. I was already stiff and shivering, in the plane.

"I MANAGED to land in a space before the temple where the pinnacles weren't too high. They would have torn the ship to pieces, if they had been solid enough. But they are somehow unsubstantial. The plane plowed through them, and sank until it was resting on the fuselage and wings.

"As soon as I landed—*they* came! I can't describe them. They are greenish. They fly. Perhaps they have no definite shape. Perhaps their bodies are half invisible. But they are cold. Cold is their very nature. And they kill with that cold!"

Adcock made a little shivering gesture, and Ferrier gave him the tumbler of hot whisky-and-water. He drained it with an intent, grateful avidity, then hurried on.

"At first they weren't hostile. Just curious. They swirled around the plane, like wisps of green mist—they were unreal as that. And they went away. As soon as they departed, I left the plane. I knew

I'd have to hurry. I was freezing already. I was determined to carry it through, and the reason was more than to get your proof, gentlemen. If you had seen that girl, as I saw her, two years ago—"

His weary voice paused, his greenish eyes flickered briefly back to the fire.

"My suit, you know, had chemical heaters and oxygen mask. And I had a pair of special snowshoes, to walk on those curious massed blue crystals.

"I stumbled out across that world of ragged frost, toward the temple. Those rugged, fantastic mountains walled me in. They held me in a blue prison of cold. There was a wind, thin and cold and high. It howled through those rocks and pinnacles with an eerie shrillness, like something under torture.

"Just in front of that temple, I stumbled over the edge of a frightful abyss. A ragged-edged pit of blue haze. It was bottomless, went all the way through the island. I came near falling a hundred thousand feet. But a ledge caught me. I struggled back, and plodded around to the portal of the temple.

"That temple . . .

"The stuff of it looks like pale blue glass, or more like pure, crystalline ice. Transparent, shining, cold. I don't know what it really is. It looked solid, but my snowshoes left deep tracks in its smooth floor.

"It's vaster than anything you can imagine. The pillars are bigger than the Washington monument. It must be a mile long. The inside of it is a cavern of dim blue mystery—of silent cold.

"Their god is at the center of it. It is made of violet crystal, colder than the blue. It isn't a human form, or like anything human. If you can imagine some master symbolic artist catching the spirit, the pure essence, of utter, deadly cold. . . . That was it! A god of frozen death!

"The girl was on the high purple altar beneath it. She's human—or once she must have been. But they've changed her, or she would have died. A normal human being couldn't have lived, as she was, two minutes.

"SHE was a goddess of the cold! Her skin was white and cold as snow. Her hair was snowy white. Her eyes were cold and blue as ice. You hardly noticed the odd, sheer garments she wore. Standing there on the violet altar, she was a thing of perfect beauty. Her bare arms were making slow, curious gestures. She was singing, her voice beautiful and cold and silvery, like ice tinkling in crystal glasses.

"Some of them were in the temple. Fleeting swirls of green vapor. They were drifting about below the level of the altar, below that violet god—worshipping. Creatures of cold, worshipping the god of cold."

Jimmy Adcock shivered again, and clenched his pale hands. His eyes burned strangely in the light of the fire.

"They didn't seem to notice me," he went on. "And under those enormous ghostly pillars, I was insignificant as a fly. I walked on down that colonnade, leaving deep tracks in the floor.

"The girl had stopped her chant before I reached the altar, and the green things swirled away. Luck was with me. That altar must have been a hundred feet high, and I couldn't have climbed it. It was too unsubstantial. But I came around the corner of it, and met the girl running down a narrow stair. She had put on a queer little green cloak, but it didn't hide her snow-white loveliness. And she didn't seem to mind the cold—for she was the goddess of cold.

"I didn't waste any time. I knew such luck couldn't last. The purple steps crushed under my feet, but I got the girl—by the ankle. She was too astonished to struggle, at first. And when she did, she seemed light and frail as the stuff of the temple.

"I carried her out of the temple, safe enough. And back into that wilderness of ghostly blue pinnacles, with the wind wailing in them like the last cries of all who ever died of cold. I went stumbling around the ragged brink of that bottomless chasm.

"The girl's struggles hadn't been effective. Now she got her voice back, and made some weird, singing call. It was like a flute of ice. And suddenly the air around me was full of—*them!* They didn't make any sound, unless it was a kind of rustling, like snow falling. They just swirled around me, shapeless wisps of greenish vapor, frozen.

"They were angry, furious. I could feel that. But they didn't know just what to do. They could have killed me easily enough— I know that. But I think they didn't know how to do it without harming the girl.

"When they first swirled close, I felt terrible cold driving through my suit. It would have killed me in another instant. But the girl called out. They drew back and the cold stopped.

"I was nearly dead when I got in the plane. I dragged the girl with me to the controls. They'd have killed me if I'd let her away from me for an instant. They were hovering about, outside the windows.

"THE plane had sunk to the wings in those blue crystals. It was frozen in. The first blast of the rockets failed to move it. And then, of a sudden, I thought I was finished! I had locked the air-tight cabin. But somehow one of those green things got in. The cold of it drove into me. My whole body went stiff. With one hand I was still holding the girl against me. With the other, I jerked the rockets open all the way.

"After that, I was too stiff and numb to move. But I heard the thin, rending scream of the shattering crystals, and saw jagged cracks running through them. And then the plane trembled and plunged down. I must have passed out, for the next I knew we were shooting down in a terrific power dive, with the rockets still on. We had fallen through the drifting island. The green Thing was gone.

"My arm still held the girl against me. But I couldn't move to shut off the rockets. The vibration was shaking the ship to pieces; the wind was a deafening scream. We were coming down like a meteor.

"I managed just in time to lurch forward, and cut off the rockets with my chin. The ship came up into a glide. And finally I recovered enough to head for the beacon here and make a landing."

Jimmy Adcock shivered again, and rubbed his hands together. His horror-glazed eyes went back to the red glow of the fire as if to a sanctuary from cold. His weary voice finished:

"And that's that."

John Lane blew the ash off his extinct cigarette, and murmured:

"Doggone me for a brasseared son of a gun And you have got proof?" Arthur Randolph turned his sharp face angrily on the lank, weary flier.

"You tell us that?" his harsh voice rapped. "You expect us to believe—"

"You asked for it," said Jimmy Adcock, gently. "The proof is in the plane."

"You mean"—Ferrier's voice was thin and eager—"you mean you have that girl still in the plane?"

"I left her there," said the pilot. "I locked the cabin." A lurking dread chilled his tone. "But They are furious. They will come for her—if they can!"

"If Mr. Adcock has any evidence of the truth of this remarkable narrative," put in precise-voiced Alan Morridon, "I suggest that we inspect it."

"Okay," said Jimmy Adcock. He unfolded his rangy body with a stiff reluctance, and shivered again as he left the fire.

Denny Trevor led the way out toward the great white plane under the starlight. Starlight, he wondered with an inward tremor, that had filtered through a weird transparent frozen world, twenty miles above?

"Here!" his quick voice rang out in the frosty night. "A window broken!"

His flashlight pointed to the shattered fragments of glass that lined one of the cabin's great windows.

With tired haste, Jimmy Adcock ran to unlock the door. He lifted himself, peered into the cabin. An inner light flashed on. And presently he descended heavily.

"She's gone!" his dull voice whispered. "Gone!"


## CHAPTER III

### The Goddess of Frost

THE lank, red-headed flier leaned wearily against the silver fuselage in apathetic defeat.

"Gone!" he muttered again. "They came and broke the glass and took her."

Trevor's flashlight flickered across fragments of glass on the ground. With a muffled exclamation, he stooped, picked up particles of glass.

"I don't think so," he said. "The glass is outside—it must have been broken by a blow from in the cabin. And here's a drop of blood. Very likely the glass was broken by a human being. If there was a person locked up in here, I think he—or she—must have escaped through her own efforts. Shall we search?"

Bristling, the financier Randolph had seized the arm of the

listless pilot.

"Adcock," his harsh voice menaced, "I don't like the look of this. I put good money into this business, a hundred thousand dollars. I suppose everybody knows I've had reverses in the past two years. My share in the association is all I have left in the world. I want more out of it than a wild tale of a world in the sky—with a little broken glass for proof."

Jimmy Adcock soberly shook his head.

"Remember, Mr. Randolph," he said, "you heard my story of the world in the sky before you invested your hundred thousand. That was the time to be skeptical. Another thing: my rocket motors and the other inventions are now the property of the association. I believe they make my investment as large as any." He turned. "Isn't that so, Mr. Morridon?"

The Boston attorney nodded his grey head.

"I'm convinced," he said, "that the patents will be worth far more than we have all invested. That is fortunate, for I think we have all had financial losses since the association was organized."

The thin voice of Ferrier interjected, eagerly: "And then, gentlemen, we must not lose sight of the scientific value of our achievement. The substantiation of my theories of the molecular behavior of gases, alone, is sufficient return—"

Trevor brushed impatiently past him, to look into the tired face of Jimmy Adcock. His greenish eyes still were oddly dead, as if the cold of horror had seared out their life.

"Adcock," he demanded bluntly, "you really left a girl locked in this plane? A girl from that ice world?"

The pilot said flatly, "I did."

"Then"—and Trevor raised his voice—"let's look for her. It hasn't been half an hour. She must be near."

"Unless," Adcock cut in, "unless they have carried her back to that temple in the sky." His voice sank heavily. "But I warn you, gentlemen. They will strike at us, if they can. And that cold of theirs—" Reeling forward, he added: "But I'll help search."

"There are more flashlights in the hangar," offered little Ferrier. "We can see the beacon for miles, so there's no danger of getting lost. I suggest we all meet here again in an hour, to report any discoveries."

"I'll have nothing, to do with it," broke in Randolph's snarl. "Any fool can see this whole affair is a hoax—a flimsy hoax! I'm going in the house. And," he added bitterly, "I've finished with the association! I'm going East tomorrow, and sell my share for what it will bring."

"MR. RANDOLPH," said Morridon's even voice, "may I remind you of a clause in our charter? The shares are untransferable."

"You mean," Randolph blustered angrily, "that I can't sell?"

"Exactly," said the attorney. "You surely understood that at the time. The association was not organized for profit. Its shares cannot be sold or inherited. It can be dissolved only by the unanimous vote of all surviving members, and then its assets, if any, shall be divided equally among them."

"Humph!" snorted the financier. "A damned swindle!"

His predatory face blotched with angry purple, he strode toward the house.

Trevor briefly sketched a plan of search, and the little group dispersed into the darkness. With an orienting glance at the green beacon winking above the hangar, the newspaperman started across the field. Twisting the head of his flashlight to throw a long, piercing beam, he probed the night ahead.

The lighted buildings became small and lonely beneath the desert stars. The thin pencil of light was a feeble weapon against overwhelming darkness. It merely emphasized the silent and mysterious desolation of the mesa. Soon he lost the lights and voices of the other searchers. He was alone, drenched in the frosty gloom.

A funny business, he was thinking.

Denny Trevor was hard-headed, hard-bodied, twenty-three. In four years on New York dailies, he had acquired a certain grim realism. He was intensely interested in Jimmy Adcock's weirdly astounding narrative, without troubling himself too much about its truth.

He liked Adcock. The pilot's manner had been convincing. Ferrier, who alone had the scientific background to enable him to judge the story, seemed to accept it. The thing was possible,

On the other hand, Trevor reserved his own private doubt. He was responding to a vast curiosity, to his hunch that stranger, more sinister angles of the affair were yet to be exposed.

Particularly, he was anxious to find the girl. He knew that *somebody* had been locked in the plane, had broken the glass to escape. And Adcock's brief description had given him a vivid image of the snow-white goddess of cold.

It was her voice that led him to her. Forty minutes had gone. He was swinging back toward the buildings. He had just scrambled up the steep, crumbling bank of a dry arroyo, and stood again upon the swarthy, starlit level. The keen air was stimulating as wine, and the night's mystery was a brooding, awful presence.

High and clear, the voice came out of the dark. Little crystal notes danced in its silvery melody. It sang a wordless song, in eerie, haunting minors.

Trevor snapped off his flashlight and ran toward it silently and rapidly. He stumbled over a loose stone, and bruised his knee. But he saw the girl against the sky as he rose, and the curse died in his throat.

She stood fifty yards away upon an outcropping of shattered granite. Her body was so white that it seemed to glow against the darkness. Her slight garments revealed all its beauty.

Her white head was thrown back, her slim bare arms were flung up to the night sky. Trevor caught the lovely outlines of brow and chin and snowy throat, almost as if they were luminous. Still her silvery voice wailed out the plaintive minors of that weird appeal.

T HE newspaperman stopped, heart thumping against his throat. In one instant, her mystic white beauty had set his blood on fire. But stronger than his swift admiration was wonder—and fear.

The goddess of cold! Was her weird chant a prayer to the god she had served in that fantastic blue temple in the sky? Or perhaps a call for aid, addressed to those green beings of cold? Was she herself as unsubstantial as that ghostly crystal world?

Trevor hardly dared breathe. The beauty of her white, slim body, of her eerie sky-flung song, wove for him a spell of enchantment. He clung to the precious moment, fearful that a word, a movement, might shatter it.

She was too lovely to be real. But she was real enough, he reminded himself suddenly, to bleed.

The song stopped unexpectedly. She looked at Trevor. She didn't seem afraid of him, yet he thought he glimpsed a look of warning on her white face. Her poise, somehow, suggested that she was prepared to vanish instantly.

Trevor began to walk toward her. She lowered her arms, and watched him with eyes that were the cold blue of unflawed ice. Again he fancied a warning in them, something that said: "Stand back. I don't want to hurt you, but I am dangerous."

"Hello," said Trevor, very softly, cautious not to startle her. "Do you understand?"

She made no answer.

Somehow his sense of warning had increased, yet Trevor still advanced. He was no longer the hard-headed, realistic reporter. Her strange beauty, singing in the starlight, had set a fever to burning in his brain. Suddenly, desperately, he wanted to touch her snowy body, to take her in his arms and claim her mystic beauty. Fear arose with the desire, fear that somehow she might escape him, that she might yet prove unreal, unattainable.

He read the warning in her face as a challenge. Blithely he accepted the challenge. Was she girl or goddess of frost?

"We'll see, kid," he breathed, and made an abrupt, desperate grab for her bare ankle. He'd soon know the truth about her.

He swayed back, gasping. His zestful daring died before black horror.

For something green had flashed before him. A shapeless wraith of frozen mist, that whispered like falling snow. And cold struck him with a merciless blade. It cleaved through him, stiffening every muscle, numbing every nerve, congealing the blood in his veins.

Blinded, rigid, breathless, he fell forward against the rock.

She had gone, when Denny Trevor came back to himself. Through stiffened lips he called to her faintly, and there was no response.

He was still sprawled against the rock where she had stood. His body was numb and tingling, still smarting from that strange, sudden chill. He sat up uncertainly an the edge of the rock, rubbing together his stiff, aching hands.

Well! If this were all a hoax, it was a most remarkable one. If it were not . . . Trevor shivered. The green, shapeless Thing had been a spectre of pure frozen horror.

## CHAPTER IV

### HORROR IN WHITE

T REVOR set his jaw and swayed grimly to his feet. The fever of the girl's mystery still flamed in his veins. He wanted desperately to know the truth about her.

He bent and fumbled for his dropped flashlight. He was thinking longingly of the wide fireplace in the adobe house, of Charlie Moon's hot toddies. But he went on when he found the flashlight. After all, the exercise would warm him.

He was stiff at first, still shivering from that inexplicable chill. But warm blood thawed his aching limbs. He walked faster, in a wide circle, flashing the light here and there in quest of the girl's mystic loveliness.

His ears were straining for her eerie silver chant. But instead, twenty minutes later, it was the voice of Attorney Morridon that he heard.

"Here!" it rang through the frosty silence. "Here, all of you! I've found her!"

The sound was from the direction of the winking green beacon above the hangar. Trevor ran toward it at once. Stumbling across a shallow dry wash he heard the girl's voice again. Silver-clear, it was a wordless half-scream, protesting, warning.

Hard upon it from the same direction came Alan Morridon's: "Oh-h-h-h!"

The tortured outcry plunged abruptly into absolute silence.

Trevor ran on. There was no reply to his apprehensive calls. But a dry, crackling noise became audible. His quivering light found a ghostly, terrible form in the dark, and clung to it.

With reluctant, horror-stiffened steps, Trevor walked up to the Boston attorney. His breath went out with a dry, whistling gasp.

Yes, this was Alan Morridon. His spare, tall body. His sharp, wrinkled face, with the high cheek-bones, the narrow forehead. His long, thin hair.

The body was rigid, stiffened in an attitude of overwhelming fear. The thin arms were raised as if to fend off some frightful menace. The sharp features were fixed in a changeless mask of utter, monstrous horror.

Alan Morridon, the realization came shuddering to Trevor, was frozen. Already his garments, his horror-racked features, were silvered with a rime of frost. His flesh, incredibly chilled, was condensing frost from the air!

As Trevor watched, breathless with incredulous horror, a white shroud of crackling crystals spread over the dead man. White frost masked his face. Gleaming white mercifully hid the horror in his eyes.

And still the crackling armor increased, until his features lost their sharpness, until he became a grotesque, shapeless snow-man.

Out of the abyss of horror, Trevor's wits came back slowly. What mad terror was loose? What dread agency could lower the temperature of a living body, in minutes only, to a point where it sucked crackling frost out of this dry, desert air?

Was Adcock's fantastic story true?

The silver challenge of the white woman's voice rang again in his ears. Had she called those green entities of deadly cold, to kill Morridon? Was she, for all her exotic loveliness, a murderess?

Trevor shook his head. But he couldn't shake out the memory of her slim and mystic beauty. Even the chill of horror couldn't quench the fire in him.

H E turned away from the grotesque, still-growing white pillar that had been Alan Morridon. Its rustling crepitation followed him across the silent mesa, a dry, papery sound, infinitely horrible.

No matter how, Morridon was dead. He must go to the house, warn the others. The hour was up; they would be coming back to report. He walked rapidly toward the green beacon. His anxiety to clear up this mystery had become a frantic urge. Uncertainty, suspense, were becoming intolerable.

And the girl . . . Murderess or not, she had claimed his thoughts with her snow-white, illusive loveliness.

Panting, almost warm again and recovered from his own chill, he came to the buildings under the beacon. His voice quavering and uncertain, he began shouting.

"Come! Everybody! Morridon has been killed!"

No voice came from the lighted hangar. No hail of flash came from the black, silent mesa.

Old Charlie Moon met him at the door of the adobe residence,

His seamed yellow face was pale and anxious.

"Glad see you, Mist' Tlevor," he said apprehensively. "Where evelybody gone?"

"Nobody here?" Trevor looked at his watch. "Funny—they should be back." He demanded suddenly: "Where's Randolph? He went back in the house?"

"Mist' Landloph go out again, light away," said Charlie Moon. "Nobody here."

Trevor shivered, and walked into the long living room. In front of the fire that had burned down to a rich bed of coals, he mixed a glass of whisky and hot water, drained it.

"They aren't coming," he told the nervous cook, suddenly. "I've got to go back."

In the doorway the silent darkness struck him like a blow. He wished that he had a gun, then wondered if it would be any use.

"Hey!" The horror-edged voice came across the field. "Come here, you guys—look at this!"

Trevor ran out across the field toward the great white stratoplane. He stopped under the vast wing with a whistle of out-driven breath. The four mechanics were standing in a little muttering group. Their flashlights played uneasily over something on the ground.

"What's this?" Trevor yelled.

"Hell, I don't know," said one of them, hoarsely. "We just came in from looking for that girl. I happened to see it. Good cripes, it looks—it looks—"

It was a human body, furred with two inches of white frost. It had shattered when it fell. The head had rolled a little apart; it was a white ball. Both arms had shattered from the trunk; they had become indistinguishable white sticks. One leg had snapped off at the knee.

"Who—who was it?" whispered Trevor,

One mechanic had kicked at a white, oblong brick of frost, uncovered a brown briefcase.

"Ferrier's," he grunted. "And that's Ferrier's cane."

Shuddering, Trevor pushed at the white ball with his foot. Cold drove through shoe leather, his toes ached. But the hat came off. Black hair, like Ferrier's, was momentarily visible before white frost filmed it.

Trevor's numb toe scraped at his face. But there was no face. It had shattered away.

He kicked the hat. Frost crystals burst from it in a white cloud. It was a black felt. He stooped to read the name in the band: "Logan Ferrier."

H E straightened, stared at the four mechanics.
"Ferrier's the second," he said. "Morridon is dead, too."
"God," muttered one of the men. "Adcock was telling us the truth!"

"It's them damned green Things," said another. "Remember he said they kill with cold?"

"Let's get out of here," urged the first speaker, apprehensively. "My car's in the garage."

Trevor made some effort to halt them, but in a moment they were careening across the field in a battered sedan. One leaned out to shout:

"If you won't come along, brother, luck to you! See you in daylight."

Ominously, another voice added:

"If you're still alive."

Watching the red light wink and dwindle on the straight desert road, Trevor stifled the quick wish that he could have accompanied the fugitives. He was frightened—he couldn't hide that from himself. Cold horror had meshed him in its clammy web. But he couldn't run away.

Intense curiosity held him, an overwhelming urge to explore every sinister angle of the mystery about him, to strip the truth free of the last black shred of baffling horror. Equally strong was his desire to see that white singer again, to learn who she really was.

What next?

He drove his bewildered brain to the question. It answered with a score of others. Where were his surviving fellow searchers, Adcock and Lane? Why hadn't they returned as agreed? Were they dead, too? And where had Arthur Randolph gone when he left the house?

Had Jimmy Adcock's story of the frozen, floating world been a hoax? Its purpose to get financial backing for his experiments? If so, was he the murderer, using the same hoax to effect the recovery of his inventions?

The girl—was she an accomplice, or herself the murderess?

Trevor shook his head. How explain the green, ghostly shape

of his weird attacker? Or the sudden, terrific cold that had frozen little Ferrier's body to such brittle hardness that it had shattered when it fell?

Find Adcock. That, he saw, was the thing to do. If the thing were really an incredible hoax, then the pilot was patently the murderer. If not, he would surely be the best leader against the real danger.

Trevor ran around the deserted buildings. His flashlight probed the still darkness of hangar, garage, shops. He returned to the dwelling where old Charlie Moon had apprehensively barricaded himself in the kitchen. He looked into every room. The house was empty.

The night seemed strangely darker when he went out again. The frosty chill of the air had increased. He heard a faint whisper. Was it the ghastly night wind, or frost growing upon a newly frozen corpse?

It wouldn't do to stand still. Or to think too much of Jimmy Adcock's story, and of what had happened to Morridon and Ferrier. But what—?

Nervously, tense, Denny Trevor struck out at random into the darkness. He crossed the level of the field, and came out again on the dry mesa.

*Snap!*

Trevor heard the warning crackle of dry brush. He spun, crouching. Tall and vague against the stars, a dark figure flung toward him. His left whipped out, went wild in the dark. Lean arms coiled around him. A heavy body drove him backward. His heel caught against a stone; he fell.

T HE newspaperman squirmed beneath his attacker. Hot breath was rushing against his throat. And a savage hand closed on it, shutting off his wind. Then a sinewy wrist was in his grasp. He snapped it back in a crude wrist-lock, began to twist.

Trevor was not a skilled wrestler. He knew that his hold would be easy to break. But he fought for breath and life, twisting grimly. He heard a gasp of pain. Perhaps his opponent was equally unskilled. He ducked his head to fend off a jabbing elbow, twisted harder.

"Okay!" came a pain-choked sigh. "You've got me."

"Adcock?" panted Trevor, surprised.

"Me," came the affirming gasp. "So you're the reporter? Sorry I jumped you. Please let go my arm! I thought you were—"

Trevor's grip tightened. "Never mind!" he said grimly. "You're just the man I wanted. And you're going to talk—straight!"

The pilot's body quivered with pain.

"I'll talk," he gasped. "Ease up, for the love of— What do you want to know?"

"The truth about what's going on here. Who killed Morridon and Ferrier? And how?"

Jimmy Adcock shook his head in the dark.

"I don't know," he whispered. "It's—it's ghastly! I was trying to find out, when I jumped you. I thought—"

"Your story!" Trevor cut in. "Was that true? And the girl—"

Adcock's imperative whisper stopped him:

*"Listen!"*

Again it floated across the dark mesa: a weird minor chant, whose cold liquid melody drew Trevor like a thin, silver cord. It was a song without words, yet full of an uncanny appeal that somehow stirred his blood.

"That's her," breathed Adcock. "Singing—"

With that word, Trevor felt the drive of a sickening impact against his solar plexus. The breath went out of him. His grip relaxed. Before he could recover, Adcock's freed arm drove a stinging blow against his chin.

His head ringing with concussion, Trevor realized that his prisoner had escaped, Vaguely, he knew that Jimmy Adcock had run away, toward the silver witchery of that eldritch song. Clenching his aching jaw, he swayed grimly to his feet and stumbled in the same direction.

At first he was too dazed to run. Twice he fell headlong. Adcock was lost in the gloom before him, and he had only the singing voice to guide him. Then the voice abruptly ceased. He heard a brief, hoarse cry. Then silence.

Trembling with a new and nameless apprehension, Trevor went on. He was leaving the level mesa, entering a tangle of dark outcropping boulders that were like the shattered tombstones of an abandoned graveyard of giants.

There he found Jimmy Adcock.

T HE pilot's hands were clenched at his sides. His head was thrown back a little, as if he had suddenly stopped. His lean face was twisted into a grimace of such horror as Trevor had not conceived until this mad night. His terror-widened eyes were no longer greenish, but white, blindly white. His red hair had now turned to white. He was a statue of utter, overmastering horror, sharply cut in pure white stone.

Trevor heard a now familiar and yet dreadful crackling sound: the rustling crepitation of fast-growing frost crystals. And the sharply outlined statue of Jimmy Adcock became furred, blurred, a grotesque and swollen mockery of a man.

Trevor stood for a moment dazed, paralyzed. It was not five minutes since this man had broken away from him, to follow the silver lure of that wordless, ethereal song. Shivering, he shrank back.

"And I thought," he breathed, "I thought it was a hoax!"

His eyes went up to the frosty stars, toward Jimmy Adcock's fantastic world above the air, where ghastly, shapeless wraiths of frozen green haunted a forbidden world of cold. Jimmy Adcock's warning ran again ominously in his brain.

"They will come—if they can. And they kill with cold!"

Then clear and low out of the darkness, as if it were very near him, he heard the plaintive silver sweetness of that crystal voice of doom.


## CHAPTER V

### COLD IS THE KISS OF DEATH!

B UT now it had words—words that he recognized.

"Come!" it whispered gently. "Come to me!"

Beside the stark whiteness of the frozen stratoplane pilot, Trevor stiffened into instinctive immobility. The chill of his one perilous encounter with the white singer was still in his bones, and his head still ran from Adcock's unexpected blow. He was weaponless. And three men, this night, had died when they answered that woman's mystic call—had died of frightful cold.

He fumbled silently for his handkerchief and wiped cold beads of sweat off his forehead. And then, with a strained and nervous haste, he went ahead in the dark. Silence had followed the low, swift call. The mesa was very quiet.

Denny Trevor was faint and trembling with the greatest fear he had ever felt. But he was glad that soon now he would know. And he was grimly determined, if he could, to stem this mad wave of horror that had swept away three lives.

And still the white singer's lure was dancing in his mind . . .

Her voice stopped him again, turned him rigid and breathless. It came from the shadow of a great rock, age-carved into the semblance of some reptilian monster bursting from the earth.

Now all the mysterious silver peril had gone out of her voice. It was low, husky with fear and pain. It whispered out of the shadow in the tongue of his own familiar world:

"Here I am."

And he saw her under the boulder. She was slim as some archaic statue in argent. Her filmy garments revealed curves of exotic, snowy loveliness. Like a frightened child she crouched against the rugged stone. The oval beauty of her face was lifted toward him, appealingly.

He stepped back alertly when he saw her. His eyes flickered in search of that ghostly green shape whose uncanny chill before had pierced him.

"Come on!" she was whispering again. "There's no danger, at least not for a moment. You must help me to stop it! . . . But who are you?"

"A newspaper reporter," said Trevor. "Who are you—or what?"

Her white face changed at his grim suspicion. She rose and came quickly to him out of the shadow. He waited cautiously alert, and let her take his hand. Her flesh was warm, trembling. She was human—no fantastic being of frost!

She tugged toward the shadow.

"Come on," she breathed urgently. "Down here where we can't be seen! And don't talk loud."

"Not," protested Trevor, "till I know who you are."

"My name is Sonia Casement," her low, throaty voice told him swiftly. "I'm an actress. You think I'm responsible for the dreadful things that have happened tonight. But I'm not!" Her voice trembled earnestly. "Truly I'm not But the man who is, is hunting for me now! He'll kill me when he finds me. And kill you, too. You must let me explain before he comes. So we can fight together!"

"Well," said Trevor, "if you can explain! It looks damned suspicious to me. I was about to touch you when something nearly froze me to death. Morridon called out that he had found you, and five minutes later he was frozen hard as iron. About Ferrier, I don't know. But your voice called Adcock to death—"

"Poor Jimmy!"

G RIEF choked her. Drawing Trevor beside her into the shadow of the rock, she swallowed, dabbing hastily at her eyes.

"I suppose Jimmy and I were doing wrong," began her cautious, racing whisper. "But Jimmy didn't mean any harm. He was just a brilliant kid. He always was reckless and irresponsible. Ever since I met him in the old days when he was flying with a carnival. He had too much imagination."

"Then," Trevor said eagerly, "his story of a world in the sky—"

"—was just a story," she finished. "Jimmy couldn't get money to finance his rocket experiments. He had read about Ferrier's theory of a layer of solid gas crystals above the stratosphere. He made up the story of the flying island to get people interested. Nobody but poor Mr. Ferrier knew about the publicity stunt. He was eager as a child about it—said he thoroughly understood the value of Interesting publicity.

"Jimmy didn't mean anything criminal, really. He knew that his patents would be worth enough to pay back the investors for everything they put in. He put the girl in his story to give it publicity value. I promised to play the girl because I needed money, and—well I always had a weak spot for Jimmy. If it hadn't been for him, I'd have never got out of the carnival."

She paused, with a little sobbing breath.

"Jimmy really made a stratosphere flight today and his inventions worked wonderfully. Then he landed off in the desert, where I was waiting, and picked me up. While he was in the house, telling his story, I broke out of the ship. We planned that.

"He had helped me make up that song. I was to sing it out on the mesa, and let one or two of you glimpse me, not too close. Then I was to hide by the road. Jimmy was going to come in a car, before daybreak, and take me back to the railroad.

"But somebody found what we were planning. Somebody—" Horror choked her. "He turned it into a horrible murder plot!"

"How?" Trevor whispered.

"He found me out on the mesa. He has a green, shining veil wrapped around his head and shoulders, and he wears black clothing under it that you can't see in the dark. It makes him look like one of Jimmy's weird creatures. Somehow, he can make terrible cold. He froze me nearly to death before I would promise to do what he said. He made me go with him, and sing. When you came, he turned the cold on you, but you escaped that time because I started to run away and he had to stop making the cold to catch me. Afterwards I saw him kill Mr. Morridon with it, and Jimmy—"

Emotion stopped her voice again.

"How did you get away from him this time?"

"After we went away from Jimmy," she whispered, shuddering, "he stopped to work with his apparatus. It is something strapped to his shoulders, under the green veil. I slipped away from him, and ran until I saw you. Then I hid and called to you."

T REVOR'S mind was swiftly Trying to fit this new information with what he had seen.

"You didn't see him kill Ferrier?" he questioned. "Back under the plane?"

"No," she said. "I didn't know—"

"Must have done that before he found you. You've no idea at all who he is?"

She shook her head. "But I didn't know any of Jimmy's associates."

"Can you describe him?"

"The veil hid his face, of course. He's about average size."

"You didn't notice anything distinctive?"

"Well, perhaps his voice. Of course it sounded disguised, but I think it's naturally harsh and low, sort of guttural."

"Randolph!" breathed Trevor. "His voice is harsh. It must be— he was furious when Morridon told him he couldn't sell his share in the association. But"—wonder stilled his voice —"how could he freeze living men—"

In the shadow the girl's quivering body shrank against Trevor. She seized his arm.

"Quiet!" she breathed. "I think I hear him! Have you a gun?"

"No," whispered Trevor. "Guess we'll have to beat it. If I knew how he kills—"

"I shall allay your curiosity."

It was a harsh, rasping whisper. Trevor saw the green shape sweep around a jutting angle of the rock. It was like a wisp of green gas frozen, a spectre of frigid death.

He surged upward, but cold struck him before he was on his feet. Out of the green cloud came a whispering, faint and ghostly as the rustle of falling snow. And cold breathed on him with the breath of death. Stiffened, numb, breathless, he fell back beside the gasping girl.

"I spared your lives," came that guttural rasp, "because your task, my lady, is unfinished. You have another man to toll. You must sing once more."

Terror-widened, dulled with that frightful shock of cold, Trevor's eyes stared up. They saw that greenish, floating thing, shapeless in the gloom. But he heard the scrape of feet beneath it. He could make out black trousers, nearly invisible.

He could see, now, that the apparition effect was accomplished by a loose veil of luminous silken gauze, swathing the head and shoulders of a man. The filmy ends of it were floating free, like wisps of frozen vapor.

Again the menacing whisper grated from the veil:

"Sing."

The girl was shivering. From her cold-stiffened lips came a quivering whisper.

"I won't—I can't! I've called enough men to death. Jimmy, oh, Jimmy!" A sob trembled in her voice. "Go on and kill me. I won't sing."

"On the contrary," rasped the whisper, "you will. After I have explained. In either case, you must die. If you will sing, and call John Lane to me here, you may have the same instant and painless death I have given the others. Refuse, and your fate will be less comfortable. Flesh frozen under the hydrogen spray is quite brittle. I shall freeze your extremities, and shatter them off. You won't bleed to death until the stumps thaw. Now"—it was a jarring threat—"will you sing?"

"No!" It was a faint, defiant breath. "I won't be your tool again!"

The white form went limp beside Trevor's stiff, useless body. Sonia Casement had fainted.

I N vain did the newspaperman struggle for some control of his numb, paralyzed limbs. So John Lane, the big rancher, was still at large. If he could be warned—

The palely shining veil drifted downward. Trevor heard a faint, rustling hiss. Again merciless cold smote his body. And the girl beside him was suddenly quivering, gasping.

"Ah," came the complacent, hellish whisper, "a breath of cold revives you. If you have become too altruistic to sing for your own life perhaps you will sing for Mr. Trevor's. He is quite unable to defend himself. Shall I freeze his hands, and snap them off?"

"No! Not that!" The girl was hoarse with horror. "No. I'll sing. Just let me get back my breath—I'm so cold!"

The green shape hung over her as she coughed and gasped to clear her throat. Trevor strained his eyes at the dark figure under the veil. He made out the grotesque hump on its shoulders. The machine of deadly cold. If somehow he could wreck it—

He tried to rub his stiffened limbs. His deadened hands scarcely responded. He knew he was unable to stand.

The harsh whisper cut into his brain:

"Sing!"

Silvery and cool again, Sonia Casement's voice lifted in the wordless minors of that uncanny chant, its crystal lure calling one more man to frozen doom.

The green shape drew a little away. It seemed to crouch. The killer was waiting in the shadow of another boulder, ready to strike his unsuspecting victim from behind.

Trevor chaffed at his useless hands. He fumbled about in blind search for some weapon, found only a tiny, useless pebble. Cautiously, he tried to clear his throat. At any cost he must call out when the time came warn John Lane.

The green shape came, drifting back.

"That's enough," the whisper said. "He's coming. I don't want you to warn him."

The muffled, grating voice was hardly changed, yet a tiny new grimness in it gave Trevor his alarm. The murderer now needed the girl no longer. And he was going to take no risk of their being able to warn John Lane. He was going to kill them both, now!

As the green and deadly spectre drifted down, Trevor made a desperate effort to reach his feet. But his numbed, trembling legs would not respond. He half rose, toppled over on his side.

He and the girl were doomed, but perhaps Lane could be saved.

"Lane!" he tried to shout. "Don't come! You'll be murdered!"

His voice was a mere hoarse gasp, hardly audible. Out of the green cloud came the ghost of a malicious chuckle.

"Probably he didn't hear you," the whisper grated. "Even if he did, he'll come on. I'll get him, while he's looking at your bodies."

And already that faint, deadly rustling had begun, the whisper of tiny jets of cold beyond conception. The stark kiss of it touched Trevor's face, congealing his flesh.

He flung the pebble in his hand. It was an insignificant missile, smaller than an egg. And it was a mere gesture of hopeless defiance, that flung it at the weird, bulging lump under the veil.

I N his dazed numbness, Trevor was surprised to hear the thin sharp tinkle of glass. He was dully amazed to see the green veil billow out, before an explosive *whuff!* of white vapor. He still did not understand when an intenser breath of cold came searingly against his body, and passed.

The green veil and the dark figure under it remained absolutely motionless. And sudden realization broke upon Trevor as the ghostly frost spread in crystals and patches and crackling films over the dark, rigid form.

"His own—medicine," he managed to tell the girl.

They were trying to sit up, as warmth and life flowed slowly back into their chilled bodies, when big John Lane came striding into the little open space. His flashlight picked out the stark, white form.

A big, flat, multiple-walled vessel of thin, silvered glass had been strapped to the shoulders, under the green veil. Beneath it dangled a thick, insulated hose, with an elaborate valve at the end. The glass was shattered now. Its contents must have spilled over the man.

"Great walls of Jericho!" gasped Lane, astounded. "Ferrier!"

His flashlight was on the thin features revealed where the frozen veil had shattered like woven glass. They were white as if carved from snowy marble. And they were the features of Dr. Logan Ferrier.

Lane was helping Trevor and the girl to their feet.

"You killed him?"

"It was half an accident," gasped Trevor. "I hit the vacuum vessel with a pebble. It shattered, and spilled on him."

"But what was in it that could freeze a man like that?"

"Hydrogen," said Trevor. "That tank was full of liquid hydrogen. He told us that. Evaporating, liquid hydrogen will chill a human body—or anything else—almost to the absolute zero. To the point where it is brittle as glass. And glass—well, when my pebble hit it it shattered."

He worked his arms to warm himself, drew a deep breath. John Lane stripped off his coat, wrapped it around the shivering girl.

"A queer murder scheme," Trevor muttered. "Not many men could have worked it. The technical difficulty of producing a sufficient quantity of the liquid hydrogen, and using it in a portable sprayer must have been tremendous. But Ferrier was a skilled scientist, the leading American expert on the liquefaction of gases. It was only a weird combination of circumstances—Adcock's publicity hoax, and all—that gave even him the opportunity."

"But why did he do it?"

"It seems," said Trevor, "that all the members of the association had suffered recent financial losses, Ferrier with the rest. I suppose he needed cash for his researches. If he could have been the sole surviving member of the association, he hoped to secure Adcock's profitable inventions."

"Hell!" exclaimed the rancher. "If that ain't Ferrier back under the plane, then who—"

"Randolph," cried Trevor. "I see it! Ferrier killed Randolph as he left the laboratory with his apparatus. He shattered away the frozen face so the corpse couldn't be recognized, and left his own briefcase and cane and hat to cause us to mistake the identity of the body."

"A fool scheme," muttered the rancher. "How did he mean to get away with it in the long run? Randolph's body would have been identified when it thawed."

"FERRIER probably meant to escape in the stratoplane, and take the corpse with him, to dispose of it permanently," said Trevor. "The mechanics had identified it as his. That would have been enough to throw the authorities off the trail. Most of Adcock's inventions, I think, were not yet patented. Ferrier must have planned to patent them as his own, under some name. But it was a crazy scheme, even if it came damned near success. Its cleverness was insane, He must have been planning it for months. I suppose he was scientist enough to see through Adcock's hoax from the start, as well as devil enough to use it for his own ends."

In the dark they had stumbled away from the rigid white horror. They came at last to the silent house. Trevor and Sonia Casement collapsed on the couch in front of the fire. John Lane routed Charlie Moon out of his fortified kitchen to bring hot stimulants, and then rolled a brown cigarette.

"I reckon," he drawled, "this sort of leaves Jimmy Adcock's patents In my hands. I don't want what ain't due me. If he has any heirs, they'll get what's coming."

Hardly listening, Trevor was staring at the loveliness that shone through the shadow of grief and weariness and horror on the girl's face.

"You said you were an actress?" he asked her abruptly.

"I've been promised the lead in a mystery thriller to open on Broadway next season," she murmured.

"If you play it like you did your part tonight," Trevor said, and grinned, "there will be a traffic jam in little old New York. Just now I've got a story to write. But I'll be seeing you—backstage, maybe."

Sonia Casement's blue eyes, glistening with tears, looked at him, but she was smiling.

And Denny Trevor felt his tired mind slipping away into a dim, pleasant, silver haze. After all, there wasn't any rush about the story. The chief might say it was too wild to print.

He reached for his steaming toddy with a little shiver of delicious returning warmth.

# The Great Illusion

*Fantasy Magazine, September 1936*

In our Third Anniversary issue we featured the round-robin story, "The Challenge from Beyond." The idea was so good that we decided to repeat the stunt for this Anniversary Number—with an important variation. This time, the First of the five authors, was asked to write the Last part of the story; the second author, to write the fourth installment; and so on. John Russell Fearn started (or rather ended) the story, leaving to be explained a number of mysteries. Raymond Z. Gallun, who was next, remarked, after completing his job, "The backside-foremost yarn was pretty badly screwed up before, and I imagine it's worse now." Next, Edmond Hamilton, said, "I will give a prize of $1000 to anyone who can tell me what the other two parts of this story are about. And I will give a prize of $10,000 to anyone who can tell me what my part is about. The thing looks like the screwiest story in the history of science fiction." Jack Williamson, who followed, briefly commented, "In my opinion, this would be a very interesting story if one knew precisely what it is all about." Finally, Eando Binder completing (or starting) the story, remarked, "I've done my best to carry the yarn on, or back, as screwily as possible, following the example of the others, and I'm sure I've done no less than the others in making it completely inexplicable. Maybe with a little more thought I could have made it Utterly Impossible for the reader to understand, but I think as it stands now it's safe from ever being unraveled." Despite the above comments, we believe the five authors have done a remarkable job. To fully appreciate their difficulties, we suggest you first read the story as it was written—backwards. Then re-read it in the normal manner, and marvel at it coherence and smoothness!

\* THE GREATEST EXPERIMENT IN HUMAN HISTORY WAS ABOUT TO begin!

Four men stood in the metal-lined cabin of the spaceship, their combined attention centered on Berringer's apparatus riveted to one wall. Korth, tall and solemn, stared with a sneer on his hawk-like face. Bradley and Forijay, far younger than the other two, gazed with hypnotic fascination, their faces pale with deep-routed fear.

Berringer reached a hand toward the mechanism's only lever. Bradley jerked forward, clutched his arm in panic. Berringer turned in impatient surprise.

"Wait—just one minute!" pleaded Bradley. "Before we go ahead with this, explain it all again. After all, there may be no return. And—"

"No return!" repeated Berringer, with emphasis. "Get that. Korth—no return!"

"Bah!" snapped the physicist. "The whole thing is a farce! There will be no return because there will be no start. Go through that mumbo-jumbo about illusion again, Berringer, for their benefit. They are scared, but they have no reason to be. Bah, again, Berringer!"

The savant deliberately turned his thin, wasted form away from the skeptical, acid-tongued Korth and addressed himself to his two young assistants of the past two years.

"Boys, listen carefully, for this is the last time I'll explain it— then we go. You remember the electrical experiment we performed two years ago which proved that electricity is life, pure and completely. You remember how by establishing communication of sorts with this basic life-essence, we learned many things—incredible things! For the Blue Beings who can live in

---

\* Beginning of Eando Binder's installment

any environment, even that of airless space, revealed that all human thought is illusion! Every theory and conception ever performed by the human mind is self-delusion!"

Berringer went on despite another disgusted "Bah" from Korth. "For instance, our mathematics, by which we formulate laws about the universe, are limited between zero and infinity, which are but ciphers in the greater ad truer mathematics. Then our five senses are so inconceivably inaccurate, and cover a pitifully small range of perception. With these limitations, it is no wonder that we cannot realize that there are no stars, no vacuum, nor anything we think we know of! Yet the Blue Beings of electricity have shown us that!"

"The machine!" muttered Bradley hoarsely. "That shaft which pierces to alien dimensions—"

"Fool!" spat out Korth. "A Big Fool to believe in that!"

Berringer ignored this bitter thrust, spoke. "My two years of daily contact with the Blue Beings finally gave me a glimmering of the Great Truth. Gave me a slight idea of the Great All that is behind this gigantic illusion of life, space, energy, and all the other droolings we humans call 'science.' I was able, then, to build this apparatus. Simply stated, it pours its 200,000 volts into what we call a vacuum and rips it aside like a veil, to reveal beyond the ultra-dimensional shaft that leads to—to the Real Universe. It's like going through a mirror and finding reality there!"

"So Alice said to the Mad-Hatter, please, sir, can I have a puff on your opium pipe?" mocked Korth.

"As for you," said Berringer coolly, facing the leering physicist, "remember five minutes from now that I said your great Einstein is like a drunk who sees double and imagines pink elephants in between."

"One more thing," whispered Bradley. "This shaft to the—the Beyond—it is navigable by a space-ship, you're sure?"

At the savant's firm "yes," the two young men looked at each other in evident relief. Berringer's weak old eyes flamed suddenly. "Navigable, yes," he went on, "but only one way! For when you reach the end, you are again at the beginning, yet it is not circular!"

"And when we reach the end, we are once again at the beginning, and therefore back in the laboratory?" asked Forijay eagerly.

"Which comes first the chicken or the egg?" sang Korth scornfully. "And where does the rooster come in?"

Berringer patted the handle of the machine reflectively before answering Forijay. Then he said, emotionlessly, "I told you from the start there was no return! 'End' and 'beginning' are human conceptions, like zero and infinity. There is no end or beginning in this shaft!"

Bradley sucked in his breath sharply, while Forijay grew paler than he was. Korth mocked the whole thing with a nasal chant about the Man with Two Minds, Neither of Which Existed.

"But enough of this chatter," barked Berringer. His thin, sharp face grew livid with a driving purposefullness. "You, Bradley and Forijay, asked to come along—pledged yourselves, in fact. I told you it was slow suicide, but I see you disbelieved that. You cast aside a chance to remain and become famous, even though that is illusion with all the rest of human endeavor. You elected to plumb with me cosmos' depths—the real cosmos—and even that is an illusion! Korth is here to observe the Outer phenomena as a learned savant, and he, too, will perceive that all is illusion!"

"Not to mention the illusion that you have." Korth winked at the two younger men. "I mean the illusion that you did not turn utterly insane two years ago."

Berringer grasped the handle of his machine. "Are we ready?" he barked, and at the same time wrenched over the lever savagely.

With a suddeness that brought a gasp to their lips, the laboratory vanished from beyond their port-windows, and was succeeded by an ultimate blackness. Their ship seemed to be in a pool of ink. There was not the faintest ray of light outside the hull, and the darkness seemed to be crawling in, trying to extinguish their overhead light.

But a moment later a faint blueness appeared in the vast distance. It brightened and resolved itself as a gigantic entity of blue, with titantic green-glowing wings wide-spread. It seemed to be approaching.

Bradley and Forijay huddled together, talking swiftly.

Korth, face astounded, raced to the side port and tried to pierce the sable curtain beyond. But all he could see was the huge green-winged monstrosity, steadily nearing. "Damn you, Berringer!" he shrieked whirling. "What have you done?"

Perfectly calm, the aged savant spoke triumphantly. "Just what I said I would. I wrenched the vacuum apart, and we are now falling—or rising, no matter—in the shaft that leads beyond earthly illusion too—more illusion! We have engines, but they are useless—I see the irony of it now. For there are no such things as motion or distance! Human conceptions—illusions! Do you know what we shall find? Professor Korth, do you?"

Berringer went on as the tall physicist shrank back, eyes wide. "We shall find that the sun is the center of everything, and it is the only star! We shall see other stars space evenly around, but bunched at one end of the ultra-dimensional shaft, and they will be illusions. The planets will be missing!

"But those are silly, meaningless things—unveiled hallucinations. The important things we shall see and discover will be the Blue Beings in their natural environment of what we call vacuum. Then, the facet-rocks of the Outer World, whose reflections we call stars. The Universal Mind which the Blue Beings fear. And finally, the Great All—the reality that will turn illusion before our very eyes!"

Korth and Berringer stared at one another, both aware of a tremendous significance behind these paradoxical words.

They did not notice that Bradley and Forijay were quietly sneaking toward the airlock. In their eyes was a glassy stare—a hypnotic determination to escape from this mad ship that was plunging to an alien universe. In their fear-palsied brains range but one thought—"Get out!"

Bradley twisted the control lever for the airlock, jerked open the first door, and duplicated this maneuver at the outer hatch. Strangely, there was no blast of escaping air as he catapulted himself madly away from the ship. Forijay followed an instant later.

They had escaped! Let death come, the way they understood death; better that than the lunatic journey to a world of insanity and illusion.

*It was very dark. There were no stars visible. Forijay shivered to the cold wind that blew out of the black silence. His hands clutched at the naked, ice-cold rocks. Even as he lay with face pressed against the ledge, his head still ached and spun with an appalling, unendurable vertigo

There are no stars!

* Beginning of Jack Williamson's installment

The words hung in his mind, a haunting, hideous enigma. He tried to remember; then the thought came that the memory must be so terrible that it would shatter his insanity.

With vast relief, he sensed another inert body near him. His eyes, becoming adjusted to the strange darkness, could now see the outlines of the desolate rocky terrain, as if by a faint luminescence. He turned toward the groan.

"Bradley!" he muttered. "What happened? Where are we?" He whispered again the sinister and meaningless answer to his questions: "There are no stars!"

Bradley sat up in the darkness, still groaning.

"It would be hard to say where we are—and when," he gasped. "But we are where Berringer will never find us. I have broken our pledge, Fo—to save our lives!" He shuddered. "When I saw that winged monstrosity of the void, it was impossible to go on! I never suspected myself a coward, Fo. But that horror—"

Forijay was rubbing his bruised forehead, dizzily.

"Still," he muttered, "I can't remember—it all like a nightmare! Tell me, Brad."

"Of course you remember," said Bradley. "But no wonder you think it a nightmare—it is one! But old Berringer's experiment—remember? He was going to prove that all knowledge is illusion. And Korth, his old rival, standing there with a skeptical smile on his hard mouth, waiting for his chance to make a fool of Berringer—"

"Wait!" Forijay's voice broke in, faint with dread. "I remember . . . The terrible dark, when Berringer started his apparatus . . . The silence . . . The shaft beneath the vanishing planets . . . The fall down the shaft, out of space, Berringer said—"

Horror choked him for a time. His dry lips moved soundlessly, whispering again:

"The stars below . . . The facets of rock like a valley of jewels . . . The central sun beneath of world that no longer existed! . . . The Blue Beings, waiting for us to come to our doom . . ."

He jerked up his head, tried to recover himself.

"But that can't be!" His jaws tensed. "Illusion of illusion. There are no stars!" he rubbed his forehead, blankly and looked into the darkness toward Bradley. "But I still don't understand why we are here."

"You have forgotten the nearer horror," said Bradley. "The monstrous entity that guards the secret of the void. It pursued us through space on wings of glowing green. Its flight was as fast as light." His voice was dry with horror. "Its eye was a triple well of purple evil."

He shook his head, as if to shake off fear. Forijay grasped at his arm.

"Berringer will find us," he said apprehensively. "We gave our word to go with him to the end—even to certain doom at the end. He won't let us break it."

"No, we're safe enough from Berringer," said Bradley confidently. "It is a thing I got from the Blue Beings. Time and space and matter are illusions. There is a mastery of illusion. We are ten-thousand miles from Berringer, and ten million years—"

His voice was cut off by a gasp of panic. Far away in the starless darkness, he heard the clatter of a stone. Presently, out of the black unknown, he saw a dark bulk approaching. Its looming outlines became human, although it remained a monstrous thing.

"A man, Brad!" gasped Forijay. "Though his head's too big—"

"Once a man," the low terrible voice came out of the dark. "But now my purpose makes me greater than a god."

"Berringer!" cried Forijay in terror.

The grotesque huge head became a helmet, as the man approached them.

"It is I. I have come to remind you of your pledge. You had the choice—you could have remained behind to reap fame and wealth from my disclosures. But you have chosen—to know and die.

"There can be no turning back. We are surely doomed. But if we go forward, we may know before we die what all men have toiled to learn, since the first savage wondered at the alternation of day and night."

"But how—" gasped Bradley. "How did you follow?"

Berringer's emaciated hand touched his strange helmet.

"This mechanism gives me contact with the Universal Mind, of which you are a part, and I am. I knew every thought of your desertion.—But we must go on. Our quest will lead far beyond the range of the Universal Mind. Korth has followed us with the ship."

The little space-ship grated on the rocks beside them. They filed aboard. Tall Korth was staring from the controls with frantic terror on his face.

"Berringer!" he gasped. "It has followed us, even here!"

His trembling hand pointed at a vision screen. There Forijay saw again the monstrous entity of the void, its glowing green wings rigidly extended against the dark of space.

"Drive back into space," ordered Berringer. "The monster is the smallest of perils before us."

The ship flashed upward through spinning, vertiginous darkness. Abruptly the stars returned. Korth, at the controls, greeted them with a mocking laugh.

"Illusion. There are no stars." He looked fearfully back at the screen. "It is gaining."

"Full acceleration," commanded Berringer grimly. "Away from the Earth."

The velocimeter needle crept swiftly upward. But suddenly alarm gongs jangled. White-faced, Korth snatched for the brake dial.

"Obstruction ahead. Invisible! But we are about to collide—"

"Go on," said Berringer.

Still the needle crept upward. The pursuing monster grew larger in the screen. Korth's staring eyes searched for the invisible barrier revealed by the detectors.

Young Forijay looked mutely at his chief.

"Ahead," said Berringer, "is the etheric shell that surrounds the earth. The mirror that reflects the illusion of the stars. Itself an illusion—"

Crash!

Forijay reeled from a stunning shock. All his body ached from a searing instant of intolerable pain. He blinked, bewildered, at the vision screen.

"The barrier is gone," reported Korth, incredulously. "And the pursuing monster also—"

"The atoms of our body have rebounded from the impact with the etheric shell," said Berringer. "If you will observe yourself, you will discover that what was once your left hand is now your right. You will now require a mirror to read your charts—"

"But—" Korth stammered bewilderedly, "the monster—"

"We were reflected back against it," said the old man, the withered mask-like face beneath his helmet grim with invincible purpose. "Our combined speeds were far in the excess of the velocity of light. Impossible, you may say. Illusion of illusions.

"But the entity has experienced the illusion of death."

\* They were shaken, these four men in the cramped interior of the speeding little space-ship. Badly shaken by what they had just seen in space, by the weird incredible phenomenon that had overturned the life-time beliefs of at least three of them.

Berringer, thin, shrivelled little man, whose aged body was a husk of a colossal brain, was the least overwhelmed of them all. Korth, the tall solemn scientist who had back on earth been Berringer's greatest rival and critic, bore on his rugged face a disturbed bewilderment.

The two younger men, Bradley and Forijay, were looking helplessly toward Berringer. In their eyes was still horror of what they had just seen, and mute appeal for knowledge, for explanation.

"Now do you believe Korth?" Berringer was asking softly. "Now are you so sure that this quest is an utterly wild and useless one?"

Korth tried to keep his voice steady. "I still see no reason for overturning all the accepted laws of human science," he stated. "What we just experienced was incredible, unprecedented, it is true. But it does not mean that everything you have told us is true, that you can actually solve the supreme secret of the universe, storm that last citadel of the unknown."

"I can, and I will!" Berringer's voice rang with a super-human resolve. "For too great a time the scientists of earth have repeated parrotlike, 'The final secrets are unknowable.' I tell you that we are flying straight toward the core of the mystery of the cosmos. We are going to know all before we die!"

"Impossible," muttered Korth, his gaunt face pale. "I would give my life to achieve it, to penetrate the last supreme mysteries of time and space and matter. I have in fact hazarded my life in coming with you, simply to prove that theory of your's wrong. For it is—it must be."

Berringer motioned young Bradley to the controls of the ship. Then the aged little scientists stepped over to his tall colleague and looked up at him with burning eyes.

He said softly, "Korth, you don't believe, even after what we just went through, because you do not want to believe. You do not want to solve the mystery of the cosmos."

His thin hand flew up when Korth made as if to protest. "Don't

---

\* Beginning of Edmond Hamilton's installment

deny it, Korth. I know your secret thoughts, and they are those of every other scientist earth has had. Science is a hunt, a perpetual tracking down of the truth, and the lure of it for the scientist is the wild lure of the chase.

"All your life, Korth, you have been engaged in that chase, trailing truth amid forests of incomprehensible facts, seeking and seeking to ferret it out and always finding that it lies still further ahead. You have said, and have believed yourself, that you really wanted to track down and finally expose the ultimate secrets. But you have only said that because you thought such a thing impossible—in reality, you would hate such success because it would end your work, your thrilling hunt, forever! That is why you shrink from believing me, even now. You fear that your great chase of truth is coming to an end."

"It is not so," Korth denied steadily, though his eyes could not meet Berringer's. "The thrill of hunting truth is great, but I am not afraid to find the quarry. It is simply that our experience just now has not convinced me of the truth of what you say."

"Then convince yourself!" flamed old Berringer. He motioned to the air-lock of the space-ship. "Out on the walls of the ship still sticks the slime from the creature we met just now. Get some of that slime and analyze it—see if it does not have dimensional strangeness I say."

Korth hesitated, looked almost appealingly toward Bradley and Forijay. The two younger men were silent, staring, held by the spell of Berringer's personality.

"I will not do it," Korth said suddenly. "I am convinced that it will not prove what you say."

Rapidly he donned a space-suit, and entered the air lock. Opening the outer door, and hanging inside the lock, he reached forth a gloved hand to scrape from the wall of the ship some of the strangely glowing green slime which had coated it ever since their encounter with the monstrous entity of the void.

Korth re-entered the ship, and carefully deposited the slime in a leaden vessel at the little laboratory cubby. Slowly he took off his space-suit, and then, without looking at the others, began a minute analysis of the stuff.

They saw his face growing paler and paler as he worked. His hands moved stiffly, his lips worked like those of a man in a dream. Of a sudden, the leaden vessel clattered to the floor. Korth had risen staggeringly, was gazing wildly at them.

"It—it is true—" he whispered, his eyes dilated as though he looked into ultimate horror. "The dimensional difference in the atoms of that thing's body—it proves your theory, Berringer—"

"Of course it proves it," shrilled Berringer triumphantly. "You know now that what I said is so, that we are heading straight to the last secrets of the cosmos, and shall solve those secrets."

"Solve them?" whispered Korth. "No—*no!*"

He had made a sudden leap back toward the table. Bradley yelled, "Stop him!"

Forijay leaped, but it was too late. Korth had grasped the ray-gun in his hand and had turned it against his own breast. He sank, a suicide.

Berringer looked down, almost unmoved, yet with a certain pity on his face.

"I knew he would do that," the old scientist said. "He could not stand the prospect of ending the hunt forever that has occupied him all his life. He died, rather than finally attain the truth he has been seeking."

The old man turned to Forijay. Silently they lifted Korth's body and thrust it into the airlock. A twist of the ship flung it clear into space, a moment or so later.

The ship fled on, toward the final secrets. Far back in space floated the body of the man who had died rather than witness the attaining of his ideal.

\* "Illusion, boys? Yes! But still, just as definitely, no!"

Bradley and Forijay both looked at Old Berriger with impassive though intense interest. They felt that they knew him very well now; and yet they were sure they could never fathom all the dark and devious channels of his penetrating genius.

There he sat before the controls of the space-ship, weird helmet on his head, his thin face shrunken and sweat-streaked, his emaciated chest heaving with his labored breathing; but his eyes alight with the glow of cosmic truth. They had respected him before, though they had doubted some of his incredible theories; but now that doubt was waning fast.

"I'm sure Fo and I will listen patiently after what we've just seen, Doctor Berringer," said Bradley quietly.

"Good!" the aged savant piped. "The whole universe is a para-

---

\* Beginning of Raymond Z. Gallun's installment

dox. Things are real that are not real—in a sense! I can give you a very simple analogy: Euclidean and non-Euclidean geometry. One teaches that parallel lines never meet; the other claims that parallel lines do meet—at infinity. And both concepts are right!

"But that is nothing. I have said many strange things before, and I say them again now. In one way, the universe is a concrete thing, composed of stars, planets, and endless seas of empty ether. Real energy flows in it, real atoms and molecules compose its substance. In another way all this is illusion—the vast, ethereal dream of some mighty Mental Essence, of which we human beings are each tiny separate parts!

"Back on earth I built a shaft that was a miniature model of the component parts of the cosmos. With it I could predict much of what the greater cosmos contains; for, by the very nature of things, the pattern of the two must be the same. In it I saw the blue electrical creatures, who are nearer in nature to the Great All than anything that can be said to exist. In one sense I brought those creatures to Earth in my experiment; in another sense I brought only their images; and in still another sense they did not and do not exist at all!"

"It seems beyond all sense and reason, Doctor," Forijay muttered. "And yet—"

Berringer's cadaverous face was crossed by a fleeting grin of elfin amusement. "Reason is sometimes a doubtful thing to stand on," he chuckled. "Look at those velocimeters. There is absolutely nothing wrong with their mechanism; their readings can be depended on to tell the truth! They register a speed of 147,000 miles per second. Yet repeated tests by trigonometry, equally reliable, show that we are not moving in space at all!"

"Then nothing is reliable! Nothing is predictable!" Bradley exclaimed.

"Quite the contrary," Berringer laughed. "I've told you that before. This helmet I am wearing gives me contact with the Mental Essence, and so I can read all the diverse branches of past, present, and future. You could not do this, for your minds lack the receptivity of mine. But if you could, you would clearly see how the factors of time, space, and energy combine to form the great cosmic pattern. Many, many, many things that are beyond description. From one angle all are the illusive parts of the intellect of the universe."

"And you are sure that we are doomed in this adventure?"

Forijay demanded.

"So I told you before we left," the savant responded. "You knew the risks you faced, but you thought we had a chance to survive, since you did not entirely believe me. We set out to probe the cosmos, and we are doing it. The very core of things is being unfurled to us. We will die, but it does not matter, for we have really lived. Isn't it so, boys?"

Both of the younger men swallowed hard. They said they thought so. Both had put the thrills of adventure above the promise of long lives. That was why they had accompanied Berringer.

Berringer smirked mockingly. He glanced at a chronometer. "In two minutes all the stars will vanish," he predicted in the tone of a seer. "A strange, airless, bitterly cold world will appear beneath us. We will land."

"And then what?" Forijay questioned.

The savant shrugged. "You will see," he said.

Berringer was unruffled, but not his young friends. Each second counted by the ticking of the chronometer was a lagging eternity.

And then there was a dizzy shifting, a momentary sensation of an impossible motion. The two minutes had passed, and the stars had vanished. Close beneath was an utterly rugged terrain, illuminated only by a faint bluish glow.

Coolly Berringer spiralled the ship to a landing. Bradley and Forijay donned space-suits.

"You will need those out there, boys, more than you would need them on the moon," said the scientist. "Remember what I told you about negative pressure?" Berringer grimaced knowingly.

"Yes," Bradley said without interest. "Aren't you coming with us?"

"It is part of the plan of things that I remain here," Berringer replied. "I have seen all there is to see, and I know that I am about the die in a strange way. Besides, the radiations of my experiments have made me ill. There is no reason why I should exert myself during these last moments of existence. Good luck, boys!"

"Good luck, Doctor," they echoed, eagerness to see more of the unknown, making them abrupt.

They left the ship. They had advanced across the rugged ground for perhaps two hundred yards when there was a mighty flash of electrical blue behind them. When they turned about, the ship was gone, dissolved by some invisible enemy.

Neither of them became outwardly excited. "Just like he said," Forijay remarked, very low. "This place, his finish—everything. Uncanny, dammit. Poor old Berringer!"

* Forijay relapsed into silence, then at a mutual nod from his companion they walked slowly and cautiously forward. It was as they walked through the midst of the hard rockery, frozen with eternal cold of absolutely empty space, that they became aware of something. Nothing tangible—just Something. A conviction of murky presences, invisible, hovering in that unbelievable temperature of absolute zero.

How long the sensation lasted they had no idea, but presently it became so absolutely insistent that they stopped and looked back towards the spot where their space-ship had been standing.

"Somehow, even though the ship's gone, I'd feel safer where it was," Bradley murmured. "We're proving Berringer too accurately for my linking. Come on!"

He turned to move, then before he could do so, something entirely invisible smote him a tremendous blow that dropped him flat on the rocks. He looked up in dazed astonishment and beheld nothing, save his companion likewise sprawling with all the wind knocked out of him.

They jumped to their feet again and made swift movements to tug the disintegrators from the belts, but before they could accomplish the feat the same unknown power held their arms tightly to their sides. They were whirled off their feet and propelled through the airless expanse at tremendous speed, perhaps for a distance of two miles or more—it was difficult to determine in that vast terrain—then at last they beheld that which they dreaded to behold, the very thing instanced in the Berringer Experiment—a mine of gigantic dimensions, sinking into bottomless profundity in the depths of this strange world. Within it, just visible to the eyes of the two as they were borne down the vast shaft, there floated lambent blue spots of flame—the blue of electricity itself.

As they sank lower and lower the two hapless earth-men thought again of old Berringer; they could not help but do so.

---

* Beginning of John Russell Fearn's installment

How deadly accurate his forecast had been; how he had been ridiculed for daring to say that there were no worlds or constellations in the sky at all! And that electricity experiment of his! And those strange occurrences on the way out here . . . The two earthmen now realized the vivid truth that had underlain it all.

Faster and faster they were borne into the depths, on the wings of the invisible, or rather, now the intense darkness prevailed, they could discern the captors as similar beings to those of the blue flame . . . Then there crept into the stupefying gloom a dim sense of light, of sun-light, rapidly increasing.

Alighting at last, they beheld the source of light. Lying flat on rocks they surveyed a circular area of unguessable dimensions.

Bradley sat up, Forijay beside him. For the first time they looked above them and from Forijay came an exclamation of profound amazement. *The stars had returned!* Incredibly far distant lay the greenish globe of Earth, but from this position they could distinctly see the sun, visible only by their looking over the cliff edge, was the exact center of everything, as well as being the source of light on this queer world.

Little by little they took it all in. The stars, the Earth—a free floating body in the strange concavity that was apparently empty space—and the tiny attendant moon. The stars had returned, yes, but the planets were still missing. And, ever more extraordinary, that stars only filled the space directly opposite to them.

Then at last the two came face to face the strange luminescent beings that surrounded them, beings that required neither air nor heat, who existed in that infinite cold of empty space upon this world . . . A world? The two earth-men pondered that, and as they did so they noticed how the light of the sun caught the myriad facets of the brightly glittering rock about them, turning them into a myriad hues of orange, green, sapphire and saffron.

Suddenly there came through the communicator the bitter laugh of Bradley. He couldn't help himself. The beings came closer.

"Forijay, if ever two guys from Earth got absolute proof of an earthly scientist's experiments, we have!" he breathed. "Everything fits in exactly, just as he said it would. The rock facets, the central sun, the floating earth, the absence of stars at the top of this inconceivably deep shaft, and yet the presence of stars at the bottom of it! These blue beings, obviously born electricity, existing under hardly any pressure. Berringer's experiment to the life!

And to think we laughed at what he told us! Why, damn it man, if we took off our space-suits now we'd blow asunder; existing under pressure common to Earth we're safe enough, but otherwise . . ."

He stopped and faced his helmeted comrade grimly. They searched each other's eyes in the varicolored lights.

"We're doomed, Fo," Bradley went on steadily. "We know that now. It's a one way passage—and according to Berringer that works out right, too. Remember his energy-flow equations and what we saw back there in space. If only we could get back now and prove that Berringer was right."

"And now?" Forijay asked quietly.

"Only this," Bradley answered steadily, and with that tugged a sharp knife from its sheath upon his belt.

Before the Blue Beings had the slightest chance to interfere he had made a lightning movement and slashed both the space-suits of himself and his companion down the center. Instantly, even as Bradley had theorized, they burst asunder, deprived of the vast pressures common to their own world.

The Blue Beings surveyed the empty space where they had been, all unaware that a supreme ultimate riddle of infinity had been solved. Then they turned their back to pursue their eternal movement in their multi-colored darkness that was their home.

THE END.

# The Blue Spot

*Astounding Stories, January—February 1937*

WIFT AND SILENT, THE COMPACT, STREAMLINED EGG SHAPE OF the aërodyne flung westward, high in the moonless dark. Ivec Andrel, alone at the controls, shivered to a little chill of ruthless apprehension. In the whisper of the wind he heard the rushing wings of doom. In the coolness of the night his excited imagination felt all the deadly rigor of the age of cold ahead.

His gray eyes fixed and solemn, he peered northward. Remote and motionless, the eternal stars burned in the blue of midnight—and newly written among them was the doom of man. Across the constellations, from Perseus to Lyra, coiled a monstrous cloud. It had the shape of an octopus, and its writhing tentacles were icy blue with a bitterness of cold beyond imagination.

Tense with a living dread, he saw again his father's face as it had been that afternoon in the bright oval of the telephore—pallid and graven with care, stern with an undying purpose. He heard again the solemn, urgent words: "'My son, the time has come. The sign is in the sky. My part will be done tonight, and yours cannot be delayed. I shall expect you by dawn."

Brief and guarded as the message was, it conveyed a dreadful meaning. There in the great lyceum of sciences, upon the green, sea-pressed Bermudas, Ivec had made hasty farewells to instructors and friends.

Now, sitting rigid in the aërodyne, he opened the motor coils to full drain upon the planetary power field. The whisper of the wind against the hull became a rushing hiss. His hard, white-skinned body leaned forward, as if to press the filer ahead. Cold sweat pearled his face. Dilated with indwelling dread, his gray eyes clung to the shapeless thing of chill blue in the north, the formless cloud of doom.

Yet a little joyous eagerness crept up beside his dread. For he might once again see Thadre Jildo. A glance, a word , a touch—a crumb of life snatched from the maw of death.

It was six years, now, since he had left her at the mountain laboratory, to take up his arduous course at the lyceum; yet the loveliness of her still burned clear in his mind. A tall girl, fair-skinned and graceful. Her copper-glinting head tilted proudly. Her blue eyes large, expressive, often imperious.

Their last meeting had ended, as usual, with a quarrel. Ivec held his breath with the memory of her, so beautiful in anger.

Deliberately, to touch her pride, on that last day, he had boasted, "I'll be back one of these days, Thadre, to be director of the laboratory."

Her fair skin flushed, at that. Her bronze head lifted; her blue eyes flared at him. For the rivalry between the families of Andrel and Jildo was almost a feud.

The Jildo Power Laboratory, established generations since to solve the myriad problems of supplying power freely to all the people of the Earth, had become a vastly important institution, its directorate an honor much coveted.

"You!" the girl exclaimed, scornfully. "You, director? When you are just a mass of muscle—and an Andrel!"

IVEC ANDREL bit his lip, repressing his own flare of anger. In an age of physical perfection, when health was universal and the average height well above six feet, he, nevertheless, possessed exceptional stature and strength. It always infuriated him to be ridiculed for his athletic prowess, with the cutting inference of mental inferiority. The girl knew his sensitive spot, from many another quarrel.

"My father is now director," he told her flatly. "So was his father and his grandfather, Delshar Andrel—"

"But before him, the director was Athon Jildo, who founded the laboratory and invented the planetary power field. Delshar Andrel was a mechanic in his shop—"

"Who revised the theory of the power field," Ivec put in, "and redesigned the generators to keep half the power from leaking away through the ionosphere, into space."

"Athon's brother, Korac Jildo," the girl said, "was the first man to reach Mars."

"Good!" jeered Ivec. "But he didn't come back."

"Anyhow," she gasped, "my uncle, Barthu Jildo, is the greatest scientist in the world—"

"Did my father tell you that?"

"Well," she conceded, "next to your father. But Barthu should be the next director. He's more than a bag of muscle—"

Ivec Andrel flushed in his own turn, and bit savagely at his lip. In many visits to the laboratory, he had come to know Barthu Jildo. A tall and powerful man, almost as fair of skin as his niece, although his hair and massive brows were black. His bearing was insolently proud. He had long been assistant director, chafing at his subordination to Ivec's father, Jendro Andrel.

"Yes, he's more than a bag of muscle," Ivec retorted, stung beyond restraint. "He's a maniac. His brilliance makes him dangerous. He should be summoned to the psychophysical clinic, for examination and treatment, or elimination—"

"I understand you, Ivec Andrel," the girl said to him, enraged. "I see the miserable cunning in your primitive brain. You know you can never win the directorate fairly, above my uncle. So you plot to have him summoned—put out of your way—"

"Thadre!" he protested, stricken. "Surely you don't believe—"

She was turning away from him, her square chin high. Her lovely face, drained of color, was cold and hard as marble. He caught her quivering arm, stopped her. She swung on him deliberately, eyes dark and stormy.

"Animal!" Her voice was low, savage. "If you can understand nothing but muscle—"

Her open hand struck his face, with a grim and unexpected violence. Ivec released her, stared after her, open-mouthed. His fingers touched the blood oozing from his cheek, and he broke into a short, ironic laugh.

Now, aloft in the aërodyne, hurtling beneath the menace of

the nebula, Ivec smiled at the memory of that quarrel. For he and
Thadre had quarreled many times since they were old enough to
understand the rivalry between their families. Each had striven
fiercely to excel the other in their studies of science. And friendship had always endured beyond hurt feelings.

IT WAS on that same day, before he left the laboratory, that his
father had told him of the nebula. Outlining the studies he was to
take at the great lyceum on the Bermudas, his father said: "We
Andrels have a task that must be done, Ivec—for the very life of
man. Delshar Andrel began it. For three generations we have
worked at it. I cannot finish it alone. But you must, my son—or it
will never be finished."

Eagerly, Ivec demanded: "What is it, father?"

His father rubbed his lean chin doubtfully.

"It is rather a terrible thing to tell a young man," he said slowly.
"But you must know, so you can be working to fit yourself for it.
Promise me to say nothing to your friends about it, for it is a
secret outside the council of science."

Vastly pleased and excited, Ivec promised. His father took him
to the wide, flat roof of the laboratory on the mountain, where
the great electronic telescope bulked black against the sky. Ivec
already knew the controls of this instrument, whose
photo-electric screens were far more sensitive than the human
eye.

"This telescope," said the old scientist, "was built by Delshar
Andrel to investigate the calcium clouds scattered through space.
His first discovery was a dusty nebula—a colossal cloud of
nonluminous particles.

"Calculating the mass, dimensions, and motion of the nebula,
he found that our Sun and its family of planets must pass through
it."

Ivec asked anxiously: "There will be a collision?"

"No," his father said. "The dusty particles are very fine, very
thinly scattered. Our Sun and planets will pass completely
through the nebula, in about one hundred years, without being
measurably slowed down."

"Then what harm—"

"While the particles are as far apart as the air molecules in a
good vacuum, ninety-three million miles of them will make an
effective filter. Most of the Sun's radiation will be absorbed before

it reaches the Earth. That hundred years will be the most terrible ice age the planet has ever known. Even the air, before the end, will freeze and fall like snow."

The youth shuddered, wide-eyed.

"But won't the weather control still warm the cities?"

"That takes power." His father smiled somberly. "Most of our power comes from the tides and the solar-electric plants. When the sea freezes, there will be no tides. When the Sun is hidden, the Solar plants will stop."

"We could dig burrows," Ivec suggested, "and go deep down until the cold is over. Volcanic heat—"

His father shook his head.

"A few might survive a hundred years," he said. "But the ice and snow would change Earth's albedo, make it reflect most of the Sun's radiation. It might never be temperate again. Low forms of life might persist. But mankind would perish in the end, miserably."

The young man looked up hopefully.

"But there is a way? You have found a way?"

His father nodded soberly. "With power enough—power independent of the Sun," he said, "we could extend the weather-control system over all the planet. We could keep it warm, in spite of the nebula. We could light the cities and the farms, run the factories—keep life itself alive."

IVEC was staring at the black, multiple barrel of the instrument.

"I was thinking," he said slowly, "of an equation Thadre and I learned: $E=Mc^2$. That is the energy equivalent of matter, when $c$ is the velocity of light, in centimeters per second. The result is about nine hundred quintillion ergs per gram.

"The material energy in the loose boulders on this mountain would light and heat the planet through all the century of cold—if we could set it free! But I beg your pardon, father. I know that can't be done."

His tall father had eagerly caught his arm.

"But it can be done," the lean scientist said. "The transformation of matter to energy is constantly going on in the Sun. The Sun's loss of weight by radiation is four million tons per second. It is taking place in all the stars. In some—the supernova—it happens very suddenly.

"Even in certain laboratory experiments, the energy of the atom—the limited portion called the binding energy—has been set free. But we were forced to abandon such direct attempts long ago, because of the very danger of success—success that would burn up Earth and all the planets and the Sun itself in the brief flame of a supernova.

"Some catalyst is what we must have—an agent to control the process. All our research has failed to discover it. Yet mathematics assures us that it must exist—that, in fact, it must be a rather simple modulation of field tensions."

The tall scientist paused to touch the telescope.

"Calculations tell us the process must exist," he said. "This instrument proves that it does."

Eagerly, Ivec Andrel demanded, "How?"

"My father," the old man said, "searched all the known planets with this telescope, for any useful clue. From Mercury to Pluto, he found no high intelligence surviving, nor anything hopeful.

"But, in the year I was born, he discovered a new planet that he named Persephone. It is a tiny world, only two thousand miles in diameter, smaller than the Moon. Four times more remote than Pluto, it keeps a mean distance of sixteen billion miles from the Sun, so far that the solar radiation takes a whole day to reach it.

"That small globe is immeasurably the most ancient of the planets. Its volcanic energy and its store of radioactive elements must have been long since exhausted. At its tremendous distance the Sun is no more than a very bright star, unable to warm it appreciably. It should be frozen, utterly dead, but a few degrees above the absolute zero.

"Most of its surface proved to be a dark , frigid waste of time-shattered mountains, airless and barren. But my father discovered a small, shining area—perhaps a hundred miles long—which he named the Blue Spot.

"An amazing discovery. The Blue Spot radiates far more energy than the entire planet receives from the Sun. Upon a world so ancient, all chemical, radioactive and kinetic sources of energy must have been exhausted ages since. But one conclusion was possible: the energy of the Blue Spot comes from the controlled conversion of matter!

"Analyzing the emanations of the Blue Spot with the electronic spectroscope, my father found proof of that theory. The blue is monochromatic—its spectrum shows a single bright line. But, far beyond the ultra-violet, he found a few quanta so powerful that, as he demonstrated mathematically, they can originate only in the liberation of material energy.

"Life and intelligence, my father believed," the old man concluded, "exist upon Persephone. It has discovered the catalytic agent that we must have, to save the Earth from cold—"

Ivec Andrel was eager, on his feet.

"Then," he cried excitedly, "somebody must go to Persephone, to learn that process."

Oddly, his father looked away for a moment, and back at him with eyes curiously glistening. He seemed to gulp, and nodded silently.

"But how?" the young man put the question. "When the penetrating radiations and high-energy particles of space destroy the bodies of men in their rocket—and when the best rocket we could build had power to take Korac Jildo only so far as Mars, where he died of his burns? How?"

"I am working on a way, Ivec," his father said solemnly. "A strange way. By the time you have finished your course at the lyceum, I may have it ready. And you must be ready to go and—"

"I?" He was amazed, vastly excited. "I shall go out to Persephone—"

"If I can prepare the way before the nebula stops my work,"

Trembling, Ivec again demanded, "How? It must be something more wonderful than a rocket?"

"I'll show you," his father said, "when you come back. It will mean effort, pain, great sacrifice. You must fit yourself for it. Follow the program I have outlined. Try to develop mental readiness, courage, endurance, strength. For the life of the world may depend on you."

"I will." His voice broke. "Father, I will."

But now, in the aërodyne slipping through the dark, Ivec shivered again. What effort of his could avail against the dark might of the nebula?

## II.

DAWN was in the sky as Ivec Andrel dropped the aërodyne toward the isolated laboratory upon its lonely mountaintop. The monstrous blue spiral of the nebula was drowned in rosy light. Like the flames of a burning world, a crimson sunrise flared up behind a ragged wall of mountains he had passed. The Sun itself, red as a drop of blood, drenched the world in sinister light.

The light was red, he knew, because the fringes of the nebula already filtered out the shorter wave lengths, which carried the greater energy. Already the dread change had begun. He shivered to the coolness of the dawn.

The laboratory stood as he remembered it, a long, windowless metal building, low and rectangular, carrying the squat bulk of the electron telescope on its flat roof.

But half a mile down the grassy ridge of the summit, he saw a structure new to him. Twin towers lifted high the silver globes of colossal resonance cells, to tap the power field. Transformers, condensers, and tuning units bulked large beneath them, within screening metal barriers. Between them, connected with snake-like power cables, a small, building rested upon tall insulating pillars.

Still shuddering to the chill of the morning, Ivec grounded the aërodyne upon a gravel plot beside the laboratory, and ran eagerly inside the long building. The ancient corridors, familiar with their chemical smell distilled from centuries of experiment, were deserted, silent.

His father's office, with the proud legend on the door, "Jendro Andrel, Director," was dark, locked. He found the door marked, "Thadre Jildo, Technician." It, too, was locked. But a light caught his eye, shining yellow and pale through the translucent panel printed, "Barthu Jildo, Assistant Director."

Ivec rapped, entered. Barthu Jildo looked up, with hostile eyes, from a desk untidy with scientific models, instruments, and papers. His massive body, unhealthily pale, stiffened aggressively. His heavy, black brows drew into a frown of disfavor.

Harshly guttural, his voice rasped out: "Young Andrel! If you want your father, he's down at the new photon laboratory." His thick lips sneered. "So you've returned to become the new director?"

Ivec bit his tongue upon an impulsive retort. Struggling to conceal his dislike, he said carefully: "No. I have been studying at Bermuda for a job my father has ready for me. I have come back to undertake it."

"Then it hasn't occurred to you that success will be rewarded.

If you go alone to Persephone, and bring back the knowledge that will save the world from cold—you don't know that any possible honor will be yours for the asking."

Ivec clenched his hands.

"When the world is in danger, I won't quarrel about empty honors," he said hotly. "If my father thought another man could do this task better than I, he would send that man. But I have spent years in training—"

"You Andrels have always plotted to keep all opportunity and honor in your own family. Now your devoted father is planning to give you a power that no man has ever had, the opportunity for such an adventure as no man has ever dreamed of.

"He has refused to give it to me, when I am assistant director and it is rightly mine." Savagely, his fist crashed to the desk. "I'll show him that Barthu Jildo cannot be scorned and ignored. I'll prove—"

His jaw set grimly. Ivec Andrel had retired through the door. He turned his back on the bitterly storming man, went out of the building and along the ridge to the photon laboratory.

THE THROBBING HUM of tremendous energies told him that the high argent globes must be draining a vast river of power from the planetary field. His father appeared at the door of the odd little room on its stiltlike insulators, pointed at a warning of dangerous voltages.

Ivec waited ten minutes before that throb of power ceased, and his father came down to meet him. Now in his eighty-seventh year, Jendro Andrel was yet almost as tall and straight as his son. A long weariness shadowed his ascetic face; but his features were yet firm, his clear eyes bright with a calm and invincible purpose.

His strong arms embraced Ivec, eagerly.

"I'm glad to see you, my son. I have had good reports of your work. You are ready?"

"I hope so, father." Troubled, Ivec glanced at the red sunrise. "Last night I saw the nebula in the sky. Now the Sun is red and cold. Is there time?"

"Not too much," his father said. "What you saw was an outlying spiral—a warning. Its absorption has dimmed and reddened the Sun. But we shall pass through it in a few weeks. It is yet four months before we shall reach the parent cloud.

"You have four months to go out to Persephone, discover the

catalyst that controls the liberation of material energy in the Blue Spot, and return to Earth with the information. If you are late, you will be lost—and the world with you—because you can't return through the nebula."

"Four months!" whispered Ivec, alarmed. "When it took Korac Jildo's rocket two months to reach Mars, at a million miles a day. And Persephone is two hundred times as far! But it isn't a rocket, of course." He caught his father's arm. "Tell me, how am I to go?"

The old man's eyes seemed suddenly stricken. He seemed suddenly lonely and helpless upon this bleak mountain ridge, fearful, crushed with a sense of tragic loss.

"You are tall, Ivec," he whispered softly. "You are fine and strong and handsome. You must love your body?"

"Why—I have tried to make it strong." Ivec was puzzled, awed. "You told me I would need strength and endurance. I guess I'm proud of it, too—even if Thadre did laugh at my strength. But why?"

His father's eyes were full of grave pity.

"Are you brave enough, my son, to surrender—your body?"

Ivec stepped back a little, with lifted hands. He swallowed, said in a low tone, "I'll not shirk my task. Tell me what it is."

"I'm glad." His father caught his arm affectionately. "Come."

IVEC followed him up into the little square room. It was crowded with massive electrical equipment. Six huge photon tubes, of a type new to him, were set up with reflectors, lenses, prisms, and filters arranged to focus their radiations upon the top of a small, black insulating pillar that rose from the center of the floor.

Upon the pillar, glowing with soft green, lay a small cube. Ivec moved to touch it. It looked real, yet curiously immaterial, like a two-inch block molded of some giant emerald's rays.

"Don't." His father stopped his hand, and found a pair of delicate insulated tongs with which to lift the cube into a padded case. "It is a frail thing, although so powerful."

His heart pausing painfully, Ivec whispered, "What is it?"

"It is a stable wave frame," his father said, "like matter, except that it is built not of electrons but of photons. It is pure light energy, fixed in dynamic balance. Half the output of all the power-field system has gone into this cube for the past year, Ivec. The energy in it, suddenly liberated, would fuse this mountain."

"What"—Ivec was dry-voiced with dread—"what is it for?"

His father's eyes came up, stricken again, tragic. The old man wet his lips, began slowly: "You know the history of travel in space. There are two difficulties that have never been completely overcome. The first is power. The velocity of escape from Earth's gravitation is about seven miles per second. No rocket propelled by known chemical reactions can exceed that very much. We have no available source of power sufficient to carry a human body on a successful voyage to Persephone.

"The second difficulty rises from the fact that the human body is very poorly adapted for travel in space. It is crushed by any violent acceleration. It perishes without bulky and elaborate provision for maintaining optimum conditions of temperature, pressure, and humidity; without heavy supplies of oxygen, water, and food. It is destroyed by the penetrating radiations and high-energy particles of space—which generate deadly secondary rays even from the lead walls designed to protect the passenger.

"The human body is deficient in sense organs for the needs of space travel, unless equipped with numerous and heavy instruments, all of which require additional power.

"Generations of effort have failed to conquer those difficulties. Most space voyagers have perished in their machines; a more successful few have returned to die on Earth, of their radiation burns."

"This green cube," Ivec put in breathlessly. "Is it—"

His grave father nodded.

"Since both those difficulties are connected with the limitations of the human body, I set about many years ago to find means to separate the essential part—the life—of a man from his body—or, if you like, to devise a body without those limitations.

"The photon cube is that body. It is pure energy; all its weight is available power. It moves easily—by the mere readjustment of vibratory axes—for motion is the very nature of photons. The theoretical limit of its speed is only the velocity of light itself."

"I—" Ivec's voice was husky with dread. "I am to be—in the cube?"

Again the scientist nodded soberly.

"Your life exists as a function of the electric energy in the cells of your body. Nerve action is a progressive electrical discharge, conditioned by the dipolar moments and electrostatic tensions within the body molecules. Your mind is essentially a configuration of synaptic resistances.

"This cube reproduces, in its intricately interwoven vortices and stable wave fields, every energy potentiality of the human body. Every free electron in the body may be represented by a static photon quantum in the cube.

"With special conversion apparatus, I can drain the minute electric charges from your body—leaving it dead—and cause the energy to reappear in the balanced fields of the cube, which will then be alive."

"So my body," Ivec whispered, "must—die?"

"It must," his father said softly. "But you will gain something to compensate the loss. You will be able to traverse space at will, and swiftly. Through field extensions, you will be able to cause physical effects in the space about you—to exert pressure, pick up and manipulate objects, set up sound or electromagnetic waves. You will be able to radiate your energy in controlled beams of almost any frequency."

Trembling, Ivec closed his eyes. His numbed fingers grasped at the cold, polished surface of a great inductance shield.

"But how, in the cube," he whispered, "will I know anything? It has no eyes or ears."

"The cube is sensitive to light, because the impact of every quantum disturbs its own quantum structure," his father said. "It can see far better than your own eyes, in which the photons must act indirectly to produce chemical effects. It is sensitive to frequencies and particles that you cannot see.

"Its delicate structure is extremely sensitive to pressure and vibration—which means to sound. Its surface has a fine sense of contact and temperature.

"In a manner, the chemical senses, taste and smell, are lacking—because the cube contains no chemical elements. Yet its radiation sensitivity enables it to detect the chemical qualities of molecules. You will be able to *see* tastes and odors."

Hardly listening, Ivec stood looking at his father. Tears filled his gray eyes. A leaden ache seized his throat, choked his whispering voice:

"So I must die—to give life to a machine?"

Soberly, his father nodded, said, "If you would put it so."

Ivec looked for a little space at the scanty grass at his feet, and then down the tumbled, rocky slope. He looked into the valley's blue haze, and upward toward the far, cragged summits, dark against the scarlet sunrise. Soundlessly, his lips said: "When?"

"I knew you wouldn't fail me," his father said, relieved. "The conversion apparatus is in the main laboratory. I must tune and adjust it. I shall be ready in—an hour."

"I'll be there," Ivec promised. He looked back at the sunrise, whispering: "An hour to live."

### III.

WHEN his father had gone, Ivec Andrel stood alone on the bare mountaintop. He sucked lungfuls of the cold, dry air. Could the cube sense the fragrance of pines? He followed the thin, white thread of a road in the distant valley, traced the minute saw teeth of trees on a far ridge. Could the cube really see?

Drawing himself erect, he ran light fingers over the smooth, swelling muscles of arms and shoulders, touched his hard, flat stomach, the firm curve of his jaw. He swung forward on the balls of his feet, joyous in the elasticity of his legs. He extended and flexed his hand. He grappled with the appalling fact: in an hour this body, that seemed to be himself, must die.

Movement caught his eye. He saw Thadre Jildo, in hiking boots and black-and-scarlet tunic, striding along the mountain rim. Her fair skin glowed from exercise; the sun flamed against her copper hair.

He knew abruptly that he loved her. All his years seemed suddenly a tragic loss. There was, now, no time for love. But he turned and hastened to meet her, swelling his chest with the cold, invigorating air, rejoicing in every fragment of sensation.

A splendid way to die, he thought briefly, in joyous strength until the end.

"Ivec!" she shouted delightedly at sight of him, eagerly advancing. "I hiked to the point to watch the sunrise. It was terrible and glorious—even though it means the nebula is near.

Her sparkling eyes scanned his lean, athletic figure.

"You look wonderful," she said. "You really are a magnificent animal." At that word she flushed a little, bit her crimson lip. "I'm sorry, Ivec," she said contritely. "I've often been sorry we quarreled before you left. Will you forgive me—for striking you?"

"Of course." He smiled at her. "It's awfully good to see you again, Thadre. Even if it's just for a little while." Despite himself, he had to gulp. "I won't be an animal much longer, you see. I have just an hour."

Her blue eyes came slowly to his face.

"Ivec," she said in a low, sober voice, "don't you think my uncle deserves the opportunity to make the trip to Persephone?"

He caught her arm. "Please don't start that," he said. "I just talked to Barthu, in the laboratory. He was unreasonable. If my father has chosen me to go, I shall."

She flushed. "The Andrels stick together."

"So, evidently, do the Jildos." He caught himself, jerked his head. "I'm sorry, Thadre. Don't let's quarrel again. You know about the cube?"

"I helped your father set up and test most of his apparatus, and filed all his notes."

"In an hour," he told her, "I must go into the cube. My body will die. Before that happens, I want to tell you something." His voice sank earnestly. "Thadre, I have always loved you, I think. Now I want—"

"I know what you want!" She tried to fling his hand from her arm. "When you have stolen the opportunity and the honor that were rightfully my uncle's, you want my sympathy, my love. You want the rewards of a hero before you have earned them."

She tried again to break away, but Ivec held her. With an unconscious strength, his hard fingers dug into her arm. She looked at him defiantly.

"Listen, Thadre," he said grimly. "You are very beautiful. I just said I always loved you. But just now I don't approve of your behavior—any more than your uncle's.

"Now, when the world is in danger, this jealous, selfish squabbling about personal honors is criminal. Pride is all right—if it's justified. You are all right. But your uncle hasn't earned the responsibility he wants—and he isn't worthy of it."

The girl stood rigid, facing him in bleak hostility. She was breathless, pale. Her attitude stung Ivec to another attack.

"Let me tell you something about Barthu Jildo. He is a coward and a maniac. He was terrified when he first learned of the nebula. He was afraid to die. He began a series of experiments with his own body, seeking to change its chemical constitution, so that it could endure the age of cold and survive forever.

"Those experiments failed, of course. More than that, they injured his body and his brain. He knows that his body is doomed, whether the world escapes the nebula or not. That is one reason why he wishes to escape into the immortality of the cube.

"His mind was disturbed by the effects of those rash experiments. My father believes that your uncle is not only useless, but dangerous to society. My father would have petitioned long ago to have him summoned for treatment or elimination—if I hadn't begged him not to, for your sake!"

Trembling with anger, the girl gasped, "Let me go!"

Ivec released her, silently.

"You are the mental defective, Ivec Andrel!" she stormed. "You've let jealousy warp your mind. You know you can never beat my uncle's brilliance fairly, so you attack his sanity. You are cruel—despicable—"

He grasped her quivering shoulders, looked into her eyes.

"You don't believe what you're saying, Thadre, honestly?"

"I do," she cried. "Let me go!"

She broke free again, and ran sobbing away from him, toward the laboratory.

IVEC sat down beside the trail. The mountain fell very sharply away beside him, its gaunt, rugged slopes scattered with stunted juniper and naked boulders. Aimlessly, his eye followed the white road in the valley, the far, serrated line of pines.

The joy had gone out of him. For a long time he sat thinking of his crowded youth, his many visits here, his arduous years at the lyceum. He had waited long for the time when he, also, could serve. Now it had come.

A slow eagerness came to him. After all, this was the supreme adventure. To assume a new and wondrous body, fashioned of light itself! To go flashing away into the void, where man had never been! To visit the Sun's most ancient planet, on an errand of unguessed peril!

Against that, what was the loss of his body? What that a girl had scorned him?

He rose suddenly to his feet. He had been sitting a long time; the hour must be gone. He must go back to his father, make ready for the conversion.

He looked upward at the sky, bluer now, sun-drenched. The waning Moon was pale and low in the west. A sudden elation throbbed in him. To go flashing out there, a being of light itself—

what could be more supremely expressive of life?

"To-day," be whispered, "I shall be going out there, past the Moon—and on!"

He was startled by the abrupt, harsh voice of Barthu Jildo.

"Not you, Andrel," it mocked him. "I am the one to go."

Puzzled, Ivec looked along the path in both directions, peered over the rim. He failed to find the speaker.

"Here I am," came the voice again. "Don't you recognize the body that your father fashioned for you?"

It dropped out of the sunlight, hung in front of his face—the small cube, shining with a pale, steady green, as if molded from the glow of translucent jade.

Ivec gasped,

"I persuaded your father that I was better entitled to this privilege than you." The cube bobbed up and down, six feet before him. He heard a mocking laugh. "He was difficult to convince—but I left him still living."

Ivec clenched his fists, voiceless with fury. His eyes abruptly narrowed. He tensed, leaped, grasped for the cube. It bobbed elusively away.

"Thadre warned me of your anger," said the voice. "But now I am stronger than you, Andrel. At will, I could release energy to vaporize your body in an instant—"

"Thadre!" Ivec choked. "She knew of this?"

"Thadre Jildo is loyal to her name," said the voice of the cube. "She ran the conversion ray, to transform me." The cube danced higher, a green jewel in the sun. "Now I must leave you, young Andrel. I must go to Persephone, to obtain the key to material energy. In this cube my life may well be immortal. That secret might make me the eternal ruler of Earth.

"And never again will an Andrel—or any other man—be placed above Barthu Jildo. I promise that!"

"Thadre!" Ivec's voice was stricken. "She didn't—she couldn't have done this—"

"But she did," said the voice of Barthu Jildo. "I promised her not to injure the body you prize so highly. But I am not responsible for the force of gravitation."

Ivec was standing nerveless, dazed. It doubled the tragedy that Thadre had been involved. He was unconscious of any contact or pressure against his body. But, suddenly, he was floating upward, as if weightless. The sensation was giddily unpleasant. He snatched vainly at the bush beside the path. His body drifted across the precipice, over the steep slope below.

"Farewell, young Andrel," came the jeering voice. "I must leave you now, to find the secret—"

"You must go," cried Ivec, urgently. "Destroy me if you will. But you must find the energy catalyst, and bring it back in time to save the world from cold!"

"Don't you think," inquired the mocking tones, "that I shall be more eagerly welcome if I return after many have perished. After all, four billion are more than I need to serve me. But farewell."

The green cube flashed upward. And Ivec Andrel fell, unsupported. He plunged forty feet, to the rugged slope. His broken body rolled limply down across the naked rocks, until it caught against a juniper snag. It hung there, quite still.

IV.

"IVEC—Ivec, can you hear me?"

The distressed voice of Thadre Jildo came to Ivec Andrel as he lay on the mountain slope. He became slowly aware of his body, one bruised mass of dully throbbing agony. He tried to move, but his body was an inert and helpless burden of pain.

He was able to open his eyes. He saw Thadre over him, her dry eyes dark with pain. The aërodyne was on a ledge behind her.

"You did—" The sobbing whisper of his voice set a new agony flaming in his chest. "You did—"

"I did it, Ivec," she said. "I converted my uncle to the cube because I believed he was the one who deserved to go. And because"—her white face went rigid with pain—"because I wanted you to stay."

She gulped; her eyes glistened suddenly.

"Forgive me, Ivec. I didn't know then that he had injured your father. And he promised me not to hurt you. I was a proud fool. Please forgive me—"

She was on her knees beside him, sobbing.

Ivec closed his eyes; his pain-grayed face was grimly tense.

"My father is alive?" came his agonized whisper. "Can he make another cube?"

"He will recover," the girl said. "But there wouldn't be time to build another. It took us a year to build No. 3. That is the one my uncle took."

"Three?" he gasped. "There are—others?"

"Nos. 1 and 2," said Thadre. "They were preliminary attempts. They are weak and unstable; the wave pattern is flawed. They can't lose much energy without breaking down. Your father said they weren't fit for the journey to Persephone."

"Take me," he whispered, "—laboratory."

As tenderly as she could, she began to gather up his limp, crushed body, to lift him into the aërodyne.

"You couldn't stand it," she said, choked with pity. "Your back is broken, and many bones. I must take you to the doctors. I'm afraid you—you're dying."

"Because of you," he gasped bitterly. Consciousness rocked to the searing pain from his chest. He coughed weakly, spat scarlet froth. "Take me—to my father."

Dark oblivion came to ease his agony as she was lifting him into the aërodyne. When painful awareness came back, she and his father were carrying him into the laboratory, on a stretcher. His father's head was bandaged, his thin face blood-smeared, haggard with pain.

The girl was saying, "—made me bring him."

Ivec caught his breath, forced out the gasping whisper: "Put me—in other cube."

His father said nothing until he was motionless in the cool quiet of the laboratory, and Thadre had made some injection into his arm that seemed to clear his fevered mind, to ease his pain a little.

"Please," he gasped again. "Barthu is selfish—mad. Wants to be—a god. He will destroy—mankind. Let me go—stop him— bring back the catalyst—"

"DON'T SPEAK," his father said gravely, standing beside him. "Let me explain the situation. I know that Barthu Jildo's mind is mad; mankind had better perish than submit to his rule. But I'm afraid that you could accomplish nothing, in either of the other cubes."

Ivec whispered, "A chance."

"I don't know," his father said. "The conversion itself is very dangerous. Even when the subject is in perfect health, it is uncertain. With an old man, or a sick one, it would surely fail. That is why I cannot go.

"Even if you survived the conversion, both the remaining cubes are very much inferior to the one Barthu took, in both energy reserve and stability. It is not certain that either of them would be able even to reach Persephone, without collapsing.

"The odds were greatly against success, even with No. 3. The approach of the nebula's energy fields will make the outward voyage very perilous. It will be impossible for even the best cube to return, after the system has actually been engulfed in the cloud.

"Don't forget that the cube is merely a construct of photons that are always tending to break out of field vortices, as radiant energy. It hasn't the stability of matter. The impact of the nebular particles, or of any high-voltage quanta, will tend to break it up."

"But let me"—Ivec gasped from his couch of pain—"try!"

His father's haggard face smiled somberly.

"Consider the difficulties, my so. I have explained those that come from the imperfection of the cube. It may not be able even to reach Persephone. I think its energy reserve is insufficient to allow it to return at all.

"Another danger is that from Barthu Jildo. The photon body he took is superior to the others in every respect. His mind is yet brilliant, for all its warp. He will certainly oppose any attempt to take away his prize. He will have the power, and the ruthlessness, to destroy you.

"But most difficult is the third problem—of obtaining the details of the catalytic process. Since atoms elsewhere in nature do not break down in the peculiar way which we observe in the Blue Spot, I am sure that the process there is being controlled by intelligence. That intelligence will probably fear and mistrust seekers of its power. I believe that it will be hostile. And in the material-energy process it has a dreadful weapon."

The old man's bloodstained face was very grave.

"I want you to understand, my son, that between the three dangers —the cube's instability, the insane hatred of Barthu Jildo, the hostility of the masters of Persephone—your chance of success is near mathematical zero."

"Still," whispered Ivec, "let me try. Not quite—zero!"

His father's haggard face was briefly lighted with a weary joy.

"No Andrel," he said, "has yet been beaten by a Jildo. I shall make ready No. 2."

## V.

IN A POOL OF PAIN, Ivec Andrel lay on a black, padded table in a darkened inner room. Massive electrical mechanisms loomed about him. A tube glowed dimly here in the shadows; there a bright surface gleamed. The sharp pungence of ozone was mingled with the smell of antiseptic from his bandages.

The photon cube rested upon an insulated stand near his bed. It was not clear like the other he had seen, but murky, flickering. It was like the ghost of a great emerald, but flawed, about to shatter under some inner strain.

His new body. Anyhow, he thought, the agony would soon be ended.

"A few moments," his father said softly. "Lie still."

His father wheeled a bulky, darkly glistening instrument over him, a similar one over the cube. Thick cables connected them, coiled away to other mechanisms.

His father whispered, "Now, steady."

A shrill, whining hum; an intermittent purple flicker of electricity. The ozone stung his nostrils. A white, blinding needle stabbed from the machine above toward his face, from the other toward the small green cube.

"A needle ray of positrons," his father briefly explained, his voice calm, soothing—yet somehow betraying a private doubt, an agony of strain. "It is deflected back and forth by magnetic fields. When a positron strikes a free electron in your body, the two are annihilated, with the creation of two-million-volt quanta. Thus your body is scanned.

"The photons are trapped in special field cells, equipoised in stable wave systems, and projected into the corresponding position in the vortex web of the cube. Thus your life is transformed from the electron energy of matter to the quantum energy of light."

The scientist had been busy with adjustments as he talked. The whining had changed, grown keener; the white needle had grown thinner, sharper.

"You are ready, my son?"

"Yes," gasped Ivec. A new wave of torture came up from his broken body. He coughed feebly, sickened by the terrible flow of blood in his torn lungs. Through scarlet foam, he whispered, "Hurry."

A rapping on the door. Then his father's voice: "It's Thadre. She wants to say good-by."

"No," breathed Ivec, bitterly. "This—her fault. Go ahead."

His father touched his hand, as the black bulk of the machine descended. The whining grew sharper still. The white needle thrust toward his head. He closed his eyes, but its blinding radiance burned through the lids. Then, a thin blade of white agony, it probed into his brain.

A darkness struck him, heavy and thick as a physical wave. It drowned his senses—all save the sharp, thin pain of the stabbing ray. The darkness was shot with patches and zigzags of colored fire. A confused roaring ebbed and flowed. His whole body floated, as if on a river of roaring power.

Once he tried to move, to escape that probing needle. But his body was numbed, powerless. He relaxed into that black river—an instant or an eternity, he never knew. Then he had a vague, brief sense of dual identity, as the darkness and the roaring slowly faded.

He was one again. Light was about him once more. The thin agony of the ray receded, and abruptly he was aware of his surroundings.

He lay, naked and without pain, upon a smooth, hard surface. The dark bulks of the machines hung above him in the gloom, but they had shifted in position, so that the second, which had been upon his right, was now on the left.

He looked beneath it for the green cube. He saw the wheeled table, instead, with his father tenderly spreading a sheet over a supine, rigid form—a shape terribly familiar—his body.

With a clearing intuition, Ivec was suddenly aware of the cube as the home of his being. Vividly, he sensed each jewel-smooth face, each straight, sharp edge. He somehow felt the tumultuous, uneasy stir of the prisoned photons within it, the pressure of restrained energy processes. He was aware of the soft radiation flowing out, of his own control of it.

He dimmed the soft green rays, with an effort of will that soon became unpleasant—like the effort, in his old body, of holding the breath. He made them flare intensely, and again felt pain, as if from exhaustion.

"Careful, son." His father stood straight, above his sheeted body. "You will soon master the control of the cube—field tensions and vibration axes are directly responsive to your will. But remember your limitations. You have but a certain stock of energy, and when that is gone you will have no source for any more.

"You must be cautious. Any violent or sustained exertion, any severe shock or strain, might disturb the delicately balanced dynamic tensions of the cube and cause its sudden disruption.

"Now try to move—at first just slightly. The effect is attained by shift of wave axes and disbalance of vector forces. But you need be aware only of the effort of will and the resulting motion."

"Thank you, father. I will try."

Ivec was aware that his effort to speak had created a vibration of the entire cube, which set up sound waves in the air to carry his words to his father.

He tried to lift himself. The cube rose with the thought—a paper thickness—an inch—three feet. He soared over the great machines, poised, settled very softly upon the sheeted, stiff form that had been his body—this morning so joyously strong, now broken, useless, dead.

But this body of photons was splendid, also. It responded to his will with the speed of light. He lifted one of the conversion machines half an inch; it must have weighed a ton. He focused a beam of energy on a metal shield, heated a little spot to cherry red. And a sharp, bright pain almost cleft the cube.

Dizzily, he was aware of his father's grave warning: "Remember, energy loss can shatter the cube."

THE DOOR flung open. Thadre Jildo burst into the room. She stopped abruptly, her fair face white and dreadful, a stiffening hand at her throat.

Her voice whispered, huskily: "It is—over?"

The old scientist nodded without speaking. She moved, came slowly across the room, her face stricken, set. She paused beside the sheeted body on the table, her lifeless eyes looking dully down at the photon cube lying like a great flawed emerald on the breast of it.

The cube stirred, quivered, as conflicting emotions surged through Ivec Andrel. He loved this girl—despite what she had done, for all that he was dead. Regret ached in him that he had refused to tell her good-by. An eagerness burned in him at her presence—and a leaden bitterness of frustration quenched it.

His voice spoke her name tremulously: "Thadre!"

She burst into tears at that, dropped beside the wheeled table. Pressing her face against the sheeted body, she sobbed wildly: "Ivec! Oh, my Ivec—"

Ivec, in the cube, rocked to the horror of ultimate frustration. Her quivering breast was against the glowing emerald surface. With a savage effort of will, he fought the dreadful yearning for the life of his own body again, to comfort the girl.

Softly, he slipped away, saying: "Good-by, Thadre, father. Good-by!"

The girl looked up at the cube with a cry of startled horror; then dropped her face again, weeping. His old father stood bowed and silent, his eyes dark with compassion.

Ivec fled away from his dead body, the weeping girl and his father. He flashed through an open window, out into the air. The sunlight was a golden river. He floated in it, drifting upward.

For a little time, high over the laboratory, he paused. It was a little rectangular block, its metal walls silver and red upon the flattened mountain ridge. But his keener senses were still aware of his father and the girl, prostrate with grief.

A throbbing ache impelled him back. But there was nothing he could do. Their grief was for his body, and his body was dead. This cube was to his father merely a complex machine, to the girl apparently a thing of strangeness and horror.

His mind came back to his mission, which was greater than himself and his private loves.

His new senses were immediately aware of the vast, dark curtains of the nebula, like an ominous storm cloud, rushing upon the solar system. He could sense keenly the relative positions of the Sun and the nearer planets, and he could perceive, even in daylight, the brighter stars.

Persephone, his unthinkably distant goal, was far beyond the ken even of his sharpened senses. But he knew its position among the visible stars—near red Antares, in the Scorpion. With a last look at his father and sobbing Thadre Jildo, in the laboratory, he lifted the cube toward it with increasing acceleration.

## VI.

STRAIGHT WESTWARD, Ivec Andrel flew, wingless, at the speed of his will. Away from the red morning Sun, toward the sinking ashen disk of the waning Moon. The laboratory, the mountain, fell away behind. His range of vision vastly increased; the Earth became visibly convex.

Yet, to the delicate light sense of the cube, visual detail remained amazingly clear and intimate. With a wistful longing, an invincible sadness, Ivec looked back at the world of man—from which he was, now, forever, an exile, yet which he must spend his life to serve.

The bright roofs of lodges, where people came for rest and sport, were numerous in the green and gray of the mountains. Upon the plain beneath spread the green fields and orchards whose delectable fruits would forever rival the synthetic products of the chemists. Irrigation canals made a silver net; between them the tending machines moved almost intelligently.

The roadways were white, straight ribbons, where endless streams of vehicles flowed. He traced the long, unbending pencil of the vacuum tube, upon its spidery supporting towers.

Above the valley, yet far beneath the swiftly ascending cube, he saw the bright teardrops of pleasure aërodynes, floating, soaring, drifting with the wind.

As far as his vision reached were scattered the industrial city buildings, each a great pyramid structure, white-walled, green-terraced, with the factory space within and beneath the living apartments.

As he flew higher—or as the curved Earth fell away from the straight line of his flight—the Pacific came into view. The vast, swelling curve of it was minutely indented with waves, like hammered metal, and the terminator beyond was a sweeping arc of darkness.

The coast crept back beneath him. He saw a great city, spread for many miles along the beaches and far up into the hills. The great communal buildings, of varied shapes and colors that formed one artistic whole, were set far apart upon green, rolling park lands.

Vehicles were thick along the streets and roadways. He sensed the busy stir of life within the buildings, the swift intercourse through tubes and beltways beneath the parks. Above all, the aërodynes were flashing, like colored drops in a living fountain.

Far out upon the sea's sun-glinting blue convexity, he saw the white streamlined shapes of freight vessels; and the white walls of the floating cities, crowned with the feathery green of palms.

Vastly high above them, but still beneath the cube, hurtled the slender, silvery hulls of the rocket stratoliners, flashing from continent to continent.

A huge, diffused elation came to Ivec, to see all these evidences of busy, happy life. Power was the key to the splendor and the life of this modern worldpower created by coöperative effort, and freely available to every man.

His vision found the endless gray dikes of the tidal power plants along the coast, the far-spreading black rectangles of the solar-electric plants in the desert lands behind him. His new senses could even perceive about him the energy of the planetary power field, that maintained all the activity he saw—that fed the life of the world.

All that was doomed, if he failed.

His mind saw the coming of the cold: The Sun grew red, was swallowed in endless night. Frost blighted the crops; snow blanketed the stricken world from pole to pole. The seas chilled and froze. The aërodynes fell, for want of power. The weather-control system failed, and icy blizzards raged upon the cities. For a time the buildings were lighted, warmed, with the small reserve of power. Then the lights went out. The planet, at last, was dark.

The dead face of Thadre Jildo was looking at him, its white loveliness frozen in a beseeching appeal. She seemed to matter more than all the world. He tore his mind from that vision of death. He must not fail. No matter what the odds, he must not.

HIS FLIGHT carried him higher. The ionized upper layers of the atmosphere dropped from about him, wrapped the Earth in misty blue. In the new hard blackness of the sky, the stars shone minute and bright. The Sun's rays and the cosmic radiation came with a stinging, painful force against the surface of the cube.

Ivec was aware of the nebula again. The nearer octopus-shaped spiral he had already seen, ice-blue with cold, reflected light; its streamers had already touched and reddened the Sun.

Beyond that, his new senses detected the major cloud—so vast that the solar system, plunging northward at twelve miles per second, would be lost in it for a hundred years. A black and ominous wall of menace, it blotted out the northern constellations.

He must return before it reached the system, or the cube, helpless amid its charged particles and tremendous energy fields, would be lost, destroyed. Ever more swiftly, he flashed ahead.

The swelling Moon had changed from a pallid, ashen disk to a sphere of blinding white, its craters and pitted plains harshly rugged. It grew swiftly. It was beside him. The frozen Earth would look like that, he thought, after the nebula was gone—cruel, bright, lifeless—if he failed.

With the Moon dwindling behind, he increased his speed again. The effort of motion now brought a gnawing, inner pain, that kept him ever conscious of the cube's instability. Every expense of energy, he knew, must increase that agonizing flaw. Yet there was no time to spare; he tried to go still more swiftly.

The sunlight, cosmic radiation, positrons and other high-energy particles made a continual painful rain against the surface of the cube. Speed increased the pain of their impacts on the forward face. Enough of them, he knew, could shatter the cube.

Mars was in conjunction—lost behind the red, diminishing eye of the Sun. He crossed its orbit, flashed onward toward the region of the asteroids. He shifted his path, to cross to northward of the ecliptic plane—knowing that a violent collision with a material object would certainly disrupt the cube into a flare of radiation.

Jupiter, which was receding from opposition, he passed within ten million miles. An object of superb splendor, its white, swift-spinning sphere oblate, dark-belted, marked with the glowing red spot, encircled with its family of swinging moons.

Ivec was puzzled briefly at the apparent rapidity of its spin, at the hurtling velocity of the moons. Then he realized that, as a result of his speed, now tens of thousands of miles per second, he was experiencing the Lorentz-Fitzgerald contraction, and the associated time extension. Precious time was rushing away, unsensed.

Saturn, Uranus, Neptune, Pluto were all far from opposition; space was now open before him to remote Persephone, which was still invisible. Again he tried to increase his rate of motion, as much as the mounting agony from the cube's instability would allow.

He was ever aware of the nebula's advance, made apparently swifter by the retarding of his own sense of time. It spread across the constellations like a monstrous living thing, its sprawling black tentacles reaching out to seize Sun and planets.

Again and again he had encountered stray wisps of its cloud—streamers of its dusty particles, whose impacts brought him dazing pain, forced him to slow his speed. But the greater danger fell upon him without warning.

He was, he knew, beyond the orbit of Neptune—although that planet, nearing conjunction, was five billion miles away. The Sun had dwindled to a minute disk that, through the haze of the on-rushing nebula, looked red as a droplet of blood. The Earth was long since lost.

Yet he was only a bare sixth of the way to Persephone. He was fighting the twin pains, from without and within, striving once more to increase his speed, when, abruptly, his orientation was blotted out.

The tiny red Sun, the cold and distant stars, were swallowed in a cavern of darkness. Seized with a river of energy that he could not resist, he was flung spinning away. Scarlet agony engulfed him, as terrific forces tugged and battered at the cube.

HE WAS trapped in a sort of cosmic whirlpool, he knew—a colossal vortex created by the motion of the onrushing nebula. He fought its mad current with all his power, struggled to maintain the stability of the cube and gain his freedom, before he was dragged into the maw of the nebula.

Charged particles, given tremendous voltages in the stupendous electrostatic fields of the nebula, bombarded him with agonizing, paralyzing force. He sensed flaming lights of weird and incredible colors. Numbed, reeling, he was lost within the mazes of the nebula.

Once, when chance let him glimpse the Sun and a few southern constellations, they flickered in strange distortion, as if seen in curving mirrors. Light itself was twisted, lost in the terrific fields that held him.

But at last, weak and faint from loss of energy, wrenched from the tremendous field strains, numbed and battered from bombarding particles and quanta, he struggled free from the great vortex. For a time he wandered, utterly lost in the vast clouds, held to a snail's pace by the resistance of the charged particles.

Then again, through a rift in the nebula, he caught the faint and reddened gleam of familiar stars. His orientation restored, he drove onward toward distant and unseen Persephone. Inimical radiations battered him. The treacherous suction of energy fields sought to drag him back into the monstrous cloud. He suffered agony from the increasing instability of the cube and the terrific demands upon its vital energy.

He was fighting, not for his own life, which had long since ceased to have any meaning or value in itself, but for the life of the Earth. Against the appalling darkness of the nebula, he saw forever the proud poise of Thadre Jildo's bronze head, her blue eyes laughing, or soft with affection, or flashing with injured pride, saw the graceful loveliness of her tall, fair body. She became to him the type and the symbol of the race of man. It was she whom he must save.

Onward he flashed, toward Persephone.

## VII.

IVEC drove at last, dazed with pain, through the outermost streamer of the nebula, and found himself close upon Persephone—the smallest of the planets, incalculably the most ancient. It was smaller and more rugged than the Moon. The blotting out of the Sun would make small difference here—for a thousand million years, to this frozen world of eternal night, the Sun had been but another star. It was black, time-scarred, dead—save for the enigma of the Blue Spot.

Against the grim desolation of jagged, frozen mountains unchanged through a billion years of dark, the Blue Spot shone like a solitary eye of evil mystery. A little oval patch of strange light, its edges were dull, misty. It was like a low-clinging cloud of blue-lighted fog. He could see nothing through it.

Ivec slipped down cautiously, far from it.

Had this bleak globe been the Sun's first cradle of life? Had warm and kindly seas once filled these black chasms of abysmal mystery? Had vegetation once softened these incredibly lofty mountains?

That seemed at first a fantastic impossibility. Yet, as his father had reasoned, the existence of the Blue Spot, with its peculiar high-energy radiations, was a certain indication of the presence of an ancient and highly developed life.

And, presently, he saw a line drawn across a rugged, riven plain. He dropped toward it. It had been a wall, he saw, a long and massive barrier of something more durable than stone. In this airless, changeless world, erosion would be imperceptibly slow—yet its dark, perdurable blocks had been shattered with the impact of unthinkable æons of time.

Its purpose was lost with the long-dead hands that built it. But it surely spelled intelligence older than the life of Earth. He left it, drifting low and cautiously toward the Blue Spot.

Two dangers, now, were paramount in his mind.

The first was Barthu Jildo. That other mind, within the swifter, stronger photon cube, crazed with the fear of death and animated by a ruthless power lust, had doubtless arrived here long before him. It might well be that Barthu Jildo had already won the prize. In any event, he would know Ivec for a rival and one of his hated rival family. An encounter would surely mean a battle to the death, fought with the flaming light energy of the cubes.

The second danger—unknown, but, if possible, greater—was from the enigmatic masters of the Blue Spot. Doubtless they would defend the secret of material energy from any invader, which was at the same time their most precious possession and the most powerful weapon conceivable.

His existence meant little to Ivec for his own sake, now—but for the sake of the world, of Thadre Jildo, he advanced with utmost caution, slipping alertly through the eternal shadows of the black, titanic mountains.

Presently, he came within view of the Blue Spot, a hundred-mile bank of haze, shining with a peculiar dull blue, rising in a vague arch against the black and frosty sky. A barrier of fog before him, shining, mysterious. It lay heavily upon black, ragged slopes. Near the edge, a few sharp, tremendous peaks burst above it. Beyond, all was hidden.

Approaching, he was suddenly aware of the tingle of strong radiation beating against the faces of the cube.

Fears, memory, purpose, sensations, all seemed strangely dulled. His strength flowed away. The cube was falling, he knew dimly, into the shining cloud. But he didn't care. It didn't matter. A faint sense of danger stung him in vain. Even his life didn't matter. Why should it? He couldn't remember—

"UP! Fly upward!"

Although very faint, that sudden, warning voice was as real as any he had ever heard. Its anxious urgency revived his failing senses. Feebly, he tried to check the falling cube. But why should he suffer the pain of effort? What mattered?

"Upward!" the voice reached him again. "Or Gogok will destroy you. And the cold will take your world; the one you call Thadre will perish. Up!"

The name of Thadre awoke his memory. Her face seemed to float above him, white and lovely in the painful blue. He battled his numbness to rise toward it, endured increasing agony. It receded above him, mockingly; he followed through eternities of agonized despair.

Then, suddenly, he was free again, floating above that long bank of shining cloud—whose radiations he now realized, were insidious death to his photon body.

The faint voice spoke again, saying, "Come to me."

Its slight vibration, he knew now, was not sound. With the analytic energy senses of the cube, he perceived that it was a very weak tight beam of electromagnetic radiation—projected waves of pure thought.

He was able to locate its origin approximately. It had reached him from a thousand miles away, far beneath the north pole of this rugged, night-bound little world. The soft, pure quality of the vibrations led him to think of them as feminine.

Free from the sinister trap of the Blue Spot, he directed a tight wave beam in the same direction, and began the thought emanation: "Who?"

"Do not speak to me now," the warning reply came swiftly. "But please come and set me free. We can aid one another—if you are not discovered." The wave was fading, very faint. "My energy is nearly exhausted. Come—"

Puzzled, and somewhat astonished that life should still exist outside the Blue Spot, on this world that—must have been within a few degrees of the absolute zero for a billion years, Ivec was delighted at the promise of aid—if a little apprehensive that it might cost too much of his meager energy reserve.

He set off at once in the direction from which the wave had emanated. The cube soared over a bleak mountain range, whose cragged, hostile peaks, Ivec thought, must lift twenty miles against the planet's feeble gravitation.

Beyond the summits, and beyond a bottomless cavern of fearful darkness, lay a vast, black plain. Upon its frozen waste reared masses of rock that had been grotesquely carved by erosion in the youth of the planet—megalithic monuments and monstrous statues to the departed life of a world long dead.

He flew many hundred miles above that fantastic cemetery, before he approached a mountain looming above it, more colossal than any he had seen. Its unimaginably rugged slopes rose fifty miles, walled with precipitous, cragged barriers of stone forbidding beyond conception.

He was hesitating, puzzled, when the faint, strange vibrations of thought reached him again: "My prison is beneath the mountain. Follow the caverns below the crater—"

Upward he soared, over hostile cliffs and the cruel fangs of minor black peaks, until he found the crater's black pit, five miles across. He dropped into it. Colossal walls rushed upward, blotting out the stars. They narrowed, like a hideous maw.

He fell, scores of miles, into the cavernous space left by the cooling of the magmas that had formed the giant volcano. The darkness became intense beyond all his experience. In a younger world, he knew, his delicate senses could have perceived the emanation from radioactive elements in the rock. But this world was so ancient that even its uranium was dead.

He was able, at last, to find his way only by emitting a thin, searching beam from the cube—at a painful cost in precious energy.

Life, he perceived, had once reigned within these enormous, frozen caves. Strange patterns were graven here and there within the black walls. He passed above the crumbled ruins of a fantastic city, now fallen into the dust of illimitable ages.

TWICE AGAIN, as he hesitated before dividing passages, the faint thought beam brought him directions. And at last, upon the farther walls of the lowest cavern he had reached, he perceived the stark outlines of an enormous metal door.

Dimly, the fading vibrations reached him: "Here I am. Release me, if you can. Give me energy—or I die—"

No lock or handle, nor any opening, was visible on the time-blackened surface of the massive door. With an effort that cost him dazing pain, and drained his energy alarmingly, Ivec generated a beam of high-frequency radiation, which penetrated the door and revealed the ponderous mechanism of its bolts and tumblers.

The dense, heavy metal tended to dampen the field effects with which the photon body was able to manipulate material objects. Pain of effort staggered Ivec as he lifted the tumblers, slid back the heavy bolts, swung out the door's weight upon hinges that had not moved for millenia of millenia.

Behind the door was a rectangular space, walled massively with the same dense, black, refractory metal. Within it lay a heavy, dark gray block.

"Within this block," came the dying wave. "Cut me free—"

He tried first to shatter the block with a field effect, but it proved intensely hard and tough. He hammered at it in vain, with fragments of rock from the cavern floor. At last he was forced to attempt to cut it with a heat ray.

Beneath the thin needle of intense radiation, it proved to be highly refractory. It glowed red beneath the ray, orange, bright-yellow, intensely white. It was too tough to crack from expansion. But, at last, the surface fused, flowed beneath the ray.

Pain from effort and energy loss rose upon Ivec like a red, numbing tide. He was sharply aware of the fatal flaw in the structure of the cube, of the instability that increased with all expense of energy. But the white face of Thadre Jildo seemed to look beseechingly from the cold, gray block; it was for her that he pushed the cutting needle deeper.

The great block, at last, fell in twain. The faint thought wave directed the making of a second, shallower cut. And, at last, the prisoner of the æons was free.

It was a sphere, less than three inches in diameter—but slightly larger than the green cube. Very feebly it shone, with a pale, milky luster, like a giant dead pearl. It lifted a little, weakly, and fell again upon the fragments of the block.

"Energy," came the faint desperate plea. "Give me energy—or I shall die."

Ivec dropped the cube into contact with the sphere, emitted a slight flow of radiant energy. In a few moments stronger, grateful emanations came from the sphere, to tell him which frequencies were needed. Then the entity of the pearly globe seemed to re-lax, drinking in the life-giving beam. Ivec increased its strength, until the pain of radiation fogged his senses with a crimson mist.

This flow of vital quanta, he knew, decreased his strength and heightened the danger of the cube's disruption. Yet his strange, new ally was obviously unable to help either of them without such aid. He was moved, moreover, by a quick sympathy for it and the desire to understand its own situation—which, sealed in the prisoning block, must have been desperate indeed.

The nacerous globe ceased, at last, to absorb his energy. Its milky light was steady now, more intense; its voice came to him, thankful and strong: "That is enough; I am sufficiently restored. You are very generous. Let us now discuss our respective situations, and decide what must be done—for we are both in deadly peril."

Ivec asked, "What is the danger?"

The sphere replied: "Our lives are threatened both by Gogok, who is the master of this planet, and by the being Barthu Jildo, who has come from your world. They are now together, yet at peace. And the outcome of their meeting bodes evil indeed for you and me—and the people of your world,"

"I must do—something," said Ivec uneasily, recalling his recent misadventure in the radiant deadly haze of the Blue Spot. "Who are you?" he inquired. "And why were you—here?"

"Call me Lakne," came the swift thought radiation from the opalescent globe. "You are Ivec Andrel?"

"I am." Ivec was somewhat surprised. "Barthu and this— Gogok—are they planning something? What is Gogok?" He hesitated apprehensively. "And what can we do?"

"Listen," said the sphere. "I must tell you something of this planet, of Gogok and myself, and of my long imprisonment here. Then we can plan what to do. Our time is short, but you must understand."

"Then," urged Ivec, "tell me!"


VIII.


THE GREEN CUBE, flawed, flickering, and the softly opalescent sphere lay side by side upon the shattered prison block, beside those time-crumbled ruins that floored that black cavern within a dead and frozen world. Intently, tortured with a straining apprehension, Ivec absorbed the thought waves of the globe.

"This planet is no child of the Sun," Lakne began the swiftly radiated story. "Ages beyond calculation past, it was born from the tides of another star. A small world, it swiftly cooled; and beneath the kindly rays of its near-by mother sun, it soon gave rise to organic life—as any planet must, when all the conditions are satisfied.

"Life in turn gave birth to intelligence, and intelligence to science. There is no time to detail the long history of the planet, as tidal forces pushed it farther out and its sun grew old and cool. But its people—my forbears—met and conquered many aspects of hostile nature. Many times they were menaced by some astronomical event, and always they survived by the triumph of science.

"But at last, as the dying world grew cold, it seemed that they must ultimately perish for want of the very stuff of life—energy. They had for ages been aware of the illimitable reservoir of power in the matter of the planet, but no scientist had found means to tap it without inviting cataclysmic catastrophe.

"The planet's people, then, had become divided into two races. The surface had lost its atmosphere and moisture, through dissipation into space, save for traces that remained in the abysmal deeps of the ancient seas. A few still dwelt there, depending for their energy needs upon the scant and decreasing radiation of the star.

"But explorers had found air and water remaining in these far-stretching caverns, which were presently colonized. The new race of troglodytes depended first upon the planet's small remnant of volcanic heat, and, when that was gone, upon the emanations of radioactive elements. In quest of vital power, they sank their mine shafts to the very heart of the planet.

"I came of the upper race. My father—for we were of two sexes, as your race is—was the greatest and the last scientist that our kind produced. We lived in a dome-armored city upon the salt-crusted cliffs above the last bitter sea. Our city was the last upon the surface, and we had no knowledge of the delving race beneath us.

"Early in his youth, Sardoc, my father, perceived that our race was near its end. Another Sun, a young, giant star, had long been observed approaching our dying system. My father's calculations revealed that this great star, during his lifetime, would pass very near our ancient Sun.

"Collision would be very narrowly avoided, he predicted, and each star would survive to resume an independent path. But our old planet, he found, would suffer extreme vicissitudes. It would be seared, half fused, by the new Sun's heat, wrenched and riven by terrific tidal stresses. It would be torn from its parent star, and finally, flung into a regular orbit about the new Sun, but at such a tremendous distance that it would soon freeze and remain forever dead.

"I was a daughter, and my father's only child." Ivec became aware of infinite age-old weariness in Lakne's voice, a leaden weight of tragic regret. "We dwelt together in that last city by the salt-rimmed lake, and I worked beside him in his laboratory.

"He told me of the coming danger, and of his plan to save his life, and mine. For he had found a means of compacting light quanta into a stable form that could serve as a vehicle for life, for mind. We prepared to trap the increasing radiations of the new Sun approaching, and build two of these spherical bodies. We were to escape the cataclysm with them, and perhaps journey, to a kinder world to live.

"We were busy with that project. I was happy for a time, in anticipation of the adventure of the change, and the experience of eternal life with my father in a wondrous body that could fly from world to world.

"But sometimes, when I walked among the despairing, terror-stricken people of the city, who knew that they and their race must die in the cataclysm, dreadfully and without hope—then my heart was touched with pity.

"THUS, once I saw a male of our race, one named Gogok. He was young and strong and handsome to my eyes. He stood upon a white-crusted cliff, and looked with tragic, baffled gaze across black waters at the flaming star of doom.

"It wrenched my being with pain to see him so splendid in his strength, yet crushed with the terror of death, helpless and sick with despair. I loved him, and I could not endure to let him die.

"I begged my father to build a third sphere of photons, for Gogok. But we had not time or sufficient energy for that. And when my father perceived that my love for Gogok was greater than my love for him, or for life itself, he resolved to perish so that Gogok might take his own photon body.

"In the blindness, the madness, of my passion, I thanked my

father, and let it be so. When the spheres were finished, and the giant, hurtling Sun was near, my father conveyed my being from my old body to one sphere, and my lover, Gogok, to the other.

"Gogok thanked my father, and I did. Father set his laboratory in order, and waited to observe the phenomena of the cataclysm, and to perish with his body.

"My lover and I were briefly happy in the freedom and the splendid power of our new bodies, in the high and strange communion that they made possible between our minds, and with the glory of the universe.

"As I have said, we had lost all knowledge of the race of troglodytes. For ages past, our fathers had been confined to the deep and narrow chasms where they dwelt, and the original entrances to the caverns had long since been covered by erosion.

"But when Gogok and I, rejoicing in the free, swift motion of our new bodies, were exploring the vast, high, airless plateaus, we entered a narrow crevice in the mountains and discovered the caverns of the other people.

"They were much changed by æons of life beneath the surface. Their eyes were enlarged, their skins pale and colorless, their bodies adapted to the toil of delving. But they were still beings of intelligence, for their minds had been developed by the eternal struggle to survive.

"We found their greatest city within this very cavern—a busy place, ancient and populous. Its huge buildings were metal and stone, and the very walls glowed with eternal, varicolored light. We entered an immense central building, and made contact with the council of five who ruled the troglodytes.

"From the five we learned the history of the delving race. It was the story of an age-long struggle for power, energy, for light and heat, for transportation, for the manufacture of food. With the depletion of the planet's feeble volcanic heat, they had turned to radioactive elements, for which their mines riddled all the planet.

"Their science, forced to meet the many problems of discovering, refining, and utilizing radioactive substances, reached a very high development. With increasing understanding and control of atomic and subatomic processes, they were able to speed the disruption first of uranium and then of a few other less-active elements.

"But at last the complete exhaustion of even those more common elements had brought the troglodytes to face a supreme crisis. Food supplies failed; the caves grew dark and cold again. Nine tenths of the race perished of famine. But lights burned on in their laboratories, when all else was dark; and their science, with its deep knowledge of the nature of matter, devised a catalytic control for the release of material energy.

"With that discovery, the troglodytes entered a millenium of triumphant happiness. No longer must their lives be spent toiling in the mines. The lifetime needs of an individual could be supplied by a pebble. Liberated science branched into many new channels. Art flowered among them for the first time. Splendid cities and monuments were built; the very walls of the caverns were cut into colossal representations of their history.

"OUR COMING signaled the end of that golden age. For all their science, the troglodytes were not astronomers; indeed, it was a dogma current among them that the universe outside the caverns was compact, of solid matter. They accounted for gravitation and the observed effects of the planet's motion by a very ingenious hypothesis of the repulsion of matter toward the open space of the caves. We brought them their first hint of the approaching cataclysm.

"Gogok's mind, I now discovered, had been warped by the fear of death. He was moved by a savage lust for life, energy, power—and by a mad and fearful jealousy of any other possessor of them. The dread of perishing for want of power that had haunted all his youth, that had first won him my sympathy and love, persisted even in the eternal security of the photon sphere.

"He determined at once to secure the secret of the material-energy catalyst from the troglodytes. But the five members of the council—who alone had been entrusted with it—refused to share the secret, lest it be used selfishly against them.

"Gogok, therefore, devised an elaborate stratagem to gain the secret. And I agreed to aid him with his plan, because I wanted the catalyst for my father and our race in the upper world.

"He and I, thereupon, parted, as if we had quarreled. I left the city, and he proceeded with the ruse. He first explained the science of astronomy to the five rulers, and told them of the cataclysm that was soon to result from the passing of the suns. But he made them believe that our planet was doomed to collision with the second Sun, and that they all must perish with it unless they escaped with his aid.

"He demonstrated the nature and the power of his photon sphere to the five, and convinced them that such bodies of light would be able to escape to another world and endure there forever. He proposed to build similar energy bodies for each of the five, in return for the secret.

"But the five were unwilling to betray their positions by giving away the secret and abandoning their people to perish. And Gogok, thereupon, called me back, with a thought beam, to play my part in the ruse.

"I came as an enemy of Gogok, and demanded the secret for myself. I displayed the destructive energies of my photon body, and threatened to destroy the cities of the troglodytes unless they yielded the secret to me.

"The energy process could have been used to destroy me. But the troglodytes were a peaceful race, somewhat softened by the generations of easy living since the discovery of the catalyst. They were, moreover, uncertain and apprehensive of the true extent of my powers. When Gogok offered to become their champion, they eagerly accepted his aid.

"He and I engaged in a mock duel, with the emanation of spectacular rays and field effects that destroyed buildings and shook the cavern walls. Gogok presently retired as if defeated. He told the five that I was a dreadful antagonist, and that they and he would surely be destroyed unless he was given the catalyst to restore his depleted energy.

"TO SAVE THEMSELVES, the troglodytes yielded the secret to the being they thought their friend. Armed with it, Gogok returned to the encounter and continued the struggle, until I fell helpless and became his prisoner.

"The five rulers now insisted that Gogok build them photon bodies, as he had offered to do before. For they were now alarmed by his possession of the secret, and wished to have these powerful bodies to protect their people.

"With a simulated reluctance, Gogok agreed. With the aid of my knowledge—for I had been my father's helper—he constructed five spheres, and conveyed the beings of the rulers into them. But, as a part of his whole plot, he had made the spheres weak and unstable. One by one, they collapsed; and the five perished.

"Since none of the surviving troglodytes possessed any knowledge of the catalyst, they were helpless to resist when Gogok declared himself their absolute ruler, as he had planned to do.

"It was only then that I discovered that I, too, had been a victim of Gogok's machinations. From the first, I had been tortured with regret that my father had given up his own eternal body that Gogok might live. I had been sometimes alarmed by Gogok's selfish thoughts and the discovery of his mad lust for power. Yet I had forgiven him—even for his ruthless treachery in destroying the five—because I knew that only the dreadful fear of death had made him so, and because I loved him.

"I was wounded, beyond expression, to find that Gogok could be as cruel to me as he had been to the troglodytes. For he had agreed to allow me to carry the catalyst to my father, so that he might use material energy to build a photon body for himself, and to enable our race to survive after the cataclysm.

"Gogok, I thought, had made our sham battle realistic beyond necessity. I had been forced to expend nearly all my vital energy to protect my very life. Now, when I begged him to repair my body and restore my energy with the catalyst, he tricked me again.

"He made apparent preparations to give me the energy, and seemed to be willing enough for me to take the secret to my father. I submitted to his power, and found myself trapped in that gray block from which you released me.

"It was a prison which not only confined my movements, but prevented my absorbing energy from any source. To make my restraint doubly secure, he forced the enslaved troglodytes to hew this vault in the cavern wall and seal it with that great metal door.

"With that, my active part was ended; I have been but a grief-stricken watcher. The gray block damped out nearly all frequencies of energy vibration. For a long time my senses were blurred and dull. But, after a slow and laborious rearrangement of the quanta in my body, I was able to perceive, very keenly, events over all this planet and beyond it.

"I watched Gogok's return to the surface world. He found that my father, ignoring caution in this extremity of peril, had inaugurated experiments of his own to find the catalytic control for material energy. Gogok was alarmed lest my father succeed and equal his own power.

"With cunning lies about the tremendous danger of the process, he infuriated the people against my father. Despite the fact that he was toiling to save their lives and the life of the race, the mobs attacked his laboratory and sought to destroy him. He was able to defend the laboratory until the danger point was passed, and successful results enabled him to promise life to the people.

"WHEN the mobs failed him, Gogok conceived another plan. He told my father that I had been attacked and overcome by the material energy weapons of the troglodytes, that I was helpless and in need of aid—as indeed I was. He thus induced my father to accompany him on a rescue expedition into the caverns; and, in a narrow place, turned upon him in sudden, cowardly attack, and destroyed him with the aid of the secret catalyst.

"My father's death left Gogok the undisputed master of the planet. But, for a time, he dared not remain upon it. The approaching Sun was now near, the planet already scorching from its rays and cracking from tidal strains. Alarmed, Gogok fled far away into space, until the cataclysm should be ended,

"The celestial events took place as my father had foreseen. The two suns, red, ancient dwarf and hot-white, young giant, swept near together, each deflected from its straight path by the other's gravitational pull.

"Each was torn by terrific tidal forces. Tremendous tides were raised upon the less-dense surface of the giant, and finally dragged, out into the long spiral arm of gaseous matter which later separated into the condensations which formed your planet and the others of this system.

"This planet, meantime, suffered all that my father had predicted. It was flung toward the flaming, tide-racked giant. The mountains upon one face were fused; the surface was riven, shattered, battered with meteoric hail. Then it was hurled away again, out of the gravitational net, and, at last, torn from its departing mother sun and left to freeze forever in this remote and lonely orbit about the second star.

"The heat and the meteors destroyed the last surface city, where I was born; but a few of my kind survived in deep excavations. Many of the troglodytes died as their caverns crumbled to tidal strains, but their greatest metropolis, here, escaped.

"As if stimulated by disaster, the survivors made desperate efforts to renew their grasp on life. The last members of my race joined the troglodytes, and the two peoples made a common cause against cold and darkness and death. They found a new reservoir of radioactive elements in the meteoric matter that had fallen upon the planet. Again they sought, with the promise of success, the lost secret of material energy.

"But when all danger was past, Gogok, the fugitive, returned, to resume his lordship of the planet. He established his dwelling upon the surface, in that guarded place which you were seeking so unwisely to enter, when I first reached you. He reduced the two races to abject slavery.

"He seemed to rejoice in the degradation of his subjects, through fear, perhaps, of any independence or originality that might threaten his own absolute dominion. He allowed life to exist only in direct service to his vanity and his power lust. He killed a living world, to fashion a monument to his selfish egoism."

THE opalescent sphere ceased its story. It lay quiet for a time, in the utter darkness of the great cave. The small, flawed green cube quivered beside it, as Ivec Andrel sensed again the immemorial antiquity of the dust-shrouded ruins where the troglodytes had dwelt, and felt the dreadful loneliness of this buried metal vault that had been the sealed prison of Lakne, the unfortunate daughter of Sardoc, the scientist, since before the Earth was born.

Keenly, he perceived the old weariness, like an illness, in the sphere, the heartbreaking regret that had been age-long torture, the agonizing tension of an ancient conflict of passionate love and bitter hatred that had never been resolved.

"And the ages have gone," Lakne resumed at last. "I have lain here, tortured by thirst for the energy that is the food of this body, wearied to desperation by the agony of restraint. Æon after æon, I have watched events without, hoping for release.

"I saw Gogok crush the people of this planet into mindless automata. I watched them slave to build the dead and empty glory of his dwelling place, and then to tend it. I saw that Gogok's fear-born selfishness had slain this world.

"When hope died here, I looked to the other planets for aid. But the nearest—which you call Pluto—cooled so swiftly that its life never emerged from its seas. A promising life form evolved upon Triton, single moon of Neptune—so swiftly that Gogok became alarmed by its advance, and went there to destroy it.

"Again Gogok obliterated a race of winged, metallic beings—splendid, vivid-colored things, whose vital energies were radio-active, and who could fly through interplanetary space—that had conquered all the moons of Saturn.

"Once more he destroyed the old fifth—planet, the one within Jupiter's orbit—shattering it into the myriad fragments you call the asteroids—when the electrostatic relation between the crystals of the cooling elements in its interior became the basis of a planetary intelligence.

"It is only recently that he visited Mars, to blot out the desert dwellers there, when their long struggle to conserve the dwindling water and atmosphere of their aging planet promised to develop minds sufficiently keen to grapple with the problem of material energy.

"Upon the same occasion he examined the life of your planet, but found that no animal had evolved sufficiently to leave the ocean. The Trilobites, then the dominant form, seemed unworthy of extermination.

"He has been aware of the more recent development of intelligence upon your planet, but has neglected to destroy it, being certain that it would be overtaken by death in the approaching nebula, which he has for some time perceived, long before it advanced high enough to discover the energy catalyst.

"He was amazed and frightened to find that your father had rediscovered the art of forming photon constructs stable and complex enough to serve as media of intelligence. Cowardly as of old, however, he dared not venture to Earth to destroy them. Rather, he chose to wait within the intricate and deadly maze of defenses he has fashioned about his dwelling, confident that your photon bodies had been devised to start a quest for the energy catalyst, and that his possession of it would surely lure them to destruction here.

"GOGOK received into his place Barthu Jildo, the traitor from your own world, who arrived here long before you. He seeks to learn as much as he can about your planet and its peoples, that he may anticipate any danger from them.

"Also, in his ancient, cunning mind is the beginning of another plan. He has come to regard this planet, because of its small size and the time-battered weakness of its structure, as insecure. He thinks now of migrating to Earth, whose relatively tremendous mass would be a vastly greater reservoir of material energy.

"He is weary of this world where he has dwelt so long. He desires new slaves to master, a new and younger planet to rule, the more splendid monuments to his vanity and the more powerful defenses of his life that he could build upon Earth.

"But in Barthu Jildo his ancient craft has a worthy antagonist. Barthu is seeking to employ the same ruse that won Gogok the secret. He brought Gogok warning that you would come behind him, and told a fabulous tale of an army of invading cubes to follow you. He offers his aid in return for the secret, and Gogok merely puts him off. Each is hoping to pit the other against you, so that he may step in to destroy the weakened victor."

As the sphere of opalescence paused again, the small green cube stirred apprehensively in the utter, frigid darkness of the ancient caverns.

Swiftly, Ivec asked: "Do they know that I have set you free?"

"Not yet," answered Lakne. "Gogok has been distracted by his parley with Barthu. But his senses are keen enough to perceive my movements, whenever he makes the effort. And when he does, both of them will surely unite against us, for their danger from the two of us is greater than their danger from each other."

"Then we must act before they discover us," said Ivec. "For they are superior to us in knowledge and energy. We should certainly be destroyed in a fight. Can we enter Gogok's fortress, do you think, and reach the place where material energy is released? Secretly?"

And, as the sphere seemed to hesitate, doubtfully, he explained: "This cube possesses a wide and delicate sensitivity to wave and radiation phenomena. It was particularly designed to undertake the analysis of the material-energy process. I believe I could learn the secret of the catalyst by studying the operation of Gogok's apparatus."

Anxiously, he awaited Lakne's reply.

"The fastness of Gogok is well-guarded." Slow thought came from the small globe of mother-of-pearl. "His cowardly craft has devised many defenses to trap and destroy intruders, as well as to warn him of their approach.

"Yet, I believe I know a way that we may enter his dwelling undetected—through the ancient mines of the troglodytes. But if we are discovered near his big secret apparatus, as we almost certainly will be, our doom will be swift and sure.

"But come," said Ivec.

The green cube quivered, as if to shake off its fear.

"Let us try it," continued Ivec. "Our energy is scant and the time is short. I must obtain the catalyst and return to Earth at once—in spite of Barthu and Gogok—or all my kind will be destroyed."

"Our perils are many," said Lakne. But she rose beside him.

The flawed cube of green and the milky sphere floated away from the broken vault, through the frozen, airless dark that filled those age-dead caverns.

### IX.

"LOOK WELL at the guarded dwelling of Gogok," came the soft, cautious thought waves from Lakne of the sphere. "For there—if we reach it alive—you will see the future of the planet Earth, as it will be if either Gogok or Barthu is victorious. You will see the inevitable issue of dictatorship, the final fate of any world enslaved to the egoism of one selfish mind."

The globe of glowing pearl and the tiny, flickering emerald cube wound silently, together, through dark, endless caverns. They passed above the dust mounds of immemorial cities, and through airless, frozen tunnels hewn æons before the Earth was born.

"We are near," Lakne warned at last. "The mines extend no higher. We must find our own way, now—and be cautious of any radiation that might be detected."

Black rocks narrowed upon them. They slipped upward through tiny rifts and crevices, extinct volcanic fumaroles, the fissures left in the surface of the dead, contracting world.

The delicate senses of the sphere found the way with uncanny accuracy, yet again and again they came to some passage that must be widened with a cutting beam of directed radiation—always at a painful cost in energy, and with the danger that Gogok, above, might detect the operation.

"Halt!" the sphere emanated abruptly, in alarm. "Gogok has set a trap here, also!"

Ivec had hardly been aware of the faint, blue radiance of the rocks; the impact of a sinister radiation had been almost imperceptible. But suddenly, even as Lakne spoke, the cube was robbed of all energy. It fell helpless on the glowing stones. And the unending pain of its inner flaw exploded abruptly into a fountain of crimson agony that drenched all his being.

Extinction was close upon him, when he felt the vital contact of the sphere, sensed the shelter of a swiftly projected counterbarrier of interfering frequencies that shut out the hostile emanations. The red pain ebbed; his numbed mind groped again for sensation and strength.

"Come," Lakne urged him, apprehensively. "And swiftly. I can guard you until we pass the danger—unless it is too long."

Again they sought a way upward, through the tortuous labyrinth of crevices. The sinister blue faded slowly from the rocks, and the sphere was able to cease the effort of maintaining the barrier wave. But it was visibly weaker from exhaustion, its milky light duller, clouded.

"We are now within Gogok's defenses," came the very faint and cautious warning. "He can detect us very easily, now—and if he does, there is no escape."

They emerged presently, through a narrow fissure in the flank of a time-shattered mountain. The valley beneath was a pool of faintly shining haze, the sky a chasm of blue mist. Cautiously alert, cube and sphere drifted out into the luminous air.

Strange plants covered mountain and valley and the opposite slope. Frail leaves shone like pale-hued gem stones, saffron and pink and soft violet, wrought into shapes of ineffable, delicate grace. For all its eldritch beauty, however, the vegetation seemed to Ivec unhealthy, lifeless, unpleasant as the dream of a diseased mind. Unconsciously, he shrank from the fragile, pallid fronds.

PRESENTLY, as the two flitted apprehensively forward, Ivec was startled to see living things. Thick-bodied, repulsive scarlet worms were feeding upon the singular pale shrubs, cropping them into neat, artistic symmetry. Small, humped violet things, like snails with spiral shells, delicately lovely as the maggotlike worms were hideous, were indistinguishable against the soft violet moss that covered the surface. They mowed the vegetation evenly, Ivec saw, or turned the soil with sharp appendages.

"There is no danger from them," said Lakne of the sphere. She paused above them, as if with pity. "These are the children of my ancient race. Once they were individuals, with lives and aims and values of their own. But Gogok's slavery shut off all original expression, and degraded them into mindless instruments of his will."

Cube and sphere flitted more cautiously ahead, keeping within the cover of the pale, repulsive vegetation. At last, in the thick copse that crowned a long high ridge, the sphere paused again.

"Beyond," said Lakne, "is the dwelling of Gogok. The mechanisms of the catalytic process are locked within the glowing dome."

Quivering fearfully, the cube slipped forward to peer through the pallid, screening leaves. Before Ivec, upon a long plateau, stupendous and lofty beneath a sky of dusted azurite, loomed a building that shook him with amazement.

Upon this black and frozen world, æon of æons dead, it was an incredible thing. From the pale, well-tended gardens of the violet-carpeted plateau towered scarlet columns. Colossal, a full mile high, they were made delicately beautiful by an exquisite perfection of proportion. Curving walls of ebon black, beyond, were pierced with tall archways that opened into inner mystery. Above black walls and crimson colonnades, Cyclopean against the blue, misty sky, loomed a dome of intensely glowing purple.

"Gogok exhausted every resource of the planet to make this dwelling for himself," said the sphere. "For a million years, every being slaved toward its completion. While the whole is immense, every individual part is far smaller than your cube—and each a perfect jewel!"

And Ivec perceived that, while the large outlines were artistically simple, the detail was infinitely elaborate. There were clustered smaller towers, intricacies of windows, many-pillared balconies, patterned niches, sculptured architraves—and every jewellike surface engraved with a minute and exquisite perfection.

The sphere was motionless for a little time, while its milky luster dimmed with the effort of sensation.

"Gogok and his guest are together," said Lakne, "in a guarded, inmost chamber, beneath the dome. It may be possible for us to approach undetected close enough for you to observe the operation of the energy process—if we are very fortunate."

Again they flitted forward, close above the pale-violet moss. The very stone beneath them, Ivec perceived, had been molded into the perfect foundation for these landscapes of exotic loveliness. They passed a hedge of shrubs, whose rose-colored sword-like leaves defended great freakish blooms of utter black. Beyond, they were among tall, yellow cones, plumed with crimson, whose low-clustered leaves were like nests of gray, hideous, flat-headed serpents.

WHEN the mountainous mass of the building was near, gleaming, wondrous, incredible, Ivec saw living creatures of a different sort. Busy little gray things were clinging to crimson columns and graven ebon walls and even to the glowing dome. They had many limbs, equipped with the suction cups with which they clung to the jewellike surface, or with brushes and polishing pads that bore their own wax-secreting glands. With an intense and mindless activity, they were cleaning and polishing interminably—the caretakers of Gogok's dwelling.

The opalescent sphere paused again, to regard them solemnly. The slow thought came: "These, also, are the children of my people. And such the people of your Earth will be, if either Gogok or Barthu wins the coming struggle—the dead-alive tools of absolutism.'"

"Come!" The green cube quivered with dread. "We must hasten."

Flitting out of the gardens, the two darted between colossal scarlet pillars, and through a pointed ebon arch into a long, colossal hall of darkness. Silently, upon swift wings of apprehension, they flashed through that tremendous dark corridor, and upward through a maze of gem-gleaming passages and of lofty empty spaces, cold with dead and austere splendor.

They paused, at last, in a well of darkness, above a lofty balcony. Beyond it was an elaborate trefoil window, whose crystal panes burned with an intense and radiant purple.

"There!" Lakne's radiation was tremulous with excitement. "That is the place we seek!"

The glowing crystal panels, Ivec perceived, were, in reality, the surface of the great purple dome, continued beneath the roof of the building. Actually, it was simply a vacuum tube, incredibly immense. Within, he sensed the vast, confusing bulks of tremendous elements, the interplay of terrific energy beams, and the white, burning intensity of the Sunlike central vortex, where matter was broken down into rivers of unimaginable power.

The green cube quivered to deep elation.

"Here it is! And it is wonderful! No engineer on Earth has

dreamed of such things as these. This will advance our technology a thousand years!" Ivec's exclamations were checked by the
stern chill of fear. "But I have no time to study all this! It will take
me weeks, months, to analyze it all, and deduce the principle of
the catalyst—simple as it probably is. Long before I can succeed,
Gogok and Barthu will probably have—"

Ivec was interrupted by a screaming vibration of frantic terror
from the sphere. With them, upon the dark, high balcony, he was
abruptly aware of a third being—a formless, many-tentacled
thing of intense white radiance, whose burning arms had already
seized his companion.

"I am taken!" came Lakne's urgent, frightened warning. "Fly!
Quickly! This is Gogok's creature—sent to take us both!"


## X.

WITHIN THE GLOOM that pressed thick upon the lofty balcony, in that vast and silent space, the green cube flashed to the
aid of the pearly sphere. The globe was wrapped, helpless, in
clinging amoeboid tentacles of flowing white flame. Ivec
struggled with field effects to tear them away, but the light
creature's strength proved far beyond his own. He directed an
intense energy beam against the shining form—a ray strong
enough to fuse any material substance. But it was deflected harmlessly away.

"Go!" Lakne warned again. "You cannot liberate me. This is a
photon creation of Gogok's. It can tap the power of the matter
converter. It has boundless energy—"

But Ivec stepped up the intensity of his stabbing beam. Without the aid and knowledge of the sphere, he knew, he was surely
doomed. Nor even otherwise would he willingly have abandoned it. But still the photon creature seemed unharmed by his
attack, and he knew that his energies were near ultimate exhaustion.

He was aware, abruptly, of a vast and increasing lassitude.
That, he realized in sick despair, was a warning of the end. The
cube's energy had been limited from the beginning. He had
drawn deep upon it on the long flight out to Persephone, and in
the desperate struggle to escape the nebula's sucking vortices.
Again he had spent precious energy, to fight free of the Blue

Spot's radiation trap, and to liberate Lakne from her prison. He had shared the scant remainder of his energy with her, had expended still more to cut their way here. The limit was now at hand.

Dread numbed him with the realization that, even if he were now free, with full knowledge of the energy catalyst, he had no strength left for the long journey back to Earth—not enough even to escape the feeble gravitation of Persephone.

All hope fled away, left him inert, leaden, paralyzed.

When a flaming tentacle reached out from the photon being, he made an effort to resist. But its strength was far greater than his own. He yielded to it. Cube and sphere were lifted in the burning, shapeless arms, carried downward through the vast and splendid spaces of Gogok's dwelling, and into a central inner room.

This chamber, beneath the power dome, was circular, lofty and immense. Ebon and scarlet gleamed darkly from the floor, in intricate inlay. The tall, slim columns were a flawless white. The vaulted ceiling shone purple, with transmitted light from the dome.

The chamber was empty, save for a massive black pillar that stood in the center of the floor. Upon its crest, as if upon a black throne, lay two shining beings. One was a globe—similar to Lakne's globe, save that it was not white, but a hot, malefic scarlet—that, Ivec knew, was the infamous Gogok. Beside it, glowing with a clear, cold green, was the small photon cube that had been appropriated by Barthu Jildo.

The thing of flowing light brought its two helpless prisoners near, floating through the air.

The green cube stirred upon the pillar, and Ivec distinguished the mocking voice of Barthu Jildo: "Greetings, young Andrel! And thanks to you for having followed me here. For it is because of your coming that I have been able to conclude, with Gogok, the master of this planet, here beside me, an agreement which allows me to carry back to Earth the energy catalyst which we sought.

"With it, I shall be master of Earth, as he is of Persephone. Men shall live to do me honor, or perish—like that!"

He paused to allow Ivec to observe a small gray being near the base of the throne, polishing at the black-and-scarlet floor with a mindless and infinite diligence. Then a dazzling ray jetted from the cube upon the throne, and the gray toiler became a mass of smoking, twitching flesh.

"You, clever Andrel," Barthu Jildo continued mockingly, "shall also perish. For it is my aid in destroying you and the rest of your proud family, which Gogok is to reward with knowledge of the secret—"

Beside Ivec, suspended helpless in the luminous tentacles of Gogok's photon slave, the small globe of Lakne stirred and flushed with opalescent color.

"Fool!" her warning thought was radiated to the green cube on the throne. "I know Gogok of old. And he seeks but to bend you to his own ends, and to destroy you, as he does all beings. He plans to cause you to exhaust your own energies in a struggle with Ivec Andrel—and then to obliterate you."

THE SCARLET GLOBE of Gogok flamed with angry color, and a burning red ray stabbed at the opalescent sphere of Lakne.

"Stop, Gogok!" The green cube of Barthu Jildo darted from the throne, poised in the path of the red ray, to deflect it from Lakne. His voice demanded, harsh with alarm. "You—can you prove that charge?"

"I know Gogok of old," the milky sphere repeated. "And I, who loved him, am the one who has suffered most dreadfully from his evil cunning. Let him prove that he is dealing fair. Ask him to reveal the secret of the catalyst, now."

The scarlet globe lifted angrily above the tall, black throne.

"Lakne is my oldest enemy," it radiated swiftly. "Your fellow being from Earth has set her free from prison. Don't you believe her lies. And let us destroy her for her liberty is a menace to both our lives."

The green cube, poised in the air, seemed hesitant, doubtful.

"If Gogok is honest with you," Lakne put in again, "he will give you the secret, now."

And Barthu Jildo demanded of the red sphere: "Reveal the principle of the catalyst, so that I may know."

The red globe made no reply, but swelled suddenly with surrounding zones of defensive radiation.

"Tell me," the green cube demanded again, or I shall join the others."

"Join them!" flamed the sphere. "And perish with them!"

A narrow blade of burning red leaped at the green cube. An invisible barrier deflected it. It cut in twain a colossal white pillar at the side of the room, which toppled with appalling deliberation.

Gogok's white, shapeless photon creature released Ivec and Lakne, flung to attack Barthu Jildo. The green cube met it with a white sword of radiance. It vanished in a flare of blinding light.

But when the light had gone, the green cube of Barthu Jildo was fast upon the red-and-ebon floor, held motionless with invisible fields of force. Gogok's scarlet sphere hovered over it, malevolently.

"Perish!" The vibrations of the scarlet sphere were cold, snarling, ruthless. "All you three who desire my power. For it is mine—forever!"

And Ivec, still hanging in the air beside the sphere of Lakne, sensed the swift up-building of terrific potential forces about the crimson globe that menaced all their lives. He tried to draw back, with Lakne, but Gogok's expanding energy fields already held him powerless.

Staggered by a deadly burden of despair, he waited. It was now too late to struggle. They were all to be destroyed by the release of material energy—a power that nothing could resist. No recourse was left.

Fleetingly, before his reeling mind, passed a vision of horror unutterable. He saw the stricken Earth, darkened and helpless before the nebula's cold, seized in the dread tentacles of Gogok's power. Saw it transformed into the mindless living death of abject slavery to this eternal tyrant. The white, dead loveliness of Thadre Jildo looked at him, the wide glazed eyes beseeching, terrible with the accusation of his failure.

OVERWHELMED by the sense of terrific hostile forces rising, he prepared to die.

Beside him, however, the nacerous sphere of Lakne struggled in the web of resistless energy fields. Her challenge flashed at the red globe, clear and strong: "Hold, Gogok! Remember that all you have, I have given you. Remember that you were afraid and mortal and about to die, beside that last salt sea, when I gave you that body of deathless energy. Remember that my father's life was sacrificed for yours. Remember that I have seen you crush my people into slavery more cruel than death. Remember the ages of imprisonment that I endured, because of my old love for you."

"I remember," the scarlet globe radiated coldly. "But you will not, any longer."

Still suspended beside Ivec, the sphere of Lakne shone with a serene and steady light.

"Destroy me if you will," it returned, "for I am long since weary of the mockery of life. And obliterate your kindred selfish being, Barthu Jildo. That will be a service to the universe."

"Gladly," interrupted the red globe, still hovering evilly over the helpless green cube on the floor.

"But you must spare Ivec Andrel, who set me free from prison and shared with me his vital strength." The voice of the milky globe seemed, now, to Ivec more commanding than entreating. "Give him knowledge of the catalyst. And restore his lost energy, so that he may carry it back to preserve his threatened people.

"Thus, you may live on here, unharmed. Ivec Andrel will give his pledge not to attack you. And Earth may, also, survive, with the catalyst secure against the menace of the nebula and against your selfish schemes."

The radiations of the opalescent were now stern, commanding—and yet, Ivec thought, somehow touched with infinite pity and blackest regret, as they finished.

"Gogok, do that!"

But the red globe had continued to build up its tremendous reservoirs of threatening energy. Its swift reply came, cold and deadly: "You are foolish to appeal to any sentiment in me. Love and generosity in others I can use, but my own weak feelings I conquered long ago, in my bitter youth by that salt sea. And yours can now serve me no longer. So die—"

The thing that happened was too swift for the senses of the cube to follow. But Ivec knew that Gogok had released his vast, accumulated tide of destructive forces. He was aware that Lakne moved quickly beside him, made some abrupt, terrific effort of her own.

Then free radiation struck him, with a violent, stunning impact. The senses of the cube were numbed. It was flung into an abysm of searing fire; it spun in endless, hurtling flight, through infinitudes of flaming radiance. Terrific forces wrenched and battered at it.

## XI.

WHEN THE LIGHT was gone, and the cube was at rest again, Ivec found that he lay upon a field of shattered, colossal boulders. The space about him was airless, frozen, dark. The sky above was black again, and half covered with the hideous spirals of the nebula.

From the degree of the stellar cloud's advance, and the positions of the distant planets, Ivec perceived that more than three months had passed since he left Earth—although the period had seemed far shorter, due to the retardation of time associated with the velocity of his outward flight, and the space-time warp caused by the terrific etheric vortices in which he had been meshed. There was now no time to return before Earth was lost in the maw of the nebula, he thought wearily, even if he had the catalyst and the energy for the journey.

But he lifted the cube, nevertheless, to take stock of his surroundings. At first he had thought himself flung to some distant part of the barren planet. Then he was aware that these shattered boulders still radiated a trace of heat. He saw the delicate curve that faced one near-by broken mass. He then perceived that each boulder was formed of myriad tiny jewels, exquisitely cut and cemented.

These riven masses, he knew then, were the fragments of Gogok's dwelling. The building had been destroyed, with its fantastic gardens and the queer, mindless slaves that tended them. The radiant haze was gone. And the glowing purple dome—with the priceless secret of material energy.

The Blue Spot was gone. Persephone was dead—as soon, now, Earth would be—

"Ivec Andrel, here I am!" He recognized the faint thought emanation from Lakne's sphere. "Come to me."

With a weary and painful effort, for the cube was near total exhaustion, Ivec rose above that boulder field of utter desolation. He caught the faint gleam of the opalescent sphere, dropped beside it. Half covered with débris, it burned with a feeble, uncertain glow.

"Ivec," it radiated weakly, "my energy is spent. I am dying."

"Share mine again," Ivec invited. "I can give you life for a time."

"No," returned Lakne. "You are too generous; you have none to spare. And it is my wish to die—for I have destroyed the one that I loved once, and hated."

"Gogok?" Ivec asked. "You killed him?"

"Yes—I killed him," Lakne said. "I have known the use of the energy catalyst from the beginning. I did not tell you that, lest you demand that I use it, or perhaps unwittingly betray me to Gogok. But the keen senses of this photon globe discovered the nature of the catalyst from observing the apparatus of the five troglodytes, even before they disclosed it to Gogok.

"I could have slain him then, or when he imprisoned me, or when he murdered my father, or at any time since—for my mastery of the process was more complete than his own, and the quanta structure and energy fields of the sphere afforded all the equipment I needed.

"Yet I spared him because I once had loved him, and because even when I hated him, his life was vital to mine. It was enough to know that he was in my power, that even from the prison I could destroy him.

"But you had risked grave danger to set me free; you had shared your very life with me; I could not allow him to destroy you. Nor did I like to see a brave young world slain to make a monument to him, as this planet was.

"Therefore, I destroyed the one whom I loved and hated. And hence my own life is done." Ivec began a protest, but the urgent, fading radiations cut him off. "I am perishing; there is no more time. Now, here is the secret of the energy catalyst, which you must strive to take back to Earth."

THE faint emanations brought him the long-sought information, the treasured knowledge of the five murdered troglodytes, the key to Gogok's immemorial power; a simple modulation of continuum field tensions, expressed in a few brief equations.

When Ivec had committed them to memory, he perceived that the small sphere, lying upon the black, shattered débris beside him, had grown dim. Its milky light was flickering feebly.

"Farewell, Ivec," came the dying voice of Lakne, Sardoc's daughter. "I am weary—glad to go. Use your power—generously—"

The outlines of the opalescent globe grew misty. It burst into a flying wisp of silver vapor. It vanished. Lakne, who had lived since before Earth was born, was dead.

The green cube of Ivec Andrel lay for a little while alone upon the broken stones, weary and saddened. It had been tragic to watch the death of a world's last being. But it came to him, slowly, that his sorrow was less for Lakne than for Thadre Jildo, whom he had left upon the menaced Earth, weeping upon his own dead body.

He stirred among the ruins, as if to launch himself upward into space. But it came to him again, with a sickness of ultimate frustration, that he had far too little energy for the return to Earth, nor time for the journey, unless the cube could be made far swifter than it had ever been.

Yet, he thought wearily, he must try—for Thadre Jildo's sake— "Stay, young Andrel!"

It was the heavy, harsh voice of Barthu Jildo—who, Ivec realized with a sickening dread, had also escaped the cataclysm. The other green sphere was suddenly hanging over him, paler now, itself flickering and unstable.

Yet even here there might be hope, Ivec thought desperately—if he could touch some fiber of reason in the mad mind of the cube. Some spark of humanity must linger in this thing that had been a man.

"Barthu," he begged, "will you aid me? I have been given knowledge of the catalyst. If I can reach home with it, our Earth may yet be saved from cold. Earth—and Thadre! With your help—"

"I knew all Andrels were fools," rasped the thick voice. "But I am not—not fool enough to give you fame and honor, and let you make all men scorn the name of Jildo. I am injured. I must soon expire—but you shall perish with me!"

A harsh and mocking laugh grated from the green cube. It was wholly insane, Ivec realized—a dread machine of doom. And this would be a duel to the death.

A white needle stabbed at him. Ivec set up a deflecting field— at an energy cost that staggered him. Fighting a numbness of scarlet pain, straining the weakened cube to the point of disruption, he generated a counterray.

The other cube turned it aside harmlessly, and agony fell like a dazing hammer upon Ivec. The black, writhing arms of the nebula swept over all the sky. Frozen Persephone dropped away, and he was lost in a void of pain.

"Die," gasped the faint, triumphant voice of Barthu Jildo. "You are the last Andrel. There is another Jildo—"

Another Jildo—that was Thadre. Her name, and the sweet memory of her, stirred Ivec to a last, grim effort. Abandoning his defense, reckless of a shattering pain, he concentrated all his energy in one intense, jetting ray.

That white needle cleft the cube of Barthu Jildo, and it vanished in a flood of blinding light.

IVEC ANDREL lay alone again upon the black, riven face of Persephone. The green cube was flawed, now, with forked lines of black, its radiance very dim, unsteady. Twice it sought to lift itself, and fell back upon the broken débris.

Ivec tried to laugh, at the bitter mockery of circumstance. The ultimate jest. The catalyst he possessed was the key to all the energy of the universe—yet he was too weak to lift the cube's remaining featherweight, even against Persephone's feeble gravity.

The warning scarlet tide of pain rose higher. Soon it would submerge all his being. The cube would shatter from its ancient flaw. Knowledge of the catalyst would be lost, as free photons scattered. Earth would fall beneath the cold and the horror of the nebula. And Thadre Jildo—

Sense of his surroundings, somehow, had grown vague. Black sky and black boulders were lost. And suddenly, altogether incredibly, the girl was beside him.

He saw again the slim grace of her tall body, her skin milk-white and clear, light glinting in her copper hair. He saw the blue of her eyes, greenish and cool, dancing with malice—and yet soft with a new, tender warmth of love.

Her hand stretched toward him in the darkness. It touched him, warm, life-giving. It lifted him. A strong, living current flowed into him from her body. He relaxed, and she supported him. Her contact eased his pain.

"Ivec!" Her voice was low and rich and anxious. "Ivec, do you hear me?"

Her voice, he knew suddenly, was no illusion. A quick flood of strength restored his senses. Again he was aware of grim, barren Persephone—and now of a green, pale cube beside him, like his own. It was the strong flow of vital energy, from it, that had revived him,

"Ivec, you are alive?"

Her voice came again, out of the cube—and he knew then that it was Thadre. Thadre Jildo, whom he had left sobbing upon his body, back in the laboratory on far-off Earth.

"I am, Thadre, thanks to you," he said. "But if you came to find your uncle, he is dead."

"I came for you, Ivec," she answered. "And I have more energy for you—enough so we may both safely return to Earth."

Gratefully, he drank it in. The cube glowed stronger, with new, throbbing strength. The pain of the old weakness grew less, ceased. A deep peace filled him. At last he was satisfied.

"This is Cube One," Thadre explained, "the first model your father made. He improved it after you were gone, made it far stronger, and supplied it with a reserve of strength for you. I brought it to you."

Her voice trembled uncertainly.

"I am sorry for aiding my uncle, Ivec. When you were gone from your body, I knew I loved you. I came to seek you, to share all your efforts and dangers, to aid you and be with you—always."

"You gave up your body?" Ivec asked. "For me?"

"I did," she said. "Our bodies now lie side by side, in a vault upon the mountain. But we can live forever, now, or so long as we will. For these photon cubes can be renewed with material energy. We can range all space together, for adventure. And our powers can do many things to aid the progress of mankind."

Beside her, Ivec mounted into a loftier rapture than he had ever known. The remarkable senses of the cube were keenly attuned, until he felt the pulsing life of every sun, knew the wondrous rhythm of every ray in space, shared the life dance of every atom through all the universe.

Thadre Jildo was beside him. She was his, he hers. And all the universe was theirs, its wonder, its mystery, its beauty—theirs to explore, to know, to love. Peril there would be yet, effort, and pain, but none greater than had passed. None too great to be spice and salt to living

"Come," Thadre was saying, beside him. "The nebula is rushing on. We have time and strength to reach Earth with the knowledge you have gained. But we must not delay."

And the twin green cubes rose up together from dead Persephone and flashed away Sunward, carrying life to the waiting Earth.

# The Ice Entity

*Thrilling Wonder Stories, February 1937*

## CHAPTER I

### FINGERS OF THE ICE

BLAKE HAD TRIED TO DISSUADE JEAN ADARE FROM UNDERTAKING the fatal journey.

"Better stay here with me, Jean," he had advised. "Here, there's a chance. Out there, on the ice, you won't live an hour."

"*Non,*" muttered the little 'breed. "I go! I know we die here. Ze wood almos' gone. We freeze, or worse—" His trembling hand seized Blake's arm. "You come wit' me, *mon vieux?*"

"No, Jean. I've got work to do." Blake's big hand had gestured at the crude bench across the end of the cabin, where the white radiance of an electric bulb fell on his delicate and tiny instruments. "If I get it done we can live without a fire."

"*Mon Dieu!* Ze ice has made you crazy. *Au revoir.* I go, before it is too late—"

"Wait," Blake protested. "Listen, man. You'll be killed—"

Later, rubbing the thick frost from a tiny window, Blake

watched Jean Adare try to fight his way south across the shining horror of the glacier, toward the Chandalar-Yukon trail. Watched him—die.

Fear had preyed upon them all the dreadful winter; and for three weeks terror had lived with them in the cabin.

The tiny building stood on ground almost level, a hundred yards above the glacier that had come down the valley of the Mannabec. The arctic barrens, southward and east, spread shining desolation. Northward the plateau lifted into ice-armored hills, cleft with the glacier gorge of the Mannabec.

Mason Blake was a big man. His wide-shouldered body was bulky with furs. His red hair was unkempt, shaggy; his blue eyes, hard with little glints of steel, shone above the winter's growth of curly red beard. His great hands, bare to the chill in the room, trembled as they handled delicate metal objects.

He strove to find forgetfulness in the details of this task that had so many years absorbed him. But the horror that had driven Jean Adare out to die still lurked in the silent room.

Blake thus far had resisted the madness that drove the 'breed to death. Yet he understood it, because it had claimed one corner of his brain. He felt nothing but sympathy for the fugitive.

In the brief summers, while they worked the rich placer deposit that was now buried under the glacier, Jean Adare had ever been a generous and gay companion. But the dark chord of fear in his primitive heart always responded to winter's bitter threat.

Always, he had been annoyed by Blake's experiments. And, at the last, when he had been terrified, he had found Blake's absorbed serenity intolerable.

*"Que diable!"* he had burst out once, angrily. "Speak to me! I cannot endure ze damn silence. Say zat you are cold. Say you fear ze ice. I t'ink you drive me crazy!"

"You never understand, Jean, what I'm doing—"

*"Non,* but I do understan'. I understan' zat you are beeg fool, yes. You try to destroy gold—"

"I can destroy gold," Blake corrected him cheerfully. "You saw the activated particles under the microcope, like golden stars burning. What I'm working on is a way to control the process—and I think the tau-ray will do it.

"What you don't understand is that energy is worth more than gold. One tiny grain would give us light and heat for all the winter. One little flake would drive a steamboat up the Yukon from the Aphoon pass to the Chandalar."

But Adare refused to catch Blake's enthusiasm. He went back to crouch miserably over the stove, his one dark eye staring solemnly at the dwindling pile of wood. The stringy, stained wisp of his beard moved monotonously as he chewed; ever and again the stove hissed as he spat upon it.

The whole winter had been a burden. But the two before had passed without tragedy. It was the bewildering, the inexplicable, the mind-crushing events of the last three weeks that had driven the 'breed upon his fatal flight.

Blake knew, he thought, more than any other man of this incredible nightmare that had seized all the world. Yet his scientific mind searched in vain for its origins.

The winter had been the coldest of history—here and throughout the northern hemisphere. The radio had brought reports of unprecedented blizzards sweeping all America. The unparalleled displays of the aurora had spread wings of terrifying flame visible almost to the equator—the result, Blake knew, of a period of extreme sunspot activity.

The cold, the aurora—all the world knew of them. But Blake and Adare had been the first to observe stranger things. They had seen a green and living light spread through the ice, an uncanny, pulsating glow that seemed independent of the auroral fires. They had seen the glaciers break and move, despite the cold, as if they flowed to the pressure of an inner purpose.

B EWILDERED, Blake had paused in his researches long enough to assemble a little short-wave transmitter, powered from the small gasoline motor-generator under the bench. For a month he had reported daily to the world all he could observe of the strange fire and motion of the ice.

His last message had carried his observations of a stranger thing: the motionless, unchanging cloud that loomed black and sharp-edged against the aurora, above the shining northward hills.

The interference of terrific electric storms had been making radio communication almost impossible, and that day Jean Adare had been abruptly seized with the obsession that this electrical interference was a deliberate attempt of the ice to cut off the reports.

"Stop it!" he screamed as Blake sat before his microphone,

patiently repeating his message against the roaring flood of static. "You tell ze secrets of ze ice. It is angry! It will kill us, unless you stop! *Que diable—*"

"Kill us? How?"

"Ze damn glacier! It creeps up ze slope. Ze green fire is in it. *Grand Dieu!* It comes to crush us—"

Rubbing away the frost to peer through the window. Blake had seen that the green and shining wall of ice, that had come down out of the hills to fill the valley of the Mannabec, was indeed nearer than it should have been.

A crash brought his eyes back into the room. He saw that the desperate 'breed had smashed his microphone. Strangely, the interference had immediately lessened somewhat, so that he was able to pick up reports of the extreme cold, of loss of life—and to hear the frantic appeals of scientists for his observations.

But the greatest puzzle, the most terrific catastrophe, was what had happened to the sun. That had been two weeks later, now three weeks ago.

Jean Adare had been waiting with almost pathetic eagerness for the sun. He had marked the passing days upon a tattered calendar, prayed for the dawn of spring.

At last came a time when the aurora flamed in a clear sky, and the bitter air was still. Jean Adare slipped into his furs and went outside the hut. Blake, a moment later, heard his eager shout:

*"Le bon Dieu!* The sun—"

Dropping his tools, he ran outside—just in time to meet Jean's exclamation of frightened wonder.

Jean was standing on the point of rock above the cabin, peering south across the weirdly shining glacier and the barrens. For three hours it had been dull daylight. A glow of rose had come into the southern sky, the dawn of the summer-long arctic day. And now Blake saw the sun, a disc of red gold, raggedly bitten off by distant peaks.

Even as Adare's cry of fear rang upon his ears the sun dulled, went out. The flush of dawn faded into strange gloom. The sky had become a changeless dome of dusky, frozen violet.

Upon the dark, rocky point this 'breed had turned to stare into the north. Barrens and mountain shone alike with terrible, ghostly green. Above the ice, like eldritch phantoms marching, were glittering shapes of green.

The black cloud that had hung beyond the hills was gone.

"See!" screamed the 'breed. "Ze ice—it grows fingers! Fingers of green fire. Zey put out ze sun. Now zey reach to strangle us! Ze fingers—fingers of ze ice—"

Babbling with terror, he sprang from the rock and started running south. Blake had caught him before he reached the glacier, brought him back to the cabin. But the next three weeks had been too much for him. The violet sky never changed. The cold grew steadily more intense. And the horror at last drove the 'breed to draw his knife, make Blake let him go.

"I'll see you," Blake called as they parted, "when the spring comes."

Jean Adare said grimly, "Spring, she nevair come!"

He cracked his whip and shouted to the shivering huskies. Blake closed the door regretfully, and watched through the frost on the window. The 'breed drove the cringing, unwilling malamutes straight south, toward the ragged green waste of the glacier whose slow, inexorable advance on the cabin had so terrified him.

Blake watched green fire flowing in the ice, pulsating like luminous, blood. Numbed with horror, Blake saw insidious green fingers clutching at the man, the huskies.

He saw them dragged down. He shut his eyes and turned away when he knew that the ice had conquered.

Grimly, hands stiff with cold, brain paralyzed with the impact of alien menace, he drove himself back to his task.


## CHAPTER II

### Fire of the Golden Atom

M ASON BLAKE once had felt himself the happiest man in the world.

It was now four years ago since, taking an advanced degree in technology, he had published his thesis, *Theory of Atomic Activation*. It had won him the recognition that turned a wild dream into glorious possibility. His father had made him vice-president of the struggling little Blake-Maddon Electric Company, promised him laboratory and funds for his atomic research. Jane Maddon, tall, grey-eyed daughter of his father's deceased partner, promised to marry him.

But Ellet Frey read the thesis, and sent for Blake. Blake didn't go—his father's little firm had been crippled, more than once, by the ruthless activities of Frey's colossal Planet Power Corporation; Blake shared a proud resentment.

Frey came at last to Blake's laboratory. A gaunt, gigantic man, with bright, cold eyes.

"You've got something I want, Blake. Atomic power. I'll give you a contract at two hundred thousand a year, for five years, to work it out for Planet."

"It's worth nothing, now," Blake told him. "It isn't even a toy—because to play with it is too dangerous. If I do get it worked out it will be worth a million times your offer."

The power king smiled.

"I'm glad to see your confidence. My offer is doubled."

"I've nothing to sell," Blake said, flatly.

"Won't sell, eh?" Frey's eyes glittered frostily. "I get what I want, Blake. I'll take it."

Blake had smiled his defiance, until incredible disaster struck.

His father, trying to make the little firm safe from Frey's operations, had contracted for large stocks of copper, had borrowed funds to fit up Blake's expensive laboratories. Learning of the situation, Frey dumped huge amounts of copper on the market and used his vast influence to force the unwilling creditors to call their loans.

When Frey's newspapers managed to color the ensuing bankruptcy with criminal charges, Blake's father shot himself in despair.

Frey, taking possession of the firm's assets, seized Blake's laboratory. But no practical application of Blake's theories had been completed; and Frey's engineers, recalling a casual observation of Blake's, that gold activated by his process would be roughly 829,440,000 times more active than pure radium, cannily refused to make any attempt to carry on the work.

Chagrined, Frey then charged that Blake had stolen records and apparatus from the laboratory. He demanded that Blake perfect and hand over a workable process of gold-disruption.

Despairing of establishing his innocence in the courts, Blake had fled to escape arrest. In happier summers, when he vacationed with his father in Alaska, Jean Adare had been their guide. Blake had grub-staked the half-breed, and a scrawled letter now brought him word of Adare's rich strike on the Mannabec.

Thus it came about that Mason Blake had spent three years in the arctic, digging gold through the summer, toiling through the long winter to perfect a process for the controlled disintegration of its atoms. Success meant power to clear his dead father's name, meant freedom to return to the world—to Jane Maddon.

He had kept in touch with Jane. Left penniless by the disaster, she had found employment as assistant to Dr. Mark Lingard, a distinguished scientist and electrical engineer, for whom the old firm had manufactured experimental equipment. He knew that she was waiting.

Blake turned back to his bench, after he had watched Jean Adare die on the glacier.

He rested his numb fingers on a switch. His blue eyes rested on a golden fleck, almost invisible, lying on the insulated stage before the concave anode of his tau-ray tube. Had he failed again?

Radium, disintegrating, uses up half its bulk in some sixteen centuries. Gold, activated by Blake's discovery, was half gone in fifty-nine seconds. What he sought was a way to control the terrific force he had liberated; for such power, unharnessed, was a monster set free.

If he had failed again, the quartz stage would be fused and shattered with resistless atomic flame.

H E covered his eyes with his big hand, closed the switch. No fire seared him, and he looked. The metal flake was burning on the disc of quartz like a golden star. With trembling fingers, he varied the intensity of the tau-rays. The star obediently waxed and waned.

Blake sighed with a deep, weary gratitude, and held his stiff fingers in the radiant warmth of the star.

"Done!" he whispered. "Gold has been master of man, through all history—and made him into things like Frey. Now man is the master of gold." His tired eyes closed. "Done—if it had been three years ago—"

The golden light still flooded the room as he pried a board from the bunk, and split it up to make a fire. He made tea for himself, ate, slept. The fire was dead again when he woke. But the gold star still burned; its rays had warmed the room a little:

He sat up on the bunk, and stared at it, with a new light in his blue eyes.

"The world is freezing," he whispered. "Somehow—freezing. But if men had portable heat, portable light—"

He made another fire, and went back to the bench. Chairs and rough table went into the stove as he worked. The wood from the bunks. But the fire went out before he had finished, and silent freezing death came back into the cabin.

But the thing at last was done: a little cylinder two inches thick, a foot long. It held the tiny mechanism of the activator, the delicate little tau-ray tube with its minute coils and condensers. And half a pound of gold.

He twisted at a little stud, and a warm golden light shone out of the tube. It drove the darkness from the cabin, thawed the rime of frost that had crept through the walls. He fed the shivering, whimpering dogs again; then, cold and exhausted, he lay down in the golden beam.

Sleep presently pressed upon him, ridden with nightmares of the green fingers of the ice.

## CHAPTER III

### THE LIFE OF THE ICE

THE throb of a motor broke that last nightmare. Numb with the cold that had crept into his body, despite the golden warmth of the ray, Blake ran eagerly out into the frigid violet dusk. Green fire flowed and danced in the wild glacier that filled the valley of the Mannabec. Above it, he saw the plane, a dark fleck drifting in the sky.

Trembling with the breathless hope of contact with man, he held the disrupter like a flashlight, swept its beam back and forth. A white flare answered from the plane. Soon it dropped toward him in a long glide.

There was landing space, he thought, on the snow-covered plateau behind the cabin. He clambered hastily upon a point of rock, poured the golden flood across it. The plane sank low over the glacier. Then:

"Look out! For God's sake!" The scream burst uselessly from his lips. "The fingers of the ice."

The pilot seemed to sense his danger. The plane shot upward. Blake's muscles tensed as he watched the battle. He trembled to the roar of the motors that fought to save the ship.

Green ropes of fire had flowed up from the ice. Serpents of green flame coiled about wings and fuselage, tensed straight, pulled the machine to relentless destruction. Blake's breath went out in a long gasp of silent pain as he saw the ship strike, crumple as it flopped grotesquely over, saw the first lurid streamer of yellow flame lick upward from the wreck.

He saw the quick motion of a little figure near it, a survivor. Remembering the fate of Jean Adare, he thought he would be too late to help anyone. But with the disrupter, perhaps there was a chance.

He plunged down from the rocky point, hitched the dogs to the sled, and raced toward the flaming wreck.

Under a sky of chill violet, the glacier burned with unearthly living green. He was amazed again at its nearness to the cabin. Its motion was too slow to see. But in a few more days—

He mounted the ragged edge of the glacier. The green throbbed and flowed beneath him, like blood of cold fire.

The point of granite that marked the cabin became a small dot behind him. The plane, now, was close ahead. It lay across a ragged fissure, the broken landing gear pointing into the amazing sky. One wing was twisted and splintered.

Like a golden blade, the flame was thrusting ever higher. Was he too late?

Something gripped his fur-booted ankle. He sprawled on the ice, but his fingers clung to the sled, and the racing huskies, with a tug that wrenched his big body, jerked him free.

Running on, he looked back at the green writhing tentacles. Sick, incredulous fear mounted higher in him.

Fingers of the ice! Half insane, Jean Adare had screamed of them. Blake had seen them drag the 'breed down to death, He had watched them wreck the plane. Now they were clutching at his own body, at the dogs. The huskies leaped from them, yelping with pain.

Blake was so near he could hear the crackling flames, when he was caught again. The sled jerked onward, his numbed fingers slipped. He fell against the ice, and found an astounding, half-invisible net about him. Desperately he fought the chilling, strangling meshes.

The dogs were snarled in the harness, fighting the bands of terrible, living light—and one another. One had his fangs in the other's throat, and both were being crushed in the green coils.

Above their yelps, Blake heard the increasing roar of the conflagration. In the motionless air the flame was rising swiftly, fanned with its own draught. The orange light of burning gasoline flickered over the ice. Abruptly he was free. The green tentacles seemed to recall from the flame. The ice beneath him was now black.

He stumbled on toward the plane. The fuselage was a roaring furnace. No human being could be alive within it. But he had seen a figure moving, outside—

"Help! Here—"

The faint voice drifted out of a crevice in the ice. He stumbled, came upon two human figures beside a tapered cylinder of shining steel. One was limp, unconscious; in spite of the bulky flying togs, he could see that it was a girl.

"Here!" the man called again, nervous, urgent. "Help me get her away. Bombs in the plane!"

H IS voice was a husky gasp of pain. His small head was bare; one side was a bloody smear. His right arm flapped limply against his body.

Beside him, Blake bent over the girl. The first glimpse of her white face set a confusion of surprised delight and agony to roaring in his head.

"Jane!" he whispered. "Jane, how did you—"

The little tanned man, with his good hand, was unscrewing something from the end of the steel cylinder.

"Carry her away," he rapped, hoarsely. "Think I can make it by myself, with this detonator. But hurry! The bombs—"

Blake ran with the girl back to the sled. Although the green fire of the ice had retreated, the huskies were still rolling in deadly battle. With Jane here, the plane wrecked, they might mean life itself. He cuffed them, stopped their wolfish struggle.

He was untangling the harness when the little brown man came reeling up, his left hand grasping the little brass cylinder of the detonator from the bomb.

"Had to save it," he gasped. "You'll need the bomb." He thrust it at Blake. "Go on!" he urged. "Leave me. Miss Maddon will tell you what to do. Hurry! Sigma-bombs in the plane. Equal a hundred tons of nitro—"

Blake seized him, tumbled him on the sled beside the girl. His whip cracked.

"Mush, fellows!"

The flaming wreck was a mile behind when sudden radiance shone blue upon the glacier, and the little man gasped through white lips. "Down!"

Blake steered the sled into a crevasse, dived after it. The ice jolted to a shattering concussion, followed by an air wave that flattened them like a crushing hand. Ice-pinnacles tumbled down about them.

When Blake lifted his ringing head, the glacier was black. The green fire was gone.

"Come on," he said. "If we can make it to the cabin—"

Then he saw that the little man's lips were moving, realized that he was deaf. The little man pulled himself and the inert body of the girl off the sled, held up the brass detonator, pointed back across the glacier. Blake bent in the roaring silence, faintly heard the screamed words:

"Get the bomb—while the ice is dead."

He drove the frightened huskies back toward the crater where the wreck had been. He found the shining cylinder of the sigma-bomb beyond it, half covered with shattered ice. He lifted it onto the sled, started back.

Endless serpents of green fire were creeping beneath him in the dark ice, when he got back to the little man and Jane. He put her back on the sled, beside the bomb.

Green snakes were darting at them, above the surface of the ice, before they came to the edge of the glacier. But Blake had learned a lesson. He twisted a stud on the side of his cylinder, and its golden beam grew more intense.

"An atomic ray," he shouted at the other man. "Light seems to kill the ice. I've stopped it up to ten kilowatts."

The yellow flood drove back the creeping tongues of green. They came safely off the glacier. Blake helped the man and the girl into the cabin, propped the cylinder in a corner so that its warming golden ray fell across the room.

When Blake had examined Jane's bruises, set the little man's arm and bandaged his head, they talked.

"I'm Mark Lingard."

"I see," said Blake. "I knew that Jane had been with you!"

Lingard smiled through his bandages at the quietly breathing girl.

"A splendid assistant, Miss Maddon," he said. "Fine scientific mind. It was her intuition that suggested my investigation—"

"Tell me," interrupted Blake. "Do you know what has happened? The ice?

Awkwardly, with his left hand, Lingard fumbled for his pipe. Blake filled and lighted it for him.

"Life has been born in the ice." His voice was deliberate, low. "I say life—that's the only word I know to use. Certainly it is something very different from animal life, and even that is a little difficult to define.

"A NYHOW, it is pretty obvious that the ice has something that we must call mind; and mind seems to me the essence and the measure of life. Just what gave birth to it, I can't say. But I believe that it is the establishment of a relationship between the ice crystals, analogous to that between the neurone cells in the brain.

"Probably a matter of electrodynamic potentials. The origin of it I conceive to be associated with the winter's phenomenal displays of the aurora; the impact of electronic and electromagnetic influences from the sun.

"How its energy is derived again I cannot say with certainty. Probably, however, by the diversion of heat into other energy forms. That accounts for the increasing cold.

The fact remains that it displays energy: by luminescence, by the extraordinary motion of the ice, by manipulation of objects and forces outside the ice, And the release of that energy, again, is patently directed by intelligent purpose. Such discrimination in energy release is the very fundamental of life."

He was fingering the sling that held his useless arm.

"Its purpose," he said, "is evidently directed toward the annihilation of mankind. Its intelligence promises to be sufficient to accomplish it."

"You mean—the sun?"

Lingard's brown, bandaged head nodded soberly.

"Was that a blow at mankind?" Blake asked.

"I think so—an incidental one. The ice is intelligent enough to know fear, and it has showed that it fears man—even by wrecking our plane. But the sun itself, of course, was a greater menace then man."

"Of course. It would have melted the ice."

"The danger was more immediate than the melting of the ice," said Lingard. "The sentience of the ice is a matter of delicately balanced electromagnetic potential differences. The sun gave it birth, with the strange effects associated with the aurora. But the powerful actinic radiation of ordinary sunlight would upset those delicate balances, kill it."

"I see," said Blake. "That's why light drives it back." His voice sank. "But how—how did it put out the sun?"

"My experiments have proved," Lingard said deliberately, "that the upper atmosphere is flooded with a strange ultra-short radiation. It is of a type that excites fluorescence in helium molecules under certain conditions, and I am certain that it is the secondary radiation they emit that has shut off the sunlight, by the interference of exactly synchronized wave frequencies."

"That radiation?" Blake asked breathlessly. "Where does it come from?"

"I approximated the position of its source," said Lingard. "By directional methods, and triangulation. It is not far from here. North—probably beyond the mountains. We came north in the hope that with your aid we could locate and destroy the source—"

"And bring back the sun," whispered Blake. "It must be done." His shaggy head lifted. "You had just the one plane?"

"We were lucky to have that," said Mark Lingard, bitterly. "I think you know Frey—Ellet Frey?"

Blake bit his lip; his bearded face twitched with pain.

"I do. Because I wouldn't sell him the disrupter, he destroyed my father's business and his life. For three years I've been hiding from his trumped-up charges!" His blue eyes were savage. "What has Frey done?"

"A strange thing, Blake. You see, something has happened to Frey."

G INGERLY caressing his broken arm, he explained:
The success of my investigations, Blake, is due largely to your radio reports. When I put our observations together, and with Miss Maddon's aid, formulated a theory of the menace and a plan to avert it, I laid all my work before the president. He promised me every support. Funds, assistants from the Bureau of Standards, and the aid of the army in carrying out whatever campaign I could plan.

"But your messages had been rebroadcast all over the world. Five weeks ago, when they suddenly ceased, there was a storm of popular interest in you. At its climax, Ellet Frey announced that he was undertaking a privately financed rescue expedition."

"Strange," muttered Blake. "Unless he hoped to get the disrupter— But go on."

"Two weeks ago, with four planes and twenty-eight men, he flew north across from Spokane. Miss Maddon and I were then in Seattle, organizing our own expedition. We had ten new army bombing planes, with a splendid corps of picked officers and scientists. The military part of the expedition was in command of a friend of mine, Major Wade Cameron.

"The day before we were planning to take off, Frey came back across Canada, with one battered plane, alone. I don't know what had taken place, Blake. But something had happened to him—to his mind."

Lingard's low voice sank.

"He gave the newspapers a most absurdly fantastic story, Blake. He told them that it was you who had extinguished the sun."

"I?" Blake was breathless. "I?"

"His story was ridiculous; it would have been incredible to a sane world. He told how his expedition had been met by a fleet of strange black planes, shot down. He was captured, he said, by a group of fanatic cultists, and found you their leader.

"It was your discovery of atomic energy, he said, that had been used to put out the sun. Your purpose, he said, was to crush civilization, kill all humanity save your chosen handful, and then establish some grotesque anarchistic society. Your radio messages about the living ice, he said, had been merely a blind for the plot.

"He escaped from you, he said, fled in the plane to warn the world."

"And people," whispered Blake "people believed him?"

"The world isn't sane," said Lingard. "Men are afraid—horribly afraid of the life in the ice. They were eager for a chance to call the appalling truth a lie, glad to cast the blame on a human being, on something they could understand.

"The president accepted his story without question. Major Cameron received orders immediately to halt the expedition. And we learned that Frey had come to Seattle with a group of Federal men, with warrants for the arrest of Miss Maddon and myself as accomplices in the alleged plot.

"We should have failed utterly but for the faith and courage of Major Cameron. Miss Maddon had come to me at the airport. Major Cameron pretended to arrest us, announced that he was taking us to Washington for trial, and flew north with us instead.

"Frey was outwitted for the moment. But when Cameron ignored radio orders to turn back, we learned that Frey himself had taken off in another plane to follow us. He is only a few hours behind, and he has threatened kill us on sight. A whole squadron of army planes took off as soon as it could be organized, to follow and aid him to destroy us.

"We have not only the ice to fight," Mark Lingard said solemnly, "but man as well."

He limped to the window.

"Back in the States," he whispered, "it seemed incredible that the ice was alive—that's why Frey's story was so promptly accepted. We must kill the ice, Blake. If we fail, human life won't last very long. Already people are dying by tens of thousands, as supplies of food and fuel run out. Frost has reached the equator, the living glaciers are pushing down.

"It is a new ice-age dawning. The ice will overwhelm forests and cities, until the continents are covered with living green. Even the oceans will freeze; green fire will spread through them, until the planet is one green globe of endless frozen night, ruled by the entity of frost."

"We must not fail," Blake was whispering grimly, when he heard Jane's low voice, and went eagerly back to the waking girl.


## CHAPTER IV

### THE FIEND OF THE FOREST

IT was four hours later that the three set out through the still violet dusk, across the living ice. Jane Maddon had declared herself able to follow the sled.

The five lean huskies were running before the sled. It carried the sigma-bomb, and Blake's carefully selected equipment.

Following were the three: Blake with his long whip and the disrupter; Jane Maddon, still white-faced with pain; the brown little scientist with his slung arm, limping awkwardly on unfamiliar snow-shoes.

The disrupter, set to give an intense hot golden beam, burned a path across the snow, into the mysterious menace of the frozen barrens.

"Your batteries—" Jane had asked as they started, "won't they burn out?"

"They are half a pound of gold." Blake told her. "They would last a thousand years."

"Your atomic discovery?" she cried eagerly. "Oh, I'm so glad, Mace!"

"If we win, Jane—if life goes on," he whispered, "it can give us—everything. It will clear Dad's name, and make us safe from Frey—"

Beneath the fur parka, her grey eyes shadowed.

"But Frey's after us, Mace," she whispered. "In the north, something's happened to him. I saw him, after he came back—" Her voice trembled with dread. "He's mad—he's a fiend. He's still after us, Mace—with the green of the ice in his eyes!"

In the changeless violet dusk, the motionless air seemed to congeal about them. Numbing, bitter, insidious, its cold penetrated their furs. A terrible silence closed in on them—the stillness of a world without life.

Jane refused to ride the sled, until, with a little gasping cry, she collapsed on the ice. Blake was putting her on the sled, when Wolf, the great lead dog, went mad. He whirled in the traces and crouched for an instant, with a singular wailing howl. The green of the ice, Blake thought, was oddly reflected in his eyes.

Out of the crouch, he sprang savagely back upon the other dogs. Two were injured before Blake could snatch up the rifle to kill him.

At the foot of the long, steep ascent to the pass, the exhaustion of the dogs forced a halt. The suffering animals gulped their frozen fish, buried themselves in the snow. Blake pitched the tiny tent, melted water for tea over the primus stove, thawed bread and dried meat. Hot food revived Jane. She and the crippled scientists crept into their sleeping bags, in the warming beam from the disrupter.

Blake's exhausted companions still slept when he heard a distant droning, saw a dark speck hanging in the south above the trail. The plane was drifting low across the green glaciers, but fingers of the ice did not attack it—the ice, he thought must know it for a friend.

Blake leaped instinctively to the disrupter, cut its output down to one kilowatt. But even the weakened beam, he realized, left them clearly visible. He dared not cut it down any farther, for already the green tentacles were writhing nearer. Piercing cold sank into him.

"It's Frey," said Lingard, roused. "That's his plane."

"I cut down the ray as much as I thought safe," said Blake. "But it will still give us away."

"Better turn it up again," advised the little scientist. "We'll freeze, without it. And those green things are coming pretty close—they might snatch it away."

Blake increased the output again. Then he tried the mechanism of the rifle, found it immovable.

"Oil frozen," he muttered. "Maybe I can thaw it in the ray."

T HE plane wheeled above them, dived. Above roaring motors Blake heard a rattling sound. He saw a line of white puffs march across the ice, toward the tent.

"Machine-gun!" Lingard gasped.

Blake snatched the rifle out of the warming beam, tried it again. It leaped and roared in his hands. He flung it to his shoulder and began firing at the plane.

It passed, rose and wheeled and dived again. The ice leaped into white spray under the machine-gun. Standing upright in the golden beam, Blake slipped his extra clips into the rifle, fired until the last shot was gone.

"Gun's empty," he muttered. "Guess we're finished—"

Then he saw the bright yellow ribbon rip backward from the fuselage. He saw the plane slip aside, dive, level, crash against a pinnacle of ice. For a little time the tangle of wreckage was dark. Grey smoke drifted out of it. Then a yellow flame was mounting.

"Got it!" he whispered, savagely exultant. "Gas tank—and maybe the pilot. We can go on, until the others come—"

He turned then, and his triumph gasped and died. Mark Lingard was lying on the ice behind him, a bullet hole through his bandaged temple. Dead.

Bullets had ripped the top of the tent. Quivering with abrupt new apprehension, Blake flung back the flap, peered at Jane. She was very silent. He lifted the fur that was frosted with her breath, saw her weary face peaceful with sleep.

Blake carried Lingard a little away, and left him lying on the snow in his furs. He heated food, and then wakened Jane. They ate, watching the burning plane, while Blake told her what had happened.

"Mark?" she whispered, whitefaced. "Dr. Mark dead! And I didn't even wake." She winced with pain.

"Don't mind that," said Blake. "But now it's up to us."

He dug the dogs out of the snow. Only three remained. Blake got into the traces himself, ahead of them, to break the way. Jane plodded behind.

He fell once, and his foot twisted under him. As Jane came to help him rise, his face was white with agony.

"We'll never make it," he gasped bitterly, staring at the ragged summits ahead, that flowed with unhallowed life. "We're mad."

But for hours, again, they toiled toward the pass. Then the gaunt-grey malamute, Amberjack, fell dead in the harness. Blake cut him out of the traces, dragged his lean body out of the way of the sled. His mittened hand caressed the shaggy, frost-crusted head, just once.

Jane, looking back, gasped and called out:

"Mace! I see something—*something*—following!"

"Couldn't be," Blake said. "Nothing alive nothing but the ice. Even the wolves were all dead or gone, months ago."

But his blue eyes, searching, found the follower. A tiny figure, lonely and dark, it was still far out on the green-glowing barrens. He bent over the sled, found the binoculars. The ruddy glow drained out of his face as he lifted them; he trembled to a new chill.

"Frey! It's Ellet Frey," he whispered. "He wasn't killed, when his plane fell. He's walking after us, over the ice. His face is white, like frozen flesh. His eyes are mad, and shining green." He lowered the glasses. "His furs are light. I don't know what keeps him from freezing."

J ANE was quivering, whitefaced.

"He's not a man any more," she whispered fearfully. "He's a fiend—a fiend of the ice. The ice did something to him, when he was lost in the north." She crept close to Blake. "The ice has a mind," she said apprehensively. "Do you think—do you think it could hypnotize, or somehow dominate, another mind?"

Blake tugged at the ice in his red beard.

"That must be it," he said somberly. "I've been sure of it ever since Wolf went mad, with the green of the ice in his eyes."

Jane was pointing at the rifle. "Can you stop him?"

Blake shook his head. "No ammunition."

"I'm afraid, Blake. Afraid!"

"We must go on," said Blake. "He has no burden, but perhaps we can keep ahead."

When he turned back to the dogs, one was crouching, with a terrible green flaming in her eyes. She launched herself savagely at his throat. He went down under her. Only the thickness of his furs kept her fangs from his jugular, until his hunting knife had found her heart.

Watching the green die in her glazing eyes, he whispered:

"That was the ice."

Now Flash alone was left. Jane came silently to take the dead husky's place in the harness. They went on up the slope, often looking back. Sometimes they couldn't see the tiny lone figure of their pursuer; but when they did, he was always nearer.

"Do you know what he will do, when he catches us?" Jane whispered once, when she had looked with the binoculars at their gaunt, green-eyed Nemesis. "He'll stop us first, because he is a tool of the ice. He will destroy the bomb. But he will do more—"

Her voice hushed; she shuddered.

Climbing unendingly, at last they dragged the sled into the narrow rocky gorge of the pass, and through it to the point where they could see beyond the range.

Blake stopped, when he saw the machine. Reeling with fatigue, Jane dropped to her knees in the snow. Behind her, Flash, the last husky, gave a short, hoarse bark, and fell dead in the harness, of sheer exhaustion.

Presently Blake laughed—a bitter, short, ironic sound, He limped back past the dead dog to the sled, and sat down on it.

"And we came to smash *that!*" he whispered. *"That!* With one little bomb!"

Inert, trembling in the snow, Jane Maddon stared at it. A dull, wondering horror came slowly into her grey eyes.

Mile upon mile ahead of them, beyond a barren plain of ghostly snow, the thing loomed unbelievably gigantic upon the green, dully shining ice. Incredible, colossal, it towered into the eternal vacancy of violet twilight.

Creation of a mind utterly alien to human understanding, of a life that had in common with human life little save the will to live, it was incomprehensible.

Part of it was black. Part of it was metal. Part of it was a machine.

Blake could grasp that much. But the form of it eluded him at the same time that it numbed him with shadowy horror. It was spidery, grotesque, as if it might be constructed of fourth dimensional entities. The black, colossal parts of it—he could find no fitting words for them—were silently moving.

Other parts of it, higher, not black, not metal, were nothing that could be termed mere machine. Their color was merely analogous to blue. They seemed somehow intangible. In material shape, and function, they were beyond the grasp of the human mind.

The fingers of the ice coiled about the thing. Green arms reached up from the crested ice-waves of the surrounding glaciers, as if to move and adjust its enigmatic parts.

Blake had promised himself that they would rest in the pass. But they waited merely to make tea again, and warm a little food.

"It's too big," Jane whispered dazedly. "Too big! We can't do anything. But we must try."

"Try—" agreed Blake. "Until we are dead—"

T HEY rose beside the sled. He bent to cut Flash out of the traces, and they pulled the sled onward. The slope now was downward, and it ran easily. Limping ahead in the slack traces, Blake warmed to a sudden hope that was like a steaming drink.

"We'll make it, at this rate!" he called. "If we could explode the bomb at some vital point, it might put the thing out of commission, big as it is."

"If we could stop it long enough to let the sun shine just a moment," Jane said, "I think that would kill the ice."

They had emerged from the narrow pass, upon the broad, snow-swept slope that fell toward the machine. In marching legions, the phantoms of green flame met them. Blake was breaking the way. Jane, behind him, carried the disrupter. She swung it back and forth, and the curling, questing tentacles fled from it— and ever returned. Green, swirling fingers circled the sled, moved with it, struck, recoiled, lurked, waited—

Sometimes Blake looked back, while they rested. Once he lowered the binoculars with a hand that trembled.

"I see him," he said. "Just stalking out of the pass. A gaunt, terrible giant—with the green of the ice in his eyes."

They were hastening on when far thunder rumbled through the frozen summits behind them. Bewildered, they paused to gaze back up the dark, rugged slope, that burned with the pale, ghostly light of the ice. Blake felt Jane's hand close convulsively on his arm.

"Mace!" she screamed. "The ice—"

Already he saw the motion above them. A vast green-white wave was gathering on the slopes. It was sweeping down upon them.

Then his wild eyes saw the little mesa beside them, an age-flattened point of black granite.

"Run!" he screamed to Jane. "If we can get on the rocks, there—"

Jerking the sled about, they drove themselves into a lurching run toward the safety of the mesa. Distant cannon boomed across the glaciers; they shattered with crashes like collapsing cathedrals of glass. The ice quivered and rocked beneath them.

But they were on the slope beneath the little black plateau.

"Come on!" Blake shouted. "We'll make it—"

The warm golden light of the disrupter went out behind him. He stopped and whirled and saw that Jane had turned out the beam, flung down the little cylinder in the snow. Her face was queerly white. She had paused, with her body straight and tense. Her eyes were glittering strangely.

With a frantic desperate haste, Blake plunged for the disrupter. It was in his hands when Jane sprang upon him, savage and silent. Her bloodless face was a terrible mask, and her grey eyes were shot with a green that was like the green of the ice.

"Jane!" It was a tortured scream. "Jane—"

She was fighting for the precious tube. He held it from her clawing hands, tried to drag her up the rugged slope, toward the little table-land. They were tangled in the harness of the sled. The roar of the avalanche was deafening. Blake felt a sudden, piercing breath of frigid wind.

And a monstrous, freezing black paw crushed him down into roaring dark.

## CHAPTER V

### ICE AND GOLD

B LAKE was floating in a green sea and time passed him by
like a wind. His body was tired; it was good to float so rest-
fully and forget the wind of time. Yet some nagging problem
tugged at his rest, while ages roared above. And at last he knew
the trouble: the green sea was cold. It was freezing; green ice was
grasping his body.

He battled the hardening frozen fingers, and strove to fling
himself up into the wind of time. For there was a task he must do.
The world was sinking into the green sea—and a girl. He alone
could lift them back into the life of time.

He fought until something tensed in him, something snapped,
and suddenly he was wide awake.

He was lying on the flat point of granite that had split the
avalanche. Numb wrists and aching ankles refused to move.
Hands and feet were bound, he saw, with leather thongs cut from
the dog harness.

A low groan, shivering, piteous, twisted his head. He saw Jane
Maddon on the ledge beside him, similarly bound. A little of her
face was exposed beneath the parka, blue with cold, drawn with
pain.

Beyond her, a little cliff dropped from the ledge where they
lay, and the greenly shimmering slopes fell away from it, toward
the colossal enigma of the machine that had extinguished the
sun.

The girl moved. She was sobbing. "Sorry, Mace!" she gasped,
bleakly. "I couldn't help it—I couldn't! The ice made me do it—
the ice—"

"I know," he whispered. "Don't you worry!"

Deep relief flooded him, to know that she was herself again.

"Frey?" he breathed. "Frey—"

"He came," she sobbed, "after the ice struck us. He dug us out,
and tied us. I think he's going to kill us. But now he's digging
again."

Blake twisted his shivering, stiffening body, to look in the
other direction. Beyond the rocky level he saw the pit, where

they had been buried in the green wave of snow and ice.

Ellet Frey was in the pit. A haggard, gaunt, tremendous man. His skin, beneath his thin furs, was white as if already frozen. Digging at the rubble of snow and broken ice with white bare hands he was uncovering the sled. He came at the bright steel cylinder of the sigma-bomb.

Blake watched with sinking heart as he unscrewed the little brass detonator from the bomb, and brought it and the empty rifle out of the pit. He laid the detonator on a flat rock, twenty yards away. Deliberately, with an appalling superhuman strength, he snapped the stock off the rifle. Gripping the barrel, he brought the breech mechanism down like a hammer on the detonator. It exploded sharply with a vivid blue flash.

Despair fell like a leaden hand on Blake. That bomb had meant the life of mankind. Grimly he had hoped, somehow, to escape and use it. But without the detonator it was as inert and useless as two hundredweight of stone.

Ellet Frey came stalking across the little mesa to his two prisoners. His bare, craggy face was utterly white. His eyes glowed green. He stopped on the black rock above them, and a dull, strange voice came out of his throat. It was like the voice of some monstrous thing, Blake thought, roaring far-off in a fog.

"Man—" it whispered thickly. "Your life—life of warmth and light—must die— Cold is conqueror—"

The gaunt, gigantic figure pointed one stiff white hand into the north. Blake looked again down the slope of glowing ice. Colossal and incredible beneath the eternal violet night, he saw again the thing that had put out the sun.

The uncanny voice, strange as the aurora whispering through a frozen fog, came again:

"Ice—reigns—"

Green light flamed in the mad eyes beyond the frozen mask. It was a mask—no longer a human face. And that dull, foggy voice was not the voice of Ellet Frey. It was the voice of the ice.

If the supernal, dreadful mind of the ice could speak to men, could it understand them? A sudden trembling seized Blake's big body. If his mind could meet the mind of the ice, through this thing that had been Ellet Frey, then here was a way to attack.

T HE voice was saying, "Man—must die—"
Blake jerked his head toward Jane.

"Maybe he must!" he said, in a low, swift whisper. "But Frey didn't find the disrupter. It's still buried beneath the ice. And when I saw that the avalanche would overtake us I set it like a time bomb. It will go off after half an hour. Eight ounces of activated gold—"

"What!" the girl gasped with astonished wonder. "I didn't—"

"Hush!" whispered Blake. "He mustn't hear—might smash it—"

But the green fire had already flamed up in the hollow eyes of Ellet Frey, like dreadful panic burning. The gaunt tremendous figure whirled, ran back into the pit. Furiously, bare white hands dug into ice and snow.

Blake's hope trembled before sudden fear. Could the ice match his cunning with cunning enough to suspect? Or could its strange mind read man's mind? He must carry on.

"I didn't tell you," he told Jane. "We must escape before it explodes. Any minute—"

He writhed toward her, tugged with his teeth at her binding thongs. The frozen leather seemed hard as iron. His teeth ached to the chill. The knots were drawn tight; he accomplished nothing—

"He has it!" Jane's voice was sudden, fearful. "He's bringing it out of the pit!"

Striving to conceal his elation, Blake glanced at the giant form stalking with the little tube to the rock where he had smashed the detonator.

"Can't manage the knots," he gasped. "Got to go over the ledge. Any second now—"

"I can't—" Jane sobbed faintly. "Can't move—"

Blake caught her frozen furs in his teeth; writhing, he inched his way toward the ledge, dragged her beside him. Behind him, with the lifeless precision with which a robot might move, the tall haggard thing laid the tube on a rock, and lifted the barrel of the broken rifle above it.

In the last, frantic instant, Blake flung himself off the ledge, dragging Jane after him with his teeth. They slipped twenty feet down the face of the little cliff, into deep soft snow that buried them.

"Shut your eyes!" Blake whispered urgently against the smothering snow. "Cover your face, or the explosion might blind you—"

The universe turned into golden flame. Blake thrust his head deeper in the snow, pushed the fur parka down over his eyes. He tried to twist his body to shelter Jane's head.

Even through snow and fur and eyelids, the light came in a merciless, penetrating flood. Sudden heat was in the air, for an instant grateful, then terrible. The air was too hot to breathe. The snow melted above them. Water drenched them, cold at first, then steaming.

An eternity of flaming agony that slowly grew tolerable.

And a time came when they could uncover their eyes and sit up at the foot of the little cliff that had sheltered them. For many yards the snow was gone, the rocks hot and dry.

Bewildered, Jane asked faintly, "What happened?"

"There was no other way." Blake muttered. "I couldn't move; it was my mind against the mind of the ice. And I think I had a right to do it, after what the ice did to you. It was just, anyhow, that the human slave of the ice should destroy it."

"But what did you do?"

"I said that the disrupter was a bomb," said Blake. "I made Frey smash it. And when he smashed the tau-ray tube it left eight ounces of gold free to disintegrate at the full rate—half the atoms breaking down every fifty-nine seconds.

"I think the radiation wasn't good for the ice!"

Anxiously, his streaming, half-blind eyes were peering into the north. Glaciers and snowfields were grey and white: the green of alien sentience was gone. The green streamers of flame no longer tended the fantastic machine.

"See!" Blake breathed exultantly. "That break in the rhythm of its motion! The ice is dead, and the machine is running wild—"

The hot rocks shivered abruptly. Roar of terrific grinding crashes came rolling up the slope. And suddenly the incomprehensible upper parts of the thing, looming so monstrously against the violet sky, seemed to twist and crumple. They vanished in a blinding flicker of colorless energy.

THE violet sky brightened, then, into the hazy blue of an arctic day. A flood of rosy light washed the slope below.

"The sun!" Jane was sobbing with hysterical joy. "It's the sun!"

Wet from the melting snow, their leather bonds stretched. Blake slipped his hands free, untied himself and Jane. Though the low sun still burned through the mists on the horizon, the air grew cold again as the atomic flame died. Stiff and weary, they climbed back to the little mesa.

Where Frey had laid the disrupter to smash it a ten-foot pool of molten rock still glowed dull red. Creeping up to its grateful heat, Blake saw that the black rock beyond was smeared with the white lime from an incinerated skeleton.

"Frey," he said, "must have died instantly."

"I think that he died days ago, when he was lost on the ice." Jane shuddered. "I think the ice had stolen his body—"

That gaunt, green-eyed, frozen mask came back to Blake like a haunting thing. He shut his eyes. His bearded face twitched. Seeing his pain, Jane said hastily:

"I'm sorry the disrupter is ruined. Can you build another, Mace?"

"Not here," he said gloomily. "Guess we're finished, Jane. We're lost here, without much food, or any way to travel. We can keep alive till the rock gets cold—"

His voice ended abruptly. He stared into the south, away from the colossal ruin of the black machine. The dull saffron sun hung low in the mist above the ice-clad range.

"There!" Jane cried joyously. "Look!" The music of motors grew louder and louder. "It's the army planes that followed Frey. They must have seen the light when your tube exploded. They see us, already! They'll take us back—"

Then she was in Blake's arms. Looking into her wide grey eyes, so near, Blake saw little gleams of green—like the green of the ice. Had they been there always? Or—

He shivered, and kissed her.

# Spider Island

*Thrilling Mystery, April 1937*

### CHAPTER I

#### THE THING THAT SCREAMED

WELDON GRAIL STIFFENED WHEN HE SAW THE STRANGER. Every muscle of his long, lean body tensed to that scarlet intuition of terror and death which had never betrayed him.

But this was not the jungle. The subconscious warning seemed out of tune to the slumberous tropical peace of Havana's shady Prado. He tried to ignore it. He held his lazy-seeming sprawl on the stone bench, merely narrowed his alert grey eyes at the approaching stranger.

The man didn't look alarming. Stocky, florid, he was chewing calmly at a dead cigar. His reddish head was bare; he wore boots and riding togs. His eyes met Grail's, blue and frank. He threw the cigar away; his broad red face smiled genially. Yet Grail still sensed the chill shadow of danger.

"Weldon Grail?" The heavy man's voice was richly jovial. He put out a soft, well kept hand. "Scoville's the name. Charlie

Scoville, of Hollywood. Know how I found you?"

He held out a Miami paper, folded. His stubby finger found an item:

### AMERICAN FLYER RETURNING

The young American explorer, Weldon Grail, reached Havana yesterday in his flying boat, from Yucatan, where his aerial survey revealed new Mayan ruins. Flying to New York, Grail admitted that he is going to enjoy a new taste of civilization.

"New York!" A smile softened Grail's weather-seamed brown face. "After a year of heat and mosquitoes and no ice water—" That instinctive warning chilled his enthusiasm. He said, "Well, what?"

Charlie Scoville took the paper, turned it, said: "Read this."

### MOVIE PARTY MAROONED

Radio dispatches from the schooner *Cathay,* under charter by a motion picture company, state that yesterday she sprang a leak at sea and was forced to run ashore on the Caribbean island of Fuego.

Bound for Venezuela, where they were to make a film, the passengers included the Hollywood actress, Crystal Verrill; the noted character actor, Hugo Letz, and Lorin Key, actor and scenarist. Also aboard was a technical staff, and Mark Johns, publicity representative for the company. No injuries were reported, although the party will be marooned until the vessel is repaired.

It is rumored in Hollywood that Miss Verrill and Key are to be married in South America.

"Crystal Verrill!" Grail said softly. "I know her—knew her. Years ago, in a country town, in Kansas. We were both planning to go on the stage. I was going to be a magician."

He smiled wistfully. Then that shock of warning stiffened him again. He looked keenly at stocky Scoville.

"Where do I come in?"

"I want you to fly me to that island—today."

The lean explorer smiled. "I had a hunch you meant trouble." He shook his head. "No, I'm fed up with insects and jungles. I hanker for bright lights and music—"

"They're in trouble, on that damned island,'" the other broke in, earnestly. "I'm their director—an independent producer, you know. Scoville Productions. I was to join them in Venezuela. But now it's up to me to help them out."

"Trouble?" repeated Grail.

Frowning with worry, Scoville, dug into his breeches.

"This came last night, from the *Cathay's* radio—seems they've beached the schooner, for emergency repairs. Read it."

CHARLES SCOVILLE
MIAMI, FLORIDA
BRING PLANE TO TAKE US OFF ISLAND STOP FOR GOD'S SAKE HURRY STOP HELL IS LOOSE IN JUNGLE STOP ALL LIVES IN DANGER
MARK JOHNS

Grail's eyes narrowed slowly. "Crystal Verrill in danger," he muttered. "And the man she loves." Decision hardened his tanned jaw. "We can take off in forty minutes!"

F UEGO ISLAND was a lonely tri-angular peak, jutting abruptly from an indigo sea. Green jungles blanketed it mysteriously. Two sides sloped up sharply to the small cup of the central crater. The north slope was less abrupt. White beach shone between jungle and sea, The *Cathay* lay some distance off the beach, aground.

Weldon Grail, at the wheel of his big flying boat, quivered again to that warning chill of peril that he had learned to accept as fact, without attempting to explain it. It was near sunset. Ominous shadows already drenched the island. Menace seeped like blood from the brooding jungle.

"I'll land off the beach," he told Scoville. "I see a boat!"

He dropped the plane on smooth water, taxied in, released his anchors.

"I see Mark and the rest," said Scoville, eagerly. "Coming!" he yelled.

Above the beach was a long, low dwelling. Ancient, neglected, it was half buried in gay hibiscus, purple bougainvilleas. A little group of people left its sagging veranda, hurried down to the beach. Three men came out in a skiff to meet the plane.

"That's Mark Johns," said Scoville, smiling. "The cleverest publicity man in Hollywood. To play up the danger of this trip, he got the company to take out a million dollars' worth of temporary life insurance policies, on myself and our three principals.

"That story got our new film a hundred thousand dollars" worth of free advertising, before a foot was ever shot.—Mark! Is everybody safe?"

Mark Johns stood up in the boat. He was briskly active, stout-ish, dressed in rough khaki. A black patch covered one eye. His left arm was white with bandages, slung.

"Charlie!" His voice was loud with relief. "Glad you turned up. They're all afraid to stay ashore another night. And the schooner's still aground, where a breath of wind would make a death-trap of her."

"Afraid—of what?" Scoville was asking as they climbed down into the skiff. Anxiously, "What hurt you, Mark?"

Mark Johns touched the slung arm tenderly. Horror greyed his rugged face, rather sinister beneath the black eyepatch. He shrugged.

"I don't know, Charlie," he said. "I wish to hell I did."

One of the oarsmen spat in the water, muttering:

"If ye ask me, that scientist feller, Hacklyn, is at the bottom of the devilment."

"Hacklyn is a sort of hermit scientist," Mark Johns explained. "Seems to be the only inhabitant. He owns the house, but lives in his laboratory, somewhere in the jungle. He tried to keep us from landing, but finally said we could stay in the house."

His good eye stared moodily past the few leaning scraggy palms on the beach, at the jungle's forbidding barrier.

"Mark," Scoville insisted, "what happened to you?"

The publicity man, still staring, said in a low, quiet voice.

"I was attacked, Charlie. Last night when I was sitting on the veranda. Something came scuttling out of the jungle, knocked me out of my chair and gave me a nasty scratch on the arm."

Sharp-voiced with concern, Scoville demanded:

"But what was it?"

The good eye still peered at the jungle-clad slopes.

"Something loose there," Mark Johns said slowly. "Some wild, savage thing—had no provocation to attack me. Didn't see it very well. Dark, you know. But it looked like—rather like—"

Grail prompted, "Like what?"

"It was big," said the low, reluctant voice. "Heavy enough to knock me out of my chair. It looked like—well, a spider."

"A spider?" echoed Scoville, incredulously. But Weldon Grail, staring at the brooding menace of the jungle, listened gravely.

## CHAPTER II

### The Masters of Horror

A LITTLE group met them on the coral beach, each person anxious, tensed against nameless, implacable dread.

"Hugo Letz," said Mark Johns. "They call him the 'Master of Horror.'"

Hugo Letz was a stooped, heavy man, bullet-headed, gorilla-limbed. Some queer stiffness made Grail think of a corpse walking. His skin was pale, waxy. None of his features—the big, thick-lipped mouth, the heavy flat nose, the large, bloodshot, bulging eyes—were particularly deformed. Yet his face somehow shocked Grail; it was hideous beyond words.

"I have played horror rôles," his thick, croaking voice explained. "I have been billed as the ugliest man in the world."

He laughed. It was a gasping, bubbling sound that made Grail turn quickly away.

"And Lorin Key," said the one-eyed publicity man. "Author of *Death and the Devil.*"

Lorin Key was a tall man, suavely handsome. He had cynical dark eyes, a lean, sophisticated face. Strong white teeth flashed, as he smiled, beneath a minute, well tended black mustache. His face was a mask, Grail felt, covering something cold, ruthless, mysterious.

"Is he that bad?" Grail thought. "Or am I jealous?"

"Lorin, in his own way, is a master of horror," said Johns. "He writes the pictures in which Hugo stars."

Grail was quick enough to catch the look between the handsome man and the hideous one. It was hatred, stark and undisguised.

The others on the beach were technicians; they had set up a camera to film the landing.

"Crystal Verrill?" asked Grail, disappointed. "Where—"

Then he saw her, hastening down from the jungle-smothered dwelling. She had been the ideal of Grail's dreams. Beyond her slim physical perfection lay the true grace of a quick and generous mind. It hurt him to see that her glorious vitality was also burdened with an overpowering fear.

Weldon Grail waited, smiling, anxious. After six years, would she remember, or had dreams made a fool of him?

"Weldon!" She smiled with relief and pleasure. "It's really you! I was afraid you'd be lost in some jungle, before I ever saw you again!"

Tall, handsome Lorin Key moved beside her, possessively, saying unnecessarily:

"Darling, you know Mr. Grail?"

Horror fell again upon the creamy oval of her face. Her hand went tense.

"You've came to take us off this horrid island?"

Grail nodded. "I can carry six," he said. "But no heavy baggage."

Charlie Scoville asked, "Can we get off tonight?"

"If necessary," Grail said. "But night flying is dangerous."

"Let's stay overnight," suggested Lorin Key. "In the morning we can shoot a few sequences on the plane that will work into the picture."

"But, Lorin!" protested Crystal Verrill, urgently. "We can't stay here another night! That thing in the jungle—"

Her brown eyes looked at Grail, wide with a mute, frightened appeal.

"Never run until you know what you are afraid of," he said. "If you do you carry the fear with you always. Let's stay, tonight."

The girl nodded, whispered, "Thanks, Weldon. I was in a panic."

"Fool," came the hoarse voice of hideous Hugo Letz. "If we stay one of us will die! I *know* it—"

"Be still!" whispered Lorin Key. "Here comes our host."

G RAIL saw a tall, singular man striding out of the jungle. He was gaunt as a skeleton, clad in weirdly patched rags. His leathery face was massed with a stained white beard. His eyes were deeply sunken, strangely burning.

His stringy arms were burdened with a long, double-barreled shotgun. Stopping a little above the group on the beach, he raised a harsh, menacing voice.

"I give you warning," he said. "When you had no way to go I

tolerated your presence. Now you have the means, go immediately—or die!"

Without waiting for any reply, he turned. Implacable, gaunt and stern as Death himself, he stalked back up the jungle path-

"That's the scientist, Hacklyn," Mark Johns said to Grail, swiftly. "I'm going to follow him back to his laboratory, and see what he's up to. I don't like him. You keep the others together. Watch for trouble—"

He hastened up the trail. The rest went out to the house, a strained, silent group.

"A horrid, empty, dusty old place," said Crystal, nervously. "No servants. A man comes from the ship to cook, but we keep our own rooms."

The sun touched the sea, and tropic night fell like a wall of horror. Dim oil lamps flared in the creaky old house. Its emptiness whispered eerily.

Grail sat, with Crystal and Charlie Scoville, on the broad veranda. Key and Letz had excused themselves.

"Why doesn't Mark come back?" The girl peered into the hostile wall of the dark jungle. Her voice chattered with apprehension. "I'm afraid—*listen!*"

Grail heard it. A scream, infinitely high and thin, with a scratchy quality that lacerated the nerves. It was somehow human, agonized—yet far too shrill, too keen, to come from human vocal organs.

Grail leaped to his feet, tugging out the revolver he had brought ashore. Crystal was beside him, trembling.

"Let's go in," she gasped. "We heard that horrid sound last night, before poor Mark was attacked."

But Charlie Scoville remained in his chair. "Probably some sort of tropic bird," he said. He drew on his pipe.

Grail retorted, "I never heard a bird—"

Then it came, a shadow flitting from the jungle's fringe. A scratch of horny feet. The malevolent glow of saucer-huge eyes, purple, phosphorescent.

Grail snatched Crystal behind him. He fired twice, straight into the thing. Then it struck him A heavy, hairy body, cold, infinitely horrible. Its odor was sickening—a strange charnel musk. Flung against the girl, he tripped. They sprawled together on the floor.

"*Ugh!*" He heard Charlie Scoville's gasp. The movie producer was horrified, yet incredulous. "What—"

The voice merged into a scream of horror and agony. Again the quick scuttle of horny feet crossing the veranda, departing. Scoville was cursing, struggling, shrieking with pain. From the jungle's edge came his faint, desperate appeal:

"Help! It's carrying me! *Oh-h-hh-h!*"

"Crystal!" Gasping with dread, Grail set the girl on her feet. "Are you—all right?"

She stood like a white statue, wide, terror-filmed eyes staring into the tropic gloom.

"I saw it," her dry whisper came unbelievingly. "It touched me. A spider bigger than a man!"

"Let's get inside." Grail took her arm, found it cold with horror-sweat. "I'll call Key and Letz. Two of us will go after poor Scoville."

An oil lamp flickered in the long central hall. Grail wondered momentarily why Hacklyn, the solitary hermit of science, had built a house of a dozen rooms. Weird echoes mocked Grail's fear-choked shout.

A FTER a delay that seemed endless, Hugo Letz came from his room in the right wing. The stiffness of the grave was still in his limbs; horror like a mask on his waxen, livid face. This abandoned house upon the jungle-ridden island, Grail thought fleetingly, was an ideal stage for the man's dread genius.

"What alarmed you?" His bulging eyes, bloodshot, mismated, fell upon the slender, frightened loveliness of Crystal Verrill. "At least, my darling," he croaked, *"you* are safe!"

The girl quivered beside Grail, bit her full lip.

"Where," Grail said, "is Key?"

Black hatred twisted the horror-actor's features. "I don't know," he rasped savagely. "In hell, I hope—"

The tall, handsome actor-scenarist appeared behind him in the hall. "On the contrary," Lorin Key said suavely, "I was in the bath." Patting his neck-tie, he came to the others.

"What excited you, Grail, my dear fellow? You should be accustomed to the noises of the tropics."

"It was more than a noise this time," Grail said grimly. "Something—it resembled a huge spider—came on the veranda. It knocked me down and carried off Charlie Scoville.

"We've got to find him. Probably too late to help. But he was still alive at the edge of the jungle. Anyhow, we must try. If one of you will come with me, the other can stay with Miss Verrill."

Pale, his eyes bulging fearfully, Hugo Letz objected: "Isn't there somebody else?"

"No," Grail said. "Johns hasn't come back. And the men all rowed out to the schooner, at dark. It's up to us." His grey eyes narrowed.

"If you don't care to go, perhaps Mr. Key will volunteer—"

The anxious girl called Grail aside. "Don't leave me here with Hugo," she begged, wide-eyed, afraid. "I'd rather go with you!"

"What?" Grail's jaw hardened. "Has he been—"

"I see." Grail turned briskly. "Key," he said, "You are elected to be Miss Verrill's bodyguard. Letz, will you get any weapon you have, and come with me?"

"He hasn't done anything. I just can't stand him." She shuddered. "I know he—wants me. He hates me, because I don't care for him. And he hates Lorin, because—"

The hideous, waxen face twitched and went pale. But Hugo Letz nodded stiffly. His glassy eyes looked from Key to the girl with a dreadful intensity. His thick lips quivered, as if about to scream out hatred. Man and girl cowered back from his deadly menace.

He turned, shaking. With a curious, drunken walk he went to his room and returned with a flashlight and a long, ugly-nosed Lüger. He followed Grail out on the veranda. As they passed handsome Lorin Key, smiling possessively down at Crystal Verrill, Grail heard the hoarse, gasping intake of the horror-actor's breath, the grinding of his teeth.

The darkness, outside, fell upon them like a shocking force of tangible evil. Hugo Letz was muttering under his breath.

"She hates me!" His harsh bitterness was sudden, violent. "She hates me, because my body is ugly. She loves that damned Key, for his handsome body, though he has the devil's soul. I should kill him!"

His gorilla-body quivered; his teeth ground. "I beg your pardon, Grail," he said. "I shouldn't talk so. But you can't conceive what it means to be ugly. A hideous face makes a hideous life, a hideous soul?"

He shuddered, peering into the dark, whispering jungle. "What do you think we shall find?" His dread seemed suddenly childish, pathetic.. "Do you think there really is this large spider?"

"There is something," Grail said. "A savage monster, strong

enough to carry Scoville away. It looked like a spider. I have seen fossil remains of spiders two feet long. It is possible that a new species has originated on the island—a strange evolutionary mutation—"

## CHAPTER III

### "IT ONCE WAS HUMAN!"

A LERT apprehension silenced Letz's voice as the trail led them into the jungle. Their feeble lights flickered against grotesque masses of ferns, like monsters crouching. They flickered on massive boles of gigantic trees, choked, throttled with coiling, snakelike lianas; on weird grey festoons of moss and parasitic orchids.

Intuitive dread sank cold talons into Grail's throat.

"Death!" Hugo Letz's voice was hoarse, croaking with fear. "Death may wait within six inches of us, and we shall not know, until it strikes. In this dark—"

A thin wail of pure agony seeped through the black jungle like blood from a rotting corpse. Grail stopped beside Letz, listening, trembling with instinctive horror. It came again, a bleating whisper of pain.

"Help—help me! The spider—it—it—"

Grail stiffened, fighting the scarlet madness which fear had kindled in his leaping heart. Cocking the revolver, he crept grimly forward, whispering:

"Scoville—his voice!"

The black, smothering curtains of the jungle pressed close. Its dank breath was the reeking musk of an ancient tomb. Leaves brushed them like ghostly hands. Serpentine creepers grasped at their bodies like monstrous tentacles. The sodden muck quaked beneath them, as if with noisome buried life.

"God!" Scoville moaned again. "Let me—die—"

Grail lifted his revolver, drove his stiff, unwilling body toward the sound. He thrust through a curtain of ferns, snapped on his flashlight. What he saw froze his sweat-drenched, shuddering limbs.

The thin pale beam fell upon a contorted, swollen, stricken

thing—a thing that had been a man. Over it, feasting unthinkably, crouched sheer nightmare.

A spider whose hideous, bulging black body was larger than a man. Its stiff, angular legs covered with black fur, spread ten feet. But it was the fanged head that chilled Grail with uttermost horror. Jutting from that bulbous body, the head was also round, covered with the same black hair.

Its eyes were huge, purple, aflame with evil hate. The long, savage fangs were red, dripping with fresh blood. For all that head's uncanny monstrosity it somehow suggested the human. That, to Grail, was most horrible.

The giant spider crouched for a moment over its motionless prey. It uttered that eldritch, papery ululation—that anguished shriek so thin it rent the nerves. Slowly, moving as if of independent volition, the eight black hideous legs gathered under it. Then it leaped.

Grail's hands were stiff, nerveless. He forced them to level the gun. He fired twice, straight between those fearful purple eyes. But the thing came on.

He tried to gasp a warning, but already, with a sickening, incredible speed, it was upon them. Its powerful hairy weight struck him. He tripped against a vine, went down into the jungle muck. His senses reeled to its nauseating, reptilian musk.

Struggling to get up, he was aware of a brief sharp struggle above him in the darkness. The Lüger roared deafeningly. He heard that thin, agonizing shriek, and then a low, gasping cry of pain from Hugo Letz.

A quick rustling in the ferns. Then, as he recovered flashlight and gun, ominous silence. He snapped on the flashlight, wiped mud off the lens.

The colossal spider was gone. Hugo Letz was lying in the muck, doubled with agony, groaning. His hand clutched his left arm, where blood drenched the sleeve.

"The thing's gone," said Grail. "Let's see your arm."

The horror actor sat up. He was white, shaken, sick.

"It got me!" he groaned. "It pains like fire! I'm poisoned— poisoned—"

His body slumped, quivering. His voice became a wail of agony.

Grail flashed his light toward the spider's inert prey. His breath went out in a long, dry gasp of horror. It was a man, or had been a man. The director, Charlie Scoville. The boots and riding breeches were evidence enough of that. But the flesh looked like nothing human. It was enormously and hideously swollen, purple-black.

"Scoville!" Grail's voice was faint with sickening dread. "The spider was *eating—*"

T HE shirt was in crimson ribbons. From upper arm, shoulder, breast, the flesh was ripped to red bones. There was no face. Retching, goose-pimpled, Grail lifted the intact arm. He dropped it, gasping with relief. This scarlet thing had found the mercy for which it wailed—death!

"Dead!" sobbed Hugo Letz. "As I shall die."

He was a quivering jelly of agony and terror. Grail ripped off his shirt. The arm was fearfully gashed from elbow to shoulder, discolored, swiftly swelling.

"Come on," he said briskly. "A little permanganate will pull you through."

"Fire in my veins," gasped the actor. "Burning—burning—"

His teeth ground fiercely. His blood-smeared face twisted into a hideous mask of pain. He quivered, sagged again. Every breath was a hoarse, heaving sob of agony.

"Dying," he moaned. "And Key will live to take the woman I love." Scarlet teeth bit through his thick lips. "If I could strangle Key—"

Stiffly hooked fingers clawed savagely at his own throat. He began a croaking laugh that ended in a bubbling scream of agony.

"Murderer!" he shrieked, hysterical. "It was Lorin Key that killed me!"

"Brace yourself and come to the house," urged Grail. "That's impossible!"

The actor struck madly at Grail's lifting hands. "Key did it," he sobbed.

"He's cunning. His brain is warped, steeped in evil. His face is handsome—but you have seen his plays, master works of clever, diabolic horror.

"He hated me because I was billed above him, because I was the 'Master of Horror.' He hated me because I loved Crystal Verrill. His devil's brain designed the horror on this island. He brought me here—to die "

The croak became a sobbing rattle. Grail caught the sagging body. It stiffened convulsively in his arms, then a spasmodic struggle flung him away. It arched, hurled itself heavily backward into the jungle muck. A faint soft cry, like a baby's happy coo, came through the torn, scarlet lips. The ugly head remained set unnaturally, horribly; the face rigid and dreadful.

His greatest scene, Grail thought fleetingly, shuddering.

He stiffened. Again, far off, he heard the thin, semi-human shriek of the giant spider. Northward, it sounded. Toward the dwelling—toward Crystal Verrill!

*　　*　　*　　*　　*

What ghastly freak of evolution, in the jungle's dank, rotting womb, could have given birth to the monster spider? The question haunted Grail as he hastened back along the jungle path. And whence the hint of humanity in its fanged head? Why the undertone of human agony in its scream? Was it—he shuddered—akin to man?

The jungle-shrouded house was dark, silent. Panic closed his throat. Could there be truth in the wild accusations of the dying actor? He somehow mistrusted Lorin Key. To his relief, Crystal Verrill came to open the door.

"Weldon!" she cried anxiously. "Have you seen Lorin?"

In the glow of the lamp in her hand, her slim beauty was like a white flame. Suddenly Grail wanted terribly to take her in his arms, kiss away her fear, claim her for his own. His body tensed. Jealous fool, he thought.

"You're all alone?" he said. "Where's Key?"

"He left right after you and Hugo did," the girl said. "I told him I wasn't afraid to stay alone. Did you find Charlie?"

Grail looked away from the lovely pale oval of her face. "We found him," he said. "Too late. He was dead. The thing was still there. It attacked us. Letz was—killed."

She gasped, shuddering. "Oh, it's so awful!"

"Key?" Grail asked again. "Where did he go?"

"Lorin went to look for Hacklyn's laboratory. Up toward the crate."

"Why?"

White, strained, Crystal Verrill's face looked up at Grail. He saw that she was trembling. Fine globules of sweat pearled her fair skin. She looked sick with fear.

CRYSTAL said faintly, "Let's sit down."
Grail helped her to a chair. She collapsed in it, covered her face with quivering hands.

Gently, Grail insisted, "Tell me, if you can."

"I can." She looked up as she spoke. A quiet strength had come into her faint tone. It was very steady. "I hadn't wanted to, Weldon, because it is so terrible. And we didn't really know—"

Her eyes closed for a moment. The pale mask of her face was rigidly composed—as lifeless, Grail thought, shuddering, as if she had been dead.

"It is something," she whispered, "that Mark found out."

"Mark Johns!" Grail exclaimed softly. "He has never come back from following Hacklyn?"

"No," the girl said. "Lorin went to see what had happened to him."

"But what was it he found out?"

"Hacklyn has been here for years," Crystal said. "Mark found out that he has a mine back in the crater. He has been refining the ore in his laboratory. It's radium, Mark says. He had been using the radium to perform experiments." Her eyes dilated. "Dreadful experiments."

Grail stared mutely at her pallid, horror-struck face.

"Hacklyn must have had men with him when he came here,'" she went on. "One man couldn't have built this house. What became of Hacklyn's assistants?"

Hoarse with dread, Grail repeated, "What?"

"Mark had a theory," the girl whispered. "He talked with Hacklyn in the jungle. He found out that Hacklyn was once a well-known biologist, in England. Mark is a clever amateur scientist. He could understand what Hacklyn was up to, and he explained it to me."

Her frightened brown eyes looked up at him intently.

"You know about the *genes*—the tiny bodies in the chromosomes of the germ cells that control inheritance? And you know how the *genes* can be affected with radiations—such as radium rays—to cause mutations?"

"I know," whispered Grail, rigid with mounting horror. He had read of the astounding experiments of Loeb, Morgan, and other master biologists, in which bombardment of the parent calls with rays had caused a second generation of weird and horrible monstrosities.

If rays could cause uncanny variation in fruit flies, why not in men? He shuddered.

"Radiations can change the individual, as well as its offspring," Crystal went on, husky with dread. "You know about the endocrine glands, how their secretions—the complex chemicals called hormones—control the growth of the body? Rays can stimulate those glands, depress them, change their secretion."

Grail nodded, and again he shuddered. He recalled experiments in which science had created giants, dwarfs, monstrous things that had to be quickly destroyed. He knew that the hormones could change sex characters, cause a woman to grow a beard and develop a masculine voice and manner.

Such mastery of life wag a blessing In the hands of medicine. It enabled doctors to correct abnormalities due to malfunctioning glands. But in the hands of a strange hermit, perhaps a madman, what might it lead to?

"Don't you see?" Crystal Verrill's voice was a papery rustle. "Don't you see what happened to Hacklyn's assistants? He changed them, with his ghastly radium experiments. The thing that killed Scoville and Letz—the spider-thing—was once a *man!*"

"I see!" Grey horror rode his whisper. "That was what Hacklyn meant when he warned us. His hideous creations are roaming the jungle—perhaps spawning others—"

He looked at Crystal Verrill, saw her pale lips open and close, saw her swallow convulsively. Puzzled, he said:

"Isn't that what you meant?"

"Mark thought we were in greater danger," she whispered. "Something more dreadful than the monsters. He thought"—her voice stuck, she shuddered—"that perhaps the experiments aren't ended!"

## CHAPTER IV

### THE WEB OF HORROR

G RAIL sprang to his feet, recoiling from the cold touch of horror.

"You mean Hacklyn wants more subjects—wants to change—
*us?*"

"That's it," the pallid girl admitted. "You see, he believes the
*Cathay* wasn't really leaking. He thinks the crew was bribed to
turn water into the hold, and tell us she was sinking, and land us
here."

"Get your things." Grail's lean face was hard with decision.
"I'm going to take you aboard the plane, right now."

Relief left her pale face, but Crystal Verrill shook her head. "I'd
like to—but we can't leave Lorin, and Mark."

Grail bit his lip at the concern in her voice. "Of course we can't
take off without them. But you'll be safer on the plane. I'll come
back to look for them; they must be somewhere about Hacklyn's
laboratory."

Crystal Verrill brought a little overnight case. Grail examined
his flashlight and the revolver with its three remaining shots. He
extinguished the kerosene lamp, and they hurried out of the old
house.

The darkness struck them like a wall, actual, ominous. The
jungle was a crouching, whispering menace. Colorlessly brilliant,
the tropic stars burned far off and strange. Black water brushed
the beach with chill, ghostly luminescence.

Breathless, fleeing from the jungle's leering horror, they hurried down toward the boat.

"They're there behind us," the girl whispered fearfully. "Spiders larger than men—spider-things that once were men, crawling through the jungle. Watching us with their terrible bright
eyes. Hungry. I wonder what they eat?"

Grail thought, shuddering, of Charlie Scoville's face. He said
nothing.

"I wonder where Lorin is?" the girl broke out, nervously. "He
should be back."

They stopped above the dark water.

"The boat should be along here," Grail said. "But what's that?"

Across the restless dark water came the grinding whir of the
plane's inertia starter. A motor coughed, burst into drumming
thunder. Red exhaust flames burned on the water.

"The plane!" Grail was sick with helpless fear. "Somebody is
taking the plane!"

The second motor roared. The dark bulk of the flying boat
moved. Flaming streaks of phosphorescence raced toward the

open sea. Grail lifted the revolver, dropped it hopelessly.

"Probably those damned cameramen and electricians from the schooner," he muttered. "They were afraid to stay." He swallowed. "Now we're marooned here. God knows for how long! Nothing for it but to go back to the house."

"*Weldon—*"

Frantic with agonized terror, the girl gripped his arm. Close after her scream came another—a thin shriek, mind-shattering with its human agony, yet too shrill for a human throat to utter.

Drawing Crystal close to him, Grail crouched and turned. He leveled the revolver, waited. In a moment a dark shape came scuttling from a mass of brush. His flashlight picked it out: the huge and hideous spider-shape, hairy and black. The head was hideously fanged, its eyes saucer-large and purple, yet it carried a soul-searing suggestion of humanity.

Grail braced himself against the mad black river of his fear. The thing's stark horror was a shattering blast at his very sanity. Yet he held his body steady. He spoke softly to the limp, terror-stricken girl beside him.

And very carefully, with a supreme demand upon his skill, he emptied the revolver. One, two, three shots he placed accurately, straight between those frightful eyes of avid evil—

His world dissolved into nightmare sickness. For the shots had no effect! The spider came on. Grail was stiff, frozen with utter horror. The hairy body plunged against him. He was overpowered with its queer charnel musk. Its rushing weight hurled him to the ground. Something struck his head, viciously—

And he plunged into a void of freezing darkness, where numberless pairs of bright purple eyes stared at him, hungry, unutterably evil.

CRYSTAL VERRILL was gone.

The realization struck Grail like a numbing blow. He called her name twice, his voice hoarse with fear. A faint mocking echo came back from the whispering, ominous wall of the jungle.

The spider had carried her off. Memory brought him a picture of the bodies lying in the jungle, of the faceless thing that had been Charlie Scoville. Dread squeezed his throat shut, so he couldn't call again.

For a moment he was too stunned to move, his head still ringing from the concussion of his fall. Then he was on his feet, trembling with a wild, superfluous energy. He forgot his throbbing head.

Find her, the thought hammered at him; find her! Mutely, frantically, he prayed that he might not be too late. He would search toward Hacklyn's laboratory, he decided swiftly. If the strange scientist had really created the monster, that should be the most likely spot. Then Key and Mark Johns had gone that way; he might find them, enlist their aid.

He ran up the beach. In front of the old house he paused, balancing the empty revolver—he had fired his last shot, vainly, at the spider. But he knew of no weapon in the house, and there was no time to spare. His jaw set. He went on, running up the jungle path that Hacklyn and Mark Johns had taken.

"Crystal!" he shouted at intervals, hoarse with anxious dread. "Crystal!"

There was never any answer other than the slithering whisper of the dark, mystic jungle that seemed to have its own hostile sentience.

Although narrow, the path was clear, well trodden. Grail ran stubbornly, gasping for breath. He dripped with the sweat of effort and terror. In the glow of his flashlight, gigantic boles rose dimly, like pillars in some ghastly cathedral of evil. Coils of snakelike lianas wound them chokingly.

Once he stopped, quivering with exhaustion—and dread. Far-off, ahead, he heard that screaming: ear-splittingly keen, horrible with its undertone of grisly human agony—the cry of the giant spider!

Running on, spurred with his fears for Crystal, he came suddenly into a clearing. He crouched back. His light disclosed a dark rude building, alone in the jungle. Shadowy leaf-masses seemed to creep upon it, like sentient monsters.

No sound came from it. He slipped forward, flashed his light inside. It was one long room of rough lumber sheathed with galvanized iron. The door had been battered in. The interior was in fantastic confusion.

Tables and benches had been overturned. The floor was scattered with broken glass and wrecked scientific instruments; a smashed motor-generator; overturned storage batteries, spilling their reeking acid; broken condensers, transformers, electron tubes; copper vats upset to spill more fuming chemicals.

"Hello?" Grail called anxiously. "Crystal? Johns? Key?"

No answer. He entered, stepping through spilled chemicals and broken glass. He coughed in the strangling fumes. The place was deserted, although the wetness of the splashes showed that the vandal had not long been gone.

Hacklyn had lived here, he saw. At the farther end of the room was a rusty little stove burdened with grimy pots. Beside it was an overturned cot, a heap of soiled blankets. Grail stopped. His eyes narrowed.

On the floor, where it had been secreted under the cot, was a cheap cash box of thin Japanned steel. Bright chisel marks showed that it had been pried open. It was empty.

Had robbery been the vandal's motive?

P ASTED inside the open lid was a yellowed sheet of paper. Grail glanced at it, whistled with amazement. It bore the ink-printed legend:

*Dr. Chas. Hacklyn, grams pure radium extracted.*

Beneath was a long column of dates and weights, in ink of varying blackness. With each entry, the weights had been totaled. The last total was:

*109.6 grams.*

Grail's eyes were wide. The world's total supply of that most precious metal, he knew, was only about six hundred grams. At fifty thousand dollars a gram, he calculated swiftly, one hundred grams would come to five million dollars!

It was the dread power of this radium, more than any other scientist had ever commanded, that had transformed one, or more than one, of Hacklyn's assistants into gigantic spiders.

That seemed probable enough. But who had robbed the laboratory? Could the raids of the great spider be planned by human brains, part of a deeper plot? Had the movie people been deliberately stranded on the island, as Letz believed?

What of Crystal Verrill? Her safety was the burning thing. Did this robbery cast any light on her fate?

Grail's frantic eyes searched the littered floor for some clue. He saw a broken fountain pen beneath the cot that the vandal had overturned to get at the cash box. It bore the initials, *L. K.*

Lorin Key! Were Letz's mad charges true? Key had been here. What of Mark Johns, who had followed Hacklyn earlier? Where was Hacklyn himself?

Grail caught his breath. Who was it that had taken the plane?

The frightened technicians, he had supposed. But either Johns or Key might have reached the beach with the radium, rowed out to the plane. Or Hacklyn might have wrecked his own laboratory, and fled.

Staring at the broken pen, Grail went rigid again. Sweat beaded his face. Once more he heard the hideous rasping shriek of the giant spider. Farther inland, it sounded, toward the crater. Nothing here. That sound might lead him to Crystal.

Shuddering at a vision of her fair body ripped by those spider-fangs, poisoned, swollen, he ran out of the building. His dimming flashlight followed the crowding jungle wall, stopped at a break that another eye might have missed. He thrust aside the screening vines that hid another trail.

Swiftly he pushed along it. The jungle pressed against him, hostile, smothering. It whispered with slithering life. Loops of serpentine vines caught at him.

The way led upward, over firm-trodden, red, volcanic earth. He was nearing the crater, he knew—

A pang of terror stopped him. Something rustled beside him. Grail's agonized senses beheld the gigantic spider: black, bulbous body, the long, angular, hairy limbs; the dreadful semi-human head, hideously fanged.

He waited, gripped his empty gun. A quick rush. A flashlight stabbed at him. A weapon exploded, ear-shattering against the close-pressed foliage.

Grail gasped with relief. His assailant was a man, anyhow. He flung himself into the leafy tangle, lifted the clubbed revolver. A second shot crashed against his ears.

His clubbed gun struck metal. There was a gasp of pain. The flashlight went out. Grail grappled in the dark, caught a human body. It went down beneath him. He fended gouging fingers from his eyes, doubled up from the sickening blow of a knee against his groin. His savage fingers sank into the soft flesh of a throat.

The man beneath him relaxed. A voiceless outcry uttered its strangled protest. Grail released his grip cautiously, demanding:

"Who are you?"

"Key," came the husky answer, gasped from a bruised throat. "You're Grail—I thought you were Mark Johns!"

"Why jump him?"

"Don't you see?" gasped the movie writer. "Johns is at the bottom of this. I don't know all his plot—whatever it is. But I do know something!"

W ORDS rushed from Key's bruised throat. "You saw Johns follow Hacklyn into the jungle. Did you see what he did to the old man's laboratory?"

"I did," said Grail. "And if the paper in that tin box means anything, somebody got away with about five millions in radium—and my plane."

"Mark Johns is still here," insisted Key positively. "Let me up, and come on. I want to show you something—something you wouldn't believe."

"All right," Grail agreed. He released the scenarist. "And hurry, if you love Crystal Verrill!"

"Crystal!" Key exclaimed. "I left her safe at the house!"

"She isn't there now," Grail told him. "I was about to put her on the plane, when it took off. The big spider attacked us on the beach, and carried her off."

"Mark Johns!" muttered Lorin Key. "This is *his* work!" Imperatively he caught Grail's arm. "Come on up to the crater. Quiet!—or we'll be next."

Grail followed up the jungle path, between whispering dark walls. The incline became steep, uneven. Lorin Key stopped suddenly with a muffled gasp. Ahead, once again, Grail heard that agonized, semi-human wail—the cry of the spider.

"Damn!" breathed the actor-writer, hoarsely. "If Crystal is there!" His hand touched Grail, trembling. "Slow, now. And for God's sake, keep still!"

Key examined the gun which he had fired at Grail; it was a flat black .45. The trail had leveled again. They entered a little open space, crept across it. Lorin Key silently parted a curtain of brush, looked fearfully through.

Grail stepped up beside him, peered through—into horror's pit!

They had come to the crater's rim. Beyond the screening bushes, the rugged hollow fell, a hundred feet deep. Its sheer cragged walls glowed weirdly with a ghostly, shimmering luminescence, greenish and blue.

"Radium!" he breathed. "That is radium, burning in the rocks! No wonder Hacklyn was sleeping on millions!" He gasped in amazement.

## CHAPTER V

### THE MONSTER'S MATE!

H ORROR choked off his voice. Peering deeper into the crater, he saw something else—a web! Thick white cables
were strung from point to point of the unearthly, shining rock,
forming a vast symmetrical web.

At the center of the web hung the monster spider, a clotted
mass of black and hairy horror. The pointed bulb of its body was
fearfully huge. Its black legs spanned the web for many feet.
Burning with the same ghost-fires as the rocks, its eyes were great
wells of purple evil.

"There!" Horror thickened Key's involuntary scream. "There is
*she—*"

Agonized, Grail leaned farther through the bushes. He saw
Crystal Verrill. Caught in the sagging web, her body was bound
with many silken strands. She was almost nude; her satin skin
seemed to glow in the terrible light from the cliffs. Scarlet
scratches crossed her slim torso, her white thighs.

"Is she dead?" he whispered, voiceless with fear. But he saw
her limbs struggle weakly; heard her faint, suffering moan. She
was entangled, helpless, only a few yards from the fangs that had
eaten the face of Charlie Scoville.

"What can we do?" Grail was sick with despair. "You could
shoot, but if you don't get it the first shot, it might attack her. Can
we get closer—"

He ducked at the sudden rustle beside him in the brush, tried
to cover his head. But too late. A blow crashed against his skull,
hurled him into a world of darkness and cliffs of ghostly fire, from
which purple eyes glared malignantly.

One vague thought he carried with him: why had they lured
him here?

\*       \*       \*       \*       \*

Grail's head was a chaos of thunder and red pain. Throbbing,
roaring agony seemed to swell it like a balloon. He put his hands
up, weakly. They found a swelling laceration on his temple, came

away sticky with blood.

Dread memory came back dimly—of Crystal Verrill, helpless in the giant spider's web. He must help her. The thought drummed through his pulsating agony. He lifted himself on hands and knees, came reeling to his feet.

Only then did he become aware of two bodies struggling furiously beside him. In that last instant, he had thought Key his attacker. But now the scenarist was battling another man. Who? Mark Johns?

Grail groped for his flashlight, then decided it must have fallen over the rim when he was attacked. He struck a match. The yellow spurt showed two men rolling on the ground. Neither had a gun. But Grail saw a long rusty shotgun at his feet, the butt red-smeared as if it had been used for a club.

Hacklyn's, of course. As the struggling, groaning pair turned again, he saw that the other man was indeed the stringy, white-bearded scientist. Infuriated by his wrecked laboratory; perhaps seeking his lost radium.

"Hold on," Grail gasped, staggering forward. "Let's have some explanation—"

A low, sickening snap checked his voice. As his match flared out, he saw the old hermit's lean body grow suddenly limp, heard a long, slow sigh of exhaled breath.

"That fixed him," said Lorin Key briskly. He stood up, brushing lean hands together. "Jiu-jutsu. Got the trick from a Japanese valet in Hollywood. Snapped his spinal column—"

That sharp, confident voice oozed away into a shriek of consuming fear. Lorin Key threw up his hands, stumbled backward. Grail saw a white rope flick out of the darkness, coil about the man's feet, fling him helpless to the ground.

Grail ducked his head, shuddering. He tried to move. But the nerve-searing shriek of the giant spider, so close behind him, held him for a moment, lifeless, paralyzed.

He half recovered, thought of Key's automatic. What, in the confused mêlée, had happened to the weapon? He bent frantically to grope for it. And a sticky, viscid rope coiled about him.

IN vain, Grail leaped away. The rope drew tight, bound his arms to his sides. He grasped it. His hands adhered to it, useless. A second loop wrapped itself around his throat. It drew tight, merciless, strangling.

Then the giant spider, vague and hideous in the darkness, came scuttling out of the brush. Huge purple eyes burned malignantly in its frightful, semi-human head. It crouched a moment over Key as if securing his silken bonds, then lifted him, ran away over the edge of the crater.

"Don't—" the writer was moaning in a weak, sick voice. "Don't—"

Left alone, Grail fought vainly at the adhesive strands that wrapped him. His struggles merely tightened them, increased the suffocating pressure in his throat. He tossed his whole body about, still searching for Lorin Key's automatic. It seemed not to be on the ledge.

That shriek, dreadful with its undertone of human agony, again shredded his nerves. Horny feet came clattering back. The giant spider was over him, deftly securing his sticky bonds. Its musky fetor nauseated him.

Grail was half conscious when it lifted him. It carried him through the brush to the crater's rim. There—it dropped him! He tumbled down, giddily. In ghastly anticipation, he felt himself crushed, shattered upon the glowing rocks below.

But Grail struck the great white web! It swayed beneath him, flung him up, caught him again. Its adhesive cables stuck to his silken bonds. Now he was caught fast in the incredible web.

He twisted his head, gasping, half strangled with the coils about his throat.

"Weldon!" Crystal Verrill's voice came to him, a dry breath of terror. "Weldon—please!"

He flung his head back. Beneath the jagged walls of the pit, glowing with strange blue and devil's green, he saw her bare white body, quivering, helpless in the web.

"Please, Weldon," begged her agonized voice. "Have you a knife, or a gun? Weldon, can't you kill me?"

The word burst hoarsely from his tortured throat: "Why?"

"Once the spider was a man, Weldon." Her voice was a clotted sob of horror. "The radiations from the rocks changed him, while he was mining radium for Hacklyn. He—it is keeping me alive, so I will change, too— Because it wants a *mate!*

"Can't you kill me, Weldon?" she begged.

Grail fought for breath. He was numb and voiceless with dread. The idea seized his mind with resistless black tentacles. He saw Crystal's white, slim-curved loveliness thicken, become hairy and dark, put forth frightful limbs. The shining rocks became mirrors of dread. Even now their ghostly rays must be influencing her body's subtle chemistry, beginning that frightful transformation.

"No!" he heard the sharp protesting voice of Lorin Key. The web trembled. He saw the movie writer, bound helpless, a few yards away, where the giant spider had dropped him into the silken trap. "Listen, Grail!" His voice was low, swift with fear. "I was about to tell you—"

Then the thin shriek of the spider. It had followed its victims down into the crater. It came running with an uncanny, frightful agility across the swaying web. From Crystal came a bubbling gasp of pure horror.

*"Mark Johns!"* Key shrieked, as it approached him. "Mark—don't!"

Grail shuddered, ill with fear. The black monstrous shape crouched over the helpless, screaming man in the web. The hideous fanged head came down. Grail heard ripping cloth, another sobbing shriek:

"Mark! Why did you do this thing?"

Grail fought savagely at his bonds. He tore his fingers loose from the coils they had grasped. But his wrists were still pinioned against his sides; still he dangled helpless in the web.

T HE aviator looked down, frantically. The rugged, weirdly glowing rocks were ten feet beneath him. Among them he saw a feeble, dying glow of red. The flashlight, he realized, suddenly, which he had dropped in the crater when Hacklyn attacked him. An idea struck him; a mad, desperate plan. He caught his breath, tensed for effort.

At that moment, hoarse and terrible, came the voice of Hugo Letz—the voice of the great horror actor, who had died in the jungle from the giant spider's venomed bite. Thick and strange, it came from the crater's upper rim, reverberating uncannily against the blue and greenish walls.

"Stop!" rolled the dead man's voice, with croaking overtones of blood-freezing menace. It was thick, clotted, muffled with the horror of the grave. "Stop, before you kill another man!"

The gigantic spider became motionless above whimpering Lorin Key, alertly rigid. It seemed, Grail thought, astonished—frightened.

"Your poison is still in my veins," the death-thickened voice rasped on. "I can never live again. Yet I am not wholly dead. And neither is my companion in death, Charles Scoville—"

The gigantic black spider moved abruptly. It darted away across the yielding web, scuttled swiftly up the glowing crater wall toward the dead man's croaking voice.

"Hugo Letz!" came the shocked, terrified cry of Crystal Verrill. "I thought he was dead!"

He is!" Grail called swiftly, imperatively to Lorin Key: "Quick! Tell me about Mark Johns!"

"That's he!" gasped the writer. "The spider! It's Mark Johns, in a sort of machine."

"It is?" Grail seemed doubtful. "How come?"

"It was all my idea in the first place," the author explained in a quick, frightened voice. "You see, I had written a horror scenario—it was the story of giant spiders that come out of a cavern world under the jungle for a frightful invasion of civilization, We were going to shoot most of the picture here, on location.

"It's always hard, in a horror film, to maintain the right atmosphere. It occurred to me that the other actors might play their rôles more convincingly if they thought they were facing a real menace. I persuaded poor Scoville, our director, to approve my scheme. We told Mark Johns, and he was enthusiastic—said it would make swell publicity material. But Crystal and Letz didn't know.

"We made a preliminary expedition here," he went on, "to daub this luminous paint about the crater—it is supposed to be the entrance to the spiders' world—and string up this web. Silk cords, doped with a special glue. Our engineers—Hollywood engineers are the real modern masters of illusion—had built the spider machine. The operator carries it, stooping, looking out through slits below those painted eyes. A clever whistle makes that screaming. We left the machine in the crater.

"On the *Cathay,* we let the others think the boat leak was real. Of course, the cameramen were shooting all the time. When we came ashore, Johns slipped off and got into the suit. We kept the cameras set up, and when he appeared, I was to guide Crystal and Letz into saying the right lines. Johns faked the attack an himself.

"Of course, we were going to explain it, after a few days, and then shoot the necessary sequences to finish the picture. A good laugh for everybody, and a swell news story for Mark Johns. That's what we *thought!*

"But the moment you landed with Scoville, Johns turned the hoax into a ghastly murder plot. He has a hypodermic filled with some frightful poison—probably snake venom. He carried Scoville into the jungle, and killed him with it. Just now, he was about to inject it into me, when—"

WELDON GRAIL cut him short, "What reason did Mark Johns have for doing all—"

"The radium!" cried the scenarist. "We had been told that Hacklyn was a harmless lunatic, who believed he had a fabulously rich mine. When Mark Johns found that the radium was real, he invented the scientific angle of the hoax—the theory that the emanations of the radium had changed Hacklyn's former assistants into giant spiders.

"He took the radium, and planned to kill all who were in the original hoax. That left the apparent responsibility on Hacklyn."

"Very good," said Grail. "Except there is *no radium!*"

"No ra—" gasped Key. Terror choked him. "He's come back!"


CHAPTER VI

DEATH DIES HARD

THE master of the web came scuttling down the crater slope again. Now Grail could see that it was really a stooping man, within a cleverly designed fabric. A coat of some oil, perhaps, kept it from adhering to the sticky cables. While the thing seemed uncannily lifelike, Grail saw that the hideous limbs didn't really grasp the web.

After all, he reflected grimly, that fact did not lessen the reality of its menace.

"Mark!" Lorin Key shrieked again. "For God's sake, don't—"

But it came on, without any sign of comprehending humanity. Grail had been fighting his sticky bonds as he listened, eyes on the red, dying flashlight below. He caught his breath again, abruptly.

Mockingly, from a different angle of the rim, came the dead voice of Hugo Letz:

"You cannot kill me." A ghastly croak, eerie, gloating. "I shall follow until you are dead as I. But I am not wholly dead—and neither is Charles Scoville."

The spider-form paused until it ceased, and then went scuttling up toward the rim again.

Grail dangled between two cables. He fought to tear himself free of them, drop upon the glowing rocks beneath, where the flashlight lay. Urgently he called to Key:

"Who was interested in your company, besides Scoville?"

"Nobody," gasped the writer. "Charlie was Scoville Productions. Always worked on a shoestring."

"His heirs?"

"I don't know of any— Yes, he mentioned a brother in Alaska!" Terror broke his voice. "Can't you do something?"

Faintly, Crystal Verrill sobbed, "Oh, Weldon—"

"I'm doing my best," he gritted through clenched teeth.

A savage jerk brought his shoulders free. His body swayed down, pendulumlike. His legs straightened, kicked. The sticky cable released his knees. He plunged down toward the glowing rocks, head foremost.

Desperately he twisted to save his head. His shoulders struck with cruel force. A moment he lay gasping for breath. Then he began squirming toward the flashlight.

"Weldon!" came Crystal's thin, warning scream. "Behind you!"

He heard the hideous spider-form drop through the web. It ran after him. Despair stretched him flat on the rocks. He looked back, caught a sobbing breath.

Again, the thick voice of Hugo Letz croaked out behind the spider.

"Stop! I can see through your mask. I know you, Scoville!"

The ghastly command of that grave-muffled voice stopped the spider-form, while Grail hurled his body forward again, toward the dim flashlight. His bound hands grasped cold metal.

After one moment, the spider came on menacingly. Grail flung himself on his back, sat up. Red flame spurted abruptly from his bound hands. A heavy report against the cliffs.

Checked by the bullet, the black, giant spider reared up. The spider part was flung back, a discarded shell. A man—in Mark John's rough khaki, with the black patch over one eye—leaped forward.

Grail shot again, from his bound hands. The man reeled forward, staggered, fell beside him.

"That gun—" he sobbed. "Where—"

"Lorin Key's automatic," Grail said. "He dropped it over the rim, as I did my flashlight, when Hacklyn attacked us. I knew the gun must be near."

"Damn Hugo Letz!" gasped the dying man. "I thought I shot enough venom into him to rot him in five minutes."

Grail said, "You did."

"If he's dead!" Terror chilled the whisper; the man shuddered, died.

At last Grail tore himself free of the sticky cords, and most of his clothing, too. Smearing his hands with an oil-soaked sponge he found in the spider-suit, he liberated Crystal and Lorin Key. Beneath the weirdly glowing cliffs, they stood beside the dead man.

T HE girl shivered in the handsome actor's coat. "That horrible voice! I don't understand."

"I told you that was Mark Johns!" cried Lorin Key. "See, the patch on his eye."

Grail bent to lift the patch, revealed the features of Charlie Scoville.

"Charlie!" gasped the actor. "But I saw him dead."

"You thought you did," said Grail. "Scoville brought the poison hypodermic with him. He allowed Mark Johns, in the suit, to carry him into the jungle-part of the original hoax. Then he killed Johns, changed clothes with him, destroyed his face to prevent recognition."

Shuddering, Crystal Verrill looked intently into Grail's haggard face. Her lovely head nodded. "You already knew it was Scoville. But how?"

"Several things," Grail told her. "The actual murders began right after his arrival. He was the only one who had an opportunity to tamper with my revolver, which he loaded with blank cartridges. You see, Scoville brought blank cartridges with him to put in the guns which he knew were on the island.

"Fortunately for him, my gun was just the right calibre for his blanks. As for the murders, he was the only one who stood to profit by them. When I first met the man, I had a hunch there would be trouble. Then, I realized there was no radium—"

Lorin Key broke in, "How do you know there wasn't?"

"Hacklyn was as crazy as he acted," said Grail. "If there had been a hundred grams of real radium in that tin box under the cot, Hacklyn wouldn't have been alive to worry about it. I knew that when I had time to think. Deadly stuff. Must be kept in lead containers."

"I see," the actor muttered. "But then what did Charlie want?"

"The million dollars in life insurance. Scoville Productions wasn't prosperous; he was closing out. The brother in Alaska who would have received the money was Scoville!"

"But that dreadful voice?" Crystal Verrill shivered again. "If Hugo Letz is really dead—"

"A little counter-hoax of my own, to gain time," admitted Grail. "You remember when we were kids, planning to go on the stage together, I used to practice vocal imitations."

The handsome actor laughed with relief. "Well, Grail, if you ever get tired of exploring, come to Hollywood!" He took Crystal's arm. "Let's get out of here."

A droning reached them in the jungle trail. They reached the beach in time to see the grey flying boat drop out of the dawn sky. Five shame-faced men came ashore.

"Sorry, Mr. Grail," said a cameraman. "We sort of lost our nerve last night, and took your plane. When we had time to think, we turned back." His face was brick-red.

"That's okay," Grail said absently. He turned to the actor and Crystal.

"Well, I guess this is the—finish." A lump in his throat broke his voice. "Fly you two anywhere you want. And—the very best of luck—"

"Look here," interrupted suave Lorin Key. "Don't take poor Mark's publicity too seriously!"

Grail blinked at the girl. "You mean—you *aren't* engaged?"

"No! Unless you want to be—"

And Crystal Verrill was crying, too, in his arms.

# The Mark of the Monster

*Weird Tales, May 1937*

### 1. The Brooding Horror

EYOND THE MISERABLE POVERTY OF CRESTON, ITS SQUALID IG-norance and its rotting antiquity, there is something more appalling—something that has always seemed to me like a colossal, invisible spider, gloating over the broken victims in its intangible, unbreakable web. I had escaped it once; now I dared it again to set free Valyne Kirk.

Brakes shrieking, the antiquated bus pitched down the rutted mountain road. Carrying away all the sanity of the modern world, it left me alone and oppressed amid the sinister shadows of the time-crushed village.

I shuddered, for I felt that Creston was the unhappy ghost of a town, sprawling dead in this desolate vale. Its narrow, high-peaked houses were bleached and gray as decaying skulls; their broken windows leered like vacant eyeholes at the gloomy, frowning hills.

The spirited young all have fled from Creston. No children laugh in the ancient, cobbled streets. And I found nothing new in the years since I had gone—unless it was this spirit of festering evil, come to haunt the old town's tomb.

Valyne Kirk had promised to meet me; for I had come with seven years earnings, to take her away from Creston, for ever. Eagerly I looked for her, up and down the unkempt squalor of the narrow street. After seven years, the sweet memory of her burned still like a sacred flame within my soul. The picture of her quiet, violet-eyed face, framed in dark and shining hair, remained etched into my heart.

But she didn't come. And somber premonitions rose to cloud my joy. For in my pocket was that strange letter from Doctor Kyle, my aged adopted father. Upon my very heart was graven its puzzling and sinister warning:

> My son, you write that you are coming home to marry Valyne Kirk. I shall not, I dare not, tell you why—but may God in his mercy forbid that so monstrous a crime should be!
>
> Have you never felt the strangeness in you, Clay? Have you never sensed the stain upon your soul? Are you never conscious of the black venom flowing in your blood?
>
> Much as Sarah and I long to see you, we both prefer that you should live and die in your new foreign home, than that you should wed Valyne, and drench her life in terror.
>
> Heed this warning—you must sense its truth, like a cold serpent coiled around your heart! And accept all our congratulations upon your new prosperity.
>
> Your Second Father

The ominous enigma of that message, woven into the strange memories of my youth, and my old nameless fears of hill-girdled Creston, still shrouded me with dread. But it had merely hastened my return from the Orient. For if there were any real reason why I couldn't marry Valyne, then the toll and peril of seven years had been in vain.

SHE didn't meet me.

I walked up the cobbled street, past grim, silent houses that I had known when I was a child. Some hoary evil, I thought again, had come down out of the forests to haunt them, since I had gone.

Gaunt, hoary-headed men peered at me from sagging doors. I knew the names of some; but their dull, rheumy eyes returned my greetings with stares of hostile dread. Even haggard, one-eyed Dud Morrow, the postmaster, who must have handled all my letters to Valyne, and all of hers to me, did not know me until I spoke. Then he started and seemed to shrink from me, as if I had been afflicted with some fearful contagion.

"Valyne Kirk?" he mumbled hastily. "Why, since the old woman died in the summer, she lives at Doctor Kyle's house. Just half a mile up the hill."

He gestured as if to hasten me. And as I went on, I sensed a furtive murmur behind me in the narrow street, as if swift, unpleasant things were whispered.

Valyne had written of her mother's death, but not that she had gone to my foster-father's house. I wondered briefly at her silence.

Up the muddy road I hastened, through gnarled trees older than Creston, toward the house of Doctor Latham Kyle. No need to ask the way! I knew each turning, each battered oak, each moss-stained boulder. But I felt again that some secret evil had come down from the hills, to grasp this vale in tentacles of slithering horror.

An old, insidious fascination drew my eyes up the gloomy slopes of Blue Squaw Mountain. The tangled, monstrous trees of its forbidden fastness had filled my first nightmares. Often in childhood, driven by strange instinctive impulses that overcame my trembling fear, I had ventured into its immemorial wilderness. And once, in a desolate glade near the summit of the mountain, thick-walled with gnarled, gigantic trees, I had come upon a great circle of monolithic upright stones, that ringed a low stone altar black with fire and blood.

When I stood before that hidden sylvan altar, a singular, exhilarating terror had clutched my heart. I shook to the wakening of elder memories, more wonderful, more dreadful, than any I had known. Some savage compulsion made me kneel and strike my forehead against the altar stones until a jagged point was bright with blood.

But as soon as I left the circle of crude pillars, a frightened, utter revulsion had seized my sensitive, childish soul. Terrified and bewildered, I had ran back to tell Doctor Kyle what I had found.

His thin lips had tightened strangely as he listened. The dark eyes deep beneath his shaggy brows had peered into mine, as if probing to my soul. Solemnly, his deep and hollow voice had warned:

"Son, if you want to save your life, your sanity, your soul, never go back to that circle of stones! And never tell another human being that you have found them. Forget. Promise me you will forget."

And I—then I must have been no older than six—I promised him. But I never forgot. I had never gone back; but that strange, instinctive dread clung still, a web of insidious evil that meshed my soul.

I strove to push that ancient, haunting memory from my mind, to think only of the beauty of Valyne Kirk. And her smiling image was clear in my mind, as I went up the hill toward the old stone house. But she came to me before I had passed the last turning.

I heard her voice from among the trees, on a dim wood road that ran a short way up the somber, forested slope of Blue Squaw Mountain.

"Help—"

She must have recognized me when I paused; for her voice came again, gasping and breathless, but with an eager joy crowding upon its fear.

"Clay!"

For my name is Claiborne Coe, and she has always called me that.

"Clay, is it really you? Oh, help me—"

Through the twilight under the trees, I saw the gigantic shape lumbering after her. I ran to meet a great, bearded hulk of a man. His faded overalls were dark with dried blood. His broad face, dark above the rusty beard, was twitching with lust. His eyes were bulging and glazed.

Valyne was at my side, panting:

"Oh, Clay, stop him—"

I called to him, "Stop!"

He mouthed some bestial sound, and came on, ignoring me. His great hands were twitching, as if already shredding the clothing from Valyne's lovely body.

I stood before him. He swung at me carelessly, with one great hairy arm, as if to brush me out of the way. I ducked under his arm, and slapped his bearded face.

"Stop it, man," I said sharply. "You don't know what you're doing!"

For the first time, then, his glassy, protruding eyes seemed to focus on me. In the hoarse, cursing rasp of his voice I read the words:

"My gal. . . . Git out of the way! . . ."

His great arm swung at me again. I didn't move, and the open-handed blow jarred me to my feet.

I heard Valyne's quick voice, low and distressed:

"Clay! Don't let him hurt you. He's a beast! I was coming down to meet you, when I saw him on the road. I hid. But he must have seen me. He found me, chased me—"

Muttering in the tawny beard, the man came at me, now in earnest, with his hairy fists balled.

I fought him, then.

Always, since I was a child, I have sought to avoid physical combat. The reason is more terrible than cowardice; for a red demon seizes my body, with the first blow I strike. Blind destroying fury overwhelms all restraint. And afterward, when the calm of sanity returns, a crimson fog dulls the memory of the fearful things I may have done.

It is as if some malevolent fiend wakes in me, to fight. . . .

A .45 automatic was slung under my armpit, but that mad demon had neither knowledge nor need of the weapon. I was conscious of an unseeing, savage fury that flung me at the giant. Then scarlet chaos ruled my brain. . . .

When it ebbed away, Valyne was pulling at my shoulder with frantic hands.

"Come, Clay!" her urgent voice was pleading. "You've done enough to him. Too much—"

Her voice released the cold shock of sanity.

The bearded man was lying in the muddy road, gasping hoarsely for breath. Fresh blood, now, was mingled with the dry on his overalls. His lips were crushed to a crimson pulp, and two of his front teeth were gone.

A FAINT sickness came into me, to see what I had done. Once in Singapore two Macanese attacked me in a dark alley, with knives, and when my mind had cleared of its scarlet madness, their heads had been almost severed with their own weapons. Since then I have walked in dread of that indwelling fiend. . . .

But the bearded man was able to stand up, when I aided him. His bulging eyes stared at me, and then at Valyne, without any expression that I could read. He cleared his throat, and spat a scarlet stream of teeth and blood. He pulled out a big, nickel-plated watch, that ticked like a clock, and looked at it sullenly. Then, without a word, he went down the road toward the village, reeling like a drunken man.

I wished that he had cursed or blustered. There is deadly menace in the silence of a beaten man. His glassy, inscrutable eyes had given no hint of what hellish thoughts might be passing through his twisted, brutish brain.

Valyne called for my handkerchief, and bound it around my bleeding knuckles.

"I'm sorry," I told her. "I'm not myself, when I fight. I might have killed him—"

She looked after the staggering figure, and her violet eyes were dark with dread.

"I'm glad—glad you beat him," she said, in a small, shuddery voice. "It was terrible to watch. But I've been so afraid! He's so strange, so dreadful! Perhaps now he'll let me alone.

"He's Jud Geer," she added, "the butcher."

I remembered Jud Geer, the butcher's son. He had been a queer, slow-witted bully. We smaller boys had dreaded him. It had been his perverted delight to torture us with gruesome objects from his father's shop, as when he bound and gagged little Tommy Lanning with the entrails of swine, and left him lying in night in a pool of blood and offal, where the rats came. . . .

When Valyne had done with the bandage, I grasped her small hands. She smiled at me. A queer, sharp little pain came into my throat, for her beauty was more exquisite than all my memories and dreams. I yearned to brush the haunting shadow from her pale face, to keep this strong lamp of joy burning for ever in her violet eyes.

"He doesn't matter," I told her, "Valyne darling."

It was sheer delight to be calling her that again, after seven grim and bitter years.

"He doesn't matter, for we shall soon be gone." I caught her precious warmth close to my heart. "Let's go—now!" I urged her, on a sudden impulse. "We can hire a car in the village, to take us down to the railroad."

"Clay—" she began, and hesitated doubtfully.

"I'm afraid of Creston," I told her. "I don't know why. But I've always dreaded returning—as much as I love you, Valyne! Every minute here is a torture to me. Let's go—today—right now!"

I could find no words for the singular dread that was seeping into me from the town's somber antiquity, from the forbidding gloom of these immemorial forested hills. I yearned to shake off the squalid poverty of Creston, its desolate, haunting decrepitude. I hungered far the lights and the bustle and the laughter of a city that was alive.

But my feeling was more than that. It was horror of the brooding evil that lurked like an invisible spider in this vale of desolation. And Valyne shared my dread. Her hand grew tight on mine.

"I'm glad you've come, Clay!" she whispered tremulously. "I'll be so glad to get away. You can't realize what it has been to wait, these last few months, in Doctor Kyle's house! The terror—"

With a little frightened gasp, she checked the words.

"But we can't go tonight, Clay. The doctor and his wife will want to see you, after all these years—"

"We must," I said. "Doctor Kyle doesn't want us to marry, Valyne—"

Her face had grown paler, and Her violet eyes looked down at the road.

"I know," she whispered. "I know! And I have promised him that I won't marry you, until you have come and talked with him."

"If we must," I yielded. "But there can't be any sane reason, Valyne—I know it!"

Hand in hand, we walked slowly up the steep, rutted road, toward the old stone house; slowly, for we were laying bright plans. I told her again of the small fortune I had brought back from the Orient, of the good position now promised me with an importing firm. We were planning our escape, for ever, from Creston's brooding horror. Slowly, too, because we were both heavy with unspoken forebodings.

But at last the gray bulk of the old stone house loomed up before us in the dying twilight. Pale yellow lights winked malevolently at us from the narrow, squinting slits of windows. Valyne opened the heavy, iron-studded oaken door, and we entered.

How often have I wished that we had slammed that accursed door, and fled into the haunted night!

## 2. "FEAR IS CALLING FOR YOU, CLAY!"

THE stone house was old. It had been old when I was a child; but now it had changed. Now it seemed to me that nameless evil had sprung, since I had gone, from festering roots sunk deep into its grim antiquity. For the age of it then had been mellow, aloof, austere, even kindly; now it was a leering, gibbering horror. It was as if the house had died since my departure, and was now a restless specter, haunting its own hollow corpse.

Sarah Kyle met us in the hall, standing motionless under vast, grimy roof-beams two centuries old. Seven years had changed her. Her teeth were gone. Her face was narrowed, sharpened, shriveled. Her eyes were sunken, curiously bright. She was stooped, until her posture suggested some queer, bright-eyed bird.

She took my hand in her horny claw, and welcomed me with a cackling laugh. Then she began to make apologies for the poverty of her house, and to hint transparently for news of my business in the Orient.

"May I see the doctor?" I said.

Her bird-like eyes fixed me, with their uncanny glitter.

"You had better see him, Clay, if you have come to marry Valyne," her cracked voice shrilled. "And ye had better take his warning. Don't walk too near the edge of hell!"

I stepped back, startled, demanding:

"Mother Kyle! What do you mean?"

"Latham will tell you," she said, "if your own strange blood hasn't written it on your soul!"

"Where's the doctor?"

Her white head jerked sharply.

"Latham's still at work," she told me, "in his study in the attic. He's busy on his great book."

"His book?" I said, wondering.

"He is writing a history of the demonolatries of Creston."

"I want to talk to him right away."

"You can see him after supper." Her thin nose jerked at me emphatically, like the beak of a bird. "He'll give you reason enough why you can't marry Valyne, and drag her soul to hell!"

Valyne rescued me from her cackling strangeness, and led me

up to my old room.

There I met the two servants of the house. They, Eben Hand and his wife Josepha, were setting up my bedstead.

Eben Hand was a fat, panting man. There was no color in his blond hair, his vague pale eyes, or his pasty skin. Mute, he expressed himself very swiftly to his wife with white, pliable fat hands.

She was a big, dark woman. Her eyes were wide and sharp and black. Her raven hair was coiled into glistening, oily ropes. Her upper lip bore a thick, dark fuzz. She was doing the most of the work, issuing commands to her silent husband in a coarse, mannish voice.

She bowed to me, oddly, as I entered with Valyne and set down my light bag. Her dark avid eyes remained fastened on my face, while she told her husband:

"Eben, this is Clay. Ye remember little Claiborne Coe, Eben, that used to run through the village. Well, this is him, come back to take our Valyne away. Clay got rich, Eben, in them furrin parts!"

At that last sentence, Eben Hand's small, pale eyes shifted suddenly from his wife to me. They searched my person, and seized upon my modest gold ring. His white fingers made some swift, covert reply.

When they had gone, I said to Valyne:

"I don't like them—or this house! Can't we stay somewhere else, tonight?"

"There's no hotel in Creston," she told me. "And it would look strange if we went away tonight. Besides, you must stay to talk with Doctor Kyle. I promised him."

But even the electric warmth of her kiss couldn't thaw out the chill of my forebodings.

D OCTOR KYLE came down at last from his attic room. He was a big man. Although his body and his limbs remained massively powerful, his head had become curiously fleshless. His yellow cheeks were hollow, his dark flaming eyes were very deeply sunken. His head had become almost completely bald, so that it gave the disconcerting impression of a yellowed skull.

We met at the foot of the stairs. His hand was very cold, as if he had been working too long without a fire in his attic study.

No smile broke the solemn preoccupation of his cadaverous face.

"You are welcome to your old home, Clay," said his deep, hollow voice. "I'm very glad to see you, but"—his shrunken face changed curiously—"I had hoped that you would heed the warning of my letter, and never come for Valyne."

"I have come for her," I told him bluntly. "And I'm going to take her away, in spite of anything you tell me."

His gaunt head shook.

"Clay," he said, "you were always queer and reckless. But I know that you aren't reckless, madly selfish, enough to drag Valyne away to a living hell! Not after you have heard; for there must be one drop of human blood left in your veins!"

"Of course I wouldn't hurt Valyne," I told him. "Go ahead and tell me; I've had enough vague hints."

But Josepha Hand was setting supper on the table, and Valyne came toward us at the foot of the stair.

"Doctor," she said, smiling, "you've worked too late again! You know you shouldn't—"

Her light voice was swept away by his hissing whisper:

"Later, Clay. But it is a crime that God forbids!"

Valyne caught his arm, and mine, and drew us toward the table.

Sitting beside Valyne, so that sometimes my arm touched the firm warmth of hers, I wondered vainly what he could have to say. What demoniac purpose sought to bar me from her? What eldritch madness lurked in this ancient house?

As we ate, the man Eben Hand appeared suddenly in a doorway. He looked disturbed, his white hands fluttered agitatedly at his wife. And she called in a tone of startled dread:

"Doctor! You must go, Doctor! He can't get it quiet!"

Doctor Kyle's yellow, tight-skinned face grew a little paler. He rose hastily and followed Eben Hand through the doorway which, I remembered, led to the cellar stair.

Silently, the doctor's toothless, wrinkled wife watched the door with her too-bright eyes. She listened. Presently we heard a sound from below. It was a low scream—of tortured, animal agony.

When she heard it, Sarah Kyle relaxed as if with relief. Her bright eyes came back to the table; her brown, claw-like hands buttered a piece of bread. Her thin voice asked me:

"Clay, what business was ye in, in China?"

"One and another," I told her, absently. "The last was copper and tin, in the province of Szechwan."

I was looking at Valyne.

Her violet eyes were on her plate; her face was very pale. She was trembling; her even teeth were sunk deep into her full red lip.

"Valyne!" I whispered. "What is it, darling?"

She merely shook her head a little. She didn't speak or lift her eyes.

"Copper and tin?" Sarah Kyle's cracked voice was repeating. "And ye found it profitable?"

Doctor Kyle silently resumed his place.

His wife asked some inaudible question, and I caught his whispered reply:

"It's restless—hungry, perhaps. Jud is late, today."

His dark, brilliant eyes looked across at me.

"I must beg your pardon for this mystery, Clay. Please finish your supper. Later you will understand." Then he asked, as if to launch a conversation, "Have you any collection of Chinese art?"

"No," I said jerkily. "Yes, a few pieces of good jade."

I had too much else to think about.

B EFORE the meal was done, there was a rapping at the back door. Answering, Josepha Hand called:

"Doctor, it's Jud."

His haggard face was relieved.

"Let him in," he called. "Let him take it down to Eben."

The man Jud Geer passed across the end of the room, carrying a milk can. There was more fresh blood on his overalls. A stained bandage was wrapped around his head, to cover his lips where my fist had pulped them.

His glassy, bulging eyes rolled toward me. They rested for a moment upon Valyne's still-bowed head, and I caught a lewd glitter in them.

He went out toward the cellar. The doctor and his wife listened anxiously. I heard an eager, bestial whining, and the sound of thickly splashing liquid.

Jud Geer came back into the room.

He stopped by Doctor Kyle's chair, so close to me that I could hear the tick of his cheap watch. He held out his great, reddened hand, and muttered something through his bandage. But his filmed eyes were looking not at the doctor, but at Valyne.

Doctor Kyle dropped some coins into his palm, and he put them into his pocket, without taking his eyes off the girl.

Josepha Hand had opened the back door. At her impatient word, the gigantic butcher abruptly jerked his eyes away. He picked up his milk can, and went out.

It was after he had gone that I looked at the floor where the can had rested. On the bare pine boards was a circle of dark red. I knew that its contents had been blood.

Before I had time to digest that disturbing discovery, Eben Hand appeared again. His puffy face was strained and ashen; his colorless lips were twitching; his fat fingers nervously spelled out some hasty message.

"What is it?" Doctor Kyle's hollow voice was apprehensive.

"He says it won't touch it," said Josepha Hand. "It won't taste it, And he can't get it quiet. It keeps whimpering. He thinks it knows *he's* in the house. He thinks it's calling for *him.*"

With that last word, her dark head jerked at me.

Doctor Kyle's deep-sunk, flaming eyes came wonderingly to my face.

"It couldn't remember," he whispered faintly, as if to himself. "It couldn't know Clay, after all these years."

Again, from the cellar, I heard that eager, feral whining.

"It does," whispered Josepha Hand. "It wants him!"

And I perceived suddenly that all eyes were fixed upon me, glazed and distended with horror, as if I had been some ghastly apparition. In that abrupt and fearful silence, Valyne's fork rattled shockingly on the floor.

### 3. "Your Father was—Horror!"

WHEN the meal was finished, Doctor Kyle took me apart to the end of the room, and lowered his hollow voice.

"Clay," he said solemnly, "I beg you to trust me, as if I were your true father. I want you to leave Valyne—to go away, without making me tell you the secret of your life."

"Why?" I demanded, bluntly impatient.

"I love you, Clay." His voice quivered faintly with emotion. "I love you as my own son, in spite of what I must tell you. That is why I have never told you, and why I am unwilling to tell you now.

"If you go away from Creston, Clay, you may find some happiness. I beg you to go, and to heed my warning—never marry!"

I seized his arm. Despite his age, it felt hard and powerful as Jud Geer's.

"I'm not going," I told him flatly. "Life without Valyne wouldn't be life. And why shouldn't I marry? I'm healthy, without any stain that I know of."

He bowed his yellow, cadaverous head, resignedly.

"I see that I must tell you. It is better for my words to wreck your life, than to let you and Valyne plunge unwarned into the horror waiting—"

His voice stopped suddenly; his dark eyes flew toward the cellar door.

From below I heard a hoarse scream, thick, maddened; the clanking of a heavy chain; the shriek of rusty nails being drawn; the crashing of splintered planking.

The doctor stood voiceless, ashen, trembling, until Eben Hand burst again into the room, mouthing incoherent sounds, fingers flying.

"It's breaking out!" cried josepha Hand. "It's coming to *him!*"

Her dark eyes darted to me again, terrible with an undisguised and savage odium.

Abruptly recovering himself, Doctor Kyle picked up a heavy chair and ran through the cellar door. His wife scurried after him, with her astonishing bird-like agility.

"Let me, Latham!" her thin voice shrilled. "Let me! It always heeded me."

The two servants followed them apprehensively.

Valyne was standing at the other end of the room, staring after them with stunned tragedy in her shadowed violet eyes. I walked to her hastily, and grasped her cold hands.

"Valyne," I said urgently, "you tell me! What have they in the cellar? What makes this house so strange? Why does the doctor want us not to marry?"

Her eyes, looking back at me, were dark and wide with dread. Her cold hands trembled.

"You're afraid, darling!" I cried. "Tell me—what do you fear?"

But a terrible intuition had already given me the answer.

"You're afraid of me!"

She looked at me in mute agony, without denial.

"I know only what he told me, Clay."

Her voice broke, and her eyes gleamed with tears. Her warm arms were suddenly around me, clinging with the pressure of urgent need.

"Remember I love you, Clay!" she sobbed. "Whatever you may be, remember that I love you."

S HE was still in my arms when Doctor Kyle came back up the stairs, walking with a hasty, shaken step. His voice quick and nervous, he called:

"Clay, will you please come with me for a moment? And hurry! I think our lives are all in danger, if you don't."

Doubtfully, I said, "But why?"

"You'll understand when we have talked," he said, "but now there's no time. Come!"

I drew away from Valyne, and followed him. Unobtrusively, I loosened the .45 under my coat. I found no need of the weapon, however—then.

The great cellar of my memory had been cut in half with a heavy wall of new masonry. There was a massive connecting door, studded with iron bolts, pierced with a small opening thickly barred.

Eben Hand and his wife were waiting at the foot of the steps, beside Sarah Kyle. Hand's fingers were moving rapidly, as his wife watched them in the light of a kerosene lamp on a rough deal table. On the floor was another red circle, where the can of blood had rested.

The three were silent as I came down the steps. They retreated from me, as if I had been somehow—dreadful.

Doctor Kyle led me to the grating, and I became aware of a peculiar odor from beyond. It was an animal scent, powerful, acrid, unpleasant, yet certainly the scent of no animal I knew.

Through the bars came a whining, low, eager, bestial.

"Speak to it," Doctor Kyle told me, swiftly. "Doesn't matter what you say. Just use a firm, friendly tone—"

As I hesitated, some fiend of fortuity thrust into my mind Poe's macabre lines:

They are neither man nor woman—
They are neither brute nor human—
They are Ghouls.

As I spoke it, a stronger wave of that feral effluvium came through the grating. It rocked me with nausea. I heard the clatter of a chain, the shuffling of some great, clumsy body.

And stark horror peered through the bars, with eyes like twin scarlet pits of flaming hell. Its half-glimpsed face was monstrous, swollen, livid, queerly hairy, without a nose. It was the face of nothing sane or right or normal.

One fearful glimpse brought home the fearful aptness of my quotation. Then I heard a massive body drop in jangling chains upon the floor beyond. There was a low, singular sound, not unlike the contented purr of a gigantic cat Then the sound of lapping. . . .

When I looked at the others, in the lamp's yellow glow, their apprehensive tension was gone, although they still, looked askance at me.

"It's satisfied," said Josepha Hand, looking at her husband's fleeting white fingers. "Now it's willing to feed."

I swung upon my foster-father.

"Now," I pressed him, "you've got to tell me!"

His fleshless head jerked toward the steps.

"Come to my room." And when we were on the stairs, his hollow voice added: "Try to keep a grip on yourself, Clay, when you know. And pray to God that no other demon may ever be born into this accursed house!"

T HE bare and ancient rafters were low upon his locked attic room. It was cold, and his two lamps could not dispel its sinister gloom. There were chairs, and an antique writing-desk. The shelves were heavy with dark and massive volumes in age-discolored bindings, whose titles, a glance told me, had all to do with the history of witchcraft, occultism, lycanthropy, demon-ology, and darker lore. A tall glass cabinet held crystal globes, grotesque little idols and figurines of wood and wax, parcels of dried herbs, and a few stained and rusted weapons.

"My study and museum," Doctor Kyle boomed, as I shivered from the musty chill. "Here I have carried on my research into the evil practises that have festered in the hills of Creston. Knowing these people, I have gained access to precious material. Clay, even now there are hideous forbidden rites of demon-worship being—"

"Doctor," I broke in, "if you really have anything to say, say it."

"Sit down, Clay," he said.

But I was too much concerned to sit. I stood behind a chair, gripping the back of it with my hands. Doctor Kyle paced up and down before me, two or three times, running his lank fingers nervously across his bare yellow scalp, as if to flatten invisible hair.

"I suppose you don't remember your mother, Clay?" he asked at length, as if seeking an easy way into a difficult subject.

"No," I told him. "She died, and you brought me here, before I was two years old."

"We told you that she died," his voice rumbled, suddenly hoarse and low. "And you never knew of your twin?"

"You told me I was the last one of my family."

His flaming eyes stared at me, and his voice pealed solemnly:

"Your mother died only a few months ago, Clay. And your twin brother is still living."

Questions thronged my mind. But the stinging dust of horror had suddenly filled my throat. I could only listen, as that hollow voice went on, like a booming chant of doom.

"I shall begin, Clay, with the early history of your family." His lean hand gestured at the dark, heavy volumes on the shelves. "I have here the library of your grandfather, Eliakim Coe. From his private papers I have learned a great deal of the secret history of Creston—and of your people.

"The first Coe in America came with a cloud upon his name—the Church had almost obtained his conviction on charges of demonolatry. The Henry Coe who founded Creston was a fugitive from the witchcraft trials of Salem, and in this inaccessible wilderness he carried on the evil worship that had roused the Puritan ire.

"These dark forests have hidden fearful things, Clay! It may shock you to learn that for four hundred years every generation of your family has dealt in every manner of Satanism, black magic, and demon-worship.

"Your grandfather, Eliakim Coe, was the last and the most powerful of a line of wizards. But he paid a fearful price for his power. He paid his daughter, Elizabeth, who was your mother."

"My mother!" I was bewildered and shocked.

"Your true father, Clay," continued that ringing, hypnotic chant, "was not the distant cousin, Esmond Coe, who married your mother over your grandfather's protests, and was found stabbed to death beside her on the morning of the bridal night. No! That crime was but the beginning of a frightful ceremony. And Eliakim Coe took his daughter, on the night following, to a circle of stones about an ancient altar on the summit of the mountain—"

"Once," the shuddering whisper was wrung from me, "I saw that altar!"

"And there," that dread, compelling voice throbbed on, "that diabolical ceremony was carried to its blasphemous completion. Stripped and bound, the virginal body of your mother was laid across the blackened altar. In response to the esoteric forbidden rituals of the wizard, a Dark Power came to claim the offering.

"And Eliakim Coe brought his daughter back, crippled and maddened, to give birth to you, Clay—and to your twin!"

"What"—I forced out the faint whisper—"what do you mean?"

Doctor Latham Kyle snapped his jaws together. His yellow lips were tight and hard as a mummy's. His deep eyes flamed at me. The boom of his hollow voice was startling.

"Clay," he said, "there are forces, powers, entities, that science has never glimpsed—because they are too colossal. But you must sense the tremendous shadows that fall upon our tiny earth from the frigid voids of space. Clay, you must know the fearful rulers of the fourth dimension! Your own dark blood must whisper to you—"

I had to nod, in spite of the outraged protest clamoring in my brain. For in the mystic Orient, as well as in my strange childhood, I had seen things that science and sanity could not account for.

"Then—"

The dry, husky whisper crept like an odious reptile past my lips.

"Then—my father was not a man? And I'm not entirely—human?"

The yellow skull nodded solemnly; the hollow voice intoned:

"That is the hideous truth, Clay, that I have feared to tell you."

Panic was rushing through my heart, like a black and frozen wind.

"So that's why," I breathed, "I've always felt—different! That's why I've always been a stranger among men! It's that evil blood that seizes my body when I fight, like a destroying demon—"

"Yes," the low, booming voice caught the word. "The demon in you." The flaming eyes lifted. "Through some accident of inheritance, the dark blood is recessive in you, Clay. Physically, you appear quite human. Psychically, you are also, save for the shadow of strangeness that you feel, and for the waking of the demon when you fight.

"But I'm afraid for you, Clay!"

The terrible voice sank lower.

"Passion will awake that slumbering demon. It will transmute that shadow into reality. You must walk with care, my son, or you will lose all humanity, in a hideous reversion to the dark blood!

"If you married, you might become as monstrous as your brother. The strange blood was dominant in him. Tonight, in wishing to see you, he—or it—was displaying a fit of human emotion as rare as your fits of evil. For the most part, your twin is a mad monstrosity—"

"TONIGHT!"

My mounting terror seized the word, and I reeled under an avalanche of dread. Icy sweat drenched me. Sick, quivering, I sank against the back of the chair. It was a little time before my lips could form the faint query:

"Tonight? The thing in the cellar—that wanted me? That is my—my *brother?*"

Doctor Kyle nodded. His dark eyes looked quickly away, as if with pity. His voice throbbed to me faintly through the gray mist of dread:

"Your own brother, Clay. Its blood is your blood. Passion will cause your reversion to its form. What is equally dreadful, if you should marry Valyne, or any other woman, your children would probably be such things as it is!"

The chill gloom of the musty attic chamber was spinning around me. Fainter, ever receding, still I heard the booming tones:

"I attended your mother when you and your twin were born. I wanted to destroy the other, but neither she nor her father would allow. There was a strange perversity in her love. And Eliakim Coe desired the monster in the practise of the dark art that was overwhelming him.

"As the strange being grew, your mother saw that it could never be reared in the world of men. When you were two years old—when Eliakim Coe died, a victim of the fearful powers he had summoned out of space—she left you in this household, and took the other into the forest.

"Clay, it was a dreadful, secret life that your mother led, for the next twenty years and more, in these dark mountains above Creston! She sacrificed herself for her monstrous son. She kept it in a cave, on Blue Squaw Mountain.

"She had no contact with the world, save for her infrequent midnight visits to me. But many a time, Clay, until the year when you left Creston, she stood beside your bed at night, and even touched your hair. But always she went back.

"A few months ago she came to me, ill. I told her that she was going to die. On the last night of her life, she coaxed your strange brother down from the cave, and gave it into my keeping. Since then we have kept it in the cellar.

"I still feel that it should be destroyed—as I wanted to destroy it when it was born. But I have preserved its life because of my promise to your mother, and because it will be a living exhibit to prove the authenticity of my book: *A History of the Sorceries and Demonolatries of Creston.*"

Fast in a frozen sea of dread, I dimly knew that Doctor Kyle was turning toward the door. I could scarcely hear him say:

"You may go back to your room, Clay. You see why you can never marry Valyne."


## *4. At the Mercy of—Monstrosity!*

B ACK in my own frosty room, I collapsed on the bed. I tried to think. But red chaos ruled my brain. Only one clear thought emerged: If I couldn't marry Valyne Kirk, then I must die.

I tried to doubt what Doctor Kyle had told me. It was hideously incredible, and belief in it meant death. But the sober, convincing manner of his telling, the strangeness that had shadowed all my life, the lurking dread that festered in Creston, the hideous monster in the cellar—these combined to bring me maddening conviction.

I tried to think it a lie. But what reason had Doctor Kyle to lie to me, to whom he had always been a second father? What motive could he have for a deception calculated only to drive me away from Creston, a crazed and hopeless fugitive, for ever? And what lie could have darkened all my life, and set me apart from men, even in the distant East?

No! I could not escape the clutching intuition of horror. Strange and fearful blood burned through my body. In all the world was no being of my own kind—none save that chained monstrosity! And my love for Valyne could give birth only to terror, madness, and death.

Distantly, from below, I heard a sound like howling, and a chain clanking, and wood splintering. The monster—my twin—

Cold, trembling, I sat up on the edge of the bed. It was struggling; perhaps it would escape. A terrible resolve steadied me. I would never see it again.

I strode grimly to the window. Outside was night; the silent, immemorial forests of Creston; the gloomy, tangled slope of Blue Squaw Mountain, whose summit was crowned with that altar of frightful sacrifice.

Shrinking from the darkness and the horror of it, I was suddenly conscious of the weight sagging against my chest. There was a surer way. . . .

With a hand now steady, I slipped the automatic out of its holster. It was heavy and cold and black. Its grim steel efficiency was a match for all the festering evil of ancient Creston. I snapped back the slide and watched the bright, blunt cartridge leap into the chamber.

I thrust the hard muzzle resolutely against my temple, hardly conscious of the quiet, swift rapping upon my door. But it was flung open, and Valyne rushed to me. Her urgent hand jerked my arm away.

"Clay! Clay!" gasped her terrified whisper. "I came because I was afraid you would!"

She stood before me. Her trembling hand still held down the gun. Her breast was fluttering to her quick breathing. Her violet eyes, wide, glistening with tears, held my face. The live, pulsating beauty of her slim body stung my own eyes with tears. Every soft line of it was infinitely precious. My resolution found new steel.

"Why shouldn't I?" I rasped the hoarse demand. "You know what I am! You know why we can't marry! And that the sooner I die the less likely I am to revert to—to something hideous!"

"I know what Doctor Kyle says." Her eyes probed to the back of my brain. "And you believe it, Clay?"

"I—I do. I tried not to. But my whole life points to the truth of it—even to the rage that struck down Jud Geer!

"You must go away, Valyne," I said. I pushed her toward the door. "You must let me kill that fiend in me before it injures you."

Her body stood tremulously firm against the pressure of my hands.

"You don't understand, Clay," she told me, and a ringing strength was in her voice. "Even if it's true, I can't let you die— alone! For I love you, Clay."

I returned the gun to its holster, and caught her hands in mine. For I had been touched and elated by the sudden conviction that our love was a pure flame that could burn all the tainting horror from my blood.

Her warm hands clasped mine, and she whispered:

"Clay, promise me that you will live as long as I do! Promise me that you will never again surrender to that horror! Just promise. And we will go away from Creston, in the morning, as we planned. Perhaps we can find a way to happiness. At least we can be together for a while—and together when we die!"

I promised. I thought we might consult some psychiatrist or occultist. . . .

THE glory of her love seemed for a little time to banish the sinister chill of evil from the room. I begged her to stay with me; for the dread that still haunted me was stronger than my regard for convention. And perhaps she would have stayed; for she too was strained and white with unuttered forebodings.

But there was a light, hurried knocking on the door, and old Sarah Kyle hobbled into the room. Her dark, pointed face was bloodless. Her small, bright eyes darted about the room, and a thin, anxious whisper lisped from her toothless mouth:

"Have ye seen it, Clay? Have ye heard it?"

"You mean—" I wet my lips. "You mean the thing in the cellar?"

Her glittering eyes met mine, veiled with unspeakable dread.

"Your brother," shrilled her tremulous whisper, "has broken his chains and gone."

I swayed, and caught Valyne to me, as if an icy dark wind had sought to drag her away.

The cracked whisper insisted:

"Have ye heard it?"

"Half an hour ago I heard the chain rattling, and the sound of breaking wood."

The thin lips came together, like strips of dried leather.

"That must have been when it escaped. God knows where it went!"

Valyne whispered, into the fearful silence:

"What will it do, Mother Kyle?" Her big violet eyes came to me, with a naked horror pleading in them. "One day," she whispered, "I went down into the cellar, and it saw me through the bars. It wanted me, Clay! It tried to break out. For days it howled, and wouldn't touch its food.

"I'm afraid, Clay."

Her tense, trembling arms slipped around my neck, and her frightened eyes went back to Sarah Kyle.

Her thin lips still were pursed.

"I don't know what it will do," her thin voice said slowly. "It is cunning, and aflame with demon lusts. You're in danger, Valyne. Go back to your room, and lock the door. The rest of us must try to find it. The doctor and the servants are searching, now.

"And you must be careful for yourself, Clay. It was friendly, a while ago—it knew its own blood. But if it learns that you love Valyne, its affection will turn to jealous rage. . . .

"*Listen!*"

The whispered warning fell suddenly, and for a moment we were silent in the frosty room.

"I thought I heard it," said Sarah Kyle. "We must hasten. You must keep with me, Clay. The doctor thinks it will come to you."

In a shivering voice, Valyne said:

"Let me go with you."

"No, darling," protested the old woman; "you must keep out of its sight. Remember, once it went mad at sight of you. If it saw you again, we could never quiet it. And it might harm you."

Valyne acquiesced, and we took her to her room. She kissed me, and her lips were cold.

"Remember your promise, Clay," she whispered. "And tomorrow we shall go away together. Don't let it harm you!"

We heard the lock snap in her door, and went down the stairs.

Sarah Kyle took a kerosene lamp from the dining-table.

"We shall go to the cellar to begin." Her bright, sunken eyes darted at me suddenly. "Have ye any sense for it, Clay? Any intuition from the common blood? Do ye think that ye could trail it?"

"I don't know."

My dazed brain was still spinning blindly along the black, swift river of horror.

"The doctor says it will come to you," she was saying. "And when it comes, I can calm it. It ever heeded me—"

"It won't come to nobody," put in the flat, mannish voice of big Joseph Hand, who had just appeared out of the dark hall. "It wants that girl! It smelled the odor of her on him, when he came to speak to it. It broke out to git her, and it won't come to nobody—"

S ARAH KYLE led the way down the steps, and I carried the lamp into the walled-off cell. The heavy door had been crushed outward, torn from its hinges as if by some terrific projectile. A broken length of rusty iron chain lay across the threshold. Beyond was a rude wooden trough, which had been overturned, to spill dark, clotted blood across the foul stone floor.

Suffocatingly strong in the room was that acrid, animal stench. Reeling with its nausea, I stumbled back toward the door. But an idea had struck me. The others had seemed unaware of the odor; perhaps I had an abnormal sensitivity to it. If I could follow the trail—

Faintly, then, I heard Valyne's scream. I ran up the two flights of stairs to her room, vainly cursing the blind folly that had left her alone. Sarah Kyle came clattering along behind, carrying the lamp.

"Valyne!" I gasped, at the door. "Valyne, are you all right?"

The answer was the bang of a loose shutter.

The door was still locked. I kicked it twice, thrust my arm through the hole to twist the key that she had left in the lock The yellow flicker of Sarah Kyle's lamp showed that the room was empty. The bed was turned down; a filmy pink nightdress was laid across the pillow.

The window was open; the unfastened shutter banged again.

Ashen-faced, Sarah Kyle was staring out into the frosty dark.

"It was outside," she whispered. "It climbed over the tool shed, and broke through the window. It has carried the poor darling out into the forest."

Her voice became a thin, fervid scream.

"I wish to God my husband had killed that fiend when it was born!"

"Where"—the wild whisper leapt from my lips—"where are the others?"

I heard her say, "Searching—"

Then my frantic voice was ringing through the gloomy halls:

"Doctor Kyle! It has taken Valyne!"

Ghastly echoes gibbered at me.

"Where could they all be?"

"Searching," said Sarah Kyle. "They must be outside."

"God! I can't stand here wasting time! Where could it have taken her?"

The stooped old hag came suddenly toward me and thrust the sputtering lamp into my face. The skeletal fingers of one claw-like hand sank savagely into my arm. Her piercing eyes transfixed me. Her high voice sank to a strained and husky whisper.

"Don't ye know, Clay? Doesn't your own sleeping demon whisper it to your own stained soul? Won't your own dark blood draw ye there?"

Instinctively jerking back, I demanded:

"What do you mean?"

Her fingers clung to my arm with a terrible strength, and her voice rasped on with its unthinkable accusation:

"Have ye never felt the call of the elder dark beings that are your kin, Clay? Are ye never drawn to the black altar on the mountain, where your evil father came to your mother? Have ye no sense of the secret power of that circle of stones—"

"You mean"—the gasp broke from my lips—"you mean it has taken her—there?"

Her shriveled head jerked to a quick, sinister nod.

"It knows the place," she said, "for your mother often took it there. She told me it was ever most content in the occult power of that mystic circle. It must have taken Valyne there. And may she die before the demon-child is born!"

## 5. THE BEAST IN THE BEAST

I THINK that Sarah Kyle tried to follow me up Blue Squaw Mountain. But desperation had lent me frantic wings. Her shrill voice fell behind, screaming:

"Wait for me, Clay! I can calm it! It always understood—"

The night was moonless and frosty and still. It was very dark beneath the gnarled and ancient trees, upon that rugged mountain slope. And it was many years since I had trod it. Again and again I sprawled and fell in the thorny tangles of under-growth, or blundered heavily into the boles of gigantic trees. And once I rose, fingering my lacerated, bleeding face, to realize that I was lost. But grim urgency brought back youthful memories with the effect of preternatural vision. And obscure instincts brought me at last, breathless and fearful, to the leafy edge of that forbidden glade that since childhood I had apprehensively shunned.

There horror struck me motionless.

Red tongues of malevolent flame set lurid shadows into a fantastic demon dance against the surrounding dark wall of forest. Glowing sinister scarlet outlined the circle of rough-hewn monolithic stones, standing twice a man's height. Within that cabalistic circle I could see the low, blood-darkened altar—burdened with madness and terror!

Valyne Kirk lay across it, on her back, between two wan and ghastly fires. She was stripped nearly nude; her alabaster loveliness was bare to the red, mounting flames. Her wrists and ankles were bound with rope. She was motionless, and, I thought, unconscious.

Crouching over her, looming colossal and grotesque and hideous in the sinister gleam of the altar fires, was the monster I had glimpsed in the cellar dungeon—that dread creature of my own dark blood. It brought back those haunting lines from Poe:

> They are neither man nor woman—
> They are neither brute nor human—

It was gigantic, yet vaguely man-like in outline. It was horned. Its long, angular legs ended in cloven hoofs. Its body was heavy, bulging, hideously gross. It was covered with coarse, dark hair.

The stench of it came to me where I stood, an odor overwhelmingly nauseating as that of a reptile's den.

The red flames burst higher, on either side of Valyne's helpless body, and suddenly I saw its face. To my mind came that other line:

They are Ghouls.

There are things that words cannot describe, even by suggestion. I can say that its face was grossly broad, and yet made savage with an angular gauntness; that it was noseless, queerly hairy, livid; that its eyes were crimson lakes of flaming hell.

But the demon that glared from it escapes the words.

It is enough to say that when I looked into that creature's face, and knew that its blood was mine-then I realized that my promise to Valyne had been mad folly. If the blood of that beast was in my veins, then it must be spilled before its pollution touched another human soul.

It was curiously just, I thought, that one fiend should destroy another. For once I was conscious of no shrinking from combat. I was frankly glad of the red and dreadful rage that swept me into the fury of destruction.

As I leapt past the circle of tall stones, I saw that the twin fires were burning close to Valyne. Their crimson tongues would soon be licking her naked flesh—unless I won.

The monstrosity saw me. With an uncouth, bestial snarl of surprize and rage, it lumbered toward me. Its hairy, taloned, foul-smelling hand slapped at me. The blow flung me to the frosty ground, at the foot of the black altar.

I stumbled back to my feet, plunging blindly toward it. . . . The gun under my coat was forgotten. And all the details of the fight have been fogged with that red madness. I know that I fought that being, body to body. I know that I staggered with the sickness of its nauseating effluvium. I remember being crushed in its powerful, hairy arms, being flung to the ground and kicked with its cloven hooves. I dimly recall that it battered at my head, with a great black stone from the altar. . . .

But when the shock of returning sanity struck me, it was slumping to the ground. I reeled over it, swinging a last desperate blow. It went wild; I stumbled groggily to my knees.

T HE gross, hairy bulk lay before the black altar. It quivered a little, and ceased to move. The mad horror of its face was hidden, for which I was thankful. I saw a little dark hole in the side of its long, flattened head, saw dark blood gushing out. That surprized me, for it was a bullet wound, and I didn't remember having drawn my gun. But in that crimson chaos—

Valyne moaned. I lurched to the low black altar, and lifted her from between the two licking fires. I untied the ropes. She was shivering. Her violet eyes looked at me, and it sickened me to see their mute and shrinking terror.

"The thing"—she choked—"the thing—"

"It will never frighten you again," I promised, "Valyne darling."

I carried her a little away from the inert horror by the altar, and wrapped my coat around her. My arms clung to her. The last embrace. . . .

From the moment I glimpsed that hideous face, my purpose had been dear. Hope and doubt alike had died before the grim resolve that never should another such demon be born into the world. Not if my death could prevent it. . . .

I was glad when Valyne seemed to drop again into unconsciousness—from shock and fear, I was certain, rather than from any injury. It was better that she shouldn't see me go.

I left her, and reluctantly touched the gray, motionless bulk of the monster. Its limp weight and the rush of blood from the little wound assured me that it was truly dead.

Resolutely, then, I strode toward the dark wall of forest that would hide my body, fumbling under my coat for the automatic.

"Clay!"

The strong hollow voice boomed from beyond the circle of stones, and gaunt Doctor Kyle stalked into the crimson light. His powerful hand gripped a hunting-rifle. Gray smoke was curling from its muzzle. He stood for a moment between two red-lit pillars, and in the scarlet flickering his head looked more than ever like a skull.

He nodded to my voiceless question.

"Yes," he said, "I shot your brother, Clay—I should have killed him the day he was born. You were unarmed; he was getting the better of you. Sarah," he explained, "told us where you had come.—Valyne! is she all right?"

I turned for a moment to look at her motionless body. It wavered and faded with my tears, and my voice was husky when I said:

"She isn't harmed, Doctor. And you needn't fear that I shall wreck her life, or that there shall be born another of my blood. For I'm going—after my brother."

The sunken eyes that flamed from that gaunt, skeletal head were abruptly crimson in the firelight. Through thin lips came the ghastly rasp:

"Perhaps—perhaps that is best."

And I strode on, away from the twin red fires of the blood-stained altar, through the tall silent stones, toward the dark forest waiting to drink my blood. I was reaching again for the cold, comforting grip of the automatic. Its swift flame would burn all the horror and the madness from my brain. When I was dead, I thought with dim gratitude, I should be at last like other men. . . .

"Clay—"

It was Valyne's voice, faint, but urgent, frantic.

But I dared not stop, lest my love and her tenderness should sweep me into the black pit of a crime too hideous to name. I strode on, into the shadows that would hide and comfort me for ever.

"Clay!" It was a terrified gasp. "Come back to me. Remember your promise—"

But rasping against my brain was Doctor Kyle's fearful warning:

"Passion will wake your slumbering demon, Clay. You must walk with care, my son, or you will lose all humanity, in a hideous reversion. If you married, you might become as monstrous as your brother."

I heard his hollow tones addressing Valyne:

"Peace, my child. God has ordered it. I will care for you—"

I hastened on, lest my purpose fail too soon. . . .

The faint, desperate appeal came again:

"Clay—listen! It's all a trick. A ghastly hoax! *Listen!*"

A hoax! That word brought me back at a run. My outraged sanity had fought grimly against belief. But there had seemed no escape. What could have been the motive for so frightful a deception?

"My child!" Amazement boomed in the voice of Doctor Kyle. "What are you saying?"

"Listen!" repeated Valyne. "To that!"

She struggled to sit up, pointing at the dead monster. Wonderingly, I moved toward it, stooped. And abruptly, in the still, frosty air, I heard a familiar sound: the jangling tick of a cheap watch.

"It's Jud!" her faint voice said. "I heard his watch, when he was carrying me."

I flung back the hideous head, and tore at its ghastly face. It came away in my hands, a painted mask of wax and soft rubber adhesive. Beneath, dark with oozing blood, was the broad, bearded face of Jud Geer. The glazed, protruding eyes, still open, leered up with the fearful grin of death.

"Jud!" exclaimed the hollow, surprized voice of Doctor Kyle. "How could he—"

I ROSE abruptly to face him.

"You needn't act, Doctor," I told him, grimly. "This thing is your planning—though God knows what you hoped to gain by preventing my marriage to Valyne—"

"Clay!" he interrupted, still protesting. "Are you mad? Sarah and I have loved you since you were an infant. I was desolated at the thought of your suicide—"

"Suicide!" I grasped the word, with sudden understanding. "That's it! You were trying to drive me to kill myself. It's all part of a monstrous plot—everything from that letter you wrote me months ago, to Jud carrying Valyne up here. You were all trying to drive me to insane suicide! But, in Heaven's name, why?"

"I'll tell you, Clay." A hard ring came into his hollow voice. "We are poor in Creston. We live and die in bitter, grinding poverty. And we knew that you had made money in the Orient; that if you died, before your marriage, that money would be ours.

"The servants were ready to aid us, for a share. Jud Geer was useful, because he wanted Valyne. I shot him because I saw you were getting the better of him; I feared you were about to unmask him. Besides, he was becoming too impatient for his reward.

"My studies in the dark secret history of Creston supplied material for the hoax. Some of your forefathers really dealt in the black arts, Clay—some of them must actually have had a hand in the building of this altar.

"But out of respect for the dead"—and a twisted smile of terrible mockery crossed his gaunt, skeletal face—"I should tell you that your grandfather, Eliakim Coe, was no more than a common lunatic. He murdered your father in his bed, true enough. And he wrecked your mother's life, if in a manner a little less picturesque than I told you.

"And your own youth, in the shadow of that crime, was strange enough to give some color to my account."

He smiled again in the red firelight, hideously.

"The details should be dear enough, if I mention Jud's private entrance to the cellar—"

The rifle lifted a little in his tense grasp—

"It was a fair plan, Clay." His voice rang grim and cold with triumphant menace. "And even now it shall not fail me!" His tone sank. "It is known that you and Jud were rivals for Valyne. It is known that you have fought, and that you both are violent men. I shall remove from Jud's body this artistic creation of mine, that made him your brother. And who will be surprized to find the three of you together, dead?"

Very abruptly, his rifle snapped to the level. Its barrel flamed red in the glare from the altar, with a companion light to the twin fires of hell in the sunken eyes. Sparks burst from the muzzle, and the report shattered against the pillars of stone.

For once, then, I was completely thankful for that swift, deadly response to danger that has ever been independent of my conscious mind. I was myself surprized to feel the hard abrupt recoil of the automatic in my hand.

And Doctor Kyle had never learned of the weapon in my armpit holster. I think I had fired before he saw the gun; I am sure that he was dead before his aimless contracting finger pulled the trigger of the falling rifle.

Valyne and I have never returned to Creston. In the darkness we went down the farther slope of Blue Squaw Mountain, and morning found us in a green and peaceful meadow, whose sunlit fragrance washed away the horror of the night.

# The Devil in Steel

*Thrilling Mystery, July 1937*

IGHTIER THAN ANY MAN, THE IRON GIANT CAME CLANKING through the darkness. The building shook beneath its quarter-ton of metal. Menacing blue rays shot from its photo-electric eyes. Its steel face was a staring mask, inhuman, sinister! Puny men cowered before its crushing advance.

For they saw the monster of a new Frankenstein. They saw the soulless might of the robot turned against its makers. They saw all humanity crushed by the vengeful power of revolting machines—saw a dead world turned to a thundering hell of metal monstrosities . . .

A swell lead for his newspaper story, thought Jimmie Beckland, scribbling rapid shorthand. Nor was it all imagination! His tall lean hody was already half shuddering. The mechanical giant certainly looked uncanny enough, marching stiffly beside its maker into the long laboratory.

A queer contrast, Beckland thought between robot and man. For Dr. Runyon Daker was thin, stooped, colorless. He stood a bare five feet, against the robot's towering seven. He must have created it as a sort of compensation for his own bodily weakness.

He was quivering with pride as the great metal giant moved obediently to his high-voiced commands.

Shuddering horror abruptly stopped Beckland's flying pencil.
Melanie Doyle swayed to her feet beside him, a shriek of pure
terror torn from her lovely throat. The little group of watchers sat
paralyzed with consternation. For something was frightfully
wrong!

An ominous clashing grated from the steel-armored robot. It
swung with ponderous menace upon its proud demonstrator. A
great blue arm flailed upward, struck savagely! Dr. Runyon Daker
sprawled limply at the iron feet of the monster he had made,
blood oozing from his head!

It was half accident that brought Jimmie Beckland to witness
that strange tragedy in the lonely island laboratory. He had come
to Scimitar Lake, high in the heart of the Rockies, on vacation
from his metropolitan daily. Or so the resort village thought. It
had seemed but chance that Delcrain met him the day before, on
the pier above the lake.

A NDREW DELCRAIN was the tall soft-spoken president of
Effo Electric. Beckland had once called at his ornate Man-
hattan office to get the details of a million-dollar merger, and
Delcrain knew him now.

"Why, Beckland! How are they biting?" he shouted jovially.
"I'm here to kill two birds with one stone," he explained, offering
an expensive cigar. "Business and pleasure. —Say, Beckland, you
don't want a good story?"

"I came here for trout," Beckland said. "But a scoop's a scoop.
What's up?"

Delcrain spoke confidentially.

"You've heard of Runyon Daker, the robot inventor?"

"Sure!" Beckland spoke eagerly. "I did a feature, couple of
years back, on his new electronic ear. Specialize in scientific stuff,
you know— What's he got now?"

"Daker has been working the past two years at his private
laboratory out on McTee Island," said the tall executive. "He has
perfected a complete electrical man.

"If it's all he says, I'm going to pick up the patent rights. He's
going to put on a demonstration, tomorrow night. I could arrange
for you to see it—we can always stand a little good publicity."

"You're on!" Beckland cried—and his eager voice didn't carry half his delight.

McTee Island was five acres of rugged granite jutting from the farther end of deep, cold Scimitar Lake. Gigantic, ancient trees grew wherever there was soil enough. The big, dilapidated log dwelling stood beneath great pines, beyond the half-rotted boat landing.

Jimmie Beckland felt his first chill of sinister foreboding when the hired motorboat left him beside the tall financier on the sagging landing. They were to be guests until the boat returned next day. Already the sun had gone beyond far, snow-swept peaks, and the icy waters of the forest-walled lake turned blackly forbidding. The newshawk shuddered with a sense of dread imprisonment.

That was forgotten, however, when Melanie Doyle came running down to welcome them. Daker's niece, she was a tall girl of twenty, athletic and lovely in a tweed sports suit.

"Jim Beckland!" Surprised pleasure rang in her voice. Her grey-eyed face lit with gladness. Beckland moved very eagerly to take her offered hand.

"Two years since I saw you," he told her. "I hoped you'd be here!"

"I have to look after Uncle Runyon." Trouble stained her lovely face. "I'm afraid—afraid he has gone too far!" Her tortured eyes moved to Andrew Delcrain. "I hope you buy the robot and take it away, Mr. Delcrain. The thing is horrible—monstrous!"

"A poor sales talk." The financier smiled gravely. "But I'll make him a fair offer—if it is a practical invention. Where's Dr. Daker?"

"At the laboratory," she said, "getting ready for the demonstration."

They went up a narrow, tree-walled path, beyond the old dwelling. Dusk had already fallen beneath the pines. The laboratory stood alone, across the little island. It was a square, white-walled modern structure. Some powerful machine was throbbing within it—yet Beckland shuddered to a feeling that it was somehow tomb-like.

The door in the bright-lit entry was a green-painted studded panel of steel, its knob a modernistic cube of ruby glass. Delcrain paused in the pool of light, fumbled for it with an odd hesitation.

Beckland reached past him to open the door, followed him into the long room. The walls were lined with metal-working power tools. A great motor-generator was thrumming at the farther end.

"Franz," the girl called to a shambling, gorilla-like figure In grimy mechanic's coveralls, "tell Dr. Daker that we're all here.'"

S HE introduced two other waiting spectators, seated in folding chairs.

Tony Marvis was a dark, sullen-looking youth. His flashy checked suit was expensive but unpressed. His sallow, haggard face was purple, unshaven.

Jeff Kelly was a thin, bald man, with a twisted leering face. Gold teeth chewed at an unlit cigar. Yellow claws of hands toyed with a pair of glittering, gem-set gold dice that he wore for a watch fob.

"Tony's another member of the family," she said. "Dr. Daker's step-son. But you had better watch Mr. Kelly, Mr., Delcrain!" She laughed. "He is a rival bidder for the invention."

Franz Roth, the mechanic, appeared again, opening an inner door. His staring face was dull with an ox-like expression of stupidity—was that a mask, Beckland wondered, to hide a secret cunning?

"We are ready," pronounced his flat, nasal voice. "Dr. Daker brings you—Roxar!"

Clanking into the room, followed by its little stooped builder, the seven-foot robot looked as mighty and stern as a stone-chiseled Assyrian god.

"Roxar!" Daker's high, feeble voice was almost a squeak. "Halt!"

The robot stopped in the middle of the floor, like a futuristic colossus of bright blue steel. The sparrow-like scientist cleared his throat, said shrilly:

"Gentlemen, let me present the first complete robot automaton—my Electromaton Model 99! The robots of which you read in the newspapers are mere ingenious machines. This is more! My new electro-neuronic cells give it an electrical brain. It can remember—think—reason!"

The little scientist paused, looked proudly up at his weird creation. Writing swiftly in the silence, Jimmie Beckland looked around at the others. They all had gasped with shock at the robot's alarming aspect.

But now Delcrain's face was poker-smooth. Kelly's hard little eyes were glittering with greed. Tony Marvis's haggard face was a sullen, bitter mask of hate. Franz Roth's features were the same stupid blank.

"Electromaton Model 99," the high voice resumed, "is a complete operating unit. My new storage batteries, charged from the generator here, give it self-contained power." He cleared his throat importantly. "Now for the demonstration! I begin by addressing the robot by the name to which its electronic ears are tuned—Roxar!"

Jimmie Beckland started, at that loud thin shout. And the robot also came to life! It clanked and jerked suddenly about to face the little scientist, stopped motionless again.

"Roxar!" Daker commanded. "Brush your hair!"

A massive metal arm lifted, flailed noisily at the armored head. The robot had no hair. Beckland felt vaguely that the towering steel-visaged body was too grimly menacing!

"Roxar!" its master demanded, "what is seven minus four?"

The great metal hand reached stiffly out. One long cruel gleaming metal claw lifted. Another. And a third!

It wasn't very wonderful, Jimmie Beckland tried to tell himself. But he shuddered. Again he looked at the others. Melanie Doyle's oval face was a white pool of dread. Tony Marvis stared with dull, brooding hatred at the robot and its master alike.

A white scar of fear showed above Delcrain's thin lip. The greed in Kelly's beady eyes had turned to dread. Only Franz Roth was still ox-like, unmoved.

P UTTING himself across the room, Daker now held up a green silk handkerchief, called:

"'Roxar! What does this mean?"

The robot clanged and swung and lumbered toward him. It stopped abruptly when he pocketed the green handkerchief, held up a red one in its stead.

"Now, Roxar!" Daker commanded. "Remember! What was my first order?"

The metal body jerked and shook again. Steel talons rattled against the armored skull, grotesquely brushing hair that did not exist. It should have been funny, Beckland thought. But he shuddered to the same outraged dread that he saw in Melanie Doyle's clear eyes.

"Roxar," Daker shrilled again, "that is all!"

The robot stood frozen to a gigantic hideous statue of steel, eyes gleaming weirdly blue. The thin little scientist stepped forward.

"That is enough, gentlemen," he said, "to prove that the Electromaton can think, reason, remember!" His pale spectacled eyes glittered, oddly like those of the robot.

"My robots can do the work of all the world! Think of it—a world of metal slaves! Metal men toiling in mine and field and factory, doing all the work. Every man can be an emperor, with his own robot-slaves!"

"Caution, Doctor!" It was a low, harsh whisper from dull-faced Franz. "Roxar hears!"

"The Electromaton is worth any sum I could name." Daker jerked his head impatiently. "But I'm not greedy. I ask only a nominal reward."

His pale eyes flashed avidly from face to face. "All my inventions are for sale—at the modest price of one million dollars."

In the startled silence, Jeff Kelly caught his breath. Tony Marvis gulped. Delcrain deliberately blew the ash off his cigar. The little scientist stepped anxiously forward, shrilling:

"Well, what do you say?"

Delcrain shook his head.

"Your figure is fantastic! Effo Electric manufactures appliances of proven value. Frankly, I fail to see any scientific or commercial value in your demonstration. Honestly, I'm disappointed. Of course, if you have any discoveries of practical value—"

Jeff Kelly came abruptly to his feet, explosively spitting his half-chewed cigar toward the wall.

"Practical be hanged!" he sputtered. "It's a great stunt, Professor! Me, I'm in the side show supply business. I don't give a damn about the scientific end. But your electric giant's a cinch to pack a tent! Tell you what—I'll give you ten thousand for the exhibition rights."

Daker stepped back toward the robot, hesitant, considering.

"I need the money," he muttered. "And you don't want my patents?"

"Sell 'em to the man in the moon!" grunted Kelly. "I just want your iron man, whatja call him, Roxar!"

"I'll do it," agreed Daker. "Sold!"

At that word, the great robot came abruptly to lumbering, grinding life. Humming and clanging, it swung ponderously toward Daker, its thick-lensed eyes flashing ominously blue.

"Roxar!" he shouted fearfully. "Halt!"

But it swayed swiftly toward him, its mighty tread shaking the laboratory floor. Melanie Doyle screamed again. Deep and solemn came the warning voice of Franz Roth:

"Roxar is angered! Tell him he will not be sold!"

The agitated scientist sprang toward the steel breast of the charging robot.

"Something wrong!" he shrilled. "Got to open the plate, disconnect—"

Jimmie Beckland caught his breath with dread as the great metal arm lifted stiffly, fell. It struck Daker's head. He collapsed at the robot's feet. Abruptly motionless again, it stood above his lax body, stark and grim as the carven god of some forgotten evil cult.

With a soft cry of pain, Melanie Doyle ran to the fallen man.

"Uncle Runyon!" she sobbed. "Can you hear me? I was so afraid—"

J IMMIE BECKLAND helped her carry Daker to a cot by the wall. In a moment he sat up, peering about with pale bewildered eyes.

"That offer," Jeff Kelly muttered uneasily. "Forget it. I don't want to buy the devil in a machine!"

"Just a short somewhere," protested Daker. "I can fix it."

He stood up, tried to walk toward the grimly looming robot.

"Not now!" Melanie objected nervously. "Let's get away from this horrid—monster! Come on up to the house. Jake and Liza will have dinner ready."

Beckland took Daker's other arm, and they returned along the uneven woodland path to the dwelling. The sky had turned very black. Far thunder rolled warningly against the peaks that walled Scimitar Lake.

"A storm!" Melanie's voice was shuddering. "They are quick and terrible, here on the lake."

When they reached the house, Daker let her bandage his head, but refused to lie down. When the negro couple served the meal, he ate a little. But he kept talking, in a high, incoherent voice, of the wonders of a robot-manned world. When dinner was over, ignoring the girl's protests, he started back to the laboratory with Franz Roth.

"Just a simple adjustment," he said.

"The electro-neuronic equilibrium is very delicate. If I wait, the robot's whole mind may become deranged!"

"Can you feature that?" demanded Jeff Kelly. "A machine gone mad?"

He seemed to mean it for a joke, but nobody laughed.

Old Jake had kindled a log fire on the big hearth, for it was cold. For a while the party sat before it—all still silent from the horror of the striking robot. Melanie shuddered abruptly.

"I'm so afraid—for Uncle Runyon!" she whispered. "If the thing should turn on him again—"

"I'll stroll down and see if he's all right," offered Andrew Delcrain, sympathetically. "Let me go with you," Jeff Kelly volunteered hastily. "That robot would be one smash attraction—if he could keep the devil out of it!"

Sullenly announcing that he was going to bed, Tony Marvis climbed the broad stair. Jimmie Beckland was left alone before the fire, with Melanie. He knew, now, that he had really loved her, these last two long years. He had a vivid sense of menace dogging her, a poignant urge to defend her.

Fear still haunted her oval, grey-eyed face.

"Jim" she whispered, "why don't some of them come back? Something must have happened!"

"Shall I go down?" he offered.

"Let's both go," she said. "Before it storms!"

But the storm struck before they came out on the old veranda. Purple lightning seared across the black, cloud-massed sky. Rain drummed down in great icy drops.

"Better let me go alone," Beckland said, and pushed back the shuddering girl.

The mad wind tore at him. He was drenched in an instant, chilled to the bone. Guided by the flicker of lightning, he stumbled along the trail toward the laboratory. Relief sobbed from him when he saw its white cube. He was calling out, anxiously, when he stumbled over something sickeningly soft—and fell plunging into black horror!

On his knees in the roaring darkness, he felt the thing. It was sticky, sodden-warm! Sharp ends of broken bones jutted out of it. Through the rain, a sickening smell came to his nostrils. Half the acrid smoke of smouldering cloth-and half a peculiar penetrating pungence that was dreadfully familiar!

Hardened newshawk that he was, Beckland turned faintly

sick. His tortured mind painted again all the well-rehearsed horror of an electrocution—the death-chamber filled with that same suffocating stench of seared human flesh!

*Who?*

C HOKED with the horror of that question, he waited for the next flash of lightning. But the body was beyond any recognition. Limbs and torso were crushed to bloody pulp. The head was sheer nightmare, a broken jelly of bone and brains, the surface burned black. The face was—obliterated!

Only the clothing answered his question. The blood-drenched suit had a loud stripe. A pair of jeweled golden dice still dangled from the watch pocket. It was the hard-bitten side show man, Jeff Kelly!

But what devil's mill had pulped him? What searing horror burned him?

Himself sweating in the icy rain, trembling and ill, Beckland staggered back to his feet. Melanie Doyle was first in his mind. He had left her alone, undefended against this horror that stalked the island! Wiping crimson fingers on his handkerchief, he started running back toward the dwelling.

The girl met him, stumbling against the roaring downpour.

"Jim!" she gasped. "I came—I was afraid-for you—" She clung to his arm. "Find anybody?"

"Kelly," he said. "Dead!"

Lightning showed him her face. "Jim, what—"

Horror strangled her. Her hand went rigid on his arm. For a thin, shrill scream of mortal dread had cut through the storm! It was lost beneath a loud brazen clangor!

Shuddering, they peered back along the trail. Lightning flared blue to reveal the tragedy. A man came running from the laboratory—little Dr. Daker, his thin legs working like pistons of fear! Behind him came—horror in steel!

The seven-foot robot came plunging, glistening blue in the lightning. Evil gleams shot from its wide-lensed eyes. Clanging, clashing, it moved with a stiff, awkward, mechanical deliberation, Its speed, nevertheless, was appalling!

Darkness again. Melanie clung against Beckland's arm, gasping with dry-throated dread. Daker's quavering shriek ripped once more through the veiling rain. The clangor of the robot was nearer, a hellish alarm.

"It has gone wrong-mad!" sobbed the girl. "It will kill him! I was so afraid—"

Beckland's tense arm slipped protectingly about the shuddering girl. Hoarsely, he demanded:

"Is there a gun in the house?"

"I don't think—yes, Tony's rifle! Do—"

Her voice stopped. Lightning flashed again. The first flicker stopped the two figures motionless, yet in violent action—like a single frame from a movie film. The fleeing scientist had stumbled; caught motionless in the very act of falling. And the robot was upon him!

Darkness fell, with splintering thunder. Daker screamed. It was a thin, bleating sound, like the cry of a wounded rabbit. The drum of cold rain drowned it.

Another flash of horror! Daker was helpless on the ground— and steel feet tramping him! His cries abruptly ceased. The robot bent stiffly, lifted him in crushing arms.

Beckland swung the mute girl away, himself sickened by the dull snapping of broken bones. He saw abrupt electric sparks, crackling purple about the robot's claws. Then its dead maker, crushed and burned, was cast to the side of the trail.

Shuddering, Beckland dragged the girl swiftly behind a tree. The monster stood motionless for a moment above its victim, then went crashing blindly through the storm-torn undergrowth toward the lake.

Careless of the pelting rain, Beckland ran ahead of the girl to pick up the body. He staggered back with it to the house, laid it on a couch in the living room—and felt ill again when he saw it in the light!

"Don't look!" he gasped hoarsely at the girl. "Call Tony, and get his rifle! The thing is still loose God knows what it will do!"

RUNYON DAKER had been mangled beyond recognition. The stamping metal feet had destroyed his face. The steel levers of the arms had crushed flesh and bone to crimson pulp. Electric fire had seared it, cooked skin was falling away. Beckland coughed to the strangling reek of smouldering cloth and burned flesh.

He spread a rug over the dripping horror, called the startled negroes from the kitchen, told them to secure doors and windows.

Melanie Doyle came back down the stairs.

"Tony's gone," she whispered. "And his rifle!" Her voice sank. "Jim, Tony hated Uncle Runyon—because Uncle had called him a shiftless no-good, threatened to disinherit him."

"Eh!" Beckland rubbed his lean chin. "And there's no weapon in the house?"

"Not sep' dis, boss!"

The trembling old negro, Jake, brought from the kitchen a rusty old long tom shotgun, with one lonely buck-shot cartridge. Beckland tried the action skeptically, loaded it, handed it to Melanie.

"If the thing comes here," he told her, "wait till it's within six feet. Then shoot into the middle of it. That ought to stop it! I'm going out to see what happened to the others."

"Don't—" protested the girl, fearfully. "Or, anyhow, take the gun!"

"Oh, Lawdy!" wailed old Jake. "De debble-thing's a-comin' back!"

Above the drumming of rain and the thunder magnified to an endless reverberation against the walling peaks, Beckland heard the robot's brazen clangor. The girl thrust the shotgun back into his hands, ran apprehensively to a window. Beckland followed.

Lightning ripped the sky again. They saw the steel giant plunging back through the swaying trees—horrifying as some monstrous invader from Mars!

"De good Lawd save us!"

Jake fell on his knees to pray; fat, white-aproned Liza collapsed whimpering in a chair.

Her white face brave and quiet, the girl stood staring from the window. The monster itself became invisible in the darkness, but its huge, blue-shining eyes, weirdly sinister as those of some jungle-monster, moved swiftly toward the house. The ponderous tread crashed across the old veranda. The robot was at the door!

Beckland leveled the rusty shotgun, set himself in the middle of the room. Cold chills rattled his teeth. This wasn't funny-trapped by a mad metal giant!

A steel fist crashed against the door. The lock creaked ominously. Liza shrieked and slid out of her chair. Jake's prayer died in his throat. Melanie turned silently to Beckland, her bloodless face agonized with a terrible question.

"Wait!" he called softly. "The door's locked—"

His words were lost in a tremendous crash. The time-rotted panels burst into flying splinters. Oil lamps flickered to a wind cold as death—swirling ahead of the lumbering robot!

Its blue steel mass filled the opening. Smouldering hideously blue, its eyes moved back and forth with its stiffly jerking head. Suddenly it whirred and plunged ahead again—its fearful red-stained metal talons clutching for Melanie Doyle!

Heavy with the sickness of terror, Jimmie Beckland stepped sidewise. He stopped in front of the horror-frozen girl. Trying to steady jerking muscles and pounding heart, he lifted the ancient gun.

The metal giant lumbered swiftly toward him. Its flailing arm caught a table, tipped it, sent a glass lamp crashing to the floor. Beckland waited until it was four feet from the gun's wavering muzzle, aimed at its blue breast, pulled the trigger.

The response was an empty click.

A steel arm swung wildly at him, purple sparks crackling from cruel-taloned fingers. Beckland side-stepped, lifted the gun like a club, struck fiercely at the great armored skull. The rusty barrel crashed to its mark—and Beckland's whole body jerked to the rending agony of a powerful electric shock!

D IMLY he knew that the ancient gun had exploded In his hands, with a terrific blast. That Melanie had collapsed on the floor behind him. That wild swift flame was spreading from the shattered lamp. But blackness overcame him.

Icy rain brought back his consciousness. He was lying on the ground under a tree, his head in Melanie's lap. Jake and Liza were crouched near them, drenched and whimpering. The storm still howled and drummed against the pines—and beneath it roared a conflagration!

"Jim!" the girl was sobbing. "Oh, Jim—speak to me!"

He groaned, sat up dizzily. Yellow light flickered against great boles. The old log house was a roaring furnace. Beckland rubbed his wet head with blistered hands, looked anxiously at Melanie.

"Afraid I'll live," he muttered. "You're all right. Tell me—what happened? Where's the—robot?"

"The gun blew up in your hands," whispered the girl. "You fell as if you were dead—"

"Half electrocuted!" Beckland muttered. "Daker's storage battery is a wonder, sure enough, for portable power—that thing must pack a thousand volts! But where did it go?"

He looked hopefully toward the roaring flames, but the fearful girl shook her head.

"I don't know." She shuddered. "At first I thought you had put it out of commission. It stood swaying a minute, over you—almost fell. The fire swept toward it, on the spilled oil. Suddenly it moved, and went out in the storm again. We just had time to carry you outside."

"So it's still free!" He shook his throbbing head. "You haven't seen Tony or Delcrain or Franz?"

"No." It was a shuddering, voiceless whisper. "I'm afraid—afraid it killed them all!"

Beckland reeled unsteadily to his feet.

"We can't stay here," he gasped. "The thing may have thought we'd be finished off in the fire, if it can think that far. But it may come back—and we're defenseless! Let's go to the lab. It will be a shelter, anyhow; and there is a chance we'll find the others."

The girl nodded voicelessly, called to the whimpering servants. She walked very close to Jimmie Beckland, along the rugged trail. The black sky sluiced blinding, chilling rain. Lightning seared their vision. Thunder rolled incessantly down from the peaks.

The white cube of the laboratory came into view at last, coldly tomb-like in the rain. Beckland was reaching for the door-knob, in the bright-lit entry, when Melanie pointed trembling into a dark mass of shrubbery behind them, gasping:

"Look, Jim! *There—*"

Beckland reeled shuddering to peer at the shapeless dripping thing flung like a bundle of red rags into the brush. It was pulped and seared like the others, not easy to identify. Faint and nauseated, he picked a sodden leather cigar-case out of smeared blood and entrails.

"Delcrain," he whispered hoarsely to the girl. "Kelly—Dr. Daker—now Delcrain! That leaves Tony and Franz—"

*"Hush!"* came the girl's warning breath. "There's somebody in the laboratory. I heard—something!"

Beckland moved silently to the door. A moment he paused, weakened by horror. Then he turned the red glass knob, stepped quickly inside.

The powerful motor-generator still throbbed against the farther wall; bright electrics still glowed among the dusty roof-girders. Warily, Beckland scanned machines and benches. The room seemed empty.

"Someone has been here," whispered the girl, beside him. "Rummaging Uncle Runyon's papers. See!"

She pointed to a tall green filing cabinet. Its battered drawers were sagging open, empty. Papers and blue-prints were scattered about the wrecking-bar beside it on the floor. "But he must be gone—"

B ECKLAND heard a little sound behind the door, spun swiftly. A man was crouching there a massive, powerful, black-bearded stranger. The newshawk was in time to see a heavy black automatic descending toward his skull—but too late to defend himself!

He tried vainly to thrust up a shielding arm. The flat black gun struck his temple with shocking agony. Not quite unconscious, he sagged to hands and knees. Fighting red waves of pain, he swayed back to his feet.

The bearded stranger was backing swiftly through the open door, menacing them with level gun. Pausing against the stormy dark, he shouted harshly:

"I warned Daker not to steal my idea! You see what happened to him!"

Then he was lost in the rain. Beckland staggered groggily to shut the door. He tried to lock it, shook his throbbing head.

"Lock is broken," he muttered. "Forced." His blurred eyes looked at the trembling girl. "Know him?"

"Name's Birkhead—Leland Birkhead," whispered Melanie. "Used to be Uncle's assistant. They quarreled. He accused Uncle of stealing his ideas. He wrote threatening letters, and said he was building a robot of his own. He may have come to steal plans—"

Beckland caught his breath.

"I wonder—" he whispered. "Could he have done something to the robot, while we were all at dinner—to make it go wrong and cover up his theft?" He rubbed his chin. "Anyhow, let's look for Franz and Tony. And some weapon! For Birkhead may come back—or the robot!"

Dripping icy water, he walked swiftly through the three connecting rooms. In one doorway he rocked back to a blow of instinctive horror. Before him stood a whole monstrous line of staring robots!

"Preliminary models," explained the girl, following. "They didn't work."

He found a dry coat in a locker, put it around her shivering body.

"Nobody here," he said. "And I don't see any weapon."

"Oh, Lawdy!" Old Jake's quavering, terrified cry called them back to the main room, where the generator throbbed. "De debble-thing!"

Cold dread ran through Beckland's veins, as he, too, heard the brazen clanging of the great robot approaching through the storm. The girl's grey eyes looked at him, sick with consuming fear. Her dry lips asked soundlessly:

"What shall we do?"

"I don't know." The newshawk rubbed his throbbing head. "The door won't lock, and we can't find a weapon—maybe it will go away."

The girl shook her head.

"It won't!" Her whisper was a dry horror-husk. "Not till I am dead! It is after me because I'm Uncle's kin—"

Her voice faded to the heavy clangor outside the door. The green steel panel rattled violently on its hinges. Beckland shuddered to a nerve-severing scratching, as if metal fingers fumbled for the knob!

"Can't we hold the door?" sobbed the girl.

"No," said Beckland. "The steel would transmit current to electrocute us—"

His voice died, oddly. His eyes narrowed at the panel, his lean head inclined. Still that queer fumbling went on.

"But—" he whispered, *"listen—"*

Suddenly he snatched a coil of heavy copper wire from a bench, flung it like a thin serpent across the concrete floor, ran back toward the thrumming generator—

H E was frozen by Melanie's shriek. The glass knob had turned. The steel door flung open. The robot came lumbering into the room. Seven feet of towering bright steel, dark with running stains of human blood. Its bulging armored head swung stiffly back and forth. Sinister blue-glowing eyes fixed upon the girl.

Her strength went out, then, in a little sigh of agony.

Ashen-faced, too terrified to run, she sank down on her knees. The metal giant lumbered swiftly toward her, merciless red-stained talons of steel clutching for her helpless white flesh.

"Stay back, Jim!" she sobbed. "It's I that it wants!"

The trembling newshawk stood back against the wall. His eyes tried to follow the glistening ruddy wire laid like a lasso across the green-painted floor. Dimly he saw the monster about to pass the end of it—then everything dissolved in a picture of Melanie's fair body crushed and seared like the other hideous human remnants he had found.

"Stop!" He had tried to shout, but his voice was a dry, hoarse whisper only. And the robot clanged on. He rasped: "I know that E. E. is two million in the red!"

At that, the steel giant abruptly halted. The metal head jerked back and forth until the glaring blue eyes found him. The robot lunged toward him, flailing out with crimson, purple-sparking talons.

Beckland waited, breathless and shuddering, beside the generator. He saw one metal foot tramp down upon the copper wire—and threw his strength against a massive switch. The hum of the dynamo changed. Blue sparks showered. Suddenly inert, the colossal metal body toppled slowly forward. Out of it came a thin shriek of mortal human agony!

"Red on green," whispered Beckland, staring out of a dazed weakness. "He didn't see the wire."

The deputy sheriff from Scimitar, a little later, hammered on the laboratory door. Beckland and Melanie, clad in dry coveralls they had discovered in a locker, let him in. He was followed by Franz Roth and a little posse of the villagers. Amidst them, in hand-cuffs, glowered heavy black-bearded Leland Birkhead.

"Roth, here, rowed to the village after us," announced the deputy. "He says he found a tin suit in a boat, and figured something was wrong. I reckon he was right! We found Kelly and Delcrain dead outside or what's left of them! And this guy trying to sneak away in another boat!"

"I'm no murderer!" Birkhead protested sullenly. "I came here merely to find what Daker was doing with my stolen invention."

"He isn't the killer," agreed Beckland. "There's the suit of armor." He pointed toward the fallen robot-shape. "You'll find the murderer inside—electrocuted!"

"Marvis, eh?" said the deputy, as his men labored to pry open the steel contrivance. "He's the only one not accounted for."

"An ingenious thing!" Beckland muttered. "Designed like submarine armor, though of lighter metal. Storage cells in the shoulders, high-tension coils in the head, and insulated cables running to the claws. Light-bulbs for eyes. See how the arms are built—such a terrific leverage!"

The breast-plate came open at last, and the deputy peered inside.

"Andrew Delcrain!" he gasped. "But we found his body outside—"

"That's Tony Marvis, outside," Beckland told him. "He must have been suspicious, and come down to investigate. But Delcrain got him, first. His clothing and rifle are in a locker, here. Delcrain put his own garments on the burned and mangled corpse, so that it would be identified as himself.

"Delcrain probably meant to sink Tony's garments in the lake, together with his robot-suit. When Franz appropriated his boat, to go for help, it broke up his plan."

"Delcrain!" whispered the wondering girl. "So that's what you meant!" E. E. stands for Effo Electric!"

"It does," said Beckland. "My paper had a tip that he had looted his company from inside. I was covering the story—tailing Delcrain in case he tried to scram. That supplies half the motive for his plot—he hoped to be reported dead, so no search would be made.

He must have planned it long in advance. He had seen the robot, probably photographed it, and had the suit made to imitate it. Daker probably gave him the storage battery to test. He must have invited me here because he wanted a competent witness to his faked death.—Poor Kelly, by the way, must have seen or guessed too much."

"You knew," the girl whispered again, "when you called out, and made him turn from me toward the charged wire! But how?"

Jimmie Beckland paused to smile at her.

"Delcrain was color-blind," he said. "Couldn't distinguish between red and green. I noticed that when he couldn't see the red glass knob against the green door of the lab. The real robot could distinguish colors—you remember Daker's demonstration. But the mad monster, breaking in here, had the same difficulty that Delcrain did."

"One thing,'" demanded the bewildered deputy. "Where's the

real robot?"

"It's standing in the lab, together with that row of unsuccessful models. It's quite a tricky contraption, but the valuable thing about it is the light, powerful storage battery that runs it. Delcrain meant to steal that invention—which is why he was trying to kill every one who might know the secret of it!"

He turned back to the girl, smiling again.

"That discovery is worth a fortune, Melanie. And now it's yours."

She looked a long time into his eager face. Her grey eyes misted.

"No, Jim," she whispered. "Not mine—ours!"

# Released Entropy

*Astounding Stories, August—September 1937*

ELLO, UNIVERSE!"
The newscaster's brisk voice, carried out on the hyperchron beam, crackled simultaneously from ten billion receivers on ten million inhabited planets.

"I speak to you from the Hall of Worlds, on Melchonor, capital planet of the G. U. I. R. (Galactic Union of Interstellar Republics). For the Galactic Council is assembling to-morrow, in the first session of this new year, 104,293 C. S. (Conquest of Space). And a battle of giants is in promise!"

The crisp words were emphasized by the animated play of the announcer's features, across the fluorescent screens of ten billion hyperchronoscopes.

"The first item on the calendar is the famous Gyroc Experiment. This proposed research, which has been hotly debated in scientific and legislative circles for many years, is coming up for final action.

"Seru Gyroc himself—discoverer of the Omega Effect and the Gyroc Tensors, the basis of the proposed experiment—is going to speak in defense of his tremendous plan to prevent the universe from running down.

"Seru Gyroc is already acknowledged the greatest living scientist of the galaxy, with nearly two hundred years of brilliant achievement to his credit. Among the latest of his triumphs is a modification of the old triterium-water longevity treatment, which is expected to add another full two centuries to the useful span of human life.

"We salute you, Seru, a giant of science!"

The newscaster bowed, on billions of screens.

"But if he wins again, universe, it won't be an easy victory! For opposed to him is another giant! The famous space cruiser *Silver Bird* is now plunging toward Melchonor. Aboard, racing to reach the Hall of Worlds in time for to-morrow's debate, is Ron Goneen, captain general of the Galactic Patrol, and late commander of the Andromeda Expedition—

"We salute you, Captain Goneen, a giant of exploration!"

"A battle of giants indeed, universe! Of giants who once were friends! For Ron Goneen, in the Galactic Academy, got his first scientific training under Seru Gyroc. Now he is returning to join battle with his old professor.

"Ron Goneen holds that the Omega Experiment, if performed, will result in immediate, universal cataclysm. He is making this desperate race, in his faithful old ship—so he believes—to save the galaxy!"

The clean-featured face of the newscaster, in the billions of glowing screens, looked briefly down as he caught his breath and scanned his notes.

"Now, universe!" he cried. "Our next surprise!

"We bring you a dramatic incident from the Andromeda Expedition, enacted in our own studios under the super-vision of a group of the surviving officers.

"In the three years since its return, the history of the expedition has been told many times. All humanity knows how Captain Goneen planned the *Silver Bird*—the greatest and the swiftest space vessel ever designed! How his intrepid courage found support and volunteers for the undared voyage to the Andromeda Galaxy! How the great new vessel left the yards of the Galactic Patrol, here on Melchonor, over one hundred years ago! How it reached that distant island universe after a perilous voyage of more than thirty years!

"A thousand volumes have been written of Ron Goneen's adventures during forty years of exploration among the planets of

Andromeda. His discoveries there have already created a dozen new sciences. His life was in danger ten thousand times!

"BUT NOW we depict for you the last stirring episode of that forty years, before the *Silver Bird* returned."

The animated face vanished from the screens. In its stead appeared the tapered, silvery hull of a mile-long kappafield space cruiser, driving across a black sky whose brilliant stars were ranged in strange configurations.

"There you see the *Silver Bird,*" the brisk voice resumed its narrative, "plunging ahead on the final tour of exploration, into the Gamma Quadrant of the new galaxy. There Captain Goneen encountered a new high type of intelligent life—"

Suddenly, on the myriad screens, the space about the long ship was aswarm with flying objects. They were intricate nine-pointed crystals, each many yards in diameter. Their polished planes shone with white, mirrorlike radiance. Every point carried a clinging globe of colored luminescence that spun and changed as the crystal moved.

"These beings were gigantic crystals of eternal metal. Their intelligence life, Captain Goneen believed, was a function of intermolecular electrostatic tensions; vital energy probably being derived from controlled radioactive disintegration.

"Able to cross interstellar space without the aid of machinery, they had spread over ten thousand planets in a great globular star cluster. Once—so Captain Goneen believed from the colossal ruins he saw—their civilization had been high; but their culture had long since fallen into a vicious decadence."

The screens showed the *Silver Bird* landing upon the surface of a planet, still attended by that glittering, crystalline host. On a high, age-carved plateau, against a greenish sky, loomed a weird, colossal city of crimson cones that were shattered and truncated with immemorial time.

"The metal Andromedans displayed great cleverness in their efforts to establish communication. This was soon accomplished through a radio hook-up, the crystals being sensitive to ultra-short waves and able to generate them.

"But here you see Ron Goneen himself, in conversation with a leader of the Andromedans!"

A broad-shouldered, powerful man, darkly tanned by many

suns, the space captain stood on the barren ground beside his ship. Oxygen apparatus was slung about his shoulders, but his big, rugged head was bare, red hair tangled. He was speaking into a microphone. And before him, floating in a many-colored, luminous mist that clung most densely about its points, mirroring in its facets the greenish sky, was a monstrous nine-pointed star.

"At first the Andromedans pretended friendship," the staccato voice hastened on. "They brought amazing gifts, revealed the secrets of their half-lost science, and urged Captain Goneen to come with an expedition to the underground city of their rulers."

THE silvery crystals were shown bearing to the ship shining jewels, unfamiliar implements of metal, and fantastic works of art. Then, with a lonely little band in the trim green of the Galactic Patrol. Ron Goneen was seen marching away from the ship.

"It was all a treacherous plot against the explorers!" barked the newscaster. "For a simultaneous attack was made on the cruiser and the party lost beneath the surface!"

Thousands of the crystals, flying flat-wise, dived slantingly at the unwarned *Silver Bird.* Jets of colored flame spurted from their points—arrowed annihilating rays that consumed scores of the luckless crew, who were caught outside the vessel. The survivors took off hastily, in the great vessel, in an effort to defend themselves.

Deep in the planet, then, the screens showed the attack upon the other party. The Andromedans shone in the darkness—stars of mirrors, floating in cloudlets of many-colored flame! Multihued rays, lancing from their points, ruthlessly cut down the ill-armed, helpless men as they stumbled toward the shelter of boulders and crevices.

"The few survivors," the announcer went on, "were carefully taken alive, and carried by the Andromedans into a tremendous, rock-hewn temple, many miles beneath the surface, which was the center of their degenerate worship."

The screens showed an immense dim place, with colored stars floating amid vast columns that towered into boundless darkness. Ron Goneen and a few other men, haggard and bloodstained, were kneeling in chains before a stupendous altarlike structure. Before them, set on the apex of a black cone, was a small orb of brilliant white, shimmering like some wondrous pearl.

"Proving that they had lapsed into superstitious barbarism," the newscaster rushed on, "the Andromedans chained their captives as an offering before their most holy object—a singular small round stone, which shone with a steady pale glow.

"However, they underestimated Captain Goneen!"

Slowly, the swarming crystals departed, leaving the temple dark and empty. Only the pale reflection of the jewel showed the mighty arm of Ron Goneen, as it wrenched a massive block from the altar, shattered the fetters of his companions and himself. Then the announcer continued:

"Their escape was discovered immediately," the announcer hurried on. "But Ron Goneen led the few left with him out of the temple, into a labyrinth of narrowing caverns, where the crystals were able to follow only by blasting obstacles out of the way.

"Time is lacking to detail their hardships and escapes. Flight and hiding from the pursuing crystals! Incredible privation! Desperate struggle for food and water. Respiratory difficulties from an irritating atmosphere!

"Lost for many days in the dark caverns, they made torches from a seepage of crude petroleum. Ron Goneen ingeniously contrived a compass and a barometer to guide them—from a fragment of iron ore and the hollow shell of a dead organism! When, at last, they reached the open air, he used sheets of mica to make a heliograph with which to signal the *Silver Bird!*"

The screens, again, showed the great cruiser landing beside a narrow, dark rift in the planet. Swarms of the bright crystals, wheeling high in the greenish sky, were now puzzlingly fearful of attack. The refugees, naked, weary, bruised, staggered triumphantly aboard.

And the space captain proudly held, in his great, scarred palm, a small white stone.

"The Jewel of Dawn!" cried the newscaster. "That is what Captain Goneen called the holy stone, because its pale radiance had helped guide his men through the caverns. For he had taken it from the sacred place of their captors!

"It is said that he carries it still, in a pouch under his tunic, as a memento of that most desperate adventure. Upon the expedition's return, all the other specimens and data accumulated were given to the Galactic Museum. But, although curious savants clamored for it, Captain Goneen refused to give up the stone from Andromeda!"

A great sphere, shimmering like an illuminated pearl, vanished from ten billion hyperchronoscope screens. The newscaster's face appeared again.

"That, universe." his voice crackled, "is the history of the Jewel of Dawn. To-morrow we will take you to the Hall of Worlds, where Seru Gyroc is to speak for his proposed experiment, and Captain Goneen—if his racing ship arrives in time!—against it.

"What will be the outcome, universe? Will the Galactic Council listen to the foremost scientist of humanity, with his promises of incredible wonders to be done with the Omega Ray? Or will they give heed to this intrepid space commander and his warning of galactic doom?

"Till to-morrow, universe!"

And the ten billion screens went briefly dark.

## II.

"MY OPPONENTS have said that this thing is dangerous. I grant them that unguessed perils may lurk in the unknown realms of nature which we propose to explore, but I submit that the prize justifies the risk. Man did not conquer the galaxy through fear of new discovery!"

When the white-robed speaker gravely paused, silence hung for a long instant in the vast, green-columned Hall of Worlds. Then a tremendous sea of applause rolled upward from the representatives of many interstellar dominions.

Seru Gyroc was a slight, straight man, with brilliant dark eyes and very black hair. With thin hands folded in his severely simple robe, he stood with bowed head upon the speaker's dais until silence was restored.

Quietly then, yet with a dignity supported by his supreme achievements, he resumed, "Besides that possible danger inherent in any attempt to master the very creative force of nature, the Omega Experiment will involve vast expense and will require the best efforts of our most brilliant minds—perhaps for several centuries!

"My opponents argue that it is sheer folly to undertake a project so costly in both materials and brains, so fraught with unknown peril, and—from their point of view—so needless.

"Yet, to me"—the white-robed scientist paused; his dark eyes lifted solemnly above the green colonnades, to the vast blue dome above, pricked with golden stars—"it is worth all that cost and risk to win the goal we seek—to save the universe!"

Once more wild applause rolled against the columns; and, before the thousands had resumed their seats, a powerful figure came striding through the portals: a tall man in the green of the Galactic Patrol, with stern objection written on his rugged face.

Seru Gyroc looked down with a brief smile of recognition.

"Entering is my greatest opponent, a man who was once my most brilliant student. It is strange"—and his thin face was almost sardonic—"that the fearless captain general of the Galactic Patrol should be afraid of a mere laboratory experiment! But it seems that he is. And you shall hear his reasons—and you shall judge."

RON GONEEN found a seat and sat listening, with a grim expression on his dark, weather-beaten visage.

"I respect the opinion of Captain Goneen," Seru Gyroc continued. "It was at his request, transmitted over the hyperchron beam from intergalactic space, that ceased my preliminary experiments with the Omega Effect, thirty years ago.

"I have waited patiently for the formal approval and support of the council, because the matter is very grave.

"It is true, as Captain Goneen pointed out in his request to me, that the fate from which I seek to save our universe is very remote. Yet I venture to say that every one of you has felt the painful pressure of it! For it is supremely tragic to any thinking being to know that all his cosmos must ultimately die, even if his own life is not immediately affected.

"Our universe is running down. Eventually it must stop—die! My opponents can point out that the energy of disintegrating matter still feeds the suns, whose radiation still warms the planets with the rays that sustain all life. But they cannot deny that every phase of that vital process, being subject to the second law of thermodynamics, must at last cease to be.

"In the end, they must admit, all matter—even to the last barren fragment of the last sunless planet—must dissolve into free energy. And that energy, 'decaying' into the feeblest dark vibrations, of longest wave length, must at last be uniformly distributed through an infinitely expanded space.

"Picture that ultimate end of the universe! A void of utter darkness, of cold almost absolute, in all of which there is no possible change, no motion, no life, no thought! Even time itself must cease to be—for time is mathematically determinable only by the direction of entropy increase.

"Doesn't that vision of utter and illimitable death fill you with abiding horror—even if the reality does not touch your own lives?

"Can mankind ever be truly triumphant, living in a doomed universe?" Seru Gyroc swept his listeners with keen, dark eyes, in which burned a pressing challenge. "I feel that we cannot!

"I feel that the conquest of entropy is the supreme task of the human race, worth any cost, any risk short of sure disaster!"

When he paused, an awed and breathless silence filled the columned hall. His solemn eyes lifted slowly to the starflung dome, and an uncertain patter of applause swept the floor. He waited. It swelled slowly to a tremendous ocean of sound, beating against the green colonnades.

Only Ron Goneen kept his seat, with the same grim expression behind the red beard on his unshaven face.

At last, when Seru Gyroc held up his arms for silence, the uproar subsided reluctantly.

Only one doubtful question rang from the floor: "Can it be done?"

### III.

"IT CAN be done," said the white-robed scientist gravely. "Entropy can be mastered."

His dark eyes caught the stern, forbidding look on the face of Ron Goneen, below. He paused as if disconcerted, then caught his breath and abruptly resumed: "The first law of thermodynamics is our assurance that the dissipated energy of a run-down universe still exists. For, although energy may be expressed in many forms, from the complex atoms in the core of a young sun to the feeble, dark radiation of a dead universe, its sum total is always the same.

"It is the second so-called law of thermodynamics which informs us that any universe will run down. Yet that law has long been recognized to be merely statistical, not absolute. It is merely a statement of probability.

"Consequently, its circumvention has been the most tantalizing dream of human science. Inventors since the dawn of knowledge, vaguely sensing the hidden truth, have labored vainly to perfect machines of perpetual motion.

"There is a tradition, moreover, that a theoretical solution was imagined by an investigator whose name is now lost, at the very beginning of the Era of Science, before the race had ever left the mother planet.

"Considering the problem of a gas in a partitioned chamber, this early genius* conceived the idea of an entity he called a demon, who should be able to operate an ultramicroscopic door in the partition, in such a manner as to allow only the swifter-moving molecules to pass through in one direction, and only the slower-moving ones to enter the other end of the chamber.

"Thus this entity, so extraordinary of sense and agility, would be able, without doing any physical work, to accumulate fast molecules on one side of the partition, and slow ones on the other. In other words—since molecular motion is an expression of heat, of energy—the demon begins with a uniform or most probable distribution of energy, and he accumulates it, against the thermodynamic gradient, in one end of the chamber.

"This remarkable being, that is, reduces the entropy of this system of gaseous molecules. Without doing any work, he collects heat in a part of the system, and cools the rest. He reverses the normal flow of energy, to increase the organization of his system, and to make its energy once more available for useful thermodynamic interchange.

"How this unknown investigator pictured his demon," continued the white-robed speaker, "it is now impossible to say, for any other meaning of the word is lost.

"And for a hundred thousand years this elemental problem has

---

*This "early genius," of course, was Clerk Maxwell.

A technical definition of entropy (Swann):

"The change of entropy from one state of a system to another is the integral of dH/T from the first state to the second, the integral being taken along a reversible path, with dH representing the element of heat added at the temperature T."

A statistical interpretation of that definition is that every energy change in a system tends to proceed in the direction of maximum probability. That is, in the case of the confined gas, it follows from the conditions of probability that the molecole's will tend to reach an average state of equally distributed energy in all parts of the system.

When a piece of red-hot iron is plunged into a bucket of cold water, it is not "impossible"—according to the classical laws of molecular dynamics alone-that baffled all science. The present very highly organized—and hence, statistically, extremely improbable—state of our universe has been tantalizing proof of the existence, somewhere, at some time, of this demon. It is evident that there must have been a winding up of the universe, a building, a creative process, in which the amount of its entropy was reduced. Yet the search for it always failed.

"The first clue, I think, is to be found in the tensors I evolved less than a hundred years ago. They constitute a complete mathematical description of that demon. They apply, I am convinced, to a real phenomenon possible in the material world, which I have termed the Omega Effect.

"New forces are involved, which I have termed, again using that ultimate symbol from an ancient alphabet, the Omega Radiation. I have not yet dared to release them. That waits for your approval. And their nature, therefore, or the system of laws they will follow, is yet unknown.

"Only this much is certain: the Omega Effect will alter the conditions of real probability, in whatever part of the universe in which it occurs, in such a manner that the second law of thermodynamics will no longer apply. What was formerly a state of maximum probability will become one of minimum probability, and thermodynamic processes will be altered in conformity to the new statistical situation.

"But that is enough to show the technical possibility of the experiment."

SERU GYROC paused again. His burning eyes scanned the thousands of his listeners, beneath the golden-starred dome.

---

the molecules of iron should continue to absorb energy from the molecules of water, until the water is frozen and the iron fused. That remarkable occurrence would involve, however, a decrease of the entropy of the system. Statistically, it is very improbable, because the energy present can be distributed among the molecules in an immensely greater number of ways when the water and the iron have both reached the same average temperature. And any blacksmith can testify that, actually, it seldom happens!

Crudely conceived, then, entropy is the measure of chaos, confusion, dissipation, of spent and useless energy. As clocks run down and rain falls and coal burns and the sun shines and your car is braked to a stop and your eye reads this page, the entropy of the universe is being increased. All energy runs down a hall, up which, without the aid of something like Maxwell's demon, it can never return.

Ringing eagerly now, his low voice resumed: "And think what success would mean! Freedom from the old limitation of entropy: that energy must always be lost, wasted! Our fuel and power problems solved forever!

"A man could draw heat from a mass of ice to cook his dinner! He could collect energy from the air to run his planes and vehicles—the very same energy that they had dissipated through friction—and travel forever without any cost in fuel!

"Our children—if your courage allows me to perform this experiment—can gather dark waste radiation from the void, and condense it into matter again. They can build themselves new worlds and new shining suns—forever!"

Once again the white-robed scientist waited while tremendous applause reverberated against the green columns.

"That is my plea," he finished quietly. "This thing can be done. I grant that it will be costly; I grant some element of danger. But I am eager for your permission and your aid to do it. It is a grave matter; consider it well. Please listen now to my opponents. Then—the decision is yours!"

He went slowly to his seat.

And Ron Goneen, recognized by the presiding officer, stalked grimly forward. The mighty, red-bearded explorer of space stood for a moment silent on the dais.

"I am sorry that I must oppose this plan of my friend and teacher," his deep voice rolled against the dome. "I am sorry to oppose any brave effort to increase the greatness of man. Perhaps it seems strange that I do; But I have been long away from the sheltered planets of the galaxy, and I have felt the blind, terrific might of the cosmic forces with which Seru proposes to tamper."

Soberly, his deep-set, narrowed blue eyes scanned the multitude.

"I am proud of mankind," he said. "For a hundred thousand years the human race has marched steadily upward. We have conquered all the galaxy. From a 'minor phenomenon of planetary decay,' as one ancient cynic put it, man has become the dominating intelligence of an entire galactic system. He has won a freedom, a power, a longevity, a perfected happiness, that would amaze his less fortunate progenitors."

His great scarred hands knotted earnestly at his sides.

"Are we then to risk all this advance—everything that our race has ever accomplished since the first terrestrial beast rubbed two pieces of wood together and discovered fire? Are we to gamble all that upon one turn of an unknown wheel?

"And for what?"

The deep voice was husky with desperate urgency.

"To prepare against a doom that will not be imminent for a million million years? Isn't that sheer folly?"

His rugged, stern face looked to the white-robed scientist in his seat, and back to the thousands. "Or to gain needless, fantastic powers? What is the need to cook on stoves of ice, or to collect the waste energy of friction, when we have reservoirs of atomic power to last a billion years?"

His voice rumbled deeper. "What is the need to build new worlds, when Andromeda and a million million other island universes lie waiting for the explorer and the pioneer? Is there no room for triumphant adventure, without tampering with the very foundations of the universe?"

His solemn face lifted to the vault of stars. "Since the dawn of terrestrial history, man has struggled through superstition and religion and science to solve this ultimate problem: the riddle of creation. He has never done so—and it is well that he has not!

"For our own lives are among the phenomena of increasing entropy! Let us not seek to overrun the balance of the universe, and set time itself to flowing backward—lest we perish with our success!"

Ron Goneen stepped a little backward; his voice sank lower.

"That is all I have to say. It should be enough. Think well before you act. For the future of humanity—the very life of the universe—is in your hands."

He sat down abruptly, grim-faced as ever.

THE presiding officer again recognized Seru Gyroc, who resumed the dais to say: "Yes, the life of the universe is indeed in your hands! For, if your decision is against the experiment, I shall destroy my notes.

"And let me say that it was but a singular chance of reasoning that led me to discover the Gyroc Tensors. They are an anomaly in this universe of increasing entropy. No phenomenon guides the mind to them. It is safe to say, on grounds of mathematical probability, that my tensors will not be discovered again in this universe."

His voice was suddenly loud and clear.

"The supreme privilege is yours! To vote for eternal life, for the power of creation itself, for the ultimate victory of mankind—or for retreat, failure, and inevitable, everlasting, changeless death!"

The presiding officer again looked inquiring at Ron Goneen. But the weather-beaten space captain sat rigid and impassive in his chair, with mighty arms folded and narrowed steel-blue eyes staring bleakly ahead, as if at some awesome vision.

Seeing that the president was about to call for the vote, Seru Gyroc rose hastily to make a final plea: "Personally, I believe that the danger of the Omega Experiment has been very much exaggerated. I would not willingly endanger other lives than my own, even in the cause of science.

"And let me assure you that if the council approves the experiment, it will be performed with every precaution for safety. All my fellow workers will be carefully protected. And the actual research will be done at some point far outside the galaxy."

The presiding officer looked again, a little anxiously, at the space captain. But Ron Goneen still sat mute, staring—as if he already perceived the horror of the disaster of which he had spoken warning.

Somewhat reluctantly, the president called for the vote. Each member pressed a button on his desk. Tabulated automatically, the result was instantly flashed on a huge screen at the end of the chamber.

"The Galactic Council," the sonorous and somewhat regretful voice of the official reverberated against the green columns, "has declared its approval of the plan!"

As his voice echoed and died away, a hushed restraint filled the Hall of Worlds, as if the thousands felt a stricken apprehension at what they had done.

Ron Goneen rose quietly in the silence, made his way to Seru Gyroc. He bowed, took the hand of his old master. "You have won," he said. "It is to be. I hope my fears prove to have been without foundation. And let me be the first to volunteer my aid—for, come success or disaster, this will be the greatest adventure of man's history."

Seru Gyroc was trembling, with tears of emotion in his eyes.

"Thank you, Ron," he gasped. "I am glad to have you with me again, and your aid will be priceless. And I hope"—his voice was very grave—"I hope man never regrets this day!"

Suddenly, then, a wild and tremendous wave of cheers broke through the silent Hall of Worlds.

## IV.

THAT SAME DAY, the enthusiastic Galactic Council passed the necessary measures to authorize and finance the Gyroc Research Expedition, "Dispatched for the purpose of discovering a method for the controlled decrease of entropy."

And Ron Goneen offered the use of the veteran *Silver Bird*. Stained with the corrosion of many atmospheres, battered with the accidents of two million light years of space, scarred from the attack of the Andromedans, it was still the most powerful existing ship.

In the busy yards of the Galactic Patrol, beneath the red-and-blue binary sun of Melchonor, it was completely refitted, and provisioned with supplies to last the expedition, if need be, for half the fifteen centuries of a normal lifetime.

Vastly elaborate machine shops and laboratories were set up aboard, equipped with many pieces of apparatus designed by Seru Gyroc that were completely new to science.

Ten years had passed when the preparations were complete, and the twelve hundred selected members of the expedition gathered on the dock beside the *Silver Bird*.

Before any came aboard, Seru Gyroc appeared in the entrance valve, looking frail and thin in his severe white robe, yet animated with indomitable purpose.

"One word, before we depart," he said. "You are mostly young men and women. You represent the galaxy's best. You were selected from millions who volunteered. You have much to lose: youth, vigor, genius! Are you prepared for great sacrifice?

"I must tell you that our destination is the tiny, sunless planet of Pyralonne, discovered by the Andromeda expedition. It lies two hundred thousand light years from the limits of the galaxy. We have selected it to minimize the danger of the experiment.

"You must all realize that our research may be fatal to some or all of you. Even otherwise, you must be prepared to spend several centuries upon dark, frozen Pyralonne, toiling in a grim, exile of science. There will be no later opportunity to return. Let any who wish now withdraw. The rest will please come aboard."

The twelve hundred pressed eagerly forward, cheering. Ron Goneen strode forward silently from among them. His tanned, rugged face very grim. He strode up the gangway, clasped the thin hand of Seru Gyroc, and entered the vessel without a word. The chosen hundreds followed, marching out of the purple twilight.

The long hull was sealed at last. Ron Goneen, standing beneath the transparent dome of his bridge, gave the order to rise. Gigantic atomic generators fed power to the kappafield coils, and the *Silver Bird* was off!

The red sun and then the blue rose again, as the globe of Melchonor fell behind. They dwindled to tiny disks—to a ruby point and one of sapphire. The two points merged into one, and that was lost in the silver clouds of the galaxy.

YET, swift as was the *Silver Bird*, plunging through millions of miles in a second, drawn into a tiny subspace of her own by the field warp of the kappa coils, seven years had passed before she approached her destination.

Little larger than the ancient Moon of the mother planet, Pyralonne had been flung by some unguessed early cataclysm from the gravitational embrace of its own parent sun.

Adrift among the stars, it had acquired, through millions of years, by the rule of equipartition of energy, the terrific velocity appropriate to its own tiny mass. Until at last, a freakish "runaway" world, it had burst free to go plunging forever into the dark gulf beyond its mother universe.

Overtaking it, the *Silver Bird* slanted down across cragged, barren ranges that had not changed in a million million years, to land upon a plain. Once that bleak plateau may have known the brief flash of life. But since before the birth of Earth it had been sunless, changeless, the silent abode of frigid and eternal night.

Armored against the complete vacuum and cold nearly absolute, men emerged beneath a sky utterly black, sunless, starless. In one quarter was the vague, silvery spindle of the galaxy— visible with light that had left it two thousand centuries before. Opposite was the dim tiny spiral of the Andromeda Galaxy, four times more distant.

Undismayed, however, the explorers set to work at once.

With stone quarried from that bleak plain, using tools and materials from the ship, they at once began erection of the laboratory: a great solitary tower, crowned with an immense flat dome.

The ship itself, connected with the tower through a long tunnel, served as auxiliary workshop and living quarters for most of the expedition.

FOUR MORE YEARS had passed before the actual research could be begun, with Ron Goneen in command of personnel and Seru Gyroc in charge of the laboratory.

Already many members of the party, oppressed by the weight of cold and darkness, and recalling Ron Goneen's dire predictions, were beginning to regret their early courage.

For, as the slender scientist had foreseen, the conquest of the Omega Effect proved a long and arduous task. As the years grew into decades, Seru Gyroc himself sometimes admitted discouragement.

Even on Pyralonne, however, existence was not absolutely cheerless. Sometimes, under favorable conditions, the hyperchron beam brought news from home; and the great ship provided facilities for rest and recreation.

The expedition included a few hardy and daring women. Among the most brilliant and the most beautiful of them was tall, regal Karanora Quane, who had been for many years Seru Gyroc's assistant in his biological research.

The members of the expedition spared little time for love, and few cared to bring forth children who would know only this grim world. But Seru Gyroc and his lovely assistant were married before the first century had passed, and a daughter was presently born to them.

The child was named Lethara. Many were grateful for her golden-haired presence among them, for the difficulties of the research had begun to seem insuperable. The smiles, the laughter and the songs of Lethara enlivened many weary decades.

Discontent grew bitter, as the second century slipped away, until a company of mutineers attempted to seize the *Silver Bird*. They blocked the tunnel leading to the laboratory tower, and welded the bulkhead doors upon those aboard who refused to join them.

Ron Goneen, however, was on the bridge. He held it, single-handed, for twenty hours, until Lethara, now a grown and beautiful woman, came in a space suit from the tower to tell the mutineers that her father had made a hopeful new discovery. She joined Ron Goneen, and together they induced the rebels to surrender.

MORE YEARS PASSED, however, and the second century had turned before the supreme day of the actual experiment. The tower had been carefully insulated against the Omega Radiation, and the apparatus was set up under the dome. Ron Goneen and Seru Gyroc alone remained with it, sending all the rest aboard the ship.

Karanora Quane and her lovely daughter were the last to leave the tower.

And tears glistened suddenly in the steel-blue eyes of Ron Goneen, speaking to Lethara—in the eyes of Captain General Goneen, who had stalked a thousand planets and two galaxies, with never a second glance at any woman!

Lethara clung to his bronzed form suddenly, her violet eyes dark and big.

"There is danger, Ron?" she cried. "So much danger?"

"So I said, two hundred years ago, said Ron Goneen. "And so I still believe."

"Then why—why do you go on?" she demanded. "When there is so much to live for in the world that is! I wish so much to see the things I have never seen—sunshine and blue skies and green things growing, everything back there!"

"I wish, Lethara," Ron Goneen said softly, "that I could show you all the worlds that I have seen. Lethara—"

Softly, she whispered, "What is it, Ron?"

"Lethara," he said again, "if I am alive after this experiment is done, I shall have something to tell you. But now you must go!"

Her eyes were suddenly wide and deep with dread. She clung to the great arms that pushed her away.

"Alive— Oh, Ron!" she gasped.

"Do you mean—"

Her father took her arm, drew her toward her queenly mother.

"Don't be alarmed, my dear," he urged her. "We have taken every precaution. The only risk is the unforeseen—"

The girl's frightened eyes looked away from him, back to the rugged, bronzed face of Ron Goneen, grim again with his forebodings.

"Smile, Ron!" she begged him. "And promise you will live—to

tell me that!"

The rugged, weather-beaten features of the space captain creased into a slow, stiff smile, even while sudden unwanted tears shone in his deep-set eyes. His voice came, at the second effort, a deep hoarse croaking, "I promise—Lethara that—"

And she was gone.

Having locked and sealed the tunnel door, Seru Gyroc turned to cry exultantly, "Now we conquer entropy!"

V.

ALONE in the tower, the two men climbed back to the floor beneath the dome, where the apparatus had been erected. In the center of the room was a small metal pier. Bearing upon it, arranged in an ominous-looking circle, were the gigantic barrels of the seven ray projectors whose interfering frequencies were expected to generate the Omega Radiation.

With thin fingers trembling a little, Seru Gyroc set a glass beaker of water on the pier. From a glass rod across its top he suspended a little globe of silver, so that it hung in the water.

One by one, he began to focus the great barrels upon the tiny argent button—

Ron Goneen had gone to one of the little armored ports. He shaded his eyes from the light within, looked out across the frigid, dark plateau. In the distance, beneath the slanted, silvery disk of the galaxy, he could see the red-and-green beacons at the landing field, and the flying lights of the *Silver Bird*.

The latter rose, as he watched, like colored stars in the black sky, diminished, then vanished at last above a bleak mountain range. The ship was gone, with Lethara— He closed the insulating shutters.

"Well give them two hours," he told Seru Gyroc. "I ordered them to stand off ten billion miles, in case of any—accident—"

He stood bleak-faced, watching, as Seru Gyroc finished his List fussy adjustments, and stepped back at last to look with a nervous impatience at the tiny silver bead suspended in the water.

"It's ready." Gyroc sighed. "The heterodyning beams should set up the Omega Effect in the silver ball. The normal conditions of energy probabilities should be reversed. The silver should absorb beat and freeze the water to ice."

"I'm going to close the key!"

"Wait," said Ron Goneen. "The two hours—"

The little man looked at him sharply.

"You aren't still afraid, Ron—of so small a thing?"

"It's big enough," the space captain said solemnly, "to threaten the equilibrium of the universe! I had meant to say nothing more, Seru; but, saying good-by to Lethara, I suddenly saw all the glory of life. It is far too wonderful to put into jeopardy—"

HIS GREAT HAND caught the shoulder of the scientist.

"Seru, I beg you," he said urgently, "for the sake of our old friendship, for the love of Karanora, for the youth and happiness of your daughter—give up this thing! Even now!"

"We are risking so much—so needlessly! Let us simply destroy the apparatus, and report that the experiment failed!"

"No!" The hard power of Seru Gyroc's voice was suddenly like the vibration of a great dynamo. "We shall not turn back. If you are afraid, captain, you should have gone with your ship."

"It is not for myself," said Ron Goneen, "but for the others, for the universe, for Lethara! I beg you—"

The dark eyes of the scientist flashed to a chronometer. "The two hours have gone, Ron," he said quietly. "We begin! Stand by the safety controls, if you like—"

The tall space captain stepped suddenly forward, his great hands grasped abruptly for the other's shoulder.

"I am sorry to do this, Seru," his deep voice began, "after you have worked so long. But I am going to stop you! The risk is too great—"

With a surprising agility, however, the black-haired little scientist stepped swiftly back. A thin hand flashed into his white mantle, came out with the deadly little pointed rod of a positron gun.

"No, you won't stop me, Ron!" His dark eyes were flaming, his narrow face wild with a fanatic elation. "Mankind must perish, in the end, or rule the tide of entropy. And to-day—by myself—is the issue decided!"

"Stop!" gasped Ron Goneen. "You are mad—"

"Stand back!" the cold voice rasped. "Or I shall report that you perished in the experiment—"

"Go ahead," boomed Ron Goneen. "That would be your smallest crime. For you are about to murder mankind—about to wreck the very universe!"

His narrowed eyes fell to the tiny, bright needle in Seru Gyroc's unwavering hand. He knew that its beam of pure positive electric flame could sear and destroy a human body in an instant. For some distracting ruse—

His long, tanned body suddenly tense, he peered at a tiny port above Seru's head. "A ship!" he cried. "It must be the *Silver Bird*, returned—and it is ramming the tower! I knew they would find a way! Look out!"

The bleak eyes flickered briefly aside, as he leaped. But they came back to him, cold and dark as the sky of Pyralonne, flaming with a mad determination, merciless.

At that moment, for the merest terrible instant—and the thing was to become a fantastic enigma, to haunt all his latter life with its mad dilemma—he thought that the ramming ship was no ruse. A cold, silvery projectile indeed was smashing into the tower!

But golden fire, jetting from the cruel, steady needle, struck him with an avalanche of agony. That brief insane impression was burned away. In a last frantic effort to reach Seru, he lurched forward against the merciless flame, crumpled—

## VI.

RON GONEEN was swimming through a void of terrible darkness. Far ahead of him, somewhere, were flickering gleams that seemed to mean warmth, life itself. Swimming, walking, flying, crawling, he struggled aways toward them. But they fled away, like mirages. A cold cloud of darkness followed after him, implacable in its alien sentience. At last, however, pursuing one gleam of mocking flame, he came up to it. He thrust his stiff arms about it, tried to warm himself. But the flame turned black before him. And somehow it drained the warmth from his body, so that he was fearfully cold.

Still, he somehow knew, the black flame was hot. But its heat was selfish, useless. It radiated no warm rays, but seared him instead with bitter cold and then danced away like a malicious, mocking being.

He groped toward another. But the pursuing darkness was becoming thicker; it began to press upon him like some heavy, viscid liquid. The numbing ache probed deeper into his bones.

He was freezing. The flame was there before him, but it gave no warmth.

The big space captain woke, then. He was lying, shivering, on the floor of the laboratory. His left shoulder was blistered. The cloth of his green tunic was still smoldering around the edges of a small hole, where the positron ray had struck.

But what was this cold in his bones?

A shadow passed over his face. He opened his eyes, sat up with a painful effort. Then he saw Seru Gyroc—and he shuddered to a cold shock of bewildered dread, as painful as the ray!

This was no longer the confident, black-haired, still-vigorous experimenter. It was an old, old man!

For Seru Gyroc: was stooped and shrunken. His pale hands trembled weakly. His white face was a lax, shriveled mask, deep-lined with some unutterable horror. His dark eyes, strangely hollowed and sunken and glazed, were the eyes of one who has looked into a forbidden, searing hell. And his long hair, so dark before, was now completely white.

His quivering hands tried vainly to help the injured man to stand.

"I'm sorry, Ron—so terribly sorry!" His gasping voice was thin, quavering, cracked. It was the voice of an old, a fearful, a shattered man. "I have been utterly, criminally wrong! Please—oh, please try to forgive me! I shot you down in utter madness!" And the dreadfully aged man dropped on his knees, sobbing.

THE SPACE CAPTAIN got stiffly and slowly to his feet, drew the haggard scientist up beside him. He looked fearfully at his own huge, scarred hands, saw with relief that they looked as young and powerful as ever.

"No, you escaped the main force of it," that broken quaver assured him. "You were lying behind the shields, and I think the positron shock partially immunized you."

"What happened?"

Bewilderedly, Ron's blue eyes swept the broken, twisted apparatus about the shattered metal pier. There was no trace of the silver bead or the beaker of water in which it had been suspended.

Still sobbing, the experimenter so strangely shattered and old was peering mutely, blankly, at his broken apparatus.

"The experiment!" urged Ron Goneen. "Did you try it?"

"I did," said that aged voice. "I finally got the projectors synchronized to generate the Omega Radiation in the silver ball. I stood here, watching—"

"And what happened?"

"At first," gasped the old man, "I thought it was successful. The ball turned black, as radiation and reflection ceased. The thermometer showed that the temperature of the water was falling, as its heat was absorbed."

His tangled white head shook sadly.

"Yes, for a moment I thought I had won the power of that old investigator's demon. I could make heat flow from the cold water into the hot globe, and refuse to let it return! But then—" His voice stopped, with a shudder of his emaciated frame.

"Then?"

"Then I felt it!" whispered Seru Gyroc. "The black globe became suddenly a cold and deadly eye. I felt the chill of it all through me—a horrible cold something, the deadly enemy of life itself!

"I was suddenly stricken, numb, all but helpless. Sweat of horror was on my face, and I felt suddenly that it would freeze—that that horrible globe was sucking the heat out of everything in the room. And then, Ron—"

THE THIN MAN flung himself against the space captain's shoulder, sobbing bitterly.

"Then I did it! I don't know why. I didn't know what I was doing. The globe had begun to shrink. Normally, it should have become larger, expanded with heat. But it was contracting—the utter reversal of nature!

"And still it was like an eye—a dead-black, hypnotic eye! There was life in it. Not the human sort of life, nor the soft we have found on any planet—but an alien, hostile other life.

"And that other life commanded me!

"I was trying to reach the switch. The thing that I did seemed as vague as a dream. I hardly knew that I had done it. The water in the beaker was now frozen to ice. Thick, white frost was crusting over the glass. The room was misty with particles of congealing ice. My fingers were so numb that I could hardly feel the key.

"But at last, with a frightful effort—still fighting the terrible pressure of that eye—I shut off the projectors. There was an explosion, a flash of blinding flame. The apparatus was smashed, as you see it. I was knocked senseless."

"An explosion, I see," said Ron Goneen. "But how?"

"The silver must have reached a temperature of many thousands of degrees," explained Seru. "It had drawn heat out of the water, out of all the room—out of our bodies, even. That concentrated energy was suddenly released, as the thermodynamic interchange resumed the direction of increasing entropy—"

Eagerly, then Ron Goneen seized his arm, shook him. "So it's all over?" Ron cried. "Finished? And no harm done, except the smashed equipment, and—" he voice stuck in his throat, as he looked at the bleached and shriveled form of the little scientist.

"I know that I am changed," whispered Seru. "I saw my reflection on the instruments."

"But you stopped it?" Ron Goneen went. "And the *Silver Bird* will be coming back! And we can take Lethara back, to see all the worlds at home—"

His voice choked again, at the increasing horror that glazed the sunken eyes of Seru Gyroc.

"What's the matter?" he gasped. "Didn't it—stop?"

The dreadful hollow eyes of the shattered man flickered toward a port. And Ron Goneen saw with a start of horror that the inner, insulating shutter had been slid aside, leaving only the transparent window.

The old man shook his strangely white head.

"That is what I did," he mumbled. "I opened the shutter—because that other life commanded it! I hardly remember doing it. Honestly, Ron—I was helpless, hypnotized! That strange, dead-black, freezing eye—"

Quivering to a cold shock, Ron Goneen opened his mouth and tried in vain to speak. His nerveless hand closed weakly on Seru's thin shoulder.

"No, Ron, it didn't stop," the old man quavered at last. "At first I didn't understand. But I think I see it now. When I broke the circuit, the accumulated Omega force poured out through that open shutter. It must have gone out in a spherical wave—its velocity almost infinite!"

Ron Goneen swallowed, wet his dry lips. "Then what—what will happen?"

Seru's dreadful eyes went back to the port. "Look outside!" he gasped.

## VII.

WALKING UNSTEADILY to the unshuttered port, the big space captain peered apprehensively out—upon a thing madder than his dream of horror.

The stark, immemorial mountains of Pyralonne were no longer utterly black. An eldritch, bluish radiation flickered about every jagged summit. And across the lifeless, frozen plains swept fantastic shapes like the phantoms of his dream—like the wraiths of black flame that had seared him with their cold.

He shuddered; their dread cold pierced him, even in the insulated tower.

"Do you see them?" the hollow, sepulchral voice of Seru Gyroc, behind him, was demanding. "The creatures of destruction, born already! The hordes of doom—cold spawn of the Omega Radiation!

"Can you feel their eyes of darkness, staring through your body—like the eye that commanded me? Can you feel their fingers reaching to destroy us? Fingers of cold flame!"

"Yes," Ron Goneen whispered hoarsely. "Yes, I feel them. But what are they?"

"They are life—the new life!" spoke the hollow voice behind him. "With your warning, I should have foreseen—had I not been blind with egotism!

"For our kind of life is a phenomenon of entropy increase. These beings are an alien part of the opposite process. We have set energy to flowing up the hall—and they were born to ride the current! They suck up radiation, simple atoms, all forms of energy. They exist through integration: the building of complex atoms.

"They are vampires! They take; they give nothing. They are actually vortices of intense heat. But they only absorb; they radiate nothing, so that they seem black and cold to us. They drink up the precious force of life itself—"

"Look!" cut in the deep voice of Ron Goneen. "There's a ship—a strange, battered ship!"

His horror-widened eyes followed it, dropping out of the black sky athwart the weirdly blue-crowned crags of Pyralonne. Its hull was rusty, corroded, scarred as if by ten thousand meteoric collisions.

And it brought a disturbing memory.

"Queer!" he muttered. "But I thought—in the last instant before you shot—I thought there was a real ship ramming the tower!"

"And you fooled me!" the old man admitted. "For just an instant of helpless panic." And, bitterly, he added, "I wish something had struck us, to stop my madness—"

"But—there!" Ron Goneen's narrowed eyes were still upon the ancient space cruiser approaching. "It's out of control!" he gasped. "Falling—"

THE VESSEL sagged drunkenly. It veered unexpectedly toward the tower, so that Ron Goneen caught his breath for fear that singular feeling should prove to have been a premonition. But its mighty prow crashed against the weirdly gleaming plateau, two miles away. It rolled half over, very deliberately, and lay still.

Ron Goneen's breath went out in a long gasp of pain. "That—that's the *Silver Bird!*" he breathed hoarsely. "But look at it—battered as if it had been drifting ten thousand years. And it left here, three hours ago, shining like new!"

Behind him, the hollow voice croaked, "I have done this, also! For time has gone mad, along with entropy—because the one is the child of the other."

Still watching from the port, Ron Goneen's rugged face was grim and drawn with horror. For a valve of the fallen ship had opened. His eye caught the motion of tiny figures.

Could one of them be—his heart leaped with hope and fear—Lethara?

He groped for a pair of binoculars hanging beside the port, lifted them. The harsh landscape seemed to leap at him: naked, black rocks, every jagged point limned with pale-blue fire.

It was as if some electrical energy were being drawn out of the planet, he briefly thought, and sucked away into space.

He found the running figures. They were only a score in number—of the great ship's twelve hundred. Their leaping bodies were bulky in the space armor, heads visible in egg-shaped, transparent helmets. Every face was haggard, drawn, horror-twisted.

They were fleeing across that weirdly shining desert. And behind them, pursuing, came the shapes he had seen—the phantoms of black, freezing flame.

He saw one straggler fall behind. The spinning phantoms overtook him—or her, for Ron had failed to see. The figure stiffened, fell. Blue flame played briefly over it. It left the rocks, lifted into a whirling column of darkness. It was gone—consumed—

"The other life devours them," said the hollow voice of Seru Gyroc. "It absorbs their heat, consumes their lives. Integrates their atoms—"

Ron Goneen was suddenly rigid with hope and horror. For his staring eyes had found one familiar face, and then another—familiar still, although terrible with agonized dread.

"Lethara!" he gasped. "I see Lethara and her mother!"

The taller form of Karanora seemed weak, stumbling. The girl was aiding her. They were falling to the rear of the fugitive group.

Ron Goneen dropped the binoculars, ran toward the stair.

The lean, quivering fingers of Seru Gyroc clutched his tunic. "Wait!" the old voice quavered. "What are you doing?"

"I'm going to help them," gasped Ron Goneen. "Let me go. Lethara needs me!"

The thin fingers closed hard on his arm. "You can't live outside," warned Seru. "Your body heat will draw the other life—"

"I must," said Ron Goneen. "For Lethara—"

He broke free, stumbled down the steps toward the air lock. Swiftly, he flung himself into a suit of insulated pressure armor, slipped the transparent helmet over his head, let himself out of the valve into an explosive puff of freezing air.

THE dark, rocky waste stretched before him, every ragged point still shining with eerie and ominous blue. Far in the distance he saw the little group, each frantic figure outlined in a terrible aura.

He came shuddering against a strange wall of cold. Despite the insulation of the suit, he felt as if chilling fingers had reached through to probe his body.

This was the same piercing cold he felt in the dream.

Fighting it, he ran toward the distant group. They still fled before the black phantoms. One and another, as he watched, stiffened and fell—and the things swept down upon them, lifted and consumed their bodies.

Not half the original score were left when he plunged into a depression that was a vale of shining horror, a cup of cold, blue dread.

Panting, breathless, sweat-drenched and yet shivering, he mounted the burning slope beyond. Cold fear smote him. Only three of the fugitives were left. And one of them, as he looked, grew stiff and fell.

For a moment it lay still, the core of a blue shimmer. Then a tentacle of spinning blackness touched it: it whirled upward like a leaf in the wind: it was gone.

Ron Goneen stumbled onward, toward the two.

They saw him. One of them beckoned in wild appeal for aid. The other made a frantic gesture as if to warn him to go back.

Then he could see their faces, through the blue glow surrounding their helmets. They were Karanora and Lethara. The girl was still aiding her mother. It was she who had beckoned him back.

The mother suddenly stiffened, as the others had done, and fell. With another frantic, warning gesture at Ron Goneen, the girl bent over her, tried in vain to lift her.

Staggering, his body stiff and leaden with penetrating cold, Ron Goneen came up to them. The once lovely form of Karanora Quane lay stiff upon the shining rocks. Her face was already blue and lifeless, a frozen mask of horror unutterable.

Anxiously, the younger woman touched the arm of his suit. "Oh, Ron!" she cried. "My mother! Help my mother!" Her own face was pinched and white with cold, her violet eyes wide and strange with uncomprehending dread.

"It's too late," Ron Goneen gasped into the tiny microphone before his half-frozen lips. "Karanora is dead—and there's just the barest chance for us! Come—"

But she tried with her feeble strength to push him away. "Then go back," she begged. "Save yourself, Ron! I'm too weak to go any farther—too cold!"

He held her unwilling arm, pulled her toward the tower at a stumbling run.

BUT his stiff body ran like an ill-oiled machine. Every step took an age of effort. He ached with fatigue, with the queer, numbing pain of this penetrating cold. The blue flame was denser about him.

He fastened his dimming eyes upon the black tower. Squat

and immense, it seemed an infinite distance across the shining waste.

"Go on, Ron," the girl was sobbing. "Leave me. It was brave of you to come. But it was no use. Death is in me, already. The black, freezing flames— They sucked out something. Leave me, Ron. Just remember that—I loved you!"

Her hand went rigid in the insulated glove. She fell.

Ron Goneen bent, picked her up in his great, numb arms and ran on. All his body was dead now. It seemed that it was not he who moved, but some lifeless machine—that he merely watched.

The machine stumbled and fell. It picked itself up, lifted the girl, staggered on.

Behind came whirling black pillars of darkness; vampires hungry for the little heat left in the machine, for the atoms that formed it.

Again the machine toppled forward. This time it could not rise. It pushed stiffly forward on hands and knees, dragging the stiffened body of the girl.

The black base of the tower was near, the square entrance of the air lock outlined with glowing blue. Warmth! And a haven from the destroying phantoms!

Struggling grimly for mastery of the dead machine, Ron Goneen felt suddenly the tiny pressure of a little round object, under his tunic—the singular bubble of light that he called the Jewel of Dawn: the luminescent holy stone of the Andromedans, that he had taken for a torch, had carried since as a badge of triumph. No, carrying the jewel, he couldn't give up!

The leaden limbs moved stiffly. The machine inched forward, dragging the girl. And at last they were inside the black, square chamber. Darkness came again, as his fingers closed over the control wheel.

VIII.

WHEN Ron Goneen awoke—or came slowly back to a drugged half wakeness—he lay in the dark cubical space of the air lock. And Lethara was still inert beside him, very quiet in her bulky armor.

The inner valve had been opened, however. The air about them was not bitterly cold. And their transparent helmets had been removed so that they could breathe it.

Wondering how long he had lain unconscious, the space captain sat up painfully. His big body was still cold and stiff, and a leaden depression filled his mind. He shook his shaggy head, tried to rouse Lethara.

The girl would not completely wake, however, although she stirred uneasily and called his name in a low, half-eager, half-anguished tone.

He got awkwardly out of his own space armor, removed hers, and carried her in his arms up to the living quarters on the second floor of the tower. Still she slept, as he laid her in a bunk. Her oval face looked thin and pale.

He returned to pull the covers up about her shoulders, touched her pale-golden hair, and then hurried away to find her father, his bewildered mind full of this dread enigma.

Seru Gyroc was wearily pacing the wrecked laboratory above, running shivering fingers through his strangely bleached hair. His shriveled, haggard face, his glazed and sunken eyes, made a living mask of horror and despair. He started nervously.

"Ron, this is you?"

"It is!" The deep voice tried to sound cheerful. "I carried in Lethara. She is sleeping. I think she's all right. But Karanora—" Ron spoke gently. "I couldn't help her."

The white head shook wearily.

"It makes no difference, about anybody," whispered Seru. "Doesn't matter—dead or alive—"

"But it does matter!" boomed Ron Goneen. "We'll keep alive—somehow. We've got to keep her alive. The ship is wrecked, of course. But there's a life tube here in the tower. We'll manage to get back to the galaxy. We can do it—somehow!"

A ghastly, stricken figure, Seru Gyroc came unsteadily to stand in front of him and peer into his face with terrible hollow eyes.

"Don't you realize, Ron? When I opened that shutter and stopped the apparatus. I turned something out—something that hasn't stopped."

Ron Goneen gripped Gyroc's thin shoulder with huge, anxious fingers. "There's no way to stop it?"

"None. The Omega Ray went out faster than light! Faster than time—because it destroyed the meaning of time!" The white head shook. "There is nothing we can do, although the insulation of the tower will probably preserve our lives for a while—a little while."

Ron Goneen searched his terrible face.

"How far will it go?"

"To the bounds of the universe—growing ever stronger! Because, like the force of cosmical repulsion, its effect varies directly with distance."

Ron Goneen dropped his big hand and staggered back. "Then all," he whispered, "all the galaxy—all humanity is—"

Great tears shone in the hollow eyes of Seru Gyroc. "All humanity," his dry voice rasped, "all our cities, all our planets—" His silver head bowed. "What happened to the *Silver Bird* and those aboard has happened everywhere—"

"Has happened?" gasped the space captain.

The stricken scientist nodded. "Sooner, probably, in the most distant galaxies than in our own," he whispered. "Probably"—he swallowed with an effort, and went on in a dry, leaden tone—"there is not a human being left alive, save us in this tower!"

Trembling, his thin hand pointed, at an unshuttered port.

"Look!" he quavered. "Look at the sky! You can see—already—"

RON GONEEN swayed to the tiny port, put his face to its heavy lens. Against the darkness above a ragged wall of blue-crowned summits, he could see the galaxy, a long spindle of silver spanning many degrees.

But it had changed! It was changing, incredibly, as he looked! The spinning rotation of its spiral arms was visible. In a second he saw the normal motion of a thousand centuries! And it was reversed, turning backward!

"What is it?" he gasped breathlessly. "What is happening?"

That terrible voice behind him croaked again, "Look at Andromeda! Look at the rest! Our galaxy, being nearest, was the last to change—"

Ron Goneen staggered across the wrecked laboratory, pushed aside the shutter from another port. He saw that the Andromeda Galaxy was also visible in its motion, and turning backward.

And it was shrunken!

The spiral arms were drawing in. And its silvery glow had darkened to an eerie, bluish hue, like the luminescence that covered the frozen rocks of this stark world.

"Beyond!" quavered Seru Gyroc. "The rest!"

He thrust a pair of powerful binoculars into Ron's stiff hands. Peering through them into the dark chasm of the empty sky, the space captain saw myriads of spinning, bluish motes, all rushing toward him, all shrinking and growing dark as they came.

"What is it, Seru?" he demanded again. "I knew that there was some danger—but I can hardly understand why—"

"Space itself is contracting," echoed that doomed voice. "All stellar and galactic motions have been reversed. The nebulæ are contracting in the direction of their original condensations. Their radiation is being drawn back, absorbed, reintegrated into heavy atoms."

"But how can we see it?" Ron Goneen demanded. "This light by which we see them was emanated a million or a hundred million years before the experiment was begun!"

The scientist shook his haggard white head.

"Time and the words, 'before' and 'after' no longer have a meaning—except for events that take place in this insulated tower. For time is only our consciousness of the continual increase of entropy, a measure of the running down of the universe. And entropy—except in here—is nowhere increasing."

Ron Goneen stared out again. The blue glow, he thought, was fading from the rocks; the blue, spinning motes of doomed galaxies were fainter in the sky.

"It will soon be dark," Ron whispered, hoarsely. "Everything—gone—" He closed the shutter upon the mind-staggering doom without. Swaying heavily, like a man dead drunk, he stared at Seru Gyroc. His hoarse voice asked faintly, "And what will be—the end?"

THE stricken scientist had resumed his weary, aimless pacing. His thin, quavering reply came in disjointed fragments, "We set the current of entropy to flowing backward. No stopping it— The universe is winding up again. All matter will be condensed again into a single superatom. Even this in the tower, after the insulation fails. Our bodies—

"No energy is ever created, ever destroyed. But we have undone all the work of time. Perhaps, eventually, the balance will be turned again—although not, I think, without the intervention of intelligence. The other life may do it—

"And the superatom will disintegrate again—disperse its matter through a space once more expanding, in galaxies, suns, planets. The river of entropy will flow down the hill again—"

Ron Goneen lurched forward protestingly.

"So man many be born again!" he muttered bitterly. "If the word 'again' has any meaning when time has been destroyed! He may again conquer the galaxy, and again attempt to master entropy, and again destroy himself and—"

His narrowed blue eyes, savage and brooding, stared at Seru. Gyroc. "Tell me, my old teacher!" he demanded hoarsely. "Is that cycle of birth and struggle and doom, of birth and struggle and doom, of winding up and running down, of eternal, senseless repetition—is that less horrible than the single, inevitable death that might not have come for a billion billion years?"

The thin man stopped his restless pacing, bowed his bleached head. "It is more horrible," he whispered. "It is infinitely more horrible. You were right, Ron, from the beginning. And I was a fool, an insane egomaniac. Your words were the truth. I have murdered mankind!"

His stricken voice sank. "I have murdered the universe!"

## IX.

RON GONEEN slept for a long time, but not without dreams.

He thought that the armored tower, containing himself, Seru Gyroc and Lethara, was somehow cast loose from desolate Pyralonne. He thought that it was spinning end over end, forever, through an illimitable, starless chasm of frigid darkness. He thought that vampire hordes followed it—spinning, shapeless shadows of black flame, that sought to enter, to suck away their warmth, their lives, their bodies.

When at last he awoke—lying still dressed on the couch where he had flung himself when he came down from the laboratory, exhausted with fatigue and cold and the horror of universal doom—his body still had a dull, leaden numbness. He felt a lingering, vague nausea, as if that vertiginous dream had been half reality.

"Ron, dear, you are—are well?"

He sat up with a start of eager joy, for it was Lethara's soft voice. She was standing beside his couch, with a tray of steaming food.

"Oh, my darling—"

The eager greeting stopped in his throat. For his clearing eyes had seen her face. For a shocked, bewildered moment she seemed a terrible stranger. Like her father, the girl had been—changed!

She was thinner. Her oval face was haggard, and it had an ominous bluish cast. Her lips were pale and dry. Her violet eyes were darker than they had been, and hollow. They were wide pools of horror nameless and unutterable. And her wavy golden hair had turned, like her father's, completely white.

Ron Goneen lightly touched her hand, tried to conceal the shock on his face. He tried to make his deep voice gay. "How is the most beautiful woman?"

She shook her white head, with no answering smile. "Father has told me I am the only woman," she said. "Therefore, I must try to live—though I can feel the cold of death still in me.

"But do not say that I am beautiful. I know that I am changed. And I saw the dread in your eyes—"

"Nonsense, my darling!" He took the tray out of her quavering hands, set it down, and gathered her in his arms. He kissed her, and her lips were very cold. "I know you had a terrible experience outside," he told her softly. "But you will get over it. You must! It means so much—"

"I know," her dry voice said dully. "And I'll try, because it means so much for the race to go on—"

He held her cold, trembling body closer to him. "Because it means so much for you to go on, my darling! You must get well, and laugh again. You must forget—"

"I can never forget," she said solemnly. "And I feel that something is dead in me—forever!" She clung to him for a moment, with a desperate, shuddering strength, and then pushed out of his arms. "You must eat, and then my father wants you in the laboratory." She pushed the tray toward him.

"It was good of you to bring it," he said. "But you must take care of yourself. Have you eaten?"

"I couldn't," she said. "I wasn't hungry."

He picked her up in his great arms, carried her, laughingly protesting to her own bed, and made her lie down while he fixed her a hot drink. When she had sipped a part of it, he left her and climbed back to the room beneath the dome.

THE THIN, shattered frame of Seru Gyroc was still pacing its endless, tortured circuit about the wrecked apparatus. His whitened hair was wildly tangled, his hollow eyes red for want of rest.

"There's no way?" Ron Goneen greeted him heavily. "No possible way?" His mighty, bronzed body stiffened suddenly; his scarred fists clenched. "We must find a way, Seru—for Lethara's sake!"

The bleached head nodded. "I know. For the sake of mankind—"

"And for her own sake." The space captain's deep voice was low and solemn. "She is very ill, Seru. Those things of black fire came too near her. It's too dark for her here—too cold! She needs the warm air and bright sunlight of a young, living world."

"This universe is dead, Seru. Life—our kind of life—has become an anomaly since entropy is reversed. And she feels the death. Perhaps it is the other life creeping into her!"

"We must escape—and very soon!"

"If we could escape!" quavered the hollow voice of the stricken scientist "But there is nowhere to go. The Omega wave has spread ruin to the limits of our universe. There may be others: my mathematics indicates that probability. But even if other closed space-time continua exists, we have no gate, no key—" His thin shoulders shrugged hopelessly; he resumed the aimless walking.

Ron Goneen stood for a little time silent, staring at the scientist, his red-bearded face grimly desperate. His great hand reached slowly, absently, into his tunic, and brought out a half-inch bubble of silvery light.

"I wonder—" his deep voice grated huskily. "You say there could be—another universe?"

He tossed the shimmering droplet on his palm, caught it and tossed it again. His narrowed eyes stared down at it. Seru Gyroc stalked wearily by him, making no answer.

"I call this the Jewel of Dawn," his deep voice rumbled. "It was the most sacred object of the Andromedans. They had told us something of it, before the massacre—"

"Eh?" Sera Gyroc had halted, suddenly listening.

"It was the heart of their barbaric religion," said Ron Goneen. "They held that it was itself another universe—or at least the door to one. They believed that one day, when they had reached a certain level of perfection, all their race would be allowed to migrate into it.

"I shouldn't have taken it," he added, "but for their treacherous murder of half my men, and because I thought that carrying it would give us some protection.'"

"What is it? Not just a pearl?"

"No," said Ron Goneen. "It is harder, more perfectly round; and it emanates a soft, steady light. I've never seen anything like it on any planet. I've never attempted to analyze it, because I didn't want to destroy it."

The dark, hollow eyes of Seru Gyroc were suddenly flaming. "Hard?" he whispered eagerly. "Perfect? Constant luminescence without excitation?" Trembling, his thin hand grasped for it. "It's just possible— The theory of interpenetrating space time manifolds—"

He dropped the jewel, fell on his knees to scramble for it furiously. Ron Goneen caught up its shimmer as it rolled away, returned it to him.

"—just possible," he breathed, "that the Andromedans were right!"

## X.

AS THE OLD MAN worked with trembling hands and feverish eyes at his tests upon the jewel, Ron Goneen again opened one of the shuttered ports to look from the laboratory tower.

All was darkness now. The last bluish ghosts of the contracting nebulæ had vanished. The bleak, frigid landscape of Pyralonne, if still beneath them, had lost its eerie radiance. The black phantoms ruled supreme.

He shuddered, slammed the shutter. His senses reeled from the shock of an alien other being, without. Black tentacles of freezing flame, he knew, had sought to reach him through the port.

Numb again, trembling to a sense of overwhelming dread, he went back down the stair to where he had left Lethara sleeping. She lay very still. Her thin face, framed in her silver-white hair, looked terribly bleak and cold.

She shuddered in her sleep, as he watched. The leaden shadow of horror fell heavily on her face. Her pale lips parted, and out of them came a dry, gasping sob of utter fear.

"My poor, poor darling," whispered Ron Goneen.

He went softly to her, smoothed her cold forehead with his palm, and took her cold, blue hand in his. The tiny, frightened ghost of a smile came then to her sleeping lips, and her hand clung to his fingers.

He left her sleeping more easily, and returned anxiously to the laboratory, where Seru Gyroc was still working feverishly over the stone from Andromeda.

"Well," he gasped. "What have you found?"

"Very strange!" the old scientist quavered. "Perdurable. No wonder the Andromedans worshiped it! Its hardness seems perfect. Nothing will scratch it. X ray and electron diffraction patterns reveal no crystalline molecular structure—no molecules at all. Its surface is a perfect mirror; no radiation will penetrate it. It is not affected by the cold of liquid hydrogen or the heat of the atomic furnace. It is not a conductor of electricity, nor permeable by a magnetic field."

"Then," demanded Ron Goneen, "what is it?"

"There is one possible explanation," the old man said: "that the Andromedans were right! The negative result of all my experiments can mean only that it is walled off from our space—that it exists in its own closed continuum!"

"Another space?" Ron Goneen gasped eagerly. "Then is it possible—by any means at all—for us to enter it? To escape?"

The old man shook his head.

"Hardly. The existence of a universe of such dimensions is mathematically conceivable. Our own will doubtless contract to such a size, or smaller, since the reversal of entropy. If," he added, "one may speak of the size of one universe in the scale of another!"

Again, he shook his head.

"But each galaxy in such a universe would be no larger than one of the atoms of our bodies. How, then, could we enter it? Still," he suddenly interrupted himself, "there is the Kardishon Effect! Contraction of size is theoretically possible, through electronic acceleration and energy compensation along the time axis."

WEARILY, he shrugged.

"But actually, with our limited time—for the tower will not protect us much longer, before the insulation fails—or before we are crushed by the contraction of space outside—"

"You are the galaxy's best scientist," Ron Goneen urged him. "You are working to save mankind! You must try—"

"Yes," the old man said soberly. "We must try to save the seed of mankind from the horror that I have wrought." He, gulped. "Yes, we must try— But even if we could master the Kardishon Effect," he objected, "we should require a complete ship, able to navigate empty space.

"We have one of the *Silver Bird's* life tubes here in the tower," Ron Goneen reminded him. "It is supplied and equipped to voyage two hundred thousand light years. If we could install size-changing apparatus aboard it—"

Seru's red, hollow eyes were staring at him, with a new light in them. "There is a possibility—" he breathed huskily. "The barest possibility! The apparatus would consist of the Kardishon oscillator, transformers and field coils. The installation would be difficult."

"I'm a fair technician," said Ron Goneen. "Let's get to work!"

"I can design the field coils," Seru yielded, "and you can be installing them. But it will all be useless," he warned, "unless I can solve the problem that floored Kardishon, in the oscillator. For all the matter that he tried to contract began to disintegrate, because the shrinking atoms became unstable." He shook his head. "I don't know—"

"We'll try, anyhow!" said Ron Goneen.

"Until we die."

The haggard scientist turned to a workbench, and began to sketch plans for the coils that were to take form under the unsuspected expertness of Ron Goneen's big hands.

The life tube, seated into a rectangular chamber in the base of the tower, was a small craft, not a hundred feet in length. Lethara—when at last she awoke and came down to where Ron was desperately at work wiring up the new coils—named it the *Life of Man.*

She seemed ill and depressed. Ron Goneen paused to fix food, which she could not eat, and made her lie down again, she was unwilling to leave him to go back above.

The two men labored on almost without pause for food or rest. The big space captain knew that time was becoming very short. For into the tower was seeping a penetrating cold, a chill of half-tangible horror, that defied all their lights and heaters.

And a time came when Ron's task was almost done. He was

inspecting the last connections, and Seru was still up in the laboratory, at work on the vital oscillator, when he heard Lethara scream.

He ran back to her little cabin, amidships, and found her sitting bolt upright in her bunk.

Her eyes were wide black pools of horror, her face ashen. Her dry voice was sobbing: "They've broken in! The others—the things of black fire! I can feel them. They have come for us. They want our warmth, our lives, our bodies. We must go, Ron! Go—"

He was trying to soothe her.

"We can't go quite yet," he told her. "The Kardishon apparatus isn't finished or tested—"

"Oh-h-h-h!" her thin, agonized scream cut in. "They've got my father, Ron—"

Her voice rose on his name to a shuddering wail of utter horror. She stiffened. Her skin queerily blue, she fell rigidly back on the couch.

Trembling to a sick chill, Ron Goneen knew that the other life, indeed, had entered the tower. And to his ears came the stricken shriek of Seru Gyroc—trapped outside the vessel!

## XI.

RON GONEEN left the girl an ran to the air lock of the little vessel. A wall of bitter cold met him. The air in the long, chamber glittered with crystals of frost. White rime was forming on the walls.

And his spine tingled to a chill more deadly than cold—to the instinctive, overwhelming dread of an alien presence: the other life of the reversed universe!

Numbed and sickened, still he didn't hesitate. Seru, he knew, had been on the floor above, finishing, the precious oscillator. Catching a deep breath, he plunged into that sea of frozen menace, ran up the steps toward the dome.

The invader, he knew suddenly, was in the laboratory. For a terrible, shrinking dread increased in him, until it took gritted teeth and all his will to mount each successive step.

A strange darkness filled the room beneath the dome, when at last he fought his way in. The lamps still shone, but their radiance had contracted to little feeble moons, outlined with ghostly blue.

Stumbling forward through that thick, frigid barrier of dark, Ron Goneen found the scientist sprawled on the floor. His stiffened body was shrouded in a dreadful aura of shimmering blue. Clutched in his lifeless fingers was the tiny, bright tube of the vital oscillator.

Ron Goneen picked up the rigid form. Before he could move with it, however, something came toward him out of that dense darkness. It was dark also, shapeless. It was nothing that he could see; it made no sound—yet he was horribly aware of it.

Numb and stiff, he reeled back from it. Carrying Seru, he staggered back down the stair and into the silvered hull of the *Life of Man*. Gasping with relief, he closed the valves.

The scientist was still living, although pinched and blue with cold. His face was a mask of strain and horror, his pulse very slow and weak. Ron Goneen covered him up in a bunk, then hastened to the generator room to install the oscillator.

As he finished the task, some little sound made him look up, and he voiced an involuntary cry of startled apprehension. For Seru Gyroc stood swaying before him, a very specter of dread. His white hair was loose and wild, his shrunken body bloodless and violently trembling. His dark eyes were dilated and glazed with uttermost dread.

"We must hasten, Ron," the thin voice rasped from his fear-dried throat. "There is no time for any test. They are seeking now to enter the ship. We must try it, to escape—or perish!"

RON GONEEN led the way to the tiny bridge. It was bitterly cold, even within the vessel. And the strange, thick darkness had come into the chamber outside. The lamps were gone. He could just distinguish the dim, silvery sphere of the Jewel of Dawn, which he had laid ready on the bench across the end of the chamber.

He remembered its shimmering beauty, which he had rolled so often in his palm. Could it be actually a minute universe, complete, a haven for a new mankind? That seemed incredible, but still—

"Start it!" gasped Seru. "Now—or they might take the jewel! Now! To freedom—or death!"

The space captain touched a key. The atomic generators responded with a soft humming; the meters indicated that half their output was flowing into the Kardishon oscillator.

But he felt nothing, no change of size. He shook his red, shaggy head at Seru Gyroc. "Nothing," he whispered. "I guess we've failed—"

"No. There's no disintegration." Then the other's cracked voice was suddenly sharp with excitement. "Look! The walls—"

Ron Goneen peered through the observation ports. The walls of the sealed chamber had become visible again, shining very palely with a familiar, eerie blueness. They seemed very far away—still receding.

"The room seems larger!" he cried. "No—of course, it is we who are smaller!"

"One way of putting it is as true as the other," said Seru, "remembering the relativity of size."

"But it worked—it really worked!" the space captain rumbled eagerly. "We didn't disintegrate! We're safe!"

"We're growing smaller," admitted the little scientist. "But we aren't saved yet! First, we don't know that the Kardishon Effect can be carried on infinitely. Second, we don't know that we can actually enter the smaller universe. We may be lost outside it! Third, there is no assurance that its planets—if it is a universe and has planets—will satisfy the conditions of human life."

Steadily, as he spoke, the bluish walls receded. Their hue changed to a dull, sinister red, and then was lost in darkness—through a relative change in the wave length of light.

Only the gem from Andromeda remained visible: an expanding bubble, always shining with the same silvery white, floating in a chasm of darkness.

"Better keep near it," warned Seru, "or we'll be lost in size. Our old inches are growing into light years!"

The big space captain started the kappa-field drive. The diminishing vessel lifted from the now invisible floor—lifted upon the strange, interminable voyage from universe to universe. The silvery sphere hung in black and utter emptiness, always growing. Steadily, he drove the *Life of Man* toward its surface. And steadily grew the intervening space, so that the voyage began to seem like a fantastic flight to nowhere.

MANY HOURS, Ron Goneen was thinking, had already passed on that uncanny flight—when it came to him that time, as well as space and size, had its meaning strangely twisted on such a voyage as this.

He left the controls with Seru, after the old man had rested, and went to look after Lethara. He found her awake again, lying quietly in her bunk. Some of the horror had gone out of her eyes, but she seemed very pale and tired.

He tried to put a little cheer in her.

"We're voyaging to another world, my darling!" he whispered. "When you see the light of a sun, and smell the clean air of some warm, blue sea, and watch green cover the hills of a new planet in spring—just wait and see how good you'll feel!"

Her white head shook weakly on the pillow. "Ron, my dear," she breathed, "you don't understand. I tried to live—but I'm too old. Somehow the other life made me old. I'm older than any human being ever was! And I desire nothing but rest. Kiss me, and let me sleep—"

He kissed her lips, and they seemed icy cold again.

The haggard, gaunt form of Seru Gyroc, when he returned to the bridge, stood rigid before the instruments.

"We are near the crucial point," he said. "We must break through the shell while we are yet relatively large—while there is power enough. The kappa lines interact with the geodesics of the other universe. We must make he field strong enough, to merge them. Speed, up the generators!"

Still the *Life of Man* plunged through uttermost darkness toward the silvery bubble—which now had become infinitely huge, so that its surface was like an illimitable flat mirror.

Ron Goneen increased the power of the generators, until their soft humming became an ear-piercing whine. The vessel leaped forward, toward that mirror film. And it bent before them, yielding like an elastic sheet.

"More power!" cried Seru. "And hold fast! There must be a shift of dimensional axes. We see now only a three-dimensional section of the other universe. The merging world lines must rotate our fourth axis into it!"

Grimly, Ron Goneen pushed the control lever forward all the way. The tiny ship shuddered and rang to the vibration. His feet stung on the deck. He felt a sudden, apprehension for Lethara and—

Then that yielding elastic film seemed to snap toward him—and it was gone! At the same instant the ship lurched queerly, in some direction that was neither to right nor left, up nor down.

Giddy from that unexpected, oddly disquieting lurch, he clung to a hand rail, peering bewilderedly about for that shining barrier. It was not behind them. It was nowhere.

And the vessel was plunging, with generators screaming at full power, through a featureless void of utter darkness. He groped hastily for the control levers, shut them down to cruising speed.

"So we're through?" he gasped incredulously. "We're in the other universe? And nothing to do but find a nice friendly galactic system, and a good solid planet of the right chemical order?

"I must go tell Lethara—"

THE space captain's eager voice stopped suddenly, with a little gasp of apprehension. For Seru Gyroc had made no reply. His eyes were lifted to the twin lenses of a compact binocular telescope.

Ron Goneen bent to gaze into Seru's haggard face, saw it etched with new despair. Fearfully, Ron demanded, "What is it, Seru?"

Still the scientist made no response, except for a weary hopeless little jerk of his white head.

Anxiously, Ron Goneen peered through another port. "Why is it so dark?" his husky whisper rasped. "The thermometers show almost absolute zero. Why? Why are there no stars, no galaxies—anywhere?"

His big hand seized Seru Gyroc's thin shoulder, spun him away from the telescope. "Tell me!" he demanded. "Is it because we are yet too large to see!"

"No," came the dry, weary breath. "We are small enough. But we have failed." His white head shook very slowly. "We should have expected it, from the relativity of time. For time obviously must have flowed much faster in this tiny universe—so long as it had any time!"

The space captain's big body sagged wearily back against the bulkhead. "Time—" his dry lips said soundlessly. "Too late—"

"Too late," quavered Seru, "by a billion, billion years. This universe has reached the fate from which the Omega Effect experiment was designed to save our own. It has run down. It has reached a state of thermodynamic equilibrium, a state of maximum entropy.

"Its stars have all been disintegrated into energy. And the energy has wasted itself, in ever-longer, ever-weaker waves, though an infinitely expanding space. Its smallness, after all, was only in our own perspective."

He sighed again, hopelessly.

"No, this universe is what it looks—frozen, dark, dead. There is no longer any change, not will there ever be, unless the conditions of energy probability happen to be reversed. Even time, determined by the arrow of entropy, has ceased to flow."

Ron Goneen's blue eyes, dull and bloodshot, stared wearily out into empty, boundless darkness.

"So we have failed," he whispered. "Failed Lethara—"

"That is so." The old scientist nodded. "We have come from one extreme to the other. We can drive the ship onward until our fuel is gone—until we perish of old age—and never meet anything but darkness and cold and changeless death."

Beside him, then, Ron Goneen went suddenly tense. "But look!" he gasped. "I saw— I saw—" He leaped to the oculars of the powerful little telescope.

## XII.

BREATHLESSLY trembling, too fearful to let himself hope, the big space captain stood with his eyes fastened to the lenses. Using the full aperture of the instrument, he searched the void ahead. For a long time he saw only cold, black emptiness.

Then, it came again: a gleam of purple light! It was infinitely tiny, infinitely remote, infinitely brief—like the flash of a single, bombarded atom he thought, in the spinthariscope.

Tugging vainly at his mighty arm, Seru Gyroc was demanding, "What is it? What do you see?"

"Wait!" Ron Goneen was still peering intently. "It seemed so faint. I can't be sure!"

Another cruel eternity of darkness—and then it winked again!

"It is a light!" he cried eagerly. "A tiny flashing light!"

Seru Gyroc ran startled fingers through his strangely whitened hair. "That is very singular!" he whispered. "A light in this universe that seemed so dead! What could have kept alive, against the current of entropy, so long?"

"There it is again!" called Ron Goneen from the telescope. "A purple spark that winks like a signal beacon!" He moved suddenly toward the controls. "I'm going to set the ship toward it. We'll find out what it is."

"Caution!" The old man's trembling fingers closed on his big shoulder.

"No natural phenomenon could have survived to cause the intermittent emanation of light in a universe so old as this. That flashing represents intelligence—intelligence that has endured for æons beyond conception!" His cracked voice was hoarse with awe.

"To have survived at all, when all else is dead, it must be supremely great. And it must have survived by defending itself. It may destroy us!"

The space captain shook his shaggy, reddish head. "No risk is too great now. For we have nothing to lose—no other hope. And there is everything to gain! A haven where Lethara can recover, a home for the race to come—" His big fingers dropped to the dials.

"If that intelligence is so great, perhaps it is great enough to share its knowledge. I believe that the signal was meant for a welcome and a guide."

"Or a trap," said Seru. "But go ahead. As you say, there is nothing else."

Ron Goneen lifted and swung the prow until that flashing atom of purple fire was dead ahead. When they were driving toward it, he left Seru at the controls and went back to the galley to prepare a tray for Lethara.

She was sleeping when he entered her cabin. His light step roused her, however, and she called to him before he could withdraw.

"Ron!" her voice was feeble, yet deep with an indwelling dread. "Ron—please come and hold my hand. I had such a fearful dream!"

He set the tray down beside her.

"Here my darling. Drink this. It will make you warm. And forget your dream."

"But I can't forget it!" Huge and dark with abiding terror, her violet eyes fixed on his face. "It was too real to forget. It was more real than you are, standing here beside me."

Her thin body shuddered on the couch; the dilated eyes stared away, as if at some ghastly thing beyond the walls.

"Hold my hand, Ron!" she whispered. "I don't want to leave

you. Hold it tight!"

Her haggard face smiled a little, at the pressure of his fingers. Her great eyes stared up into his face, suddenly serene and calm, with the enigmatic simplicity of a child's.

"I thought in the dream that I was dead," she said. "And the *Life of Man* came down out of dark space, upon some cold, dead planet. You and my father dug a grave in its frozen rocks, laid me in it, and filled the grave. You took the name plaque from the ship and left it at the end of the mound, under that starless sky. And you went away. And I was dead and alone in that world of death, forever—"

Her husky whisper died away. Her thin, cold fingers, which had tightened in a grip almost convulsive, slowly relaxed. Her great, dark eyes closed, and her pale body lay motionless.

Ron Goneen leaned over her, frightened. "Lethara?" he breathed. "My darling—"

Her eyes opened, then. She smiled at him wanly. He sat beside her, holding her cool fingers in a grasp almost fearful, until she had gone quietly to sleep again.

"RON!" the thin voice of Seru Gyroc quavered through the speaker system. "You had better come back to the bridge."

He slipped away from the girl—still smiling faintly in her sleep—and hurried forward, demanding, "We are near?"

"The photometers show that the brightness of the flashes has increased four hundred times," the old scientist reported. "Which means, by the inverse square law, that we have come nineteen twentieths of the distance."

Ron Goneen was peering with narrowed blue eyes through a port, when the strange beacon—if it were a beacon—ceased its blinking and became a steady purple point.

"See it!" whispered Seru. "That shows intelligence—aware of our approach!"

The big space captain towered alert at the controls. The solitary star became swiftly bright, and he decreased their speed accordingly. Still it was but a tiny, burning atom, alone in a gulf of empty blackness.

"We are near," Seru announced from the photometer. "A few miles more and—"

Eyes now against the oculars of the telescope, Ron Goneen watch the beckoning point. Slowly, it expanded to a tiny, reddish-purple moon. Dimly, at last, he could see its light cast on other objects.

"A great black sphere!" he rumbled. "Like a tiny, armored planet— The beacon is on a metal tower!"

"Armored!" Seru caught up the word. "Yes, it must be armored—against the loss of heat! For available energy is very precious here—even the stored energy of matter itself! Do you see any entrance?"

The *Life of Man* still slipped toward the light. Ron Goneen studied that black, armored ball. Several miles in diameter, it was yet tiny, he thought, to be the sole citadel of life in all a universe.

"No—yes!" His voice was suddenly tense and eager. "A slit is opening at the base of the tower—a great valve! A pale light is shining through."

"Some intelligence is opening it for us!" cried Seru. His hollow, bloodshot eyes darted sharply at the space captain. "It may be a trap!" he said. "Remember: the very matter of the ship and even of our bodies is precious, in this universe! Worth any crime—"

"I remember," said Ron Goneen, quietly. "But we shall enter. There is nothing else—"

Pale-white light, dimly reflected from the walls of the passage, showed the sphere to be of metal, not in reality black, but polished to a brilliant, silvery luster.

Now fully open, the mighty valve revealed a cylindrical well nearly a hundred feet in diameter. Without hesitation, Ron Goneen nosed the *Life of Man* gently into it.

"Strange to think," he said suddenly, "that all this is happening inside a half-inch jewel that I used to carry in my pocket!"

"But is it?" said Seru. "Remember our rotation of axes, and the relativity of size—" His cracked voice broke off, to gasp, suddenly, sharp with alarm, "But look! In the periscope—behind us!"

Ron peered into the tube, saw that the disk of blackness behind them was swiftly vanishing. The two halves of the great valve swung together as he watched, to for a solid wall of silvered metal.

"Trapped!" gasped Seru.

Ron Goneen's rugged, red-bearded face remained impassive. His steady fingers guided the little ship onward through the tube, toward another massive valve that closed the way ahead. Calmly, his deep voice rumbled, "We shall see."

## XIII.

AS THE big space captain's tanned fingers brought the *Life of Man* to a stop, a line suddenly cleft the metal wall ahead. The two halves slid ponderously black, to reveal another section of the silvered passage.

Again he sent the little vessel forward, until they were once more stopped by a third barrier. The substance of it was unfamiliar, dead-black, lusterless.

As they waited before it, Seru said, "Whatever intelligence may dwell here is well shielded, indeed, against the loss of energy. Otherwise it must have perished a billion years ago."

The black wall also divided, in its turn, and they glided through into the last section of the tube. In view beyond its mouth lay an extraordinary space: the hollow interior of the armored globe.

Fully a mile in diameter, as Ron, Goneen estimated, it was crowded with enormous enigmatic machines, nearly all of silver-white metal that was polished to mirrorlike perfection.

"The high polish conserves light and heat," commented Seru. "You perceive that the actual illumination is very feeble. Energy is precious here—so precious that I fear for our own!"

Conscious of some strange depression, Ron Goneen struggled to analyze it, as he sent the vessel gently ahead toward the circular opening of the passage. It came to him suddenly.

Turning to Seru with a little shudder, he said, "This place is queer—dead! There is no sound. There's no whir or throb of energy. Those big machines don't move; they haven't turned for a million years!"

But the old man shook his haggard white head. "No," he quavered, "the flashing of the beacon and the opening of the doors is evidence enough of life. There is simply no energy to waste on friction and vibration. Eh—"

He stopped with a gasp, and Ron Goneen reached abruptly for the controls. For the gently gliding craft had come abruptly to a halt.

"We've struck something!" Puzzled, Ron Goneen shook his red head. "Some invisible barrier across the opening—" His deep voice went suddenly tense. "But, look! There's something moving—coming toward us!"

Drifting across the pale silver intricacies of the giant machine, across the mazes of supporting girders, immense sealed rotors, and snakelike enigmas of armored cables, came the floating object. Anxiously, Ron Goneen turned the telescope upon it.

"It's almost a sphere," he reported excitedly. "Its a greenish, and patterned with strange convolutions. It's almost like—like a great brain! It is flying toward us through the air—if there is air—"

The approaching object passed through the unseen wall that had halted them, entered the passage.

"It has stopped outside the air lock!" Seru's voice, from the periscope, was shrill with anxious emotion. "Shall we go out to meet it? The risk—"

"It took a risk of its own, letting us in," said Ron Goneen. "Come!"

HE LOCKED the controls, ran back along the corridor toward the valves. Pausing a moment outside Lethara's cabin, he saw that she still slept quietly, the faintest ghost of a smile on her lips.

"I'll take my positron gun!" panted Seru. "In case it has planned to attack—"

"No," rumbled the space captain. "Leave the weapon."

In feverish, trembling haste, they helped each other into two of the bulky suits hooked to the wall, clamped on egg-shaped, transparent helmets. Ron's gloved hands reached for the valve wheel.

Seru caught at his arm, with a warning whisper, "Consider—"

"I have considered," said Ron Goneen. "We are helpless. Lethara is asleep—unwarned. But there is no other way."

His own great hands trembled in the insulated gloves, as they gripped the wheel. But they heavy outer valve slipped aside, and they stumbled fearfully out, toward the ridged, green mass of the thing waiting.

The little vessel had drifted against the silvered wall of the great passage. Almost weightless, here out of the ship's gravity field, they settled slowly to the shining floor. Their weary eyes stared apprehensively through the helmets.

The corrugated greenish mass—it was some three feet in diameter—approached them a little, hung motionless before them. Seru's bulging suit waddled back anxiously. Ron Goneen did not retreat, but his mighty body was rigid, beaded with sudden sweat. Unconsciously, he held his breath, and every muscle instinctively tensed for some effort of defense.

At last, however, when nothing happened, he turned to the old scientist with a little strained smile.

"See?" His awed voice spoke huskily into the little microphone before his lips. "It means no harm, Seru. It must have come to establish communication."

"Communication," quavered Seru's voice from the phones of the little ultra-wave radio set. "But tell me how! The alien heir of an alien universe! We can't just speak to it. Even if there were air enough to carry sound, it has no ears, no vocal organs. We don't even know how it senses us. It has no eyes that I can see. Ugh!"

His voice became a gasping cry. His gloved fingers clutched convulsively at Ron's bulging arm.

"Look at it!" his broken voice sobbed. "I warned you! I wanted to bring a weapon. Watch it—*change.*"

Ron Goneen stated silently through his helmet, open-mouthed, staggered.

For that rugged green mass had suddenly lost distinctness. Its surface dissolved into a greenish haze. And the cloud of haze narrowed, elongated, swiftly flowing into another shape. It became an upright pillar, nine feet tall. The pillar bifurcated into two supports; which touched the silvered floor. Twin appendages flowed out from its upper part.

THEN, suddenly, the haziness vanished, and Ron Goneen saw that this singular being had taken the shape of a man.

It was a gigantic form, standing nine feet tall. It was unclothed, and the greenish color of it resembled the patina of some age-tarnished metal. It was like some splendid, colossal statue, representing superhuman strength and manly beauty. Then it moved, and Ron Goneen gasped.

"Ron!" came the choked, incredulously protesting cry of Seru Gyroc. "That is you!"

The giant smiled, and Ron Goneen staggered backward. For the smile, save for some disturbing hint of immemorial despair, was his own!

That supernal, majestic form—save that it was naked, greenish, and some nine feet tall—was a reflection of himself!

The two men stepped back in the clumsy suits, breathless,

speechless. That splendid green figure advanced one step toward them across the curved, bright floor. Its arm thrust out in an odd, arresting gesture.

And a strange voice, supernally deep, reverberated from the headphones in the two helmets, speaking their names: "Ron—Seru—"

The space captain's rugged, red-bearded face was grim with amazement. His narrowed eyes stared. He swallowed twice, and his husky whisper spoke into the microphone, "You—how do, you know us?"

The green giant still smiled disarmingly. "I know words," that deep voice boomed promptly. "Speak words! I know words you speak."

Seru shuffled forward suddenly, nearly helpless by reason of the slight gravitation, and picked at the sleeve of Ron's suit. His dry voice whispered from the phones, "I think I see it! He can understand what we say! He must somehow pick up the radio waves, and—somehow—perceive the images in our minds. That's it—it must be!"

"That's it," echoed the deep voice, startlingly. "I perceive the waves of your minds." The great green arm lifted commandingly. "Speak! I pick up words."

"Talk to him, Ron," whispered the scientist, urgently. "Tell him how we got here."

"Talk," parroted the amazingly deep reverberation. "Tell me!"

Ron Goneen gulped and wet his lips. "We are wandering fugitives from another universe, infinitely larger than this one," he began. "Because we have destroyed our own, in an experiment with entropy—"

The tanned space captain paused and swallowed again, staring through the helmet at his gigantic green simulacrum. "Do you understand that?" he demanded incredulously. "Do you know what entropy is?"

The shaggy, green-bearded head nodded solemnly. "I understand your words," the deep voice assured him. "Speak!"

Ron Goneen blinked and continued his narrative. The green giant listened intently, nodding from time to time in Ron's own characteristic manner.

A pleading earnestness came into the explorer's voice, as he, at last, concluded, "There is another with us—a girl. She is very ill. We seek a young, friendly planet, with warm sun and invigorating air—which will make her want to live again!"

He leaned forward urgently in the bulky suit, fear forgotten. "We have seen no stars in this universe—no worlds save this place of yours. Tell me—is there a planet left where our kind can live?"

Desperately, his eyes searched that rugged green face which was the replica of his own. "We must find it, if there is! Because Lethara alone can be the mother of the new race. And because— we love her!"

His heart sank, then. He shuffled backward wearily.

For the giant had shaken his head. "There is no habitable world left in all this universe," rang the deep voice. "Nor any living thing surviving, save myself."

Ron Goneen's body sagged heavily in the bulky armor. "Then we have failed at last?" he sighed. "There is no hope at all?"

"You will find no home in this universe," his nude, green likeness assured him. "But," the deep voice went on, "I admitted you here for a reason. You have something that I need. If you will listen, I wish to propose a fair exchange."


## XIV.

RON GONEEN shuffled quickly forward. His narrowed eyes stared searchingly up at the gigantic green image of himself. Suddenly he caught his breath. "There is a way?" he whispered anxiously. "There is some haven for Lethara—a new home for the race of our children?"

The shaggy, greenish head nodded, in the abrupt, decisive manner characteristic of Ron himself. The deep voice boomed in the phones, "That is possible—although not a certainty—through the use of my greatest treasure. And I would gladly put it at your disposal, if you will perform a certain service for me."

Ron Goneen stepped back a little, his rugged face grim. "What is that?" he demanded. "How can we possibly aid you, when your powers are so immense?"

"I shall tell you," answered the green giant. And now Ron Goneen first noticed a rather disconcerting thing: that the green lips no longer moved as that supernal voice came through the phones!

"We'll give you anything you ask," Ron said. "If you need matter—our spare stores and instruments, even parts of the ship—"

"Matter is indeed precious to me," the great voice echoed in their helmets, "but I do not ask for that. I will tell you my request—but first you must know a little of myself."

The space captain moved forward a little, eagerly listening, as the mighty voice went on: "You may know me as Orthu. As you have guessed, I am the last survivor of my kind. The fathers of my race came into being in the youth of this universe. Like your own kind, they presently mastered space, spread from planet to planet and from galaxy to galaxy.

"Not without disaster and defeat, they at last attained a supremacy threatened only by the death of this universe itself. They became, as I am, beings almost eternal. They slowly acquired a voluntary control over molecular structure: that ability to dissolve into a gas, to flow like a liquid, to condense into any solid form, that you found so amazing in me.

"They evolved, at the same time, a means of direct contact with space. It is that which enables me to move myself and other objects without the use of any cumbersome appendages. It is that, also, which enables me to create the radio waves by which my thought is conveyed to you,.

"A new sense came to them with that advance. I am aware of the world lines of objects and forces in space and time, without the interfering aid of any cumbersome organs of special sense. I fully and immediately perceive every atomic process in both your brains.

"I tell you this because I have observed your own curiosity, and to point out the height to which my kind was once advanced. Their development of the art of living was equally great. In truth, such material achievements seem insignificant beside their latter intellectual triumphs.

"YET, for all their greatness, they never conquered time. Despite every effort at conservation, matter crumbled ceaselessly into energy, as the ages passed, and the energy was wasted through space.

"The life of a universe is long. All the suns had ceased to shine many ages before I came into being. Yet, by collecting matter and accelerating its disintegration, we were able to survive. My life has covered half the whole time span of this universe.

"At last, however, dwindling resources forced us to attempt the one last and most important task of the intelligent life of any universe, the one which you performed in your own prematurely: the reversal of entropy.

"This laboratory was constructed for that purpose, with our last resources. I was chosen to attempt this fatal but necessary task, and the last of my fellow beings, since their places were no more, passed on.

"And for ages beyond memory I have labored at this task. The outlines of the problem have been clear from the beginning. But there is an elemental difficulty that I have never mastered. That, but for sheer chance, I never could—"

"True!" whispered Seru Gyroc. His haggard white head nodded in his helmet. "The elimination of the infinity factor!" his thin voice quavered. "I realized that pure accident alone led me to the correct solution. . The mathematics of chance assured me that if I failed to perform the experiment, no other mind in our universe would stumble upon the Omega Effect. That realization, with my mistaken pride, was what led to the fatal blunder."

The green giant moved eagerly a little toward him—not walking, Ron Goneen observed, but floating a few inches above the curving silver floor.

"So you know it?" the deep voice boomed. "You can solve my problem—give me release from this task of bitter ages?"

"I can." But the little man's quaver warned him: "If you release the Omega Radiation here, this place will be very swiftly destroyed, and your own life."

"That is well," the deep tones reverberated. "For I am long since weary of my task, and weary of being."

Ron Goneen shuffled forward, objection written grimly on his rugged face. "We should be destroyed also," he said. "We should never find any haven in this universe. It would become as deadly as our own."

"That would not be well," agreed Orthu. "For your race is yet young and has not yet achieved its full fruition. I should, therefore, gladly open the way for you into another universe—into one that is young, in which you may find a pleasant dwelling for the one of you who is ill.

"You will make the exchange?"

"We will," said Ron Goneen, promptly. "Only show us the way and give us time to escape, before you release the Omega Ray."

"Then it is done," said the deep voice. "If you will reveal the information—"

"Hadn't we better wait?" Seru's apprehensive eyes came to Ron Goneen. "We should have evidence of his good faith."

"We have evidence enough, said Ron Goneen. "Tell him."

A LITTLE UNWILLINGLY, the old man launched into an exposition of the Gyroc tensors, and the formulas, apparatus, and processes involved in setting up the Omega Effect. The green giant listened for a time intently, then cut him off with a sudden gesture.

"That is enough," the deep voice said. "Your thought has covered all the problem. You are indeed fortunate, Seru Gyroc, to discover that secret so securely hidden by the laws of increasing entropy."

"Unfortunate!" breathed the old man. "It destroyed our universe—"

"Now," Ron Goneen broke in abruptly, "the way to that other universe—for Lethara is very ill!"

For answer, the being Orthu raised a mighty bare arm, as if to point toward the maze of silvered machines in the vast space beyond the passage. Ron Goneen looked after his arm, saw an object approaching.

It came flying, apparently unaided—Ron recalled what Orthu had told them of direct control of the warp of space—and settled to the curving argent floor, near their feet.

It was a curiously designed oval chest or coffer, very massive. It was made of some bluish metal, and had evidently once been covered with singularly patterned red-and-black enamel. It was worn, however, scarred and battered, as if by the impact of immemorial ages.

"That box is older than I am," said Orthu. "The treasure in it is older than my race."

A heavy, queer-looking lock snapped open, as if to the turn of an invisible key. The thick lid lifted, as if of itself, and Ron Goneen bent forward to peer into the chest. He groped in amazement for Seru's arm.

"Look!" he whispered. "Another crystal like the Jewel of Dawn!"

Breathless, he was trembling to a sudden incredulous awe. Could this be another, yet smaller universe? Already they had once come into the infinitely small—could it be possible to become as much smaller, again?

"It is possible," that always startling voice filled his helmet again. "You must be aware of the relativity of size?"

"And we may enter it, to seek a haven?"

"You may."

"But wait!" quavered Seru, anxiously. "You said it was older than your race. May it not be dead also?"

"There is a relativity of time," boomed Orthu. "I have looked into it. It is such a universe as you seek."

If it's young, and you had it all the time," the old man demanded suspiciously, "why didn't your race migrate to it? Why don't you go there yourself?"

"Your children will know the answer to that question," the solemn tones replied, "when your race is as old as mine! Now go, if you will, so that I may finish my ancient task, and also depart."

"Farewell, Orthu," said Ron Goneen. "And thank you." He shuffled back toward the *Life of Man*, and assisted Seru Gyroc into the entrance valve.


## XV.


BACK in the little bridge room, he started the Kardishon oscillator, and their second interuniversal voyage was begun. The walls of the cylindrical passage receded. Orthu, the doomed last survivor of a dead universe, expanded into a vast, dark cloud that still had the shape of a majestic, watching man.

The space captain lifted the dwindling vessel, guided it into the ancient chest, which still rested at the feet of the expanding giant. They glided down toward the second jewel: a growing bubble of shimmering white, lying on something like black velvet.

The chest became a monstrous chamber, filled with increasing gloom. The supernal statuesque figure above was lost in darkness. Presently only the silvery sphere was left, growing always, drawing away.

Leaving Seru at the controls, Ron went back to Lethara's cabin.

Her pale body didn't move when he entered. But her faint voice, called. "Come to me, Ron. I need you now, my dear—and I shall not need you long."

He came and took her hand. "Don't think of giving up, my

darling," he whispered. "We are flying—now into a new, younger universe. We will find some friendly planet there—a home for you and our children."

Her white head shook very slightly.

"I don't need a home, Ron," she breathed. "No home but your heart. And we shall have no children. Her great dark eyes were on his face, serene, unafraid. "The dream came again while you were gone. It was the same. I know I am going to die!"

His fingers tightened desperately on her hand. "But you can't die—you mustn't!"

Her huge eyes were suddenly shadowed with remembered horror. "Those things of cold black fire, on the rocks of Pyralonne—they drank away my life. This with you, Ron, is only a pale ghost in my body, soon to perish also." Her tragic eyes closed. "I am very sorry," she breathed faintly. "Because—because I love you, Ron!"

Her white body lay very still. He could barely detect the motion of her breathing, the slow throb of the pulse in her wrist. He still sat beside her, fighting a deadly and ultimate fear, when he felt a sudden, disquieting lurch of the vessel.

"RON!" quavered Seru's voice from the speaker. "Come! For we are through—and there are stars!"

The sleeping girl seemed undisturbed by that abrupt, giddy plunge from universe to universe. He left her, hurried to the bridge.

Seru Gyroc stood weary and haggard over the controls. "The reflecting barrier yielded as before," he reported, "until the field effect rotated us into the fourth axis."

Peering eagerly into the dark space without, Ron Goneen saw a long spiral of silver dust, splendid with innumerable many-colored points of diamond light that burned through green streamers of nebulium.

"There!" His cry was a deep sob of joy. "There is a galaxy—one like our own that was destroyed! There are suns in it. There must be planets—a place for Lethara—"

The old man nodded gravely. "Yes, a home for my daughter," he said. "For your children, and the new race to come. Orthu played fair."

"It is strange," Ron Goneen whispered suddenly, "to think that we are now so infinitely small—that all this universe must be smaller than the smallest particle of our old one!"

"But is it?" questioned Seru. "We have spent none of our mass. Remember the relativity of—"

Ron Goneen had ceased to listen. His rugged, red-bearded face was suddenly grim with agony. In a choked, apprehensive voice, he sobbed, "Lethara! She called me—"

There had been no sound. He could not define the manner of his impression. But dread was cold in his heart as he ran back to her small cabin,

"My darling, I am here—"

The words stuck in his parched throat. He walked slowly toward her bed, looked down. She lay still. Her eyes were closed. A quiet, strangely peaceful smile touched the corners of her lips.

Gently, almost reverently, he picked up her cool, lax hand. But already he knew that she was dead.

## XVI.

LETHARA IS DEAD! Again and again the words throbbed through Ron Goneen's numbed, stricken mind, like hammers of leaden pain. Lethara was dead—and with her his heart—and the race of man.

He gently folded the cold, small hands on her breast, and covered her face. Kneeling beside the bunk, he thought aimlessly of the grim, strange life the girl had led since her birth in their exile on dark Pyralonne, of her shattered chance for happiness.

He stayed there until Seru called from the bridge: "Come, Ron! Quickly!"

Purpose and vitality had died in Ron Goneen. A dull automaton, his big body rose stiffly and reeled mechanically forward.

The emaciated little scientist was tinkering excitedly with the vessel's long-range hyperchron receiver. His thin hand jerked tremblingly toward the telescope.

"Look!" he cried. "At the suns in that galaxy!"

"But it doesn't matter, Seru," Ron told him wearily. "It's no use now. Nothing is any use!" His tanned hand dropped sympathetically on the old man's shoulder. "Because, Seru—" He gulped. "Because Lethara is dead."

But Seru Gyroc's bright-eyed excitement was not affected by that statement. Heedlessly, he pushed Ron's hand away, went on with his feverish efforts to tune the hyperchronoscope. Thinking dully that this greatest mind must at last have cracked under the awful pressure of cosmic disaster, Ron caught the shoulders of the old scientist, swung him away from the instrument.

"Don't you understand, Seru?" his grave voice said. "I told you that your daughter is dead."

The old man struggled desperately; "But she isn't!" his cracked voice sobbed wildly. "Not yet! Let me go, Ron!" He twisted free, sprang back to the receiver. "Look in the telescope!" he begged. "Go ahead—look! I'm not insane!"

The space captain staggered heavily at last to the little instrument, put his lusterless, bloodshot eyes to the oculars, scanned the luminous whirlpool of that distant island universe.

And all his grief and apathy were suddenly gone!

"What is it, Seru?" His voice was deep and tense again, electric. "What did you see? Why does that galaxy look so much like our own?"

The old man's voice jerked brokenly from where he bent over the receiver.

"Remember the relativity of size? Magnitude, like space and time, is cyclical. We have completed the cycle of change, and come back to our starting point.

"Yes, that galaxy is our own!"

"But our universe is destroyed!" rumbled the bewildered objection of Ron Goneen. "Our galaxy perished with the rest. We saw it!"

"But remember," the old man mumbled, still busy with the dials, "the direction of entropy is the arrow of time. When the Omega Effect reversed the current, we were flung backward—"

THE HUM of a carrier way came suddenly from the hyperchron receiver, then a snatch of military music. The once-familiar features of a newscaster appeared on the rectangular screen.

His brisk voice barked: "Hello, universe! I bring you the latest hyperchron dispatch from the Goneen-Gyroc Expedition, on the far-off planet Pyralonne. After two hundred years of work in exile, Seru Gyroc is about to make the crucial test in his great Omega Ray experiment.

"Success will open the door to a new age of wonder. Mastery of entropy, Gyroc believes, will make anything possible—even to cooking on ice!

"But if it fails?

"Well, two centuries ago, in a speech before the Galactic Council, Captain General Ron Goneen made some dire hints of cosmic disaster. That same day, he joined the expedition!

"Listen to-morrow, universe, for the latest—"

The old man's trembling fingers spun a dial; voice and image faded. "That proves it!" he cried. "We are back in our own universe, a few hours—or perhaps only a few minutes—before the moment of our fatal experiment!"

Ron Goneen's deep-set blue eyes were staring at him in anxious bewilderment. "Then they—we—are all still alive on Pyralonne," he gasped. "Even *she* is still alive—Lethara? Our experiment has done no harm?"

"Not yet," said Seru, gravely. "But it is about to be performed. You heard the announcer!" A strange, fanatic elation of despair burned in his bloodshot eyes. "We have returned to witness the doom that we wrought! And to perish, fittingly, by our own act! For the jewel is left behind. There is now no way to any other universe!"

The space captain's rugged face was suddenly stern with purpose, his blue eyes narrowed and grim. Low and hard, his quick voice rapped: "Then we must stop our own experiment! How far is it to Pyralonne? The charts—"

"Only a few light years, probably," said the terrible-eyed oldster, "since, according to the principles of inter-continua dynamics, we tended to return to the point we left. But the experiment cannot be stopped!"

"It must be!" Ron Goneen was already over the controls. "To save the universe!"

The old man shook his haggard head.

"Impossible!" he shrilled., "The chain of events is now inevitable—for the experiment resulted in our being here. Logically, a result can never change a cause!"

Ron Goneen's narrowed eyes scanned the charts, while his long-practiced fingers set up their position on the automatic control board.

"I think," his deep voice said gravely as he worked, "that the direction of entropy increase is the only objective distinction between causes and effects. And we have reverse entropy—"

He moved swiftly to the telescope. "There it is—cold, dark

Pyralonne!" he whispered. "We shall see if there is time—"

THE soft humming of the generators rose again to a painful, ceaseless screaming, as the *Life of Man* flashed into that last desperate race through the void. Wearily pacing the tiny floor, Seru Gyroc clutched suddenly at Ron's green tunic.

"If it should be possible," he gasped, "to undo my crimes! To save my daughter, and Karanora! To spare mankind—"

He was interrupted by the clanging of a detector gong.

Still tense at the telescope, Ron Goneen distinguished a familiar pattern of red-and-green lights drifting far away, athwart the faint, flattened spiral of the Andromeda Galaxy.

"The *Silver Bird!*" he whispered hoarsely. "Already it is standing away from Pyralonne. The two of—of *us*—are now alone in the tower—about to begin the experiment. Time is short!"

"Yes," quavered Seru, "our time is short. This time we are to be destroyed, by our work, forever. That is cosmic justice—"

Ron Goneen was standing rigid at the controls. His great body, wet with sweat, gleamed like a statue of bronze. His narrowed eyes peered resolutely ahead.

"Pyralonne!" he whispered again, hoarsely. "The only world Lethara ever knew— There's the tower, the landing lights!"

His eyes probed the eternal darkness that lay upon that cragged, frozen plateau. He could make out the squat bulk of the laboratory tower, faint gleams filtering from its shuttered ports.

It was strange—maddening!—to know that he and Seru were *there* in the dark tower, setting in motion a force that would destroy the universe, yet also *here,* racing desperately to avert that doom.

His intent eyes were watching the tiny stars of red and green that outlined the rectangle where the *Silver Bird* had rested. They went suddenly dim.

"The lights—" It was a sob of agony. "The current drain, when the apparatus started! They—*we* are just beginning! There is no time—" The old man shook his tangled, hoary head. "I told you we must fail—must perish for my cosmic crime! For logic allows nothing else—"

"No!" The space captain's voice was a rumbling drum. "We can't fail!" His quick fingers flung the little ship into a dive; tortured generators shrieked again. "I'm going to ram the tower!"

"You can't!" shrilled Seru. "For if you destroy us then, we can't exist now, to do it—"

But the cruel plateau of frozen crags, the squat night-shrouded bulk of the tower, were rushing upward. Still steady, Ron Goneen's long, bronzed fingers moved to aim the ship accurately at the flat dome. His big body braced itself for the impact. Calmly, in that last mad moment, his deep voice was saying: "When the law of entropy has been overturned, there is no *then*, no *now*—"

## XVII.

RON GONEEN was dreaming again. It *had* 'to be a dream he knew. It *couldn't* be real! It was strange enough even that he dreamed, it came him; for he had expected to perish in the ramming ship.

But it was a very, satisfactory dream, he felt—even if all his body up to his eyes seemed to be wrapped in bandages, and his first effort to move brought a series of dull, vague pains.

It was becoming curiously real and persistent for a dream, of course. And yet it *must* be! For he had seen Lethara dead, had folded her cold hands and covered her pallid face.

Now, however, she was sitting beside his bed, and smiling down at him. And she looked radiantly well—as utterly beautiful as she had been before the fateful experiment. The glory of her hair was no longer white, but golden again. Her oval face was serenely young. Her violet eyes no longer held any horror, but only sympathy, concern for him, a bright hope.

"Ron?" her soft voice was asking. It was thrillingly familiar, thrillingly real—alive! "Can you hear me? Can you see me? Is it too painful to speak?"

"No." The voice that came through his bandages was very weak and low. It set a sudden dull aching in his strapped chest, that, so experience told him, meant a few cracked ribs. "Where—am I?" he whispered. "Is this—no dream?"

"No dream at all," the huskily sweet voice of Lethara assured him. "You are in the hospital of the *Silver Bird*. And don't worry!" She touched his bandaged shoulder, very softly. "You're going to be all right, Ron, dear—and so is father."

"But what—happened?" he breathed the painful words. "You are—alive?"

"Of course I am, darling," she said. "But it's just luck that you are!" Great and dark, her violet eyes were suddenly glistening. "I was so afraid—" She bit her full trembling lip, swallowed. "Anyhow, you're going to get well!" She was smiling gloriously through the tears.

"But I think," she added, "that the great experiment is ruined."

Ron Goneen took a cautious breath and whispered two words: "What—happened?"

Her cool, soothing hand touched the little bare streak of his brow, very gently. "Don't ask any more—it hurts you too much. Just keep quiet, and I'll tell you. Of course you and father didn't have time to realize what hit you—"

"What!"

"Quiet!" she commanded. "I promised not to disturb you."

He liked the soft stroking of her fingers on his forehead. He waited obediently.

"We were standing off into space to wait for the experiment," she told him. "But suddenly our detectors revealed a large meteoric object—and showed that it was hurtling toward the tower!

"We raced back into the *Silver Bird,* to try to deflect it and save you. But we were one minute too late. The thing—whatever it was—struck the laboratory, shattered it!" Her great eyes were briefly solemn and disturbed.

"It seems very queer that a meteor should strike here, so far outside the galaxy, and just in time to stop the experiment! The officers have been talking about a conspiracy of nature to protect the law of entropy—" Her golden head shook; her eyes were again smiling.

"ANYHOW, we were in time to pick you and father up out of the wreckage. You were both pretty badly battered, and, of course, nearly asphyxiated. And something—queer—must have happened to father." Her voice was grave; puzzled dread shadowed her violet eyes.

"His hair has turned to white," she said. "And he seems suddenly so very old!"

"I know." Ron Goneen caught his breath, made the effort to speak again. "No other—bodies."

The girl stared at him, questioningly. "Of course not. How could there be? You and father were alone in the tower." She bit her full lip absently, and added in a puzzled voice: "It was a queer thing, that we couldn't find an atom of that meteor!

"It went through the floor beneath the dome, to the life tube in the safety chamber. We found you and father near it. But there wasn't a trace of the meteor left."

Ron Goneen shut his eyes and tried to think. Entropy. Reversal of time. Annihilation of cause and effect. Three who had lived twice—and returned to destroy themselves. Where were the missing bodies? His head began to ache a little. Lethara's hand was very comforting on his forehead.

"Oh, yes—Ron!" the girl's soft voice came to him suddenly. "Father sent you a message. I don't know about it. You might want to hear. He seems a little—well, out of his head. Mother is with him, now."

Ron breathed, "Message?"

"Wait," she said, "and I'll tell you the exact words." Her smooth brow wrinkled with effort, as she repeated slowly: "'The closing of our world lines in space and time, when the cycle was completed, created an independent subspace manifold which is therefore detached from our continuum. What happened to us is real in that new subspace, but not in this universe.'

"That's it," she said, "if it means anything!"

"It does—" he gasped. "Everything!"

"Somehow, father has changed his mind about the experiment," she said. "He told the men not to try to save any of the apparatus. He's giving it up."

Her dark eyes looked at him suddenly, regretful. "There's another thing—that I know you'll be sorry about," she said. "The stone from Andromeda—the Jewel of Dawn—was gone from the pouch in your tunic. I asked the men to search, but they couldn't find it anywhere."

"Doesn't—matter!" breathed the space captain. "This universe—good enough—now." He took a careful breath. "Because—of you—my darling!"

"Don't talk," she commanded.

And Ron Goneen, captain general of the Galactic Patrol, he who had taken the Jewel of Dawn from the warrior crystals of Andromeda, obediently closed his eyes.

Her lips were cool against his forehead.

# Dreadful Sleep

*Weird Tales, March, April, May 1938*

N INITIAL APOLOGY SEEMS TO DUE TO THE READER OF THIS history. For I, Ronald Dunbar, am not a man of letters. Three of the books that bear my name—those entitled *Antarctica I, II,* and *III*—are merely the necessary scientific records of my various polar explorations. And the popular abridgment of them called *An Odyssey of the Ice* was no more than an effort (which turned out very happily) to wipe out the deficit of my third expedition.

It happens however, that no accomplished literary historian was present to observe those mind-crushing events that made the year 1960 the most terrible in human history. I am the only surviving witness to much of that hideously enigmatic catastrophe. Despite my disqualifications, therefore, as well as the natural reluctance of an active man to spending some months confined to an unaccustomed desk, I feel it my duty to set down a plain, simple account of what happened. If without much literary embellishment, it will at least be accurate and clear.

The event of June 11-December 24, 1960, is already recognized to be the most astounding and terrifying phenomenon that ever overtook our world. It was high noon over America, on June

11, when the summer abruptly vanished and the chill blackness of a wintry midnight fell, soundless but infinitely appalling. At the same instant, in the eastern hemisphere, night was turned incredibly into day.

Amid the stunned shock and panic that followed, astronomers swiftly perceived that the earth had moved half around its orbit. In a split heartbeat, six months had somehow gone. The Christmas season fell, unwarned, upon a world too staggered and fearful for merriment.

For, inexplicably, the disaster had cost thousands of lives. From office and home and street, in that dazing instant, the victims had abruptly vanished. Bewildered survivors, found themselves addressing empty air, or passing food to a vacant plate. The vanished left no clue.

The bodies were never recovered. Near New York, however, which had suffered most heavily, a sinister thing was found. Upon the Jersey Pallisades lay a queer gray area of lifeless desolation, and near its center, where lovely Alpine Park had been, was a wide circle of strange squat earthen mounds.

The mounds were swiftly crumbling. But apprehensive explorers, venturing into the unpleasant labyrinth of burrows beneath them, found a few gruesome relics identified with the missing persons. No single human fragment, however, had been found when the tunnels caved in.

The world has had no explanation of this amazing tragedy. The astrophysicists, it is true, put their learned heads together, called up the shades of Einstein and Minkowski, and spoke sagely of a flaw in the space-time continuum. The press caught up their magic words, and the whole planet was soon informed that it was a Time Fault which had made six months seem like the winking of an eye. Neither savants nor newspapers, however, could account for the vanished thousands, or explain the grisly mounds in that queerly devastated park upon the Palisades.

I am the only surviving man who knows that actual cause of the Time Fault, who experienced all the nerve-shattering horror of those six lost months, or who met face to face the incredible menace that stopped all the world. I found courage, then, to go ahead, believing that the inherent interest of what I have to tall will make up for any lack of literary adornment.

## 1. The Different Doctor Harding

ON THE morning of February 10, of fateful 1960, Doctor Aston Harding came into my room at the Aero Club. I was just three days returned from that season's very successful polar flight; clangerous New York still seemed a shining paradise, and any old acquaintance a welcoming angel. I greeted Harding like a brother—before I discovered that he wanted me to fly him back to the Antarctic, the very next week!

I put the answer to that in pretty plain words.

"We can't do that, Harding! There's just about six weeks of twilight left at the South Pole, before six months of winter set in. I know what it's like—I've just come from there!"

I ignored the set determination on his blank face.

"I'm fed up with silence and ice and frostbitten feet. What I want is jazz bands, and my ice in a frosty glass, and feet tapping on waxed hardwood. Sorry, Doctor, but it simply can't be done—not this season. Now, if you can wait until November—"

Harding set down the whisky soda I had mixed for him, and rose deliberately to stand over my chair. He was a tall man, his broad shoulders a little stooped but powerful; he had a ruddy skin and yellowish hair. A few years older than I, but still under forty, he was already distinguished in both philanthropy and science.

I has always like Harding, for a quick generosity and a spirit of genuine fellowship, almost as much as I admired the girl he had married: lovely Jerry Ware. I was indebted to him, as director of the Planet Research Foundation, for substantial aid to my polar flights. He had been a good friend—and I was deeply shocked, now, to see the change in him.

His pale blue eyes fixed me with a penetration that I found disquieting, and his low voice, a new strange hardness in it, rapped:

"Yes, Dunbar, you're going to fly us to the Pole—this season!" His eyes, always before so genially mild, were suddenly sharp as gimlets. "An explorer, you want fame: you want to advance science: you want money for another expedition. You've got a price, Dunbar—what is it?"

A very rude reply was on my tongue. But my respect for the

old Doctor Harding, my old friendship for Jerry Ware, rose up in time to check the words. And Harding stabbed at me with an almost menacing forefinger.

"We've got the biggest proposition you ever had a nibble at, Dunbar," his harsh voice crackled at me. "We're going to reclaim Antarctica. We're going to thaw the ice cap with atomic power!"

He paused a moment to let that sink in, his keen pale eyes boring into my face.

"An invention of Meriden Bell's," his rasp went on. "You know him. This is confidential, Dunbar; I trust you. We've formed a syndicate. Five of us. My wife and I, Bell and Tommy Veering—and yourself."

At last I swallowed my amazement, and:

"Thaw the ice!" I blurted. "Harding, you don't know what you're talking about. I've spent years there. Remember what Antarctica is: five million miles covered with ice up to a mile deep, with temperatures seventy to a hundred below! Thaw—*that?*"

"It can be done!" he rapped. "You talk to Bell. And there are millions in it. Billions. For all five of us. I've put you down for four per cent, plus expenses." His tone became unpleasantly dictatorial. "Get ready, Dunbar, to fly us down in your *Austral Queen*—by the end of next week."

"If that's all you want, Harding—"

I bit my tongue, and held open the door. Something, some indefinable quality in his bearing, made me want desperately to hit him. It was his old friendship that held my arm, and Jerry Ware.

I WAS still hurt and puzzled by this harsh dictatorial insolence in a man who had been the most patient and generous of my friends, when the phone rang again that afternoon, and I was surprized to hear the voice of Harding's wife.

A discord of anxious worry marred its old sweet music.

"Ron!" she cried eagerly. "How are you?"

Jerry had been, and was, perhaps the friend held closest in my lonely life. But I must make it clear, against possible misunderstanding, that I did not love her, nor she me. I had sincerely congratulated the Hardings on their marriage, believing them perfectly mated. The change in her husband distressed me deeply, for I knew what it must mean to Jerry.

Her voice was quivering, now, pleading.

"Ron, if Aston's way provoked you, I am sorry. I must explain about him. He had an—illness, two years ago. He had been working late in his office at the Foundation—some Government research, on account of the Pacific War. And one night he—disappeared.

"I was frantic. The police couldn't find him. I was afraid he was—dead. It was two weeks before he came to himself, stumbling along a highway out in Jersey.

"It was amnesia. Still he can't remember what happened. There was evidence that somebody had broken into his office. The police thought an Asiatic spy might have attacked him, to get some secret. But he doesn't know. And since—"

Her low voice caught, choked.

"Since, he seems different—sharp and impatient—sometimes cruel. And still there are lapses in his memory, details he can't recall. I have to help him. For he's still"—she choked again—"still dear to me. And promise me, Ron, that you'll forgive him, bear with him."

"I promise, Jerry," I told her.

"Oh, thank you." It was a glad, eager cry. "And, Ron, will you come out to dinner tonight? There's to be a meeting of the syndicate, afterward, to discuss the expedition."

"I'll be there, Jerry, to see you. But I warn you, I'm not flying back to the Pole—not this season."

Her gay little laugh ignored that last.

"Thanks, Ron," she said. "Doctor Bell will pick you up at seven."

Meriden Bell—old "Merry" Bell! I was eager to see him, and yet dreaded the encounter. I had known him well when he worked at the Foundation, before the terrible events that shattered his career and estranged him from the world.

His genius had been a flame in him, in the old days. Radiant good spirits had sparkled in his eyes. I knew that things were different, now. I had hardly seen him for two years, but the outline of his tragedy was familiar to me: it is part of the blackest chapter in American history.

Three years before, a day came back to me, when I had called on Bell in his biological laboratory at the Foundation, which then occupied a gray old building at the edge of the Jersey meadows. Harding had already hinted that Bell's bacteriological research was the greatest of the century, but I was nevertheless surprized.

All that long-past summer afternoon came back: the air in the laboratory a little stuffy, unpleasant with a vague odor of formaldehyde; the north light gleaming on microscopes, incubators, centrifuges, and specimen jars; Bell, a tall blue-eyed man, young and slender in laboratory white, eagerly busy over a spectroscope.

He came to meet me, turned to point dramatically at a test-tube that held a few drops of an amber fluid.

"My triumph, Ron!" Eager elation rang in his low voice. "That is my Culture V 13—the perfect bacteriophage! It is a filterable virus that will destroy any living thing, any bacterium, any malignant organism. When I have developed the control—a specific protection for the cells of the human body—it can eradicate all disease!"

"All disease!"

Awed by the might of this slender man's genius, perhaps a little incredulous before his sudden promise of universal health, I reached out gingerly to touch the tube in its rack. Bell swiftly caught my arm, and:

"Don't!" his tense voice warned. "If one drop touched you, Ron—or the millionth of a drop—until I have developed the specific control."

I turned somewhat apprehensively—for those few brown drops seemed suddenly more terrible than all the blizzards and Antarctica—and came face to face with the most dreadful man I have ever seen.

## 2. FIVE AGAINST THE ICE

DREADFUL—no other word so fits that human monstrosity. Wearing a stained laboratory smock, he stood less than five feet tall. His back was horribly hunched, and his great gnarled hands slung forward like the limbs of a gorilla. Beneath sleek black hair, his face was a yellow, V-shaped mask. His eyes, set deep beneath dense, bushy dark brows that sloped to make a smaller V, were black, also—and his most appealing feature.

They held me, his eyes, in a sort of shrinking fascination, because they were—hideous. One was oddly red-flecked around the contracted pupil, with an evil, glittering red. The other was strangely dilated, a fearsome inscrutable midnight orb that seemed to have no iris.

Those dark, mismated eyes were fixed on the yellow liquid in the tube with an intensity somehow terrifying. Beneath the ugly blackness of the yellow, pointed face I sensed a sinister storm of suppressed emotion; a mad black yearning, a bitter, burning hatred, a savage and triumphant gloating.

I started back, appalled as if some bottomless crevasse had abruptly snapped open before me. Bell made a hasty introduction:

"Ron, this is Doctor Kroll. Captain Dunbar, meet Doctor Dawson Kroll, who is assisting my biological research."

The hunchback had started also, and all hint of that yearning and hatred and gloating was instantly gone from the yellow V of his face—though he couldn't erase its stifled, searing fury from my mind. The hand he gave me was unpleasantly cold.

"Doctor Bell has made a remarkable discovery." Kroll's voice was oily and yet grating, unpleasant as his breath. "One the world will not forget."

The horror to come must have been already in his twisted mind—perhaps I had seen its birth. But only afterward did I see the sardonic second meaning in his words.

The Pacific War was fought during my next polar expedition, ended before I knew of its beginning; for the censored radio carried no news.

The American air forces, supported by the fleet, had already won a swift and brilliant victory, when Bell's "Culture V13" fell mysteriously into the hands of the enemy. Nevertheless, by the last vengeful order of a defeated and mortally wounded commander, three surviving Asiatic planes sprayed the bacteriophage along the Pacific coast. From Seattle to San Diego, it took a million and a quarter lives, hideously.

Hideously—for every droplet that touched a human body started an incurable sore, a bleeding crater of agony that spread implacably, swiftly destroying skin and flesh and bone, until not life alone but every vestige of the corpse was consumed.

On that terrible morning, when a whole nation was stunned with horror and death, high military authorities called on Meriden Bell at his laboratory. His skill could do nothing: the dead were dead, and Asiatic vengeance satisfied. Bell admitted that his bacteriophage must have caused the deaths, but could not account for its possession by the enemy. He was arrested, tried by court-martial, convicted of treason—then suddenly exonerated, when the guilt was pinned upon Mawson Kroll.

For Bell's assistant had taken flight, leaving a trunk filled with Asiatic gold. In the intercepted communications of the enemy were found letters in which Kroll demanded, as payment for his treason, to be made Emperor of America.

The fugitive hunchback was arrested two weeks later, on the Mexican border. Stupidly he denied his guilt, even his own identity. An alienist pronounced him criminally insane. Tried in a military court, he was convicted by the overwhelming weight of circumstantial evidence, shot by a firing-squad.

Bell abandoned his experiments, destroyed his records and various cultures at the Foundation, by military command. His brilliant mind, it seemed for months, had been shattered by the disaster. He was forcibly restrained from suicide, committed to an asylum.

His tortured brain had assumed the guilt of a million murders. The psychiatrists, if they failed to unburden his altogether of Kroll's crime, at least convinced him that he might best make atonement by living. He had come back to the Foundation before my last expedition, to begin research in a newly opened field of sub-atomic physics.

N OW, when Bell came to meet me in the winter gloom that filled the halls of the Aero Club, I saw that he had never escaped the shadow of that tragedy. He was frail and thin, his blue eyes dark with brooding. His white pinched face looked as if it never smiled. The eagerness of his eagerness, however, was almost pathetic.

"Good old Ron," he whispered, and felt the muscle of my shoulder with his pale fingers as it we were schoolboys again. "You must thrive on cold—you're looking like a red-headed Hercules."

"But I've had enough of winter for this season, Merry," I told him. "What I'm looking for is warmth and women and laughter." And I asked hopefully, "Harding wasn't possibly joking, about this project to thaw the ice cap?"

"No, Ron." Bell's pale thin face was abruptly serious, almost grimly resolute. "We're going to do it, all right. The equipment will be ready in a week. And you are the only man with experience enough to take us where we want to go, at the season.

We're going to the Stapledon Basin—"

"The Stapledon Basin—right across the pole!" That got me. "Surely, Merry, you haven't considered how difficult—or impossible—it would be to thaw a continent of ice!"

His dark eyes came gravely to my face, and in them was some commanding power, some deep reflection of his old supernal genius, that silenced my protests.

"But I *have* considered, Ron," he said quietly. "And I have developed an atomic battery that will supply ample power—it is still secret; what I tell you is confidential."

"Atomic power?"

He nodded.

"It is a hydro-helium vacuum cell. We call it the Atom-Builder. It builds hydrogen atoms into helium. Four hundred grams of hydrogen gives you three ninety-nine of helium, plus one of pure energy. A gram of energy is a great deal, Ron. A few tons of water will be all the fuel we need. We shall burn ice to thaw Antarctica!"

I was speechless to that. Merry went on gravely:

"Your plane will carry all the equipment we need. I have designed a heat-beam radiator, transformers, tower—everything. Harding has formed a syndicate to put up the money. We are all meeting tonight—"

"Listen, Merry," I started to object. "Harding is taking just a little too much for granted. So far as I'm concerned—"

His white fingers caught my arm.

"But, Ron, old man, you don't understand." His voice was hoarse, quivering. "This is the chance for me to make up for what I have done. One discovery of mine took a million lives. If another could open up a new continent, where millions could live, it would help settle the score."

He gulped. His tortured eyes searched my face.

"That's all I've been working for, Ron, since I—came back. You won't stop me—will you?"

No resisting that. "All right, Merry," I told him.

His thin hand wrung mine.

"Thanks, old man!" He was almost sobbing. "We'll be ready to fly by the eighteenth. You can have the *Austral Queen* in shape? There will be five of us going, and no others."

"But Jerry Harding!" I protested. "She isn't going—not into such hardship and danger. Some of my men might be persuaded to return—"

"No others!" An old bitterness was hard in Bell's voice. "This thing is secret—there won't be another Mawson Kroll!" His dark eyes stared at me, so terrible that I looked away. "And Jerry will hear of nothing else but going," he went on. "There'll be just the five of us, against the ice."

### 3. THE DWELLER IN THE PYLON

W E FOUND the Hardings at their uptown apartment, and Tommy Veering. Jerry Harding was her old self; slender, gray-eyed, charming; yet I could see her deep concern for her husband. She hovered anxiously near him, twice came swiftly to his aid when his memory seemed to stumble upon a momentary blank.

Veering was a slim, slick-haired young chap, whose smiling brown eyes held a diffident appeal. A new protegé of Harding's, he had been with the Foundation since his graduation. For all his youth, he was already distinguished in electronic engineering.

He listened intently as Bell briefly outlined the momentous plan, after we had eaten. Keen enthusiasm lit his boyish face. Eagerly, he gripped Bell's hand.

"Wonderful, Doctor Bell! It—it's great. You have given the world another world!" And he began a question: "Your precise sub-atomic formulæ—?"

"If I have revealed enough to convince you," Merry Bell said gravely, "I shall reserve the rest until we have reached the site of operations." Old bitterness shadowed his voice again. "So there cannot be another—" He bit his thin lip. "I have listed the equipment we shall need."

Veering's enthusiasm ended indecision. We went on to plan the expedition: plotted a schedule for the flight to the frozen Stapledon Basin, that would be a race against the swift-falling polar night; listed our essential supplies and the nine tons of Bell's equipment against the maximum capacity of my loyal old plane, the *Austral Queen*.

It was two o'clock when I got back to my room at the club, elated with this mad dream of conquering the polar world, yet troubled with vague apprehensions inspired by the change in Doctor Harding. I was thinking moodily, too, of the mockery in Bell's old nickname, for if ever I had seen a man walking alive in hell, it was surely he. It was worth all the risk and folly of the flight, I thought, to alleviate his torture. I went to bed, and, of old habit, fell immediately asleep.

From this point it is difficult for me to go on. Much of the remainder of this history must deal with facts and beings that will appear incredible in the severe light of established science.

I share the reluctance of the orthodox scientist to admit anything not proven by objective observations and beyond all doubt, for I know too well the possible subjective vagaries of the human mind. I am sensitive, too, of any charges of sensationalism or mistreatment of the truth.

Yet it is my obvious duty to omit nothing that happened, however fantastic or ill-supported that account of it may seem. To leave out anything would distort the whole. Perhaps it is to be expected, after all, that the circumstances leading up to the incredible phenomenon of the Time Fault should appear equally astounding.

I WOKE suddenly in my dim-lit room. The city had grown almost quiet. The illuminated hands of the electric clock showed five minutes past three—I had been sleeping no more than an hour.

The sound that had waked me was totally unfamiliar—unless perhaps it suggested the song of some tiny, exotic tropical bird. Its plaintive keenness held a wail of lonely despair, yet somehow it was heart-piercingly sweet.

I sat up in bed abruptly, less frightened than merely startled although my heart was thudding. My hand went toward the light. Before I touched the switch, however, I saw what was in the room. And all movement left me.

My incredible visitor was floating a yard off the floor, beside my bed. It shone with a pale light of its own, so that I had no need of the electrics. A brief high note came from it again, keen with lonely longing, and somehow telling me not to be afraid.

A being beyond conception, supernal! An exquisite rosy shell, floating upright, flushed with a living light, Its fluted spirals tapered to a point, below. Its gleaming lips, flared out like a vase of pearl, held the bust of an elfin woman.

Maru-Mora!

Her tiny shoulders were covered with a fine golden down. Her delicate head was—or seemed—the head of a pigmy queen. But the golden plates that crowned it, I knew, and the plumed scarlet crest above, were living part of her.

Her small pointed face was whiter than alabaster, and imperial in its pride. Her eyes were huge, purple, limpid. They were round and sober with the innocence of a child's; they were inscrutable with ageless wisdom; they were dark wells of agony, ancient and ageless.

Her lips were a tiny crimson wound. They were full, almost sensuous. They smiled at me, with a faint twist of malice.

Maru-Mora. I knew she was nothing human. Yet my fancy ever made her so, for eyes and lips and even the impudent flirt of her crimson plume held all the essence of humanity: wisdom and the vain yearning to forget, pride and bitter defeat, hot passion and long frustration, hope and despair, bright courage and consuming fear, living joy and ultimate, final agony.

Against all that, it mattered not if she had a golden carapace instead of hair, if her great eyes were lidless, if her facial economy seemed to provide no nostrils. Bodily, she might have more in common with the mollusk than with man, but some chord in her spirit touched the human, none the less.

Altogether, elfin bust and pearly vase, she was lass than four feet tall. And the flying shell, I knew, was as much a part of her, as much alive, as the shining crest or her purple eyes.

I sat in the bed, staring at her, bewildered, incredulous. She should have been a dream. The fastened window—for the room was air-conditioned—had not been disturbed; the door was still locked. But here she was. And I was as wide awake as I had ever been. I heard the distant thunder of an elevated train.

The red lips pouted, the keen voice came again, like a whistling, saying, as I sensed its wordless meaning: *Do not be afraid.* The shining being drifted a little toward my bed, settled toward me. Over the lip of the shell reached a slender arm, bright with golden fur.

The hand that reached for me was tiny, infinitely delicate, seven-fingered. It was thumbless, the middle finger longest. The nails were narrow, pointed, crimson. For all its golden strangeness, it was beautiful, and, to me, a hand.

The keen piping, so lonely, so sorrowfully sweet, wailed again. I looked into the infinite wells of those purple eyes. And something made me put up my own big hand, grasp those tiny furry fingers.

Instantly, incredibly, I was snatched out of my body.

I know how utterly fantastic, impossible, that must seem. But I had an instant's impression of my body left behind in that dim room, sitting bolt-upright and motionless in the bed. Then we were plunging upward, outside, above the dark building and the restless city.

Southward we soared—that shining being beside me, drawing me by the hand, for my form was still the same, even if my body lay behind—across slumbering continents and over dark whispering oceans.

We swept into the frigid gray twilight that lay upon the polar lands. I recognized the very Mountains of Despair, of which my party had made an aerial survey on the last expedition, and lying vast and desolate beyond them, the Stapledon Basin.

And down we sloped again, across gray crevasse-riven glaciers, toward a towering transpolar range that I had glimpsed in the distance, called the Mountains of Uranus, but had never reached.

As we dropped toward those black granite peaks, bleakly stark, frost-shattered, yet rearing so majestically from the eternal ice, I was amazed to see what seemed a building, with twin hexagonal towers, projecting above the naked wind-swept ledges of a rounded summit.

This structure—I hardly know a name for it—seemed deeply anchored in the living granite. Its material was unfamiliar: ice-clear and richly purple, like some unimaginable colossal amethyst. Its low massive outline somewhat suggested those towered gateways of the ancient Egyptians that archeologists call pylons. But it had no opening; it appeared doorless, windowless, one solid block of flawless crystal.

Near it, however, a side fissure cleft the black summit. Worn stone steps, freshly swept free of snow, led down into it. At their foot was a massive door of black metal, battered and corroded as if by the impact of ages.

W E SETTLED down upon the barren ledge above the fissure. I stood upon the snow-patched granite—or it seemed that I did, for I was still aware that my body lay back in New York. And the shining being floated beside me, the golden tendrils of her fingers still grasping my hand.

A weirdly unforgettable scene. The stark black mountain beneath us towering above the gray infinity of ice. The midnight sun burning low and ominously red in the misty distance. The immemorial mass of that towered crystal block, strange with deep-cut glyphs, looming above us like the enigmatic monument of some lost and forgotten race.

But the being at my side was looking down at that ancient black door. A little time went by. Then a girl opened the door, and came running lightly up the steps.

She was beautiful—slender, tall, filled with the glory of young womanhood. Her trim clothing was strangely cut from some pure white fur. The one strand of hair that escaped her close-fitting cap was a gorgeous ruddy gold. Her oval face was very fair, the forehead high and white. Her wide blue eyes were burning with some new-born eagerness.

Beautiful. . . . My stumbling words could never convey her perfect loveliness. I looked at her, drank deep of her vital splendor, for some old, haunting thirst was being satisfied. She held some elusive perfection that I had sought, for many weary years, in many lands, even in my polar explorations, and never glimpsed before.

Beautiful. . . . I knew instinctively that I wanted her, to possess and to serve, to love, for ever. And I knew, bitterly, that this was only some strange dream, that I really lay still—or my body did— back in New York City.

"Maru-Mora!"

The girl ran to the flying being, with that eager greeting on her tongue. She embraced those golden shoulders, lightly, gently. A tiny golden-furred hand stroked her head, affectionately. Then the keen thin piping of Maru-Mora came again, and the girl turned eagerly toward me.

"I know your name: you are Ron Dunbar," she said, surprizingly. She spoke English. Her voice was low, faintly awkward, as if she were little used to speech. It was soft, deeply rich, delicious. "I am Karalee," she said. "Maru-Mora brought you here to her dwelling—or a part of you—so that I might speak to you, for her."

I—or the "part of me"—stood drinking in her sheer, glowing loveliness. Swift admiration had conquered my old diffidence with women, even my present amazement. I stood merely looking, delighted, until suddenly I was afraid that my gaze might offend or discomfit the girl.

"I'm glad that she did," I said. "And I wish that she had brought all of me, so that perhaps I could stay."

Deep and serene, the girl's clear blue eyes looked into mine. Her full lips quivered suddenly; her white nostrils flared to a deeper breath; her deep bosom lifted.

"I wish, Ron Dunbar," her low voice said simply, "that you could stay."

Afterward, I was surprised at my swift surrender to a woman in a dream. But that incredible experience, seemed more direct and clear than common. Some old restraint was left behind.

"I'll come again," I found myself promising the girl. "Now I know the way. I'll fly back to these very mountains. Next time, all of me—for you."

Eagerness shone bright on her face.

"You will come, Ron—for me?" Gleaming tears misted her eyes. "And sometime—we can go out together—out into the World?"

The sweet exotic piping of Maru-Mora came again then, swiftly urgent. The girl Karalee looked up at the supernal being, and back to me. And all the eagerness had gone from her face. It was a pale, bleak oval, stricken. The tears were gone. Her eyes were dry, dark with pain.

"No, Ron, you must never come back." Her voice was steady and low. "That is what Maru-Mora brought you to hear. You must never fly your machine into this land again. You must promise that."

I looked at her, sharing all the agony written on her white face.

"But I'm coming back," I said, "before the sun is gone. I'm coming to take you away, Karalee—"

Her face brightened for a moment, to a tortured eagerness of longing. She looked up again at the silent fantastic shape of Maru-Mora.

"No, Ron Dunbar," her voice came slow and heavy with regret. "You must not come to this land again." Her tone quivered. "Never—not even for me. Maru-Mora forbids it."

I looked up at the shining being that still held my hand in her tiny furry fingers, demanding:

"Why?"

## 4. "They That Sleep"

A GAIN that eldritch, plaintive piping sobbed from the elfin woman's head, gold-crowned and scarlet-plumed, above that flaring opalescent shell. Again the fair girl Karalee, so lovely in her trim white furs, rendered translation:

"It is true, Ron Dunbar, that you are planning to fly here again, with new companions, before this sun is gone?"

"It is," I said, surprized.

"It is true," Karalee gave the next question, "that your purpose is to thaw the ice from all this world?"

Perhaps I shouldn't have been amazed at that. After all, Maru-Mora had come to New York after me. I suppose, that she now displayed knowledge of what had occurred there, that evening, in Harding's apartment.

For an instant, however, I was speechless. A strange fear chilled and shook me, until I looked up into those great purple orbs. They came down to my face, and I felt a warmth of supernal peace. The fear was gone.

"That's right," I said. "We're going to use atomic power. Doctor Bell hopes to make the whole continent temperate, and open it up to settlement."

"Then you must give up the plan," Karalee rendered the swift reply. "For the ice must never be thawed. . . . Death is sleeping under the ice, Ron Dunbar—the death of all the world! Take care lest you rouse it."

"Death?" I demanded. "What do you mean?"

Then took place the strangest and certainly the most terrible part of all that incredible adventure.

We still stood together beside that colossal pylon, on the naked granite of that frozen peak. Red as blood, the midnight sun burned low in the horizonless distance, where the gray illimitable desert of ice merged with the gray and featureless sky. A bitter wind howled and moaned about the towers of the pylon. I was insensible of any cold, but the girl Karalee was already pale, shivering. She had gestured toward the steps that led down to the door in the rock.

"Let us go down into my rooms," she said. "It is warmer there."
Dark with longing and regret, her eyes looked at Maru-Mora, and

back to me. "If you are forbidden to return, at least—"

Maru-Mora's piping cut her off. As if answering a command, the girl stepped quickly to the flying being. She held out a mittened hand. Tiny golden fingers clasped it.

"Come," the girl translated. "Maru-Mora is carrying us to see the peril that you must not rouse. It is They That Sleep."

We rose again. I had the briefest glimpse of Karalee left standing on that frozen ledge, her arm rigidly extended. Yet she was with us also, drawn by Maru-Mora's other hand—drawn out of her body, as I had been.

W E THREE soared swiftly through chill gray mists, descended upon a rugged ice-plain from which jutted great boulders of granite, black, naked, shattered with the frost of ages. We stood at the brink of a dark crevasse. Karalee pointed across it.

Her lips moved twice before she could speak, and her voice came muffled, breathless, choked with horror.

"There," she said. "One of Them. It is the Watcher."

I shuddered at sight of that monstrous thing. It stood upright upon a cragged boulder, and it did not move. The body of it was black, covered with great scales, a swollen elongated thing shaped like an immense barrel. It stood upon three black tentacular limbs, whose extremities had coiled like mighty serpents to grasp the granite.

Head, it had none. But the bulged upper end of the black body was broken with a great sharp triangular projection, which looked like a hideous snout. Three scaled triangular flaps, just about its swollen equatorial belt, might, I thought, cover strange organs of sense.

This creature was utterly horrifying, in a sense I can hardly define. Its horror held nothing familiar. If Maru-Mora was clearly non-human, it was certainly non-terrestrial. It chilled me with an elemental, absolute revulsion.

I knew that the girl was sick and cold with dread. I heard her make a pleading little whistle: her human imitation of the voice of Maru-Mora. Her strained hoarse whisper came to me, urgent:

"Look swiftly, Ron, so that we can go, I do not like these things. But Maru-Mora says you must see—"

The black monstrosity, indeed, held my gaze with a fascination of utter terror. It had been there, motionless, a long time. The great black scales were silvered with frost. Snow was banked beyond it. The ice had climbed up over the coils of its ophidian limbs.

The boulder was cracked, I saw, shattered. Time had splintered the granite since those giant tentacles first grasped it. Only their frozen pressure held it from crumbling. How many centuries?

Surely, after so long, I thought, it must be dead—and I knew that it was not. Nothing dead could inspire such resistless fear. I sensed—or fancied—a slow, implacable beat, like a pulse of evil, measured, menacing, mind-shattering.

I flinched suddenly, turned away, hid my eyes with a trembling hand. I fought a strange and elemental sickness, a newborn horror that gnawed worm-like at the marrow of my bones. It brought a flood of vast relief when:

"Come," said Karalee. "We go to see the others."

We left that stark eternal black sentinel overlooking the glaciers. We soared swiftly through the leaden mists, came down upon ridged and fissured ice.

"The others," said the girl, "are all about their ship, beneath the ice."

Driven by a fascinated compulsion to see all I could, even though the horror of it should consume me, I was striving in vain to peer down through the gray-white obscurity of the ice—when suddenly we were beneath it!

Down through the darkness of the glacier we plunged, as swiftly as through the air above. The ice was all around us, like a blue-green liquid.

And suddenly we were standing again on a long ridge of granite. We were far beneath the glacier, which was like a thick green-black mist above us. I could see little at first, but gradually my vision sharpened—or perhaps Maru-Mora in some manner shared her own strange senses with me—and I perceived the great valley beyond and below us.

Dim in the green haze of the ice, I presently distinguished a cyclopean machine. Resting on tremendous skids which lay far along the floor of the valley, it was all of darkly gleaming red-black metal. A colossal bulging hull, surrounded with a confusion of struts and braces, masts and booms and metal arms, mysterious rods and vanes, towered even above the ridge where we stood. It was like the bloated body of some monstrous spider, crouching with folded limbs, set to spring.

Here and there about those crimson planes and arms, frozen motionless in the green mist of ice, I saw black and hideous beings like the Watcher: scaled bodies headless and bulging, supported on triple ophidian limbs.

An alien horror touched me, as we stood on that black ridge beneath the ice. It was the stark menace of the Outside; the terror of worlds strange beyond conception, of powers and entities supernal, monstrous, utterly alien. That stark, wondering, elemental dread—some dim instinctive inkling of it, I think, is at the basis of many primitive religions—is the most terrible emotion a human being can feel.

D IMLY through the numbness of my dread, as if I dreamed within a dream, I heard the piping of Maru-Mora, and Karalee spoke:

"That is the ship that came from—Beyond. And They are the Tharshoon. They came to conquer Earth. That was in another age, before the ice came here. This was a fair world, then, and my people ruled it. Man was not born."

I knew that this was Maru-Mora speaking, through the lips of the wide-eyed, terror-gazed girl.

"The Tharshoon brought fearsome weapons: giant needles that poured out terrible red flame. Even their eyes could stare us into—nothingness. And we had none. We had been a people of peace.

"The invaders attacked our white cities, overwhelmed them in horror and death. We were without defense, until I, the Seeker, who had long since given up my body on the altar of science, discovered a power that made them sleep.

"By that time, it was too late to save my people. They all had perished. But I lived—when rather I had died. I stopped the Tharshoon, in the hour of their victory. And I have stood guard upon them, whom I could not destroy."

The half-chanting voice of Karalee—speaking, I knew, the thoughts of the strange elder being—had become oddly like the piping of Maru-Mora. It was plaintively sorrowful, weary with age-old loneliness, piercing with a yearning beyond words.

"The world has changed its axis. The ice has come to bind the sleepers more securely. Your race of man has risen from the northern jungle beasts. And still I wait and watch. . . . And the

Tharshoon shall not wake!"

However amazing that scrap of Earth-history, it was, in my singular mental state, somehow credible. I knew Antarctica had once been tropical; it is rich with coal seams; our survey had revealed a rich Jurassic fossil flora of ferns, conifers and cycads, within fifty miles of the pole; I was familiar with the various theories of axial shift and continental drift. For the rest of it, the hideous forms of the invaders and the Seeker's exotic beauty were here before my eyes.

Yes, I accepted it without question, then. And the ray of understanding merely increased my shocked and reeling dread. Maru-Mora was piping again, and the girl said anxiously:

"Come. We must return. Maru-Mora's strength is low. Should it fail, we all must perish."

For myself, I was eager to escape. The green mist of ice was suddenly crushing, suffocating. And I was sick from the overwhelming horror of that ship and its monstrous crew.

But the tiny golden figures tightened on my hand, and the girl's. We left the black ridge beside that vessel from "Beyond," drive upward through the malachite haze of the ice. We swept over the glaciers again, toward the towering black range and the time-battered summit where the purple pylon stood.

I glimpsed the girl's body waiting, rigid in its furs—not a muscle had moved since we left. Then we were beside it, and there was but one Karalee. Blue with cold, shuddering, she began beating her mittened hands stiffly against her sides.

The Seeker piped again, and she turned to me, gasping:

"You have seen them now, Ron Dunbar. The eternal Sleepers—if they are waked, your world will die! Let them sleep—do not try to thaw the ice—and don't come back again."

"But I am coming back." I tugged toward her, against the strange strength of Maru-Mora's hand. "For I love you, Karalee."

The shivering girl started toward me, eagerly. But the eery voice of Maru-Mora stopped her. The white oval of her face went starkly rigid. Her wide blue eyes turned dark with dread.

"No, Ron, don't come back!" she sobbed. "For you will die, and I, and all the world—"

The Seeker piped again, imperatively. The girl turned slowly, as if in reluctant obedience. Her dry eyes looked back at me, blank with tragedy, mutely imploring. She tried to speak, and could not. She went stiffly, at last, down the steps in the fissure, and through the black door.

"Karalee—" I called after her, vainly. The door closed ponderously. I was still staring at it when I felt the Seeker's tiny fingers tugging at my hand.

She drew me toward the side of the pylon. The purple transparency of it towered sheer out of the black granite. Frost of ages had splintered and crumbled the stone, blizzards of ages carved it grotesquely. That cyclopean crystal, however, remained diamond-hard, diamond-polished; it was deeply graven with the lost runes of a world dead before the coming of the ice.

One moment she paused against that amethystine wall. Wondrous being! A fluted spiral vase of opalescent pearl, holding flower-like an elfin queen, golden-robed and golden-crowned, crimson-plumed. Last and greatest of a people lost! Maru-Mora, the Seeker!

The deep purple wells of her immense eyes regarded me soberly, as if with unuttered warning. Her delicate seven-fingered hand gestured toward Karalee's door. Her scarlet mouth pouted to a single admonishing note.

Then her furry fingers released me. As easily as we had entered the ice, she drifted through that adamantine wall, into the crystal pylon. She seemed to relax. For an instant I watched her still, sinking peacefully through its pellucid depths.

Then I turned. I tried to walk back toward the crevice in the rock that opened to Karalee's abode. But the world splintered about me. I was crushed beneath a black, appalling avalanche of pain. . . .

And then I was in bed again, back in my room at the Aero Club.

## 5. Beyond the Pole

EVEN now, writing these words, I am overcome with a black tide of guilt. For the warning in that singular vision had been explicit, unmistakable. Had I been wise enough to heed it, what untold horror and death might have been averted!

The silent hands of the electric clock, when I looked, stood at three-forty. My body, which had lain thirty-five minutes uncovered and motionless, was stiff with cold, yet strangely damp with sweat. A blinding headache splintered through the back of my brain. Clambering uncertainly out of the bed, I found myself trembling with nervous exhaustion, sound heart fluttering as if it had come through some terrific strain.

At first I could hardly stand, but I felt better as movement restored circulation. I wouldn't, I decided, call a doctor; what I wanted was a chance to think over what had happened. After a few turns around the room, I took two aspirins, smoked out a pipe, and went back to bed—but not to sleep that night.

For my mind was still too full of Maru-Mora's supernal wonder; of the immemorial ice-drowned horror of the Sleepers; of Karalee's young intoxicating beauty. Desperately I wrestled with the terrible question: had it been real, or a dream?

It all had been absolutely convincing as it passed; doubt had only come afterward. It had seemed too perfect in detail, too strangely coherent, too fearfully alien, to be a dream—for the dreaming mind commonly reflects only the familiar patterns of the day, creating nothing new. But the stiff orthodoxy of my scientific training balked at accepting it as anything more than a dream.

Could the human mind exist outside the body?—fly ten thousand miles and back in half an hour?—dive a mile beneath the ice cap?

That was childish superstition; any enlightened savage would know better.

The Seeker—was she possible? A pre-human being as high as mankind—or higher; ageless dweller in a crystal block; flitting intangibly over the planet at the speed of thought! Who would believe my tale of Maru-Mora?

The Tharshoon—could such monstrosities be? Could sentient invaders have crossed the gulf from some imaginable Beyond? Assuming that they came when a tropical wilderness covered the present polar continent, could they have survived ten or a hundred million years beneath the ice? The scientist in me answered those questions with an outraged "No!"

Moreover, at the risk of greater blame, but for the sake of honesty, I must confess that even if I had been fairly convinced of the reality of that experience—still might I have gone. For a kind of foolhardiness—or it may be only egotism—had made me ever seek danger rather than avoid it. No that I am fearless, at all; merely that great peril has a resistless fascination, even when it terrifies me.

And then, besides, I had seen Karalee.

That is all my apology. I merely hope the reader will try to understand why I chose to ignore that singular warning—why I strove to credit it, in my own mind, to a heavy supper and my worries about Doctor Harding and our flight to the south.

I SAID nothing at all to my associates about that astounding dream. Our preparations were completed with little delay. On the afternoon of the February 21, the last bulky crates of Bell's atomic apparatus were stowed aboard the *Austral Queen,* moored in San Francisco Bay. The next morning we took off for Antarctica, via Honolulu, Suva, and Dunedin.

We were five. Remembering the loyal faith of Jerry Ware, I might have known that no husband of hers would go into peril without her by his side.

A strange haze the forewarned of an early blizzard met us, as we came down across the dark polar sea. In the pale light of the low sun reddening behind us in the north, it shimmered with a curious pellucid saffron radiance. The towering white-crowned icebergs loomed out of it with a suddenness always startling.

Flying low, no more than a frail mote lost in the ominous immensity of this ice-walled sea at the bottom of the world, the *Austral Queen* soon battled a freezing headwind.

A big, four-motored amphibian transport, she had served me loyally through two previous expeditions. But she was too heavily laden, now, with the five of us, our winter's supplies and equipment, and the nine tons of Bell's apparatus.

The blizzard, as if to give warning of the grim night to come, met us with savage fury. Sometimes it drove us perilously close to the fangs of the ice; sometimes its opposing violence held us motionless.

Tommy Veering had spelled me at the controls, while I got a little sleep back on the dunnage that filled half the cabin, but he called me forward as the wind grew worse, in the sixties. I was tired—for all the flight had been a desperate race against the polar night. Yet, back at the controls, I found an old elation. I shared the victory of the ship as she defied the teeth of the ice and the sea's cold maw, and met the blows of the bitter wind.

Floes and bergs became more frequent, and at last the white pack was beneath us. The desolate Balleny Islands were behind. We veered a little eastward, around Cape Adare, and battled our way along the grim coast of South Victoria Land.

Dim-shrouded in the blizzard, the dark masses of Mount Erebus and Mount Terror crept down to our right, and at last the Ross Barrier came marching out of the ever-thickening saffron mists, a black and hostile wall towering hundreds of feet to the white desert of flying snow.

Jerry Harding had come up into the cockpit, after Veering went back, bringing hot coffee. Her brave gray eyes scanned the wall of ice ahead; then she looked at me, and her voice came quiet and grave:

"We are flying very low, Ron. Do you think—"

"I've been trying to keep under the wind," I said. "The ship is heavy, but she'll climb—she has to climb eighteen thousand feet to cross the passes into the Stapledon Basin. But she'll pull through."

"I hope so, Ron," Jerry said. "Aston has staked everything. . . . So much depends on us—a whole new world!"

The blizzard screaming off the ice shelf, as I brought the ship up, struck like the hand of a demoniac giant. She shuddered like a stricken thing, and plunged down again into the mist of ice crystal whipped off the frozen barrier.

Harding's wife stifled her instinctive cry of fear, but her white small hand went convulsively tight on my shoulder. Her gray eyes looked at me, big with that terrible question.

"It's all right, Jerry." I tried to get some calm into my voice. The *Queen* has never failed me yet. She's brave—as a woman!"

And she didn't fail me then. She came up again, with motors thundering wide open, through that flying spume of frost. She hung, evenly battling the wind, for a heart-breaking moment above the frozen blade that edged the ice plateau. She sank— lifted—leapt ahead.

"And here we are—on the world we've come to conquer."

Jerry Harding caught a breath of relief, and her hand relaxed on my shoulder. She leaned across to peer down at the polar world, thickly misted with blizzard-whipped snow, savage-fanged with hummocks and pressure ridges, black-scarred with abysmal crevasses.

Then again something happened that it is difficult to account for in the cold rational light of established science. A small thing in itself, perhaps—merely the inexplicable sensation of an in-stant—but terrible in its significance.

I had looked aside at Jerry's frail loveliness, her pale lips now parted with a little smile. And some warning tentacle of cold reached suddenly into the insulated cabin, to touch my spine. Something, I know, made me shudder, made my trembling hands knot hard on the wheel.

It was a thing I could not explain, any more that the dream of the Seeker. But in that instant, as surely as if I had seen her lying in her coffin, I knew that Jerry was doomed.

She knew it, too. She felt the same ghastly intuition—that was the terrible part. Otherwise I should have ignored it, set it down to fatigue and my own vague fears, for I haver never been ruled by hunches.

Her face went abruptly paler. She caught her breath, and her white lips set. For a moment her whole thin body was rigid. Then her gray eyes looked at me, suddenly dark, dreadful, shadowed with the doom I knew they had seen.

"Quite a bump, we passed," I said, as easily as I could. "Made me giddy for a moment, and nearly got the controls."

For a long, terrible moment, her tortured eyes looked into my face, straining as if to read some awful secret. I tried not to let her know I had shared that fearful premonition. At last she swallowed uneasily.

"Ron," she said uncertainly, "if—if anything should happen to me, please look after Aston. He needs someone. He isn't—he's not quite himself."

And she left me, in a moment, and went back to her husband.

I TRIED to deny or forget that disturbing, uncanny sensation. But it clung and grew in my brain, like something evil and alive. And the difficulties ahead seemed suddenly a more terrible barrier than the wall of ice we had passed. Where lay any hope of success? What impress could four men and a woman make upon this eternal citadel of winter?

The tense hours passed. We drove on into the blizzard, above the featureless white surface of the Barrier. As our load of fuel was lightened, I fought for altitude to gain the passes of plateaus before us.

The barren summits of the Commonwealth Range behind, we flew up the long inlet of the Barrier, beside Queen Maud's Range. The Austral Queen labored bravely upward, battled the shrieking wind that hurled her at the black crags that walled a glacier-carven pass, and we were at last above the polar plateau.

We passed seventy miles to the left of the Pole itself. For two hours we fought the tempest that raged down beside the Mountains of Despair, across beyond the Pole, before we reached the only pass. It was the highest on the flight, and there we met the most savage wind. I had to drop half our reserve tanks of gasoline, before the ship found courage to lift above the barrier.

Beyond we came down into the Stapledon Basin: the site the Bell had chosen for our attempt to thaw the ice. It was an ice-clad plateau nine thousand feet high, walled on all sides with dark tremendous ranges towering above the glaciers.

Far across it, a hundred and forty miles away and invisible in the hazy fury of the blizzard, rose, I knew, that mighty unexplored transpolar range that I had glimpsed and named the Mountains of Uranus—on whose summit, in the dream, I had seen the purple pylon of the Seeker.

I had resolved to discount the dream. But now I found myself straining my eyes through the bleak gray mist, wondering, dwelling even upon the bright memory of the girl Karalee—until a jutting rocky ridge broke the ice beneath us, and it was time to land.

Wind and altitude made that landing difficult. The heavy-burdened plane came hurtling down far too swiftly. A black granite boulder loomed suddenly out of the blinding drift-snow whipped along the surface. Our skids crashed against the ice crust. The ship bounced, lurched awkwardly around the boulder, buried her nose in the drift beyond.

The flight was ended.

### 6. The Haunted Camp

I OPENED the hatch and dug my way to the surface. Merry Bell followed me up into the blizzard. It had moderated to a mere fifty-mile gale, but still at nine thousand feet, at forty below, it could pierce our furs and sear our lungs.

A welter of dark outcroppings of shattered granite and fantastically carved white drifts surrounded us. The desolate rugged ice beyond was like a wild sea congealed in the midst of a furious storm. The dark ranges that walled the Basin, fifty to eighty miles away, were lost in lead-gray mist.

Bell was staring about, shivering.

"This ridge is the summit of a mountain, buried under the glacier," I told him. "Our survey showed the ice over most of the Basin to be three to five thousand feet—"

His tortured thin face was suddenly warm with enthusiasm.

"It's just the spot I wanted, Ron," he was saying eagerly. "We'll set up the tower on the ridge. The atomic beam itself will reach to all these mountains. And the Basin, when it is warmed, will serve as a sort of furnace to moderate all the continent, with wind-convection, and warm rivers flowing down through the passes."

The breathless wonder of his dream caught me for a moment. I saw lush verdure replace the white desolation of ice, saw green forests blanket the black flanks of those mountains that had known no life for ten million years. I saw busy cities, even, rich plantations spread beneath the summer-long day, mines, railroads, factories.

"Once this land was warm," Bell's quick voice had run on. "Coal forests, in the Permo-Carboniferous—"

That brought back my haunting dream: the fantastic beauty of Maru-Mora, and the alien horror of the sleepers. Jerry Harding's voice reached me faintly from the plane, and I recalled the grim premonition that had struck me as we crossed the Barrier. I shuddered, and tried to forget.

"Our first problem is to build living-quarters," I told Bell. "If we don't—well, this is mild summer, compared to what is coming."

And we set to work at once, to establish a winter camp. For the plane we cut a sort of hanger in the ice, covered it with protecting blocks of snow. Our living-quarters also were hewn in the glacier, walled with the packing-cases that held our supplies, roofed with snow packed on tar-paper.

That occupied the most of our time until late March—until the sun, wheeling ever lower and redder and huger and colder, peered for the last time through a pass in the Mountains of Uranus, and did not return.

None of the others had had any previous polar experience. All but Harding were willing to follow my leadership in building the camp. But he made himself difficult, to put it mildly.

He wanted Bell to begin erecting his atomic battery at once. But Bell said that three months or half a year might pass before the installation could be completed. And during that time, I knew, without good living-quarters we must perish. Bell and

Jerry did their best to convince Harding of this necessity, but he remained sullen and unwilling.

Harding's disturbing change of manner seemed always more extreme. There was no visible physical difference in him—unless, as I sometimes thought, his pale blue eyes had turned a little darker. But something had totally changed his nature. Had I been superstitious enough to credit such a thing, I should have thought him literally *possessed*.

For many years he had been a close friend of mine. The long ruddy face beneath his untidy mess of yellowish hair was still unmistakably familiar. Yet sometimes, as I caught the new ruthless hardness in his eyes, I thought I looked upon a stranger.

He became increasingly dictatorial, quarrelsome, even vicious, He was savagely rude, even cruel, to young Tommy Veering. He cursed him, made rough jokes at his expense, ridiculed his youth and timidity. Twice I saw him knock Veering down, when they were at work together, with no excuse at all.

And the thin young engineer, through some quirk of dog-like meekness, accepted all Harding's offensiveness without any show of resentment. Indeed, so far as I could tell, he liked the big man all the better for this abuse. He kept Harding's company, and came to side with him in any argument.

What most distressed me about Harding, however, was his unkindness to Jerry. He developed a way of saying sharp cruel things to her, displaying a venomous malevolence that I had never suspected in him.

One day at table, for example, saying that his tea was cold, he flung it into Jerry's face, and began cursing her savagely. I should have hit him, then, but Jerry ran to me, wiping the scalding liquid out of her eyes, caught my arm, and begged me not to strike him.

T HE rude dwelling finished at last, we unloaded Bell's equipment and carried it to the chosen site: a bare out-cropping of living granite, just above the camp. Working beneath a canvas shelter—for, since the sun had gone, it was growing bitterly cold—we began drilling holes into the rock to anchor the legs of the tower.

As we cleared the crust of ice from this ledge, Tommy Veering made a curious discovery. In a crevice he found a number of tiny fossils: lichens, several small ancient spiders, two minute degenerative hymenopterous insects, and a small ammonite. The specimens were not so remarkable as their state of preservation. For every tiny limb and segment was intact, diamond-hard.

Veering showed the find to Harding, who became oddly excited over it.

"These are the original bodies!" he exclaimed, peering at them with a pocket microscope. "There has been no mineralizing, no substitution as in ordinary petrification. They have been just somehow—frozen!"

Mere heat, however, did not thaw them. The effort seemed sheerest folly—for the presence of the extinct mollusk alone was proof that the things had existed unchanged through geological ages—but Harding and Veering, in our rude little laboratory, made continual effort to revive the fossils.

"But they aren't fossils, at all," Harding insisted. "There has been no change or deterioration since they were alive. The microscopic structure is perfect, ever cell intact!"

His weeks of work only deepened the puzzle. It was about this time, incidentally, that he began to wear colored glasses, saying that the long hours at the microscope strained his eyes.

"The newer physics," he told me once, "would say that these creatures are in a space-time *stasis*. The spectroscope shows that the characteristics of space about their atoms has been altered, warped, so that no change or motion is possible—not even any time!"

Behind the dark lenses his eyes glittered with a strange excitement.

"If we could reverse that warping force, unlock the stasis, they would live again, unaware that even a second has passed." His voice was feverish, husky, terrible. "And that secret, if we learn it, will be a weapon greater than the Gorgon's head."

Frankly, I thought the project mere folly if not insane delusion, for I had increasing doubts of Harding's mental balance. But I did not discourage it, because it occupied his time and left his less troublesome.

The erection of Bell's automatic apparatus, meantime, went steadily forward. Veering proved himself a skilled and brilliant technician. By midwinter, it seemed, the battery might be in operation. All the ice would be thawed from the Basin, Bell promised, by the coming of the sun.

It is hard to give a true record of those weary, dragging months of winter night. The shadow of dire catastrophe had overhung us from the first. My old irrational conviction of approaching tragedy had slowly deepened. Life in the Antarctic is a grim enough business at best, and Harding's increasingly evil nature made it, at times, almost insupportable.

But, aside from all that, there had been something else—something that Bell, and perhaps even Jerry, must have sensed more keenly than I.

When I say that the camp was haunted, it sounds like superstitious nonsense. Yet, almost from the day of our arrival, I had a curious, uneasy feeling that it as—that some strange intangible Presence hung about us, alertly watching every move we made, listening to every word we said.

Bell and Jerry, I think, were more conscious of it than I. For I often saw them silent, with cocked heads and strained intent faces, listening.

"It's nothing, Ron," Jerry said once, when I asked her what she listened for. Her tired face tried to smile. "I'm just nervous, I guess, worried about poor Aston. He had changed so, grown so much worse—have you noticed?"

And Bell, as we worked together about his tower, often paused to peer away across the ice. He laughed when I spoke about it, but his white face remained very grave.

"Just a feeling," he said, "that Something is watching us—trying to speak to us, perhaps." His thin frame abruptly shivered. "I've a queer feeling, Ron," he confessed, "that we shouldn't thaw the ice. I'm somehow afraid." His dark tortured eyes stared away again; his voice sank low. "Yes, afraid—of what we might uncover."

The warning of that singular dream came to me again. I felt an impulse to tell Bell about it, but checked my tongue. He was troubled enough already; I didn't want to increase his anxiety.

For still I believed it a dream. I dared not regard it as anything else. Sometimes I found myself staring northward, toward the Mountains of Uranus, wondering if the Seeker's purple pylon might indeed stand on some summit there. But I could never see it.

MARCH had gone, and most of April, when the thing happened that crystallized all my vague apprehensions and shattered the routine of our life at camp—that started the dread avalanche that did not end until all the world had been overwhelmed in horror.

The whole camp was asleep, after a long shift spent bolting together the sections of Bell's tower. I started suddenly awake, alarmed, yet not knowing what had roused me. For an instant I lay still, listening.

The wind, which had blown steadily for many days, had died. At first I could hear only a soft, weird rustling—the whisper of the aurora.

But suddenly, mingled with that eery sussuration, I caught another sound—a sound terribly familiar, and yet incredible: a thin far wailing, infinitely sweet and infinitely sad. It held all the heart-broken loneliness of the world, caught in slow eery minors, so faint they mocked the ears.

It was the piping of the Seeker of my dream. The voice of Maru-Mora! Or had I merely dreamed again? For it had ceased.

Breathless and trembling, uncertain that I had heard anything at all, I donned furs and hastened up out of our ice-burrow, into the polar night. The unutterable, appalling splendor of it caught me, held me for a moment motionless.

Complete calm had fallen. The air, curiously brilliant with frost, was absolutely still. The clear sky was purple-black, the southern constellations pale beyond the most brilliant auroral display I ever witnessed. Pure silver, crystal green and living rose, its curved rays sprayed from beyond the pole. Its rustling, bannered hosts marched endlessly, whispering immemorial secrets of outer space.

With an effort I broke the aching thrall of its beauty. I stumbled up to the ledge beside Bell's unfinished tower, and peered away across the snow. It lay glittering and brilliant, dimly flushed with auroral color, drifts massed fantastically.

Painful as the ring of glass to a violin bow, I heard that sound again: an eery minor threnody, a resistless call of provocative promise.

And far away, beyond black grotesque hummocks of bare ice, I saw an incredible thing. Above the silver snow, plain the aurora's radiance, it drifted. Flew—wingless! A tapered spiral, flaring upward. A woman's bust, golden-furred, cradled in it shimmering cup. An elfin woman's head, golden-crowned, proudly scarlet-crested. Slim golden arms that beckoned.

It was Maru-Mora, the Seeker of my dream!

And the dream, then, was real. The purple pylon did tower

somewhere from the peaks beyond the ice. And lovely Karalee, to whom I promised in the dream to return, must be living reality!

A cold tide of horror flowed suddenly over my soul; for the black Tharshoon, the scaled and monstrous Sleepers of the ice, must then be real also—and waiting to be wakened, if we should thaw the polar ice.

I had ignored the Seeker's warning, and Karalee's tearful appeal. What, now, was to be the penalty?

Manu-Mora's piping came again, alluring with its uncanny haunting sweetness, terrible with immemorial pain. The aurora flooded the sky again, and once more, far away, I glimpsed the alien beauty of the Seeker.

She flew low but swiftly, calling, golden arms beckoning. And beneath her, stumbling frantically after her, was—a man!

Caught in a queer paralysis of fascinated dread, I watched as he toiled up a slippery bank, tottered perilously along the brink of a black crevasse. The shining alien siren fled away before him, mocking, elusive. He followed her over the flank of a gleaming drift. They both were gone.

It was a moment before I could recover myself, put down a sense of outraged unreality. Then I shouted, ran along the ledge toward the drift where they had vanished.

What the Seeker might be, dream or illusion, phantom or alien living being, I knew not—but I did know that only terrible death could await any man luted out across the ice. Was that her way to stop our work?

The aurora dimmed suddenly. In the starlit darkness I saw nothing beyond the drift. Thin echoes from the ice were the only answer to my calls. The eery song had ceased, the singer and her victim vanished.

Shivering, from the shock of eldritch horror as much from the bitter cold, I stumbled back to the camp. My shouts had roused the others. Jerry Harding, bewildered, anxious-eyed, met me as I came down into our burrow.

"What was it, Ron?" she whispered apprehensively. "What happened? I woke with the most dreadful feeling. And where is poor Merry?"

"Bell?" I gasped.

"He's gone from his bunk," she told me.

And I knew that it was Meriden Bell who had followed the Seeker across the snow.

## 7. For Love of Maru-Mora

ONE thing was clear. Bewildered dread still fogged my mind. But I knew that Merry Bell had wandered out alone across the ice—knew that, without aid, he soon would die of cold. I told the others that I was going after him.

Aston Harding looked at me oddly. The dark glasses that he had worn since he began research on Veering's crystal fossils gave his long ruddy face a curiously sinister look.

"Yes, go after him, Dunbar," he rasped unpleasantly. "He's got to finish his job here. Then he can go where he likes."

Jerry Harding winced from the tone of that.

"You must find him, Ron," she begged compassionately. "Poor Merry—he has had no experience on the ice. He'll suffer. He has seemed so anxious lately—somehow tortured."

Whether it would take an hour or a week to find, Bell, I didn't know. Still following that eldritch siren, he had vanished beneath the fading aurora. I could only follow in the same direction. Hastily I put on trail clothing, while Jerry packed a little food for me, and a tiny alcohol burner. In ten minutes I set out, the light pack slung on my shoulders, carrying a flashlight and a compact little Hamlin gryo-compass. A grim impulse turned me back at the doorway, to pick up my automatic pistol.

Striking out northward, along the ridge, I was pondering the riddle of Maru-Mora, the dark enigma of the Tharshoon, the haunting question of Karalee's reality. Soon, however, the difficulties of the trail were enough to claim all my attention.

The going was not at all good. The ice was cracked and fissured, heaved into jutting masses. Over all was sifted the white drift snow that might here be half an inch deep, there hide a hundred-foot crevasse.

I was able, for the first half-mile, to follow the trail of Bell's boots. The dying witch-fires of the aurora still gave a little aid. The thin beam of the electric torch cut a small disk of flickering silver from the gray, ghostly starlight.

The trail ended, however, at the edge of a long steep slope of clear, wind-swept ice. Beyond, some stray gust may have covered it with snow. I couldn't find it again.

I pushed on northward, at last, following only the compass.

The Mountains of Uranus lay in that direction, seventy miles away, a week's march, perhaps, over this rugged, treacherous ice—farther, I knew, than Bell could ever make it.

It was an uncomfortable and perilous business. Even in the calm, numbing cold seeped into my furs. One false step could hurl me to death—perhaps in the same frigid chasm that already had swallowed Bell. If a blizzard should rise, there was small chance the we could retrace a way through its blinding fury back to camp.

I pressed on steadily, however. During the months at the Pole my old friendship for Merry Bell had deepened. I understood the torture of guilt he felt for Mawson Kroll's old crime. And I had come to share his eager hope of thawing the polar world.

Sometimes I called Bell's name into the frosty silence, but there was no reply save some brittle echo from the ice peaks. The hours passed, and my hope ebbed away. Glancing back, I saw an ominous bank of haze blotting out the poleward stars.

A blizzard was on the way.

DESPAIRINGLY, I was about to turn back when I saw a tiny gleam of light, far off to the left. Thinking that it was Bell, perhaps helpless, making a signal with his flashlight, I turned toward it.

Half an hour of stumbling effort brought me to the beacon. It was Bell's pocket light, lying on top of a lofty hummock and weighted with a block of ice. But he was not with it. The wavering trail of his boots led on across the snow, northward, toward the Mountains of Uranus.

But he must have left the light for a signal. Why?

The answer was a fluttering sheet of paper, pinned under the light. I snatched it out. A sheet torn from Bell's notebook, it was written awkwardly with ice-numbed fingers, addressed to me:

Dear Ron:

I can see the reflection of your light. I know you must be following. Please come no farther—it will only endanger your life. Let me go in peace.

You may have seen her—the wondrous being who came for me. It you did, you can understand. If you did not, no word of mine can tell you.

She is Maru-Mora, the Seeker, the last survivor of an elder people. She has wisdom older than the human race, and powers that science has not dreamed of. And she is alone.

She has come to me often, Ron, while I slept. She has taken me three times out of my body, to her dwelling on the mountain. Now she has called me again.

For ever.

This may be hard to understand, Ron. But I hope you will try, for we have been friends. I love Maru-Mora. I know she is non-human. Ours is no physical love, but a calling of kindred minds. And we are to be together.

I know already that this will cost my life, Ron. That is a small price, and I will pay it cheerfully. I feared that you and the rest would think me insane. That is why I have said nothing. But please understand.

For I love the Seeker as I could never love any woman. And life holds nothing more for me—you know that Mawson Kroll murdered my soul.

There is another reason, also, why I must go. I once hoped to thaw the polar ice, but that can never be. Maru-Mora has showed me the unthinkable horror that dwells beneath, waiting its chance to overwhelm the world. She says she warned you, Ron. For the sake of humanity, heed that warning!

Therefore I go, taking the secret of atomic power with me, lest it should fall into the hands of another Mawson Kroll. I beg you to watch Harding. The change in him is more diabolical than you suspect.

I am getting cold. Can't write more.

BELL.

THAT paper trembled as my hand held it in the silver funnel of light. With a strange mixture of feelings, I read it twice.

Maru-Mora! All the golden beauty of the elfin bust in its opalescent shell came back to me. I could see how such a man as Bell, lonely and estranged, might love that alien being with a passionate devotion.

Yet, Bell was a dear friend of mine. I could not see him surrender to an emotion so tragic, so hopeless. Ignoring the threatened blizzard, I followed his trail on into the north.

The surface for a space was more level. The tracks in the snow were clear. They showed that Bell was exhausted, reeling, staggering. This wild march had been too much for his unaccustomed strength. I knew that it would be difficult to get him safely back to camp before the blizzard struck.

It must have been an hour later when I saw—the Seeker!

Silently, she rose from a point on the trail ahead—a golden woman, scarlet-crested, flying in a vase of shining pearl. High and swiftly she soared away, straight toward one black rounded peak in the far-off Mountains of Uranus.

I stumbled fearfully ahead. At the spot from which she had risen, I found Merry Bell, lying motionless where he had fallen from a twenty-foot ice cliff. Dull red stained the snow about his head. His extremities were already frozen, but warmth was still in his body. I knew that he had lived until a few minutes before— until about the time I had seen the weird shining being fly back toward her mountain.

I cursed the Seeker, then, despite all that Bell had said of loving her, of giving his life willingly. For he had been a friend, and she had lured him out to die. . . .

I covered his body in a shallow grave, with a cross cut into the ice above his head, and whispered the Lord's Prayer over him. Bell had not been religious, nor was I. Yet the strangeness of that alien being, flying away from his dying body, had made me shudder with a superstitious fear.

Grief was heavy in me, and my senses dulled with a wondering dread, as I left the grave and turned wearily back toward camp. Bell's death, of course I thought, had ended the attempt to thaw the ice. I supposed that, as soon as the weather permitted us to level space for a takeoff, we should fly back toward civilization.

That ominous bank of haze rose swiftly before me, however. And the blizzard struck, with insane sudden violence, before I had covered a fourth of the distance. Savage wind hammered me. Cold pierced like probing needles. Whipped ice-crystals blinded and stung.

In the teeth of it I struggled on. I was soon reeling with fatigue, but, already numb with cold, I dared not stop to rest. Wind whipped the drifts into strange configurations. I could not retrace my steps. Blundering along, blinded, I slipped into a black pit.

Snow fell with me, buried me, suffocating. I floundered about to escape the chasm. Then I was dismayed to find that the compass, as well as my gun, had been lost in the snow.

The wind had grown harder, and, I thought, shifted. Without the compass, I knew, there was no hope of finding camp. I was lost in the blinding storm.

## 8. The Thing in the Snow

T HE remainder of that march is like an evil dream: bitter cold, draining effort, screaming wind piercing through my furs, driving snow a cruel blinding mist. My body was numb. Sensation became vague. Sense of time and reality were gone.

Without the gyro-compass, there was small chance of finding the camp again. It was little more than the old stubborn will to live that kept me on my feet. My dulled mind, however, felt no surprize when the up-tilted wing of a plane loomed dark in the flickering cone of my light.

It was the *Austral Queen,* I thought, uncovered and blown out of her hangar by the fury of the storm. She would have to be moored and covered again. Dimly, I wondered if she had been damaged, if our ice-hewn shelter had survived the wind.

The others—Jerry, Harding, Veering—might be in need of aid. But the thin beam of my light, smothered in flying snow, revealed no familiar landmark. I didn't know which way to search. And I was too far exhausted for any continued effort.

Dazedly I staggered up the last frozen slope, against that blast of stinging blinding ice, pried open the frost-locked door, and stumbled gratefully into the shelter of the slanting cabin.

I remember no more: I must have fallen immediately asleep. The wind had moderated a little when I woke. However cold, stiff, and weary, I was still alive. Reluctantly I stirred, to search for the others.

The plane lay on one side. The cabin was a confusion of broken instruments, equipment, and wreckage, covered with sifted snow. I clambered outside to investigate the extent of the disaster. The light's white finger played over the wreck. My heart sank, It was hopeless. One wing was altogether crushed. The plane was beyond repair.

The catastrophe staggered me. I couldn't understand it. Our ice-hangar had been constructed with habitual care. I had thought the plane safe from any possible freak of the wind.

My searching light quivered, stopped. There was something unfamiliar in the cambre of the intact wing, in the design of the crushed fuselage.

This wasn't the *Austral Queen* at all!

Lost, I had stumbled by sheer accident upon the wreck of some other plane. And I was still lost. In the gloom I clambered over the wreckage, found the shattered propeller, the motor hurled forward from its mount. I identified the ship: it was an old Albatross monoplane, twenty years out of date.

I scraped the crust of frost from the side of her crumpled fuselage, traced with the flashlight the painted letters: *Elida L—*

Elida Lee! I thrilled to a shudder of wondering dread. My boyhood came back, and the newspaper stories that first turned my mind to flying. Those had been the pioneer days of aerial exploration, when the exploits—or, too often, the deaths—of Lindbergh, Will Rogers, Wiley Post, Amelia Earhart, Amundsen, Ellsworth, Byrd—of them and many more, filled the front pages. And the "Flying Lees," as the papers called them, had been the bravest of that daring band.

I remembered their last flight. It was twenty years ago, when I was fourteen. Emulating the feat of the Russians, in making a highway of the top of the world, they had left Capetown, planning to fly to New Zealand across the South Pole. Their radio had failed as they came over the ice-blocked coast of Enderby Land. The last interrupted message stated that they had decided to go in, on spite of the trouble. And they had never come back.

This shattered wreck, then, must be the coffin of those gifted flyers, man and wife, Wilbur and Elida Lee, whose dauntless skill had thrilled my boyhood!

Searching through the snow in the fuselage again, however, did not find the gruesome things I expected. I uncovered navigation instruments, a hunting-rifle in its case, empty food cans, a little gasoline stove, blankets, and finally the frost-stiffened brief-case that held their records.

I saw that they must have survived the accident, living on in the poor shelter of the cabin. In the brief-case I found the diary of Wilbur Lee. Breathlessly, numb with the horror of that old tragedy and yet trembling with increasing amazement, I read the brief, inadequate notes the doomed flyer had written:

M ARCH 18, 1939. Wrecked two days ago. Both well enough, but for my crushed foot. But there is no hope of rescue or escape, so late in the season. We must face that.

I was a fool—I see it now. And Elida was too good a sport to tell me so. This flight was a reckless thing. We were going to retire. This was the last throw.

It was the landing that cracked us up. We came down to examine a thing we saw on the snow. It looked like some per-historic monster. It is near, though a drift hides it now. I shall examine it when my foot permits.

*March 19.* God knows why I write this. The odds are a thousand to one that no other eye will ever see it. Rescue is impossible. Yet there is a satisfaction in pretending to carry on.

Elida is brave. We should have been prepared for this. But we aren't. We had a trust in our luck. We never looked straight at the horrible reality. It couldn't happen to us. But it has happened—as surely as if we were already dead. There are supplies for two months. After that—

*March 26.* A week's blizzard. I had no heart to write. I tried to comfort Elida, though the truth may be that I am the more dependent on her calm strength. I was never made for such a trial as this. If it weren't for my foot—

*March 27.* We are weak already, from trying to conserve our rations though why the urge to prolong our hopeless existence, God knows. We have the rifle. Two quick shots would solve our problem. Is that the better way?

Still I have not seen the Thing. I spent yesterday improvising a crutch, meaning to go. But this morning I found excuses to stay. Am I afraid?

*March 28.* Last night's wind removed the drift. The thing can be seen from the plane. It is incredible. Surely the earth never gave birth to such a monster. Did it land here, a visitor from Space, and freeze in the ice? So Elida suggests.

Alive, it must have stood twenty feet tall. God! it must have been frightful. Fortunate, if Elida is right, that it came down here, not in civilization.

*March 30.* Two days of blizzard. Bitter cold. We suffer. But it is a blessing, for drifting snow shuts out sight of the monster. That would drive us mad

*April 2.* Last glimpse of the sun yesterday. We shall not see it again. Weak and hungry. What is the use?

*April 3.* Elida today confessed her state. A shock to me. She knew before we left Capetown, but said nothing because she didn't want to disappoint me about the flight. It makes no difference now, for we can only die. But the tragedy is doubled.

*April 4.* Last night I did not sleep, considering the possibility that Elida, alone, might survive the winter. Surely another expedition will come with the sun. I have only to walk away on my crutch, while she sleeps. Perhaps it is my duty, for the sake of the child. Yet what hell it would be for Elida! Very scant rations, even for one. And she fears the monster more than I.

*April 5.* Elida must have read my mind. She begs me not to go --- not to leave her alone with That. Better die together, she says. And so I gave my word.

*April 15 (?).* I have lost track of the terrible days. Weak. Delirium. One vision most persistent. Haunts the plane like a ghost. I have seen it three times. Elida also. Collective hallucination? Or are we going mad?

It appears like the head and shoulders of a tiny golden woman, rising from a conical shell. The shell flies, above the snow. She sings. Elida says she is calling us to follow her across the snow. But it is death to leave the plane.

*May (?).* Food half gone. I insist we eat enough. No benefit in hours of agony. An effort at resignation. Would it be better to walk together into the blizzard? There is no hope. Yet Elida's love is a joy. She was praying today.

*May (later).* Maru-Mora came again. Elida calls her that. She sang again. It is a terrible thin crying, yet musical. Elida wanted to follow her. I restrained her by force. Maru-Mora will give us food, she says, and shelter. That I know is delirium.

The scaled black thing is still outside on the snow. It is real. I kept looking to see if it had moved, until Elida covered the window. I wonder whence it came. And when it was alive.

*Later.* The thing is still alive. It never moves, but I feel life in it. An indwelling horror. I know that it is waiting for us to die. Waiting. God! can it take us after death?

I want to take all our food and leave the plane. No hope of escape—I am helpless on the crutch. But I want to get as far as possible from the thing. I don't want to lie dead here beside it. For I have dreamed twice that we were lying stiff and cold, and it woke and stirred and came to eat our bodies. I have not told Elida that.

*Later.* Elida is gone. Maru-Mora was here again. She was singing, calling to Elida. I slept—it was because of this damned weakness; I had been putting food back. When I woke they both were gone.

I feel stronger now after eating. I am going to search for Elida. Probably I shall not find her. I know I can't go far on the crutch. But at least I shall die farther from the thing in the snow.

F AINTLY scrawled in a trembling hand, that was the last entry. Foreseeing his fate, Wilbur Lee had left his diary and gone to seek his wife, as I had followed Merry Bell. That was twenty years ago.

Maru-Mora! what manner of being was she? Splendid in her alien beauty, how many had she lured to death on the glaciers? Could she lead some vampire-life, feeding on those who followed her?

The diary had warned me of the thing waiting beside the wreck. I should have been prepared for it. Its stark reality, however, came with an impact of shattering violence.

The dark sky was almost clear again, although the bitter wind till swept a few wraiths of cloud across the wheeling stars. Like dying embers sprinkled with some chemical, the aurora burned with feeble, changing, many-colored flames, beyond the poleward range.

The questing white finger of my light found the thing that had brought the Lees down to die, sixty yards from the wreck. Huge and monstrous, it loomed appallingly above the wind-carved drifts. I staggered a little way toward it, until amazed terror stiffened me.

For it was incredible.

And it woke all the horror of my most dreadful memory.

Barrel-like and hideous, the black-scaled body of it towered colossal above the ice. Thick tremendous cables, snake-like, its three giant limbs coiled fast about the projections of a shattered granite boulder.

Unmistakably, it was the Watcher! The same fearsome frozen being that Maru-Mora had shown me in that weird experience that I had tried to believe a dream, when she had also carried me down beneath the ice to witness the frightful horde of this monster's fellows, rigid in the ice that held their cyclopean ship.

The Watcher of the Tharshoon! I needed no more support of Maru-Mora's warning that the unthinkable invaders, now held motionless by her weapon of sleep, might wake again to attack the world.

Bitterly, vainly, I regretted my blind folly in bringing Harding's expedition to the Pole. And I was glad, in the rigor of horror that gripped me—almost glad—that Merry Bell was dead, so that his discovery of atomic power could not be used to thaw the ice.

I wanted to go closer to this frozen creature, to examine it in detail. But an inexplicable, overwhelming fear had come into me at the first glimpse of it. My heart was pounding. I had to put down an insane urge to run, a trembling fear that the monster would wake to pursue me.

Utterly irrational as I knew that dread to be, all the knowledge-thirst of the scientist in me could not overcome it. I did, nevertheless, examine the being as well as possible from where I stood.

A curious smooth ridge, black, glassy, and about two feet wide, belted the middle of it. Above were three curious protuberances, equally spaced, which, I imagined, must cover organs of sense. A hideous triangular snout projected above the great scales of its bulging upper hemisphere.

I noted a curious socket about each of the three limbs, below that glassy belt, which suggested that they had been retractable into the scaled black shell, so that the entire being was encased in the scaled armor of its elongated spheroid.

Its connection with any known order of terrestrial life was not apparent. I recalled, shuddering again, the suggestion on the diary that it had come across the gulf of space—and Maru-Mora's statement in the dream that the invaders had come, geologic ages past, from "Beyond."

I was glad to leave the thing. Yet alien horror crept behind me, as I started back to search for camp. Knowledge that it had not moved for long eons was inadequate defense against a disturbing childish fear that somehow it might wake and follow.


## 9. The Eyes of Mawson Kroll

A DISQUIETING thought came to hasten me—that Veering's crystal fossils might have been solidified by Maru-Mora's weapon of sleep, that Hardings' efforts to revive them, through some ghastly accident, might wake the sleeping monsters.

Still I was lost.

I had found no serviceable compass in the wreck. My watch

had stopped, I found, crushed; and, although the sky was now clear, the stars, wheeling eternally above the pole, gave no hint of either time or direction.

The outcropping boulder, however, convinced me that I must be somewhere upon the same ridge upon which the camp was situated. For most of the Basin, I knew, was covered with many thousand feet of ice. If I could follow the ridge, then, and in the right direction, I might come upon our base.

Looking for the next visible granite ledge, in the direction, I hoped was south, I struck out toward it. I had no hope of aid from camp, unless perhaps a light should be hung in Bell's tower. In fact, for the safety of the others, I had asked them not to leave camp for any cause.

Hour after hour I stumbled on, searching out one projecting ridge and then another. Hidden as they were by ice and drifts, it was never easy to identify them. And they became less frequent as I went on, so that I began to fear that I had taken the wrong direction.

I stopped once, made scalding tea on the alcohol burner, and thawed a little of the concentrated food in my pack. Struggling on again, I slipped into a numb, drugged fatigue in which my personal fate seemed to matter very little. Some aching restlessness had kept me ever wandering, searching. The black peace of death, it came to me, now so near, might be the goal I had sought. Still, however, a bitter rebellion rose against that idea, with thought of the dream-girl, Karalee.

If Maru-Mora were real, she must be also. And I loved her. It was the beacon of her white beauty, at the end, toward which I struggled.

I had expected no search to be made for me. I was surprized to see the ghostly flicker of a searchlight, far across the ice. Stumbling toward it, beckoning with my own light, I was distressed and alarmed to hear the terrified voice of Jerry Harding. Pain was in her weary calls, as well as horror.

My own troubles vanished before concern for her. I hastened to meet her, but she slipped down on the ice before I came to her.

She was unconscious. I carried her down into a little declivity where the wind struck less keenly, swiftly examined her. Plainly she was exhausted from her struggle across the snow. But more than that was the matter with her.

She had been mistreated, brutally. My blood boiled at sight of her injuries. One arm was dragging limply, broken. Blood was clotted inside her furs. Disfiguring her white face was the print of a boot, whose ice-calks had cut through lip and cheek to the bone.

Harding, the black suspicion came to me, must have gone completely mad, attacked her.

Her condition was alarming. She had internal injuries, I thought. Her pulse was very slow and weak. Her hands and feet were already white and stiff with frost.

Hastily I dug out a little shelter beneath the crust of a drift, carried her inside, and walled it up with blocks of snow. I did everything my small skill made possible: set the arm, put antiseptic on her lacerated face, rubbed her hands and feet, made hot tea over the little alcohol flame.

And she regained consciousness at last, gulped a little of the tea I held to her lips. Her gray eyes flickered open. She tried briefly to smile. Then her face went waxen pale again with pain and remembered horror.

"Ron, dear!" she whispered. "I knew I'd find you. I had to—"

The effort of speech seemed to exhaust her. Her eyes closed. Her head fell back on its pillow of snow. But I couldn't repress the savage question burning in me.

"Who did it?" I demanded. "Jerry, who hurt you?"

Her stricken eyes opened again, dark, distended, staring. Low and hoarse and terrible, her voice whispered the blackest name I knew:

"Kroll did it—Mawson Kroll!"

That grim name brought me a start. But I thought she must be out of her head.

"Don't try to talk, Jerry," I urged her, soothingly. "Just drink some more hot tea, and rest. You shouldn't have come—but I'll get you back to camp. Everything will be all right."

Wide and glazed with horror, her great eyes stared up at me. Quivering with pain, her blood-clotted lips moved again, whispering:

"No, it won't be, Ron. And I'm not delirious—I wish to God I were! After you were gone, Ron, I found out. And he saw. He tried to kill me—he did kill me.

Her dark eyes flickered with agony. She gulped painfully, went on:

"But I got away from him. I came to warn you, Ron, so that you can stop him. For he's a monster, Ron. He's not human. He's something—hideous! He lives only to crush and destroy. To kill, as he killed me—"

H ER dreadful eyes closed again. Her face was very white. "Quiet, Jerry." A lump was in my throat. "And don't you worry about Mawson Kroll. He is dead, you know that. He was Bell's assistant, who sold the bacteriophage to the Asiatics. He was caught, executed."

Her filmed, staring eyes came open again.

"No, he wasn't executed," she whispered. "He lives on, Ron—more terrible than ever. Before, with the bacteriophage, he murdered a million. Now, utterly mad, he plans to murder all the world!"

"But Jerry—"

I was trying to calm her, but:

"Wait, Ron," her tortured whisper begged me. "Let me explain. I haven't—long."

Agony closed her eyes as she swallowed again. Her slender body quivered on the snow. In a moment, however, she looked at me again, caught a gasping little breath, and went on:

"You know how—how Aston has been changed?"

"Of course," I said. "Since his amnesia."

She shuddered.

"Many things he couldn't remember," she said. "I helped him carry on. His nature seemed strangely—ill. But I tried to bear with him."

"I know, Jerry."

For a little time she lay silent, gasping, in that tiny space beneath the snow. The alcohol flame had warmed it a little, now. My light cast a pale disk of silver on the roof. The wind was a far merciless howling.

Jerry Harding went on:

"His eyes—you know how he has said his eyes were weak, and worn dark glasses all the time? Well, after you had gone to follow poor Merry, he went on working over his crystal fossils, as if he didn't care whether either one of you came back. This morning I went into the laboratory—I was so lonely and anxious. Aston—*he* was working over the microscope, without glasses. He looked up at me, with some sharp word.

"And I saw his eyes—"

Jerry Harding's torn bruised face was suddenly paler. Her eyes closed again. Her breath was a slow, tortured gasping. I waited, wishing in vain agony that I had the medical skill to aid her, until she sobbed:

"His eyes!"

"They weren't Aston's eyes at all. They were hideously—changed! Aston's eyes were blue. And these were black. One of them was necked with a queer terrible red all around the iris. The other had no iris—it was just a pool of terrible black.

"I had seen those eyes before. Once when Aston took me to Merry's laboratory, to hear about the bacteriophage, we met Mawson Kroll. He was a horrible little hunchback. He stared at me, and something made me sick with fear. I could never forget his eyes—they haunted my nightmares."

Her voice was a faint, hoarse rasp:

"Ron, these eyes, in my husband's face, were the terrible, mismated eyes of Mawson Kroll!"

## 10. The Stasis Ray

FOR a long time after she gasped those incredible words, Jerry Harding lay white-faced and silent in that tiny chamber under the snow. Her strength was ebbing. Certain that she was bleeding internally, I thought she might not speak again. But her slight form held an extraordinary strength; her desperate trek across the snow had already proven that.

An hour must have passed when she opened her eyes and looked at me again. Her small cold hand, which I had been rubbing, closed upon my fingers with a strong grasp. Her low voice, calmer now, steadier, went on as if she had not paused:

"A cold horror fell on me when I saw those eyes. I crouched back toward the door. And, before I could think, I gasped out that name:

"'Mawson Kroll!'

"He looked startled, when I said that. His face—Aston's dear familiar face—went a little pale. Then slowly he began to laugh. It was Aston's laugh that I knew so well, but there was a terrible hard new ring of evil in it.

"And he spoke to me in a ghastly mocking voice.

"'Well, Mrs. Harding,' he said, 'I've been wondering when you would find it out. The grafting of the optic nerve was impossible. My eyes were disguised, but they are my own.

"I couldn't believe what I had seen, Ron. Or what he said. I tried to ask him if this were some dreadful joke.

"'There was a joke, Mrs. Harding,' he told me. 'But it was on your husband—when they shot him for Mawson Kroll!'

He laughed a ghastly laugh, and I managed to whispers

"'You aren't—aren't really—Kroll!'

"'But I am, Mrs. Harding.' His voice was gloating. It made my flesh crawl. He grinned at me—it was Aston's old dear smile, with a hideous leering twist. 'You have served me very usefully,' he said. 'But I have no further need of you. And now, while Dunbar is out of the way, is a very good time to dispose of you.'

"He started toward me. Fear had taken my voice. But I had to stop him. I managed to whisper:

"'What do you mean? And how could you be Kroll?'

"And I stood there in the little laboratory under the ice, cowering back, while he told me the horrible thing. His smile—on my husband's face—was cruel, mocking, mad.

"'You aren't deformed, Mrs. Harding,' he began. 'You don't know what it means to be a cripple—not yet. But I know,' His voice was terrible, bitter. 'The world made me suffer, Mrs. Harding. And I determined, when I was still a child, that the world would pay for every slight and sneer and insult.

"'I bargained once to be made Emperor of America. But I was betrayed. The Asiatic command was too chicken-hearted to use the bacteriophage—until it was to late for victory. And that defeat is another thing that must be avenged.

"'The frightened human vermin wanted the life of Mawson Kroll. But I wasn't to ready to die. Not unavenged. And I was able to turn that defeat into a victory.

"'For one of the Asiatic secret agents, who had aided me in the matter of the bacteriophage, was a doctor, famous in his own country—famous for an experiment he had performed publicly only upon animals, but secretly, and with entire success, upon human beings.

"'That was the transplantation of living brains. He had developed a radically now technique, using Zymoff's vitacolloids. His Government had sent him to America so that this skill might serve his country. In a New York apartment was a secret operating-room, where he had put Asiatic brains in the heads of two American officers—who became most valuable spies.

"'You must remember the body of Mawson Kroll, Mrs. Harding. It was not a desirable abode. Often I had admired your husband's splendid physique—as I had admired you.'

"He snickered then, Ron, with a dreadful leer.

"'It was all very simple,' he said. 'A spy reported the arrest of Meriden Bell. I knew that suspicion would fall on his assistant. So our machinery went into action.

"'Your husband had the habit of working late at his laboratory. One night two of our agents removed him to the secret operating-room. I had prudently gone there already, having planted the necessary clue. My distinguished Asiatic colleague, glad of another chance to try his novel technique, removed our two brains, and transferred each to the other skull!

"'Convalescence, in each case, was swift and satisfactory. Mawson Kroll—with your husband's brain in his skull—was carried to the Mexican border, drugged, and released. One of our agents won the confidence of the American Government by aiding in his capture. Surgical precautions had been taken against his being able to give a very intelligent account of his identity—a few cubic inches of brain-tissue mislaid! You know what happened to him.

"'As for myself, as soon as skull and scalp were healed, I walked along a highway and said I didn't know who I was. You identified me, Mrs. Harding. You were very kind. You took me into your home. You gave me your husband's position, his fortune, and—yourself.'

"He laughed again, with a gloating satanic triumph.

"'You made it possible for me to regain the confidence of Meriden Bell, to secure the advantage of his second great discovery, which is even more wonderful than the bacteriophage—"

AGHAST at that, I interrupted the low weary voice.

"But he hasn't got Merry's atomic discovery," I protested. "Because Merry is dead—and he took the secret with him."

The terrible dark eyes of Jerry Harding looked up at me, from her cold bed in that tiny snow-cavern. She coughed when she tried to speak again, and I saw dreadful red on her lips.

"But he didn't," she whispered. "He left all his apparatus. It wasn't finished. But Tommy Veering is very brilliant, Ron. And he serves Kroll like a dog. He has studied the equipment, already, and worked out the principles of it.

I heard him promise—*him*, that he, could go ahead and thaw the ice!"

That was a terrific jolt to me. It meant that Bell had died in vain. It raised danger that the monstrous sleepers might yet be wakened. But I tried to conceal my shuddering fear, tried to calm my voice, as I asked:

"Then what happened, Jerry? How were you—hurt?"

Her face, save for its wound, was white again with agony. She made an effort to speak, and coughed again, terribly, spitting red froth. I wiped her lips, and she lay back for a long time, almost motionless, with her eyes closed. It must have been half an hour before she breathed my name:

"Ron?"

"Don't talk, Jerry," I urged her. "It hurts you too much."

"I must tell you these things, Ron," she whispered faintly. "That is why I came. Then I can rest."

Her tortured eyes looked for a long time up at my face, with a pleading in them that was heart-rending, almost as if they tried to convey her thought without the agony of speech. She went on at last, laboriously:

"He—Kroll in Aston's body—told me that he was going to kill me, Ron. 'Because you sneered at me when you saw me in my own body, Mrs. Harding,' he said. I told him that wasn't true. I had only pitied his deformity. But it made no difference.

"Because Kroll—Kroll's brain—is mad. Insane!

"I was too terrified to move. He came at me, slowly, horribly, like some gaunt beast stalking me . Fires of hell were blazing in his black, mismated eyes. Once he laughed a little, hideously.

"At first I couldn't make a sound. But finally I screamed for Veering, who was working up at Bell's tower. He came to the door and looked in. Kroll cursed him, and he went back again. He is Kroll's creature."

Jerry Harding's eyes were closed again. Her gasping, bubbling breath was agony to hear. It was a long time before she could go on.

"He took me in his hands. He has a terrible strength, for Aston was a powerful man. He—he twisted me. I didn't scream again. I knew it was no use, and I didn't want to give him that satisfaction.

"I don't know all that he did. Twice I lost consciousness. The second time I came to, I was on the floor. He was gasping and grunting like some mad beast, kicking and trampling me. Then Veering came in again—but not to help me. He had news for *him*.

"'I've got it, Harding!' he was shouting. 'I've got the wave-formula for the stasis ray. The space-warp projector will run, with adapters, off Bell's atomic battery. I can create the stasis, or unlock it. A reversible reaction. And I've revived the fossils— see them crawling!'

"He paid no attention to me, lying on the floor. He was holding out his hand, with those tiny things creeping over the palm— he had made them come alive!

"Kroll seemed queerly excited at that. He left me, and hurried with Veering back to the tower. I heard them say something about having the stasis ray ready for you, Ron, if you came back.

"I guess they thought I was helpless, dying. And I was—almost. But I knew that I must warn you, or they would do something terrible to you when you came back—with that ray. And I had to tell you about—Kroll."

Her voice was very weak, now. I was leaning forward to catch the gasping words.

"When they were gone, I made myself stand up. I got into my furs, and found a light. I had watched you go after Merry. I started in the same direction. It was hard to walk, Ron. One arm is broken, I think. And I—hurt—inside.

"I knew that I was dying, Ron. But I came on. On—"

Her darkened eyes flickered shut again. She slipped back into unconsciousness. Trying to do something for her injuries, I shuddered with a black rage against Mawson Kroll. All her poor body was evidence of his savage cruelty. It had taken fortitude beyond all telling for her to come to meet me.

For many hours I watched beside her, tried to keep her warm. I knew that her life was flowing away, but I had neither skill nor equipment to do anything for her internal hemorrhage. I had not expected her to speak again, but her eyes fluttered open at last, while I felt her failing pulse. Faintly she whispered:

"Promise me, Ron—"

She coughed weakly, gasped terribly for breath. I wiped the red foam from her lips, waited. An agony of urgency was burning in her glazing eyes. Finally:

"Promise, Ron," she breathed again, "to kill this monster—in my husband's body—before he uses this new power—for something more dreadful!"

"I promise, Jerry," I said.

Her face relaxed, then, The dark shadow of horror went out of her eyes. Beneath that cruel laceration, I saw a smile almost gay—the old smile of Jerry Ware. And suddenly I realized that she was dead.

## 11. THE WAKING OF THE WATCHER

WHEN I had done all that I could do for Jerry Harding, I left her there in the rude little ice-cave in which she had died, and set out to keep the promise I had made her; or a least to try, so long as I lived. For, summing up the odds, I saw their balance against me.

Kroll, as I shall call him now, and Veering were both strong men, equipped with firearms as well as this new weapon, and desperately bent upon whatever incredible scheme Kroll's mad brain had conceived. Jerry had made it clear that they already planned me harm.

And I was below par, physically. For perhaps two days and nights I had hardly slept at all, nor eaten adequately. I was exhausted from continual effort and nervous strain. And both my feet, from prolonged exposure, had become somewhat frostbitten, making walking very painful.

Moreover, I was unarmed. Now, however, I recalled the hunting-rifle I had seen in the wrecked *Elida Lee.* For all its twenty years on the ice, it had looked to be in good condition. And I decided, now, to return to the wreck and get this weapon.

Our camp lay a few miles to the south of me. The cracked-up plane was some greater distance back north along the ridge. I thought that I could get the rifle and reach camp, if the weather turned no worse, within forty-eight hours.

I had never killed a man, and a faint shudder ran through me at thought of it. But memory of Jerry Harding's injuries kept my resolution hard.

My feet made travel difficult. The weather remained clear, although a shifting bitter wind blew constantly. Huge glittering diamonds, the stare wheeled endlessly about the zenith. The sky was a frozen bowl of luminous sapphire. Green and mysterious, the living tongues of the aurora australis leapt up unceasingly beyond the dark and distant mountains.

Utter exhaustion forced me to stop long before I had come to the wreck. I cut through the frozen crust of a drift, excavated a little room, slept there, and ate the little food left in my pack.

The wind had fallen when I emerged. Savagely cold, the air itself seemed to glitter with frost. The stars immense and brilliant in a dome of purple-blue. I was limping on again, when I saw the glimmer of a lantern ahead of me, far in the north.

Perplexed, I waited in the shelter of an ice hummock. At last I could make out two men, one of them dragging the sledge. They came toiling nearer. I saw that the lank, gigantic man who stalked ahead was Mawson Kroll. And it was Tommy Veering dragging the rude sledge, like a willing beast of burden.

They must have been out to search for Jerry, I thought, and were now returning. My first impulse was to hide and let them go by. But something in me rebelled at such cowardly skulking.

I had promised Jerry to kill Mawson Kroll. I meant to keep that promise. But I had no intention of trying to get him from ambush. When the time came I would see that we both were fairly armed, speak my accusation to his face, and let the best man win.

Another thing: I could not believe that they were prepared to kill me on sight. Kroll would not know that Jerry had talked to me. My polar experience and my skill as a pilot certainly would make me more valuable alive than dead. And I still hoped to make some successful appeal to Tommy Veering's humanity.

Such considerations prompted me to abandon my first plan of getting the rifle from the wreck. It had been by no means certain, anyhow, that I had strength left to carry it out.

W HEN they had come within a hundred yards of me, then, I flashed my light—it was the one Jerry had brought—and called out:

"Harding! Veering! This is Dunbar!"

The instant reply was the orange-red flare of a gun. A shattering blow struck my shoulder. The light went spinning out of my hand. I staggered backward, trying to get my balance, and pitched into a ten-foot crevasse. My head struck the ice a stunning blow.

I lay there, half covered with the snow that had fallen with me, too numb with pain to move. Through the stinging air, I heard frost crackling under cautions feet. The white blade of a flashlight stabbed into the fissure, found me.

I heard Tommy Veering's flat nasal voices

"Here he is, Doctor Kroll! You got him!"

Doctor Kroll! So Veering knew the truth—and was willing still to serve his infamous master. Other feet grated on the ice, and I heard the voice that had been Harding's:

"Well, that's an end of Captain Dunbar. We saw where he buried Bell. And Harding's slut must be dead by now."

Veering's voice said:

"Then it is just we two."

"We two," I thought that other familiar voice had changed, like the eyes, until it was strange with the intonation of Mawson Kroll. "We two—against the world!"

"And now I have power, Veering. Bell's atomic beam, and the stasis ray, and now these others, as we rouse them."

A dreadful triumphant ring of madness had come into that altered voice.

"Power enough! There'll be an end of mankind, Veering. How I hate the verminous breed! Now these others shall have their chance. And I'll rule them with the ray."

"Yes," began Veering, "we'll rule—"

Harshly strident, Kroll's voice cut him off:

"Get to your traces! Quick, now!"

Frost crackled again as they walked away. Their voices dimmed: Kroll's sharp and loud, Veering's grovelingly acquiescent. I caught some puzzling reference to a guest they expected, but the rest of the sentence was lost.

I lay a long time there in the crevasse, after they had gone, dazed as much by Kroll's mad plan to destroy mankind as by the blow on my head. At last I struggled dazedly upright.

The bullet, I discovered, had glanced from the leather pack-strap; my shoulder was merely bruised.

Reeling with my still-throbbing head, I climbed painfully out of the fissure, and limped on toward the wreck. A wall of black despair had risen before me. There seemed small chance indeed that I could stop Kroll's mad scheme. But I must not give up.

It could have been no more than half a dozen miles to the wreck. Yet, foot-sore and exhausted as I was, it was a heartbreaking march. I slept once on the way, but had nothing more to eat.

TWENTY hours must have passed, when I came into the vicinity where I had left the shattered plane beside the frozen monstrous form of the Watcher. The sky was still clear, the circling stars great diamond sparks in a haze of sapphire frost. A brilliant arch of the aurora stood below the Southern Cross, like the façade of some unimaginable palace of crystal light.

In its soft radiance, I made the terrible discovery.

I recognized the shattered black rock upon which the gigantic hideous form of the Watcher had stood, frozen through so many ages. But it was vacant—the monstrous shape was gone.

Was the doom already begun? Had Kroll and Veering been already to wake the creature, with their newly discovered equipment, when I met them on the ice?

Feverishly, with that question battering at my sanity, I searched for the *Elida Lee*. But it also was gone. Where it had been I found a curious hollow in the ice. Lying in the bottom of it were a few blackened and corroded scraps of metal—fragments from the engine-block and landing-gear of the wrecked plane.

Of the gun I had come to seek no visible trace was left.

What happened to the plane? Numbed and bewildered, stunned by the impact of alien dread, I was still standing on the brink of that inexplicable pit in the ice, when I saw another astounding thing.

Incredibly strange against the colored wings of the aurora, it came flying above the white ice-scape—an immense black balloon-shape, elongated, and belted with a wide band of violet fire cold as the aurora.

It dropped a little, swerved toward me. There was a strange slow pulsation In that frozen girdle of purple light, and the thing lifted and fell a little as it flew, to the same queer rhythm, so that I thought the belt of light must be its organ of locomotion.

Heavy and dull with a fascinated and incredulous dread, I stumbled back from it, without taking my eyes from it to watch where I went, until I realized with a start that I had come to the brink of a narrow black crevasse.

Swiftly it swept toward me. I saw the hideous, triangular snout that projected from the top of it, saw the immense black scales that covered its bulging armor. And understanding came to me like a black flood of horror.

This was the Watcher!

The black frozen monster of the rock, come to fearsome life! The great tentacles had been retracted, so that the thing was all contained in the black spheroid which flew through the unguessed agency of the shining belt.

Above that band of frigid violet, a black-scaled flap lifted suddenly. Behind it was a huge, triangular pool of ice-green fire. A malevolent eye, luminous and pupilless!

Dread had held me hypnotized. But motion came back to me, at the unveiling of that eye, with a shock of panic fear. I flung myself flat behind toward the shelter of the crevasse behind.

That frightful triangular eye, however, must have seen me. It had been already luminous, and now a strange ray of pale green poured out of it. It struck the ice where I had stood. A queer little cloud condensed there, out of the beam—a swirling mist like dust of malachite. It thickened, and the ice shone green beneath it. It settled, faded. And the hummock was there no longer.

Many cubic yards of ice were gone—destroyed.

It was the green eye of the Watcher, I knew now, that had obliterated the *Elida Lee.*

Cold with horror, shuddering, helpless. I pushed myself deeper into the narrow fissure that concealed me. Curiously, even in that desperate moment, my brain seemed to take refuge from horror by pondering the cause of that dread annihilation. Atoms were practically all vacant space, I recalled; and Bell's own experiments had proved that their fragile energy-lattice could be collapsed, destroyed. Was that the explanation?

The thing hung motionless for a moment. I ceased to breathe. The thump of my heart and the rush of my blood seemed alarming sounds, so loud they must betray me. But the creature lifted in a moment, the flap falling again over that triangular eye.

Rising and sinking a little, to the pulsations of the purple band, it flew away southward, toward our camp—toward Mawson Kroll—its master?

After that, I didn't know what to do. Utter defeat was upon me. Strength and hope were both exhausted. It was all my fault. I thought bitterly, for not heeding Maru-Mora's warning. But no use in thinking that. No use in anything.

It seemed to make no difference when a lurid wall of cloud rolled like an overwhelming wave across the purple sky, and flying snow out my face with a savage whip. I knew that I could not survive another blizzard. But that didn't matter any more. For I had failed.

## 12. THE COMING OF KARALEE

I MUST have wandered for some time after the blizzard struck. I set out at first to return to camp, vaguely planning some surprize attack. But I was lost before I had gone a dozen yards. I staggered on, upon feet so numb I could feel their agony only dimly, trying merely to keep the blood moving in my veins.

Faintly I remember plunging into some unseen crevasse, then struggling vaguely to extricate myself, before surrender to fatigue and despair.

Then there is a singular dream.

I thought that I floated somewhere off in space. There were splendid stars, remote and cold in the abyss of velvet black; and the earth was a small globe beside me, misty and greenish. Down upon it came the Watcher.

Swift and monstrous, that violet-belted barrel-shape seemed large as the very planet. Suddenly, as it approached, the three black tentacles were thrust out of their sockets, and grasped the earth.

They impaled it upon the hideous triangular snout that crowned the headless entity. The planet shrank, like a fruit from which the juice is sucked. And it was consumed.

Then the monster came toward me, flying through the black vastness of space. Its purple belt was shining. A green huge-eye, like a triangle of fire, stared from the upper hemisphere. It held me in a fascination of horror, so that I could make no effort to escape.

The black whip of one long tentacle reached again from its socket, and coiled about me like a snake, and dragged me helpless toward that impaling, sucking beak.

But something came to save me, ere I died. A yellow star moved amid the diamond hosts, and sped toward me. It was Maru-Mora's the golden elfin queen, flying in her pearly shell. Her eery piping quavered through the void of space, and the black monster was suddenly congealed again into the rigidity of stone.

I slipped out of that suddenly frozen tentacle, and fell through the dark abyss. The stars swept up about me like dust motes in a draft. They were gone. I was lost and alone in universal night.

The darkness was cold. An icy rigor crept into me, and I knew that I was dying. But a voice called to me through the emptiness. It was the eery piping of Maru-Mora, and it aside *Awake and rise up!*

I did awake. I lay on the bottom of the ice-fissure into which I had fallen. The sheer dark walls rose ruggedly about me, and above, in a streak of purple-black sky flushed now and then with the aurora, I could see the faint stars of Octans.

The cold was reality. It had stiffened all my body. Movement was sheer agony. But yet, such was the urgent pressure of that command in my dream. I dragged myself up out of the snow and clambered painfully from the crevasse.

Peering about over the ghostly waste of the glaciers—wondering bewilderedly if I could really have heard Maru-Mora singing—I saw a glowing point coming toward me from the north.

I waited, curious and somewhat apprehensive. The sky was clear again, though without moderation of the bitter cold; and faintly, far beyond the approaching light, I could see the Mountains of Uranus.

Had it come from there?

The point became presently a little cloud of golden radiance, creeping over the snow. And within it, as last, I made our a queer-looking sledge, with a white-clad figure running behind it.

The strange vehicle came swiftly nearer, its runners making a clear ringing sound on the ice. Its motive power was not visible. The little cloud of light that surrounded it, moved with it, was equally puzzling.

But my eyes were upon the trim, white-furred driver, who sometimes ran behind, guiding the sledge by an upright handle at the rear, and sometimes, when the ice was smoother, stepped on to ride.

Blood was beginning to thump hard in my veins. For the sledge came from the direction of Maru-Mora's pylon. And that slim figure, running in the fog of coruscating golden atoms, was thrillingly familiar.

She was—Karalee! Karalee, whom I had seen only in that warning vision, whose very reality I had tried for bitterly.

After a speechless, incredulous moment, I ran stumbling to intercept her, wildly shouting her name, She saw me. She stopped the sledge, in its haze of golden light, and came running to meet me.

Her tall slender body was all in pure white fur. A wondering eager gladness shone in her deep blue eyes. She was more beautiful than I had dreamed her.

S HE stopped before me, and a mittened hand caught at her heart.

"Ron Dunbar!" she carried softly. "You are alive—alive! Maru-Mora promised me that I should find you by the way. But I was afraid you would be dead."

The choking pain in my throat would not let me speak.

Trembling, faint with an eager joy I had never felt before, I put my arm around her shoulders. I drew her to me, and kissed her lips. Warm, quivering, they answered. It seemed right, inevitable, that our greeting should be thus. For we were not strangers met, but old friends—yes, lovers—reunited.

She held me back from her, when we had kissed, and regarded me with great compassionate eyes.

"Ron, my darling! You are so white and weak. I'm glad that I hastened."

I stood reeling before her, but trying to look as fit as possible.

"Come," she urged. "Warm yourself. And we shall eat."

I limped, with her aid, into the golden cloud that clung to her sledge. It filled my body with an immediate, deeply penetrating warmth—its diathermal effect must have been similar to that of high-frequency Hertzian waves.

Relaxation came with that warmth. I wanted to sleep again. Yet a sharp concern touched me: fear for Karalee. For we were near my former companions and the monstrous thing they had awakened.

"Where are you going, Karalee?" I asked, and warned her: "Ahead of you lies danger."

"Wait, Ron," she said. "You must eat."

From somewhere under the white tarpaulin which covered the bulky load of the sledge, she drew a great metal urn, and from it filled two crystal bowls with a hot thick fluid. One of them she gave me, with a handful of brown wafers. It was a concentrated soup, with a pungent flavor of mushrooms. Eagerly I sipped it, and another bowl.

A vast lazy realization filled me, as we leaned back against the tarpaulin, in that strange warming mist. But my sense of danger persisted, and I asked the girl's mission again.

"From her place on the mountain," she told me, "Maru-Mora saw the waking of the Watcher. She perceived the doom which she had foreseen close upon her and all the world.

"She sent me down to deal with the man who has the body of another. And she came after me, while I rested by the way, and told me that you were about to die. She showed me where you lay fallen In the snow, and gave me permission to pause and save your life."

"She did?" I broke in, wondering. "But this has happened because I ignored her warning. Has she—forgiven?"

"She has need of you," said Karalee, rather enigmatically.

"You say you are going to deal with Kroll?" I demanded. "How?"

For answer she rose to loosen the tarpaulin that covered the sledge, and laid it back in a manner almost reverent, saying:

"This is Maru-Mora's treasure."

It was a huge, strange-looking chest that she had uncovered. Eight feet long by three in width, it was massively constructed of golden-yellow metal. It was enameled with strange figures in red, blue, and black, among which predominated a curious spiral emblem. These designs were half obliterated, however. The chest was worn, battered, and stained with a greenish patina—the scars, I knew, of ages beyond comprehension.

"It is older," the girl whispered solemnly, "ten times older than the race of man."

From inside her clothing she produced a massive time-stained key of the same golden metal, and turned it in the lock.

"These are the priceless things that Maru-Mora has kept from her own world," Karalee said, "which was here before the ice."

I helped her lift the great battered lid—and my breath went out in a gasp of awe. For this coffer held the wealth of a lost world. The golden rays that bathed us shimmered back redoubled from such splendor as I had never dreamed of.

There were pearls, bushels of pearls, many-colored, larger and more perfect than I had ever seen. There were shells of a delicate nacreous beauty, and wondrous jewels fashioned into the likeness of shells—Maru-Mora's people, I thought, must have risen from the sea.

There were jeweled robes of spun silver, and a great splendid sword of hard yellow metal. There were strange heavy cylinders, which I knew from their blue-white color to be platinum, inlaid with the blue of lapis lazuli in intricate spiral patterns.

There were figurines of beings like Maru-Mora, the fluted conical shells of silver-white metal, queerly human-like busts of yellow gold, crests of blazing ruby. There were odd-shaped vessels out from jewels—from monstrous diamonds, sapphires, and emeralds; utensils, and some, I thought, lamps.

There were other things, strange in shape or half hidden beneath the rest, that I had not identified when Karalee lowered the massive lid. My imagination was staggered, my eyes blinded by those precious scintillations.

The mere intrinsic value of jewels and metal, would be tremendous. And the historical, the archeological value of what I had seen was beyond all calculation.

"These things," the girl was saying gravely, "Maru-Mora has preserved in memory of her world, that is lost. But now she has sent me to give them up for her, that the evil Tharshoon may not be wakened."

"Eh?" I muttered, still staggered with the mental impact of that treasure. "What's that?"

"I am taking it to the man Kroll," she said. "It is all to be his—if he will let the Watcher sleep again, destroy his apparatus, and depart for ever from this land."

I LOOKED for a long time, wonderingly, into the clear blue light of her eyes, and then beyond into the purple north, where in the dream I had seen the Seeker in her pylon. Such an effort to buy peace. I knew, meant surely that she had no weapon against the evil power Kroll had gathered.

"It's a large reward," I said. "But how does she know that Kroll will play fair?"

"No man," she said, "having Maru-Mora's treasure, could desire more."

"He shouldn't," I said. "But I think Kroll will."

The girl's blue eyes looked at me squarely—they were warm kind human eyes, but deep in them was something remote and alone, some reflection of the Seeker's purple orbs.

"That problem is yours," she told me gravely. "For you are to go with me, to aid me in dealing with him. And you are to return with him, to your own land, and see that he does not come back."

"That shows a touching confidence in my abilities," I said rather doubtfully. "But we can try."

"Now we must go on," she said. "Maru-Mora warned me to hasten, before Kroll has carried his plan too far to abandon it. But before we start, Ron," her voice was suddenly soft and low, "I have a gift for you."

She slipped off the gauntlet of white fur that covered her slim lower arm, and took from her wrist a little trinket, which she handed to me.

It was a little oblong block of argent metal, heavy as silver, but faintly self-luminous. Cut in the top of it, filled with red enamel, was the curious spiral design which appeared to be the Seeker's emblem. Its pierced ends were attached to a flat metal chain.

Seeing from the way the girl handled it that it was precious to her, I hesitated to accept it.

"Karalee," I protested, "you mustn't—"

"Put it on." Her voice was husky, gravely urgent; her blue eyes bright with tears. "If you love me—wear it, Ron.

Promise me you will never take it off."

"I promise, Karalee."

Quivering, her fingers fixed It on my wrist. I kissed her again, tenderly. Her eyes were filled with joyous tears.

*Karalee, my darling! If I had known the meaning and the cost of that gift—*

## 13. Blue Star of Doom

W E STARTED on at once toward the camp.

When Karalee saw how I limped, she made me take off my boots and smear my frostbitten feet with a gray ointment she gave me, which eased their pain immediately.

Despair rode with us, from the first. It was clear that Kroll's mad ambition, aided by Veering's strangely devoted genius, had already seized overwhelming forces. Our mission was Maru-Mora's last desperate play, and one foredoomed to fail.

Yet I clung to the desperate hope of some odd chance to strike. If Kroll let us open the great chest in his presence, the heavy golden sword lay just beneath the lid. If I could reach it, one second—

Karalee showed me how to control the sledge, with two small

levers on the upright. We took turns, one steering it while the other rode seated on the tarpaulin that covered the chest.

It was a remarkable vehicle. Its method of propulsion I never learned, but it must have been some directional repulsion between the silvery runners and the surface beneath. The snow in its track was compacted, and left shining with a pale silvery phosphorescence that endured for several seconds—doubtless the residue of whatever radioactive or sub-atomic reaction it was that drove the sledge.

Its speed on smooth ice might have been twelve or fifteen miles an hour. Over this welter of hummocks and fissures, however, we made no more than three. The warming golden mist, Karalee told me, came from a square black box under the tarpaulin. She showed me how its intensity was regulated by the turning of a knob.

"We must hasten," she said again. "Kroll is embittered with mankind. He thinks to give the planet to those others. Once he has awakened them, we can never turn him back."

We toiled on. The sledge pitched and labored over the hummocks. Sometimes we both had to push and steady it, to get it safely past a crevasse. Sometimes it glided smoothly on ringing runners, and we both could ride.

"Karalee," I asked hesitantly, once when I was steering and she rode before me on the chest, "there is something I want to ask—if I may?"

She smiled and waited. Her smooth white face was bright and beautiful, her blue eyes almost gayly inquiring. But it was queerly difficult to frame my question.

"How long, Karalee—how long have you—known Maru-Mora?"

She looked at me wonderingly. White teeth flashed in the starlight, and suddenly she laughed.

"All my life, Ron."

"Then are you—"

Dread closed my throat, but she laughed again.

"But I'm not so old as she, if that's what you mean."

Relieved, but still wondering. I demanded:

"How did you come here? Where did you learn English?"

The smile vanished, her face was wistfully sad.

"I learned it from my mother," she said. "Maru-Mora guided my mother across the ice, to the dwelling of those who served her in the old days. I was born there. My mother lived and cared for me, until the going of the twelfth sun. Then—then there was only Maru-Mora. But she was kind. She taught me many things."

The girl had been fumbling in the breast of her furs again. She drew out a worn little make-up compact, and snapped it open.

"Here is my mother."

Carefully she handed me a tiny snapshot. Faded and yellowed, it showed a woman whose lean, laughing, reckless features seemed somehow faintly familiar. I turned it over. On the back of it, in fine script, was written:

"To her lonely daughter Carol, from Elida Lee."

Elida Lee! Slowly, numbed again with the horror of that old tragedy of the ice, my mind filled out this fantastic ending to the story of the "Flying Lees."

Karalee was Carol Lee!

That did not end the wonder of her—nothing ever would. But it removed some little barrier of strangeness, made her humanity complete.

"I saw the machine that brought your mother here," I told her. "And I knew of your parents when I was a child. They were brave and famous flyers. The world will make you welcome, Carol, when we go back. If—"

An aching constriction stopped my throat.

"Carol," I whispered, "if you—"

She must have read the question in my eyes. For her own were suddenly misted with tears, and said softly:

"Yes, I'll go with you, Ron. Maru-Mora has promised. If we can deal with Kroll—"

And she had leaned to kiss me again, when the blue star flamed out ahead. It was miles away, on a summit of the long granite ridge that jutted here and there through the ice. It flickered once, and when it dimmed I could see the tall metal tower that supported it.

"What is it, Ron?"

The girl's eyes were dark with apprehension.

"It is the atomic radiator that Merry Bell invented," I told her. "Bell is dead. But they have finished the machine. Kroll has started it—to thaw the ice."

"And to wake the Tharshoon!" Her low voice was hoarse with dread. "We must hasten, Ron—or we shall be too late."

W E KEPT the sledge plunging on across the rugged ice, as fast as it would go, tolling and straining to guide it safely. The tiny orb of blue ahead became no larger, but its radiance became searing, terrific. All around us the ice was brilliant with it, the frost splintering its rays into unimaginable sapphire splendor.

The light shone poleward to the Mountains of Despair. Northward it lit the black distant peaks of the Uranus Range, and the nameless rounded summit where Maru-Mora dwelt.

The air became warm, as we struggled desperately on. Carol turned off the golden radiance of her heater. Our furs became uncomfortable . The fairy sheen of the frost was lost, as it began to melt, leaving bare black ice.

And still that fearful, blinding radiance increased. It blistered our faces, inflamed our dazzled eyes. We had to replace our discarded furs—now as protection against the heat.

For Meriden Bell's great invention was proving successful beyond his wildest dreams. It seemed fantastically incredible that such terrific heat could come from the hydrogen atoms in a few pounds of ice. But the glacier retreated almost visibly from the ragged black teeth of the granite ridge. Pools of slush soon flowed together, in deepening icy torrents.

Still we labored on.

One great boulder, when we struggled by it with the wallowing sledge, proved to be no boulder at all, but a tremendous monument of gray stone, which must have been set upon this buried mountain before the coming of the ice. The long eons had shattered it, but still we could distinguish the massively sculptured shell and crusted bust of a molluskan being like Maru-Mora

When Carol saw it, her lovely face set with fearful desperation.

"The ice is going fast," she sobbed. "We must hasten. The dead cities of Maru-Mora's people will soon be uncovered, as the destroying Tharshoon left them. And then the victorious ship of the invaders, and the hideous mound city they were building. And they will wake, as the Watcher did. And we shall be too late!"

We went on. Even before the thawing started, our progress had been slow enough. Now it was exasperating. Whatever propelled the sledge, it would hardly function on the slushy surface of the exposed ice. When it slipped into a pool, or one of the increasing icy torrents, we had to wade or swim and drag it.

The slush remained ice-cold, although the air was now heated to a searing wind. We were frozen below, blistered above, exhausted with desperate effort, taut with fear of the danger ahead.

There had been only a few miles to go, however. And at last, faint and reeling with fatigue, we came over a ridge near the camp. Bell's spidery metal tower stood now on a stark, naked peak of granite supporting that small blue orb of terrific flame. Our ice-hewn shelter, of course, was already gone. A white tent had been pitched below the little sheet-metal shelter which covered the atomic battery.

The *Austral Queen,* I saw with relief, had been drawn up out of the slush, on the bare black rock. If Kroll should accept Maru-Mora's amazing offer, I thought—or if he gave me an opportunity to use the golden sword—we might soon be aboard her, flying back toward civilization, all this horror no more than an evil dream. Carol and I. . . .

Then I saw the Watcher.

I T ROSE up from behind the white tent, the monstrous black-scaled spheroid of it belted with pulsating purple. One huge malefic eye, a cold triangle of terrible green, stared from beneath its uplifted flap.

Carol, beside me, stiffened and gasped with unutterable terror. And I was cold with fear of the pale beam of dread destruction that I had seen strike from that baleful organ.

But the creature dropped back again, to the tent. Beside it, gesturing to it, I saw the lank powerful body that had been Aston Harding's, clad now, against that searing radiation, in white lines, dark glasses, and pith helmet. The huge green eye winked evilly. A black tentacle whipped out of its socket, seemed to gesticulate, seized a pencil and marked upon an easel. Man and monster, incredibly, were allies, had already evidently worked out some code of communication!

Kroll peered at whatever his strange companion had drawn on the easel, and then stood watching us as we labored up the last slushy slope. I saw slim Tommy Veering, beyond, tending the humming mechanisms at the base of the tower.

We stopped the sledge twenty yards from Kroll and his appalling ally. He saluted us, with a sort of mocking courtesy, and said:

"Well Dunbar. Hello, Miss. What can I do for you?"

I said, "We have a proposition to make, Doctor Kroll."

He started when I called that name. Keen-edged, harsh, his voice demanded:

"Well, what is it?"

"We want you to stop Bell's ray," I said. "Put your strange friend back to sleep. Break up all your apparatus. And leave Antarctica, to stay. We'll fly you, in the *Queen*."

His harsh voice—so like Harding's and yet so different—rasped:

"The human race was a biological mistake, Dunbar—and you're part of It. I'm going to rectify the evolutionary error, I'm going to take over the planet and give our visitors from Saturn a chance."

His terrible eyes flickered up to the swollen black monster, and came back to my face.

"What could induce me to accept your preposterous suggestion?"

I knew that we were beaten—I had known if from the first. But I tried to hold a steady voice, a poker face. One second, with that golden sword . . . . .

"Something we have here, Doctor Kroll." I gestured toward the sledge. "A greater treasure than you can earn with all your schemes. Accept our terms, and it's yours. Look it over."

Carol had flung back the tarpaulin. We opened the chest. Bright metal and jewels shimmered in the intense blue light. The yellow blade was just beneath my fingers.

But Kroll came no nearer. His long arm made a contemptuous gesture.

"I don't bargain for what is already mine."

"But it isn't yours," I said, "—yet."

I groped for the ancient sword, measuring the distance between us. But he stepped alertly back, and waved his hand to Tommy Veering, who was watching from beside the tower.

"Veering!" he rapped the command. "The stasis ray!"

"Yes, Doctor Kroll."

The thin pale youth held up something that looked like a small movie camera. The intense blue orb on the tower flickered, went dim, as its energy must have been diverted. And another ray flashed toward us, from the little object in Veering's hands—a narrow beam of radiant energy, of a pale magenta color.

It struck through me, painful, stunning, blinding. I tried to move, to snatch and hurl the sword. But my numbed body was arrested, starkly rigid. In that last frozen instant, before shattering darkness fell, I realized the overwhelming horror of this catastrophe.

This was the stasis ray, that had frozen the crystal fossils and the Watcher. Maru-Mora's old weapon of sleep, now turned against her!

Carol and I had been congealed, struck into the eternal hardness of adamantine stone.

## 14. The World Below the Ice

H OW long my mental being was lost in that black and featureless abyss, outside of Time itself, I have no certain way of knowing. But consciousness, if it failed at all, recovered long before my body did.

For timeless eternities, it seemed, I dwelt alone in darkness. I had no awareness of my body, no fatigue or pain. Yet my mind became clear. I knew that Carol and I were petrified, at the mercy of Mawson Kroll. And the hatred of him lived and grew in me.

Silent ages passed: eons of flat darkness. I lived all my life again. Boyhood, when I was first filled with the desire to fly. College years, when I was absorbed in the modern science of exploration. My polar expeditions, and the small unsatisfying fame they won. The first strange dream of Maru-Mora, in which I saw Carol, and loved her, and knew that I had glimpsed the supreme goal of my life. And all the weird grim tragedy that had met us at the pole, up to the very flash of the stasis ray.

The body that I could not feel was eternal crystal now, I knew, more than diamond-hard, perdurable. Permanent as Time, it could endure unchanged for a million years.

I wondered if I might live and be awake for ever, and never able to move, even until this drifting continent sank beneath the sea again, and I was covered with the ocean's ooze, and the mud hardened to stone, and the stone crumpled upward again to form a new mountainous land, and the mountains eroded and washed back into the sea again; so that in the end I should be left uncovered and alone, a luckless immortal, lying on some dead frozen desert when the sun went out.

At first I had had no physical awareness. But at last, as the black ages fled, sensation began to return. Still my body was rigidly motionless. But faintly to my deadened ears came some whisper of sound—it might be the crashing of some volcanic eruption, I thought, after a million years And dimly, then, my fixed eyes began to perceive a glow of light.

I waited, and still millennia crept away. Desperately I strained to move, to hear, to see—to wake, even if it should be alone, on a dead world; even if Carol should be standing sill beside me, a statue yet locked in that eternal sleep; or even if she had been waked, by Kroll, and her body dust a million years. Desperately, I wanted to know.

Still my body was rigid as iron. But the gray mist of light grew steadily stronger before my eyes. Vague shapes in it slowly took form. And at last I was able to see what lay straight ahead, though I could not turn my eyes.

At first I thought that indeed I must have survived to some far-off, fantastic future age. For my adamantine body, its tense pose unchanged since Kroll had congealed it with the stasis-ray, stood upon the barren summit of an unfamiliar lofty mountain.

Before me, in the expanding cone of vision, a dark slope tumbled sharply down. Beyond and below, for scores of miles where the glaciers had lain a mile deep, spread a vast strange valley.

On a gentle hill at the foot of that wild slope stood—the white city, a city like a garden of the sea. Its low walls were milky mother-of-pearl. Its towered gates were graceful with the curves of racing waves. Its lofty, wide-set buildings were great shells of opalescent white, lifting spiral cones and fluted domes from paves like shining sand. Silver bridges arched the flowing curves of a thousand wide and mirror-like canals.

But it was a dead city. Nothing moved on pavement or bridge or canal. Gaps loomed in the nacrous wall. Fallen bridges clogged the canals. Exquisite opalescent buildings were shattered, crushed—as if by millennia of abandonment.

Its dead white beauty set up a ache of grief in my heart. Trying in vain to look away from its silent desolation, I discovered, beyond—the other city.

It lay beyond the area of my clear vision, so that I had not observed it at first, and now could not see it clearly. But it was a low, dark city, built, it seemed, all of squat dome-shaped mounds of red-black earth. It was hideous, strangely repulsive, as the other had been beautiful.

And it, too, was dead—a necropolis of evil.

Beside it, and almost beyond the cone of my vision, loomed

something red, tremendous, glittering darkly. I strained to distinguish its outline with the corner of my eye. And appalling recognition came to me abruptly.

It was the ship of the Tharshoon—the same colossal machine that Maru-Mora had shown me in the dream, locked beneath the ice! And that squat red city was the city of the monstrous invaders from Saturn. And now the ice was gone, ship and city free again.

Dimly, I thought, at the very edge of my vision, I saw black shapes moving about that cyclopean ship.

Were all the hideous invaders, then, awake?

I could not be sure.

The first city, it came to me suddenly—that canal-woven wonder of shell-curved fairy white—had been a metropolis of Maru-Mora's ancient race. Its exquisite beauty was dead because the invaders had ruthlessly slain it.

This was no world of the distant future, below me, but the world of the age-dead past. The atomic fire of that hot blue orb had thawed the ice as I slept—for weeks, perhaps, or even months; but surely not for years or geologic ages—and the water had flowed down through the eastern pass, uncovering this ice-locked valley of the forgotten past.

W HERE, I wondered, was Mawson Kroll? How far had he gone with his monstrous plan to extirpate mankind? And what of Carol, whom the congealing ray had caught here at my side?

My ears, then, caught the thunder of aero motors. Still my body could not move. But at last my own plane came into the fixed cone of my vision: the *Austral Queen.* It taxied to the end of a tiny level shelf that broke that rugged slope, and turned, ready for a take-off.

Aiding the motors were two monstrous things: headless swollen bodies, black-scaled and belted with purple. They flew like balloons, tugging at the plane with mighty triple tentacles.

Two!

So I knew the Kroll had waked another besides the Watcher—probably all the invading horde.

It was young Veering who stepped out of the plane as the motors died. Mawson Kroll stalked down to meet him—gaunt and powerful. He stood on a ledge, giving orders, while Veering and the monsters loaded the plane.

They first put aboard the dismantled tower and Bell's atomic battery. Then one of the creatures came flying, carrying in its tentacles the great golden chest that Carol had brought: Maru-Mora's treasure.

Kroll gesticulated. Then monster laid down the chest, and came sailing back, directly at me, its tentacles dangling like immense black pythons. It settled above me. A black limb whipped in front of my face. I thought it had come for me. But when I could see it fully again, returning to the plane, it was carrying Carol.

Caught by the stasis ray, her limbs tense with dread, and horror a stark mask on her lovely face, the girl had been instantly congealed. She was a statue of consuming dread, executed by some master of terror.

Moving swiftly to Kroll's harsh-toned command, Veering opened the ancient treasure-chest. Dark tentacles dropped the petrified girl into it: another jewel amid the matchless gems of Maru-Mora.

Veering closed and locked the chest. Living black cables swung it aboard the plane. Veering clambered after it, as if to secure his cargo, and Kroll came stalking toward me up the barren slope, tall and haggard, almost gigantic in his stolen body. He still wore whites and pith helmet, although the sky had turned dark and cold since the atomic ray had stopped. I could see his eyes, hideous in my old friend's long ruddy face—one sharply contracted, its dark iris strangely flecked with evil reds the other dilated to a black well of horror.

I felt his hand on my rigid shoulder. I heard his voice—the familiar voice that had belonged to genial Doctor Harding. It was heavy with a mocking triumph.

"Well, Captain Dunbar, we're going to say good-bye. You look almost as if you could hear me, Captain. As if you could speak. But you won't move or speak Dunbar, till the end of Time."

Chuckling thickly, he drummed his knuckles on my iron-hard shoulder.

"We're going north, to take things over. Your verminous breed is finished, Dunbar. I'm going to give the Saturnians a chance. And if the stasis ever wears off, you'll wake in a different sort of world.

"Because we're leaving you for a sort of statue, Captain. A memorial of error." His fingers ceased their idle tapping on my shoulder. "A monument to the species that failed."

He turned and strolled back down the naked slope.

The sky was filled with a dim gray twilight. Faintly, low above the northern horizon, I could see white Spica in the Virgin. A wind was rising, though my rigid body could not feel its cold. Clouds were drifting from behind me, and snow began to fall over the white fantastic city in the valley below.

Again I fought desperately to move my petrified body. But I might as well have set my will against the granite beneath my feet.

Meantime, at last, Veering started the motors again, let them thunder, one by one, warming up. Kroll turned to wave me a mocking farewell—though he must not have realized my awareness of the gesture—and climbed aboard.

It would have been difficult for the laden ship to take off safely from that snow-swept shelf, alone. But the two black monsters wrapped their tentacles about the wings, flew forward with it, helped to lift it. And it soared away over the valley, toward that titanic dark-red ship.

Thickening storm-clouds sometimes hid the ship from Saturn. And it was at the very faint verge of my vision. But dimly, at last, I saw the *Austral Queen* drop like a white mote upon one of the vast flat vanes that extended from its hull. A port opened, closed again, and the plane was gone.

Then long rods projecting all about the middle of the vast red hull began to glow with an intense blue-violet incandescence. Tongues of blinding flame flared from them, joined, until the ship was belted with purple fire.

Slowly, then, it lifted, with a grotesque seeming of heavy awkwardness—oddly resembling, in flight, one of its monstrous crew. Swiftly gaining speed, it drifted northward above the abandoned red mound city, and out of my sight.

Only after it had gone did its sound come to me: a monstrous reverberation, crashing, roaring, hissing, that rolled up the mountain like a crushing wave, thunderous and appalling.

That concussion passed me and died. I was left alone, standing petrified on that stark granite peak in the frigid polar world. The brief twilight was gone, those two dead cities lost again in the antarctic night. The clouds thickened. Snow fell steadily, blanketing the dark slope below. The wind made an eery whistling about my rigid body.

For still I could not move.

### 15. THE DREADFUL CALM

A SLOW fear crept upon me, as I stood there with the unfelt blizzard whipping the snow about my ankles: a dread more terrible than death. For a time I had hoped that I was somehow slipping from the stasis. Now I was afraid that I would exist for eternities, conscious, yet unable to move, unable even to die.

That huge red ship had been gone a long time—hours or days, I do not know—when the dark scene before me flickered again with the pale magenta of the stasis ray. And again oblivion fell upon me: a second shattering blow that blotted out awareness.

Ages of timeless blackness dragged again. Then sensation, as if had before, came slowly back. No sound, this time, reached my ears. But a gray mist came into my eyes, and imperceptibly increased, and at last I could see again

It was a world queerly changed and still, in which I woke that second time. The wind had ceased to blow. The snow no longer fell. The ragged, angry storm clouds loomed against the night, dark and permanent as mountains. And a terrible silence filled the world. There was no faintest whisper of sound.

A dread suspicion struck me suddenly, with a cold impact of horror. I remembered Kroll's reckless boast, spoken when I stood like a statue before him. He must have frozen all the world, I thought, with the stasis ray.

The life of all the planet congealed, stopped! All mankind cast into rigid sleep, defenseless—helpless prey to Kroll and his fearful allies! Dread of that vision numbed me, more piercing than the congealing ray itself.

For a second interminable space I stood there, frozen in that silent frozen world. No single object before me on the surface of the planet moved or changed in any way. I stared at a picture of eternal death.

But the brief twilight came and vanished. Pale Spica crossed a rift in the frozen clouds, and passed it again. I knew that the earth still turned.

Bitterly, I thought it might be my fate to stand there, as the Watcher had stood, rooted in the snow on the mountain, and count those same stars crossing that same rift, a million times, or a million million.

But a prickling numbness was suddenly in my left hand. It spread slowly up my arm. I discovered—with amazed, incredulous delight—that I could wiggle my fingers.

Somehow, I was recovering. I could close the fingers. I could move the whole hand, from the wrist. That painful stinging crept over all my body. I gasped a deep breath, took a reeling step. I could walk again!

I had come alive, in a dead world.

For a little time I stood there on the snow, incredulous, bewildered. For nothing else had moved. The terrible calm still ruled. In all the white world about me, there was no faintest sound or slightest motion.

It was only I that lived.

Wonderingly, still dazed and numb, I looked down at the left hand that had first come to life, and started to see a pale lambent gleam—the luminescence of the little trinket that Carol had given me.

Then, with a sudden aching in my throat, I understood: it was the jewel which had restored me!

The stasis ray, I knew, had been Maru-Mora's weapon. Naturally she had prepared a shield against it. And knowing that Kroll had found the secret of the ray, she had given the shield to Carol, to guard her on her mission.

Carol had given it to me, made me promise to wear it in token of our life together, without revealing its wondrous property. Then it was because of me, I thought bitterly, that she was now petrified, amid the loot of Mawson Kroll.

Queer little brick of radiant silver, inscribed in scarlet the Seeker's spiral emblem. Examining It, I slipped it off my wrist— and at once a piercing numbness warned me that without its precious contact I should be petrified again, and forever.

Swiftly replacing it, I discovered a little slide along Its edge. Its pale light shone more brightly when I moved the knob—which must, I knew, regulate its power. It had been turned very low, I suppose to conserve its energy.

All my aching fatigue had come back in a blinding wave—for there was no rest in the timeless sleep of the stasis. Reeling. I looked about the mountain top. Kroll had left the white tent standing, and beside it lay Carol's empty sledge. Everything else was gone.

I STAGGERED through the silent world to the tent. Its fabric, when I first touched it, was stiffer than metal, hard as a diamond sheet. At first I tugged in vain at the entrance flap. But it slowly softened in my hand—as the fabric was restored to its natural state by the radiation of the little silver plaque.

I entered. The floor was littered with rubbish and sleeping-bags were piled there, against a great stack of tinned supplies. I attacked a can of corned beef. It was unyielding as a block of steel, until I held it for a few moments near the shining plaque. Then I was able to open it, and eat. I drove the stasis from a sleeping-bag, in the same way, and crept gratefully into it.

I can claim no heroism for the resolve that came to me before I slept: to follow Kroll and his monstrous allies northward, rescue Carol, and release the planet from the stasis, or to try. It seemed a completely hopeless thing; for I had no weapon against all the dread instrumentalities his mad plan had gathered. I didn't even know where to find him.

But there was nothing else to do.

I woke, ate another lonely meal, and went out to examine the sledge on which Carol had come down from Maru-Mora's mountain. At first it failed to operate, for it, too, was locked in the stasis. But its strange motive force was presently restored by the radiation of Carol's silver plaque.

Carefully, then, I loaded it with crated supplies. For thousands of miles of barren ice and polar seas lay between me and the first outpost of civilization. It would be a hard march, at best, of many weary months. At worst—

I knew how ruthless the polar world could be. But I tried not to think of the worst. The odds, I knew were overwhelmingly against me, at every turn of the game. But I had no choice except to take them.

Still, however, I clung to one hope of aid: Maru-Mora. Much as I once had dreaded her alien beauty, Carol had convinced me of her benignity. And I knew she had shared my purpose to defeat Kroll and his allies. Her strange omniscient power, I thought, might somehow aid or guide me.

When the sledge was loaded, therefore, I turned it northward, in the direction of Maru-Mora's mountain in the distant Uranus Range.

The brief glow of twilight lit the sky ahead, as I was starting. The clouds piled dark against its silver were all motionless as stone. There was no longer any faintest gleam of the aurora—for the atomic change of the stasis had transformed even the upper air.

The long bright runners of the sledge rainy musically upon the snow. But now they left no visible track upon its diamond surface. And their ringing was the only sound in that dead world of absolute calm.

Running behind to steer the sledge, or riding sometimes when the surface was smooth enough, I descended the long northward slope, and made camp on the floor of that great valley that had lain so long beneath the ice.

From the crown of a distant hill, the shattered white walls and the broken delicate spires of the ancient city of Maru-Mora's vanished race called to me, beckoned me to explore the abandoned wonders of its nacrous beauty. But I had no time for that.

T HE second camp found me half-way up the towering range beyond. And there I was halted. Carol had come down from Maru-Mora's mountain on the sledge. Since then, however, thousands of feet of ice had been thawed from its slopes. And above me towered the black granite cliffs the glaciers had formed, sheer, jutting out in knife-like salients, utterly unscalable.

For two marches I skirted the bast of that awesome ice-carved precipice. But nowhere was its sheer frowning height less than a thousand feet. Nowhere could I possibly ascend it.

Each time as I slept I had hoped that Maru-Mora would come to me, as once she had come in what seemed a dream, to guide or comfort me. But my dreams were no more than dreams—or nightmares of Kroll and the Saturnians triumphant.

No sign had come from her when I left that forbidding rampart and turned eastward the passes. Looking back at the end of the next day's march, I chanced to glimpse her pylon. It was a sharp-cut, tiny shape, on the rounded summit of that unattainable mountain. It looked black and dead, against the brief glow of twilight.

The Seeker herself might be fast in the stasis, I thought. Or perhaps the liberated Tharshoon had already turned some annihilating weapon upon their ancient enemy.

This first attempt, in any event, had failed. I could expect no aid from Maru-Mora. I was alone, against all the monstrous invaders and the mad human renegade who ruled them.

From that lonely camp, when I had slept and eaten, I turned the sledge down the unknown slope beyond the pass, toward the unthawed glaciers below, the far-stretching ice-deserts and unconquered ranges of the Weddell Quadrant, and the empty polar seas beyond.

Alone, against the madman who had stopped the world.

## 16. The Frozen Ocean

T HAT long march northward was a strange and terrible time. The radiation of Carol's little plaque on my wrist restored motion to the air about me, so that I could breathe. But outside that little sphere of safety in which I lived and toiled, nothing moved or changed.

There was no sound save the ringing of the sledge-runners. The wind never blew. There was no snow. The motionless clouds served as landmarks, like dark fantastic mountains in a world gone mad.

I drove the sledge northward until I was exhausted, rested briefly at a cheerless camp, and resumed the weary march. The season advanced as I went. The lingering dawns were ever longer. The feeble sun at last peered up above the white death of snow before me. Next day all its disk was visible. Every day it was higher.

A month, I suppose, had passed, when I came to the edge of the continental ice. That was queerly startling: to come unwarned to the brink of that rugged ice world across which I had been toiling for so many days. Its vertical precipice fell two hundred feet. Ahead I could see for scores of miles across the fissured sea-ice frozen before the stasis ray had congealed the world.

What, I wondered, of the open water beyond? Had the ray turned that to a diamond plain? And dare I walk upon it? Or must I trust to drifting northward on a floe of ice?

Such burning questions drove me ever northward, in a fever of hope and incredulity and dread. For two days I followed the dizzy rim of the barrier, until I found a sloping fracture and let the sledge go hurtling down its diamond slide to the ice of Weddell's Sea. And for many days, again, I pressed forward across it, until I came to the open polar ocean.

Never shall I forget that view. I had climbed up upon the last tumbled bulwark of the ice, shattered and piled back upon itself by the might of that world-girdling sea. Beyond, dark-blue and glittering under the low northern sun, the vast smooth billows lay solidified, absolutely motionless.

For a long time I stood there on the ice, staring across that heaving frozen plain. A numbing apprehension choked me. To venture across that congealed sea with the sledge seemed fantastically perilous.

It still seemed incredible that Kroll had petrified all the ocean. And there was no assurance that he would keep it so. I might come to liquid water—or the solidified waves might suddenly flow again, to swallow me.

Yet there was no other way.

Cold with a numbing wonderment, I pushed the sledge over that wave-heaped wall of ice, and down the slope of a sea beyond. The water was hard and smooth as polished diamond, blue and deep beneath me.

The traction of the sledge was somewhat impaired, and I found it difficult to walk upon that glassy surface. Every ascent was a desperate labor, every descent an inglorious slide.

And a fantastic peril haunted me. The surface of the waves, so long as I kept in motion, was diamond-hard. But after I had made camp as usual, eaten a scant meal from my dwindling rations, and gone to sleep, I woke alarmed and gasping to find myself drenched, the sleeping-bag floating in a pool of liquid brine—for the radiation of the plaque on my wrist had released from the stasis the water beneath me.

Thereafter I slept lying on the sledge, and kept that precious radiation adjusted to the weakest power that would prevent my own body from growing solid again. Even so, after a few hours of sleep I would wake to find the sledge sinking into an icy pool.

Still I struggled northward, and the weary weeks dragged away. My carefully rationed supplies were at last exhausted.

For two days I had no food save tea without sugar and a small tin of caviar—which I had left because I did not like caviar.

On the third day I found a fish lying on the crystal surface—a tuna which must have leapt at the very instant that Kroll's ray congealed the world. Avidly I restored It to life by contact with the radiant plaque, dispatched it again, and made several meals upon it.

The day the fish was gone I came upon a ship. She was a small

Chilean whaler, the *Esperanza,* standing upon that frozen ocean silent and motionless as the poet's-painted ship.

She had been stopped in pursuit of a whale, evidently. For swarthy men, rigid as figures of wax, stood about the harpoon gun on her foredeck. Her lean dark captain, on his bridge, was pointing intently ahead, mouth still open as if he had been bawling come command.

I clambered over the side and sought out the galley. Thawing food with the plaque, I made a badly needed meal; and then went to sleep in the captain's bed—for once without fear that I would wake up drowning.

N EXT morning I loaded the sledge again, with food and water casks. Before I departed, however, I tried an experiment. For I felt the desperate need of some ally in my attempt to wake the world. The swarthy captain looked clean-featured and intelligent. I determined to wake him and enlist his aid.

What I needed most was merely to know where I was. The elevation of the polar stars, rudely approximated with a sort of astrolabe I had made from a packing-box, gave me some idea of my latitude. Without watch or chronometer, however, I had no way of arriving at the longitude.

My little magnetic compass was useless—the magnetic field of the planet, like everything else, must have been in the grip of the stasis. Guided by sun and stars, and a rough sort of dead reckoning, I had been trying to make for the mainland of South America. For all I know, however, I might be a thousand miles too far east or west to strike the Horn, with only empty frozen seas ahead.

And the captain of the *Esperanza* must have kept her log in his head, for I could find no record that gave a clue to her position. Her chronometer, of course, was frozen, unless in this world where Time itself had stopped.

Hopefully, then, I turned up the power of Carol's plaque, and held it against the captain's swart brow. Suddenly he was alive. His voice bellowed out the unintelligible remainder of the arrested command.

Widening then, his black eyes saw his ship and crew starkly motionless against the frozen sea. They saw me—I must have seemed a gigantic, shaggy, haggard apparition. His dark face drained to a yellow pallor, and terror contorted it.

*"Madre de Dios!"* he screamed. *"El diablo—"*

He whirled and sprang away from me, in ungoverned fear, over the side of the vessel. He sprawled on the adamantine sea, scrambled to his feet, and started running across the waves, howling with terror.

Swiftly, however, the stasis returned when he was beyond the radiation of the plaque. Suddenly rigid as stone, he fell, and slipped down a glassy billow beyond my sight.

I knew, then, that the battle would be mine to fight alone.

I T WAS four days after I had left the whaler that the sledge failed. It began to falter, ran on for a time with irregular spurts of power, and then stopped altogether.

I had never understood its silent motive power. Now I took down its mechanism, hoping to repair it. The parts were few and simple. There was a hollow transparent tube down each runner, which seemed to contain a trace of some luminous gas. Nothing seemed broken. The fuel, I thought, must be exhausted.

Baffled, I had to leave the vehicle which had carried me so far. I nailed together packing-boxes to build a smaller sled, one that I could pull with my own strength, loaded it with supplies, and went on.

My progress now however, was heart-rendingly slow. The solidified billows were slippery as glass. Sometimes I had to climb a towering sea on hands and knees. And the supplies I had been able to bring on the little sledge swiftly vanished.

I found other fish—when I saw one just beneath the surface I could liquefy the water about it and catch it with my hands. But I had no source of fresh water. Blue-black rain clouds towered here and there, but no drop fell from them in this arrested world.

Rationing the little water that remained in the cask, I toiled ahead. Each night—now using a sextant which I had taken from the whaler—I took the altitude of the polar stars, and estimated the distance to Cape Horn.

Then came the dreadful night when the water cask was empty, and my observation showed that I had crossed the fifty-fifth parallel. I had missed the Horn. Should I turn to right or to left? The wrong guess. I knew, meant death upon that diamond sea—and the failure of my purpose.

I woke with an appalling numbness in all my body; the forewarning of that dread petrification. Yet the slide on the plaque was set as usual. Hastily I moved it to increase the silvery radiation—realizing, with a cold shudder of apprehension, that its power was failing.

Perhaps it contained some sort of atomic battery, which was running down. Clearly, anyhow, my time was limited. I had but a few months, at most, to find Kroll, to strike—or the rigor of the stasis would catch me again, for ever.


## 17. The Petrified World

I TOSSED a stray worn dime I found in my pocket—it seemed queerly incredible that the fate of the world might turn upon it—and struck out toward the east. I had left the sled, making a little pack of my sleeping-bag and the few scraps of food that remained.

As the sun rose higher, however, I was astonished to see a low blur of land in the north. I turned toward it, struggled all that day toward its tantalizing promise. Next morning, after a feverish night of little rest, I threw away my pack and stumbled on— toiling up endless hills of polished diamond, and sliding down again.

My tongue was swollen in my mouth. I was half delirious, still wondering if it might be hallucination or mirage, when I dragged myself over the ragged teeth of frozen breakers, and came to the shore.

It was a low, dreary coast. Sheep grazing on the scant, marshy vegetation inland had been turned to frozen blobs of wool. In the distance I saw a thatched cottage that might have stood in the Hebrides.

I knew that I had come upon the Falkland Islands. I had come up east of the Horn, rather than west. And but for the chance glimpse of land, that eastward trek could have led me only to death upon frozen sea.

Wearily I stumbled up to the cottage, and entered. The shepherd's rudely clad family had been congealed as they sat about the dining-table, before a peat fire—a fragment of emigrant Scotland, fixed in eternal tableau.

I did not disturb them, but restored the water in a tin pail to the liquid state, and drank thirstily. For a time I felt faint and ill. When I could eat, I helped myself to a leg of roast mutton and a plate of scones from the table, and then threw myself uninvited into the big four-poster bed in the other end of the room.

I made another meal when I woke, and then walked northward again, helping myself by the way to such food and clothing as I required. This island was East Falkland, I decided. On the third day, traveling deliberately as I recuperated, I came into the little town of Stanley, on the south side of Stanley harbor.

A silent village, peopled with unmoving statues. I collected supplies and equipment from the stores there, intending to build another sledge and pull it westward toward South America.

But in a hangar down by the docks I found a trim little Starling monoplane, a two-place amphibian which must have belonged to some spirited young officer at the Government house.

That discovery elated me. I didn't know whether the radiation of the plaque could shield so large an object from the stasis, or whether a plane could fly in the motionless air. But I knew that I had no time to search very far on foot for Mawson Kroll. I determined to make the attempt.

With oil congealed in its bearings, the motor was rigidly frozen. I turned the plaque up to full power—wondering apprehensively how fast that depleted its strange energy—and in twenty minutes it was possible to start the motor.

The solidified harbor supplied a flying field level as a sheet of glass. I tossed the supplies I had collected into the machine, warmed it up, and took off.

It flew smoothly enough, for the air was absolutely still. Owing to an increased resistance, however, at full throttle I could make no more than ninety miles an hour, when the normal cruising-speed of the plane must have been twice that.

Happy, nevertheless, to be flying at all, I circled once over the gelid blue expanse of Port William, and then flew westward toward the mainland. Safely, an hour before sunset, I landed at a drear little village on the great plateau of Patagonia.

Obtaining gasoline at a filling-station there, I flew up the east coast next day, and by late afternoon landed on a broad airport beside Buenos Aires.

Appropriating a motorcycle, I rode it, in the red light of sunset, into the silent city and up the stately Avenida de Mayo. This was the first great metropolis I had seen, and the sight was infinitely appalling. The streets had been densely crowded, when the stasis ray stopped everything. It was dreadful to see such multitudes, starkly motionless. I think the utter silence, when crowds and streetcars and motors should have made a humming din, was the most terrible thing.

I walked into an expensive restaurant, lifted a tray from the rigid hands of a waiter, and made myself an excellent meal.

A singular feeling of elation came to me afterward, walking through the silent, darkening streets, the one man alive. It set my blood to pounding queerly to know that any object in the city was mine for the taking, that any of these sleeping millions was at my mercy. Grimly I set my foot upon that feeling, for I knew it was akin to the madness of Mawson Kroll.

And I knew that I dared not awaken another to aid me, even if the plaque's shielding power had been ample for two. Whom could I trust, in a world where law and all restraint were dead?

I SLEPT that night in the lonely silence of a great hotel, and next morning, when I had serviced the plane, flew across the glassy Plata to Montevideo, and then northward up the coast. I planed to search all the world, trying first the more important cities, until I found Mawson Kroll and his Saturnian allies—or until the stasis seized me again.

I cast longing eyes upon a fine new American-built bombing-plane, at the Brazilian military aviation depot, where I landed at Sao Paulo. With its smart crew of six, its racks of bombs, it looked a splendid weapon. But I gave it up with a sigh, for all the power of the plaque was now required to shield my own body and the tiny sport plane from the universal stasis.

I did appropriate a ten-pound bomb, however; and relieved one of the officers of his automatic pistol, a fine pair of binoculars, and a powerful flashlight, wondering grimly what his reaction would be if ever he woke.

It was ten days later that the motor failed when I was circling over Havana. I managed a pancake landing on the Prado, and carried my weapons on a bicycle to the airport, where I was fortunate in discovering a trim little low-wing Cord.

The steady weakening of the plaque, I found, had caused the accident. Crossing to Florida and proceeding up the Atlantic coast, I was forced to travel by hops of only a few hours, stopping to let the precious little instrument recuperate at minimum power.

I had found no trace at all of Mawson Kroll, until one late

afternoon when the towers of downtown Manhattan came into view, beyond Staten Island and the glassy upper bay; and I glimpsed dimly, far beyond, a red and monstrous shape towering upon the Jersey Palisades.

It was the ship from Saturn.

## 18. The City of Doom

I DROPPED the plane at once into the shelter of Staten Island, on the diamond floor of Raritan Bay. Now that I had found the enemy, consternation staggered me. What was next?

I had hoped to rescue Carol, overcome Kroll and his allies, unlock the stasis that held the earth. But how was such a program to be carried out? The obstacles, when now I came face to face with them, appeared overwhelming.

The weapons I had—the ten-pound bomb and a pistol—were nothing against the terrific scientific instrumentalities commanded by Kroll and the Saturnians. I lacked information, moreover, to plan any effective campaign.

Did Kroll live aboard the interplanetary ship, or had the he perhaps taken possession of some luxurious penthouse apartment? Where would he keep Maru-Mora's treasure chest, and Carol—if her petrified body were still in it? Where was the projector that maintained the earth-wide stasis? How could I gain access to it, or get the skill to reverse its force? What possible weapon lay to be discovered, against all the power of the enemy?

Waiting apprehensively for the shelter of the night, I pondered those questions and many more, and found no certain answer. I could go nearer, try to see and not to be seen. That was all.

Using the binoculars as I waited, I saw dark specks moving above the skyline ahead, dropping toward New York and soaring away again. The Saturnians, I knew. But what was their business in the sleeping city?

The long dusk came at last—I had come from one winter to meet another. In the brief dark hour before the waning moon should rise, I took off again, flew across Staten Island and the upper bay and as far up the Hudson as I dared. I landed hastily when I saw moving lights in the sky ahead, and taxied across the solid river to the Hoboken docks.

Carrying the bomb, I left the plane and hastened up into the shelter of the frozen streets. The cyclopean ship still lay twenty miles away. But, across above Manhattan, I could see the Saturnians. Immense black-armored spheroids, belted with purple fire, they dropped among the sleeping towers, rose again, and soared back toward the Palisades.

Shuddering with the elemental dread those other-world entities never failed to rouse, I crouched back in an entry and fearfully lifted the binoculars to watch. Cold horror came with the impact of what I saw.

For the monsters came like black balloons, with limbs retracted. But each black tentacles was extended when they returned, each wrapped about a rigid human body!

The Tharshoon were carrying away the sleeping people. Why? But one answer came to me, and that was unthinkable.

Keeping fearfully to the shadows, I hurried back from the river. A Wester Union messenger stood congealed at the curb, beside his bicycle. That seemed a silent and inconspicuous mode of transport. I commandeered the wheel and rode northward through the Jersey towns trying to avoid the moonlight.

It must have been after midnight when I passed the low gray building of the Planet Research Foundation, where the modern chapter of this weirdly grim tragedy had begun. I followed the lonely road past its wooded grounds.

The moon shone with an eery opalescence on the fairy shapes of high frozen clouds. It glittered in crystalline splendor on the bright emerald leaves of trees turned to stone. I had turned into Alpine Park, beyond the Foundation, when a thing happened that stopped me, tense with involuntary dread.

A cricket had chirped.

It was the first sound, other than those of my own making, that I had heard for many months. It was queerly startling, unnerving.

L EAVING the cycle, I slipped forward through the park. The vegetation here was no longer diamond-hard and diamond sharp, but soft and yielding, natural. I had come, I realized, into a zone shielded from the stasis.

I pushed through an oddly murmurous grove, and came once more in view of that colossal red-black ship—and the city of the Tharshoon.

Squat and repellent, dark in the moonlight, low mud walls rose before me. The invading ship, resting in the center of the park, had been surrounded with a city of low doomed mounds—like the hideous city I had seen beyond the pole.

In its midst, looming incredibly vast against the moon-flushed sky, that dark long hull surrounded with its enigmatic rods and vanes suggested some hideous alien creature crouching.

Above the city and the ship I saw scores of the Saturnians soaring away southward, returning laden with stiffened human forms, dropping with them into those flat mud domes.

What horror waited there?

I crept as near as I dared, and lay in a clump of brush, studying ship and city through the powerful night glasses. High in that tremendous hull, lights came on beyond a row of triangular ports. Shadows moved against them. I watched, and at last glimpsed briefly a gaunt unmistakable outline.

The shadow of Mawson Kroll!

So he was still aboard. The next matter was to reach him. But how? How cross those walling mounds, and evade the monsters wheeling above? How find undetected entrance to that great ship? Or find my way through its colossal mystery, to Kroll's apartment?

I didn't know how. But I was prepared to try.

Waiting until the moon had gone behind a black pillar of the motionless cloud, I got silently to my feet, dug into my pocket for the detonator for the bomb, and started to screw it into place, preparing for action.

Suddenly, behind me, a shoe scraped on the gravel. Turning swiftly, I saw a man standing in the shadow of a tree. A faint steely gleam betrayed his gun. A low voice rasped:

"Drop it, Captain Dunbar."

The bomb, without the fuse In place, was quite useless. I dropped it obediently—and snapped a quick shot from the hip. It struck the gleam of that level gun, sent the weapon spinning into the shadows.

The gasping curse had a familiar flat nasal intonation.

"Stand still. Veering," I said. "I'm going to ask some questions."

But I saw the glint of metal at his mouth, and a whistle shrilled out.

"Quiet—"

Behind me, suddenly, another sound bellowed out: a deep and hideous baying. I had not heard the cry of the Tharshoon before. I spun, and consternation struck me powerless.

For a monstrous fire-banded shape had lifted above a mass of trees behind me. A great triangular eye opened its baleful window of lambent green flame. And a queer, numbing shudder ran through me.

I swung up the automatic, tried to pull the trigger. But the green fire of that eye was suddenly intense, painful. A freezing greenish cloud began to obscure my vision. Sudden screaming agony flashed through my limbs, and the gun dropped out of my fingers.

I must have been within an instant of annihilation by that consuming orb. But, faintly, I heard two short blasts on Veering's whistle, and that deadly mist vanished from about me.

I staggered back, reeling, blinded. I felt faint and sick. The fearful cold of that annihilating ray was still in my bones, yet my body was drenched with hot perspiration.

Veering whistled again. A tentacle darted like an immense black snake from its armored receptacle, ran toward me, whipped about my middle. Its strong, indescribable earthy pungence made me suddenly and violently ill.

Yet I knew that another tentacle had lifted Veering, at his command, set him on top of that headless body. The whistle shrilled above, and the great creature lifted, carrying me dangling in that tentacle.

In the Intervals of vertiginous sickness, I saw that we were soaring over that low wall of clustered dome-shaped mounds. Each dome, I saw, had a black central orifice, through which the flying monsters came and went.

Then the crimson-black hull of the ship was beneath us, vast as an ocean liner's, supported hundreds of feet above the ground on the limb-like struts of its landing-gear. We sank toward it. The black tentacles dropped me unceremoniously into a sort of hatchway. I fell through musty darkness, and sprawled on a bare metal floor.


### 19. The Emperor of Terror

I T WAS a cold dank space into which I had fallen. The biting pungence of the Tharshoon was sickeningly strong. As my eyes became accustomed to the darkness, I saw a great ophidian tentacle setting Veering down beside me. He held my own pistol in a bleeding hand.

"Stand back from me, Dunbar." His voice was high, quavering. "Make another play, and I'll kill you."

He moved into the beam of moonlight that fell through the hatch. I saw that he was very haggard. His skin had an unhealthy, yellowish pallor. His hollow eyes were deeply sunken. His thin hand shook with the gun.

He looked a man consumed, half crazed, with fear.

"Come along, Dunbar," his nasal voice quavered. "Walk straight ahead. Doctor Kroll will want to see you."

Fighting for time, for any possible advantages

"Wait a minute, Tommy." I said. "You are afraid. What are you afraid of? Tell me."

His flat laugh had a dry brittle ring.

"You are the one to be afraid, Dunbar, if Doctor Kroll lets them take you down to feed the grubs," Menace edged his voice. "Get on! Straight ahead."

His shaking gun made an imperative gesture, but I stood still in front of it—if I lost now, it would be for ever.

"I've known you a long time, Tommy," I said, keeping my voice as low and steady as I could. "I first heard of you when you had a paper route. You were delivering papers to old Judge Ware. And Jerry found out how you wanted to be an engineer, how you were saving money for books and experiments.

"She told Doctor Harding about you—that was long before they were married. And Harding gave you a chance. He paid your way through tech, and made you a place in the Foundation."

Staring at me with a bright anger in his eyes, Veering caught a gasping breath and started to speak. But I went on t

"This man Kroll killed Doctor Harding, Tommy. And stole his body, his position, his wife. Tommy, don't you remember Jerry Ware? Can you serve the man who tricked and murdered her?"

Veering licked his quivering lips. The gun gestured again. Dry and hard, his voice rasped:

"Don't talk. Dunbar. Move ahead. Or else—"

Standing in front of the wavering gun:

"You're a human being, Tommy," I told him. "Your parents lived in the Bronx. Your father was born Verensky. He had a little tailor shop. He's in it now—frozen—waiting for these monsters to take him. The others—"

Shuddering, he bit through his lip.

"You had a sister, Tommy—Jerry told me about her. Nada was her name. You loved her. She went to live with a man you hated, a gunman named Ricci. That killed your mother. You haven't seen your sister again, Tommy. You've tried to put her out of your mind. But you love her still. And she's out there, petrified."

Tears burst out of his bright, sunken eyes.

"Shut up!" his hard voice whipped at me. "By God, I'll drill you! Get going!"

I stood still in front of him, in the reeking, mysterious darkness of that colossal hold. Inside, I was sick and cold with fear. But I tried to keep it out of my voice.

"Go ahead and kill me, Tommy." I said. "Kill your father, and Nada. Kill your dead mother's last hope. Kill the last chance that mankind has—"

The gun came up, unsteadily. The bore of it was like a terrible round eye. It stared at me. I was cold all over, waiting for the hard impact of death. But suddenly it fell, and Veering's face drew into a white, quivering mask.

"You win, Dunbar," his choked voice sobbed. "I can't kill you. And don't think that I wanted to be Kroll's slave. But I—I'm afraid of him. He threatens me."

His slight body shuddered to gasping sobs.

"You saw the mud city, outside. Well, the things lay eggs there under the ground. They carry people, and revive them, and seal them up in the burrows. And when the grubs hatch, there is food.

"When they are grown, the grubs undergo a metamorphosis, and come out as mature creatures. They will be sent out, to establish new colonies. All the people of the earth are to be used up for food, left petrified until they are needed."

Veering tried to control his sobbing, looked fearfully behind him.

"Doctor Kroll—he bullies me all the time. He threatens that he will let them take me. I have to obey—there is no choice. And in the end he will send me anyhow—he said he would!

"I don't want to kill you, Captain. But there's nothing we could do. All the creatures obey him—they know he would turn them back to stone if they didn't. There's no use—"

"But there is," I broke in. "We can do—something." And I demanded: "Where's the stasis ray projector? If we could get to that, reverse it!"

"That's no good," Veering insisted. "It's in his laboratory, aft—where he is, now . He won't let me in it, any more. He has one of them to guard it. We can't go there."

My voice struck an the next questions

"Tommy, where—where is Carol? The girl who came with me, back at the pole? Is she still in the chest? Or is—has she—"

Thinking of those stiff victims carried down into the mounds, I couldn't finish. I felt a vast relief, when:

"She is still in the chest," Veering said. "He is keeping her under the stasis. But we can't go there. Doctor Kroll told me that if he found me there—"

"Come on," I said. "Perhaps she can help."

"We can't do anything," Veering whispered. "Doctor Kroll is the Emperor of the World. He makes me kiss his feet."

But, although trembling with fear, he showed me the way through that vast gloomy compartment. It had been planned for no puny human beings. We climbed a ladder to a circular passage. Veering manipulated a combination lock to open the way to another vast dark room—the Saturnians, of course, made their own light wherever they went.

"THERE is a stasis here," said Veering. "We must use the reactor."

He fumbled with a little metal device he wore on his wrist—it was oddly similar to the plaque that Carol had given me.

"Hold my hand," he said.

He snapped on a flashlight, and we walked into that huge, silent room. Great piles of casks, boxes, drums, and bags, cast fantastic shadows. Vast stacks of tinned food. Bales of clothing. Crates of books and scientific equipment. Heaped golden bars, currency, furs, furniture, pictures.

The loot of New York!

"Doctor Kroll and I used to walk through the city," Veering said, "Taking what we wanted." He added: "He sent me to the Foundation today, to look up references for him in the scientific library there. I happened to see you riding past on your bicycle."

His darting light had picked out the yellow gleam of Maru-Mora's ancient chest. I ran to it eagerly. The key was in the lock. I turned it, and Veering helped me lift the massive lid.

He gasped with awe as his light shone on the treasure within: pearls; gems and precious metals wrought by the dead genius of

Maru-Mora's people into a thousand unfamiliar shapes, all of haunting beauty; the heavy jeweled sword of yellow metal; and, lying rigid amid that ancient splendor—Carol.

Or Karalee, as I first had known her, strange lovely castaway of the antarctic. Beautiful and white, she lay still in that rigid pose of horror in which I had seen her frozen, months before. On my knees beside the chest, I kissed the diamond hardness of her lips, the frightened oval of her face, the white, icy column of her throat.

"Carol! my darling. Wake."

Remembering myself, I moved the slide to turn the silver plaque up to full power, held it against her breast.

"Quick!" Veering muttered fearfully beside me. "We can't stay!"

The power of the plaque, I knew, had been ebbing. For a long time, Carol made no motion. Was It too weak to rouse her?

Then I thought she stirred.

"Carol!" I sobbed. "Can you hear? Wake—Carol!"

I heard Veering's breathless gasp of horror beside me, and then, behind us, a hideous deep ululation, like the baying of a monstrous hound.

Paralyzed with dread, I turned, and saw in the circle of the doorway, the tall gaunt figure of Mawson Kroll, and, behind him, staring at us with a green triangular eye, one of the black Saturnians.

### 20. The Chamber of the Worm

"RON DUNBAR!" It was Carol's low, bewildered cry. For she was alive again. She sat up suddenly in that great yellow chest, amid the strange heirlooms of Maru-Mora. Her blue eyes stared about the great dark room, startled. Seeing Kroll and the monster she stiffened again, with one hand on my arm, almost as if she were back in the stasis.

Kroll came stalking into the room, with the invader floating like a black cloud beside him. White and sick with terror, Tommy Veering flung himself down on the floor in front of them.

"It was Dunbar, Doctor Kroll," he sobbed frantically. "He made me do it. He got the drop. For God's sake, sir, don't let them—"

That haggard face, beneath Harding's yellowish hair, smiled with an unspeakable mockery of Harding's old warm smile—

made dreadful by the black, mismated eyes of Mawson Kroll.

Speaking no word, Kroll made some quick gesture to the thing beside him—I think it was the Watcher, that I had seen brooding over the ice—and then pointed to the groveling man on the floor.

A long thick black tentacle ran like a serpent out of the fire-belted spheroid, toward Tommy Veering. Reduced by terror to a shuddering, abject thing, he began to shriek:

"Emperor! Lord of the earth! Exalted majesty! Have mercy—"

With a quickness terrible to see, the tentacle ran round and round his body, tightened, swung him off the floor and toward the black balloon. The breath came out of him in a long bubbling scream of ultimate horror, and he was limp and still.

Carol had not moved again, or spoken. Her rigid hand quivered on my arm, as Kroll stalked toward us. His black, fearful gaze surveyed us. Harding's big mouth twisted suddenly.

"Well, Dunbar," came that ironic, queerly altered voice, "I had meant to leave you two as monuments to the lost race. But you have forfeited that eternal honor. We shall select another couple for the museum. You may go with Veering—"

He gestured again to the monster, and the two remaining tentacles came racing out of their sockets, to seize us. This was the last instant, the last possible chance. I fought the paralysis of fear that held me.

I had come weaponless into the room. But before me, in the chest, was Maru-Mora's golden blade. I reached behind Carol, seized it, and hurled myself forward.

The black whip of that limb came up in my face like a striking python. I swung the ancient blade with all my strength. Its bright edge came whistling against the tentacle, half severed it.

Ghastly white blood gushed from the wound. The ophidian limb jerked back. I flung myself at Mawson Kroll, the heavy yellow blade whirled above my head again. One more instant, and it might have split those mad brains.

But Kroll's long fingers had snatched something off of his belt, a little black box like a small movie camera—his hand projector of the stasis ray. Its thin beam flashed at me, a painful sword of pale magenta.

A crashing wall of darkness struck me. I knew, in the last split second of awareness, that my body was petrified again, and Carol's. We were once more at the mercy of Mawson Kroll.

A WARENESS, as before, came back to me slowly. I was in absolute darkness. The air was close, stifling. The earthy, acrid fetor of the invaders was overpowering in my nostrils. I thought I was alone until Carol moved beside me, fearfully whispered my name.

"Here I am, Carol."

She found my hand, gripped it with the unconscious strength of desperation.

"It's so dark, Ron!" came her dry urgent whisper. "Where are we? What is this dreadful odor?"

Anxiously, I had been feeling about us. We were in a little cylindrical cell, eight feet high perhaps, and eight feet across. The walls were rough, hardened mud.

Beside us on the floor, my feet found a stiff rugged thing. I bent apprehensively in the darkness to feel it. It was longer and heavier than my body. Muffled stirring sounds came from within it. It reeked that nauseating fetor.

Carol gasped suddenly with horror, and her hand closed hard again on my fingers.

"We are under the ground, Ron," her dry whisper came at last. "We are sealed up in a little space like a grave. But what is this with us—moving?"

I had to swallow twice before my fear-dried throat would speak.

"I don't know," I said.

But the dread knowledge was already cold in me; and Carol shared it, for she said huskily:

"But I know, Ron. For Maru-Mora has told me about the Tharshoon. They make cells underground, and seal up food with their eggs. The eggs hatch into shining white-fanged worms, and the food is ready for them. We are in a egg cell, Ron. This thing will hatch into a shining worm."

With my bare hands, desperately, I attacked the clay that walled us in. But it had been hardened, perhaps with some secretion of its builders. The rough surface broke my nails, shredded flesh from my fingers. I accomplished nothing, we were trapped.

In the utter darkness we could see nothing, but the long malodorous thing on the floor stirred again, and a sharp, clicking sound came from it—like great fangs snapping.

"Let me see the gift I gave you," Carol whispered. "It gives off a little light."

I felt at my wrist for the little silver plaque. Cold fear stabbed through me when I found that it was gone.

"Kroll has taken it," I gasped, shuddering. "Now there is nothing to keep us from turning to stone again, for ever."

"Better that than to be eaten by the worm." breathed Carol. "But it is gone." Then suddenly she asked: "If that is gone, what wakened us? For we had been frozen by the ray..

Then it seemed to me that another voice spoke beside me in that tiny buried chamber. It was the voice of Doctor Meriden Bell, whom I myself had buried many months before in a shallow grave of ice.

"We hastened your waking, Ron," it said. "I, and the Seeker. To give you warning, against the worm."

I knew that Bell was dead. But I had no time to ponder the uncanny wonder of that voice, for the dry clicking sound came again from the long rough thing at our feet. It writhed and tossed in its crackling leathery envelope, flung itself against my legs. I drew the girl behind me.

"It is hatching," she gasped. "The worm—"

Suddenly, with a loud rending sound, the thing burst along one side. The split was a line of lurid white fire. It widened swiftly. With a writhing, convulsive effort, the great worm hurled itself out of its tough integument.

The thing was longer and thicker than a man, and inordinately fat. Shining with a cold white light—ghastly white as the blood of the Tharshoon—the smooth skin hung in swollen folds.

The head alone showed any kinship to the adult invaders. It was black. The hideous spear of its projecting snout was a triple jaw. Blazing balefully behind each segment was an ice-green, triangular eye.

On the back of it, behind that frightful head, was a small oval dark spot. Not quite black, it shone faintly with the same purple light that came from the radiant belts whose unguessed power of levitation carried the adult Saturnians.

The creature writhed about on the floor. Its ghostly light shone pale against the narrow dark walls that trapped us. Then its shining eyes discovered us. And they shared the deadly power of the eyes of the grown Tharshoon—for a cold penetrating numbness paralyzed me, so that I could not move.

I T CAME toward us, across the narrow floor. Slowly, awkwardly, its gross shining mass climbed over the barrier of its own empty husk.

The triple jaw opened, Three terrible fangs snapped together, hungrily. They were white and shining, terrible. They snapped again, nearer. They grazed my knee. And still I couldn't move.

Then once more, strangely, I thought I heard the voice of Merry Bell.

"The purple spot, Ron!" it seemed to cry. "The worm is vulnerable there."

"But I can't move," I gasped.

I thought I felt a cold touch, then, as if a ghostly hand had brushed my shoulder. And I was free from the dread paralysis. Catching my breath, I strove to put down panic fear. With bare hands I flung myself upon the shining worm.

The white fangs slashed again. The thing writhed to escape my hands. Somehow, rat-like, hideously, it squeaked.

My fingers groped vainly for the purple oval. The fangs caught my leg, dragged me down. The worm flung itself about, twisted, fought to guard that purple spot.

Desperately I clung to the thing, sick with its stench. Fangs slashed clothing and skin. But my fingers found that vital oval, gouged into its soft shining jelly, ripped and tore.

And the worm suddenly stopped its wild thrashing. It made a low moaning sound, like the cry of a hurt child, and stiffened, and at last lay still, with the luminescence fading slowly from its skin.

On my knees beside it, with that phosphorescent jelly still dripping from my fingers, I looked up. Pale and anguished, Carol stood above me in that tiny, stifling space, sobbing:

"Ron! Oh, Ron, are you hurt?"

But I couldn't speak to answer. For beside her, tenuous and gray. I could see, or thought I did, the outline figure of dead Merry Bell, whose advice and touch had saved me in the battle with the worm.

"Ron," it said, "do you hear me?"

### 21. THOSE ETERNAL

S CIENTIFIC training, I think, has made me as free of superstition as most men. But there is in every man, I believe, a deep-rooted horror of the Unknown which no rational materialism can eradicate. Even though I knew that our lives were due to that intangible presence, I was shuddering to an elemental dread.

"Yes, Merry," I managed to whisper. "I can hear you. But you are—dead."

"Yes, my body is, Ron," that pale form said—and I knew that its words were not actual sound, but somehow projected into my mind. "You know that, for you buried it. But I survive, through the agency of a science greater than man has dreamed of.

"Of that—and a love beyond understanding.

"I wrote you a letter, Ron, before I died, and left it for you on the trail. I told you how Maru-Mora had come to me many times, had taken me three times out of my body to the pylon where she dwelt. I tried to tell you of our love, Ron—a thing deeper and purer than any physical bond."

"I found the letter, Merry," I said.

"Maru-Mora had come for me again," that soundless voice went on. "She knew what Kroll was planning. She knew that he meant to learn the secret of the atomic ray, and then to murder me. She asked me to come with her.

"To die. And to live in her dwelling, for ever."

Actual doubt, I had none. But wonder sent the burning question to my lips:

"If you are dead, Merry, how can you be alive?"

"Still the scientist, Ron!" The dim form smiled briefly—in my own mind, I thought, and not actually before my eyes. "I can't tell you much, for time is pressing. You must try to escape, while there is a chance.

"But I must tell you something, to put your mind at ease. You saw Maru-Mora. She was born a hundred million years ago. Her strange people cared more for the art of living than for knowledge. But she was different. She was a seeker of truth. Physical life was too short to learn all she wished to know. I have ever felt the same thing—that burning thirst to know is a thing we hold in common.

"She yearned to live for ever. And she knew that her body could not. So she perfected a means to divorce mind and body.

"We were materialists, Ron. But you will admit a distinction between mind and matter. What others would term a spirit or a soul, is to the psychologist a synaptic configuration, to the biologist a function of intramolecular dipolar moments and electrostatic tensions. Briefly, mind is merely an energy pattern associated with living protoplasm.

"The science of Maru-Mora was able to free that pattern from the original bodily atoms, as a stable energy vortex in the structure of space itself. Her dwelling—the pier of purple crystal that you saw upon the mountain—was designed to shelter that abstracted vital pattern, to feed it with the energy of radioactive materials fused into the crystal.

"She had entered it, before the Saturnians came. All her people had been destroyed, before she stopped the invaders with the stasis ray. She has been alone, for a hundred million years, and lonely. When she first came to me, a bond sprang between us: a thing too deep, too wonderful, to be defined. But we loved. I followed her. My body died. But she took me into her dwelling, for ever.

"There was one task to do, before we could follow the eternal paths of knowledge and delight opened by her science. Kroll must be destroyed. We tried to reach you, Ron, to guide you. But Maru-Mora's own weapon had been turned against her. We could not penetrate the stasis, until, awakening Carol Lee, you re-established an old *rapport*.

"And even now," finished the soundless voice of Merry Bell, "we may not be able to reach you long. You must hasten to escape, and to strike."

That eery communication had come swift as thought. I stood up, now beside Carol, in that suffocating clay-walled cell, the dead worm at our feet, its white radiance swiftly departing. Desperately seeking some weapon, my eyes fell upon the fangs in the open triple jaw of the worm. I kicked and tugged at one of them until it came loose: a nine-inch blade of ivory. Vainly, again, I began to search for some opening in the hard mud wall.

"Above your head," that still voice spoke in my brain. "Try the middle of the roof."

I stepped upon the worm, drove my fist upward. A thin shell of clay shattered to the blow. Fragments showered upon us. It was sort of plug, left thin to be broken by the emerging creature.

Swiftly I broke the plug, swung myself up through the circular opening into a passage dark as the cell had been before the hatching of the worm. I caught Carol's hands, lifted her up beside me.

"To the right," came the urgent warning voice. "And hasten— one of the monsters is coming from the entrance."

W E STARTED running through the stale fetor of the tunnel. It was cylindrical, some eight feet in diameter. The darkness was absolute. We followed it only by the feel of the curving wall beneath our feet.

"Remember, we can give you no physical aid," the voice of Merry Bell warned again. "Through Maru-Mora's mastery of space, we can see you, speak to you, even share the illusion of our senses with you. But that is all, for the bridge is mental alone."

A vague purple glow began to shine on the curving walls, from behind us.

"Hasten," urged the voice. "The creature is coming to wake you, to feed the larva. Soon it will discover what you have done."

Carol gripped my hand. We ran on, gasping in that foul air. The tunnel sloped upward, ran level for a space, turned upward again. Once the door of another egg chamber shattered beneath my foot. Almost I fell in upon a shining worm wallowing amid gnawed human fragments. White fangs slashed upward at my foot. But I regained my balance, lifted Carol over the reeking pit. We ran on.

"Here—stop!" Merry Bell's voice commanded suddenly. "You must break through the wall, on the left. Quickly!"

I hammered my fists against the hardened clay, kicked. This was no thin plug, however, but a heavy wall. The effort made no impression.

Behind us, suddenly, I heard a deep terrible baying ululation. My blood ran cold. Shuddering, I must have bitten through my lip, for a salt sweetness of blood was in my mouth.

"It has found the dead larva," Bell's voice said.

Desperately I began to chisel at the clay with the worm's white fang. A dim purple reflection flickered on the walls of the tunnel. That hideous baying was louder. Carol's trembling had touched my shoulder.

"They are coming," she whispered.

I redoubled my efforts. A thin pale line of light zigzagged across the wall. I drove the fang wedge-like into the crack, kicked and tugged at it. The wall shattered. Fragments clattered down. Fresh air, incredibly delicious, struck our faces.

Carol was helping. We worked furiously. The baying had came terribly near. But the opening at last was large enough for our bodies. I lifted Carol, helped her through, squirmed after her.

We tumbled together on the ground. Overhead the stars were shining. The hole we had broken yawned behind us in the low curving wall of the mound-city. We were outside its circle.

"Run!" Bell's voice cried again to my mind. "Go to my old laboratory in the Foundation building. You must reach it before they can overtake you."

I lifted Carol to her feet. Holding hands, we ran away from that city of horror, toward the frozen silence of the petrified wood and the low gray building beyond.

Behind us the dark purple-belted balloons of the Saturnians were flying on their usual errands about the flat mud domes and the ship that bulked so vast against the stars. Soon again, however, I heard that fearful baying taken up by many. They sank close to the ground, and spread out searching.

Running desperately, we came out into the stasis. The wood was strangely still. The grass was no longer soft beneath our feet, but rigidly sharp as diamond blades. And I felt the numbing chill of the stasis ray sinking into my body.

## 22. THE CROPS OF DOOM

"THE SHIELD I gave you is gone," Carol was sobbing as she ran. "We'll be turned to stone again."

Swiftly our limbs were stiffening, as if we had come to some invisible gelid barrier. But then, again, I felt a queer, tingling touch. And I heard the voiceless words of Merry Bell:

"This is Maru-Mora's power. For the stasis ray was hers. Go on. You must reach the laboratory. We can guard you—for a time."

That paralysing numbness was abated, although it did not completely go. We ran on, through the frozen night. The waning moon glittered on the leaves of a crystal forest. There was no sound save the gasping of our breath and the baying of the hunting Tharshoon behind.

My lungs were seared with pain, I was half carrying Carol, when we staggered across the lawn to the Foundation building. We stumbled through the laboratory entrance.

"Lock the door," that still voice said, "and I will tell you what to do."

The long laboratory benches, with their orderly rows of gleaming bottles, racks of glassware, delicate balances and great microscopes—all stood neat, silent, petrified. Through whatever power had reached us from the pole, however, everything was restored to normal at our touch.

Together, Carol and I hurried to obey the swift commands that came to us: sterilizing and setting up equipment for some elaborate biochemical process. Not a very good chemist, I soon realized however that we were preparing for the synthesis of a group of complex proteins and polypeptids.

Meantime, through the high north windows, I could see the fire-banded spheroids of the Saturnians flying against the stars, searching. I had begun to hope that they would not discover us. But their awesome baying came suddenly near.

A glass beaker dropped from Carol's fingers.

"Look!" she gasped. "Oh, Ron, it is—*he!*"

She had pointed, and I saw one of the monster drop past the window. Standing upon its black-scaled body was the gaunt tremendous figure of Mawson Kroll.

In a few moments there was a pounding at the door, and Kroll's harsh voice demanded:

"Come out, Dunbar—or die."

Still obeying the bodiless voice of Merry Bell, I took a flask from a steaming water bath, poured its black contents into a filter. Slow brown drops began to fall, one by one, into a test-tube beneath.

Carol touched my arm. Her lovely face had drained white. Voiceless with dread, again she pointed.

A greenish mist had gathered about the locked door. It thickened, obscured the metal panels—as once I had seen the same green mist hide the wreck of a plane on the polar ice. It settled. It was gone.

And a vast ragged opening yawned in the wall, where the door had been!

Through it swept a black, monstrous spheroid. Blazing above

its belt of purple fire was the green triangular eye whose annihilating ray had destroyed the door.

Beneath it stalked the tall gaunt body that had been Doctor Harding's, the black dissimilar eyes of Mawson Kroll burning from its leering face with a light of hellish triumph.

"Well, Dunbar," rasped that hideously altered voice. "Die—"

A lean commanding arm lifted to that creature we had called the Watcher, and the cyclopean eye bent its green destroying stare upon us.

But then the voice of Merry Bell spoke again, soundless, yet more arresting than any sound I ever heard:

"Mawson Kroll, you killed a million with this thing you stole. You killed me with it, more terribly. You have turned another discovery of mine against all the world. Therefore, this thing I do is just."

Suddenly, as that dread voice spoke, I remembered a long-past afternoon in this same room, when Merry Bell had showed me—before the staring eyes of Mawson Kroll—the few brown drops of his deadly bacteriophage.

"Yes, Ron," that still voice told me, so much swifter than audible speech, "this is the bacteriophage." Then its command was desperately urgent: *"Throw the tube!"*

For already in Kroll's hand was the black projector of the stasis ray. Its pale magenta beam flickered out, probed my body with its terrible chill. My last act of consciousness was the effort to hurl that test-tube straight at Mawson Kroll. But I did not know if the impulse ever reached my fingers, for darkness came down like a toppling mountain.

A WARENESS came back, as always, slowly. And while I hung in that queer state of timeless suspension, there happened one of the strangest things of all. I had been alone in the darkness, but two bright figures came slowly into being before me.

Merry Bell came toward me—transfigured! Unencumbered, his tall body looked youthful and straight. His lean face wore a smile that I had not seen for many years. In his blue eyes was serenity, ineffable, complete.

Beside him was—Maru-Mora!

Golden queen of elf-land, flying in an opalescent shell. Her white pointed face, beneath yellow carapace and scarlet crest, was radiantly alight. Her great purple eyes were warm with a supernal joy, all their agony gone. One slender arm, golden-furred, reached over the shell's bright lip. And her tiny seven-fingered hand held the hand of Merry Bell.

Terribly, in the darkness. I struggled to speak. I could not, but Merry Bell seemed to sense the question that burned in me, and he answered:

"You moved in time, Ron. The bacteriophage splashed Kroll and the Watcher. And the Seeker's knowledge had gone into it, with mine; it was a thousand times more swift and deadly than the old.

"Kroll perished where he stood—I am glad that you and Carol did not see. And Doctor Harding's body can be desecrated no longer.

But the Watcher, before it died, carried death back to the rest. Seeking safety, they drove the ship back into space. But the virus was a passenger. Now the ship is an empty hulk, drifting on an eternal orbit that will carry it for ever around the earth like a second moon—and still it carries Maru-Mora's treasure.

"The virus, before it expired, swept the city. It penetrated the deepest burrow. It destroyed every living thing in the vicinity—all except those held in the safety of the stasis ray.

"Now the menace is ended. The Sleepers are dead. We are ready to left the stasis and let the world go on—but little harmed by the horror that passed while it slept."

Tears shone in Bell's clear eyes.

"All my guilt is absolved, Ron. My old debt is paid. Now I can go ahead. Thank you, Ron. And good-bye."

Beside him in the darkness, Maru-Mora's tiny face seemed almost to smile. From crimson lips came the eery music of her piping.

"She says farewell," Bell told me. "To you, and to Carol."

The darkness around them, suddenly, was no longer black but purple. I saw that they were in the crystal depths of that purple pylon, on the summit beyond the pole. And they fled away from me, into infinite distance.

Then I woke up in the laboratory. My right hand finished an over-arm sweep—the arrested gesture that had hurled the deadly tube. The force of it carried me around, and I saw Carol, waking. It was odd to watch her lovely face change from frozen horror to swift, incredulous delight.

"Ron!" she whispered eagerly. "You saw them, too? You heard

them—Doctor Bell and Maru-Mora?"

Little need to speak. She came into my arms, and I kissed her. It was good to feel the supple warmth of her body, when it had been so stiff and cold; good to feel the tremulous softness of her lips, when they had been diamond-hard.

We came out of the half-demolished laboratory, into a winter's dawn.

Northward, upon the Palisades, we found a strange broad circle of desolation, from which the bacteriophage had obliterated all life. Piled in the center of it were low crumbling mounds of clay, where the hideous city had stood.

But beyond that circle of doom, and all about us, was a world alive again. The south wind was warm as spring. Noisy larks soared on it, unconcerned, to greet the belated sun. The distant humming of bewildered New York was a vast and comforting sound.

The great silence was ended.

Carol took my hand like an eager child, and we walked toward the golden towers of the city awake in the dawn.

THE END

# The Infinite Enemy

*Thrilling Wonder Stories, April 1937*

## CHAPTER I

### Into—Enigma!

HIS was going to be a tough proposition. But Kerry Lundoon summoned a happy whistle to his lips, and walked jauntily up to the guarded gate of the Kallent Memorial Foundation.

"You get the Winship story, Lundy," his editor had ordered. "And I don't care how—bribe a guard, or bump him off. I want to know what Winship is doing inside that fence."

"Yes, chief."

"Don't 'yeschief'—get the copy! For fifteen years, Winship's laboratory has been a mystery. Ever since the atomic explosion, or whatever it was, that killed Dr. Kallent and his daughter, back in 1948. Cedric Kallent was the biggest scientist of his time. And Roger Winship seems to have carried on, behind that fence, from where Kallent left off.

"I don't know what he's got. The rumors say atomic power that could wreck the coal and oil interests, if Winship would let it go. They say gold transmuted out of zirconium, that could wreck the world's financial system—if Winship weren't too philanthropic to do it. They say a ship to fly to Mars.

"Well, I'm fed up with rumor and mystery. I want facts. Get 'em, Lundy. Or don't come back."

"Yes, chief," he had said.

The fence certainly looked formidable enough. A triple barrier, surrounding New Jersey's most inaccessible thousand acres. The outer one was of heavy steel mesh, twenty feet high. The next of glistening barb wire, hung with ominous signs:

*Danger—44,000 Volts!* The inner one was a high wall of sheet steel that shut out the view of everything beyond.

"Mr. Kerry Lundoon," he announced himself, "to see Dr. Winship." Seeing the forbidding glint in the eye of the guard, he added impressively, "I'm the science man from the *Planet,* for the interview on Dr. Winship's atomic discoveries."

The massive and muscular ex-pugilist who defended the gate uttered a porcupine grunt.

"Pass?" echoed the newshound. He patted the pockets of his immaculate dark suit. "Of course he sent me one. Here it is!"

G RINNING cheerfully, he presented the card. The big man inspected it, grunted, and dropped it into a pneumatic tube. Thirty seconds later it dropped back into the receiver. The guard read a note scrawled on it, deliberately tore it in half.

"Neat forgery, Buddy," he commented. "But the ultra-violet will tell."

"Better luck next time," grinned Kerry Lundoon.

"My advice, Buddy," scowled the guard. "Stay away."

That night the moonless sky was overcast. An hour after midnight, a silent plane dipped briefly below the ceiling, at three thousand feet. Kerry Lundoon stepped out of its cabin, caught his breath, and pulled the rip cord of his parachute.

The ceaseless throb of a great power plant came up to his ears. Floodlights poured white against the blank mystery of huge windowless buildings. Black shadows clotted clumps of trees. The forbidden thousand acres floated toward him.

"In!" he murmured, cheerfully. "And how I get out is *their* problem!"

He tugged at the 'chute's rigging, spilled air to sideslip toward a mysterious construction near the middle of the grounds. It was shaped like a tremendous wheel, one hundred feet in diameter and twenty in thickness, lying on its side. Dense shadow made a black pool within its rim. Overalled men were busy under the floodlights outside, loading tools and equipment into trucks.

"Eh?" muttered the newshawk. "Something just finished. The Martian flier, maybe? We'll see."

Uprushing air whispered softly against the cords. He side-slipped again. The pool of shadow was beneath him, expanding. He crossed his legs, relaxed for the impact. Hard metal smacked up against him, and the silk fell over his sprawled body.

"Greetings!" he whispered. "Doc Winship!"

He unbuckled the harness, kicked off the folds of the parachute, and cautiously rose to his feet in the darkness. A flat metal deck was beneath him. The rim of the wheel made a heavy metal bulwark about the edge.

"What is it?" he muttered. "But, first thing, a few good pix."

Leaning over the massive rim, a tiny automatic camera in his hand, the reporter ignored a sudden powerful throbbing that began beneath him—until an avalanche of white-hot agony struck him abruptly, hurled him backward.

He sprawled again on the metal deck. It was quivering, now, to the thrumming beneath. Blue fire of brush discharges danced above the edges of the rim.

Lundoon staggered back to his feet. He gasped for breath, felt gingerly of seared hands. The drumming underfoot was steadily louder. He blinked, stared apprehensively around him.

"What a gosh-awful jolt! Was it wired for me? Not likely. Then what? The space flier, maybe? Taking off!"

Panic gripped his heart. He reeled across the quivering deck again, to the rim. Another crushing shock hurled him back.

T RAPPED, in a wall of electric fire, on a ship taking off for Mars! Stark terror galvanized him. The parachute! Its silk would insulate a road to safety. He caught up the white folds in his arms, ran to the weirdly glowing wall, flung them over it. Blue sparks crackled explosively. Flame burst from the silk. The reporter struck at it with bare hands, Another shock flung him back to the throbbing deck.

The fall dazed him. When he opened his eyes, a light shone into them. A thick, cylindrical tower, studded with round ports, had risen from the center of the deck. The light was shining from a massive door opening in its side. A man darted out.

The reporter had struggled to his feet when the stranger reached his side, gasping:

"Come on, below! Before you're killed—"

They stumbled together back into the conning tower. Heavy double doors slid shut behind them. The circular interior of the tower was crowded with unfamiliar glittering instruments. Panting, the stranger touched some control, and a humming mechanism lowered them into the hub of the wheel.

Kerry Lundoon stared bewilderedly at his rescuer. This was a tall, thin man, whose thick shaggy hair seemed prematurely white, for his skin looked ruddy and youthful. His face was lean and haggard. His blue eyes were hollow, shadowed like wells of secret agony.

"I—" floundered the reporter. "Who—"

"I don't know what you were doing out there," said the other. "But the reversal field would have killed you in two minutes more."

Lundoon got his breath and tried to be coherent.

"I'm a newspaperman," he offered. "I was looking for Dr. Winship, for an interview about his discoveries."

A brief, quizzical smile lit that strangely haggard face.

"I'm Dr. Winship," the thin man said. "And there will be time for all the interviews you like, before we get back."

"Get back?" echoed Lundoon, with increased alarm. "We aren't going—" he had to gulp—"going—to Mars?"

"No," said the thin man.

"Then where?" Panic seized the reporter. "Stop it!" His voice was almost a scream. "You've got to let me off."

Winship gravely shook his white head and glanced at a bank of quivering gauges.

"Sorry, Mr. Reporter," he said. "But it's too late to stop." That oddly whimsical smile touched his thin lips again. "You came for news? Well, this trip will make plenty of it."

"Where?" Desperate urgency screamed in Lundoon's voice. "Where are we going?"

Winship inspected his dials again, cocked his white head to listen expertly to the throbbing machinery. He nodded at last, turned back to Lundoon.

"There'll be an hour or so," he said, "while the field is building up. After all, we're in it together, and alone. I may as well tell you." The bright hollow eyes glittered at Lundoon, excited, feverish. "The *Phantom Queen* is bound for another Universe!"

## CHAPTER II

### THE INVERSE UNIVERSE

T HE lean, haggard scientist opened the double sliding doors through which they had entered the conning tower. Now, since the tower had been lowered again, it gave into the interior of the great wheel, a circular space filled with huge, unfamiliar, throbbing machinery. Living quarters were partitioned off. Winship peered out anxiously at the immense machines.

Uneasily, Lundoon was pondering what the other had said. His mind reeled from incredulous questions. And a terrible loneliness began to haunt him, for obviously they were alone. But Winship looked at him again, with a grave understanding.

"It's strange, I know," he said. "I'll tell you about it."

The newshawk nodded gratefully.

"Dr. Cedric Kallent was the greatest scientist the world has seen," began the thin man. "You are familiar with many of his discoveries. But not with the greatest of all: the inverse Universe."

A humble awe came into his solemn voice.

"That is the supreme achievement of the human mind. But it has the simplicity of all great things. I can give you an idea of it in a few words." His keen eyes shot Lundoon a questioning look. "Of course you understand the atomic theory?"

"Of course," agreed the newshound, confidently.

"The orthodox theories of the atom recognize six subatomic particles," Winship said. "Three heavy ones: the negatron, proton, and neutron. Three light ones: the electron, positron, and neutrino.

"An ordinary atom—an atom of our positive Universe—consists of a nucleus of protons and binding electrons whose net positive charge is balanced by a number of orbital electrons.

"Kallent's geodesics of inversion established the mathematical basis for a Universe whose atoms would consist of a nucleus of negatrons and binding positrons, whose net negative charge would be balanced by orbital positrons.

"In other words, *minus* elements! A complete series, from minus hydrogen to minus uranium, with atomic numbers and chemical properties determined by the number of orbital positrons.

"And they make up a minus Universe! For Kallent's geodesics proved that the world lines of a positive and a negative atom, due to their inverse space-warp, can never intersect.

"Experiment soon confirmed mathematics. And it became Dr. Kallent's burning ambition to enter and explore that sister Universe."

Roger Winship paused to inspect the gauges, make careful adjustments on his elaborate banks of controls. Outside the tower, the mighty thrumming surged deeper again. Lundoon clenched his two hands, and fought the screaming panic in him. Trapped with a madman! Plunging into a foreign Universe! He bit his lip, waited. At last Winship went on.

"Dr. Kallent had a daughter. Her name was Venice. She and I were classmates at Tech—she had some of her father's genius. I came back with her, after graduation, to share the great research.

"S HE was a tall girl, proud and erect as a princess. She had a small, perfect face, fair skin, fine blue eyes, and honey-colored hair. Her quick smile had all the understanding humor in the world. I loved her from the moment I saw her. She liked me, but her father's work came first.

"For three years, we worked to open the door to that other Universe. The geodesics were the key. Finally we hit on the theoretical solution: a special field, of terrific intensity, whose space-warp would make positive atoms unstable, at last disrupt them, causing their energy to seek a new equilibrium in the negative form.

"The machine we built was disc-shaped, like this, with the atomic-powered field coils in the rim, although smaller and less powerful. We had it almost finished, when Dr. Kallent unexpectedly sent me to Europe to have a piece of equipment made.

"A cable from him was waiting at the hotel in Paris. It ran: 'Roger, forgive my fraud. Risk too great for all. We are going today. If anything happens; do what you can. Venice will go. She says good-by.'

"That same day I read in the newspapers that Dr. Kallent and his daughter had been killed in a terrific laboratory explosion. I was heartbroken. But I returned at once, and tried to find out what had happened. The laboratory was completely wrecked. Some imperfection of the field, I thought, must merely have disrupted the atoms, instead of transforming them.

"Working side by side with Kallent for three years, I had learned a good deal about his unpublished discoveries. Now, hoping it would help me forget, I set out to complete his work and record it for the benefit of science.

"I was having the laboratory rebuilt, when an obsession began to haunt me: the belief that Venice Kallent, somehow, was still alive! I had peculiar dreams, in which I saw her beckoning, gesturing. Her lovely face was white, strained. She was lost and helpless, trying to communicate with me.

"Dr. Kallent had done some work, years before, toward identifying thought as a radiogen phenomenon., a subatomic radiation. Following that clue, in a direction that somehow came to me in those dreams, I made the psychode."

The thin man paused again, in that small drumming space, took down a queer-looking helmet from the wall, and fitted it to his white head. A great horseshoe tube arched above the crown, its electrodes against his temples. Golden flame burned through it when he touched a knob.

"It picks up thought-energy," he explained, "amplifies it regeneratively, heterodyned upon ultra-waves, and rebroadcasts it, thus serving as both receiver and transmitter for tele-mental communication."

A strange, burning eagerness in their hollow depths, his tortured eyes peered far beyond Kerry Lundoon, beyond the walls of the metal tower.

"I put it on the day it was done," he said, "and waited." His low voice sank, until the newshound leaned forward to hear. "The white vision of Venice Kallent came to me again. And I was able, for the first time, to understand her."

T HE scientist paused a moment, reminiscent.

"'Dear Roger,' she was calling to me," he resumed, "'can you hear? I'm alive, lost in the other Universe. Father was killed. I'm all alone. It's so terrible. So strange! Can you hear me, Roger? Will you come?'

"'Yes, Venice!' I shouted, in the empty dark laboratory. 'I hear you. I'll come—if I can!'

"I thought she smiled. Then her shadow was gone."

His thin hands trembling, Roger Winship replaced the helmet on the wall. His feverish eyes inspected the dials again, peered out at the mighty drumming machines already hurling them into ominous enigma.

"That day," he said, "I began the effort to duplicate all Dr. Kallent's work, so that I could reach the inverse Universe to rescue the woman I loved. The difficulties were tremendous. The geodesics of inversion—the greatest single triumph of the human mind—I had memorized. But terrific problems rose in their application, and in avoiding the error that had caused the first disaster.

"A few times, briefly, I spoke to Venice again. She tried, fearfully, to tell me of some other being she had encountered. But she knew no more of her father's work than I. She couldn't help.

"There was a financial problem, too. Millions were needed, and I was penniless. Kallent had made me his heir. He left no money, but I was able to work out profitable applications of his brilliant discoveries. I struggled with one obstacle and another, and the years went by."

Roger Winship sighed wearily. A worn man, with the lines of agony on his emaciated cheeks. His tortured, restless eyes scanned the dials again.

"A long battle," he whispered. "But at last the *Phantom Queen* was done, ready for the voyage of rescue. Loyal men had worked beside me, for years. But they all had ties, obligations, or fears. I started tonight, alone. There was a noise on the deck." The glittering eyes dwelt upon Kerry Lundoon. "And I found you, a stowaway."

Staring, trembling, the reporter opened his dry mouth, swallowed twice. At last he could speak:

"And we're already—going—"

Eyes on the dials, Roger Winship nodded gravely.

"The atomic generators are feeding nine million kilowatts into the coils," he said. "The reversal field has already reached six billion kallent-volts. A little more—I don't know how much—and we shall undergo the atomic inversion, into the negative Universe. Or else, if I have failed, we shall be destroyed in a stupendous explosion of atomic energy."

"If—" whispered Lundoon. "If we live, what then?"

"If we are still alive," the haggard man said, "we shall search for Venice Kallent. The psychode, I hope, will guide us to her. And the reversal coils, at a different frequency, generate an unidirectional field that serves for propulsion in space."

S URGING up against the barrier of Lundoon's fear came a quick tide of sympathy for this slight man who had struggled so long toward a goal so difficult. He offered his hand.

"Here's hoping, Doc," he said, "that you find her."

Then his newspaper instincts were suddenly awake. What a story! He was fumbling for notebook and pencil, thinking sadly of his lost camera, when Winship's cry came to him, sharp and urgent: "Lie down!"

Lundoon flung himself to the floor of the conning tower. He was suddenly aware of a terrific strain that racked every atom of his body. There was a sudden appalling darkness, soon rent with searing flame. Every nerve shrieked with agony. For every atom, literally, was being torn asunder. The ship lurched and spun, as if swept before a black tidal wave.

Then it was ended. The pain receded. A soft little cry sobbed from the lips of Kerry Lundoon. He dragged himself to his feet, wiped cold sweat from his face.

Roger Winship was white and swaying, but a quiet light of victory shone in his hollow eyes. He touched a key, and the mighty thrum of the generators was suddenly silenced.

"It is done!" he whispered shakenly. "Field potential zero. We have been revibrated safely into the minus Universe." His trembling hand reached for the psychode helmet. "Now—Venice—"

## CHAPTER III

### THE GIANT OF CUBES

H UMMING motors were lifting the conning tower again, through the circular deck. Kerry Lundoon clung to a handrail, speechless, staring incredulously through a port.

For the high-fenced field was gone. He looked into a void of velvet darkness. The darkness was laced with an incredible web of shining rays. Strange worlds shimmering like jewels of a thousand colors were strung upon those threads of living light.

"The world is gone," he whispered. "Everything—gone."

Roger Winship reeled bewilderedly to a thick-barreled telescope. He kept his eyes against its oculars for a long time. His face became lax and white with dread. Lundoon's apprehensive curiosity became ungovernable.

"What—what do you see?" he stammered.

"I don't understand it," came the scientist's dismayed whisper. "Nothing bright enough to be a sun, yet all these bodies are luminous. There were no planetary systems, but queer worlds strung on shining rays."

"What can we do?" demanded the reporter. "Can we—can we go back?"

Roger Winship's thin face was stern with purpose.

"We'll search for Venice," he said. "She's here—somewhere in this madness—alone."

He adjusted the golden horseshoe of the psychode helmet on his head, and stood rigid beside the telescope. His eyes closed. It was eerily and ominously still.

Waiting, in a maddening tensity of anxiety, Lundoon peered outside again. Below and above, this strange space was the same. A lace of light woven against the darkness, sewn with tiny jewels of worlds.

He put his eyes to the telescope, and trembled to the strangeness of another discovery. These were no natural planets! One was an opal globe; but another was a white cube, the third an emerald tetrahedron, the fourth an amber rod.

A great disc of flaming magenta came across the field: a fiery wheel rolling on a ribbon of purple light. It receded and vanished. A bright green ellipsoid came back, devouring the purple road as it came. It passed, huge for a moment as the Moon, and also vanished.

What manner of Universe was this?

Staggering back from the instrument, the reporter passed a trembling hand across his forehead. Here was evidence of order, of law. But what uncanny order? What incredible law?

Roger Winship, beneath the psychode's fantastic crown, uttered a low gasping cry. Hastily, he took the thing from his head. His face looked white, stricken.

"Venice?" whispered Lundoon. "Did she speak?"

"No," said the thin man, his face still shadowed with some unutterable dread. "But a strange mind reached me. It commands us to land upon the nearest planet."

"But you won't obey!" protested Lundoon, apprehensively. "You don't know what sort of being—it may be dangerous."

"But I shall obey," said Winship. "It is the only clue."

He touched the control board. The generators started again, their throb now more gentle than upon the inter-universal voyage. The opal sphere drifted nearer.

I T was a strange ball of luminescence, perfect, many-hued. It was splendid against the velvet dark. No fewer than six incandescent threads, ranging in color from frozen blue to a dull smoky crimson, joined it to the web of worlds.

"Queer!" Winship was at the telescope again. "A perfect globe, two thousand miles in diameter. No trace of atmosphere. No mountains, no seas. Nothing like a city—no sign whatever of life or intelligence. Just a bare, shining ball."

"What—what could it have been," the reporter said huskily, "that spoke to you?"

"We shall see."

The *Phantorn Queen* proved swifter than Lundoon had thought possible. The strange world ahead grew. It was like a vast bubble of frosty incandescence, expanding.

Winship touched his keys again. The drum of the generators softened. The disc tilted, so that the planet was beneath. It dropped, toward a brilliant convex horizon.

Softly, they landed. The dark sky above was veiled with wondrous woven rays. A hard flat plain shimmered away from the ship. It was absolutely featureless, nowhere broken. A thin strand of blinding green fire leaped up beyond the flat horizon, ran straight to a tiny, cone-shaped world of red.

With a trembling hand, Winship was pointing out at that level of mingled diamond light.

"Look!" he quavered. "It's crystalline—in the cubic system!"

Peering down at the plain, as near the ship as he could, Lundoon saw that it was all composed of tiny, identical cubes, carefully laid to form a tilelike surface.

"That's so, but—"

His throat stuck. For the shimmering plain had heaved up. As if hurled by an explosive blast, a cloud of little diamond blocks came flying toward the ship. They rained down upon the flat circular deck, outside the conning tower. And they fell in a very curious way.

Lundoon had seen that each one-inch cube was joined to eight of its fellows by tiny threads of incandescence that ran from corner to corner. And they didn't fall at random on the deck, but piled themselves into a grotesque mockery of the human form.

It looked like something a child might have built, with a million nursery blocks.

It towered twenty feet tall. It was weirdly terrible.

One stride brought it to the observation tower. The ship shuddered to its weight. A thin rope of bright yellow fire ran from it back over the rail to the hole it had left in the plain, joining these cubes to the others there.

The face of it was outside the ports.

The reporter stared at it with a sick fascination. Hard bright cubes, strung together with threads of fire, made a massive nose, bulging many-faceted eyes, the square travesty of a chin. The thing looked like the creation of a surrealist sculptor gone mad. And it was infinitely horrible.

A fantastic arm of cubes came up, made some incomprehensible gesture.

"It's alive!" sobbed Kerry Lundoon. "The whole planet is alive!"

R OGER WINSHIP looked at him for a moment, with a torture of uncertainty in his hollow blue eyes. Then, slowly, he began to put on the headset of the psychode.

"I think it wants to talk to us," he said.

He seemed to listen. His thin face went suddenly white. Beads of sweat burst out, and gathered into glistening droplets that rolled down his lined cheeks.

"No," he whispered. "I won't do it! I want to find Venice. I want her more than anything. But I won't do that."

In a fever of apprehension, Lundoon caught his arm.

"What is it?" he demanded. "What does it want?"

But the scientist, absorbed in his battle with the grotesquerie of cubes, paid him no heed. And Kerry Lundoon turned suddenly to the ports again.

For that nightmare giant had stepped back across the deck. A second eruption of cubes opened a greater hole in the plain behind it. These, also, rained upon the deck. But they changed as they fell.

Bars of yellow gold laid themselves in glittering stacks. Massive ingots piled themselves, gleaming with the blue white of platinum, the blue gray of osmium, the brilliant white of pure radium. Great blocks fell into walls, flashing with the green of emerald, hot scarlet of rubies, prismatic splendor of diamonds.

That precious, incredible rain continued until the ship was laden with treasure beyond all calculation. And Roger Winship stood motionless inside the conning tower, the golden horseshoe still burning on his head, mute agony twisting his thin face.

"Millions!" gasped the reporter. "That's worth—billions! If it's real."

Still the scientist seemed not to hear him. The dull voice spoke again, gray, weary:

"No, I won't do it. All this is less to me than Venice. But I won't do it, even for her. I tell you—I won't—"

His voice had risen almost to a scream. Suddenly Winship wrenched the helmet off, dropped trembling on the stool behind the control board. Lundoon gripped his shoulder.

"What did it want?" he asked in a voice hoarse with urgency.

Dull and bloodshot, unutterably weary, Winship's hollow eyes looked up at his face.

"It wanted me to reveal the inversion geodesics," his dull voice said. "Dr. Kallent's greatest discovery: the key to the gate between the Universes."

"Why?"

Cold dread had already stiffened the journalist, when Winship spoke.

"There could be but one reason: that it desires to invade our own Universe. Therefore, I refused. It offered me all the treasure stacked outside, transmuted out of its own substance. It offered to lead me to Venice, and surrender her to me safe and alive." His voice was hoarse with pain. "But still I refused."

"Now what?" Lundoon demanded apprehensively. "Can we go back?"

Winship shook his white head.

"I don't think so. We're in its power. There would be no time to build up the reversal field. Besides, I am afraid to try. It can't discover the geodesics from any examination of the ship. But it might read them from my mind, if we tried to return—and follow."

The reporter's tongue stuck to the roof of his mouth.

"What—" he faltered. "What is going to happen?"

Winship shrugged thin shoulders, hopelessly.

"We'll be killed, I suppose. Probably not very pleasantly. The thing threatened to destroy us if I didn't reveal the geodesics.

There's nothing we can do."

The haggard head sank forward on his arms.

Kerry Lundoon turned unsteadily again to the ports. The precious stacks of metal and gems still lay on the deck, with that fantastic giant behind it. But something was happening to the treasure. A rope of white fire had run to it from the pit in the plain. At the ends of raveled incandescent threads, metal ingots and crystal blocks were flowing—changing back to hard bright cubes.

And the change didn't stop with the treasure. Bright filaments stabbed against the steel of the ship. Glowing knots formed at their ends, grew swiftly into cubes like the rest. The metal was pitted, consumed.

"It's eating the ship!" Roger Winship gasped. "We've got to get away."

A dull weariness still in him, the scientist stirred himself heavily, tapped at the control keys. The machinery throbbed again. The *Phantom Queen* lifted from that bright plain, into a flame-veiled space.

But the cloud of new-born cubes rose about them. The joining strands of fire stretched endlessly. And still the consuming threads attacked the ship. Winship dropped his white head again, hopelessly.

"We are helpless," he whispered. "There is nothing we can do."

## CHAPTER IV

### MOCK-SUN

KERRY LUNDOON turned away, shuddering, from the swift, uncanny destruction of the deck. Frantically, his eye searched the conning tower, fell upon the psychode helmet, which Winship had thrown aside after his failure to communicate with Venice Kallent.

With trembling hands the reporter set it on his head, snapped on the switch to light the horseshoe tube. He felt a curious tingling shock from the cold metal electrodes against his temples.

"Help!" he began to shout. "Help, before we die!"

Suddenly, then, crawling images of uttermost malevolence

filled his mind. Somehow they were rendered into words, perhaps by his own mind, as if a mocking, evil voice were saying:

"No one will help you, little being. For you two are alone. You know not the secret, and the other will not speak. Therefore you both must perish—unless you will cause the other to reveal the inversion geodesics."

That was the way out, Lundoon perceived. Attack Winship, beat him, torture him, force him to reveal the secret. He was amazed at the sudden, virulent hatred that filled him. Winship was a murderer, he was about to kill them both. And this being of the cubes was merely strange, not really evil.

Lundoon knew, somehow, that he was snatching a pair of heavy binoculars from beside a port. He swung them over the bowed white head. Knock him out, that was it. Bind him. Then twist his fingers. Burn his toes. Make him tell—

"Wait!"

Another strange voice seemed to speak through the helmet. It was like the peal of a silver bugle, clear, imperative.

"Wait! For I am coming."

And the thin man looked up, startled. He ducked the blow. His white head butted into Lundoon's middle. The reporter struck again, savagely. Get him! The first voice overwhelmed the other. Make him tell!

Winship's groping hand caught the helmet, jerked it from the reporter's head. Kerry Lundoon staggered back against the wall, suddenly weak and faint with the horror of what he had tried to do.

"Sorry, Doc!" he gasped. "Somehow—it got me!"

The pale, haggard face smiled at him, wanly.

"I understand, Lundoon. I met it, awhile ago." Breathing hard, he sat wearily back on the stool. Fingers fumbled automatically in his pocket. "Smoke?"

Lundoon accepted and lit a cigar. Then he remembered something.

"There was another voice. Something else—coming!"

He looked outside again. Still bright cubes swarmed above the deck, still thrust their filaments against the heavy steel, transforming it to other cubes.

But suddenly the light of the terrible swarm grew dim. Bright threads snapped. The cubes swept away from the ship like a flock of frightened birds. And another thing darted down, hung poised outside the conning tower.

No larger than a man's head, it was a mirror-polished globe. Its surface reflected in miniature the strange veil of fire across the sky. It tapped gently against a port, as if seeking entry.

W INSHIP, beside him, was staring at the sphere.

"It's all right, Doc," Lundoon assured him. "It drove away the cubes."

Winship put on the psychode. The tube flamed golden again. His haggard face smiled. And Lundoon listened once more to half a strange conversation.

"Yes," said Winship, "the thing of cubes is our enemy. . . . We came to this Universe to seek one of our own kind." . . . His voice went hoarse with amazement. "Yes, Venice Kallent! You know *her?* . . . Energy? . . . Yes, we have energy to spare. I'll let you through the lock."

His white face turned to Lundoon.

"It knows Venice," he whispered. "It says that it has escaped from a prison in which they were together."

The silver globe had vanished from the port. Winship touched the buttons which controlled the double, sliding doors. The inner one opened, and the sphere flitted into the conning tower, quick and silent as the image of a trembling mirror.

And Kerry Lundoon, standing near the yellow horseshoe of the psychode, was aware of faint thought-images, eagerly hopeful.

"Energy? Energy for me?"

"Plenty of it," Winship said. "Millions of kilowatts, from the atomic generators. But tell me about Venice."

Unconsciously, Lundoon had become aware that his cigar was extinct.

Automatically, for all his mind was filled with the wonder of that argent bubble, he thumbed a pocket lighter, raised it. He was astounded when the bubble leaped like a moth at the tiny flame. It hovered above the light, and suddenly its silvery film was hidden in a mist of rainbow color.

"A splendid thing!" came Winship's awed whisper. "A perfect parhelion."

Parhelion? The reporter puzzled at the word, recalled that it meant a mock sun, a sun-dog. Faintly, then, the thought-forms of the little being:

"Energy is good. Mock-sun is grateful. For he was starved for energy, in the prison."

"Welcome, Mock-sun!" Winship said eagerly. "But where is Venice? Tell me about her."

Lundoon could catch nothing more of the swift emanation of thought from the sphere. Rapt wonder had seized Winship's pallid face. His hushed voice asked swift questions.

"Where is the prison? What is this thing of cubes? Can we fight it?"

Lundoon waited in a fever of impatience.

"What is it?" he demanded once. "What does it say?"

But Winship seemed unconscious of him. The sphere still danced in its haze of color above the lighter's flame. It seemed a long time before it turned silver again, darted upward. Winship bent suddenly over the controls, and the *Phantom Queen* throbbed into motion again.

"Where are we going?" Lundoon questioned. "What did it tell you?"

"A great deal," said Winship's awed voice. "An amazing story." He adjusted the controls. The generators drummed louder. The far-off web of colored rays crept visibly past the ports.

I MPATIENTLY, Lundoon insisted, "Tell me!"

"This Universe was once pretty much the counterpart of our own, so I gather," Winship began. "Its matter condensed into galaxies, suns, and planets. Life was born, became intelligent, extended its sway over matter. Upon one planet sprang up a race of scientists. Two of them, brothers, became the supreme minds of this Universe.

"Grappling with the few great problems their race had not solved, they first sought eternal life. One of them—our guest, who had conveniently elected the name Mock-sun,—achieved the goal through a mastery of space and time.

"His brother being sought it in another way, through control of energy and matter. It revised its entire physical organization, and gradually made itself able to transmute and assimilate matter in unlimited amounts.

"It devoured all the others of its race, save Mock-sun. It devoured all the life on the planet. Then it transmuted and consumed the material of the very world itself. It stretched out the radiant tubes of force that might be called its nerves to other planets, even to their parent star, and transformed them also into the hard eternal cubes of fixed material energy that were its life-cells.

"Its greed was insatiable. It spread from star to star, across all the galaxy. It consumed everything it touched, from suns to meteoric dust. It reached a shining arm to the next galaxy, spread to others.

"In the end, all the matter in this Universe-continuum had been consumed—all save the body of its brother being. It attacked him, also. But Mock-sun protected himself. He created this silvery shield—walling himself, in fact, into a tiny sub-space manifold of his own.

"Mass is not always indicative of quality. The conquering entity suspected the existence of our twin Universe—and desired, in its infinite greed, to enter and devour it. But, for all its giant bulk, it was unable to discover the geodesics of inversion.

"The keener mind of Mock-sun had long since mastered them. However, recognizing the infinite evil of the other, he refused to reveal them. Demanding them, the other confined him, cut off the energy he needed to live.

"Venice, when the experiment hurled her into this Universe, fifteen years ago, was thrown into the same prison—still aboard the ship, but unable to operate it. They have been together.

"The psychode made them aware of our arrival. Mock-sun escaped—he has some power left, against the other. And he came to guide us to Venice."

Suddenly the silver bubble was darting, as if with alarm, from port to port. Looking out, apprehensively, Kerry Lundoon saw an ominous thing. The shining web that veiled the dark sky was tightening, the queer living worlds drawing in about them.

"It's closing in!" he gasped.

Hastily, Winship adjusted the psychode again. Intent with listening, his face went ashen white.

"Mock-sun says that the infinite entity has discovered his escape," he whispered in dismay, "and terminated a sort of truce they had made. Now all its power is against us."

## CHAPTER V

### Universe Lost

R OGER WINSHIP'S drawn hollow face showed no fear. An eagerness of hope was burning in his feverish eyes.

"It has been fifteen years." His low voice was anxious and wistful, "If I could only see her again, before the finish, I should ask for nothing more—"

Kerry Lundoon was peering out, fearfully.

A scene of terrible wonder met his gaze. Burning against velvet dark, bound together with cords of flame, strange worlds were crowding thick about them. Various as to shape and color, fantastic as a madman's dream.

A rope of hot red fire leaped at them suddenly, like a striking snake, from the center of a violet planetary ring. The end of it raveled out, into a million wirelike strands. These incandescent filaments shot to the deck. Bright cubes grew swiftly at their extremities, and the metal wasted again.

The reporter turned suddenly from it. He caught the silver bubble between his two hands. He chatted fearfully.

"Can you—can you help us?"

But Winship, with the helmet on his head, said hopelessly:

"We are lost. Mock-sun cannot use the power that he has. He can't, now, even guide us to Venice. And there—*the air!*"

Lundoon looked out again, in time to see a black hole yawn in the pitted deck. Outrushing air condensed into a tenuous cloud of frost. And the frost was gathered into a glittering cube; nothing escaped the hunger of the universal being.

Rigid with the terror of death, the reporter saw a bright filament stab against the port. He saw the thick quartz transformed into little hard cubes, bright with opalescent gleams. And then the port was open.

The air exploded outward. Lundoon was hurled against the wall. Breath sighed out of his bursting lungs. Agony swelled his heart. The hammer of his pulse was deafening. He felt the hot rush of blood in his nostrils, his ears, tasted its salty sweetness in his mouth.

Pressed from their sockets by fiendish fingers, his eyes went blind. Terrible fingers closed on his throat. His empty lungs labored in vain. He staggered, fell.

And, in that last terrible moment, he thought he felt incandescent filaments burning against his body—to transform it also into hard tiny cubes.

But awareness came back to him, out of a queer dream in which he was winged, soaring above the towers of New York. He could breathe again. He opened his aching eyes, and discovered Winship near him, and the silver globe of Mock-sun.

They were all floating together in a queer transparent bubble. The wreckage of the *Phantom Queen* was a little distance away. Lundoon watched its last fragment dissolve into a little swarm of bright cubes, laced together with shining wires. The strange worlds, beyond, still were gathering.

Winship, the psychode still on his head, floated up from the bottom of the twelve-foot crystal bubble.

"What—" gasped the reporter. "How—"

"Mock-sun was able to use his power, after all," the thin man said. "He made this transparent shield—it is akin to his own sub-space barrier. He filled it with oxygen, so that we can breathe. The cubes cannot enter it. And he can move it, so that we can continue the search for Venice."

E VEN as Winship spoke, the bubble darted away, at a speed far greater than the *Phantom Queen* had attained. The bright living web was brushed backward. They plunged into a gulf of darkness, so vast that the clustered worlds were lost,

"The prison," Winship rendered Mock-sun's message. "A space drained of all energy."

The bubble came, at last, to a sudden halt.

Roger Winship pointed abruptly out through its pellucid film, uttering a soft, choked cry. Staring, Lundoon saw, drifting beside them, a battered disc of steel, a smaller *Phantom Queen*.

"That's Kallent's first machine!" sobbed Winship. "Where Venice is!"

The reporter saw a woman's face looking through the round port of an air lock in the rim. A thin face, pale and anguished, its violet eyes were wells of tortured loneliness. Horror unspeakable had marked it. Yet, somehow, it was still beautiful.

"Venice!" Winship was shouting. "Venice—darling!"

The woman beckoned. The bubble floated closer to the valve.

She vanished, flung it open. Escaping air hurled her out. She struck the shimmering wall. And, somehow, it let her in.

A throbbing ache closed Lundoon's throat, to watch that reunion. Roger Winship caught the exile's frail hands, with both of his. They stared for a moment at each other, on both their faces a startled, half-incredulous wonder.

"Roger!" whispered the woman. "You came!"

She burst suddenly into tears. Winship made a little choked sound, and drew her very tenderly toward him. And abruptly they clung together, desperately.

Then the little silver ball of Mock-sun was suddenly darting about the bubble. It bumped gently against Winship's head. He turned from the woman, to adjust the psychode.

"Followed?" the scientist gasped.

Indeed, far off in the black gulf, the reporter saw a cometlike body. A bright spark, racing toward them, trailing a path of flame. Lundoon was still staring, fearfully, when Winship touched his arm.

"Get your breath," he said. "We're going back."

"Back?" Lundoon was incredulous. "Back to Earth? How?"

"Mock-sun has mastered the geodesics," Winship said. "And we are still so far away that he can shield the process from the enemy."

"When?" Lundoon gasped.

But Winship had already made a warning gesture. And the reporter was overwhelmed again with racking torture, as if every atom of his body were crushed by inconceivable forces. The agony of the reversal field. It ended. And he was amazed to find himself sprawled on the ground.

He staggered to his feet, bewildered. The sky was blue above. The genial rays of a familiar sun fell across clumps of green trees and great, white-walled buildings. Fresh-mowed grass was crisp underfoot. The warm air shuddered to the distant mundane whistle of a locomotive.

This was Earth again.

Home!

THEY were back in the well-fenced grounds of the Kallent Memorial Foundation, he recognized, from which the *Phantom Queen* had carried them. Roger Winship was helping Venice to her feet, at his side. Mock-sun was bounding about over the grass, like a silver hall.

"We're home!" sighed the weary man, happily. "After fifteen years! Venice, my darling-*ugh!*"

Lundoon heard the sudden croak of horror in Winship's voice. He turned. Consternation froze him. For the thin, white-headed scientist was retreating from the woman he had rescued. His hands were lifted, his gaunt face ashen and rigid with dread.

The woman had laughed, mockingly. The laughter changed to a sound not human. Her slim body altered suddenly. It became a fantastic grotesquerie of hard, bright cubes.

"Venice!" Winship gasped. "Why, Venice—"

Beyond them, the silver globe of Mock-sun had dissolved into a cluster of glittering cubes. Already they were feeding on the grass. Bright filaments writhed from their corners down against the turf, absorbed it to grow new cubes.

The fantastic thing that had been Venice Kallent dissolved into a swarm of little opalescent blocks, that fell like locusts on the trees and grass.

Roger Winship staggered back against the bole of a tree, wiping horror-sweat from his gray, stricken face.

"What a fool!" he whispered. "What a fool I was!"

"What—" Lundoon gasped. "What—happened?"

"A trick," came Winship's rasping voice. "It was all a hoax, designed to destroy our Universe. In the attack on the *Phantom Queen,* when we were unconscious, the entity recaptured Mock-sun."

"But Mock-sun helped us—"

"The thing that helped us, or pretended to, was a counterfeit Mock-sun, made to deceive us. It was easy for the entity has absolute mastery of matter. The counterfeit led us, not to Venice, but to another duplication. And so, unwittingly, we brought back the seed of the monster, to destroy our Universe!"

## CHAPTER VI

### INFINITE ILLUSION

THE change which overwhelmed it the world took place with a frightful and progressively increasing rapidity. Each cubic life-cell of the invader, when grown, could send out seven new filaments, from seven corners, to start new ones.

The grass and trees within the high-fenced enclosure were soon transformed to gleaming blocks. The white buildings fell, and then the fence. Trees and stacks in the distance crumbled. Inequalities were leveled. The earth, to the limit of vision, was soon a glittering opalescent pave.

The workmen and technicians employed by the Foundation, with their families, had lived in a model community village which occupied one end of the thousand acres. The fate of those neat homes was a scene of typical horror. Screaming men, hysterical women, wailing children, all fled vainly from the terror of the cubes.

Overtaken, struck ruthlessly down by conglomerate hammers, they were swiftly turned to bright cubes themselves and so rose to pursue the rest.

Lundoon had momentarily expected the death of Winship and himself. Surely their lives had no value to the entity. And, since Earth was lost, their fate seemed to matter not at all.

But they were spared. The turf was consumed beneath their feet. A shrieking mechanic, running toward them, fell and was consumed almost at their feet. But they were left at the end, standing alone on a glistening plain of diamond blocks.

The world was flat, presently, to the level horizon. Nothing broke the glittering surface. And Lundoon saw a rope of purple flame leap out across the westward sky, toward the waning moon. He watched its mottled silver change to a poison green. He saw other fiery shafts arrow from it, to consume yet other worlds.

"It is done," he whispered, "But were we spared?"

He looked at Roger Winship, haggard disheveled man, sunk in weary heart-crushed apathy. The scientist shook his white head, fantastic with the psychode still upon it. He made no reply.

Lundoon gripped his arm in sudden panic.

For the shining plain had heaved up before them. A rising cloud of cubes left a ragged pit. They clustered together to form, once more, a grotesque, gigantic manlike shape. It came toward them, still bound to the pit behind it. Standing before it, Winship adjusted the psychode, listened.

And Lundoon was suddenly absorbed by the expression on the face of the scientist. His despair and horror seemed to ebb away. A grim smile played for a moment across his lined features.

And Winship shook his head.

The gigantic thing tramped nearer. Its great arms flailed threateningly. Colossal feet crushed down, almost catching the two men. And Roger Winship smiled again.

"Nothing doing, sweetheart," he said softly.

He slipped off the helmet, and stood idly swinging it in his hand. The bewildered reporter caught his arm.

"Now what is it?" he asked.

Roger Winship made a cheerfully careless gesture at the appalling giant.

"It informs me that Venice is still alive," he said. "Still in the ship that we saw imitated so expertly. And it will carry me back to the other Universe, to join her—if only I will disclose the inversion geodesics!

"It can do no harm to spill the geodesics, now, the entity argues, because our Universe is wiped out anyhow. And still it needs them, otherwise it is forever cut in twain. It is offering, therefore, to take us back to Venice, and to let us live out our natural lives there in the ship—if only we tell.

"If we don't, torture for both of us—until we do."

L UNDOON saw nothing to be so cheerful about. His throat was rough and dry, but finally a husky whisper came.

"Well—why not tell? If it can't hurt—"

Wearily, Roger Winship smiled.

"Mass doesn't always mean quality. Among the largest brains ever weighed was that of a congenital idiot. The entity has set a very elaborate stage and produced a very impressive illusion—but there's one obvious flaw."

"Illusion?" gasped the reporter. "Flaw?"

"It is obvious," said Roger Winship, "that we have not been returned to our own Universe. Therefore we have not seen Earth destroyed."

"But we did—" began Lundoon.

"We thought we did. But we know that the entity is a master of matter. We have seen that its substance, at will, can be molded and transmuted into any form. More significant, we know, too, that the psychode, amplifying any thought, is a powerful adjunct to hypnotic suggestion."

Lundoon glanced fearfully up at the threatening monster of cubes.

"But this is—was the Earth," he insisted. "Mock-sun brought us back."

"That's the flaw," said Winship. "The real Mock-sun knew the inversion geodesics. But the counterfeit that returned us was a part of the entity. And the entity doesn't know them. Therefore, we weren't brought back!"

Lundoon gasped, his head spinning. When he looked up at the darkening sky, he saw that its flame-veiled wonder had indeed grown curiously familiar. This world might very well be the opal planet where they had first landed.

He peered in bewildered apprehension at the fantastic giant. That, anyhow, was real, menacing. But suddenly the little blocks that formed it turned black, and began to fall apart. They clattered down, like shattering black glass, upon the plain.

And the plain itself was darkened. A circle of blackness ran out like a ripple, from where the monster fell. It expanded to the flat horizon. A shadow was cast upon the veil of flame above. The colored sparks of worlds were quenched in darkness. A dim purple twilight fell upon them, and Lundoon shivered to the chill of universal doom.

"It must be dying!" he whispered. "But why?"

A disc of battered metal came plunging out of that void of deepening purple, slowed itself, settled softly toward them.

"Kallent's old machine!" cried Winship. "Or else the counterpart we saw!"

It landed beside them on the glassy, darkened plain. A valve opened in its rim. A familiar small globe of silver darted out, tapped against the helmet swinging from Winship's hand. He put it on, lit the golden horseshoe, listened.

"If you are Mock-sun," he said, "repeat the inversion geodesics. . . . Good! And where is Venice? . . . What has happened to the entity?"

Consumed with wonder, the reporter studied Winship's lean face. It went lax with amazement. It was suddenly bright with eagerness, then clouded with sorrow. Tears welled out of the weary eyes, ran down hollow cheeks.

T HE purple dusk, meantime, grew deeper. As if, Lundoon thought, all light was being quenched from this Universe. He shivered to an increasing chill. The air seemed very thin; his lungs were laboring.

And something, he thought, was the matter with Mock-sun. Little irregular patches of darkness appeared and vanished on its bright silver. At last it sank, as if weary, upon the black pave.

Winship slowly looked away, toward the machine. Lundoon caught his arm, rapped out insistent questions.

"Yes, this is the real Mock-sun, who was in prison with Venice," he said. "He has destroyed the entity—the being that was his brother. He did it with a subtle transformation of the space-warp, so that it is no longer an adequate medium for the other's vital energy.

"Mock-sun had possessed the weapon for a long time. But they, were brothers, alone together. Mock-sun, in a way that perhaps we can never understand, loved the other. He forgave it all its crimes—even his own imprisonment and torture.

"Mock-sun was near death, he says, when Venice was thrown into the same prison. She kept him alive with the heat radiated from her own body. They were together fifteen years, Mock-sun, it seems, came to feel something more than gratitude. For it was for her sake, at last, to insure the safety of the world she loved, that he killed the other being."

In the thickening purple darkness, Winship looked down at the small globe lying at their feet. Larger patches of black were flickering across its silver.

"It is difficult to follow the emotions of an alien being," Winship said. "But Mock-sun is ill—perishing. Not from any physical necessity, I think, but because his heart is broken by what he has done."

A sharp, brittle snap drew Lundoon's eyes to his feet. The silver sphere was gone. A minute naked body quivered, where it had been, and lay still. Wonderingly, they bent over it. At first it resembled the form of a tiny man. In a moment, however, it had crumbled to a pinch of gray dust.

Presently Winship got slowly and stiffly back to his feet.

"Come aboard," he said. "The ship is uninjured. We can return to Earth."

The rusted valve closed behind them. They came through the lock, into the machine. Winship stopped, with a soft cry of breathless joy, and then ran unsteadily forward.

For a woman had been waiting for him. Swaying to meet him, she looked thin and frail. Her hair was completely white. Her violet eyes were shadowed with the horror of her long exile, but happiness was a radiant right in them now.

"Roger!" she whispered. "You have come!"

Lundoon walked softly past them, into the control room of the ship that now could take them safely back. His practiced mind was searching, already, for the fitting lead for his story that would scoop the world.

# The Legion of Time

*Astounding Science-Fiction, May, June, July 1938*

HE BEGINNING OF IT FOR DENNIS LANNING—THE VERY BEGIN-
ning of his life—was on a hushed April evening of
1927. Then eighteen, Lanning was slender, small-featured, with straw-yellow hair which usually stood on
end. He commonly wore a half-diffident smile—but his gray eyes
could light with a fighting glint, and his wiry body held a quick
and unsuspected strength.

In that beginning was the same fantastic contrast that ran
through the whole adventure: the mingling of every-day reality
with the stark Inexplicable.

Lanning, that last term, shared a Cambridge apartment with
three other Harvard seniors, all a little older than he. Wilmot
McLan, the mathematician, was a slight man, grave and reticent,
already absorbed in his work. Quietly cheerful, studious Lao
Meng Shan, proud son of a mandarin of Szechwan, was eagerly
drinking in the wonders of modern engineering. Good friends
and swell fellows, both. But the one who stood always closest to
Lanning was Barry Halloran.

Gigantic red-haired all-American tackle, Barry was, first and
last, a fighter. Some stern, bright spirit of eternal rebellion he and

Lanning shared in common. Companions in everything, they had been taking flying lessons together at the East Boston airport.

The other three were out, however, on this drowsy Sunday evening, and the house was still. Lanning sat alone in his room, reading a thin little gray-bound book. The flyleaf was inscribed, "To Denny, from Wil—a stitch in Time!" It was Wil McLan's first scientific work (which he had just published at his own expense) entitled, *Reality and Change: The Nature of Time.*

Deep-hidden in its abstruse mathematics, Lanning had sensed an exciting meaning. He leaned back, with tired eyes closed, trying to complete the tantalizing picture he had glimpsed through the mist of symbols on the page. The book began with Minkowski's famous dictum: "Space in itself, and Time in itself, sink to mere shadows, and only a kind of union of the two retains an independent existence."

Was Time, then, but another extension of the universe; tomorrow as real as yesterday? What if one could leap forward—?

"Denny Lanning!"

A clear silvery voice had spoken his name. Dropping the book, he sat upright in his chair. He blinked, swallowed. A queer little shudder went up and down his spine. The door was still closed, and there had been no other sound. But a woman was standing before him on the rug.

A plain white robe swept long to her feet. Her hair, a glowing mahogany-red, was held back with a blue, brilliant band like a halo. The composure of her perfect, classic face was almost stern. But, behind it, Lanning felt agony.

Before her, in two small hands, she held a thing about the size and shape of a football—but shimmering with splendid prismatic flame, like a colossal, many-faceted diamond.

HER GRAVE EYES were on Lanning. They were wide, violet. Something in their depths—a haunting dread, a piercing, hopeless longing—choked him with emotion, dimmed his eyes. Then amazement came back, and he stumbled to his feet.

"Hello!" he gasped. "Yes, I'm Denny Lanning. But who are you?" His glance went to the locked door behind her. "How'd you get inside?"

A grave smile lit the white cameo of her face.

"I am Lethonee," she said. Her voice, Lanning noticed, had an unfamiliar musical rhythm. "And I am not really in your room, but in my own city of Jonbar. It is only in your mind that we meet, through the *chronotron,"*—her eyes dropped briefly to the immense flashing gem—"and only your study of Time made possible this complete *rapport."*

Open-mouthed, Lanning was drinking in the slim, clean youth of her, the glory of her hair, her calm, deep loveliness that was like an inner light.

"Lethonee—" he murmured, relishing the sound. "Lethonee—Dream or not, you are beautiful!"

A quick little smile, pleased and tender, rewarded him. But instantly it was gone, before the deep solemnity of trouble.

"I have come a long way to find you, Denny Lanning," she said. "I have crossed a gulf more terrible than death. Will you help me?"

A queer, trembling eagerness had seized him. Incredulity struggled with a breathless hope. A throbbing ache was in his throat, so that he couldn't speak. He walked uncertainly to her, and tried to touch the slim bare arms that held the great jewel. His quivering fingers met nothing but air.

"I'll help you, Lethonee," he gulped at last. "But how can I?"

Her silver voice sank to a low, urgent tone. From the startling whiteness of her face, the great, violet eyes seemed to look far beyond the room.

"Because destiny has chosen you, Denny Lanning. The fate of the human race is on your shoulders. My own life is in your hand—and the doom of Jonbar!"

"Eh!" Lanning muttered. "How's that?" He rubbed his forehead, bewilderedly. "Where's Jonbar?"

His wondering dread increased when the girl said: "Look into the *chronotron,* and I can show you Jonbar."

She lifted the great flashing jewel, holding its ends in her two small hands. Her eyes dropped to it. Colored rays shattered from it, blindingly. It exploded into a prismatic glare. The fire-mist slowly cleared, and he saw—Jonbar!

The lofty, graceful pylons of it would have dwarfed the skyscrapers of Manhattan. Of shimmering, silvery metal, they were set immensely far apart, among green park-lands and broad, many-leveled roadways. Great white ships, teardrop-shaped, slipped through the air above them.

"That is my Jonbar, where I am." the girl said softly. "Now let me show you the city that may be—New Jonbar—lying far-off in the mists of futurity."

BRIGHT FLAME veiled the city, and vanished again. And Lanning saw another wondrous metropolis. The green hills along the horizon were the same. But the towers were taller, farther apart. And they shone with clean brilliant colors, against the wooded parks. The city was one artistic whole; a single stupendous jewel whose beauty caught Lanning's breath.

A reverent awe was in the girl's voice when she whispered: "New Jonbar! Its people are the *dynon.*"

There were fewer ships in the air. But Lanning now saw tiny figures, clad it seemed in robes of pure, bright flame, launching themselves from lofty roofs and terraces, soaring above the parks in perfect, wingless freedom.

"They fly through adaptation to the power of the *dynat,*" breathed the girl. "It makes them near immortal, almost—godlike! They are the perfect race to come."

Prismatic flame hid the vision. The girl lowered the crystal in her hands. Lanning stepped back. He blinked bewilderedly at the reading lamp, his books, the chair behind him. From that old, comforting reality, he looked back to the girl's white wonder.

He spoke again, diffidently: "Lethonee— Tell me, are you real?"

"I am real as Jonbar is." Her voice was hushed and solemn. "You hold our destiny—to give us life or death. That is a truth already fixed in the frame of Space and Time."

"What—" Lanning gulped, "what can I do?"

Dread was a shadow in her eyes.

"I don't know. The deed is dim in the flux of time. But you may strike for Jonbar—if you will. To win or to perish! I came to warn you of those who will seek to destroy you—and, through you, Jonbar."

The rhythm of her voice was almost a chant, a prophecy of evil.

"There is the dark, resistless power of the *gyrane,* and black Glarath, the priest of its murderous horror. There are the monstrous hordes of the *kothrin,* and their savage commander, Sorainya."

The white beauty of Lethonee had become almost stern. A sorrow darkened her eyes, yet they flashed with a deathless hatred.

"She is the greatest peril." It was a battle-chant. "Sorainya, the Woman of War! She is the evil flower of Gyronchi. And she must be destroyed."

Her voice fell, and Lethonee looked at Lanning over the giant crystal, her eyes full of a tender and almost childish concern.

"Or," she finished, "she will destroy you, Denny."

Lanning looked a at her a long time. At last, hoarse with wonder, he said: "Whatever is going to happen, I'm willing to help— if I can. Because you are—beautiful. But still—what, exactly, am I expected to do?"

The words almost crackled from Lethonee's lips: "Beware of Sorainya!" Then, her rhythmic voice once more soft and musical, "Denny, make me one promise. Promise me that you will not fly to-morrow."

"But I'm going to!" Lanning cried. "Max—he's the instructor— said that Barry and I could solo to-morrow, if the weather's right. I couldn't miss it."

"You must," said Lethonee. "Or Jonbar will be slain!"

Lanning met her violet eyes. Emotion had burned away some barrier. He looked into her very soul—and found it beautiful.

"I promise," he whispered. "I'll not fly."

"Thank you, Denny." Her smile set a throbbing ache in his throat. "Now I must go."

"No!" Alarm tore Lanning's heart. "I don't know half enough. Where you are, really. Or how I could find you again. Don't go!"

"But I must." Dread clouded her face again. "For Sorainya might follow me here. And if she finds that the crisis turns indeed on you, she will strive to take you—yes, destroy you! I know Sorainya."

"But—" Lanning gulped. "But—will I see you again?"

"It is your hand on the wheel of time," the girl said gravely, "and not mine. Good-by, Denny."

"But wait!" gasped Lanning. "I must tell you! I—"

But the fire of a million sunlit prisms had burst again from the jewel in her hands. Lanning was momentarily dazzled, blinded. Then, blinking, he found himself alone in the room, speaking to vacant air.

DREAM—or reality? The question racked him. Could she have been an actual person, come across the gulf of time from the remote, possible future? Or was he going crazy?

Dazed, he picked up the little gray book, and reread a paragraph of Wil McLan's: "To an external observer gifted with four-dimensional senses, our quadraxial universe must appear complete, fixed, and forever unchanging. The sweep of Time is no more than the hand of a subjective watch; it is no more than the intangible ray of consciousness, illuminating human experience. In any absolute sense, the events of yesterday and to-morrow are alike eternal as the structure of space itself."

But the white, troubled beauty of Lethonee rose against the page. How did that fit with her tale of worlds that might be?

He flung aside the book, helped himself to a generous slug of Barry Halloran's pre-war Irish whisky, and walked blindly down through Harvard Square. It was after three when at last he came in to bed, and then he slept with a dream of Lethonee.

He wanted to tell Barry, in the morning, for they had been closer than brothers. But he thought the big redhead would only laugh—as he himself might have laughed if another had told him the thing. And he didn't want laughter at his dream of Lethonee—not even from Barry.

Half sick with a confusion of wonder and doubt, of hopeless hope for another glimpse of her, and bitter dread that she had been all illusion, Lanning waited for the fatal hour.

"Buck up, kid!" Barry boomed at him, heartily. "I never thought you'd be shaky—Max says you've got the nerves of a hawk. I'm the one that should be turning green around the gills. Come out of it, and let's go catch some sparrows!"

Lanning wanted to solo that morning more than he had ever wanted anything—until he saw Lethonee. He had promised not to fly. But what signified a promise made in a dream?

He stood up, uncertainly—and then the phone rang. He had made his own expenses, that year, covering university activities for a Boston paper—and this was his editor. It was an assignment that could have been evaded. But, listening, he saw the tragic eyes of Lethonee again, beyond her glowing jewel.

"Okay, Chief," he said. "On the job!" He hung up and looked at Barry. "Sorry, old man. But business first. Tell Max I'll be out to-morrow. And—happy landings, guy."

"Tough luck, kid."

The big tackle grinned, crushed his hand, and went out.

Lanning read in his own paper, four hours later, how Barry Halloran died. The training plane had gone out of control two thousand feet over Boston harbor, and plunged down into the Charles River Basin. Grappling hooks had brought part of the battered wreckage up out of the mud, but the body had not been recovered.

Lanning shut his eyes against the black headlines, reeling. He was sick with a dread that was almost terror, numbed with a black regret. For Lethonee had saved his own life, he knew—at the cost of Barry Halloran's.

## II.

LANNING felt no gratitude for the warning that had saved his life. Rather, a sick regret, an aching sense of guilt for Barry's death. Yet he could feel no actual resentment toward Lethonee— the tragedy seemed a terrible proof of her reality—for in her grave, troubled beauty, surely, there had been no evil.

A kind of excitement, however, buoyed up Lanning for a few days, and relieved his grief. There was a bright hope that Lethonee would return. Her memory was a haunting pain of loneliness, that would not die. Her enigmatic warnings, even the vague expectancy of peril, lent a spice to existence.

But life went on—after the funeral preached for Barry's never-recovered body—as if Lethonee had never come. Lao Meng Shan returned to China, eager to put his new science at her service. Wil McLan was off to Europe, on a fellowship in theoretical physics.

And Lanning presently embarked for Nicaragua, on his first foreign press assignment. American marines were straightening out the Sacasa-Chamorro fracas. Barry's uncle had offered him an advertising job. But a burning unrest filled him, born of the conflicts of doubt and hope, wonder and grief, dread and bitter longing. He saw no way ahead, save to break old ties, to forget.

It was on the little fruit steamer, bound for Corinto, that he first saw Sorainya! And knew, indeed, that he would never forget, never escape the strange web of destiny flung across Space and Time to snare him.

Velvet night had fallen on the tropical Pacific. The watch had just changed, and now the decks were deserted. Lanning, the only passenger, was leaning on the foredeck rail, watching the minute diamonds of phosphorescence that winged endlessly from the prow.

But his mind saw, instead, the great jewel that Lethonee had called the *chronotron,* and her slim haunting form behind it.

And it startled him strangely when a ringing golden voice, in pealing mockery of her own, called: "Denny Lanning!"

His heart leapt and paused. He looked up eagerly, and hope gave way to awed wonderment. For, flying beside the rail, was a long golden shell, shaped like an immense shallow platter. Silken cushions made a couch of it, and lying amid them was a woman.

Sorainya—Woman of War!

Lethonee's warning came back. For the long-limbed woman in the shell was clad in a gleaming, sleeveless crimson tunic of woven mail that yielded to her full lissom curves. A long, thin sword, in a jeweled sheath, lay beside her. She had put aside a black-plumed, crimson helmet, and thick masses of golden hair streamed down across her strong, bare arms.

The white, tapered fingers, scarlet-nailed, touched some control on the shell's low rim, and it floated nearer the rail. Upraised on the pillows and one smooth elbow, the woman looked up at Lanning, smiling. Her eyes were long and brilliantly greenish. Across the white beauty of her face, her mocking lips were a long scarlet wound, voluptuous, malicious.

FLOWER OF EVIL—Lethonee's words again. Lanning stood gripping the rail, and a trembling weakness shook him. Swift, unbidden desire overcame incredulity, and he strove desperately to be its master.

"You are Sorainya?" He held his tone grave and low. "I had warning to expect you."

She sat up suddenly amid the cushions, as if a whip had flicked her. The green eyes narrowed, and her body was tense and splendid in the gleaming mail. Her red mouth became a thin line of scorn.

"Lethonee!" She spat the name. "So that slut of Jonbar has found you?"

Lanning flushed with anger, and his fingers drew hard on the rail. He remembered the cold glint of an answering hate in the eyes of Lethonee, her sadly stern ultimatum: "Sorainya must be destroyed."

"So, you are angry, Denny Lanning?" Her laugh was a mocking chime. "Angry, for a shadow? For Lethonee is but a phantom, seeking with lies and tricks to live—at the cost of other lives. Perhaps you have discovered that?"

Lanning shuddered, and wet his lips.

"It's true," he whispered, "that she caused Barry's death."

The scorn had fallen like a mask from Sorainya's face. Now she tossed her splendid head, and pushed back the tumbled glory of her hair. The sea-green eyes danced an invitation, and she smiled.

"Lethonee is no more than a spectre of possibility." Her tone was a suave caress. "She is less than a single speck of dust, less than a shadow on the wall. Let us forget her, Denny Lanning— shall we?"

Lanning gulped, and a tremor shook him.

Her bare arms opened, beckoning.

"But I am real, Denny. And I have come for you—to take you with me back to Gyronchi. It is a mighty empire, more splendid than the pallid dream of Jonbar. And I am its mistress."

She stood up with one flowing movement, tall and regal in the scarlet mail. Her bare arms reached out, to help Lanning to the golden shell. Her cool, green eyes were shining with intoxicating promise.

"Come, Denny Lanning. To rule with me in Gyronchi!"

Lanning's hands gripped the rail until his knuckles cracked. His heart was pounding, and he drew a long shuddering breath.

"Why?" His voice rapped harsh and cold. "Of all men, why have you come for me?"

The shell drifted closer, and Sorainya smiled.

"I have searched all Space and Time for you, Denny Lanning. For we are the twain of destiny! Fate has given us the keys to power. Together on the golden throne of Gyronchi, we can never fall. Come!"

Lanning caught a sobbing breath.

"All right, beautiful," he gasped. "I don't know the game. But—you're on!"

HE CLIMBED upon the rail, in the moonlight, and reached out his hand to take Sorainya's.

"Denny—wait!" an urgent voice spoke beside him.

Lanning drew back instinctively, and turned. A ghostly figure in her straight white robe, Lethonee was standing by the rail, holding the prismatic fire of that colossal jewel between her hands. Her face was drawn, desperate.

"Remember, Denny!" her warning rang electric. "Sorainya seeks to destroy you!"

Sorainya stood stark upright upon the shell, her tense, defiant body splendid in the scarlet armor. Slitted, her greenish eyes flamed with tigerish fury. Strong teeth flashed white in a snarl of hate. She hissed an unfamiliar word, and spat at Lethonee.

And Lethonee trembled, and caught a sobbing breath. Her face had drained to a deadly white, and her violet eyes were flaming. One word rang hard from her lips: "Go!"

But Sorainya turned to Lanning again, and a dazzling smile flashed across the blackness of her hate. Her long bare arms opened again their white invitation.

"Come with me, Denny," she whispered. "And let that lying ghost go back to her dead city of dream!"

Lethonee bit her pale lip, as if to control her wrath.

"Look, Denny," she warned, "where Sorainya would have you leap!"

She pointed down at the black tropic sea. And Lanning saw there the glittering phosphorescent trail that followed a shark's swift fin. The shock of cold dread had chilled him, and he climbed stiffly back from the rail.

For he had touched—or tried to touch—Sorainya's extended hand. And he had felt *nothing at all.*

Shuddering, he looked at the slim, white girl by the rail. He saw the gleam of tears in her eyes, and the pain that ran like a burning river beneath the proud composure of her face.

"Forgive me, Lethonee!" he whispered. "I am sorry—very sorry!"

Her voice was small, stricken: "But you were going, Denny! Going—to *her!*"

The golden shell had floated against the rail. A warrior-queen, regal, erect, Sorainya stood buckling on the golden sword. Her long, green eyes flamed balefully.

"Denny Lanning," the bugle of her voice pealed cold, "it is written on the tablets of Time that we must be enemies, or—one! And Gyronchi, defended by my *kothrin*—by Glarath and the *gyrane*—has no fear of you. But Jonbar is defenseless. Remember!"

One sturdy foot, scarlet-buskined, touched something at the rim of the yellow shell. And instantly, like a projected image from a screen, she was gone.

Lanning turned slowly toward Lethonee. Her face, beneath the band of blue that held her red-glinting hair, was still white and stiff with tragedy.

"Please," he whispered. "Forgive me."

No smile lit her solemn face.

"Sorainya is beautiful," her voice came small and flat. "But if you ever yield to her, Denny, it is the end of Jonbar—and me!"

Lanning shook his head, dazed with a cold bewilderment.

"But why?" he demanded. "I don't understand."

THE WIDE, VIOLET eyes of Lethonee looked at him for a long time. Once her lip stiffened, quivered, as if she were about to cry. But her voice, when at last she spoke, was grave and quiet.

"I'll try to tell you, Denny." Her face was illumined like a shrine by the shimmer of the jewel in her hands. "The World is a long corridor, from the Beginning of existence to the End. Events are groups in a sculptured frieze that runs endlessly along the walls. And Time is a lantern carried steadily through the hall, to illuminate the groups one by one. It is the light of awareness, the subjective reality of consciousness.

"Again and again the corridor branches, for it is the museum of all that is possible. The bearer of the lantern may take one turning, or another. And so, many halls that might have been illuminated with reality are left forever in the darkness.

"My world of Jonbar is one such possible way. It leads through splendid halls, bright vistas that have no limit. Gyronchi is another. But it is a barren track, through narrowing, ugly passages, that comes to a dead and useless end."

The wide solemn eyes of Lethonee looked at him, over the slumberous flame of the jewel. Lanning tensed and caught his breath, as if a light, cold hand, from nowhere, had touched his shoulder.

"And you, Denny Lanning," came the silver rhythmic voice, "are destined, for a little time, to carry the lantern. And—*yours is the choice of reality.*

"Neither I nor Sorainya can come to you, bodily—unless perhaps at the moment of your death. But, through a partial mastery of Time, we can each *call* to you, to carry the lamp into our different halls. Denny—"

The silver voice caught with emotion.

"Denny, think well before you choose! For your choice will bring life to one possible world. And it will leave another in the darkness, never to be born."

A choking lump had risen in Lanning's throat. He looked at Lethonee, her slim white beauty shining pure and innocent in the jewel's clear light.

"There can be no choice—not now!" he whispered huskily. "Because I love you, Lethonee. Just tell me what I must do, to settle the thing. And if—if I can ever come to you."

Her fine head shook, in the blue halo.

"The time has not come for you to choose, Denny," she said slowly. "And the event is vague and ambiguous in the mist of possibility."

Lanning moved closer to her, and tried again to touch her arm—in vain.

"Just remember me, Denny, and what I have told you. For Sorainya still has her beauty, and black Glarath the *gyrane's* power. Beware of Gyronchi! And the hour will come."

Her eyes dropped to the jewel, and her fingers caressed its bright facets. Splintering diamond lances burst from it, and swallowed her in fire. She was gone.

Shaken with a curious weakness, suddenly aware of complete exhaustion, Lanning caught the rail. His eyes fell to the water, and he saw the glitter of the shark's black fin, still cruising after the ship.

### III.

HIS LIFE was a dusky corridor, and the present a lamp that he carried along it. Dennis Lanning didn't forget Lethonee's figure of speech. And eagerly he looked forward to discovering her again, at some dark turning. But he walked down the hall of years, and looked in vain.

Nor could he forget Sorainya. Despite revulsion from a ruthless evil he had sensed in her, despite Lethonee's warning, he found himself sometimes dreaming of the warrior-queen in the splendor of her crimson mail. Found himself even dwelling upon the mysterious menace of Gyronchi, an eagerness mingled with his dread.

The hall he walked was a corridor of war. An old hatred of injustice made him forever a grim champion against the Right of

Might. War correspondent, then flying instructor, pilot, and military adviser, he served on four continents.

He fought with pen as well as battle plane. Once, waiting for Viennese doctors to persuade an obscure African amoeba to abandon his digestive tract, he wrote a utopian novel, *The Road of Dawn,* to picture the world that ought to be.

Again, in the military prison of a dictator whose war-preparations he had exposed, he wrote an historical autobiography—the latest style among journalists—in which he tried to show that the world was nearing a decisive conflict between democratic civilization and despotic absolutism.

His scathing foreign dispatches, laying bare oppression and imperialistic aggression, closed to him the frontiers of several nations.

In all those years, he had no glimpse of Lethonee. But once, on the field with the native army in Ethiopia, he woke in his tent to hear her grave warning voice still ringing in his ears: "Denny, get up and leave your tent!"

He dressed hastily, and walked out through the camp in the thin, bitter wind of dawn. The tent, a few minutes later, was struck by an Italian bomb.

But Sorainya came to him, again.

It was a night in Madrid—the next year—where he had gone to join the Loyalist defense. He was sitting alone beside a little table in his hotel room, cleaning and loading his automatic. A queer little shudder passed over him, grimly reminiscent of the malaria he had contracted in the Chaco, covering the Jungle War. He looked up—and saw that long, shallow shell of yellow metal floating above the carpet.

Sorainya, in the same burnished, scarlet mail—and looking as if it had been five minutes since he had last seen her, instead of nine years—was lounging voluptuously on her silken cushions. A bare arm flung back the golden wealth of her hair, and her greenish eyes smiled up at him with a taunting insolence.

"Well, Denny Lanning." Her voice was a husky, lingering drawl, and her long eyes studied him with a bold curiosity. "The ghost of Jonbar has guided you safely through the years. But has she brought you happiness?"

Lanning had grown rigid in his chair. He flushed, swallowed. The sudden white dazzle of her smile caught his breath.

"I am still the mistress of Gyronchi," came the lazy caress of her voice. "And still the keys of fate are in our hands—if we but choose to turn them."

Her white and indolent arm indicated a space on the silken couch beside her.

"I have come again, Denny, to take you back with me to the throne of Gyronchi. I can give you half a mighty empire—myself, and all of it! Will you go, Denny?"

LANNING tried to control his breath. "Don't forget, Sorainya," he said in a dead flat tone. "I saw the shark."

She tossed back her head, and her hair fell like a yellow torrent across the colored cushions. And the white lure of her smile set a pain to throbbing in his throat.

"The shark would have killed you, Denny. But death alone can bring you to me—and to the strong new life the *gyrane* gives! For our lives were cast far apart in the Stream of Time. And not all the power of the *gyrane* can lift you out of the time-stream, living—for then the whole current must be deflected. But the stream has small grasp upon a few dead pounds of clay. I could carry *that* to Glarath, to be restored by the *gyrane*."

She came with a gliding, pantherine movement to her knees on the cushions. Both hands pushed the flowing gold of her hair behind her red-mailed shoulders. And her bare arms reached out, in wide invitation.

"Denny, will you come with me tonight?" urged the golden voice. "The way is in your hand."

Trembling, hot with desire, Lanning looked down at his hands. The automatic had slipped in his unconscious fingers, until its muzzle was pointed at his heart. His finger was near the trigger. One little pressure—it would be so like an accident.

Her indolent voice was seductive music: "Gyronchi is waiting for us, Denny. A world to rule—"

The white and gold and crimson of her beauty was a stabbing pain in his heart. His pulse was hammering. His finger curled around the cool steel of the trigger.

But sanity remained in one corner of his mind, and out of it spoke a voice like the quiet voice of Lethonee: "Remember, Denny Lanning! You are carrying a light for the world to come."

Carefully, he made his quivering fingers snap on the safety. He laid the gun down beside him on the little table. His voice a breathless rasp, he said, "No soap, Sorainya!"

The green eyes glittered, and her red lips snarled with rage. She flashed upright.

"I warned you, Denny Lanning!" All the indolence gone, her voice crackled brittle and sharp. "Take the side of that phantom of Jonbar, and you shall perish with her. I sought your strength. But Gyronchi can win without it."

With a tigerish savagery, she whipped out the long golden needle of her sword.

"When we meet again, it shall be at war. Guard yourself!"

A savage foot stamped down, and she was gone.

THOSE TWO antagonistic women set many a problem that Lanning could not solve. If they were actual visitors from conflicting possible worlds of futurity, he had no evidence of it save his own tortured memory. Many a weary night, pondering the haunting riddle, he wondered if he were going insane.

But a package that presently came to him in Spain contained another thin little book from Wilmot McLan, now the holder of many degrees and professor of astrophysics at a small western university. Inscribed, "To Denny, from Wil—another stitch in Time, to repair my last." The volume was entitled *Probability and Determination*.

One underlined introductory paragraph Lanning searched desperately for a relevant meaning:

"The future has been held to be as real as the past, no more different from it than right is from left, the only directional indicator being $k$; the constant correlating entropy and probability. But the new quantum mechanics, destroying the absolute function of cause and effect, must likewise annihilate that contention. There is no determination in small scale events; consequently the 'certainties' of the macroscopic world are at best merely statistical. And probability, in the unfolding future, must be substituted for determination. The elementary particles of the old physics— electrons, photons, etc.—may be retained, located probably in a continuum of five dimensions. But any consideration of this hyper-space-time continuum must take note of a conflicting infinitude of possible worlds, only one of which, at the intersection of their geodesics with the advancing plane of the present, can claim reality. It is this new outlook of which we attempt a mathematical examination."

*Conflicting—possible worlds!*

Those words haunted Lanning. Here, at last, was light. Here, in his old friend, was a possible confidant—the one man who might understand, who might tell him whether Lethonee and Sorainya were miraculous visitors out of Time, or—insanity.

At once he wrote McLan, outlining his story and requesting an opinion. Delayed, doubtless, by the military censors, the letter at last came back from America, stamped *Removed—Left no Address*. An inquiry to the University authorities informed him that McLan had resigned to undertake private research, and that his whereabouts were unknown.

And Lanning groped his way along, through the dark hall of wars and years, to 1938. Lao Meng Shan's cable found him at Lausanne, recuperating from the war in Spain, the splinter of a shell still aching in his knee. He was writing another book.

Turned philosopher, he was trying to analyze the trends of the world, to pick out the influences of good and evil. The resolution of those conflicting forces, so he believed, would either establish the new technological civilization—or hurl the race into martial doom.

"Denny, American friend," the cable ran, "humanity needs you. Will fly for China?"

Direct action had been the only anodyne for Lanning's tortured mind. And the newspapers, that day, stirred his blood with accounts of hundreds of women and children killed by ruthless aerial bombardment. Ignoring the stiffening pain in his knee, he abandoned the ancient problem of good and evil, flew to Cairo, and caught a fast steamer east.

## IV.

WINGED DOOM was awhisper in the sky. Sirens moaned warning of the *pei chee*—"flying engines." Hapless Hankow had been swiftly darkened, but already yellow bursts of ruin and death had flared above in the north and eastward along the river docks, where the first bombs fell.

*Stop the raiders!* was the frantic, hopeless order.

Limping in his game left leg, where bits of steel still made an excellent barometer of impending weather, Lanning stumbled across the field to the battered, antiquated American plane that jabbering mechanics had roaring in the line. The cool of midnight cleared the sleep from his head, and he shuddered to the drumming in the sky.

Lao Meng Shan, now his observer, was already beside the machine, dolefully shaking his watch. Solemnly, in habitual careful English, he shouted above roaring motors: "Our orders, tonight, are over-confident. For my watch stopped when the first bomb struck. That is a very bad omen."

Lanning never laughed at superstition—few fliers do. But his lean face smiled in the darkness.

"Once, Shan," he shouted in reply, "an ancient warrior named Joshua stopped the sun until his battle was won. Maybe that's the omen. Let's go!"

Adjusting his helmet, the Chinese shrugged.

"I think it means that time is stopped for us. If it is written, however, that we must die for China—"

He clambered deliberately into the rear cockpit.

Lanning tried the controls, signaled the ground crew, and gunned the motor. The machine lifted toward the thrumming in the sky. The fact that most of the defending aircraft had been bombed into the ground on the day before, he thought grimly, was a more conclusive omen than the watch.

Darkness was a blanket on the city northward. hiding cowering millions. Troop lorries and fire trucks shrieked through the streets. Anti-aircraft batteries were hammering vainly. Probing searchlights flared against the white puffs of exploding shells, uselessly seeking the raiders.

Spiraling for altitude, Lanning narrowed gray eyes to search a thin cloud-wisp above. He winced to a yellow flare beneath. For his mind could see the toppling wreckage of a splendid modern city ruined, hear shrieks and groans and wailing cries for aid, even smell the sharp odor of searing human flesh. His body tensed, and he fired a warming burst from twin guns.

The wraith of frozen mist was at last beside them. It burned white, abruptly, in the glare of a searchlight. And a dark bomber dropped out of it, swaying between the gray mushrooms of shells.

Lanning tipped the ancient plane after it, into a power dive. Shan, open-mouthed, yelling, waved cheerfully. Their machine guns clattered. The bomber swerved, and defending guns flickered red. But Lanning held his sights on it, grimly. Black smoke erupted from it suddenly, and it toppled downward.

One—

HE WAS pulling up the battered ship—gingerly—when a roving searchlight caught them, held them for a fatal moment. Black, ominous holes peppered the wings. Glass shattered from the instruments before him. A sudden numbness paralyzed his shoulder.

The betraying light had passed. But gasoline reeked in his nostrils, and a quick banner of yellow flame rippled backward. Twisting in the cockpit, he saw behind them the second enemy, diving out of the cloud still firing.

And he saw the dark blood that stained Shan's drawn face.

They were done for. But Shan grinned stiffly, raised a crimson hand to gesture. Lanning flung the creaking ship through a reckless Immelmann turn. The attacker was caught dead ahead, still firing.

A red sledge of agony smashed all feeling from Lanning's right leg. But he held straight for the other ship, guns hammering. It dived. With flaming gasoline a roaring curtain beside him, Lanning clung grimly to its tail. The tiny puppets of its crew jerked and slumped. Then it, too, began to burn.

Two—!

Explosion buffeted Lanning's head, deafening. Metal fragments seared past. Hot oil spattered his seared face. The motor ceased to run, and a new torturing tongue of yellow licked back.

Strangling, Lanning sideslipped, so that the wind stream would carry away the heat and suffocating fumes. He looked back at Shan. The crimson face of the little Oriental was now a dreadful mask. With a queer, solemn little grin, he held up something in a dripping hand—his watch.

A cold shudder went down Lanning's spine. He had never laughed at superstition. And there was something terrible, now, in this hint that something could perceive the future.

Then stark incredulity froze Shan's grin, and he pointed stiffly. Lanning's eyes followed the crimson-streaming arm. And a cold hand stopped his heart. For something was flashing down beside them.

Something—*incredible.*

It was a queer-looking ship—or the gray, shining ghost of a ship. It was wingless, flat-decked—like no ship the sky had ever seen. Its bright hull suggested that of a small submarine, save that its ends terminated abruptly with two massive disks of metal, which now shone greenishly.

A singular crew lined the rail, along the open deck. At first they seemed spectral and, like the ship, unreal. Several were strange in odd, trim tunics of silver-gray and green. But there were a few in familiar military uniforms—a French colonel, an Austrian lieutenant and a tall, lank captain of the Royal Air Force.

Lanning's mouth fell open, and a sudden agony of joy wrenched his sick body. *For he saw Barry Halloran!*

Unchanged since that fatal April day of ten years ago, even wearing the same baggy cords and football sweater, the gigantic tackle stood among the rest! He saw Lanning, and grinned, and waved an eager greeting.

The phantom craft swept closer, dropping with the burning plane. Lanning's pain was drowned in wonderment, and he ceased to breathe. He saw a thin, white-haired man—a figure puzzlingly familiar—busy beneath the small, crystal dome that capped a round metal turret, amidships. A crystal gun thrust out of the turret. A broad blinding-yellow ray funneled suddenly from it and caught at the plane.

LANNING felt a momentary wrenching pull. The plane and his body resisted that surge of mysterious force. Red mighty hands of agony twisted his hurt body, squeezed intolerably. Then something yielded. And the spectral ship was suddenly real, approaching.

Yellow flame wrapped Lanning again, for his fingers had slipped useless from the stick. He coughed, strangled, battled a sea of suffocating darkness. Searing torture bathed him. Then he was being drawn over the rail of the stranger, out of the furnace.

The ghost ship seemed real now. Quick, tender hands were laying them on stretchers. But Lanning was staring up at big, red-headed Barry Halloran, magically unchanged by ten years of time.

"Sure, old man, it's me!" boomed the once-familiar voice. "Just hold that line! These guys will fix you up as good as new—or better. And then we'll have a chin. Guess I'm way behind the times."

A spectral ship, manned with a crew of the dead! Lanning had not been superstitious—not even, in the conventional sense, religious. His faith had been a belief in the high destiny of man. He had expected death to blot him out, individually; the race, alone, was eternal. This Stygian ship, therefore, was utterly incredible—but it looked decidedly interesting.

"Barry!" he whispered. "Glad—see you—"

A wave of shadow dimmed his eyes. Blood was welling from his aching shoulder, hot and sticky against his body. A dull throbbing came from his shattered leg. Dimly, he knew that the men in gray and green were picking up the stretcher. Awareness faded.

## V.

WHEN Dennis Lanning began to be fully conscious again, it seemed that he had always been in that small, green-walled room. His old roving life, restless and haunted, seemed dreamlike, remote beyond reality—all save, somehow, the visitations of Lethonee and Sorainya.

Dimly he remembered an operating room—blinding lights and bustling men in white masks, the gleam and tinkle of instruments, Barry Halloran standing reassuringly near. Then a whiff of some strange anaesthetic.

Shan was lying in the opposite bed, quietly sleeping. And Lanning, in some forgotten interval, had met the two others in the ward. They were Silvano Cresto, Spanish ace shot down in the Moroccan war; and Willie Rand, U.S.N., missing when the ill-fated airship *Akron* was destroyed at sea.

The latter was now propped up on his pillows, inhaling through a cigarette. He grinned. "Smoke?"

"Thanks." Lanning caught the tossed white cylinder, felt a dull twinge from his bandaged shoulder. He asked, "What's up?"

Willie Rand exhaled white vapor.

"Dunno."

"What is this—ship? Where're we going?"

Rand blew a great silver ring.

"Her name's the *Chronion*. Cap'n Wil McLan. We're bound, they say, for a place called Jonbar—wherever that is!"

Wonder stiffened Lanning. Wil McLan! His old roommate, the student of Time. And Jonbar! Lethonee's city, that she had showed him, far-off in dim futurity.

"But why?" he gasped. "I don't understand!"

"Nor me. All I know, messmate, I turned loose when the wreckage of the *Akron* was rolling over on me, and tried to dive clear. Something smashed into me, and I woke up on this bed. That was maybe a week ago—"

"A week!" muttered Lanning. "But the *Akron*—that was back in 'thirty-three!"

Rand lit another cigarette from the first.

"Time don't make no difference here. The last man on your bed was the Austrian. Erich von Arneth. He came from the Isonzo front, in 1915. The one in the Chink's bed was the Frenchman, Jean Querard. He was blown up in the defense of Paris, in 1940."

"Forty!" whispered Lanning, softly. Was to-morrow, then, already real? Lethonee? And Sorainya?

A brisk man in gray and green hastened into the ward, gently removed their cigarettes and replaced them with odd-looking thermometers. Lanning took the instrument out of his mouth.

"Where's Barry?" he demanded. "I want to see Barry Halloran. And Wil McLan."

"Not now, sir." The rhythmic accent was curiously familiar—it was like Lethonee's! "It's time for your last *dynat* intravenous. You'll be able to get up when you wake. Now just lie back, sir, and give me your arm."

He put back the thermometer. Another man rolled in a wheeled instrument table. Deft hands bared and swabbed Lanning's arm. He felt the sting of a hypodermic. And quiet sleep came over him.

When at last he woke, it was to a new, delicious sense of health and fitness. The bandages were gone. His shoulder, his shattered leg, felt well and whole again. Even the steel no longer ached in his knee.

Shan, he saw, was gone from the opposite bed. In it lay a big man, swathed in bandages, regarding him with dark, stolid Slavish eyes. A silent orderly came in, thrust a dozen little glowing needles into the Russian's bandages, and laid Lanning's old uniform, cleaned and neatly repaired, beside his bed.

"Boris Barinin," he gave brisk information. "Soviet rocket-flier. We picked him up near the pole in 1942. Smashed, starved, frozen. The *dynat* repair-hormone activators will take him through, however. You may go above, sir."

LANNING put on the uniform, elated with his new sense of

well-being, and eagerly mounted a companion to the deck of the *Chronion*. It was seventy feet long, between the polished faces of the great metal disks, broken only with the domed turret amidships. Some mechanism throbbed softly below.

The ship must be moving. But where?

Looking about for a glimpse of the sun, or any landmark, Lanning could see only a curiously flickering blue haze. He went to the rail, peered down. Still there was nothing. The *Chronion* hung in a featureless, blue abysm.

The flicker in the azure mist was oddly disturbing. Sometimes, he thought. he could almost see the outline of some far mountain, the glint of waves, the shapes of trees or buildings—incongruous, impressions, queerly flat. Two-dimensional things piled one upon another. It was like a movie screen, he thought, upon which the frames were being thrown a thousand times too fast, so that the projected image became a dancing blur.

"Denny, old man!"

It was a glad shout, and Barry Halloran came to him with an eager step. Lanning gripped his hand, seized his big shoulder. It was good to feel its hard young power, to see the reckless freckled grin.

"You're looking fit, Barry. Not a day older!"

The blue eyes were wide with awe.

"Funny business, Denny. It's ten days since they picked me up, trying to swim away from that smashed crate in the Charles, with both legs broken. But—you've lived ten years!"

Lanning shook his fine-chiseled head, bewildered.

"What's ahead of us, Barry? What's it all about?"

The big tackle scratched the unkempt tangle of his red hair.

"No savvy, Denny. Wil has promised us a scrap, all right. And it's to save this place they call Jonbar. But what the odds are, or who we're going to fight, or how come—I don't know."

"I'm going to find out," Lanning said. "Or try. Where's Wil McLan?"

"He's on his bridge. I'll show you the way."

They met four men in the gray and green, just coming on the deck carrying two rolled stretchers. Following them was the little group of fighting men in their various uniforms. Lao Meng Shan grinned happily to see Lanning, and presented the rest.

They were the Spaniard, Cresto; Willie Rand; the lank British flier, Courtney-Pharr; hard-faced Erich von Arneth; dapper little

Jean Querard; and Emil Schorn, a blue-eyed herculean Prussian, who had been taken from a burning Zeppelin in 1917.

"Where we go?" Cresto shrugged, white teeth flashing through his swarthy grin. *"Quién sabe?* Anyhow, *amigos,* this is better than hell! *Verdád?"* He laughed.

"We are fighting men," rumbled Emil Schorn, grimly smiling. "We go to fight. *Ach, 's ist genug!"*

"Quite a gang, eh?" Barry Halloran led Lanning on, to a small metal door in the turret. Inside, another man in gray and green waited alertly behind a bulky thing like a cannon with a barrel of glass. "You'll find Wil up under the dome."

Lanning climbed metal steps. Standing behind a bright wheel, under the flawless shell of crystal, he came upon a slight, strange little man—or the shattered wreck of a man. His breath sucked in to the shock of sympathetic pain. For the stranger was hideous with the manifold print of unspeakable agony.

THE HANDS—restlessly fumbling with an odd little tube of bright-worn silver that hung by a thin chain about his neck— were yellow, bloodless claws, trembling, twisted with pain. The whole thin body was grotesquely stooped and gnarled, as if every bone had been broken on a torture wheel.

But it was the haggard, livid face, cross-hatched with a white net of ridged scars, that chilled Lanning with its horror. Beneath a tangled abundance of loose white hair, that face was a stiff, pain-graven mask, terrible to see. Dark, deep-sunken, the eyes were somber wells of agony—and of a deathless, brooding hatred.

Strangely, those dreadful orbs lit with recognition.

"Denny!" It was an eager whisper, but queerly dry and voiceless.

The little man limped quickly to meet him, thrust out a trembling hand that was thin and twisted and broken, hideous with a web of scars. His breath was a swift, whistling gasp.

Lanning tried to put down the wondering dread that shook him. He took that frail dry claw of a hand, and tried to smile.

"Wil?" he whispered. "You are Wil McLan?"

He choked back the other, fearful question: *What frightful thing has happened to you, Wil?*

"Yes, Denny," hissed that voiceless voice. "But—I've lived forty years more than you have. And ten of them in Sorainya's torture vault." Lanning started to that name. And the old man stiffened as he spoke it, and something flared in his hollow eyes—the baleful fire of hate, Lanning thought it was, that kept his shattered body alive.

"I'm an old man, Denny," the dry rasping ran on. "I was fifty-three when the *Chronion* was launched on the time-stream, in 1960. The ten years in Gyronchi—" The seamed face went white, the whisper sank. "They were a thousand! And the last four years, in Jonbar, I've been preparing for our campaign."

His gnarled body came erect with a tense and desperate energy. A grim light flamed in his sunken eyes.

"An old man!" he husked again. "But not too old to fight Gyronchi! The *dynat* has given me life enough for that."

A sudden eager hope had risen in Lanning, above his wonder and dread.

"Jonbar?" he cried. "Then—then have you seen a girl named Lethonee?"

Desperately, he searched that scarred and tortured face. A painful pulse was throbbing in his throat. The tension of his hope was agony. Was it possible—possible that that "gulf more terrible than death" could now be crossed?

The old man nodded, slowly. The stern strength of hate seemed to ebb out of him, and the bleak grimness of his face was lit with a stiff little smile.

"Yes, Denny," his whisper came softly. "Indeed I know Lethonee. It is she who set me free from the dungeons of Sorainya. It is for her, and her people, that we must fight—or Gyronchi will obliterate them."

Lanning caught his breath. Trembling, his fingers touched Wil McLan's twisted, emaciated shoulder.

"Tell me, Wil," he begged. "This is all a riddle—a crazy, horrible riddle. Where is Jonbar? Can I go to Lethonee, help her? And, Sorainya—" Dread choked him. "What—what did she do to you?"

"I'll tell you, Denny—presently."

McLan's hollow eyes flashed to the dials of a bewildering instrument board. Moving with a swift precision that amazed Lanning, his gnarled fingers touched a series of levers and keys, spun a polished wheel. He whispered some order into a tube, peered ahead through the crystal dome. An alert, surprising strength moved his shattered frame.

"Presently," his hoarse whisper came aside to Lanning. "As soon as this task is done. Watch, if you like."

STANDING wonderingly behind him, Lanning stared out through the crystalline curve of the dome. The blue, enveloping haze flickered more violently. Bent over a creeping dial, McLan tapped a key. And the blue was gone.

The *Chronion* was flying low, over a gray, wave-tossed sea. It was late of a gloomy afternoon, and thick mists veiled the horizon. The little craft shuddered, abruptly, to the crash of mighty guns.

Lanning looked questioningly at Wil McLan. A twisted arm pointed, silently. And Lanning saw the long, gray shapes of battle-cruisers loom suddenly out of the haze, rocking as they erupted smoke and flame.

McLan tapped the keyboard beyond the wheel, and the *Chronion* slipped forward again. The turret revolved beneath them, and the crystal gun thrust out. Below, the stretcher crews moved alertly to the rail.

Peering through the fog of battle at the reeling ships, Lanning distinguished the Union Jack, and then, on another vessel, the German imperial standard. Suddenly, breathless with incredulous awe, he fitted this chaotic scene into his knowledge of naval history.

"The *Defense* and the *Warrior!*" he gasped. "Attacking the *Weisbaden!* Is this—Jutland?"

Wil McLan glanced down at the dial.

"Yes. This is May 31, 1916. We await the sinking of the *Defense.*"

Through the haze of acrid smoke, the *Chronion* slipped nearer the attacking British vessels. Suddenly, then, the German cruiser fleet loomed out of the mist, seeking with a hurricane of fire to cover the stricken *Weisbaden.* Two terrific salvoes rocked the doomed flagship *Defense,* and it was lost in a sheet of flame.

The intermingled battle-cruisers of both fleets were still plunging through the clouds of battle, great guns thunderously belching smoke and death, as Wil McLan brought the *Chronion* down where the *Defense* had vanished. Shattered wreckage littered the sea, rushing into a great whirlpool where the flagship had sunk.

A long helix burned incandescent in the crystal gun, and a broad yellow ray poured out into the drifting smoke. His sweater stripped off, Barry Halloran leapt overboard, carrying a rope. He was dragged back, through the ray, towing a limp survivor. Dripping blood and brine, the rescued sailor was laid on a stretcher, rushed below.

Courtney-Pharr was poised to dive, when the steel prow of the disabled *Warspite* plunged suddenly out of the blinding smoke. He stumbled fearfully back. Lanning caught his breath. It had run them down!

But Wil McLan tapped a key, spun the shining wheel. Green radiance lit the great terminal disks. And the battling fleets were swept away into blue, flickering twilight. The broken old man sighed with weary relief, and rubbed tiny beads of sweat from his scarred forehead.

"Well, Denny," he whispered. "One more man to fight for Jonbar."

"Now!" demanded Lanning, breathless. "Can you explain?"

## VI.

LEANING against the bright rim of his wheel, Wil McLan pushed back the snow-white shock of his hair. Then, as if arranging his thoughts, he began fingering with twisted broken hands the white scars that seamed his face, and the pendant silver tube.

"Please forgive my lack of a voice, Denny," his hoarse whisper came at last. "But once in the dungeon, when I had had nothing to drink for a week but the blood of a rat, and was delirious and screaming with thirst, Sorainya had molten metal poured down my throat. And not even the *dynat* can grow new vocal cords. She'll pay for that!"

Hate had flared in the sunken eyes again, and drawn the gnarled body to a taut rigidity. But the old man seemed to make an effort to compose himself. He unclenched his hands, and his twisted face tried to smile. He spoke more deliberately. "Time was always a challenge to me. When science lived in a simple continuum of four dimensions, with Time the fourth, its conquest appeared relatively simple—through some application, perhaps, of the classical Newtonian dynamics.

"But Max Planck with the quantum theory, de Broglie and Schroedinger with the wave mechanics, Heisenberg with matrix mechanics, enormously complicated the structure of the universe—and with it the problem of Time.

"With the substitution of waves of probability for concrete particles, the world lines of objects are no longer the fixed and simple paths they once were. Geodesics have an infinite proliferation of possible branches, at the whim of sub-atomic indeterminism.

"Still, of course, in large masses the statistical results of the new physics are not much different from those given by the classical laws. But there is a fundamental difference. The apparent reality of the universe is the same—but it rests upon a quicksand of possible change.

"Certainty is abolished.

"Let a man stand on a concrete floor. It is no longer certain that he will not fall through it. For he is sustained only by the continual reaction of atomic forces, and they are governed by probability alone.

"It is merely a very excellent statistical probability that keeps the man from radiating heat until his body is frozen solid or absorbing it until he bursts into flame. From flying upward into space in defiance of Newton's laws, or dissolving into a cloud of molecular particles.

"Mere probability is all that is left. And my first actual invention was a geodesic tracer, designed for its analysis. It was a semi-mathematical instrument, essentially a refinement of the old harmonic analyzer. Tracing the possible world-lines of material particles through Time, it opened a window to futurity."

The hoarse whisper paused. and old Wil McLan limped to the side of the dome. His scarred, trembling hands lifted a black velvet cover from a rectangular block of some clear crystal mounted on the top of a metal cabinet.

"Here is the *chronoscope*," he said. "The latest development of the instrument. Scansion depends upon a special curved field, through which a sub-etheric radiation is bent into the time-axis, projected forward, and reflected from electronic fields back to the instrument. A stereoscopic image is obtained within the crystal screen, through selective fluorescence to the beat frequencies of the interfering carrier waves projected at right angles from below. But I'll show you Gyronchi."

THE OLD MAN snapped a switch, manipulated dials at the end of the crystal block. It lit with a cloudy green. The green cleared, and a low cry escaped Lanning's lips.

For, microscopically clear within the crystal, he saw a miniature world. A broad, silver river cut a fertile green plain dotted
with villages. Beyond the river rose two hills.

One was crowned with a tremendous castellated citadel. Its
frowning walls and mighty towers were gleaming red metal.
Above them flowed banners of yellow and crimson and black. A
massive gate opened in the foot of the hill, as he watched, and an
armored troop poured out.

"Watch the marchers," rasped McLan.

Lanning bent closer to the crystal block. Suddenly it seemed
that he was looking through a window, into an actual world. He
found the soldiers again, and uttered a muffled cry.

"They aren't men!" he gasped. "They're—insects!"

"They are ants," came the whisper of McLan, "hypertrophied
mutations produced by the *gyrane*. They are the *kothrin,*
Sorainya's savage horde. That is her castle on the hill, where
she—held me. But look at the other hill."

Lanning found it, topped with a temple of ebon black. The
building was vast, but squat and low, faced with endless colonnades of thick, square columns. From the center of it rose a beam
of *blackness,* of darkness thick and tangible, that widened into
the sky like the angry funnel of a vast. symmetrical tornado.

"The temple of the *gyrane,"* husked Wil McLan, "where
Glarath rules." He was adjusting the dials again. "But watch!"

A village of flimsy huts swam closer. The marching column of
gigantic, upright ants was swiftly surrounding it, driving the villagers—a fair-skinned, sturdy-looking folk, although ragged and
starved—before them from the fields.

"This happened while I was in prison," the old man rasped.
"The offense of the people was that they had not paid their taxes
to Sorainya and their tithes to the *gyrane.* And they had no grain
to pay them, because Sorainya and her lords—hunting a convict
for sport—had trampled and destroyed the fields."

Armed with heavy golden axes and short thick guns of crimson metal, as well as with frightful mandibles, the six-limbed
force made a terrible ring about the frightened village. And now
an armored tanklike vehicle came down from the red citadel, and
through the line of ants. A hot white beam flickered out of it, and
miserable buildings exploded into flame. The wind carried a wall
of fire across the village.

A slim human figure, in black-plumed scarlet armor, sprang from the tank to join the great black ants. A thin yellow sword played swiftly, cutting down the men and women and children that fled from the merciless flames.

The slaughter soon was done. That figure turned away from the smoking desolation, flung up the crimsoned sword in triumph, slipped back the helmet. A flood of yellow hair fell across the scarlet mail.

Lanning's breath sucked in, and a bright pain pierced his heart.

"Why, that—" he gasped, "that's—Sorainya!"

"Yes, Sorainya," whispered Wil McLan. "The warrior-queen of Gyronchi."

HE SNAPPED a switch, and that grim scene dissolved in the pellucid transparency of the crystal block. His hollow eyes lifted slowly to Lanning, and in them was rekindled the slumberous flame of hate. His gnarled hands knotted and relaxed, and lifted once more to fondle the little, worn, bright cylinder of silver that hung from his throat.

"It happened," the hoarse voiceless gasp went on, "that Gyronchi was the first future world, out of all those possible, that the *chronoscope* revealed. And I saw Sorainya, splendid in her armor, flying on the back of a gigantic winged ant.

"You have seen that she is—well—attractive. And at first, the range of the instrument was limited to her youth, where scenes of—barbarity are less frequent. Remember, Denny, I was thirty years younger when I first saw her, in 1945. Her glorious beauty, the military pomp of her empire—they seemed very foreign to my old scholar's life. But I—" the old man gulped, "I— loved her.

"Neglecting other possible worlds that I might have explored, I followed her, for months—years. I didn't know, then, the fatal change the temporal ray was causing." His white head bowed. For a moment he was speechless. "But no process whatever can reveal the state of an electron without *changing that state*—a consequence of indeterminism. Even the sub-quanta of my scanning ray were absorbed by the atoms that reflected them. The result was an increase in the probability factor of Gyronchi—that is the root of all the tragedy."

The scarred face made a grimace of pain.

"The blame is mine. For—before I was aware of it—the absorption had lessened the probability of all other possible worlds, so that Gyronchi was the only one the limited power of my instrument could reach. And that blinded me to the crime that I was doing.

"I hope you can understand my passion for Sorainya."

Lanning's hoarse and breathless whisper was an echo of his own: "I can."

The sunken eyes flamed again, and McLan fondled the silver tube.

"I watched her, with the *chronoscope,*" the rasping words ran on. "Sometimes I was driven to despair by her remoteness in Time and probability—and sometimes to desperate effort. For I resolved to conquer Time, and go to Gyronchi.

"In 1952, after seven years of effort, I was able to communicate. By increasing the power and focal definition of the sub-etheric temporal radiation, I was able to project a speaking image of myself to Sorainya's fortress."

Agony stiffened McLan's scarred face. His lean jaw set. His breath came in rasping gusts, and it was half a minute before he could speak again.

"And so I made suit to Sorainya. At first she seemed puzzled and alarmed. But, after I had made several bodiless visits to her apartments, her attitude changed suddenly. Perhaps she had got advice from Glarath!"

His clenched hands cracked.

"She smiled," the old man rasped. "She welcomed me and asked me to return. And she began to ask about my discoveries— saying that perhaps the priests of the *gyrane,* being themselves able scientists, could solve my remaining problems. If I could come to Gyronchi, she promised, I might share her throne."

Lanning bit his lip and caught a gasping breath. Memory of Sorainya's visits mocked him. But he did not interrupt.

"A mistrust of the priests, fortunately," McLan went on, "kept me from divulging very much. But Sorainya's bland encouragements, her lying smiles, redoubled my frantic efforts.

"THERE IS a terrific resistance to the displacement of any body in time. For the geodesics are anchored in the future, as well as in the past. The removal of a living person—which might warp all futurity—is impossible. And even to dislodge inert matter requires tremendous power.

"Nothing less than atomic energy, I soon perceived, could

even begin to overcome that resistance. I set out, therefore, with the searching ray of the *chronoscope,* to discover the secret of the atom from future science. And there I met a curious difficulty.

"For the instrument—which, after all, can only analyze probabilities—sometimes queerly blurred the fine detail of script or printing. I studied the works of many future scientists—of John Barr and Ivor Gyros and many more. But essential words always faded.

"There is a law of sequence and progression, I found at last, operating along the fifth, rather than the temporal dimension, which imposes inexorable limits. It is that progression which actually creates reality out of possibility. And it is that higher law which prohibits all the trite absurdities met with in the old speculation about travel in Time, such as the chronic adventurer who returns to kill himself or his grandfather. The old logic of cause and effect is by no means abolished, but merely elevated to a higher dimension.

"The principle of the atomic energy-converter came at last only through independent research based on various scraps of knowledge. I built the first successful working model in 1958. It developed eight thousand horsepower—and I could carry it in one hand! But listen."

He paused, leaned his haggard, scarred head to hear the soft thrumming that pulsed up through the deck. His hollow eyes shone with a weary triumph.

"There you hear the power of three hundred Niagaras, fed from the merest trickle of water. For each gram of matter converted yields 900 quintillion ergs of energy—enough, if it escaped, to turn the ship into a puff of highly incandescent gas.

"The very absorption of the temporal ray, which had so troubled me, now provided a resistance against which reaction was possible. An adaptation of the special field gave me a definite moment along the time axis.

"Those two discoveries—driving power and reactive medium—made the *Chronion* possible. For two years I worked on it desperately. Designed only for travel in time—not for a fighting machine—it was finished in June, 1960.

"At once, from my lonely laboratory in the Colorado Rockies, I set out for Gyronchi." The rasping whisper fell raw-edged, bitter. "Fool, blind with passion, I hoped to reach Sorainya and share her throne!"

A spasm of agony racked the white, tortured face.

## VII.

THE GASPING whisper paused, The old man limped swiftly about the dome, reading dials and gauges. His gnarled, scarred hands deftly set controls, moved the shining wheel. Aware of the soft, steady thrum of the atomic converters beneath, Lanning realized that the *Chronion* was moving again, through the blue flickering chasm. On another incredible flight through Time?

Wil McLan at last looked back to him, with hollow, haunted eyes.

"I went alone," resumed the painful rasp. "The *Chronion,* with all her millions of horsepower, could not have drawn a crew of sound men from their places in Time. Even alone, I had difficulty. An overloaded field coil burned out. The laboratory caught fire, and I was badly injured. The very accident, however, so weakened my future geodesics that the converters could pull me away. And, at the very instant the burning building collapsed, the *Chronion* broke free into the time-stream."

The dark, smouldering eyes stared away into the shimmering abyss beyond the crystal dome. The old man shuddered.

"You have seen Gyronchi, in the *chronoscope.*" The husky whisper was slow and faint. "And one look at my body can tell you enough of what reception I had from Sorainya, when at last I came to her red citadel."

The lean, white-wealed face went hard again with agony and hate. Great tears burst suddenly from the sunken eyes. The broken, bloodless claws of hands came up again, unconsciously, to the bright enigma of the tiny silver tube. Lanning looked quickly away, until the hoarse whisper went on:

"Excuse my self-pity, Denny. I shall spare you the details of Sorainya's treachery. But, the instant her smiling greeting had lured me from the deck of the *Chronion,* she commanded her warrior ants to seize me. She mocked my audacity in desiring the queen of Gyronchi, and then demanded that I surrender the secrets of the ship.

"When I refused, she threw me into the dungeons beneath her fortress, and turned the *Chronion* over to the priests of the *gyrane.*" The whisper had become a dry, terrible sob. "For ten years, in her torture vaults, Sorainya tried to make me talk. And the priests studied the ship—

"It was Lethonee who set me free," whispered the shattered man. "You have seen Lethonee."

A little tremor of eagerness and dread ran over Dennis Lanning. He tried to speak, made a little gulping sound, and nodded. Listening eagerly, he waited.

"She came to me in Sorainya's dungeons," softly whispered Wil McLan. "She was white and beautiful, holding in her two hands the jewel of her *chronotron*—that is another geodesic tracer, similar in principle to my *chronoscope.*

"Lethonee forgave the unwitting injury my experiment had done Jonbar. She planned my escape. She searched Time for the hour when the disposition of the guarding ants would make it possible. She examined the locks, and brought me measurements of the keys. I carved them from the bones of a previous occupant of that cell.

"WHEN THE chosen night came, she guided me out of the dungeons, across the body of a drunken, sleeping ant. Sorainya had that beast roasted alive when the escape was discovered. Lethonee picked out a safe way for me down the cliff, and across Gyronchi to the black temple.

"Glarath and his priests had carried the *Chronion* there. Apparently they had dismantled and re-assembled all the mechanism. Perhaps they had not understood it completely, however, for they had not ventured into Time. But, utilizing the principle of the *chronoscope,* with power supplied by the *gyrane,* they had made a golden shell—"

Lanning caught his breath.

"I've seen that!" he gasped. "Carrying Sorainya!"

"Or the projected image of Sorainya," corrected Wil McLan. "But Lethonee guided me into the temple." His whispered narrative went on. "The alarm was spread. The pursuing ants roused the priests.

"With seconds to spare, I got safely aboard the *Chronion,* started the converters, and escaped into Time. I returned to the early twentieth century. And then at last, guided by Lethonee down the fainter geodesics of her possible world, I came to Jonbar."

"Jonbar—" Lanning interrupted again, with a quick gesture at the crystal block of the *chronoscope*. "Can we see Jonbar, in that? And—Lethonee?"

Very gravely, Wil McLan shook his white, haggard head.

"Presently, we shall try," he whispered. "But the probability factor of Jonbar has become so small that I can reach it only with the utmost power of the scanning beam, and then the definition is very poor. Jonbar is at the brink of doom."

His broken fingers touched the thin white cylinder that hung from his throat.

"But there is still one chance." A stern light flashed in his dark sunken eyes. "Jonbar hasn't given up. It was Lethonee's father, an archeologist digging in the Rockies where my laboratory used to be, who found there the charred notebooks and age-rusted mechanisms from which he rediscovered the secret of time.

"He constructed the *chronotron;* and, with it, Lethonee soon discovered the menace born of my unwitting tampering with probability. And she brought me to Jonbar to aid the defense. That is why I have been picking up you and your men, Denny."

Lanning was staring at him, frowning. "But I don't understand," he muttered. "What can we do?"

"These two possible worlds—each armed with the secret of Time—are engaged in a desperate struggle for—no, not survival. Perhaps existence, would be better.

"Denny," the whispering husk of voice grew confused and troubled, "it is almost impossible to explain, or tinderstand. Time involves the fourth dimension, and its fixation and ultimate determination involves the fifth-dimensional progression of the continuum. It is as difficult to grasp the inter-weaving actions of the geodesics, as to picture mentally that necessary phenomenon of the fourth dimension; that a body may rotate not around a point, as in two dimensions, nor about a line, as it would in three, but about a *plane*.

"I have not time now to show you the mathematics of the geodesic interactions. But this is the meaning in practical things: neither Lethonee nor Sorainya is fixed in that fifth-dimensional progression. In that sense, neither is yet real. Neither Jonbar nor Gyronchi. Somewhere, there is a turning in the Path of Time that leads, one way, to Jonbar. The other branch leads to Gyronchi.

"THE CRUX of it all is this: If Jonbar exists, *Gyronchi can not*. And equally, if Sorainya exists—Lethonee never comes to be.

Each of those cities—each of those women—represents a possible future, a possible epoch. And—they represent different possibilities of *the same epoch.*

"Each has the secret of Time. But neither can, by any means whatever, reach the other! They can see each other—but they cannot reach or affect each other. Those doctors of Jonbar aboard the *Chronion*—they cannot reach Gyronchi, even though this ship goes down the geodesics that lead there. They cannot—for Gyronchi and Jonbar, and all things of either city are *mutually exclusive.* Either is possible—*but not both!*

"Each is possible—but because of my blundering, I know now that the geodesics of Gyronchi are far stronger. The probability of Gyronchi is far greater."

"But we can help!" Desperately Lanning clutched the thin, old shoulder. "What is our part?"

"No direct geodesics link Jonbar and Gyronchi," rasped McLan. "Therefore they have no common reality. They are contradictory. They can explore each other's trains of probability, but there can be no physical contact, remember, because the existence of each is a denial of the other. *Their* forces, therefore, can never come to grips.

"But our contemporary world is joined by direct geodesics with all possible worlds. It has a common existence with *both* those possible—but mutually impossible—worlds of futurity. That accounts for your place in the picture, Denny."

"Eh," Lanning leaned forward, desperately urgent. "Lethonee and Sorainya both talked of destiny. You can tell me what they meant?"

The blue, haunted eyes looked at him steadily, from beneath that startling shock of snowy hair. "Yours is the key position, Denny," the whispering husk responded. "Your triumph alone can save Jonbar. With your failure—it fails."

"And that's why they both came to me!"

The old man nodded. "Sorainya sought to cause your death in a way we could not restore. The life-giving powers of *dynat* are great—but we could not restore life to bomb-shattered flesh, or to a shark-torn body. And that type of destruction would insure her victory. Had you, instead of Barry, flown that day, the plane would have exploded. Lethonee took it upon herself to watch over you, until such a time as Fate ruled your death in a way we could restore. Then we could take you aboard the *Chronion.* And only then."

"Death—" Lanning whispered the echo. "Then we are a Legion of the Dead."

"I came back to find you and a band of your contemporaries to serve Jonbar," McLan whispered gravely. "Since it is impossible to draw a sound, living man from his place in Time—to do so would warp the whole continuum—we had to wait until the moment when each of you was actually dead to draw you aboard through the temporal ray.

"THERE ARE two civilizations for the future, and while neither yet exists to us, each exists to its inhabitants. For in the fifth-dimensional view, all things are co-existent, some more fixed than others. Like the exposed film of a camera, wherein the images already are. Part of the long scroll of film—Time—has passed into the fixing bath of the fifth-dimensional progression, and may not be changed. Part—that we call the future—has not, and the film is yet sensitive to change.

"But to those future beings, their yet-to-be civilization is real. And—they are fighting for it. But to do so, they must fight through us, they must reach us and influence us. *Those two futures must fight over a modern, since they cannot fight each other.*"

"And—we are the dead!" whispered Lanning.

"Not dead now," the husked whisper of the old man came. "Jonbar has provided the corps of surgeons and doctors to revive you immediately as the temporal ray drew you aboard the *Chronion.* The *dynat* can revive any reasonably whole man."

"*Dynat?*" Lanning caught at the term. "I heard Lethonee use that word, and the doctors, What does it mean?"

"It is the vital scientific power upon which the whole civilization of Jonbar is based," said McLan. "The slow evolutionary adaptation to the use of its illimitable power is what will give birth to the *dynon,* the perfect race that may exist—if you win for Jonbar!

"The *dynat* is as important to Jonbar as the *gyrane* is to the Gyronchi. But there's no time for that. I've explained the situation, Denny. What about it?"

The dark, hollow eyes searched his face with a probing keenness almost painful. Wil McLan thrust his white head forward. The hoarse whisper rasped, desperately: "Will you accept the championship of Jonbar—knowing that it is a nearly hopeless battle? Will you set yourself against Sorainya, and give up all that she may have offered? And remember, Denny, an act of yours must kill Sorainya—or Lethonee!"

A COLD shudder passed over Dennis Lanning, and a choking ache closed his throat. The serene white image of Lethonee was before him, holding the jewel. And the proud, red-mailed splendor of Sorainya pushed it away. He couldn't, he thought, endure the death of Lethonee. But could he—even if he would—destroy Sorainya? An agony crushed his heart, but slowly he nodded.

"Yes, Wil," he said. "I accept."

Broken fingers gripped his hand,

"Good for you, Denny," gasped Wil McLan. "And now I give you command of our Legion of Time."

"No, Wil," Lanning protested. "I've earned no right to command."

"Gyronchi must be destroyed—and even Sorainya." A stern bitter light flashed in the hollow eyes again, and the gnarled fingers; touched the worn silver tube. "And I'll do my part." The whisper quivered. "But I've no knack of leadership. My life has been spent too much with abstractions. But you're a man of action, Denny, and in the crucial place. You must command."

Lanning met the tortured eyes.

"I will."

A scarred hand lifted in a salute almost gay.

"Thank you, Denny. Now I suggest that you go down and lay the situation before the men, in the way you think best. They have this choice: to follow your command, or to be returned to where we found them in Time."

"Which would mean—death?"

Wil McLan nodded. "There is no niche for them in Time—alive. If we win, a place can be made for those who survive, where the fifth-order progression has not yet fixed the continuum—in Jonbar. If we fail, there is death—or Sorainya's torture vaults."

"In Jonbar—" repeated Lanning, huskily. "Can I go to Jonbar, if we win? To Lethonee?"

"If we win," the old man told him. "Now, if you will go down to your men, I'll try to pick up Jonbar with the *chronoscope.*"

Eagerly, Lanning asked, "May I—"

A solemn twinkle flashed briefly in McLan's hollow eyes.

"If I get Lethonee," he promised, "I'll call you. But it's very hard to get Jonbar."

Lanning went back down through the turret to the deck, and requested Barry Halloran and Lao Meng Shan to call the rest together. Facing the expectant little group, in their oddly assorted uniforms, he began: "I've just talked to Wil McLan." He waited for the flash of eager interest. "He has gathered us out of Time, saved each one of us from certain death. In return, he wants us to fight, to save one world that is struggling for survival against another. I know the cause is good.

"He has offered me the command. And I must ask you either to follow me, or to be returned to your own place in Time—to die. That may be a hard choice. But it is the only one possible."

"Hard?" shouted Barry Halloran.

*"Nein!"* grunted Emil Schorn. "Are we craven, to turn back from Valhalla?"

*"Viva!"* shouted Cresto. *"Viva el capitán!"*

"Thank you." Lanning gulped, blinked. "If we win, there will be a place made for us in Jonbar. Now, if you will follow me, repeat: *I pledge loyalty to Jonbar, and I promise to serve dutifully in the Legion of Time."*

The eight men, with right hands lifted, shouted the oath. And then, led by Willie Rand, roared out a cheer for "Jonbar and Cap'n Denny Lanning."

ONE OF THE orderlies from Jonbar beckoned to Lanning, and he returned hastily to the bridge, his heart thumping.

"Did you—" he asked breathlessly, "did you—?"

Wil McLan shook his haggard head, and pointed to the cabinet of the *chronoscope.*

"I tried," he whispered hoarsely. "But the enemy have moved again. One more triumph of Sorainya is fixed on the fifth axis. And Jonbar is one step nearer extinction. The image flickered, and went out. And that is what I got."

Looking into the crystal block, Lanning once more saw Gyronchi! But it was strangely changed. Sorainya's proud citadel on the hill had collapsed into a heap of corroded, blackened metal. The black temple of the *gyrane,* on the other eminence, had fallen to a tremendous mound of shattered stone. Beneath, upon the denuded wastelands where fields and villages had been, was a desolate, untrodden wilderness of weeds and brush, leprously patched with strange scars of white, shining ash.

"Gyronchi?" breathed Lanning. "Destroyed?"

"Destroyed," rasped Wil McLan, "by its own evil! By a final war between the warlords of Sorainya's class and the priesthood of the *gyrane*. Mankind, in the picture you witness, is extinct."

His hoarse whisper sank very low.

"If we fail—if mankind follows the way of Gyronchi—that is the end of the road." Wearily, he snapped off the switch, and the bleak scene vanished. "And now it seems that that road has been chosen. For the geodesics of no other remain strong enough for the instrument to trace."

His hands knotted impotently, Lanning stared bewildered and helpless out through the dome, into the haze of flickering blue.

"What—" he demanded, "what could have happened?"

Wil McLan shook his head.

"I don't know. Gyronchi has done something. We must try to discover what it is, and undo it if possible. We had best return to Jonbar, I think, to secure the use of the new geodesic analysis laboratory that Lethonee has organized—if we can!"

Anxiously, Lanning gripped his thin shoulder.

"If—"

"It may be," Wil McLan whispered, "that this latest move has so far attenuated the probability of Jonbar that its geodesics will not serve to lead the *Chronion*. That—we can never again reach it!"

"But we can try," Lanning snapped with a sudden fierceness.

"Yes, try." The old man shook his head slowly. The fumbling, broken hands twisted at the shining wheel of the *Chronion*.

VIII.

BORIS BARININ came up from the hospital ward. Then two Canadians, lean silent twins named Isaac and Israel Enders, who had been taken aboard, before Lanning left his bed, from a shell hole on the Western Front. And at last Duffy Clark, the British sailor from Jutland.

Willingly taking the oath, they made twelve men under Lanning. He organized them into squads, made big, fearless Emil Schorn his second in command, and began drilling on the deck.

There were arms, he found: a dozen Mauser rifles, two dozen

Luger pistols, four crated Maxim machine guns, several boxes of hand grenades, and a hundred thousand rounds of assorted ammunition, which McLan had taken—along with a stock of food and a few medical supplies—from a sinking munitions ship.

"The first precaution." the old man rasped. "We located a torpedoed arms ship when we first came back from Jonbar to collect supplies and weapons—and test our technique of recovery. Weapons from Jonbar, you see, wouldn't function against targets from Gyronchi—mutually impossible! And men who had been eating food from Jonbar, in a raid on Gyronchi, might find themselves—well, hungry."

Lanning superintended the unpacking, inspection, and assembly of the weapons, served out the rifles and automatics, assigned crews to the machine guns. Since McLan's assistants from Jonbar would be unable to enter Gyronchi, he detailed Clark, Barinin, and Lao Meng Shan as crew for the *Chronion,* and himself learned something of her navigation.

And the time ship drove steadily down the geodesics of Jonbar. The atomic converters throbbed endlessly beneath the deck. Sometimes Lanning relieved him, but Wil McLan seldom left the control dome.

"The world we seek is now all but impossible," he rasped. "The full power of the field drives us forward very slowly. And at any instant the geodesics of Jonbar may break, for they are weak enough already, and leave us—*notime!"*

Once, in his tiny cabin aft, Lanning woke in his bunk with a clear memory of Lethonee. Slim and tall in her long white robe, she had stood before him, holding the flaming splendor of the *chronotron.* Despair was a shadow on her face, her violet eyes dark pools of pain.

"Denny," her urgent words rang clear in his memory, "come to Jonbar—or we are dead."

Lanning went at once to the bridge, and told McLan. The old man shook his white head, grimly.

"We are already doing all that can be done," he said. "The geodesics of Jonbar are like microscopic wires drawn out thinner and thinner by the attenuation of probability. If the tracer loses them, or if they snap, Jonbar is—lost."

Helpless, Lanning could only return to the drilling of his men.

TWO WEEKS passed, by the time of the ship—physiological

which the span of life moved relentlessly toward its end, regardless of motion backward or forward along the time dimension. And at last the *Chronion* slipped silently out of the blue, shimmering abyss. Lanning, waiting eagerly on the deck, saw beneath them—Jonbar!

The ship was two miles high. Yet, so far as his eye could reach in every direction, stretched that metropolis of futurity. Mirror-faced with polished metal, the majestic buildings were more inspiring than cathedrals in their soaring grace. With a pleasing lack of regularity, they stood far apart all across the green parklike valley of a broad placid river, and crowned the wooded hills beyond. Wide traffic viaducts, many-leveled, flowed among them, busy with strange, bright vehicles. Coming and going above the towers, great silver teardrops swam through the air about the ship.

Lanning had glimpsed it once before, through Lethonee's jewel. But its majestic reality was new. The staggering vastness and the ordered splendor of it shook him with a kind of awe. Hundreds of millions, he knew, lived here, labored, loved, rejoiced in the happiest estate that mankind had ever known—or, he realized, he should put it, might ever know. And all the wonder of this world, the incredible fact came to him stunningly, was faced with absolute annihilation.

Trembling with eagerness and dread, he hastened up to Wil McLan.

"This is Jonbar!" he cried. "Then it's still—safe? And we can find Lethonee?"

The bent old man turned solemnly from the polished wheel, and shook his scarred white head.

"We're here," came his grave, voiceless whisper. "But only the geodesic analyzers can measure the degree of Jonbar's probability. It hangs by a strand weaker than a spider's web. Lethonee will doubtless be at her new laboratory."

The *Chronion* was gliding swiftly down to a mile-high argent spire—that soared from a wooded height—propelled in space, McLan had explained, by the same special field that moved it in Time. A vast doorway slid open in a silvery wall. The little ship floated into an immense hangarlike space, crowded with stream-lined craft. A green light beckoned them to land on an empty platform.

"This is the world we must fight to save," Lanning told the

men.

"*Ach!*" rumbled Emil Schorn. "It is a good world, well worth fighting for."

Leaving the big Prussian in command, and warning him to be ready for instant action in case of emergency, Lanning and McLan left the ship. An elevator in a great pillar shot them upward. They emerged into the cool refreshment of open air, amid the gay verdure of a terrace garden. A sliding door opened in a bright wall beyond. Tripping eagerly out of it, to meet them, came Lethonee.

Instead of the long white robes in which Lanning had always seen her, she wore a close-fitting dress of softly shimmering, metallic blue, and a blue band held her dark ruddy hair. Something of the grave solemnity of the apparitions was gone. She was just a lovely, human girl, joyously eager to see him—and trying, he thought, to hide a tragic despair.

She came quickly to him, through the bright garden, and took both his hands in an eager grasp. And Lanning felt a queer little shiver of joy at the warm reality of her touch.

"DENNY LANNING!" she whispered. "At last you have come. I am so glad—"

Her weary, troubled eyes went to scarred old Wil McLan.

"Gyronchi has carried out some attack," she told him gravely. "A warning came from the *dynon,* and now—they are gone. The full power of the *chronotron* will not penetrate forward, beyond tonight."

Her voice was hushed and shaken; in her eyes was the shadow of doom.

"I have been with them twenty hours in the laboratory. But we could discover nothing. Only that this is the last possible night of Jonbar. Unless—"

Her haunted eyes clung desperately to Lanning's face.

"Unless the tide of probability is changed."

Wil McLan limped toward the sliding door, breathing huskily. "I'm going up to the laboratory."

Lanning lingered, and his thirsty eyes caught the girl's.

"I have done all I can, there," she said. "And, if this is the last day of Jonbar, I should like to spend an hour of it with you, Denny. Perhaps the only hour we shall ever have together."

"I'll send for you, Denny, if we discover anything," rasped

McLan. "You can do nothing, until—unless—we find what action Gyronchi has taken."

He turned through the sliding door.

Alone on the terrace with Lethonee, Lanning was overcome with a sense of incredulity. He looked wonderingly at her grave quiet beauty, framed in the greenery, asking, "How can I believe that you aren't real? What is the difference between reality and such a seeming as this?"

The universe of reality, determined by progression on the fifth axis, is simple and complete," the girl told him solemnly. "All the branching geodesics of possibility tend to pick up energy; all possible worlds strive for reality. But only one line, at each bifurcation, can win. All energy is withdrawn from those other, half-formed worlds, as the world lines of the victorious one are fixed in the fifth dimension. And it is as if they had never been."

Her white face was very sober.

"In a manner of speaking, all the seeming reality of Jonbar— even I—was given creation by the atomic power of the *Chronion,* bringing you down the geodesics. We are only an illusion of possibility, the reflection of what may be—a reflection that is doomed!"

Abruptly, then—and Lanning knew that it took a desperate effort—she tossed her lovely head, and smiled.

"But why need illusions talk of illusion?" The silver voice was almost gay. "Aren't you hungry, Denny? Gather flowers for the table, and let us dine—on illusion!"

WITH HER own hands she set a small table at the rail that edged the terrace. The huge white buds that Lanning picked bathed them in a delicate perfume. Beyond the rail, and a mile below, stretched the green parklands. Other silver pylons shimmered magnificent on distant hills. The genial sun was setting from a serene sky, of a blue clarity that Lanning had never seen above a city. A cool wind whispered across the garden, in a silence of ineffable peace.

"Nothing can happen to you, or to Jonbar, surely," whispered Lanning, sipping a glass of fragrant wine. "Perfection cannot die!"

"But it can." Her voice shuddered. "When the whole continuum is tortured with forces in conflict, who can foretell the outcome?"

Lanning caught her hand. "Lethonee," he said huskily, "for ten years of my life, since the first night you came to me, I have lived in hope of finding you. Now, if anything should take you—"

An iron grasp closed on his throat.

The girl moved closer, shivering. "But we know," came her dread-chilled voice, "that this is *the last night of Jonbar*. The *chronotron* can discover no possible tomorrow!"

The blue dusk turned to mauve and to purple-black. The far towers of Jonbar shone like pillars of fire. And the roadways, sweeping through the dark woodlands, were broad, brilliant rivers of flowing light.

Shadows filled the terrace. Some night-blooming shrub sent out a flood of intoxicating sweetness. Slow music came softly from somewhere below. Close to Lethonee, Lanning strove vainly to forget the torturing pressure of peril, sought to grasp and hold her threatened reality with the strength of his arms.

Suddenly the girl's hand stiffened in his, and she caught a gasping, frightened breath.

"Greetings!" rang out a voice of golden mockery, "Queen of Nothingness!"

LANNING looked up, startled. Above the terrace, floating as he had seen it before, was a long, shallow, golden shell. Sorainya stood in it, proudly erect in a long-sleeved shirt and kilt of woven scarlet mail. Beside her stood a tall, angular man—gaunt-faced, with dark, sullen eyes and cruel, heavy lips—robed to his feet in dull, stiff black.

Glarath, the latter must be, Lanning knew, high priest of the strange *gyrane*. His sunken black eyes smouldered with a malevolent flame. But Sorainya's greenish glance held a mocking amusement.

"Best taste her kisses while you may, Denny Lanning," she taunted. "For we have found a higher crucial factor. I didn't need you, Denny Lanning, after all—Glarath, with the *gyrane,* took the place I offered you. And now the struggle is won!"

The black-haired hand of the priest clutched possessively at her strong, bare arm. He snarled some guttural, unintelligible word, and his dark eyes burned at Lanning, terrible with hate.

Sorainya whipped out the thin golden needle of her sword, and drew it in a flashing arc above the dark city. And she leaned into the black priest's arms.

"Farewell, Denny Lanning," pealed the mockery of her shout.

"And take warning! All Jonbar—and the phantom in your arms—will be gone before the wind. We have come to watch the end."

With the hand that held the sword, she flung him a derisive kiss. Her foot touched some control, and the shell soared upward and vanished in the sky of night.

White-faced, shaken, Lethonee was on her feet. "Come to the laboratory!" Her voice was dry with alarm. "I hadn't meant to stay so long."

Lanning followed her to the sliding door. Beyond it, he glimpsed a vast tower room. At endless tables, hundreds of men and women were busy with mathematical instruments: calculating machines, planimeters, integrators, and harmonic analyzers. Beyond was a huge bulwark of intricate mechanism, resembling a magnified version of a product integraph Lanning had seen at the Massachusetts Tech, capable of solving problems too complex for the human brain. Beyond, in a far wing, pedestals supported scores of huge crystals like the *chronotron* screen Lanning had seen in the hands of Lethonee. Swift activity hummed everywhere.

BEFORE they had entered, however, Wil McLan came to meet them at a frantic, limping run. His white hair was wild, a desperate urgency strained his haggard face.

"Back, Denny!" It was a rasping, whispered scream. "Get back aboard. Jonbar is—going!"

Lanning swept Lethonee with him into the elevator. McLan tumbled after them. The cage dropped toward the hangar. Lanning held the girl in quivering arms.

"Darling—" he whispered. "You are coming with us!"

She shook her tragic head. "No, Denny. I am part of Jonbar." She clung to him, desperately.

The elevator stopped. Lanning caught Lethonee's hand, and they ran out across the hangar, toward the *Chronion*. Ahead, Lanning saw a welcoming throng of gay-clad people gathered about the time ship, tossing flowers to the deck. Dapper Jean Querard stood by the rail, making a speech.

But a curious dim, silver light was beginning to steal over the crowd and the teardrop ships and the walls, as if they were beginning to dissolve in a silver mist. Only the *Chronion* remained clear, real.

Lanning sprinted.

"Hurry!" he sobbed. "Darling—"

But Lethonee's fingers were gone from his hand. He stopped, and saw her still beside him—but dim as a ghost. Frantically, her shadow beckoned him to go on. He tried to catch her up in his arms. But she faded from his grasp. She was gone.

McLan had passed him. Lanning caught a sobbing breath, and fought a blinding pain, and stumbled on— But what was the use, demanded bitter agony, if Lethonee was gone?

Everything but the *Chronion* was dim now. Beginning to flicker like the blue abysm in which the time ship rode. He saw Wil McLan scramble up a ladder. But the floor was giving way. His running feet sank deep, as if its metal had been soft snow—

And it was gone. Lanning caught his breath, and clutched out desperately, and fell. The last wraith of the building flickered away. Jonbar was gone. Beneath, under the empty night, lay only a featureless dark plain. And Lanning was plunging unchecked toward it, a cold wind screaming up about him.

A malicious golden voice pealed: "Farewell!"

And Lanning saw the long yellow shell flash by, Sorainya and Glarath lying together on its cushions. He fell past them, and the icy wind took his breath.

Then the *Chronion* shot down beside him. The yellow ray flared from her crystal gun, and drew him headlong to the rail. And Barry Halloran, laughing, hauled him safely aboard.

## IX.

THE SHIP, in a moment, was back in her timeless blue abyss, driving through the ceaseless flicker of possibility. Lanning hastened to join Wil McLan beneath the crystal dome, and asked a breathless, tortured question: "Lethonee is gone—dead?"

The sunken, haunted eyes looked at him solemnly.

"Not dead," rasped Wil McLan, "for she was never born. Jonbar was merely a faint probability of future time, which we illuminated with the power of the temporal ray. This last triumph of Sorainya has—eliminated the probability. The reflection, therefore, vanished."

"Sorainya!" gasped Lanning. "What has she done?" He clutched a twisted arm. "Did you discover anything?"

The white head nodded.

"In the last hour, before the laboratory was obliterated—"

"You did!" Lanning quivered with impatience. What was it?"

"A moment, my boy," came the whisper. "It seems that the priests of the *gyrane* must have learned more from the study of the *Chronion* than I thought. Sorainya's golden shell, as you know, is merely an image projected by the temporal ray. But now Glarath has built an actual time ship!"

"Eh?" muttered Lanning.

"It is similar to the *Chronion,* but heavier and armored. And it carries a horde of Sorainya's fighting ants."

"And they used that, against Jonbar?"

"They went into the past," said the voiceless man. "Back to the turning point of probability. They found something there—it must have been a small material object, although we failed to glimpse it with the *chronotrons*—which was the very foundation of Jonbar. Using the power of the *gyrane,* they wrenched the thing, whatever it was, out of its place in time. The resulting warp of the geodesics extinguished the possibility of Jonbar."

"What did they do with the thing?"

"They kept it concealed, so that we could get no sight of it with the temporal ray. And they carried it back to Gyronchi. It is guarded, there, in Sorainya's fortress."

"Guarded?" Lanning echoed. His fingers twisted together in a sudden agony of hope, and his eyes searched McLan's wealed face. "Then if we took it—" he gasped desperately, "brought it back—would that help Jonbar?" Urgently, he seized McLan's thin shoulder. "Can—can anything bring back Lethonee?"

The haggard white head moved in a tiny nod.

"Yes," came his slow, hoarse whisper. "If we can recover the object; if we can discover where they found it, in Space and Time; if we can put it back there; if we can prevent Gyronchi from disturbing it again until the turning point has passed—then Jonbar will again be possible."

Lanning's fist smashed into his palm. "Then we must do that!"

"Yes," whispered Wil McLan, very softly, "we must do that." A solemn light came into his hollow eyes, and his broken hand softly touched Lanning's arm. "Yes, this is the task for which we gathered your Legion, Denny—although the details have not been clear until now."

"Then," Lanning cried eagerly, "let's go!"

"Now we are retracing the faded geodesics of Jonbar," the old man told him, "back toward your own time. There we can pick up the branching world lines of Gyronchi, and follow them forward again, to seek that guarded object."

"And let Sorainya beware!"

BUT McLAN caught Lanning's arm again, with a firmer grasp.

"I must warn you, Denny," he whispered. "Don't be too hopeful. We've need of every bit of caution. The odds are all against us. Fourteen men, we must fight all Gyronchi, Sorainya and her battle ants, the *gyrane,* Glarath and his ship of Time.

"And Jonbar can help us no farther. Even the surgeons we had aboard vanished with all the rest. Twice seven—against a whole world of futurity."

"But we'll take 'em on!" muttered Lanning, grimly.

"We'll try—"

An old slumberous fire burned again in McLan's haunted eyes, and his seamed face drew into a grim and rigid mask. His whispering voice fell hoarsely.

"It's thirty years since I saw Sorainya." He spoke, it seemed, to himself. Broken fingers touched the worn silver tube that hung from his throat. "A glorious flame that lured me across the gulf of Time. I—I loved her."

Tears burst into his hollow eyes, and his gulp was a startling little sound. Lanning looked away, out of the dome, and heard nothing for a full minute.

"Fifteen years—" came the slow whisper at last. "Fifteen years since I found that she is a demon. Lying, treacherous, savagely cruel, as near a female devil as could be. And still—beautiful. Somehow, glorious!" Some deep-hidden agony throbbed in his whisper.

"I hate Sorainya!" It was a savage rush. "She tricked me, tortured me, maimed me forever! She—she—" Something seemed to choke him. At last came the voiceless sigh: "But still—for all her hateful evil—could I kill Sorainya? Could any man?"

Lanning's fists were knotted into hard balls. "I have seen her," he gasped hoarsely. "And I don't know." Then he strode suddenly across the room and back, moved by a tearing agony. His voice quavered thin and high: "But we've got to—if we can! To save Jonbar."

"Yes," whispered the man she had broken. "If we can."

A week, ship's time, had passed when the dials registered

1921.

"Here," Wil McLan told Lanning, "the last broken geodesic of Jonbar joins reality. In this year, it is just possible, we may find the apex of that cone of probability formed when Glarath took the object out of time—if we ever come back from Gyronchi."

The *Chronion* came briefly out of her blue, flickering bourne, high above the brilliant blue Pacific, where the circle of an atoll glistened green and white about a pale lagoon. In an instant they were gone again, back through the blur of multitudinous possibility, down the geodesic track of Gyronchi.

Lanning and Schorn were drilling the men "daily" on the deck. But the first brush with Gyronchi came as an utter surprise. It was jaunty little Jean Querard, leaping from his place in the line, who screamed the warning. *"Grand Dieu!* A ship from hell!"

Turning from the little rank, as he pointed, Lanning saw a black shadow in the shimmering blue abyss. It vanished, reappeared, flickered, was suddenly real. A great black vessel.

THREE TIMES the *Chronion's* length, it was thick and massive. Its ends were two immense square plates, which shone with the same greenish glow as the *Chronion's* polar disks. Black muzzles frowned from ports in her side, and the high bulwarked deck was crowded with a black-armored horde of Sorainya's gigantic ants, aglitter with golden axes and thick, crimson guns.

On a lofty quarter-deck, Lanning thought he glimpsed the black-robed angularity of Glarath. But it disappeared. And, a moment later, a dazzling white beam jetted from a projecting tube. A two-foot section of the *Chronion's* rail turned blindly incandescent and incontinently exploded, flinging out searing drops of molten metal.

"Lie flat!" ordered Lanning. "Fire at will!" He shouted to Schorn: "Get the Maxims going!"

But what—the question racked him—could lead avail against that beam of terrible energy? Rifles and machine guns crackled as he ran to the speaking tube that communicated with McLan.

"Wil!" he yelled. "What can we do?"

The white sword flashed again behind him. And Israel Enders, kneeling to fire, collapsed in a smoking heap. There was one dreadful scream, agony-thinned. And then bright flame burst up from the pile of burnt cloth and seared flesh and fused metal that had been a man.

With an answering scream that was the echo of his brother's, Isaac Enders fed a belt of ammunition into his Maxim, and sprayed lead at the far rank of hyper-ants who were leveling their red-metal guns. Projectiles spattered the *Chronion.*

The hoarse, tortured whisper came back from Wil McLan. "The *Chronion's* no fighting ship. We can't meet the ray of the *gyrane.*"

"What then?" It was a gasp of agony. "They've got Israel Enders, already—"

"Outrun them!" came the voiceless husking. "The only hope. The *Chronion's* lighter. Hold them off. And maybe—"

Blinded by blood from a wound on his forehead, the Austrian, Arneth, was fumbling with his jammed Maxim.

Lanning ran to take the gun, seared his fingers freeing the hot action, and trained it on the port from which the ray had flashed. Perhaps, if it came from some sort of projector that could be broken—

He hammered hot lead at the black-armored ship. It was drifting nearer. Another volley from the ants screamed above. The white ray flashed again. One of the Maxims exploded, spattered fused metal. Willie Rand, behind it, rolled moaning on the deck, beating with blackened hands at his flaming garments.

This couldn't go on! Shuddering, Lanning fed another belt into his smoking gun. A few of the great ants had fallen. But the battle was hopeless. He listened. Was the throb beneath the deck a little swifter?

The great black ship was close when his gun clattered again. Swinging their golden axes, the mighty ants lined the rail. Were they preparing to board? Lanning tilted up the Maxim, to rake them.

A thick black tube crept down, stopped in line with him. His breath caught. It was time for that flaming ray. A stabbing, blinding flash—

BUT THE TIME SHIP had flickered, like a shadow of black. And it was gone in the shimmering abyss. Dazzled, reeling, Lanning left his hot gun and stumbled to the speaking tube.

"Wil?" he called, shakily.

"We've outrun them, Denny," came the voiceless rasp. "Though it took our full field potential. We can keep a little ahead, along the time dimension. But they'll be back to Gyronchi ahead of us, by a seeming paradox, to warn that we are coming.

"What are our casualties?"

Lanning turned to survey the littered deck. The tall, grim-faced Canadian was on his knees beside the smoking remains of his brother, sobbing. Barry Halloran was dressing von Arneth's wound. And Willie Rand, blackened, his clothing still smoking, was groping his way about the deck, cursing in a soft, weary monotone. Lanning saw his eyes, and chilled to a shock of horror. For, staring wide and blank from his red-seared face, they were cooked white from the ray, blinded.

"Israel Enders dead," he reported to McLan, in a sick voice. "Arneth wounded. Rand blind. And one Maxim destroyed. That terrible ray—"

"That was the *gyrane,*" rasped McLan "And but a hint of what the *gyrane* can do. The odds are all against us, Denny. We must avoid another battle—if we can. But now that they are warned—"

The whisper faded, on a note of tired despair.

Wrapped in a sheet, to which was pinned a tiny Canadian flag and the silver star of Jonbar, the remains of Israel Enders and his fused rifle were consigned to the shimmering gulf of Time— where, McLan said, having the velocity of the ship, they would drift on into ultimate futurity.

The deck was cleared, the broken rail mended, the guns cleaned and repaired. Atomic converters throbbing swiftly, polar plates shining green, the *Chronion* plunged on down the track of probability, toward Gyronchi.

Erich von Arneth came up from the hospital, with a new grimness on his lean dark face and a livid white scar across his forehead.

Asking for a Mauser whose lock was broken, Willie Rand sat for long hours on the deck, bandaged head bowed, whetting the gleaming bayonet and testing its keenness with his thumb.

On the bridge, Lanning and Wil McLan peered for long hours into the crystal block of the *chronoscope,* using its searching temporal ray to scan Gyronchi, seeking an opportune moment to check the time ship, for the raid. Some strange force, however, made it impossible to look actually into Sorainya's mighty citadel, to find the object they sought to recover.

"Another application of the *gyrane,*" rasped Wil McLan. "An interfering sub-etheric field, set up about the metal walls, that damps out the temporal radiation." A stern light glinted in his hollow eyes. "But I know Sorainya's fortress," he whispered grimly. "With Lethonee's aid, planning that escape, I memorized every inch of it."

His broken fingers drew maps and plans. He and Lanning and Schorn pored over them, hour after hour.

"It must be a sudden strike," he husked, "with the hour well-chosen. A moment lost—a wasted step—may mean disaster. The great strong room, where Sorainya keeps her treasure. is in the eastern tower. It is reached only by an elevator, through a trap door in the floor of Sorainya's own apartments. And the great hall outside, through which you must go, is guarded always by scores of ants."

And at last Wil McLan spun the shining wheel and tapped a key, to stop the time ship in Gyronchi.

## X.

IT WAS the somber dusk of a cloudy day when the *Chronion* first paused in the land that Lanning had seen in the crystal screen of the *chronoscope*. The tiny fields, the broad river dully silver in the twilight, sprawling miserable villages—and a blackened, barren patch where one had stood. The twin hills beyond, bearing the temple of the *gyrane,* with that awful vortex of black still funneling out into space above its squat and somber colonnades. And Sorainya's citadel.

Standing on the deck, Lanning scanned the fortress through powerful binoculars. Mountainous, frowning pile of eternal crimson metal, ancestral fastness of Sorainya's warrior dynasty—he knew from the *chronoscope*—for half a thousand years. Scores of the black armored ants, agleam with the gold and scarlet of their weapons, were marching in sentry duty along the lofty battlements. And Lanning saw, mounted cannonlike upon the wails, a dozen of the thick black tubes that projected the deadly ray of the *gyrane.*

*"Gott im Himmel!"* rumbled Emil Schorn at his side, awed. "Der thing we must recover is in that castle, *nein?* It looks a *verdammt* stubborn nut to crack!"

"It is," said Lanning. "One slip, and we are lost. There must be no slip!" He handed the glasses to the big Prussian. "We have only paused here to look over the ground by daylight," he swiftly explained. "We are to land after midnight on that ledge that breaks the north precipice—see it?"

"*Ja!*"

"Sorainya herself will then be gone to visit Glarath in his temple—so we saw in the *chronoscope*. And perhaps at that hour her guards will not be too alert. Our landing party must climb to the little balcony above, where the skeleton hangs—"

"*Ach, Gott!* A dizzy climb!"

"The little door on the balcony gives into the dungeons. Wil McLan has the keys he carved there, for his escape. We'll enter through the dungeons, and try to reach the great hall above. Is the plan all clear?"

"*Ja,*" he rumbled. "Clear as death."

Lanning waved his arm to Wil McLan, in his crystal dome, and the mote of the *Chronion* flashed again into her shimmering gulf.

The landing party gathered on the foredeck. Including Lanning and Schorn, it numbered eight men. A grim, silent little band—save for Barry Halloran, who tried to make them join in his roaring chant of "Jonbar!"

Isaac Enders and von Arneth packed two of the Maxims, Cresto and Courtney-Pharr were burdened with the fifty-pound tripods. The others were laden with climbing ropes, rifles, grenades. and ammunition for the Maxims.

Boris Barinin set up the remaining gun to guard the ship. And blinded Willie Rand sat silently beside him. breathing white cigarette smokeand whetting at the bayonet of his broken gun.

The *Chronion* plunged again into the blackness of a wet midnight. The overwhelming mass of Sorainya's citadel was a vague shadow in the clouds as the time ship slipped silently down to the narrow, lofty ledge. A cold rain drizzled on the deck, and a bitter wind howled about the unseen battlements above.

Noiseless as a shadow, the *Chronion* settled among the gnarled and stunted brush that clung to the ledge. Limping down from his bridge, Wil McLan handed Lanning the three white keys that he had carved from human bone.

"This is the balcony door," came his voiceless rasp. "The master key. And the inside gate. But I have none for the strong room—you must find another way." His broken hand gripped clawlike on Lanning's arm. "I've told you all I can, Denny." The whisper shuddered. "You'll pass through the prison where I lay for ten years—where we may all rot, if you fail. Don't fail!"

Lanning grasped the quivering, twisted shoulder.

"We can't fail—Jonbar."

BURDENED with Mauser, coiled rope, and a hamper of grenades, Lanning led the way over the rail and up the precipitous cliff. The mossy rock was slippery with mist. Wet cold pierced him, numbing. The wind tugged at him with icy, treacherous hands. In the darkness he could see nothing save bulking vague shadows; he had to fumble for the way.

Knives of granite cut his fingers, and damp cold deadened them. Once he slipped, and clawed at the sharp rock to catch himself, scraping flesh away. An age-long instant, heart still, he hung by the snapping fingers of one hand.

But he recovered himself, and climbed on. He came at last to a stout little oak, well anchored in a crevice, which he had marked through the binoculars. He knotted a rope to it, tested its strength, and dropped the coil to the men below.

He climbed again. A wild gust of wind tore at him. The rain, in bigger, colder drops, drenched his numb body. Pale lightning flashed once above, and he chilled with dread that it should reveal them.

He fastened another rope about a projecting spur of rock, dropped it, and climbed again. Stiff, trembling with physical and nervous fatigue, he came at last to the narrow rugged ledge where the precipice of stone joined the sheer, unscalable precipice of crimson metal. Wedging his bayonet, stakelike, in a fissure, he anchored another rope, and then began to inch his way along the ledge.

Then he heard a stifled scream beneath. A long silence. Something crashed, faintly, far below.

Shuddering, Lanning waited, listening. The storm moaned dismally about the battlements, still hundreds of feet above. There was no alarm. On hands and knees, he crept onward.

*"Ach, Gott!"* came a hushed rumbling. "This *verdammt* blackness—it would blind der deffil!"

And Emil Schorn came swarming up the rope behind him, and followed along the ledge. They came to the little projecting balcony of rusted red metal. A gallows arm projected above it. A rope hung through an open trap door, and beneath it, swaying in the wind, hung white bones in jangling chains.

As Lanning tried the thin bone key in the metal door, the other men joined them, one by one, breathless, dripping, shivering with cold—all save the Austrian, von Arneth.

*"Madre de dios!"* shuddered the Spanish flyer, Cresto. "He fell past me, screaming. He must have splashed, at the foot of the mountain! *Cabrón!* It leaves us but one Maxim."

The massive plate of the door slid aside, and a fetid breath came out of Sorainya's dungeons. The stench of unwashed human misery, of human waste and mouldering human flesh, mingled with the suffocating acrid pungence of the great ants. Clenching his jaw against the sickness in his stomach, Lanning led the seven forward.

At first he could see no light in the dungeons. He led the way by touch alone through the narrow, rock-hewn passages, counting his steps and fumbling for the memorized turns. But presently he could see a little, by a phosphorescence of decaying slime that patched the walls and floors.

Beyond the bars of cells he glimpsed abject human creatures, maimed, blinded, livid with wounds of torture. The bones of the dead, sometimes shining with a cold, blue luminescent rot, lay still chained in the same cells with the living.

A DREADFUL silence filled most of the prison. But from one cell came an agonized screaming, paper-thin from a raw throat, repeated with a maddening monotony. Glancing through a barred door, as he passed, Lanning saw a woman stretched out in chains on the floor. A crystal vessel swung back and forth, above her, pendulumlike. And drops of cold green fire fell from it, one by one, upon her naked flesh. With each spattering, corrosive drop, she writhed against the chains. and shrieked again.

The half-consumed body, Lanning thought, might once have been beautiful. Could this have been some rival of Sorainya's? A cold hate turned him rigid, and quickened his step. A muffled shot echoed behind him, and the screaming stopped.

*"Mon cœur!"* whispered little Jean Querard. "She shall suffer no more."

In another cell was a great squeaking and thumping commotion. And Lanning glimpsed huge, sleek rats battling over a body in chains, newly dead, or dying,

Once, beyond, that situation was reversed. A sightless, famished wretch had bitten his own wrist, to let a few drops of blood flow upon the floor. He crouched there, listening, and snatched

again and again, blindly, with fettered hands, at the great rats that
came to his bait.

"My word!" gasped the British flyer, Courtney-Pharr. "When
we meet that fascinatin' she-devil, she'll account for all this.
Rather!"

Lanning stopped, at a turning, and called back a soft warning:
"Ready, men!"

With a little jingle of their weapons, two of Sorainya's warrior-
insects came down the corridor. Hypertrophied ants, walking
erect on two angular limbs, eight feet tall. Their great eyes
gleamed lambent in the darkness, strange jewels of evil fire.

"Bayonets!" whispered Lanning. "No noise."

But his own bayonet had been left back on the precipice to
hold the rope. He clubbed his rifle, to lead the rush, swung it
down to pulp a compound eye. Taken by surprise, the monsters
reeled back, snatching with strange claws for their weapons.

The ants were mute. But little red boxes, clamped to their
heads, might, Lanning thought, be communicators. A black limb
was fumbling at one of them. He snapped down the rifle in a
second hasty blow, crushed it flat between stubby antennæ.

Ugly, powerful mandibles seized the Mauser's butt, sheared
through the hard wood. And a mighty golden battle-axe came
hissing down. Lanning parried at it with the barrel of the broken
gun, but the flat of its blade grazed his head, flung him down into
fire-veined blackness.

He lay on the floor, dazed and nerveless. Red agony splintered
his temple. Yet he retained a curious detached awareness. He
could see the weird feet stamping about in front of his face, on
the faintly glowing slime. The reek of formic acid stung his nostrils, burning out the nauseating effluvium of the cells. The ants
fought silently, but their limbs and chitinous armor made odd
little clicks and creaks.

THE MEN had swept forward after Lanning, with bayonets set.
They were dwarfed by the four-armed monsters. And, in a moment, the advantage of surprise was gone.

"*Vive* Jonbar!" sobbed Cresto. And the dexterous sweep of his
blade completely decapitated the nearer ant. Insect physiology
was not so quickly vanquished, however. The headless thing remained for a moment upright, and the great yellow axe struck
again, bit deep into the Spaniard's skull.

*"Dios—"*

His gaunt body lurched automatically forward, and came down on top of the ant's, driving the bayonet deep into the armored thorax.

Emil Schorn's weapon had driven into the monster Lanning had half-stunned, with a force that carried it over backward. Barry Halloran followed him, with a ripping lunge. The battle was ended.

Barry helped Lanning to his feet, and he stood a moment swaying, fighting for control of his body. Courtney-Pharr produced a silver flask of brandy, splashed its liquid fire on his temple, gave him a gulp of it. His spinning head cleared. He seized Cresto's rifle, jerked the bayonet from the great ant's body, and staggered on, following Emil Schorn.

An outstretched hand and a whispered warning stopped him in the darkness. Greenish light shone through massive bars ahead. He crept up beside Schorn, and looked into a long guard room.

A dozen of the ants were lounging in the room, and the air was thick with their acid smell. Several, at a low table, were sucking at sponges in basins of some red liquid. Two couples were preening one another's glistening black bodies. One, in a corner, was mysteriously busy with a complex-looking board vaguely like an abacus. A few were polishing battle-axes and thick, red guns.

"No hope for silence, now," Lanning breathed to Schorn. "We'll take 'em with all we've got!"

He was working with the bone key at the lock. Isaac Enders and Courtney-Pharr, beyond him, were setting up the Maxim on its tripod, the muzzle peering through the bars. The lock snapped silently. He nodded to Schorn, and began to swing the door slowly open.

The compound eyes of the farther ant glittered as they moved, and the black claws froze on the abacus. An electric silence crackled in the guard room.

"Now!" Lanning shouted.

*"Allons!"* echoed little Jean Querard. "With you, *mon capitaine!"*

The Maxim thundered suddenly, filling the room with blue smoke and whining, ricocheting lead. Lanning flung Querard and Barry Halloran diagonally across the room, to stop the other entrance.

The great ants retained a hymenopterous vitality. Even when riddled with bullets they did not immediately die. Under the Maxim's deadly hail, they abandoned their occupations, seized weapons, and came charging in two groups at the entrance.

Courtney-Pharr slammed the prison gate to protect Enders and his weapon, defending the lock with his bayonet. And the monsters in front of the Maxim began at last to slump and topple.

The defense of the other door, however, was less successful. Lanning and his companions met the charging creatures with tossed grenades and a blaze of rifle fire. Out of seven, two were blown to fragments by the bombs, and one more crippled. Four of them came on, with axes swinging, to meet the bayonets. The cripple fell back, to load and fire his clumsy gun. It coughed once, and then a burst from the machine gun dropped the ant.

But little Jean Querard was staggering forward, with blood spurting from his breast. Knees trembling, he held himself upright for a moment, propped his rifle so that a charging ant impaled itself on the bayonet. Loud and clear his voice rang out: *"Allons!* Jonbar!"

He slipped down quietly to lie beside the dying insect.

Lanning checked one of the ants with three quick shots to its head, ripped open its armored thorax with a lunge that flung it back, helpless. Schorn stopped another. But the third caught the barrel of Halloran's gun a ringing blow with its axe, leapt on top of him, and clawed its way past.

Lanning snapped another charge of ammunition into his Mauser, and fired after it. But it dropped forward and scuttled out of sight, at a six-limbed, atavistic run.

Barry Halloran staggered back to his feet, his shirt torn off and blood dripping from a long red mark across his breast and shoulder, where a mandible had raked him.

"Sorry, Denny!" he gasped. "I tried to hold the line!"

"That's all right, guy," panted Lanning, running back to open the door again for Pharr and Enders with their guns.

But already, somewhere ahead, a great alarm gong was throbbing out a deep and brazen-throated warning that moaned and sighed and shuddered through all the long halls of Sorainya's citadel.

## XI.

THE FIVE survivors of the raiding party, Pharr and Enders, Halloran and Schorn and Lanning, running with their burden of weapons, came up a long winding flight of steps, and through a small door, into the end of Sorainya's ceremonial hall, where the warning gong was booming,

It was the largest room that Lanning had ever seen. Great square pillars of black soared up against the red metal walls, and between them stood colossal statues in yellow gold—no doubt Sorainya's warlike ancestors, for all were armed and armored.

The reflected light, poured down from the lofty crimson vault, had a redness that gave the air almost the quality of blood. Most of the floor was bare. Far toward the other end stood a tall pillar of shimmering splendor—the diamond throne that once Sorainya had offered Lanning. As treacherously, perhaps, as she had also offered it to Wil McLan.

From a chain, beside the throne, hung the alarm gong—a forty-foot disk of scarlet metal. Tiny in that great hall, two of the warrior ants were furiously beating its moaning curve. And a little army of them—thirty, Lanning estimated—came rushing, down the hall.

"Quick!" he rapped. "The Maxim!"

He helped set up the hot machine gun, gasping to Schorn, "We've got to get through—and back! The door to Sorainya's own apartments is behind the throne. The strong room is reached through a trap door, beside her bed—quick! The bombs!"

"Devils!" Isaac Enders' lean face was a hard, bitter mask as he started an ammunition belt into the Maxim, dropped down behind it. "They won't forget you, Israel!"

The gun jetted flame, sweeping the line of ants, Beside him, Pharr and Barry Halloran blazed away with rifles. Lanning and Schorn dumped hampers of hand grenades on the floor, and stooped over them, snapping out the safety pins and hurling them into the rank of ants.

The ants fired a volley, as they came. The thick, crimson guns were single-shot weapons, of heavy calibre but limited range. Most of the bullets went wide, spattering on the metal wall. But one struck Enders, drilling a great black hole in his forehead.

He lurched upright, behind the Maxim. His long, gaunt arms spread wide. A curious expression of shocked, incredulous eagerness lit his stern face for an instant, until it was drowned in a gush of blood. His voice pealed out, in a joyous ringing shout—"Israel!"

He slid forward, and lay shuddering across the gun.

Courtney-Pharr tossed his body away, and resumed the fire.

It took the ants a long while to come down the hall. Or time, measured only by the sequence of events, seemed curiously extended. Lanning had space to snatch a breath of this clean air, so refreshing after the stench of the prison. He wondered how, without key or combination, they could break open the strong room—if they won to its door. And how soon, after this alarm, Sorainya herself might return from the temple, with more of her *kothrin*, to block the retreat.

A FEW of the ants, riddled with lead from rifles and Maxim, had time to slump and fall. A few more, running heedless over the tossed grenades, were hurled mangled into the air. But most of them came on, converging toward the door, clubbing crimson guns, spinning yellow battle-axes.

The four men waited in a line across the doorway, the Maxim beating its deadly roll. Schorn flung his last grenade when the black rank was a dozen yards away and snatched his bayonet to meet the charge. Saving two of his bombs, Lanning leveled his rifle to guard the machine gun, sent bullets probing to seek some vital organ.

Three of the foremost monsters slumped and fell. But the rest flowed over them in a tide of death. Diabolic monsters, fantastic in black, great eyes glittering redly evil in the bloody light, golden axes singing.

Lanning's Mauser snapped, empty. He lunged, with the bayonet, ripped open one armored thorax. But the golden blade of another monster rang against the rifle, tore it from his numbed fingers. The club of a scarlet gun, at the same instant, struck his shoulder with a sledge of paralyzing agony, hurled him backward against the metal wall.

One arm was tingling, nerveless. He groped with his left hand for the Luger at his belt, surged to his knees. sent lead tearing upward through armored, acid-reeking bodies.

Savage mandibles seized and tore away the rifle of Emil

Schorn, and the bull-like Prussian went down beneath the rush of two giant ants. They leapt on top of the drumming Maxim. Great black jaws seized the bare, blond head of Courtney-Pharr.

The gun abruptly ceased to fire, and in the breathless scrap of silence the crushing of his skull made an odd, sickening little sound.

"Fight 'em!" Barry Halloran was singing out. "Fight 'em!"

Furiously, with his bayonet, the big red-headed tackle fell upon the two monsters sprawled over the silent machine gun and the Briton's decapitated body.

The Luger was empty again. Lanning dropped it, groped for his rifle on the floor, and surged up to meet the second rank of ants. If he could hold them for a moment, give Barry a chance to recover the Maxim—

The weird, mute giants pressed down on him. But his arm had come to life again. And he had learned a deadly technique: a lunge that ripped the black thorax upward, then a deep, twisting thrust, to right and left, that tore vital organs.

Yellow axes were hissing at him. But jet-armored monsters were piled before the doorway, now, in a sort of barricade. And the floor was slippery with reeking life-fluids. so that strange claws slid and scratched for balance. Lanning evaded the blows—lunged, and lunged again.

Behind him, Barry had finished one monster with the bayonet. But his blade snapped off in the armor of the other. He snatched out his Luger, pumped lead into the black body. But it sprang upon him, clubbed him down with the flat of a golden axe, sprawled inert on top of his body.

Alone against the ants, Lanning thrust and ripped and parried. He laid one monster on top of the barricade, and another, and a third. Then his own foot slipped in the slime. Great mandibles gripped the wavering bayonet, twisted and snapped it off.

He tried to club the gun. But black claws ripped it from his hands. Three great ants leapt upon him, bore him down. His own gun crashed against his head. He slipped to the floor, beneath the ants. sobbing. "Lethonee! I tried—"

The *kothrin* were clambering over the barrier of dead. Heedless claws scratched him. He fought for strength to rise, fight again. But his numbed body would not respond. Jonbar still was doomed. And, for him, would it be Sorainya's dungeons?

THE LOUD TATTOO of the Maxim was a wholly incredible sound. Lanning in his daze thought at first it must be a dream. But the reeking body of a great ant slipped down across him. He twisted his head with a savage effort and saw Emil Schorn.

The big Prussian had once gone down, beneath the ants. His bull-like body was nearly naked, shredded, red with dripping blood. But he was on his feet again, swaying, his blue eyes flaming with a terrible light.

*"Heil,* Jonbar!" he was roaring. *"Ach,* Thor! *Der tag* of Valhalla!"

He started the last belt into the Maxim, and came forward again, holding it in his arms, firing it like a rifle—a terrific feat, even for such a giant as he.

The remaining ants came leaping at him, and he met them with a hail of death. One by one, they slumped and fell. A great, golden axe was hurled across the barricade. Its blade cut deep into his naked breast, and fell. And a flood of foaming red rushed out.

But still the German stood upright, leaning against the shattering recoil of the gun, sweeping it back and forth. At last it was empty, and he dropped it from seared hands. Wide and fixed, his blue eyes watched the last ant stagger and fall.

"Jonbar!" his deep voice rumbled. *"Uber alles! Ja—"*

Like a red and massive pillar falling, he toppled down beside the red-hot Maxim. For a little space there was a strange hushed silence in the Cyclopean crimson hall of Sorainya's citadel, disturbed only by the faint sorrowful reverberation that still throbbed from the mighty gong. And the golden colossi, in their panoplies of war, looked grimly down upon the peace that follows death.

A little life, however, was coming back into Lanning's battered body. He twisted, and began to push at the great ant that had fallen across his legs. A sudden throbbing eagerness lent him strength. For Schorn had opened the way to the strong room. There might still be time, before the alarm blocked escape—

But Barry Halloran was the first on his feet. Lanning had supposed him dead beneath the ant that brought him down. But he heard an incoherent, muffled shout—"Fight 'em! Fight! Hold that line!" It changed. "Eh! Where—? Denny! Oh, Denny, can you hear me?"

The big tackle came stalking toward him, through the dead,

his naked torso crimson almost as Schorn's. He dragged the dead ant from Lanning's legs, and Lanning sat up, clenching his teeth against the pain in his head. A flood of dizzy blackness came over him, and the next he knew Halloran was pressing Courtney-Pharr's silver flask to his lips. He gulped the searing brandy.

"Make it, Denny?"

Lanning stood up, reeling. A great anvil of agony rang at the back of his head. His vision blurred. The long red hall spun and tilted, and the golden colossi were marching down it, to defend Sorainya's diamond throne.

"Le's go," his voice came fuzzy and thick. "Mus' get that thing. Get back to the ship. Before Sorainya comes! First, the two grenades—key to the strong room."

BARRY HALLORAN found the two bombs he had saved, and then started to pick up the hot weight of the Maxim. But Lanning told him that the ammunition was gone. He snatched up a rifle, and seized Lanning's arm. They started, at a weary, stumbling run, down the colossal red-lit hall.

Lanning staggered, at first, and only Barry's grasp kept him from falling. But his vision cleared slowly, and the pain began to ebb from his head.

It was an interminable way, past the frowning yellow giants and the soaring pillars of black, down to the lofty diamond splendor of Sorainya's throne. But they ran at last beneath the undying sigh of the mighty gong, and passed the throne.

Beyond was a great arched doorway, curtained with black. They pushed through the heavy drapes, and came into the queen's private chambers. Lanning did not pause to catalog the splendor of that vista of vast connecting rooms. But he saw the shimmer of immense crystal mirrors; the gleam of delicate statuary, ivory and gold; the glitter of immense jeweled caskets; the silken luxury of great couches and divans.

Sorainya's bed, hewn from a colossal block of sapphire crystal, and canopied with jewel-sewn silk, shone like a second throne at the end of that vista of barbaric magnificence. Lanning and Halloran ran panting toward it, trailing drops of blood across shimmering inlaid floors.

Lanning ripped back a wide, deep-piled rug beside the bed. In the floor he found the fine dark line that marked the edge of a well-fitted door, and, in the center of that, a smaller square.

Barry Halloran used his bayonet to pry out the central block, while Lanning unscrewed the detonator cylinders from the two bombs. Beneath the block was revealed a long keyhole. Lanning poured the two ounces of high explosive from each grenade into the little square depression, let it run down into the lock. He thrust one detonator into the keyhole, with the safety fuse projecting. Barry came dragging a great jeweled coffer of red metal from the foot of the bed, reckless of the scarred floor, pushed it over the lock to hold in the force of the charge. Lanning took the rifle, put a bullet into the percussion cap. They stepped quickly behind the bed.

The floor quivered to the shattering blast. Glittering fragments of the burst coffer rocketed to the lofty ceiling. Jewels, exquisite toilet articles and shattered jars of cosmetic, scraps of silk and fur fell in a rain of splendor.

They ran back around the sapphire bed. A blackened hole yawned in the floor. A tough sheet of red metal had burst jaggedly upward. Lanning reached his arm through to manipulate hot bolts and tumblers.

The square section of the floor dropped suddenly, elevatorlike. Halloran, after a startled instant, stepped upon it with Lanning. And they were lowered swiftly into the strong room.

IT WAS A vast space, square and windowless. The concealed lights which sprang on, as they descended. burned on hoarded treasure. Great shimmering stacks of silver and gold ingots, mysterious piled coffers, great slabs of unworked synthetic crystal, sapphire, emerald, ruby, and diamond. Statuary, paintings, strange mechanisms and instruments, tapestries, books and manuscript—all the precious relics of the past. And, most curious of all, a long row of tall crystal blocks, in which, like flies in amber, were embedded oddly lifelike human forms—the armored originals of the golden colossi above. This was not only the treasury but the mausoleum of Sorainya's dynasty.

"Ye gods!" murmured Barry Halloran, blinking, forgetful of his wounds. "The old girl is one collector! This junk is worth—worth more money than there is! King Midas would turn green!"

Lanning's jaw went white.

"I saw her once—collecting!" he muttered bitterly. "She slaughtered a whole village, because the people couldn't pay their taxes—when she had all this!"

The dropping platform touched the floor.

"We're looking for a little black brick," Lanning said swiftly. "They covered the thing with a black cement, to hide it from the *chronoscope.*" Shuddering to a little helpless, trapped feeling, he looked back up at the square door. "And hurry! We've been a long time, and that gong would wake the dead. Sorainya'll be here, soon."

"Sure thing!" muttered Halloran. "It's a long way back, through that prison and down the cliff to the ship."

They began a frantic search for the small black brick, breaking open coffers of jewels, and shaking out chests of silks and furs. It was Barry Halloran who found the little ebon rectangle, tossed carelessly into the litter of a cracked pottery jar that had seemed to serve as a waste basket.

"That's it!" Lanning gasped. "Let's get out!"

They leapt back upon the platform. Lanning tapped a button on the floor beside it, and it lifted silently. His red hands trembling with a wondering awe, Halloran handed the heavy little brick to Lanning.

"What could it be?" he whispered. "So small and yet so important!"

Lanning looked down at the glazed black surface that hid the object stolen from the past: the object whose position meant life or death to Gyronchi and Jonbar. He shook his battered head.

"I don't know—but listen!"

For their heads had risen again into the queen's bedchamber, and he heard far-off a monstrous brazen clang like the closing valves of a metal gate, the far tinkle of weapons, and the clear, tiny peal of a woman's anger-heightened voice. His strength went out, and cold dread ached in every bone.

"Sorainya!" he sobbed. "She's coming back!"

They scrambled up to the floor, without waiting for the rising platform to come level, and ran desperately through the empty litter of the vast apartments of the queen, back the way they had come.

They passed the black hangings. Once more they came into the lofty, red-lit immensity of the ceremonial hall, where the golden colossi still towered, frowning, between the columns of black. Again they ran beneath the whispering gong, beside the high diamond throne. And there, under the moaning disk, they halted in cold despair.

For a black horde of the *kothrin,* gigantic four-armed figures tiny in the distance, were pouring into the hall. Running gracefully ahead to lead them, flashing in her red-mailed splendor, came the warrior queen.

Lanning turned to look at Barry's crimson, stricken face, and read the desperate question there. Wearily, he shook his head.

"She's cut us off!" he groaned. "There's no way out—"

## XII.

BUT ONE WEAPON now remained to the two men standing alone beside the diamond throne before Sorainya and her charging horde of giant ants: Barry Halloran's blood-stained Mauser.

"Quick!" urged Lanning. His red fingers closed hard on the precious black brick that was the very cornerstone of menaced Jonbar. "Fire! There's time enough to get—her!"

Yet, as soon as Barry raised the rifle, he was sorry he had spoken. For the queen of Gyronchi, in her black-plumed panoply, was too splendid to be slain. All the mocking, glorious beauty of Sorainya returned, as when she had come to him on the golden shell. Demon-queen! He bit his lip, and fought down a frantic impulse to snatch Barry's level rifle.

The gun crashed, and Lanning waited, with a stricken heart, to see Sorainya fall. But it was one of the great ants that stumbled and clutched with four queer limbs at its armor shell.

"I had it on her," muttered Halloran. "But they'd get us just the same. And she's a woman. Sort of—beautiful!"

Lanning reeled, and the anvil of agony rang louder in his brain. His taut fingers grasped the brick, and his dulled mind groped foggily for any possible way back to the ship, however desperate. But there was none.

And the voiceless question of Wil McLan was rasping in his ears: "Could any man kill Sorainya?"

But there was something— His dazed brain spun. Sorainya must be destroyed, so Wil McLan had said. And Lethonee had told him, long ago, that he must choose one of the twain, and so doom the other. His heart came up in his throat, and he reached out a trembling hand.

"Give me—"

But the rifle had snapped, empty. Halloran flung it down.

folded his crimsoned arms, stood waiting grimly. Lanning bent to pick up the gun, gasping: "Mustn't give up, alive! That prison of horror—"

But Sorainya had paused, leveled the yellow needle of her sword. A hot blue spark hissed to the rifle. Lanning's hand jerked away from the half-fused weapon, seared, nerveless. Too late. She had them—

The golden bugle of her voice pealed down the hall, triumphant: "Well, Denny Lanning! So you prefer Gyronchi? And the dungeon, to my throne here—"

Lanning blinked. Sorainya and her charging horde were already halfway down the hall. Beneath her crested helmet he could see that clear-cut face still white with vengeful anger; those long, green eyes cold as ice and cruel with a pitiless mockery. But something was coming between—a shadow, a thickening silver veil.

The shadow grew abruptly real. Breathless, Lanning rubbed at his eyes, shuddering to the shock of incredulous hope. For it was the *Chronion!*

The green glow fading slowly from her polar disks, the time ship's silver hull dropped to the floor before the throne. The small figure of Lao Meng Shan, on the foredeck, turned the Maxim mounted there toward Sorainya and the *kothrin*—and then fell desperately to taking the gun apart, for it was jammed.

The thin, twisted figure of Wil McLan, under his crystal dome, was beckoning urgently. After that first stunned instant, Lanning caught at Barry's arm, and they ran frantically to climb aboard.

SORAINYA screamed a wild battle cry. With a flashing sweep of her golden sword, she led the great ants on at an unchecked run. A scattering volley from their heavy guns peppered the *Chronion.*

The turret revolved beneath the dome, and the yellow ray flamed upon Lanning and Halloran from the crystal gun, to pull them into the field of the ship.

Lanning had glimpsed the blind, bewildered figure of the navy airman, Willie Rand, stark and alone on the deck. But, when he and Halloran tumbled breathless over the rail, finding Shan still busy with the useless Maxim, Rand was gone.

"Look, Denny!" Barry Halloran was hoarse with an awed admiration. "The damn blind fool!'

He pointed toward Sorainya's horde, and Lanning saw Willie Rand, going to meet them. Bandaged head bent low, he moved at a blind, stumbling, run. The broken Mauser was level in his hands, the whetted bayonet gleaming.

The giant ants paused before that solitary charge as if bewildered. Sorainya's fierce shout urged them on. Their guns rattled, and the sailor's body jerked to the smacking impacts of the bullets. But he ran on.

Lanning staggered to the deck speaking tube, gasping: "Wil, can we help him?"

Wil McLan, under the dome, shook his white head.

"No," the whisper came. "But it's what he wanted. Useless— but terrible. Grand!"

Even Sorainya halted. Her golden needle leveled and spat blue fire. Willie Rand lurched, and his clothing began to smoke. But he staggered on, to meet the yellow axes lifted.

Lanning had dropped on his knees, to help the Chinese with the jammed gun. But he saw Rand come to the rank of ants. He saw the flashing bayonet, as if guided by an extra-sensory vision, drive deep into a black thorax.

Then the golden axes fell—

But Wil McLan, on his bridge, had spun his shining wheel, closed a key. And the *Chronion* was gone from Sorainya's hall, back into the blue, shimmering gulf of her own timeless track.

Lanning reeled through the turret, where Duffy Clark was on duty behind the crystal gun, and up to join Wil McLan below the dome. The old man seized his arm, eagerly.

"Well, Denny! You got it?"

"Yes." And Lanning demanded: "But how'd you come to meet us in the hall? That's all that saved us! And where's Barinin?"

"There was an alarm," husked the voiceless man. "They discovered us on the ledge, and turned down one of the *gyrane* rays from the battlements. Barinin was caught at the gun. Crisped black—"

He shuddered.

"We had to take off; and I drove down into the future, to avoid meeting their time ship. I hadn't wanted to enter the fortress with the ship—when we couldn't explore it with the *chronoscope*. There was too much danger of collision with some solid object— with very disastrous results.

"But that was the only course possible. We had to take the

risk—and we won." He sighed wearily, mopped sweat from his scar-seamed face. "That hall was the largest room. From my plans, and a study of the ruins in futurity, I approximated its position. And we came back to where I guessed it had been. That's all. But where is—it?"

LANNING handed him the glazed, black brick from Sorainya's strong room. His hollow, blue eyes lit with an eager gleam.

"What could it be?"

"Let's open it up," the old man rasped, "and find out!" The brick trembled in his hands. "We've got to discover where Glarath and Sorainya took it from—in Time and Space—and put it back there. If we can."

Lanning lifted his eyes from the black fascination of the little block that was the foundation of all Jonbar. Anxiously, he caught at McLan's twisted arm.

"Do you think—" he gasped. "Will they follow"

McLan's hollow eyes dulled. "Of course they'll follow," he whispered. "It means life and death to Gyronchi, as well as to Jonbar. And they have the time ship—if only one. If they fail to overtake us on the way, they will surely be waiting where the object must be placed. They know the spot."

He repressed a little sigh of grim foreboding.

"And now we are only five."

But the white head came erect, and the haggard eyes flashed again, with a bleak bitterness of hate.

"But you saw Sorainya's dungeons," he rasped. "Now you know why Gyronchi must be destroyed." He handed the brick to Lanning. "See if you can break it open."

"I know," Lanning was whispering grimly. "For I've seen Jonbar, and—Lethonee."

The block was glass-hard. He tapped at it vainly, broke his pocket knife on it. then carried it down to the deck. It yielded at last to hack saw, chisel, and sledge. It proved to be a thick-walled box, packed with white fiber.

Breathless, with quivering fingers, Lanning drew out the packing, and uncovered—a thick, V-shaped piece of rusty iron.

His vague, wild expectations had been all of something spectacular. Perhaps some impressive document of State upon which history should have turned. Or the martyr's weapon that might have slain some enemy of progress. And disappointment drove a leaden pain through his heart. With heavy feet, he carried it back to Wil McLan.

"Just a piece of scrap iron," he said wearily. "Just an old magnet, out of the magneto of a Model T. And we spent all those lives to find it!"

"That doesn't matter, what it is," the old mail whispered. "It was important enough, when Gyronchi wrenched it out of the past, to deflect the whole direction of probability—to destroy even the possibility of Jonbar.

"Now, with the *chronoscope*, I must try to find its place. And then we must put it back—if Sorainya will let us!" He looked suddenly up at Lanning. "But you're tired, Denny. And you've been hurt."

Lanning had hardly been conscious of fatigue. Even the ring and throb of pain in the back of his brain had become a tolerable thing, a vague and distant phenomenon that did not greatly matter. And he felt a great surprise, now, when the dome went black and he knew that he was falling on the floor.

## XIII.

LANNING woke with his head bandaged, lying in the little green-walled hospital. Barry Halloran grinned at him from the opposite bed. The little cockney, Duffy Clark, came presently with a covered tray.

"Cap'n McLan?" he drawled. "Why 'e's on 'is bridge, sor, with hall 'is bloomin' gadgets. 'E's tryin' to find where that bloody she-devil and 'er blarsted ants got 'old of that magnet."

"Any luck?" demanded Lanning.

He shook a tousled head.

"Don't look it, sor. Wot with hall Spayce and Time to search for the spot. And the woman and the blarsted priest is arfter us, sor, in a black ship full of the bloomin' hants! We've seen it— twice, sor. A blinkin' 'ell-ship!"

"But we can outrun them!" broke in Barry Halloran. "The *Chronion* can give 'em all they want."

"Ayn't easy, sor!" Clark shook his head. "Cap'n McLan's running the fields at full potential, with the bloomin' converters overloaded. And still they're 'olding us, neck and neck. Lor, the bloody swine!"

An overwhelming lethargy was still in Lanning. He ate, and slept again. And many hours of the ship's time must have passed when he suddenly awoke, aware of another sound above the accelerated throb of the atomic converters—the hammering of the Maxim!

He tumbled out of bed, with Barry Halloran after him, and ran to the deck. The firing had stopped, however, when they reached it. The *Chronion* was once more thrumming alone through the flickering blue abyss.

But little Duffy Clark lay beside the Maxim, smoking and still, his body half consumed by the *gyrane* ray.

Shuddering, Lanning climbed up into the dome.

"They caught us," sobbed voiceless Wil McLan. "They'll catch us again. The converters are overdriven. As the grids are consumed, they lose efficiency. They got poor Clark. That leaves four."

The question burning in his eyes, Lanning whispered: "Did you find—anything?"

Solemnly, the old man nodded, and Lanning listened breathlessly.

"The time is an afternoon in August of the year 1921," whispered Wil McLan. "The broken geodesics of Jonbar had already given us a clue to that. And I have found the place, with the *chronoscope.*"

Lanning gripped his arm. "Where?"

"It's a little valley in the Ozarks of Arkansas. But I'll show you the decisive scene."

The little man limped to the metal cabinet of the geodesic analyzer, and his broken fingers carefully set its dials. A greenish luminescence filled the crystal block, and cleared. Lanning bent forward eagerly, to peer into that pellucid window of probability.

An impoverished farm lay before his eyes, folded in the low and ancient hills. A sagging shack of gray, paintless pine, a broken window gaping black and the roof inadequately patched with rusty tin, leaned crazily beside an eroded rocky field. The sloping cow pasture, above, was scantily covered with brush and gnarled little trees.

A SMALL, freckled boy, in faded overalls and a big ragged straw hat, was trudging slowly barefoot down the slope, accompanied by a gaunt, yellow dog, driving two lean red-spotted cows home to the milking pen.

"Watch him," whispered Wil McLan.

And Lanning followed the path of of the boy. He stopped to encourage the dog digging furiously after a rabbit. He squatted to watch the activities of a colony of ants. He ran to catch a gaudy butterfly, and carefully dissected it. He rose unwillingly to answer the halloo of a slatternly woman from the house below, and followed the cows.

Wil McLan's gnarled fingers closed on Lanning's arm, urgently. "Now!"

Idly whittling with a battered knife, the boy spied something beside a sumac bush, and stooped to pick it up. The object blurred oddly in the crystal screen, so that Lanning could not distinguish it. And vision faded, as Wil McLan snapped off the mechanism.

"Well," demanded Lanning, bewildered. "What has that to do with Jonbar?"

"That is John Barr." rasped the voiceless man. "For that metropolis of future possibility is—or might be—named in honor of the boy, barefoot son of a tenant farmer. He is twelve years old in 1921. You saw him at the turning point of his life—and the life of the world."

"But I don't understand!"

"The bifurcation of possibility is in the thing he stoops to pick up," whispered Wil McLan. "It is either the magnet that we recovered from Sorainya's citadel—or an oddly colored pebble which lies beside it.

"And that choice—which Sorainya sought to decide by removing the magnet—determines which of two possible John Barrs is ultimately fixed in the real universe by fifth-dimensional progression."

"But how?" said Lanning. "From such a small thing!"

"If he picks up the discarded magnet, he will discover the mysterious attraction it has for the blade of his knife, and the mysterious north-seeking power of its poles. He will wonder, experiment, theorize. Curiosity will deepen. The scientist will be born in him.

"He will study, borrow books on science from the teacher of the one-room school in the hollow. He will presently leave the farm, run away from a domineering father who sneers at 'book larnin',' to work his way through college. And then he will become a teacher of science in country schools, an amateur experimenter.

"Sometimes the flame will burn low in him, inspiration be forgotten in the drudgery of life. He will marry, raise two children, absorbed for years in the cares of family life. But the old thirst to know will never die. The march of science will rekindle the flame. Finally, at the age of fifty-five, he will run away again—this time from a domineering wife and an obnoxious son-in-law—to carry on his research.

"A bald, plump little man, mild-mannered, dreamy, impractical, he will work for years alone in a little cottage in the Ozarks. Every possible cent will go for the makeshift apparatus powered from a crude homemade hydro-electric plant. He will go often hungry. Once, a kindly neighbor will find him starving, nearly dead of influenza.

"BUT AT LAST, in 1980, a tired but triumphant little man of seventy-one, he will publish his great discovery. The dynatomic tensors—shortened to *dynat*. A radically new principle in physics, making possible the release of atomic energy under control of the human will.

"Given freely to the world, the *dynat* will soon solve many problems of power, communication, and food—although John Barr, not waiting for material success, that same year will be quietly buried by his neighbors beside a little church in the Ozarks. And presently the illimitable power of the *dynat* will be the lifeblood of the splendid new metropolis of Jonbar, christened after him.

"Nor is that all. Ennobled humanity will soar on the wings of this most magnificent slave. For the *dynat* will bring a new contact of mind and matter, new senses, new capabilities. Gradually, as time goes on, mankind will become adapted to the full use of the *dynat*."

The whisper was hoarse with a breathless awe.

"And at last a new race will arise, calling themselves the *dynon*. The splendid children of John Barr's old discovery, they will possess faculties and powers that we can hardly dream of—"

"Wait!" cried Lanning. "I've seen the *dynon!* When Lethonee first came, so long ago, to my room in Cambridge, she showed me New Jonbar, in the jewel of the *chronotron*. A city of majestic, shining pylons. And, flying above them, a glorious people, robed, it seemed, in pure fire!"

Hollow eyes shining, Wil McLan nodded solemnly.

"I, too, have looked into New Jonbar," he whispered. "I have seen the promised glory beyond—the triumphant flight of the *dynon,* from star to star, forever! In that direction, there was no ending to the story of mankind.

"But in the other—"

His white head shook. There was silence under the dome. Lanning could hear the swiftened throb of the converters, driving them back through the blue shimmer of possibility toward the quiet scene in the Ozarks they had watched in the crystal block. He saw Lao Meng Shan cleaning the Maxim on the deck below. Barry Halloran, rifle ready, was peering alertly into the flickering abyss. Duffy Clark was already consigned to the gulf of Time.

"If we fail to replace the magnet," the grave whisper at last resumed, "so that the boy John Barr picks up the pebble instead, the tide of probability will be turned—as, indeed, it is turned—toward Gyronchi.

"The boy will toss the pebble in his hand, then throw it in his sling to kill a singing bird. And all his life will want a precious spark. It will remain curiously similar, yet significantly different.

"JOHN BARR, in this outcome also, will run away from his father's home, but now to become a shiftless migratory worker. He will marry the same woman, raise the same two children, and leave them in the same way. The same mechanical ingenuity, that might have discovered the *dynat,* will lead to the invention of a new gambling device, on which he will make and lose a fortune. He will die—equally penniless—in the same year, and be buried in the same graveyard in the Ozarks.

"The secret of atomic power will now be discovered nine years later, but with a control far less complete than that attained through the perfection of the *dynat.* The discoverer will be one Ivor Gyros, an exiled Russian-Greek, working with a renegade Buddhist priest in an abandoned monastery in Burma. Calling the secret the *gyrane,* the two will guard it selfishly, use it to destroy their enemies and impress the superstitious. They will found a new fanatical religion that will sweep the world, and a new despotic empire."

The whisper paused again, gravely.

"That is the way of the cult of the *gyrane,* and of Sorainya's dark dynasty," rasped Wil McLan, at last. "A way of evil! You have seen the end of it."

"I have!"

A little shudder touched Lanning, at memory of that desolate scene in the crystal block: mankind annihilated in the final war of the priests and the kings, by the *gyrane* and the monstrous mutations it had bred. The jungle returning across a devastated planet, to cover the rusting pile of Sorainya's citadel and the shattered ruins of the vast, black temple.

Quivering, then, his hands grasped at the rusty V of the magnet. lying beside the controls of the *chronoscope.*

"And so— And so all we have to do is to put it back, where the boy John Barr will pick it up?"

"All," nodded Wil McLan. "If we can!"

Lanning started, then, and shivered to the rattle of the Maxim. His scarred face stiff with startled dread, Wil McLan was pointing. Lanning turned. Close beyond the dome, he saw the square, black mass of the time ship from Gyronchi.

"Mankind!" cried McLan. "The converters—failing!"

He flung his broken body toward the controls.

But already, Lanning saw, the decks had touched. In the face of the hammering Maxim, a horde of the gigantic ants, monstrous spawn of atomic radiation, was pouring over the rail. Leading them with the flame of her golden sword, magnificent in her crimson panoply, came Sorainya!

## XIV.

"SORAINYA!" Lanning gasped. "She's aboard!"

"Sorainya!" It was a stricken, husking echo from old Wil McLan. His broken hands came up, automatically, to the odd little tube of bright-worn silver that Lanning had wondered about so often, hanging at his throat. That ancient, smouldering hate glazed his sunken eyes again. Yet a strange agony racked his whisper. "Sorainya—must she die?"

"The ants!" warned Lanning. "Pouring aboard! Can we get away?"

Wil McLan started, and his hands fell to the controls again.

"Can try!" he rasped. "But that converter—"

A score of the great ants were rushing the Maxim on the foredeck. Lao Meng Shan was crouched behind the rattling machine gun. And Barry Halloran stood beside it, a sturdy, smiling giant of battle, waiting with his bayonet for the ants.

"Fight 'em," his great voice was booming out cheerfully. "Fight 'em!"

Grinning blandly, the little Chinese made no sound at all.

With a ringing war cry, Sorainya had turned toward the turret. followed by a dozen ants. The needle of her golden sword flashed up, pointing at Wil McLan in the dome. And her green-eyed face was suddenly terrible with such a blazing passion of hate that Lanning shuddered from its fury.

"She's coming here!" sobbed the dry, hoarse whisper of Wil McLan. "After me!" Terror flared red beside the ancient hatred and the puzzling agony in his eyes. "Ever since I refused to aid her conquest—"

Lanning was already running down the turret stair.

"I'll try to stop her!"

And the whisper rasped after him: "And I'll pull away—if the converters will stand it."

In the little turret, beside the crystal helix-gun that projected the temporal field, Lanning belted on a Luger. He snatched the last Mauser from the rack, loaded it. His eye caught one hand grenade left in the box. He scooped it up, gripped the safety pin.

The little door was groaning and ringing to a furious assault from without—for the *Chronion* had not been designed for a fighting ship. It yielded suddenly, and a great black ant pitched through.

Lanning tossed the last grenade through the doorway, and ripped at the ant with his bayonet. He reeled to the burning stench of formic acid. A savage mandible ripped trousers and skin from his leg. But the third thrust stilled the monster, and he leapt into the doorway.

Outside, the grenade had cleared a little space. Three of the monsters lay where it had tossed them, crushed and dying. But the warrior queen stood unharmed in the crimson mail, with eight more ants about her. A savage light of battle flamed in her long green eyes, and she flung the ants forward with her golden sword.

"Denny Lanning," her voice cut cold as steel. "You were warned. You defied Gyronchi, and chose *her* of Jonbar. So—die!"

Yet Lanning, waiting grim and silent in the turret's doorway, had a moment's respite. He had time for a glimpse of Barry and Shan, now engaged in a furious battle about the Maxim, holding back a murderous avalanche of ants. He caught Barry's gasping, "Fight! Fight! Fight 'em, team!"

HE SAW BRIEFLY the high, black side of the other ship, beyond. He glimpsed the gaunt, cadaverous, black-robed priest, Glarath, safe on his quarter-deck. He saw a second company of ants, aglitter with gold and crimson weapons, gathered by the rail, ready to leap after the first.

Panic gripped his heart. It was an overwhelming horde—

But suddenly the black ship was gone, with Glarath and the rank of ants. There was only the flicker of the blue abyss. The throb of the over-driven converters was heavier beneath the deck. Wil McLan had driven the *Chronion* ahead once more in the race toward the past.

But Sorainya and her boarding party remained upon the deck. The Maxim suddenly ceased to fire. Shan and Barry were surrounded. Then the eight attacking ants converged upon Lanning in the doorway, urged on by Sorainya's pealing shouts, and he had attention for nothing beyond them.

The bayonet had proved more effective than bullets against the great ants. And now, defending the doorway, Lanning fought with the same deadly technique he had mastered in Sorainya's citadel.

A ripping lunge, a twist, a savage thrust. One ant fell. Another. A third. Fallen black bodies made an acrid reek. Spilled vital fluids were slippery on the deck.

The bullet from a crimson gun raked Lanning's side. A golden axe touched his head with searing pain, where a tenderness remained from the other battle. A heavy gun, flung spinning like a club, knocked out his breath, sent him staggering back for a dangerous instant. But he recovered himself, lunged again.

Sorainya ran back and forth behind the ants, shrilling her battle cry. A cruel, smiling elation lit her beauteous face, and her narrowed green eyes were cold and bright with the lust of blood.

Once, when the ants fell back and gave her an opening, she leveled the needle of her sword at Lanning. Knowing the deadly fire it held, he ducked, and whipped a shot at her red-mailed body with the Luger.

His bullet whined harmless from her armor. And blue flame jetted past his shoulder. A jolting shock hurled him aside against the wall. Half blind, dazed, he slapped at his burning shirt, and reeled back to meet the remaining ants.

Four were left. His staggering lunge caught one. And another fell, queerly, when he had not touched it. And a hearty voice came roaring to his ears, "Fight, gang! Fight!"

And he saw that the battle on the foredeck was ended. A great pile of the dead, black ants lay about the Maxim. Lao Meng Shan was looking over the barricade, with a curiously cheerful grin fading from his still, yellow face.

And Barry Halloran, crimson and terrible with the marks of battle, came chanting down the deck. It was a burst from his Luger that had dropped the monster beside Lanning. He flung the empty pistol aside, and leveled his dripping bayonet.

Lanning was swaying, gasping for breath, fighting a descending blindness as he fought the two remaining ants. He feinted, lunged, recovered, parried, still defending the turret door.

But he saw Sorainya turn to meet Barry Halloran, and heard her low, mocking laugh. He saw the rifle shift in Barry's crimson hands, ready for the lunge that might pierce the queen's woven mail.

"Fight—"

BARRY'S chanting stopped on a low, breathless cry, astonished. The grim smile of battle was driven from his face by a sudden, involuntary admiration.

"My God, I can't—"

The bayonet wavered in his slackening grasp. And the queen of war, with a brilliant smile and a mocking flirt of her sable plume, darted quickly forward. The golden needle flickered out in a lightning thrust, drove his body through and through.

Lanning's reeling lunge caught one of the attacking ants. He ripped, twisted, recovered. He staggered back from a flashing yellow blade, lurched forward again to engage the survivor.

But his eyes went, again and again, to that other tableau, so that he saw it as a continuous picture. He saw the practiced twist that withdrew Sorainya's blade. He saw her draw it through her naked hand, and then blow Barry a malicious kiss, from fingers red with his own lifeblood.

A dark fountain burst and foamed from Barry Halloran's heart.

The admiration on his face gave way to a hard, grim hate. His hands tried to lift the rifle, but it slipped away from them and fell. And his stained face became terrible with a bewildered, helpless bafflement.

"Denny—" It was a soft, bubbling sob. *"Kill—"*

And he slipped down, beyond Sorainya.

Lanning brought his staggered mind back to the one remaining ant. It was too late to avoid the descending golden axe. But his weary muscles had time to complete the lunge. A little deflected, the flat of the blade crashed against his head, drowned him in a black flood of pain.

Automatically, the run-down machine of his body finished that familiar rhythm—rip, twist, slash. And then, slowly, it toppled down beside the dying ant.

Still, for an instant, some atom of awareness lingered. *Don't quit now!* it shrieked. *Or Sorainya will kill Wil McLan. She will take the magnet back. And Jonbar will be lost.*

But that despairing scream was drowned in dark oblivion.

## XV.

AGONY WAS still a rush and a drumming beat through all of Lanning's head. But a frantic purpose that had lived even through unconsciousness lifted him reeling to his feet.

The throbbing deck lurched and wheeled beneath him. And the black mist in his eyes veiled the flickering blue. But he saw Lao Meng Shan and Barry Halloran lying dead in the midst of the slaughtered ants.

He saw that Sorainya was gone from the deck, and the malicious triumph of her golden voice floated down to him. "You have led me a long pursuit, Wil McLan. I thank you for the pleasure of the chase. Remember, once I promised you my sword—"

A terrible scream, because it was voiceless, whispered, came rasping down from the dome. And then Lanning heard Sorainya's low, throaty laugh, pleased and pitiless.

"Perhaps you had the means to destroy me, Wil McLan. But never the will—for I know why you first came to Gyronchi! Other men have sought to slay me, as silly moths might seek with their wings to beat out the flame. They failed."

"We'll see, Sorainya," Lanning muttered under his gasping

breath. "For Barry's sake!"

His body moved stiffly, like a rusted machine. It staggered and reeled. Pain rushed like a river in his brain. A mist of darkness veiled his sight, shot with blinding wheels of red. All his body was a throbbing ache, his garments glued to it with drying blood. His whole being revolted from effort.

But he found the Mauser, picked it up in numbed, fumbling hands, and staggered into the turret that he had tried to guard where the metal stair led up to the bridge. The caressing mockery of Sorainya's golden tones came to him again, boasting.

"You were a fool, Wil McLan, to seek my doom. For, since you brought us the secret of Time, the *gyrane* can conquer death also. I may be the last of my line—but I shall reign forever! For I searched the future for the hour of my death. And it is not—"

Reeling up the turret stair, Lanning came into the bridge beneath the dome. Wil McLan was lying on the floor, beneath the shining wheel. His broken hands were set down in a great dark pool of his own blood, to lift his shoulders. His white head was thrown back, so that his scarred, thin face could look up at Sorainya. The dark, deep-sunken eyes were fixed on the woman, blazing with a beaten, hopeless hate.

Hung by its thin white chain from his neck, the little silver tube touched the spreading pool of blood.

Lithe and tall in the red splendor of her black-plumed mail, Sorainya stood facing him, crimson drops still falling from her thin, yellow sword. But she heard Lanning's unsteady step, and turned swiftly to meet him as he came to the top of the stair.

A bright, fierce exultation lit the smooth, white beauty of her face. A deadly, smiling eagerness flashed in her long emerald eyes, at sight of Lanning. And her blade cut an arc of golden fire before him.

"Well, Denny Lanning!" her suave voice greeted him. "So you would try, where the others failed? The champion of *her!* Then carry her my message, to Jonbar, in—Nothingness!"

Her ringing blade struck sparks from his bayonet.

SHE WAS beautiful. Tall almost as Lanning, and strong with the lithe, quick strength of a tigress. The woven red mail followed every flowing curve of her. Wide nostrils flared, and high breasts rose to her quickened breathing. One red hand clutched the magnet. Bright yellow hair was bursting from under the black-crested helmet. A wild, fierce smile was fixed on her face, and she attacked with the speed of a panther leaping.

Lanning parried with the bayonet, thrust warily at her gleaming body. She swayed aside. The blade slid harmless by her breast. And the yellow needle flicked Lanning's shoulder with a whip of pain.

His weapon was the longer, the heavier. And it made no difference, he tried to tell himself, that she was beautiful, for Barry's death was still a dark agony writhing in him, and he could see Wil McLan on the floor behind her, gasping terribly for breath and following the battle with hate-lit, glazing eyes.

But he fought a fatigue more deadly than Sorainya's blade. All his strength had been poured out in the battle with the ants. Sorainya was fresh, and she had a tireless energy. The rifle grew leaden heavy in Lanning's hands. His vision dulled to a blurry monochrome, and Sorainya was but a fatal shadow that could not die.

He was glad she blurred, for he could no longer see her lissome loveliness. He tried to see, in her place, the black-armored horror of one of her ants. He lunged into the rhythm of the old attack—rip, twist, slash.

But the blade slithered again, harmless, from the gleaming curve of her body. And the flash of her sword drew a red line of pain down his arm. She leapt back, with a pantherine grace—and then stood, as if to mock him, with the yellow needle down at her side.

"No, Denny Lanning!" She gave a little breathless laugh. "Strike if you will—for I shall never die. I scanned all the future for the hour of my death, and found no danger. I cannot be slain!"

"I'll see!" Lanning caught a long gasping breath, and shook his ringing head to clear it. "For Barry—"

With the last atom of his ebbing strength, he gripped the rifle hard and rushed across the tiny room under the dome. He thrust the gleaming bayonet, with every ounce of muscle, up under the curve of her breast, toward her heart.

*"Denny!"*

It was a choking sob of warning from Wil McLan. And the golden needle flashed up to touch the rifle. Blue fire hissed from its point. The rifle fell out of Lanning's hands. He staggered backward, stunned and blinded by the shock, smelling his seared hands and the burning pungence of ozone.

He caught his weight against the curve of the dome, and leaned there, shuddering. It took all his will to keep his knees from buckling. He caught a deep, rasping breath, and blinked his eyes.

He could see again. He saw Sorainya gliding forward, light as a dancer. Beneath stray wisps of golden hair, her white face was dazzling with a smile. And her lazy voice chimed, gayly, "Now, Denny Lanning! Who is immortal?"

HER ARM flashed up as she spoke, slim and red in its sleeve of mail. A terrible, tigerish joy flashed in her long green eyes. And the sword, like a living thing, leapt at Lanning's heart.

He struck at the blade, a stiff and awkward blow, with his empty hand. It slashed his wrist. Deflected a little, it drove through his shoulder, a cold, thin needle of numbing pain, and rang against the hard crystal behind him.

Sorainya whipped out the sword, and wiped its thin length on her fingers. She blew him another red kiss, and stood waiting for him to fall. Her white smile was breathless, thirsty.

"Well?" Her voice was a liquid caress. "Another?"

Then Lanning's failing eyes went beyond her. The tiny dome swam. It took a desperate effort to focus Wil McLan. But he saw the jerky little movement that broke the thin, white chain, tossed the tiny silver tube across the floor. He heard the voiceless, feeble gasp: "Break it, Denny! And her! For I—can't!"

Sorainya had sensed the movement behind her. Her breath caught sharply. And the yellow sword darted again, swift as a flash of light, straight for Lanning's heart. Even the tigerish grace of that last thrust, he thought, was beautiful—

But the silver cylinder had rolled to his foot. Desperately—and shuddering with a cold, incredulous awareness that, somehow, he was so crushing Sorainya's victorious beauty—he drove his heel down upon the tube.

It made a tiny crunching sound.

But Lanning didn't look down. For his eyes were fixed, in a trembling, breathless dread, upon Sorainya. No visible hand had touched her. But, from the instant his heel came down, she was—stricken.

The bright blade slipped out of her hand, rang against the dome, and fell at Lanning's feet. The smile was somehow frozen on her face, forgotten, lifeless. Then, in a fractional second, her beauty was—erased.

Her altered face was blind, hideous, pocked with queerly bluish ulcerations. Her features dissolved—frightfully—in blue corruption. And Lanning had an instant's impression of a naked skull grinning fearfully out of the armor.

And then Sorainya was gone.

The woven red mail, for a weird fractional second, still held the curves of her form. It slumped grotesquely, and fell with a dull little thud on the floor. The plumed helmet clattered down beside it, rolled, and looked back at Lanning with an empty, enigmatic stare.

Lanning tried to look back at Wil McLan, seeking an explanation of this appalling victory. But a thickening darkness shut out his vision, and the ringing was deafening in his head. A shuddering numbness, from the wound in his shoulder, spread to all his being. And his knees at last gave way.

XVI.

LANNING lay still on the floor of the dome, when awareness came back. The throb of the atomic converters came loud through the metal beneath his head. The anvil of agony still rang in his skull, and all his body was an aching, blood-clotted stiffness. But, queerly, the cold pain had ebbed from the sword-thrust in his I shoulder.

"Denny?"

It was a voiceless sob, from Wil McLan, husky with an urgent pleading. Lanning was surprised that the old man still survived Sorainya's stab. Despite the screaming protests of exhaustion and pain, he swayed once more to his feet, leaning against the curve of the dome. He blinked his clearing eyes, and found McLan still lying in the dark pool on the floor.

"Wil! What can I do?"

A broken hand pointed.

"The needle in the drawer," gasped McLan. "Four c.c. Intravenous—"

Lanning stumbled to the control board, found, in the drawer beneath it, a bright hypodermic and a small bottle of heavy lead, marked: *Dynatomic formula L 648. Filled, New Fork City, August, 1985.*

The liquid in the needle shone with a greenish luminescence. He pushed up McLan's sleeve, thrust the point into the radial vein at the elbow, pushed home the little plunger.

He examined the wound in the old man's breast. It had already ceased to bleed. It looked—puzzlingly—as if it had been healing for days instead of minutes.

"Thanks," whispered McLan. "Now yourself—but only two c.c.!"

He lay back on the floor, with his eyes closed. Lanning made the injection into his own arm. It seemed that a quick tide of strength and power flowed through his veins. His dulled senses cleared, the aching stiflness ebbed away. Still he was dead-tired, still his battered head ached. But he felt something of the same almost-mystical well-being that he had known when first aboard the *Chronion,* after the surgeons of Jonbar had brought him back from death.

He picked up the rusty little magnet lying on the floor beside Sorainya's empty armor. Was there still a chance to put it back, and save Jonbar? He peered apprehensively out into the gulf of shimmering blue. What if Glarath overtook them again?

The rhythmic beat of the converters beneath the deck suddenly wavered, slowed. Trouble, again. But Wil McLan, still white and trembling, pulled himself up behind the wheel, began to adjust the controls.

"Do you think—" demanded Lanning, anxiously. "Can we put it back?"

"If the converters hold out," the old man whispered, "we can—try! Glarath will guard the spot, no doubt, with his ship and the *kothrin.* And you must fight this time alone. But I'll be able to take you there. My old body is about finished, anyway, and ill-adapted to the *dynat.* But it gave me life enough for that."

The thrumming was becoming swifter again, steadier, as his broken hands touched keys and dials.

"SORAINYA—?" The question burst from Lanning's lips. "That tube I broke?" His hand touched the twisted shoulder. "Wil, what happened to Sorainya?"

The old man turned from the controls. Supporting his weight with both gnarled hands on the bright wheel, he looked at Lanning. The old hatred was gone from his sunken, eyes, and they were dark with an agony of grief.

"I loved Sorainya," came his whisper. "That tube held her life. I took it because I thought I hated her—" He caught a sighing breath. "I did hate her, for all she had done to me! But still I could never break the tube."

"But what was it?" Horror roughened Lanning's voice. "I didn't touch her. But she changed—dreadfully! As if she had some terrible disease. She died. And then even her skeleton was gone!"

Wil McLan's hollow eyes were dry, glazed with pain.

"Sorainya failed to discover the hour of her death when she searched her future," came the tortured rasping. "For it was in her past! In the year that Sorainya mounted her throne, the Blue Death swept Gyronchi—a plague born of the poverty and squalor in which oppression held the peasants. It was that pandemic that killed Sorainya."

"But—" Lanning stared. "I don't understand!"

"When Lethonee helped me escape from Sorainya's dungeons and recover the *Chronion*," the whisper answered, "I determined to destroy Sorainya. I searched her past—with the *chronoscope*— for a node of probability. I found it, in the year of the Blue Death.

"For the priests of the *gyrane* managed to prepare a few shots of effective antitoxin. When Sorainya contracted the disease, Glarath rushed to her castle with the last tube of the serum, and saved her life.

"But if the tube had been broken before it reached her, the geodesic analyzer revealed, she would have died. Discovering that, I drove the *Chronion* back through the temple to the plague year. I carried away the tube."

Lanning nodded slowly. "I see!" he murmured, awed. "It was like the carrying away of the magnet, to destroy Jonbar."

"Not quite," pointed out Wil McLan. "The magnet was carried into the future. Its geodesics skipped over the vital node. Therefore Jonbar was immediately blotted from the fifth-dimensional sequence.

"But I carried the tube back into the past of Gyronchi. It was possible for its geodesics to make a loop and return to the node. Therefore—so long as the tube was intact—she was not essentially affected. But, when you broke the tube, the possibility of her survival was blotted out."

Lanning was staring at him, numbed with a bewildering paradox. "But if"—the incredulous question burst out—"if Sorainya died as a girl, what about Sorainya the queen? The woman that imprisoned you, and haunted me, and fought the legion. She didn't exist!"

The white, bleak face smiled a little, at his bewilderment, and a thin, shaking hand touched his arm.

"Remember," McLan whispered softly, "we are dealing with probabilities alone. The new physics has banished absolute certainty from the world. Jonbar and Gyronchi, and the two Sorainyas, living and dead, are but conflicting branches of possibility, as yet unfixed by the inexorable progression of the fifth dimension. The crushing of the tube merely altered the probability factors of Sorainya's possible life."

A soft gleam of tears was in his hollow eyes. They looked down at the little glistening heap of woven mail, the empty helmet and the golden sword.

"But the queen Sorainya was real, to me," he breathed. "And, to me, she is dead."

Lanning broke in with a final question: "These wounds? Were they made by a woman who didn't exist in reality—?"

"When they were made, her probability did exist," whispered Wil McLan. "And a lot of atomic power had been spent—through the temporal field—to match our probability to hers. You will notice, however, that they are disappearing now with a remarkable rapidity."

The bright eyes lifted to Lanning. "Just keep in mind, Denny, that the logical laws of causation are still rigid—but removed to a higher dimension. The absolute sequence of events, in the fifth dimension, is not parallel with time—although our three-dimensional minds commonly perceive it so. But that inviolable progression is the unalterable frame of all the universe."

His gnarled hand reached out to touch the rusty magnet in Lanning's hand.

"The march of that progression, higher than Time," his hushed whisper ran on solemnly, "has now forever obliterated Sorainya, the queen. The sequence of events has not yet settled the fates of Jonbar and Gyronchi. But still the odds are all with Gyronchi."

The thin hand gripped Lanning's arm. "The last play is near," he breathed. "The hope—the probability—of Jonbar is all in you, Denny. And the outcome will soon be engraved forever in the fifth dimension."

He turned to grasp the Wheel of Time.

## XVII.

WIL McLAN lived to nurse his failing converters, although Lanning was stricken to see his pallor and his ebbing strength. He drove the *Chronion,* still ahead of pursuit in her shimmering abyss, back down her geodesic track until the dials stood at 5:49 P.M., August 12, 1921. He raised his hand in a warning signal, and his whisper rasped down through the speaking tube. "Ready, Denny! They'll be waiting to guard the spot."

Lanning was standing on the foredeck, peering alertly into the flickering blue. As a desperate ruse that might win a precious moment, he had donned Sorainya's armor. It fitted without discomfort. Her black plume waved above his head. One hand clutched her golden sword—the device in the hilt which made it also an electron gun was either broken or exhausted. The other moistly gripped the rusty magnet—which must be returned to the path of a barefoot boy, to save his namesake world.

His weary brain, as he waited, dully pondered a last paradox: that, while the *Chronion* had outrun the black ship of Glarath in the long race backward through Time, no possible speed could bring her to the goal ahead of the other ship. He gripped the sword, at the warning from McLan, and his body went tense in the borrowed mall.

And the *Chronion* flashed out of the blue again, into the lonely hush of that valley in the age-worn Ozarks. Everything was exactly as Lanning had seen it in the shining block of the *chronoscope:* the idle, tattered boy, indilgently driving the two lean cows down the rocky slope toward the dilapidated farm, with the gaunt, yellow dog roving beside him.

Everything—except that the great, squarish, black mass of the time ship from Gyronchi lay beside the trail, like a battleship aground. Glarath was a haggard, black pillar on his lofty deck. Ugly projectors of the *gyrane's* blasting atomic energy beam frowned from their ports. And scores of the great ants had been disembarked, to make a bristling, hideous wall about the spot where the magnet must be placed.

Whistling, the dawdling boy had come within twenty yards of the spot. But he gave no evidence that he saw either ship or monsters. One of the red-spotted cows, ahead, plodded calmly through a giant black ant.

Back to Lanning, already tensed to leap from the deck. came a whispered explanation of McLan. "No, the boy John Barr won't be aware of us at all—unless we should turn the temporal field upon him. For his life is already almost completely fixed by the advancing progression in the fifth dimension. In terms of his experience, we are no more than phantoms of probability. Travelers backward into time can affect the past only at carefully selected nodes, and then only at the expense of the terrific power required to deflect the probability-inertia of the whole continuum. It required the utmost power of the *gyrane* merely to lift the magnet from John Barr's path."

Gripping the magnet and the sword, Lanning flung himself to the ground. He stumbled on a rock, fell to his knees, staggered back to his feet, and ran desperately toward the great black ship and the horde of ants ahead of the loitering boy.

He waved the golden sword, as he ran, in Sorainya's familiar gesture. And Glarath, on his bridge, waved a black-swathed arm to answer—and then, as Lanning's tired feet tripped again, he went rigid with alarm.

For Lanning's weary gait lacked all Sorainya's grace, and the black priest marked the change. A great hoarse voice croaked a command. The wall of giant ants came to attention, bristling with the crimson and yellow of arms.

And a thick, black tube swung down in its port.

THE FIRST BLAST of the atomic ray struck a rock beside Lanning. It exploded in a blaze of white. Molten stone spattered the red mail. A hot fragment slapped his cheek with white agony, and blinded him with the smoke of his own flesh burning.

The boy, meantime, had already walked into the unsuspected ranks of ants. A cold desperation clutched at Lanning's heart. In a few moments more, John Barr would have picked up the pebble instead of the magnet, and the fate of two worlds settled forever—unless he broke through.

Strangled with bitter white smoke, Lanning caught a sobbing breath, and sprinted. Twin blinding lances of the *gyrane's* fire fused the soil to a smoking pool of lava, close behind him. He was now safe beneath their maximum depression. But the ants were waiting ahead.

Thick crimson guns were leveled, and a volley battered

Lanning. The bullets failed to pierce the woven mail. But the impacts were bruising, staggering blows. And one raked his unprotected jaw and neck, beneath the helmet. A sickening pain loosened his muscles. Red gouts splashed down on the crimson mail. He gritted broken teeth, spat fragments and blood, stumbled on.

Yellow axes flamed above the ebon ranks. He whirled the yellow sword, and leapt to meet them. For an instant he thought the ants would yield, in awe of Sorainya's very armor. But Glarath croaked another command from above, and they fell upon him furiously.

Golden blades ripped and battered at his mail. He drove Sorainya's sword into an armored, jet thorax. And a clubbed red gun smashed against his extended arm. The bone gave with a brittle snap, and his arm fell useless in the sleeve of mail. He clutched the precious magnet close to his body, and leapt ahead.

Blows rained on him. The helmet was battered stunningly against his head. A cleaving axe half severed his neck, at the juncture of helmet and mail, and hot blood gushed down in the shirt.

Yet some old terror of their queen repelled the ants from any actual contact with her mail. So Lanning, even wounded and beaten down, pushed through their close ranks to the hollow square they guarded.

He saw the ragged boy John Barr stroll unawares through the farther ranks, the hungry dog at his heels. He saw the gleam of the pebble, the triangular print where the magnet had lain, but two paces from the boy. Another second—

But he was falling. His strength was rushing out in the foaming red stream from his neck. Another merciless blow smashed his shoulder, numbed the arm that held the magnet, crushed him down.

Lanning's eyes were dim with weakness and pain. But, as he fell, he saw beside him, or thought he did, a splendid figure. The grave, majestic head and mighty shoulders of a towering man rose above a mantle of shimmering opalescence. Deep and wide and clear, the eyes of the stranger struck Lanning with a power that was unforgettable, supernal.

A bare, magnificent arm reached out of the flaming veil and touched his shoulder. That cold touch tensed Lanning's body with a queer, shocking force. A deep, hushed voice said: "Courage, Denny Lanning! For mankind."

AND THE STRANGER was gone. Numbed with awe, Lanning knew that he had been one of the *dynon,* the further heirs of Jonbar.

His hand had given Lanning a mysterious new strength. cleared the red mist from his head. And the visitation meant, Lanning knew dimly, that Jonbar still was—possible!

Glarath had bellowed another command, and an avalanche of ants was falling on his body. And the aimless boy was already stooping for the pebble.

Lanning hurled himself forward, his good arm thrust out with the magnet. A yellow blade of pain slashed down at his sleeve. The horde crushed him to the earth. But the magnet, flung with the last effort of his fingers, dropped into the triangular print.

A bright curiosity—the very light of science—was born in the eyes of the stooping boy. His inquisitive fingers closed on the V of steel. And then the warrior ants, piling themselves upon Lanning's body, were suddenly gone.

The black ship flickered like a wing of shadow, and vanished.

John Barr picked up the magnet, wonderingly discovered a clinging rusty nail that it had drawn from the dust, and went on down the slope, driving his two spotted cows through the unseen hull of the *Chronion.*

Dennis Lanning was left alone beside the trail. He knew that he was dying. But the slowing, fading throb of his pain was a triumphant drum. For he knew that Jonbar had won.

His failing eyes looked down toward the *Chronion.* He wondered if Wil McLan had been hurt again, in the battle. Puzzled dimly, he saw the little time ship flicker also, and vanish. And he lay quite alone in the sunset on the slope of that Ozark hill.


XVIII.

IT WAS a dream, all a delirium of death, a thing that could not have been. But Lethonee had been standing beside him. Tall and straight in the same simple white, with the great splendid jewel of the *chronotron* held in her hands. Her white face, under her coronal of shimmering mahogany, was beautiful, and in her violet eyes shone a tender, joyous light.

"I thank you, Denny Lanning!" her breaking silver voice had whispered. "I bring you the thanks of all Jonbar, for a thing that no other could have done."

Lanning struggled against a terrible inertia, to speak to her. But all his desperate effort could utter not even one word of his love. For he was held in the leaden hands of death.

But he saw the violet eyes turn soft with tears, and he heard her trembling breath, "Live, Denny Lanning! Get well again. And come back to me!" Her full lips quivered, and the tears sprang glistening into the jewel's soft glow. "For I'll be waiting, Denny Lanning, whenever you come to Jonbar."

He fought again the rigor of death, but in vain. And darkness blotted out the jewel and Lethonee.

As if all his life swirled in brief review, through the last hallucination of death, he thought that he was once again lying in a clean bed in the little green-walled hospital aboard the *Chronion*. The brisk, efficient surgeons of Jonbar had been attending him for a long time in the dim, drowsy intervals of sleep. The wondrous agencies of the *dynat,* he dreamed, had made his body whole again.

It had to be a dream. For Willie Rand was sitting up on the opposite bed, grinning at him, with clear, seeing eyes. Willie Rand who had been slain—blind and alone—in that fantastic, hopeless charge against the ants before Sorainya's diamond throne. He blew an expanding silver ring, watched it happily.

"Howdy, Cap'n Lanning. Smoke?"

Numbed with bewilderment, Lanning reached automatically to catch the cigarette he tossed. There was no pain in the arm that the great ant's clubbed gun had broken. He tried the fingers again, incredulously, and stared across at Willie Rand.

"What's happened?" he demanded. "I thought you were—were killed! And I was cashing out—"

Rand exhaled a white cloud, grinned through it.

"That's right, cap'n," he drawled cheerfully. "I reckon we've all died twice. And I reckon we'll all get another stack of chips—all but poor Cap'n McLan."

"But—?" gasped Lanning. "How were—?"

"Well, cap'n, you see—"

But then there was a clatter on the stair. Barry Halloran and bull-like Emil Schorn came down from the deck, carrying a stretcher. It bore a sheeted form, and behind came two of the surgeons from Jonbar, in their tunics of gray and green. A third rolled in a table of instruments. They laid the bandaged figure gently on a bed. Lanning caught the gleam of a hypodermic, glimpsed the little shining needles that gave off a healing radiation of the *dynat.*

"That's the little limey, Duffy Clark," Willie Rand was informing him. "He was the last one. He was put overboard on the flight back from Gyronchi, and sort of lost in probability and time. Took days to untangle the geo—geodesics. But they found him! He was burned with the *gyrane*—the same cussed ray that put my lights out. But I reckon that *dynat* will tune him up in good shape again, now that Gyronchi never was."

LANNING was sitting up on the side of his bed, a little shakily at first. And now Barry Halloran discovered him. The rugged, freckled face lit with a joyous grin. He strode swiftly to grip Lanning's hand.

"Denny, old man! I knew you'd be coming round!"

"Tell me, Barry!" Lanning clung to the powerful hand. He shuddered to a sudden burning agony of hope. "How did all this happen? And can we—can we—?" He gulped, and his desperate eyes searched Barry's broad, cheerful face. "Can we go back to Jonbar?"

A shadow of pain blotted the smile from Barry Halloran.

"Wil did it." His voice was deep with a sober regret. "Wil McLan. The last thing he did. After you had settled with Gyronchi, he left you and drove the *Chronion* back down to Jonbar. He was dead when he got there—dead beyond the power of the *dynat* to revive him. For even it can't make men immortal, not until the *dynon* come.

"They are building a tomb for Wil, there in Jonbar."

The big tackle looked away for a moment, with a new huskiness in his voice.

"Wil knew he was going down," he went on suddenly. "He had rigged an automatic switch to stop the *Chronion* when it came to Jonbar, and Lethonee's time. And she sent the doctors back with it, to haul us out of Time and probability, and resurrect us with the *dynat,* as they did before. Quite a hunt, I gather, through the snarl of broken geodesics."

"Lethonee?" whispered Lanning, urgently.

*"Ach!"* It was a bellow greeting from Emil Schorn. He smashed

Lanning's fingers in a great ham of a hand. *"Ja, Herr* Lanning! Jonbar is der Valhalla der old sagas promised us, where men fight and die and are restored to fight again. *Und* Sorainya—"

An awed admiration deepened the bellow.

"Der red queen of war! *Ach,* Sorainya was a Valkyrie—one of Odin's maids of battle, terrible and beautiful. There will be none like her in Jonbar, *nein!* Though the maiden waiting for you there is fair enough, and kind."

"Jonbar? Are we going back?"

*"Ach, ja!* Our own time is closed to us forever—unless we choose to perish there. We exiles of time, *ja.* But der white girl has promised to make a place for us in Jonbar. And der *herr doktors* with us say that it need not be an idle, useless one. For mankind, marching forward under der *dynat,* will meet new enemies. We may even fight again, for Jonbar." A stern eager blue flashed in his eyes. *"Ach, heil,* Valhalla!"

Lanning was standing on the deck, aglow once more with the mystical strength and elation that came from the *dynat,* when the *Chronion* slipped again from her blue shimmering bourn into the clear sky over Jonbar.

Genial sunlight of a calm spring morning burned dazzling upon lofty, silver pylons. Gay-clad multitudes thronged the vast green parks and broad viaducts and the terrace gardens of the towers, eager to greet the *Chronion.*

The battered little time ship drifted down slowly above them. The men out of the past, radiantly fit, but still—as Barry Halloran commented—a trampish-looking lot in their ragged, faded, oddly assorted uniforms, were leaning on the rail, waving in answer to the welcome of Jonbar.

ALL THE LITTLE Legion alive again: Schorn and Rand and Duffy Clark, swarthy Cresto and grave-eyed Barinin and grinning Lao Meng Shan. The two lean Canadians, Isaac and Israel Enders. standing silently side by side. Tall Courtney-Pharr, and grim von Arneth, and Barry Halloran. And dapper little Jean Querard. perched perilously on the rail, making a speech of thanks into space.

But it was one of the scientists from Jonbar who held the bright wheel under the dome. And the *Chronion* floated over a slim, new shaft of pure white that soared alone from a wooded hill. Standing on its crown, both arms reaching skyward, Lanning

saw the statue in hard white metal of a small weary man—Wil
McLan.

All the Legion saluted, as they passed, and a silence stilled the
humming of the multitudes below,

A wide valve had opened ahead in the argent wall of a familiar
tower on a hill. The *Chronion* nosed through, dropped gently
upon the same platform in the great hangar, where a smiling
crowd was waiting, cheering noisily.

Jean Querard strutted and inflated his chest. Teetering on the
rail, he waved for silence.

*"C'est bon,"* his high voice began. *"C'est très bon—"*

Trembling with a still incredulous eagerness, Lanning leapt
past him, over the rail. He pushed his way through the crowd,
and found the elevator. It flung him upward, and he stepped out
into that same terrace garden of his most poignant memory.

Amid its fragrant, white-flowered greenery, he paused for a
moment to catch his breath. His eyes fell to the wide, verdant
parklands that spread smiling to the placid river, a full mile beneath. And he saw a thing that probed his heart with a queer little
needle of pain.

For this great river, he saw, was the same river that had curved
through Gyronchi! Great pylons soared where miserable villages
had stood. The lofty monument to Wil McLan, he saw, leapt up
from the very hill that had been crowned by the squat, black
temple of the *gyrane,* beneath the awful funnel of black.

But where was the other hill, where Sorainya's red citadel had
been?

His breath shuddered and caught, when he saw that it was *this
same hill,* that now bore the tower of Lethonee. His hands
gripped hard on the railing, and he looked down at the little table
where he had dined with Lethonee, on the dreadful night of
Jonbar's dissolution.

And Sorainya, glorious on her golden shell, rose again to mock
him, as she had done that night. Tears dimmed his eyes, and a
haunting, sudden ache gripped his pausing heart.

*Oh, fair Sorainya—slain!*

A light step raced through the sliding door behind the shrubs,
and a breathless voice panted his name, joyously. Lanning looked
up, slowly. And a numbing wonder shook him.

"Denny Lanning!"

Lethonee came running toward him, through the flowers. Her

violet eyes were bright with tears, and her face was a white smile of incredulous delight. Lanning turned shuddering to meet her, speechless.

For the golden voice of the warrior queen had mocked him in her cry. And the ghost of Sorainya's glance glinted green in her shining eyes. She had even donned a close-fitting velvet gown of shimmering crimson, that shone like Sorainya's mail.

She came into his open, trembling arms.

"Denny—" she sobbed happily. "At last we are—one."

The world was spinning. This same hill had borne Sorainya's citadel. Jonbar and Gyronchi—conflicting possible worlds, stemming from the same beginning—were now fused into the same reality. Lethonee and Sorainya, also—? Eagerly, he drew her against his racing heart. And he murmured, happily—

"One!"

THE END

# Afterword

AM NEARING 94 AS I WRITE THIS IN EARLY 2002. TIME IS OVERTAK-
ing me. My sense of balance is poor. I do my six blocks
a day with a wheeled walker. I've lost most vision in
my right eye. I'm pretty deaf. Yet I feel fortunate to be
here at all. With the generous support of family and friends, I can
still live alone. In spite of failing memory, my brain is still more
alive than I ever expected. I published a new novel last year. I've
sold half a dozen short stories since it was finished. With Dr.
Patrice Caldwell, I'm team-teaching a science fiction course at
ENMU this semester.

I seldom reread my early work; the world ahead has always
seemed more inviting than the one behind. The stories here were
published over sixty years ago, most of them in *Astounding Stories, Weird Tales,* and *Thrilling Mystery*. Reading them as if I'd
never seen them, I couldn't help seeing faults, yet I'm happy to
have them remembered.

The circumstances or their birth are hard to recall. I've no idea
what suggested "The Ruler of Fate," but the idea intoxicated me.
A machine to create absolute omnipotence! A theme perhaps better suited to theology or philosophy, and pretty ambitious for the

writer I was at the time. I intended the story for F. Orlin Tremaine, then editing *Astounding*. He rejected it, with comments I don't recall. I was grateful to Farnsworth Wright, who ran it as a serial in *Weird Tales*.

"Death's Cold Daughter" was done for *Thrilling Mystery,* part of the Standard group, owned by Ned Pines and edited by Leo Margulies. Back in those more literate times before the electronic revolution brought us sit-coms and talking heads, people read for information and entertainment. The pulps were popular entertainment. Individually, most of them had small circulations, but the newsstands were stacked with hundreds of competing titles, westerns, romances and ranch romances, mysteries, war stories, air stories, railroad stories, at last science fiction. Standard had a good many titles. Margulies, I think, was paid $25 to edit each, a fair income in those days when the subway or a cup of coffee in the Automat cost a nickel.

Leo asked for stories and mailed the checks, but Mort Weisinger did the actual editorial work on *Thrilling Wonder, Startling Stories,* and *Thrilling Mystery.* He worked closely with me, discussing plots in advance and discussing rewrites of anything that violated Leo's formulas. For *Thrilling Mystery,* he wanted a shock of horror but nothing supernatural. Anything startling had to have a rational explanation.

News reporters make convenient lead characters for such stories; they have instant motives for probing into strange situations. The situation here is certainly strange enough. I wrote the story, trimmed the ending to fit. Leo bought it. I was hungry for money and his checks were quick, but I felt stifled by the limits. Writing for Leo was never much fun.

"The Great Illusion" was written for a fan magazine, for no pay at all. Ed Hamilton was a close friend. I'd met Binder, whose actual first name was Otto. He had a brother named Earl; the name "Eando" had been invented for their collaborations. Gallun and Fearn were still strangers. I don't remember who invented the story idea, such as it is, based on contrasting perceptions of illusion and reality, a theme that made Philip K. Dick's whole career.

We began without a plot. Each contributor tried to challenge the next with a new complication invented to inspire the sense of wonder reflected in the titles of the early magazines, *Amazing, Astounding, Marvel, Startling,* even *Wonder* itself. A real emotion then, if now almost forgotten.

Back then, before World War II and the A-bomb, before concerns about pollution and over-population, the wonders of future technology could still dazzle the popular imagination. Such thinkers as Wells had already foreseen the dark side of technology and the limits of progress, but the story says nothing of them. The essentials of character and theme are barely there at all.

"The Blue Spot" had vanished from my memory. Reading it like a stranger's work, I wondered why. It has nearly everything. Extrapolation based on current science, the sense of a future world in the shadow of impending doom, characters in conflict, a plot full of action. What it lacks, I think, is what Stephen King does so well, the creation of a strong bridge to lead the reader from the here and now. Typically, he opens with appealing characters at home in his familiar Maine landscape and has the reader well involved before their troubles begin. Yet Tremaine bought the story for *Astounding,* and I recall no storm of protest from the readers.

Children and primitives animate dead objects and natural forces by giving them minds of their own. More than once, I've done the same thing. "The Ice Entity" is one example. Another, one that I recall rather wryly, was a collaboration I attempted with A. Merritt. Almost forgotten now, he was editor of the *American Weekly,* the Sunday supplement of the Hearst newspapers. In his free time, he wrote serials for the old *Argosy* that enchanted me when Gernsback reprinted them. *The Moon Pool, The Face in the Abyss, The Ship of Ishtar.* My first stories had been efforts to recreate their magic.

I felt enormously flattered when he read the first installment of "The Alien Intelligence" and asked for my carbon of the second. Though Ed Hamilton made the sardonic suggestion that he only wanted to see if I had plagiarized him, he agreed when I dared ask if he would collaborate with me. I sent him an idea for a serial about an African with a living spirit of its own.

I was elated. Running in *Argosy,* "The Purple Mountain" would have brought me instant wealth and fame. Then a college sophomore, I spent the four-day Thanksgiving break pounding out 20,000 words of "The Purple Mountain," and mailed it to Merritt. Sadly, if not surprisingly, there was never a response. With no carbon copy, the manuscript is gone. I was left to make my own career. H. G. Wells soon became a better model.

"The Ice Entity" did a little better. Margulies bought it for *Thrilling Wonder Stories,* and "Spider Island" for *Thrilling Mystery.* The latter has supplied the title for this volume, I suppose because of the cover illustration. Like "Death's Cold Daughter," it was tailored to fit Leo's formula. "The Legion of Time" is a far better story, one that came out in *Astounding* with a cover of its own, but the title had already been used on an earlier reprint.

The big spiders in "Spider Island" are said to have been created by a genetic process, though unfortunately I failed to call it "genetic engineering." I've thought for years that the term was my own creation. I did use and define it in 1951, in *Dragon's Island,* but now the *OED* seems to have found it in a science paper published in 1949. My fifteen minutes of fame.

"The Mark of the Monster," too, was written for Leo and crippled by the fit to his formula. I must have been reading too much of H. P. Lovecraft. The story has too much talk of terror and too little to evoke it. Leo rejected it. Farnsworth Wright bought it for *Weird Tales* and featured it with a cover of its own. His readers, accustomed to the play of free imaginations, panned the story so severely that I've always regretted its publication.

Leo kept on asking for stories. I always needed money. He did buy "The Devil in Steel" for *Thrilling Mystery.* It might have been science fiction, but the formula required the hoax to explain it all away.

My own title for "Released Entropy" had been "Entropy Reversed." I suppose the change was meant to make it seem more dramatic, but it's nonsense. The story was an effort at actual science fiction, the extrapolations drawn from the science of thermodynamics. Like "The Blue Spot," it plunges too suddenly into a far-off future, with no bridge out of everyday human experience or familiar human problems to carry the reader there. I was never quite another Stephen King. Yet it did sell to *Astounding.*

"Dreadful Sleep" was the first story I wrote in 1937 when I got home to New Mexico after a year in Topeka, Kansas, under analysis with Dr. Charles W. Tidd at the Menninger Clinic. I had hoped the analysis would make me a happier person and a better writer. In the long run, I think it did. Dr. Tidd was intelligent and humane; he did his best for me at a fee of only five dollars an hour, for three hours a week. Stretching my limited means, I lived cheap and tried to write. The analysis worked no instant wonders. I had to break it off when my writing stalled and my money ran out. Farnsworth Wright paid me $420 for the story. I sent half of it to Menninger as payment on my debt.

A novel has been defined as a long prose narrative that has something wrong with it. "Dreadful Sleep" fits the definition. I've never been entirely happy with it. Once, years later, I set out to rewrite it for book publication and gave the project up because I wasn't certain what was wrong or how to fix it. Farnsworth Wright did buy the story, and I soon went on to better things.

One was "The Legion of Time." Nat Schachner had published "Ancestral Voices," a story where things vanish from the present time when their origins in the past are erased. That suggested that the battle for existence of two possible future worlds would make a great plot. The paradoxes of time travel have since been worked to death, but the idea seemed fresh to me then, far more exciting than trying to cut another story to fit Leo's pattern. The story went fast. My first draft was 12,000 words. Retyping brought it to 39,000.

It was my first sale to John W. Campbell. I had submitted it to Tremaine before Campbell took over as editor of *Astounding*. He had been a prolific science-fictioneer, first in competition with E. E. "Doc" Smith, writing space operas of galactic war fought with superscientific ships and weapons, then reinventing himself as Don A. Stuart, with a new sense of style and story values.

He became a great editor, recruiting and inspiring a team that included Isaac Asimov, Robert Heinlein, Sprague de Camp, Lester Del Rey and all the others who recreated science fiction in what has been called its golden age. He dictated no formulas. He was inspired instead by optimistic visions of a magnificent human future. He invented story ideas, shared them freely, and wrote useful letters of comment. He had traits that turned off a good many people, but we got on well. His *Astounding/Analog* was my best market for the next dozen years.

Jack Williamson
Portales, New Mexico
January 2002

# Appendix

# Interview with Jack Williamson

*Interview, The Science Fiction Fan, July 1936*

He is 28 years old, stands 6 feet tall, weighs 160 pounds, has black hair; eyes, a sort of gray. Born in Bisbee, Arizona. Has lived mostly in the west with expeditions here and there. Early interest in science and science fiction. First story sold eight years ago.

Q.   What do you consider your best story?

A.   My best story? I don't know. I liked "Golden Blood," in weird tales. Also liked "The Legion of Space" in *Astounding Stories*.

Q.   Who is your favorite character?

A.   Giles Habibula of "Legion of Space" fame. I have planned another story about him if the readers wish it? (What do you say, Readers?—Ed.)

Q.   What do you consider the best story of Science Fiction published?

A.   Again I don't know. Wells' "The Time Machine," "First Men in the Moon," "War of the Worlds," "Island of Dr. Moreau," have never been beaten. But the story that has affected me most is Merritt's "The Moon Pool." The first "Skylark" story was splendid in the fantasy field. Clark Ashton Smith is very fine. (Agreed.—Ed.)

Q.   Do you think the Science Fiction being written today superior to that of several years back?

A.   Certainly more scientifiction is being written today than several years back and I also believe it superior than that of the past. Sometimes it doesn't seem so interesting as the old stories did, but when I look back at the old ones I find that they have also lost something because of my changing and maturing taste.

I think it is the duty of every science fiction author to keep pace with the growth and development of science, of science fiction, of his reader audience and, of course, himself. New scien-

tific discoveries, new settings, new characters and new plots, re-
finements in literary value, improvements in technique, these can
keep science fiction alive and interesting both to writer and
reader.

JACK WILLIAMSON

(Speaking for the readers and myself, I thank you.—Editor.)

# Psychology and Characterization

*Article, Science Fiction Correspondent, November/December 1936*

Modern psychology has a good deal to offer the fiction writer. Writing, in fact, is an exercise in applied psychology—none the less so, because, like most human activities, it is best done when practice has made its skills unconscious.

The cornerstone of psychology is the law of stimulus and response. A human being never does, thinks, or feels anything purely by chance. Every act, thought, and emotion is the result of some definite stimulus.

That principle has a double application in the writing of fiction. It must be applied both to the reader, as he receives the stimuli of the story, and to the characters in the story, as they respond to stimuli provided by the writer's ingenuity.

First, with regard to the reader, the primary purpose of any work of art is the creation of an emotional effect. The law of stimulus and response leads the writer to include those stimuli which will lead to the desired effect, and to exclude those which fail to contribute, or which lead to conflicting emotions.

Here is the actual basis for the dogma of the dramatic unities, and for the laws of unity, coherence, and emphasis. They are all merely methods, governed by the nature of the human mind, by which it may be efficiently stimulated by any desired response.

The illusion of reality is the signal of successful stimulation. It means that the reader for the time being is in the hands of the writer, thinking and feeling as the writer would have him think and feel, while he ignores the conflicting stimuli which are always clamoring for his attention.

A common reason for the rejection of stories, especially those of begining writers in the fantasy field, is unconvincingness: the failure to establish and hold that precious illusion of reality. It means some defect in the stimulating apparatus of the story.

Anything at all that breaks the illusion spoils a story. It may be even a grammatical or typographical error—or the reader may have dyspepsia or an unexpected caller! A grave danger in writing science fiction is any displayed ignorance of scientific fact.

Poor writing and dullness tend to make a story unconvincing. If, on the other hand, the reader is supplied with vivid sensory impressions, if the descriptions are crystal clear, if the dramatic interest is intense, the reader will ignore things that might ordinarily shatter the illusion.

But the most important cause of unconvincingness, I think, is poor characterization. That brings us to the second application of the principle of stimulus and response, which must be supplied not only to the reader but to the people in the story.

The characters, in other words, must be shown responding to stimuli. The reader will not be convinced unless they respond in the way he thinks they would do in real life. When the writer wishes to show a person doing, thinking, or feeling anything, he must be sure to provide a sufficient stimulus to cause that particular person to behave in that way.

The primary interest of human beings is in other human beings. The rendition of character is the supreme end of writing. Every story is a character story. We hear also of stories of incident, atmosphere, and theme. But the interest of incident depends upon the characters involved; atmosphere can be expressed only by its effect upon characters; themes are statements about human life.

The steps in characterizing a person are several. The first is the description. The visual image of an actor should be not only made clear at the beginning of the story, but continually suggested so long as he appears. It should be, moreover, dynamic rather than static, since fiction is a dynamic art. In other words, rather than, "He was a tall, lean man," say, "His tall, lean body tensed with apprehension." That is, the character is shown responding to stimulus.

Manner is more important than static appearance, because it indicates underlying traits of character. Indicate whether the actor is hasty, confident, or furtive. Show gait, posture, expression, habitual gestures, tone of voice.

The "backbone" of any character is his basic traits. Remember that these traits are nothing more than habits of response, that they have been conditioned by stimuli the character has experienced in the past. They are expressed in purposes, beliefs, and habits of behavior. (Very frequently, the motives of behavior are unconscious, though perhaps that point is not very important for the popular writer.)

A fundamental problem of the writer seeking to control the emotional responses of the reader is to cause him to admire certain characters and to dislike others. This result may be achieved through following a simple rule: selfish characters are disliked, unselfish ones are admired.

In the application of this principle, however, in order to be sure that the reader will favor the hero in his struggle with the villain, the element of unconvincingness must again be considered. The reader knows from his own experience that all human beings are very complex mixtures of varying and frequently conflicting traits. Hence the villain who is too completely selfish or evil, or the hero who is excessively virtuous and brave, is apt to shatter the vital illusion of reality.

The younger and more unsophisticated the reader, generally speaking, the more the characters may be simplified toward the two essential types, selfish and unselfish. At the other end of the scale, we find much modern literature dealing with characters as the helpless pawns of life, neither good nor evil, mere mechanisms of response to the experience.

To define it briefly, a story is the unified account of one person's reaction to one situation. This reaction is in terms of emotion, purpose, and action. It carries the reader from the beginning, in which the character becomes aware of the situation and formulates a purpose with regard to it; through the body, in which he struggles inconclusively to gain that purpose; to the ending, in which the purpose is either won or abandoned, and the character is again in equilibrium. The cycle of stimulus and response is completed.

All these devices for attaining convincingness are especially important in the fantastic story. Typically, in such a story, the reader is persuaded to assume one premise: that a man can travel in time, for example, in *The Time Machine*. That one assumption is developed with the strictest logic, with careful attention to plausible characterization and a dominant emotional effect. Irrelevant flights of fantasy are restrained. The unusual, the fantastic, is emphasized by contrast with the ordinary. The unified feeling, frequently of eeriness, wonder, or terror, is the essential thing: characters, incidents, and settings must be subordinated, integrated with it.

I hope that these comments may prove helpful to someone. Many of the ideas above came from the books of Mr. John Gallishaw, which I recommend to the student interested in the psychological approach to writing.

I believe that writing can be taught, and that the writer is the better for a scientific understanding of his art. But no good story has ever been written by the mere academic compounding of a technical prescription. Science may explain the artist, bit it cannot displace him. Good writing will remain the expression of a genuine creative purpose, backed by sincere belief and deep emotion.

# Has Science Fiction a Future?

*Article, The International Observer, January 1937*

The future of science fiction, I strongly believe, is unlimited. For science is ever more important in the lives of men. The impact of modern technology has shattered age-old institutions and set men free of ancient superstitions. Most of the unrest in the world today boils down to a struggle for control of this new force.

It is the real function of literature, of any art, to fuse and integrate the elements of life, so that we may respond to the whole of them, fully, both intellectually and emotionally. At such a time as this, values are changing; the old art-forms no longer supply a valid response. The creation of a new art is a slow and uncertain business. There is much mere propaganda, much simple fantasy of escape. But such conditions not only aid but make necessary the building of a new structure of art. And science fiction, the art that welds science into the unity of life, will be increasingly, vitally, important.

Differing audiences demand different sorts of literature and the same person, in different moods, may belong to different audiences. Propaganda and fiction of escape have doubtless a real place in life. I expect science fiction to gain not only in the pulp field, but also in others. Despite its popularity today, it has no outstanding figures such as were Verne and Wells at the opening of the century. But it is noteworthy that most of its writers are young; and I feel that as they acquire literary experience and depth of vision, their work will appeal to a larger and more important audience.

Science fiction has existed as long as men have—for magic is "science" to the savage; to believers in magic, the Arabian Nights were science fiction. And so long as there is science, the complete human response to it will be in terms of science fiction.

# Polar Catastrophe

*Authorial Comments on "The Ice Entity,"*
*Thrilling Wonder Stories, February 1937*

JACK WILLIAMSON'S novelette of tragedy in the polar wastes, THE ICE ENTITY, has an interesting basis. This is what the author says about it:

The riddle of life has always intrigued me, as it must, somehow, every being that lives. Life, the ultimate mystery! Was it pure accident, mere fortuitous congregation of atoms, that brought into the universe this miraculous new entity? This substance that grows and perpetuates itself in a hostile environment, that adapts itself, that knows, reasons, feels.

Or was life inevitable, inherent in the very nature of the atom? The filterable viruses seem to be on the border-line, in some ways living, in some ways mere chemicals. The recent speculations of Jeans and others (with which I don't personally agree) suggest that the universe itself is an expression of mind, and this makes of life—of which mind is the essence—something vastly more important than an accidental scum on an insignificant speck of a planet.

I don't remember when I first came upon the idea for this yarn—it was some years ago. I like to speculate on the origin and meaning of life, and the form that vital processes might take under different conditions.

Actually, ice crystals—or snowflakes—are similar in many ways to living beings. They grow, following a general plan; yet each is individually unique. When injured, they tend to repair themselves. Their "life processes" liberate energy—the appearance of latent heat. They can propagate themselves, when introduced into supercooled water.

Ice has been important in the geologic history of Earth—there is a theory that our present temperate weather is just a minor break in the great ice-age. It is an interesting fact that the ice upon the Earth tends to perpetuate itself—with their high reflecting power, fields of ice and snow increase the planet's albedo, and lower the amount of solar radiation absorbed. Which means more ice and snow! It has been estimated, I think, that an average temperature drop of about four degrees would be enough to plunge the Earth into a new ice age, that might last thousands of years.

So much for the scientific theme. The real problem was how to present it. It is a psychological truth that people are interested only in people. Any abstract idea, scientific or otherwise, is really interesting only because it's of human meaning, conscious or unconsciously appreciated.

Psychologists have discovered that what people "know"—in the shallow conscious mind—is much less important than what they feel. To give an idea its full expression, then, the writer must appeal not only to the reason, but the emotions.

The writer must show the full human meaning of his theme. He must present not just the bare idea, but real characters responding to it in the conflict of a dramatic plot: setting and style must fit and strengthen the emotional acceptance of his basic idea.

The science fiction story— from this point of view—is then a scientific instrument, perfected by modern psychology, for the complete expression of scientific ideas. A bald way of putting it, perhaps. But the complete—and successful!—expression of any idea is called art.

THE ICE ENTITY was begun three years ago, in Key West, but it didn't thrive in that tropical atmosphere: the rigor of a New Mexico blizzard was required to get it finished.

# Science in Science-Fiction

*Letter to the editor, Astounding Science Fiction, June 1937*

Dear Mr. Tremaine:

When Mr. Duncan checks 'em off, they are really checked off, eh, what? His lively letter will remind me to look up difference between a positron and a ring nebula before I write another story dealing with either.

Seriously speaking, I share his admiration for H. P. Lovecraft. But Weinbaum was also a very skilled craftsman, in his somewhat lighter vein. There are moods when one wants to be drenched with preternatural horror, and moods when one wants merely to be amused. And isn't love also an important scientific fact?

May I comment on this question of the science in science-fiction? It isn't, as I see it, the first purpose of science-fiction merely to present scientific fact. There is, of course, a great deal of true science in all real science-fiction—which is a good thing, but more or less incidental.

Stories have been written largely to present facts or to support argumentative theses—but most of them aren't the highest type of literature. The childhood favorite, for example, "The Swiss Family Robinson," is mostly a sort of animated natural history—and rather dry reading after one has become thoroughly familiar with the facts it sets forth.

There is no need for the science-fiction writer to turn out disguised monographs. Such authorities as Eddington, Jeans, Jones, Carrel, Lemon, and Paul Karlson are constantly writing brilliant popular expositions of the latest research and theory.

But science-fiction, it seems to me, is concerned with something a little different. Its purpose, I think—like that of any art—is to create a unified emotional response to its material. It deals, in other words, not so much with science itself, as with the *human reaction* to science.

The science-fiction story would bring its reader a vicarious emotional experience, a vital illusion of reality. To cause such a response, it must present various stimuli.

True scientific fact is one necessary element. The writer must be very careful of his accuracy in dealing with known science—because any blunder wrecks the precious illusion. He should keep up with a dozen fields of science.

But speculative theories—

daring ideas yet unproven—are also important. So are realistic human characters, harmonious settings, dramatic incidents, and well-fashioned plots.

Modern science has become a tremendously important thing in the world. It's new, strange to a human mind fed for thousands of years on myth and superstition. The business of science-fiction, I fully believe, is to help our modern age make its complete imaginative and æsthetic response to science. —Jack Williamson, 235 Harrison Street, Topeka, Kansas.

# Horror Yarns—Double Action

*Article, The Author & Journalist, August 1937*

SO you want to do a mystery-terror story? Then why not try the device christened for the purposes of this discussion, the double-action plot? Several of my yarns based on it have sold to Leo Margulies. It should also click with Rogers Terrill's horror string, and the general principle could be adapted to the whole mystery field.

Don't pass the horror magazine by with a sniff of disdain. Their unique requirements are almost worthy of the abilities of an Edgar Allan Poe. To make them, you must juggle two stories at once: the emotional narrative of the hero's battle with overwhelming horror; and, cleverly hidden beneath it, the villain's plot with its final solution, which is as closely logical as an algebraic theorem. If this seems as difficult as juggling nine balls, the double-action principle will help you to do it.

First, let's review the fundamentals of the mystery-terror story—and then see how double-action helps to provide them. The basic purpose of the story, to begin with, is to give the reader a genuine thrill of vicarious terror. This feeling must come to the reader through the hero. Therefore, the whole machinery of the story must be set up to batter and drench and freeze the hero with uttermost horror.

The hero himself must be a likeable person, and engaged upon a desirable enterprise—such as seeking the safety of helpless people in terrible danger. Otherwise the reader will not be sympathetic and willing to share the hero's terror to the full extent.

The hero, furthermore, must be himself actually terrified. He mustn't be allowed to doubt the mind-crushing reality of the supernatural menace—not until the last few pages. Despite his fears, however, he must be engaged in constant, vigorous action, to protect and rescue others from the overwhelming forces of horror.

Every item of setting, characterization, and incident, should be chosen to stimulate the hero—and with him, the reader—to *fear, dread,* and *horror.* And remember that these emotions are strongest and purest when felt for a helpless loved one.

The writer should remember that he is creating an impression by the use of words, and select those associated with the effect he wishes to create; namely, such words as *fear, horror, ter-*

*ror, dread, death, grave, tomb, skull, corpse, ghost, decay, fetor, hell, cold, night, dark, storm, fury, hate, madness, insanity, sickness, pallor, werewolf, vampire, ghoul, wolf, bat, snake, worm.* A very few words denoting light and happiness will increase the effect, by contrast. One way, of course, to get such atmospheric words into the story is to choose characters, setting, and plot the depiction of which requires them. Another is to portray the subjective emotional reactions of the hero with picturesque, blood-curdling figures of speech, such as "Hellfangs of black horror ripped at the nakedness of his shuddering soul."—Rather an extreme example. This type of story for the current market may be overwritten to a considerable extent, if the emotion rings true. Restraint, however, is frequently effective, and there is a current demand for terror action and less subjective writing.

The hero must be placed in a situation rousing the greatest possible extremes of fear. This means that he and other sympathetic characters should be menaced by some overwhelming peril against which ordinary measures of defense are useless—they face the *unknown*, something weirdly astounding, apparently supernatural. There is an editorial requirement, however, that everything has a natural, logical explanation at the end.

The obvious solution is to let the villain perpetrate some hoax, involving weird or supernatural menace, in order to create a feeling of horror in the hero. He must have a convincing, sane motive for his diabolical plot—financial profit is the best. Lunatics, except for suspects, are definitely out!

The villain's connection with the horrifying phenomena, however, should be deftly concealed until the ending. There should be several innocent suspects, upon whom the reader's eye will first light when he begins to penetrate the atmosphere of supernatural horror.

The hero himself must solve the mystery—expose the hoax—through his acuity in perceiving the significance of some clue planted early in the story. This essential clue must be very carefully selected and disguised, to prevent its giving the hoax away to the reader and prematurely destroying the supernatural illusion.

A clinical example, of which I am a little proud, is the solution of my story "The Devil in Steel," to appear shortly in *Thrilling Mystery*. A scientist has invented a walking robot. The villain, scheming to obtain a valuable storage battery, dresses himself in a suit of armor designed to look like the robot, and runs amok in the island where the laboratory is located, horribly killing the other persons who know the secret of the battery.

The vital clue is that the villain, innocently entering the laboratory with the hero before the murders begin, fumbles oddly for the red glass door knob. The scientist, in his demonstration, shows that his actual robot can distinguish red and green. But the mad metal monster, breaking into the laboratory as it seeks to mangle, crush, and burn the girl in its steel arms, fumbles for the door knob in the same way—thus betraying that it has the villain's color-blindness!

It is a good idea, by the way, always to have the characters in some confined setting, such as a prison, a ship, or an island, so that they can't just walk away from the menace. And the menace must be an actual, horrible, immediate physical disaster, usually demonstrated on several minor characters.

It is quite likely that the basic psychological explanation behind the popularity of these horror thrillers is that the reader himself actually shares the gloating, sadistic lust of the masked monster engaged in orgies of gory torture. But this forbidden pleasure burdens him with a sense of unconscious guilt. The hero then cleverly unmasks the villain, pins all the guilt on him, and destroys him. The punishment of the scapegoat having thus absolved the unconscious sins of the reader, he is ready for another story.

To sum up, the essential elements of the mystery-terror formula: The *villain,* driven by a convincing *profit-motive,* perpetrates a *hoax* of *overwhelming, supernatural horror,* directed at the well-being of innocent characters. These include several *suspects* and the *girl,* who is under immediate, horrible *menace.* The *hero,* bravely fighting *unknown horror,* for her sake, penetrates the hoax through seeing the significance of an *essential clue,* destroys the villain after a final *big scene,* by his own efforts, and gives every horrifying phenomena a satisfactory *natural explanation.*

This formula fits the typical and most successful variety of mystery-terror yarn, especially the novelette length. The shorts don't run so much to formula. They are sometimes based on pure horror action, unexplained supernatural retribution, torture, etc. NOTE: it does not apply to *Weird Tales,* which fortunately doesn't have a formula and doesn't care for mundane explanations.

Now, at last, we're ready for

the double-action principle. We have seen that there is to be a weirdly amazing or supernatural hoax. That the villain should have an apparently iron-clad alibi. That innocent suspects should be apparently implicated.

Then—here it is—let the suspects start the hoax! They do it for some more or less innocent purpose, without any murderous intent. Then the real villain comes along, penetrates the first relatively innocent plot, and makes it the foundation of his diabolical horror-murder scheme!

Thus the unfortunate suspects are automatically caught up to their necks in guilty circumstances. And the villain—who was usually somewhere else in the hero's company when it all started—can readily arrange a perfect alibi.

In "Spider Island," for example—a story of mine which appeared in the April issue of *Thrilling Mystery*—a movie company has set out to produce a horror picture of giant spiders invading civilization. The hoax of the giant hunting spiders haunting the island is first invented merely to scare the actors into a better similitude of horror. Then—here's the double-action!—the producer twists it into a plot to murder the whole company, his motive being to collect insurance.

In "Death's Cold Daughter," a novelette which appeared several months ago, a young aviator-inventor, Jimmy Adcock, perpetrates a hoax of a weird world floating above the stratosphere, in order to interest investors in his stratosphere plane. Then—double-action again—one of the investors turns the hoax into a murder tool, to kill the flier and the other investors, his purpose being to get possession of the new plane. His victims are weirdly frozen, apparently by a strange invader from the world above.

It's like juggling nine balls— easy when you know how! Try it. *Thrilling Mystery, Dime Mystery, Terror* and *Horror Stories* all pay one cent and up, on acceptance.

# The Inverse Universe

*Authorial Comments on "The Infinite Enemy,"*
*Thrilling Wonder Stories, April 1938*

INTERPLANETARY stories come and go. By far, they're our favorite variety of theme. But when an author takes time out to embellish his offering with an approach that's strikingly different—well, we call the result a corker.

We hope we're not wrong in acclaiming THE INFINITE ENEMY a superior story. JACK WILLIAMSON, its author, has written many hundreds of thousands of words of science fiction. This one, we think, ranks high up on his "tops" list. His letter explaining the basis for his novelette, incidentally, is as interesting as the story itself. Here goes:

The story behind THE INFINITE ENEMY has several possible beginnings. It might begin with a letter I wrote Edmond Hamilton, about 1930. It might begin with the startling mathematical discoveries made by a man named Dirac, at about the same time. Or with the faint shining track that Anderson, in Chicago, observed, a year or so later, in a Wilson cloud chamber. Or, for that matter, it might even begin with the fact that a science fiction writer suddenly wanted money to buy a new microscope.

To begin with the letter, Hamilton's reply led to a close friendship, and the friendship to a projected collaboration. A story by two writers, we agreed, ought to be twice as good as one by either. So we set out to plan a universal ad-venture, to be called ROVERS OF INFINITY.

The project, I suppose, was a little too ambitious. And collaboration is, we discovered, a difficult art. We abandoned the story. Left in my files was a description of the infinite entity, which I had planned to use in one of my episodes of the **opus magnus.** Hamilton claimed no interest in it, and somehow it stuck in my mind, too interesting to be forgotten.

My files contain hundreds of story ideas, in various stages of progress. Often a promising idea is turned over and developed a bit, every now and then for several years, before the yarn becomes real and complete enough to be actually written. The old unconscious, I think, does part of the work.

At last, anyhow, I had a story of adventure in another

universe. But where find room for a new universe? Dirac and Anderson came to the rescue.

For the minute historic streak that Anderson observed was the trail of condensing vapor left in the ionized track of a positron. That elusive particle, never observed before, had been predicted by the mathematical genius of Dirac—a pencil-and-paper feat as remarkable as that of Adams and Laverrier in discovering Neptune.

Dirac's conceptions of negative mass and negative energy, thus so amazingly verified, seem as fantastic as any science fiction plot. The more power you apply to drive a particle of negative mass in one direction, the greater its velocity in another!

It was now the famous "Dirac hole"—which has been defined as the **want** of a particle which is negative of mass and of charge, and identified as the positron—that suggested the **minus** universes of the story, which became the abode of the infinite entity.

The infinite possibilities of life have always been, to me, a favorite topic of speculation. They must be, I think, to any living—and speculating—being. There is a kinship between the animistic savage who attributes life to rocks and winds, and Sir James Jeans, who sees that hand of a Mathematician in the structure of the Universe.

And the potentialities of life are, literally—infinite!

# Acknowledgments

"The Ruler of Fate," Copyright © 1936 Popular Magazines, Inc., for *Weird Tales,* April, May & June 1936.

"Death's Cold Daughter," Copyright © 1936 Beacon Magazines, Inc., for *Thrilling Mystery,* September 1936.

"The Great Illusion," Copyright © 1936 Julius Schwartz, for *Fantasy Magazine,* September 1936.

"The Blue Spot," Copyright © 1937 Street and Smith Publications, Inc., for *Astounding Stories,* January & February 1937.

"The Ice Entity," Copyright © 1937 Beacon Magazines, Inc., for *Thrilling Wonder Stories,* February 1937.

"Spider Island," Copyright © 1937 Beacon Magazines, Inc., for *Thrilling Mystery,* April 1937.

"The Mark of the Monster," Copyright © 1937 Popular Magazines, Inc., for *Weird Tales,* May 1937.

"The Devil in Steel," Copyright © 1937 Better Publications, Inc., for *Thrilling Mystery,* July 1937.

"Released Entropy," Copyright © 1937 Street and Smith Publications, Inc., for *Astounding Stories,* August & September 1937.

"Dreadful Sleep," Copyright © 1938 Popular Magazines, Inc., for *Weird Tales,* March, April & May 1938.

"The Infinite Enemy," Copyright © 1938 Better Publications, Inc., for *Thrilling Wonder Stories,* April 1938.

"The Legion of Time," Copyright © 1938 Street and Smith Publications, Inc., for *Astounding Science-Fiction,* May, June & July 1938.

COVER REPRODUCTIONS

*Weird Tales.* Copyright © 1936, 1937, 1938 Popular Magazines, Inc. Used by permission of Weird Tales, Ltd.

*Thrilling Mystery.* Copyright © 1936, 1937 Beacon Magazines, Inc.
*Thrilling Wonder Stories.* Copyright © 1937 Beacon Magazines, Inc.
*Thrilling Wonder Stories.* Copyright © 1938 Better Publications, Inc.

*Fantasy Magazine.* Copyright © 1936 Julius Schwartz.

*Astounding Stories.* Copyright © 1937 by Street and Smith Publications, Inc.
*Astounding Science-Fiction.* Copyright © 1938 by Street and Smith Publications, Inc.
Used by permission of Dell Magazines, a division of Crosstown Publications.

# FIRST EDITION
## 2002

SPIDER ISLAND, THE COLLECTED STORIES OF JACK WILLIAMSON, VOLUME FOUR, was published by Haffner Press, 5005 Crooks Road, Suite 35, Royal Oak, Michigan 48073-1239.

One thousand trade copies, and a limited edition of one hundred numbered and slipcased copies signed by the author, have been printed on 55# Natural from Adobe ITC Garamond and ITC Kabel. The printing was done by Edwards Brothers of Ann Arbor, Michigan. The custom binding cloth is Eshbach Blue.

**DATE DUE**

| MAR    2004 | FEB 1 9 2004 | |
|---|---|---|
| | | |
| | | |
| | | |
| | | |
| | | |
| | | |
| | | |
| | | |
| | | |
| | | |
| | | |
| | | |
| | | |

GAYLORD      #3522PI      Printed in USA

1  *Weird Tales*, April 1936
   "The Ruler of Fate", Pt. 1
   art by Margaret Brundage

2  *Weird Tales*, May 1936
   "The Ruler of Fate", Pt. 2
   art by Margaret Brundage

3  *Weird Tales*, June 1936
   "The Ruler of Fate", Pt. 3
   art by Margaret Brundage

4  *Thrilling Mystery*, September 1936
   "Death's Cold Daughter"
   art by Rudolph Belarski

5  *Fantasy Magazine*, September 1936
   "The Great Illusion"
   art by Clay Ferguson, Jr.

6  *Astounding Stories*, January 1937
   "The Blue Spot", Pt. 1
   art by Howard V. Brown

7  *Astounding Stories*, February 1937
   "The Blue Spot", Pt. 2
   art by Howard V. Brown

8  *Thrilling Wonder Stories*, February 1937
   "The Ice Entity"
   artist unknown

9  *Thrilling Mystery*, April 1937
   "Spider Island"
   art by Rudolph Belarksi

10  *Weird Tales*, May 1937
    "The Mark of the Monster"
    art by Margaret Brundage

11  *Thrilling Mystery*, July 1937
    "The Devil in Steel"
    artist unknown

12  *Astounding Stories*, August 1937
    "Entropy Released", Pt. 1
    art by Howard V. Brown

13  *Astounding Stories*, September 1937
    "Entropy Released", Pt. 2
    art by Wesso (H.W. Wessolowski)

14  *Weird Tales*, March 1938
    "Dreadful Sleep", Pt. 1
    art by Margaret Brundage

15  *Weird Tales*, April 1938
    "Dreadful Sleep", Pt. 2
    art by Virgil Finlay

16  *Weird Tales*, May 1938
    "Dreadful Sleep", Pt. 3
    art by Margaret Brundage

17  *Thrilling Wonder Stories*, April 1938
    "The Infinite Enemy"
    art by Wesso (H.W. Wessolowski)

18  *Astounding Science-Fiction*, May 1938
    "The Legion of Time", Pt. 1
    art by Charles Schneeman

19  *Astounding Science-Fiction*, June 1938
    "The Legion of Time", Pt. 2
    art by Wesso (H.W. Wessolowski)

20  *Astounding Science-Fiction*, July 1938
    "The Legion of Time", Pt. 3
    art by Howard W. Brown